Lost in Taiwan

ABOUT THIS BOOK

This book was edited by Andrea Colvin and designed by Ann Dwyer. The production was supervised by Lillian Sun, and the production editor was Lindsay Walter-Greaney. The text was set in CC Wild Words Lower, and the display type is Better Times.

This book is a work of fiction. Names, characters, places, and incidents are the product of the author's imagination or are used fictitiously. Any resemblance to actual events, locales, or persons, living or dead, is coincidental.

Copyright © 2023 by Mark Crilley

Cover illustration copyright © 2023 by Mark Crilley. Cover design by Ann Dwyer.
Cover copyright © 2023 by Hachette Book Group, Inc.

Hachette Book Group supports the right to free expression and the value of copyright. The purpose of copyright is to encourage writers and artists to produce the creative works that enrich our culture.

The scanning, uploading, and distribution of this book without permission is a theft of the author's intellectual property. If you would like permission to use material from the book (other than for review purposes), please contact permissions@hbgusa.com. Thank you for your support of the author's rights.

Little, Brown and Company
Hachette Book Group
1290 Avenue of the Americas, New York, NY 10104
Visit us at LBYR.com

First Edition: May 2023

Little, Brown and Company is a division of Hachette Book Group, Inc.
The Little, Brown name and logo are trademarks of Hachette Book Group, Inc.

The publisher is not responsible for websites (or their content) that are not owned by the publisher.

Library of Congress Cataloging-in-Publication Data
Names: Crilley, Mark, author, illustrator.
Title: Lost in Taiwan / Mark Crilley.
Description: First edition. | New York : Little, Brown and Company, 2023. | Audience: Ages 12 and up | Summary: When Paul becomes lost in Taiwan, he meets Pei-Jing, who teaches him about the local culture as she helps him find his way home.
Identifiers: LCCN 2022022317 | ISBN 9781368040884 (hardcover) ISBN 9781368040990 (paperback) | ISBN 9780316385251 (ebook)
Subjects: CYAC: Lost children—Fiction. | Taiwan—Fiction. | Friendship—Fiction. | Graphic novels. | LCGFT: Graphic novels.
Classification: LCC PZ7.7.C75 Lo 2023 | DDC 741.5/973—dc23/eng/20220712
LC record available at https://lccn.loc.gov/2022022317

ISBNs: 978-1-368-040884 (hardcover), 978-1-368-04099-0 (paperback), 978-0-316-38525-1 (ebook), 978-0-316-38535-0 (ebook), 978-0-316-38545-9 (ebook)

PRINTED IN SINGAPORE

COS

Hardcover: 10 9 8 7 6 5 4 3 2 1
Paperback: 10 9 8 7 6 5 4 3 2 1

To the people of Taiwan,
who are truly among the kindest
and most generous people
in the world

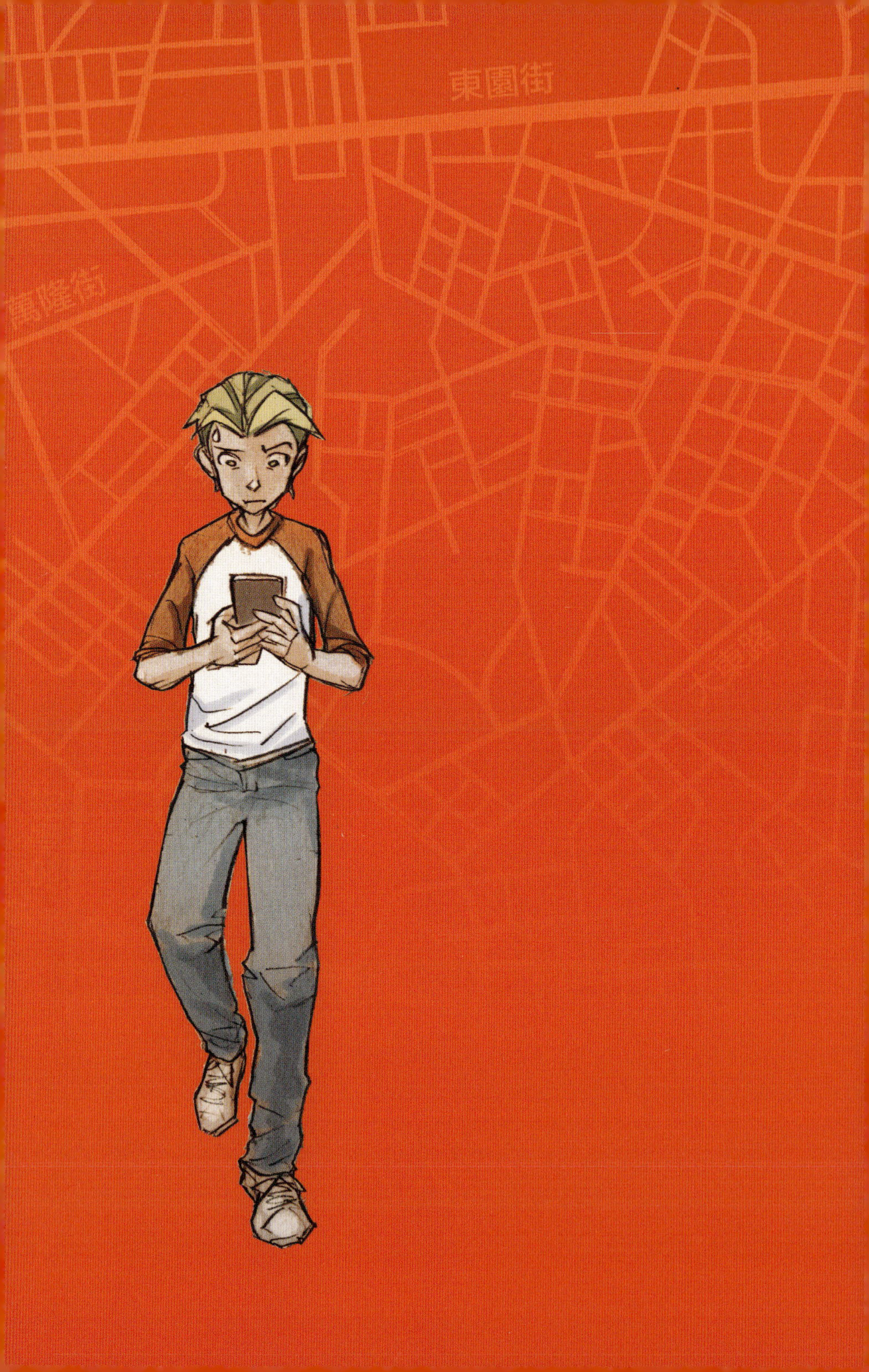
東園街

Lost in Taiwan

MARK CRILLEY

LITTLE, BROWN AND COMPANY
NEW YORK BOSTON

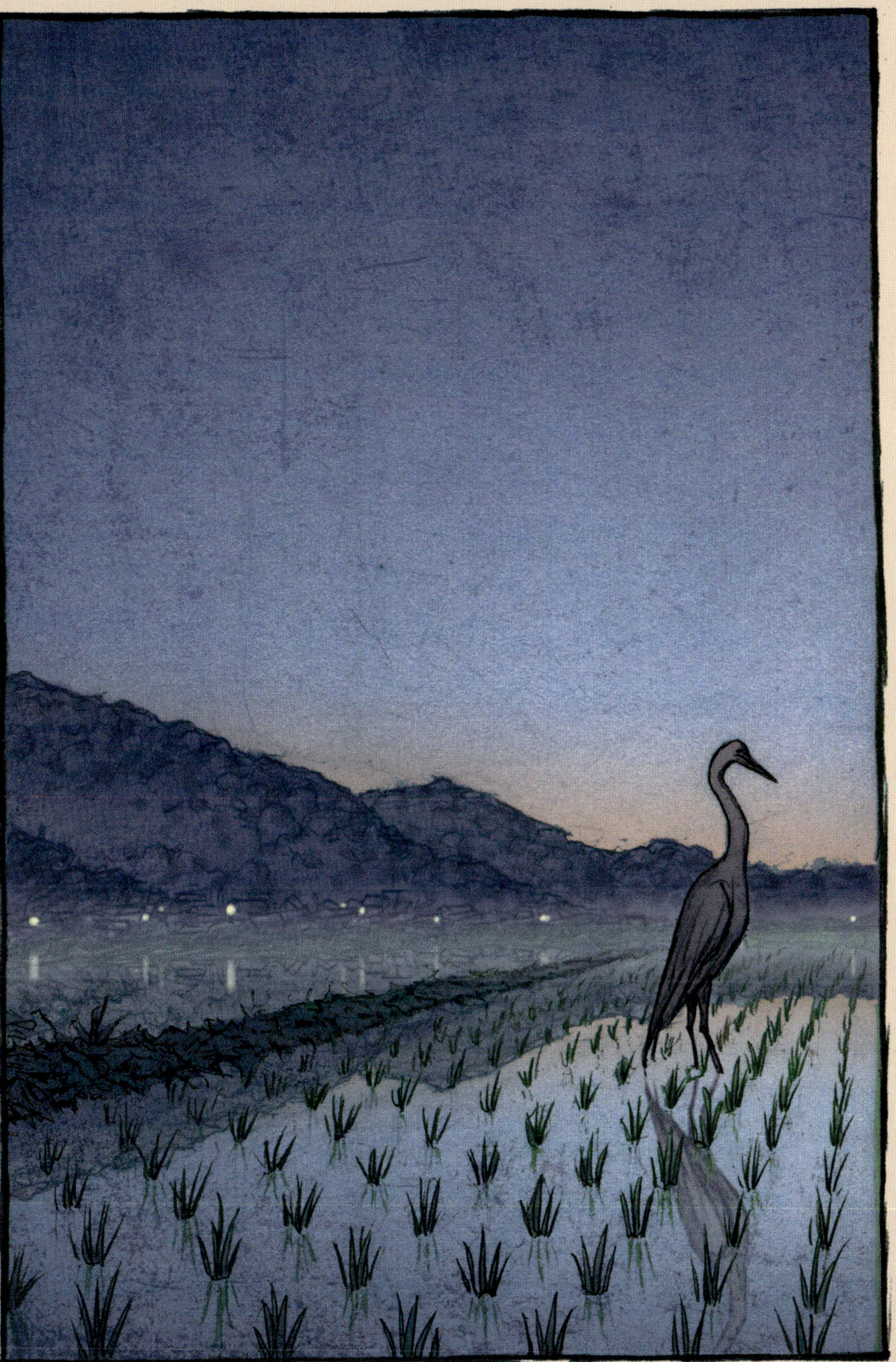

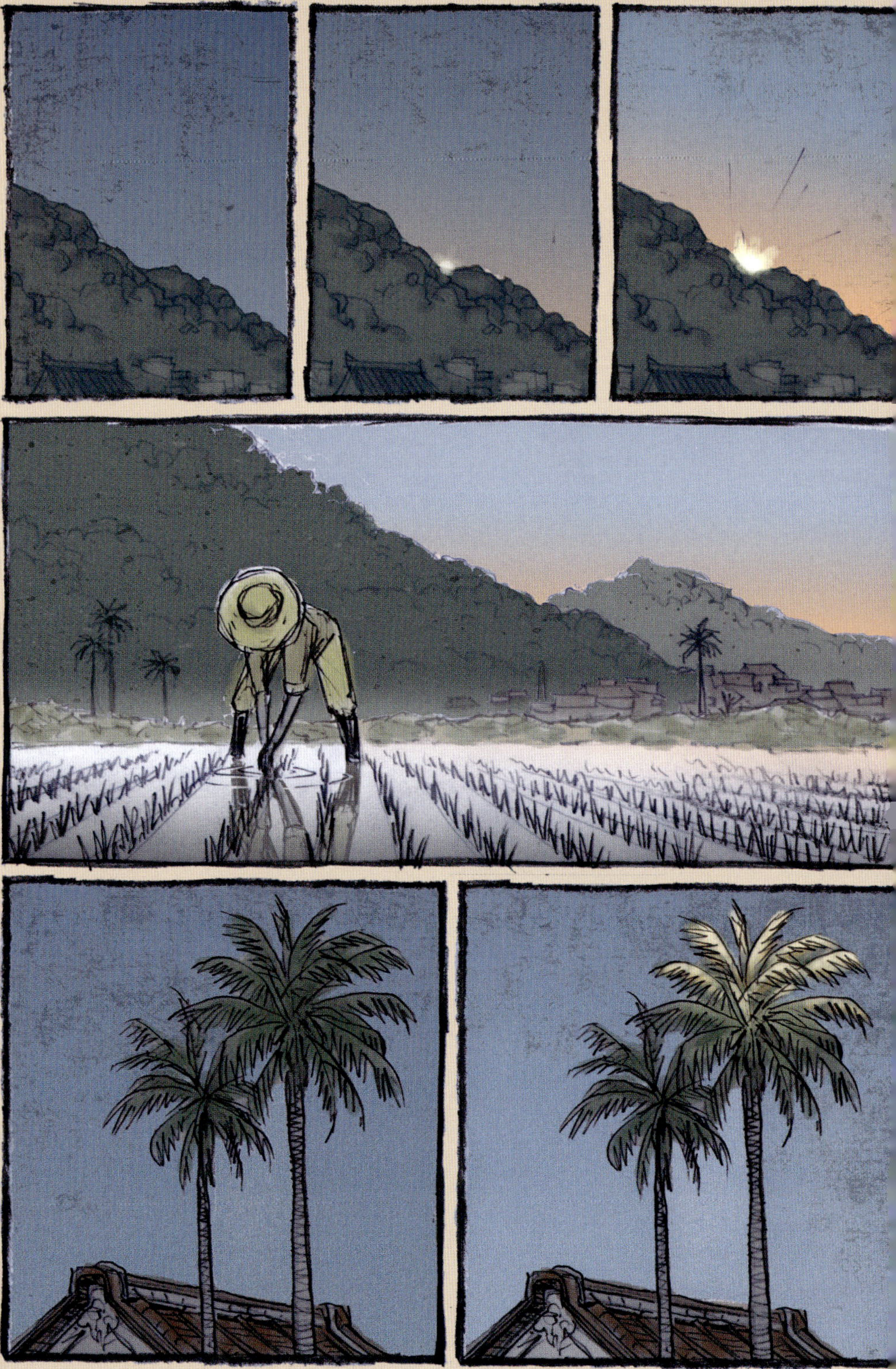

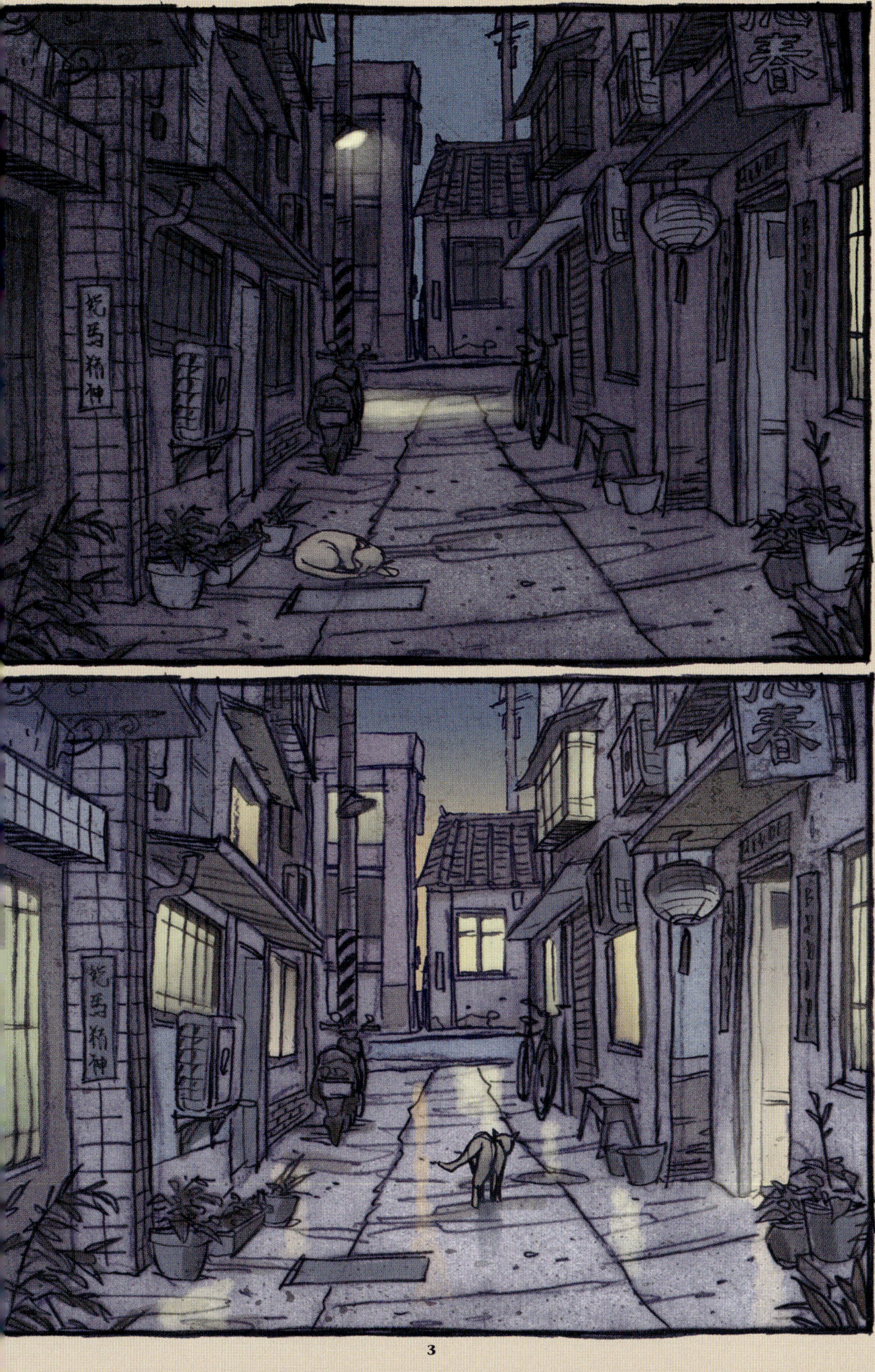
春

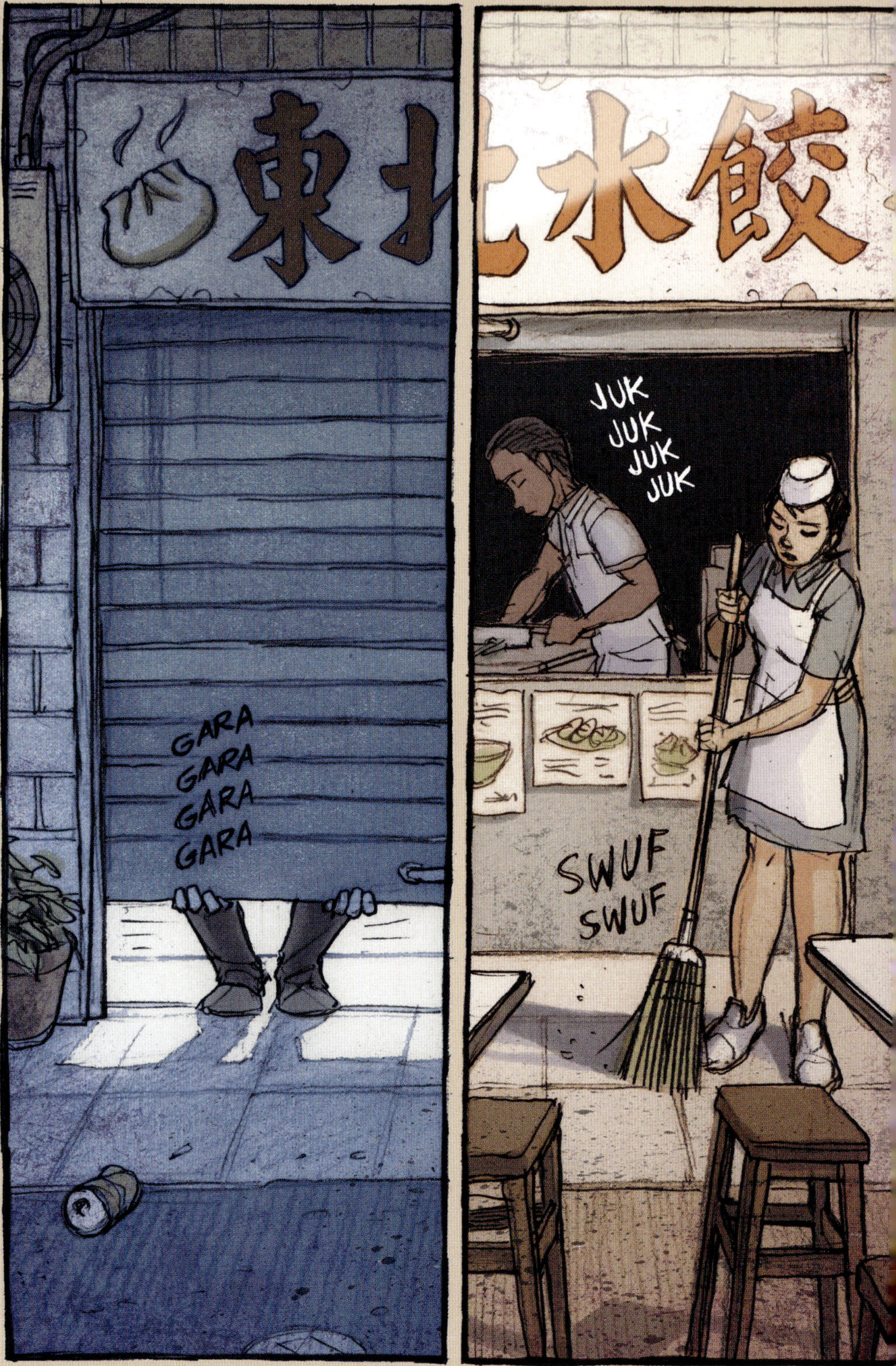
東北
GARA
GARA
GARA
GARA
北水餃
JUK
JUK
JUK
JUK
SWUF
SWUF

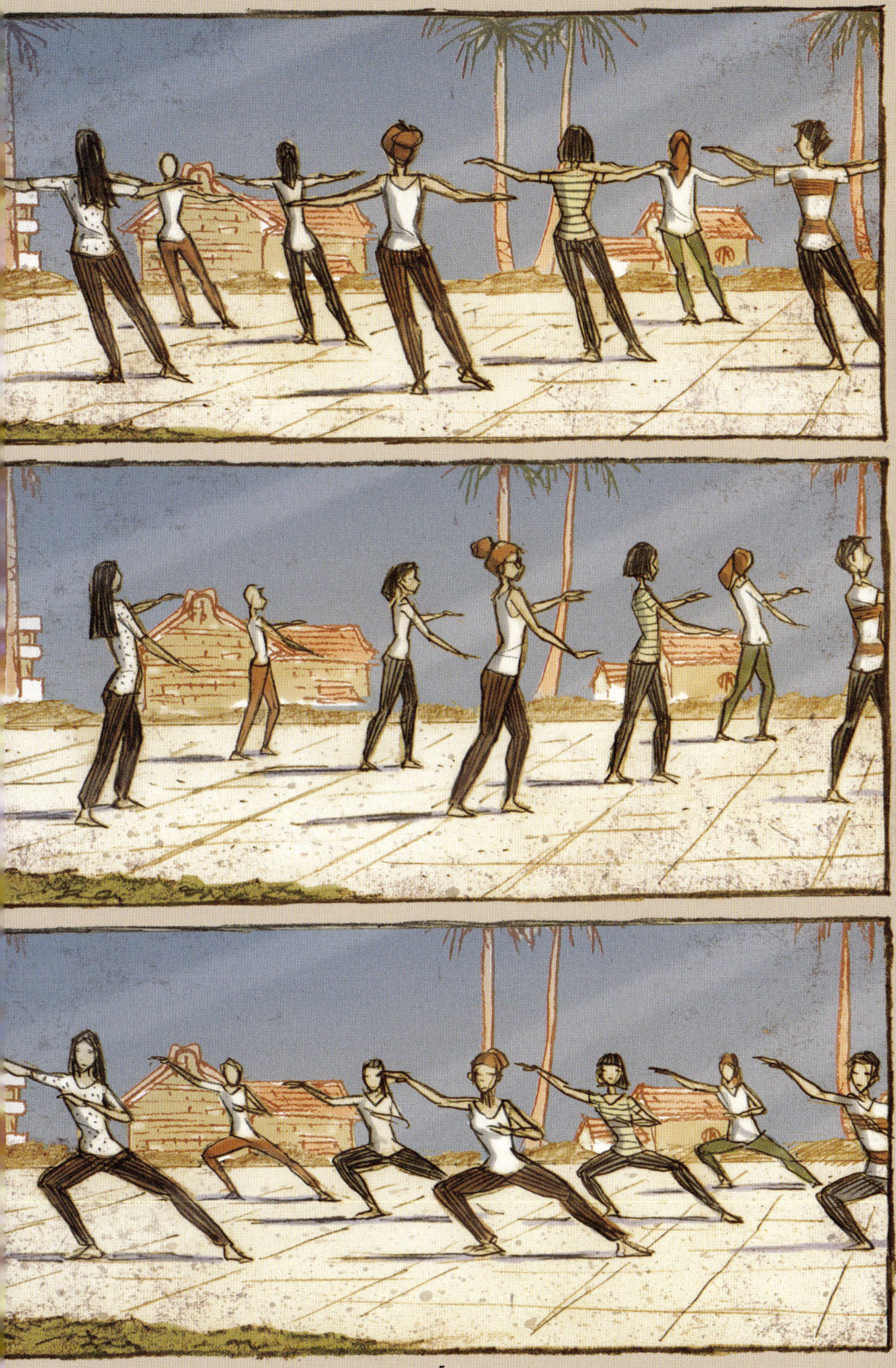

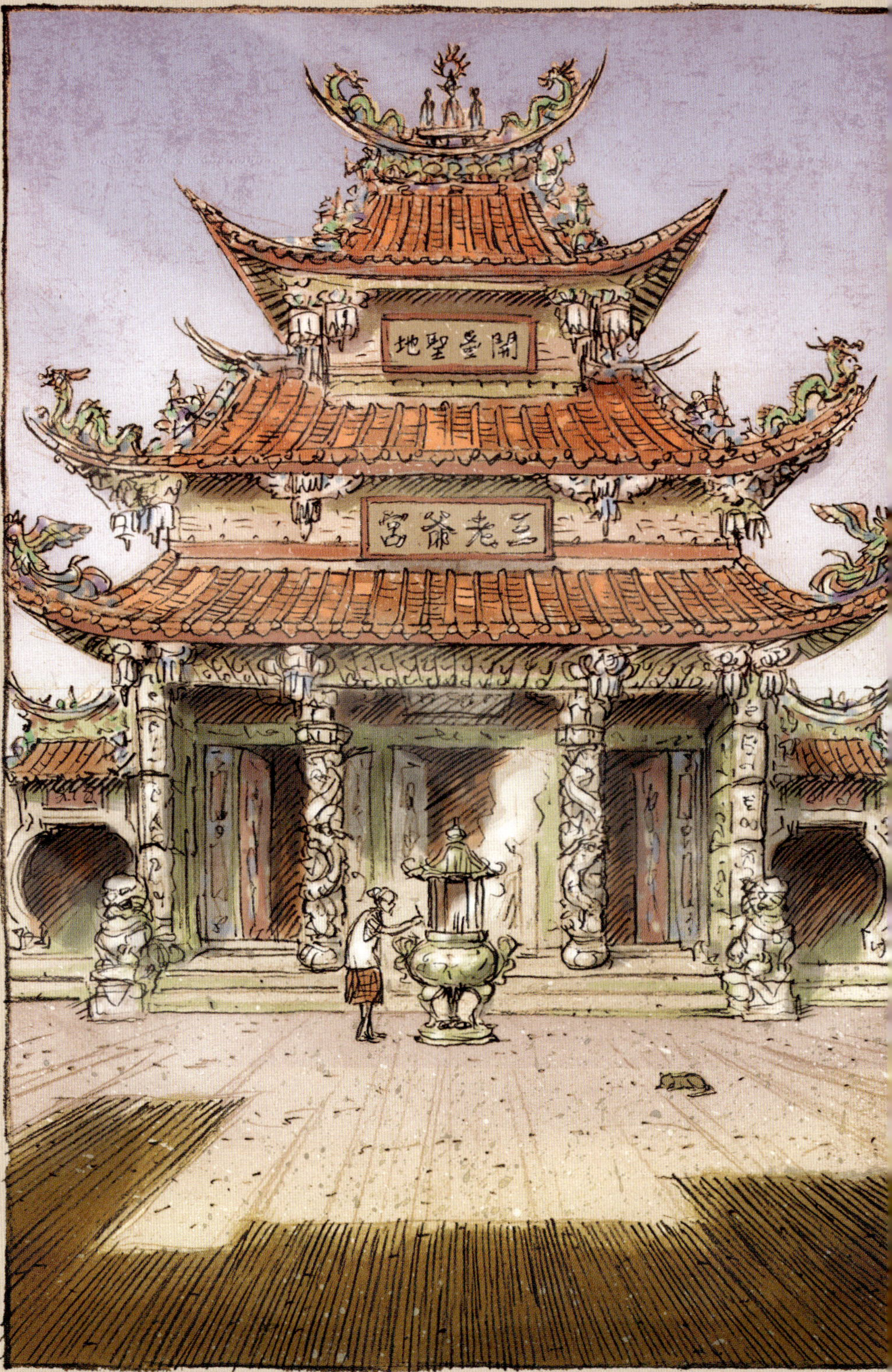
開臺聖地
三老爺宮

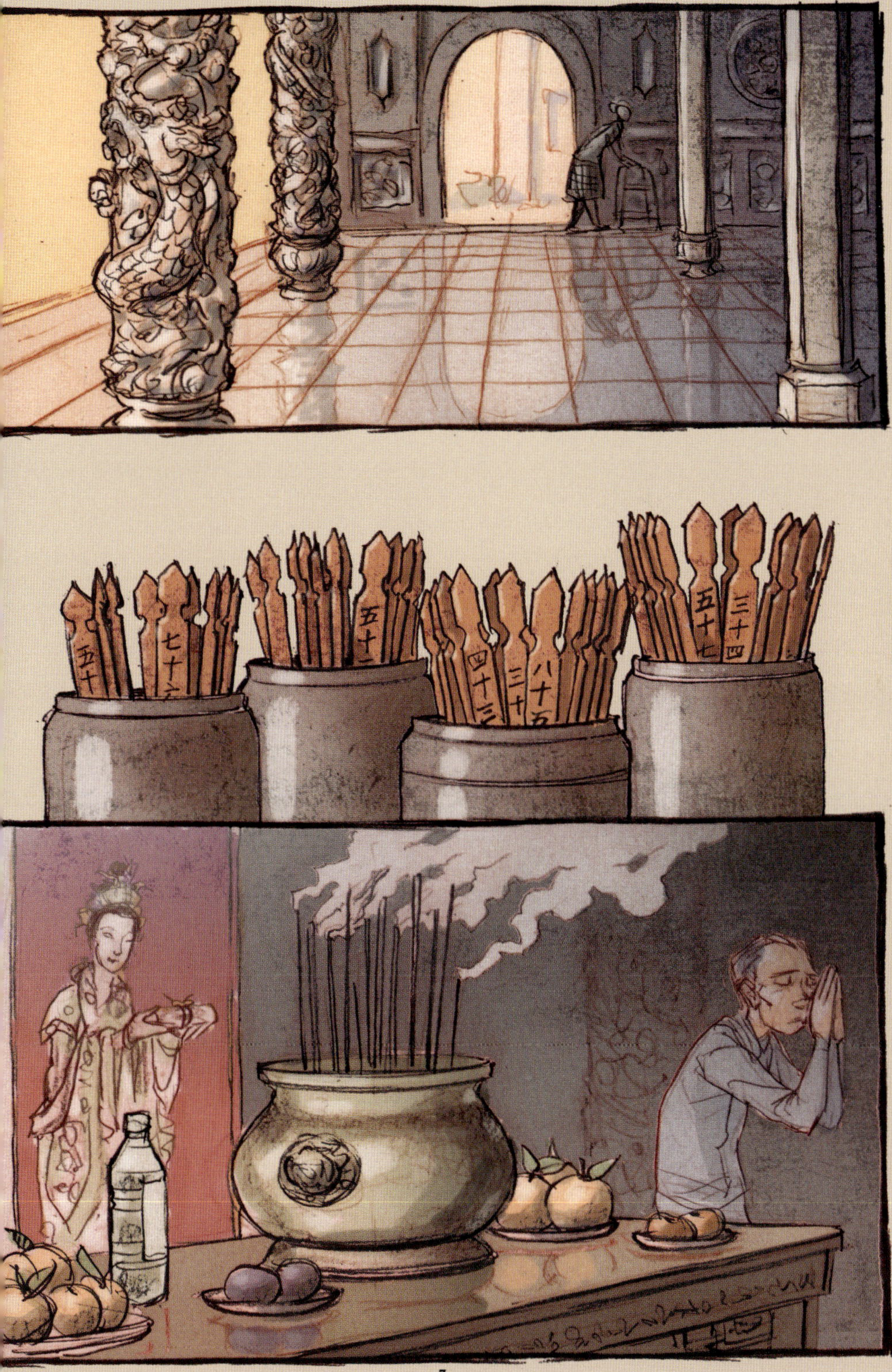
五十
七十
五十
四十三
三十
八十五
五十七
三十四

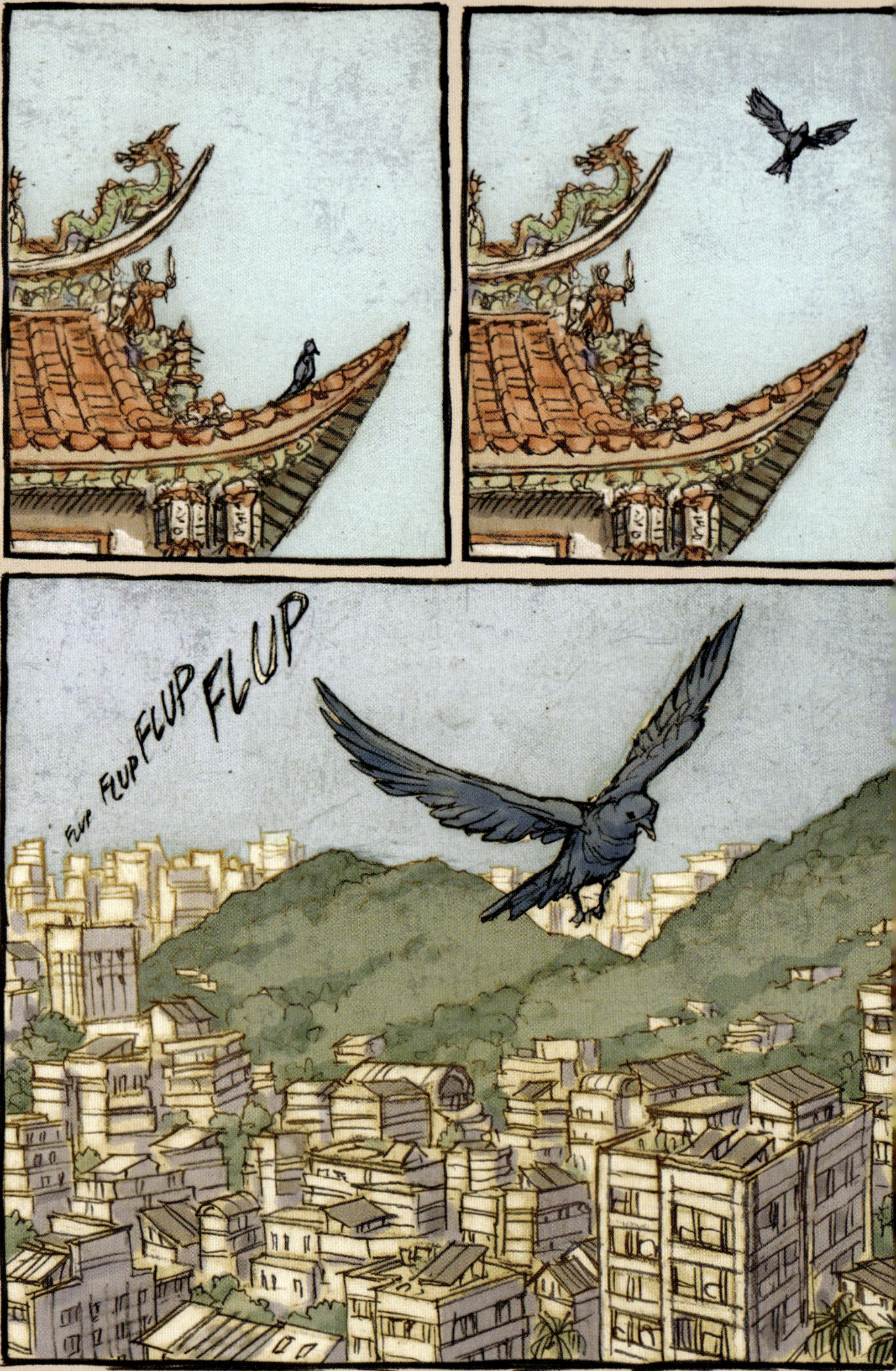
FLUP FLUP FLUP FLUP

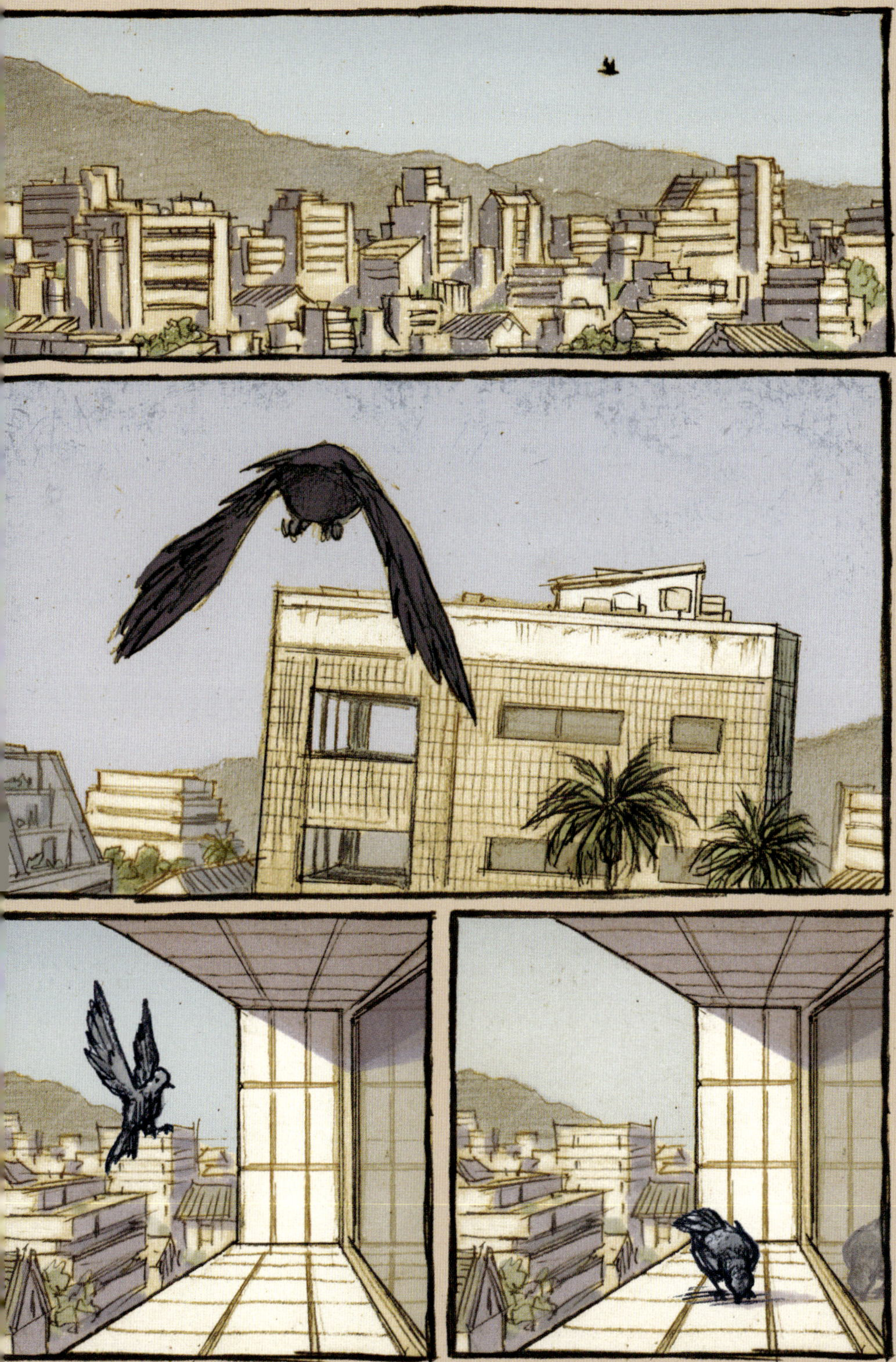

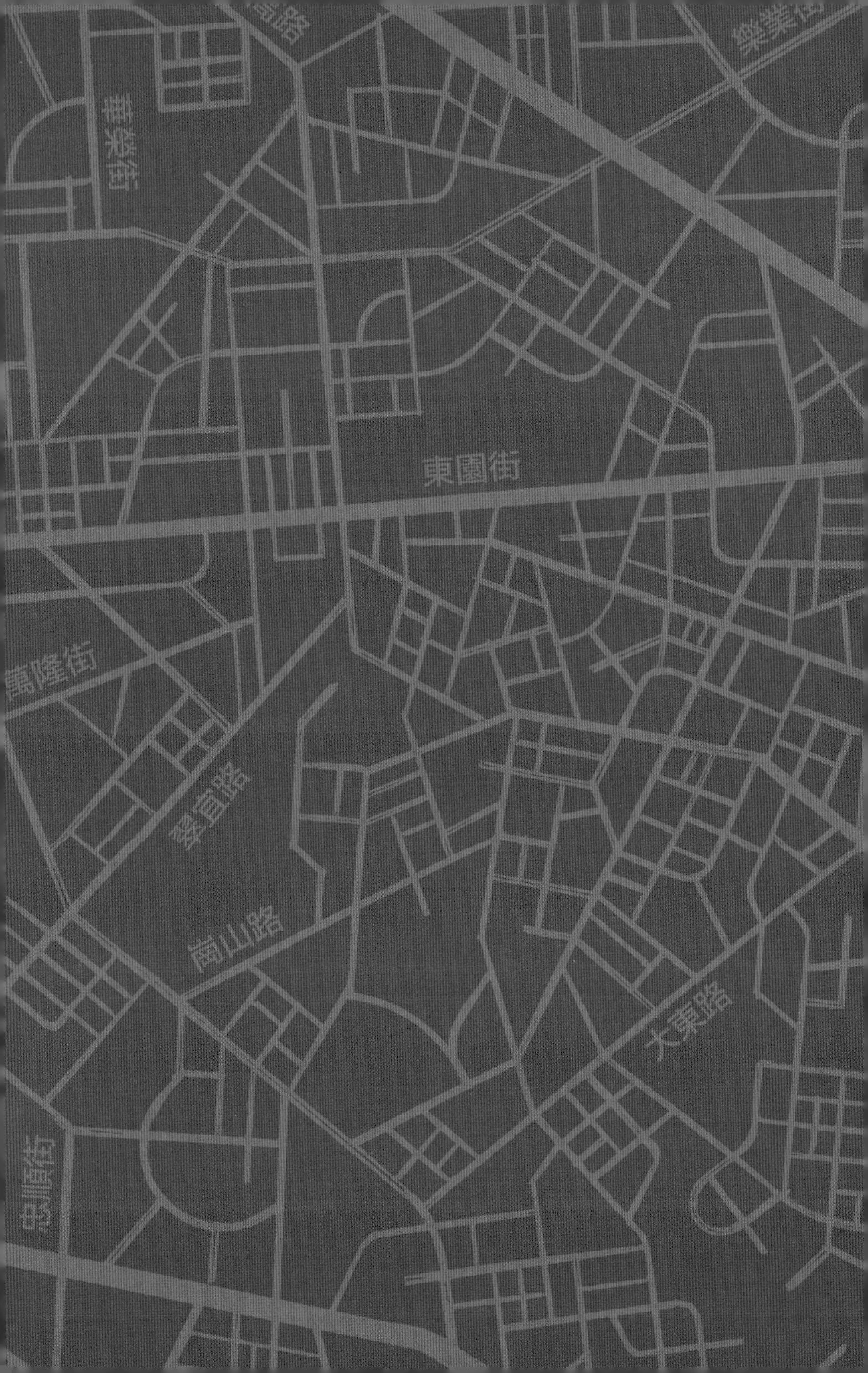
華榮街
東園街
大東路
忠順街

CHAPTER 1

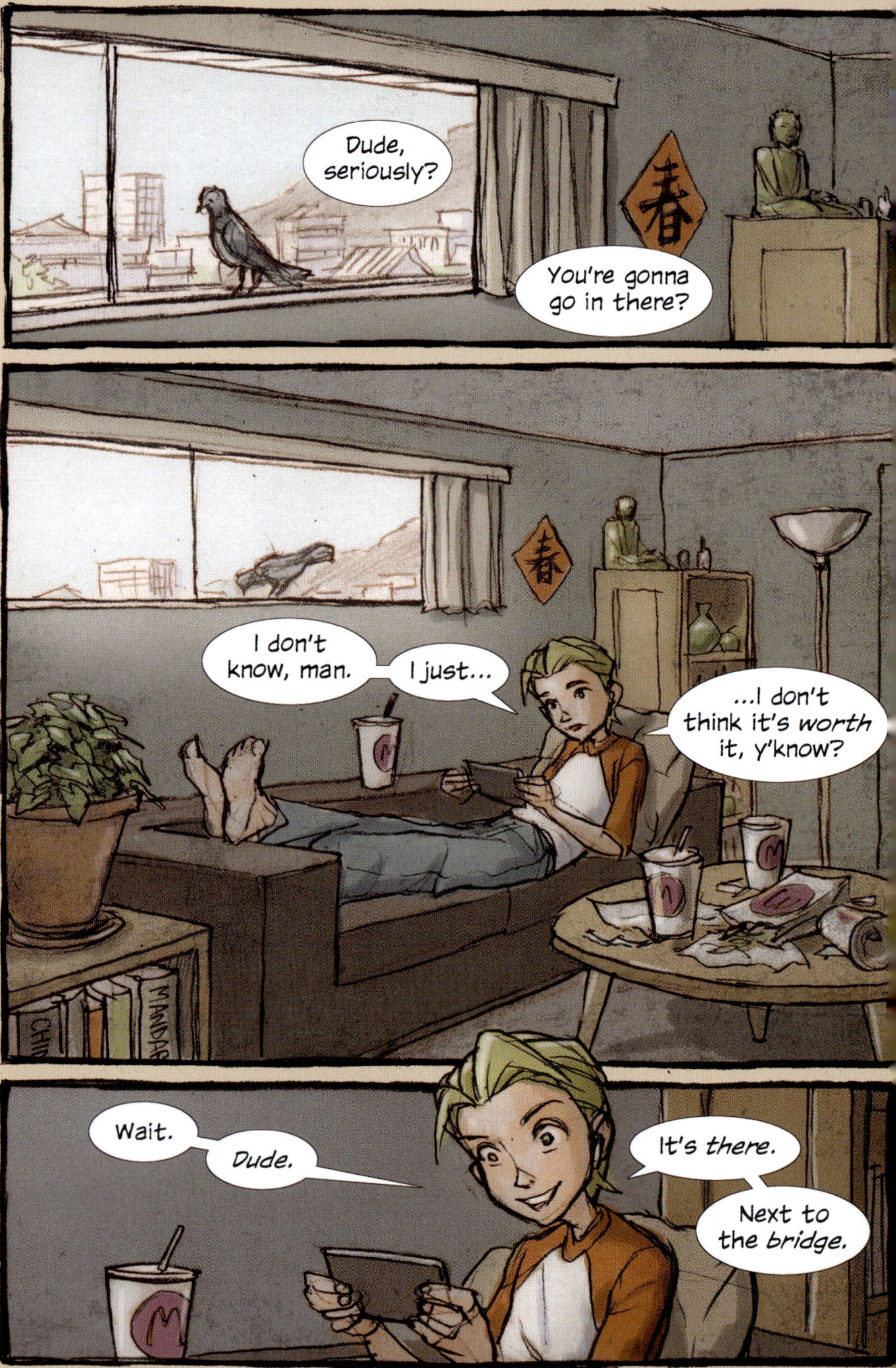
Dude, seriously?
You're gonna go in there?
春
I don't know, man.
I just...
...I don't think it's *worth* it, y'know?
Wait.
Dude.
It's *there.*
Next to the *bridge.*

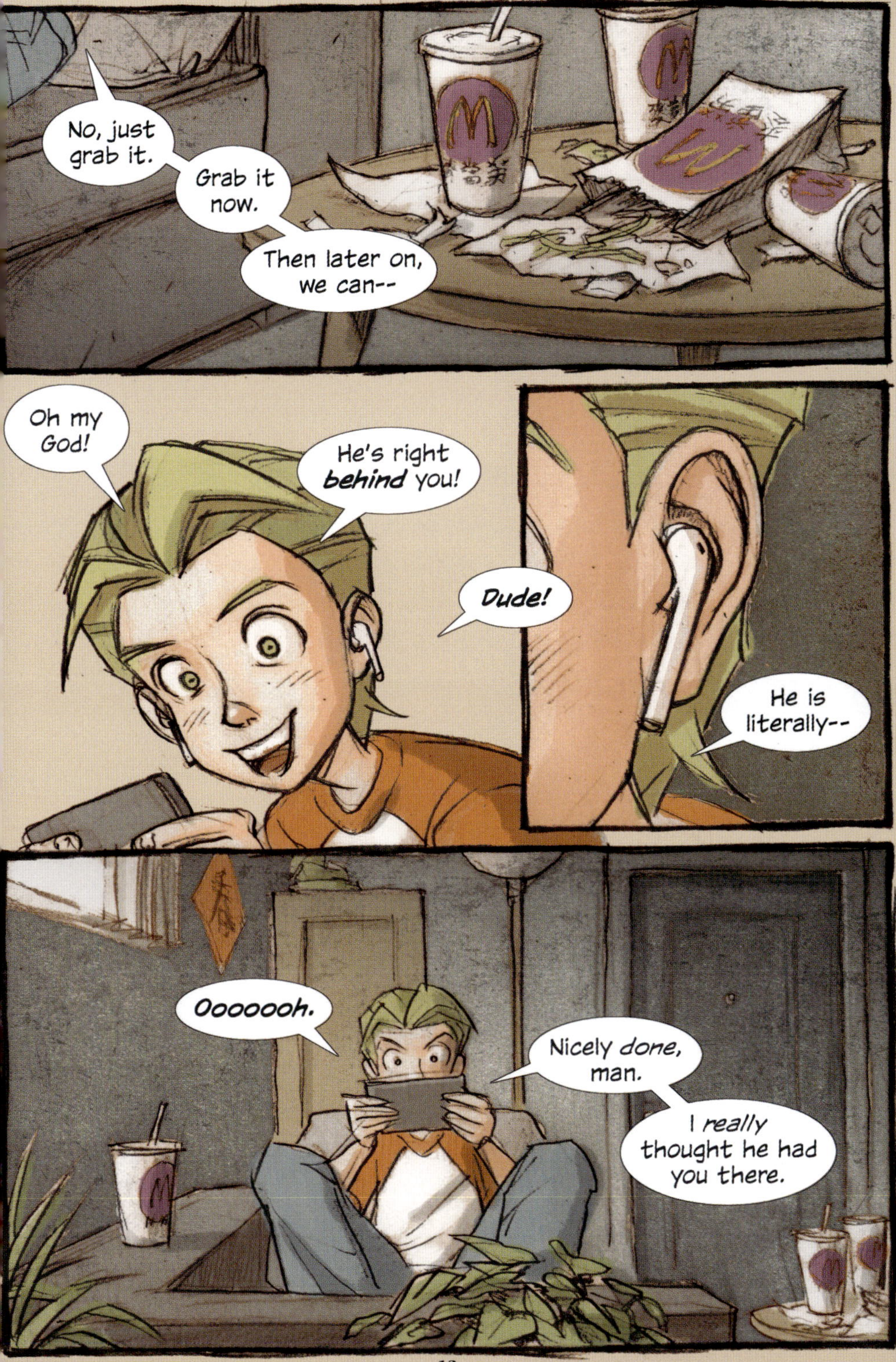
No, just grab it.
Grab it now.
Then later on, we can--
Oh my God!
He's right *behind* you!
Dude!
He is literally--
Ooooooh.
Nicely *done*, man.
I *really* thought he had you there.

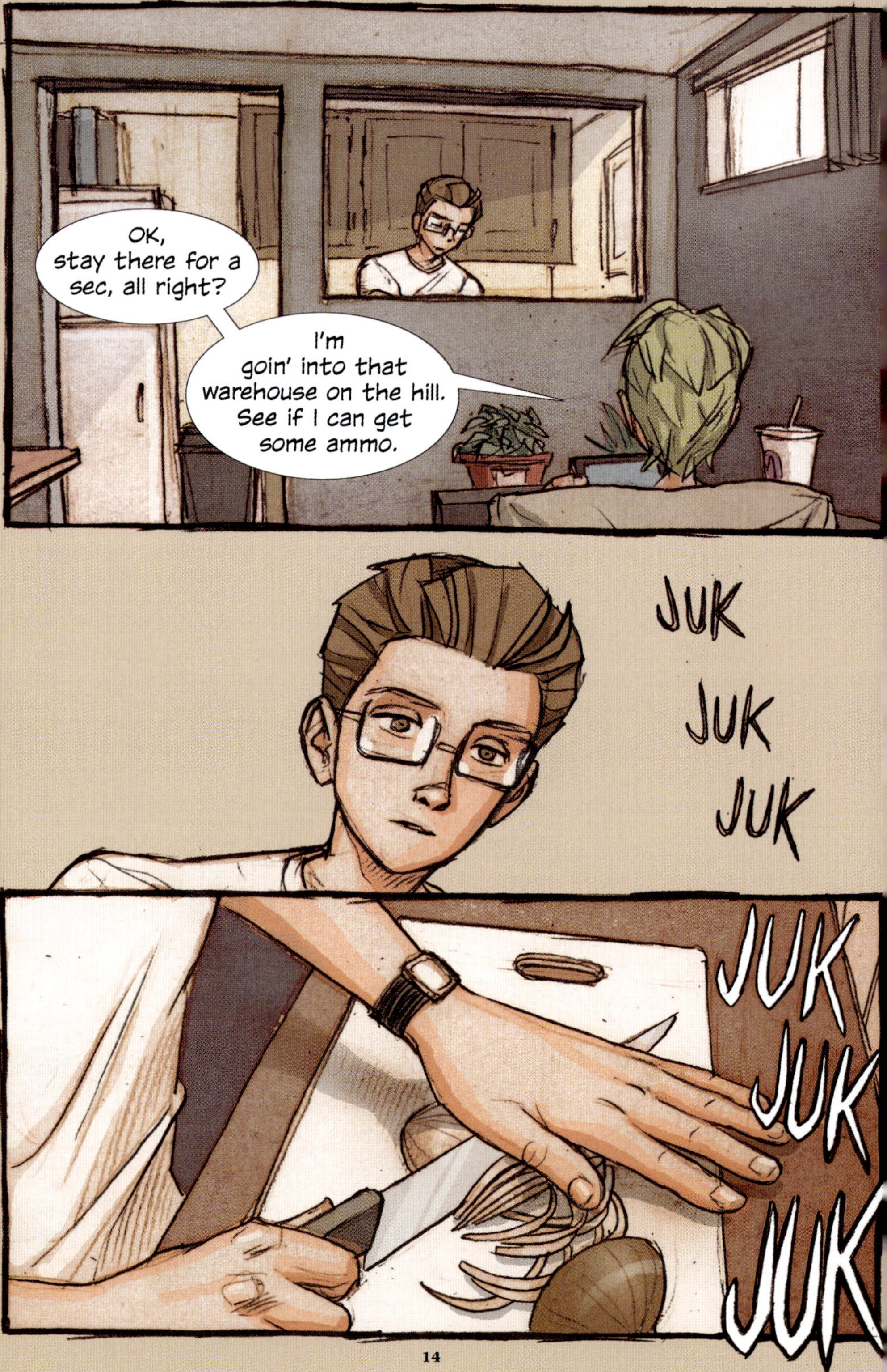
OK, stay there for a sec, all right?
I'm goin' into that warehouse on the hill. See if I can get some ammo.
JUK
JUK
JUK
JUK
JUK
JUK

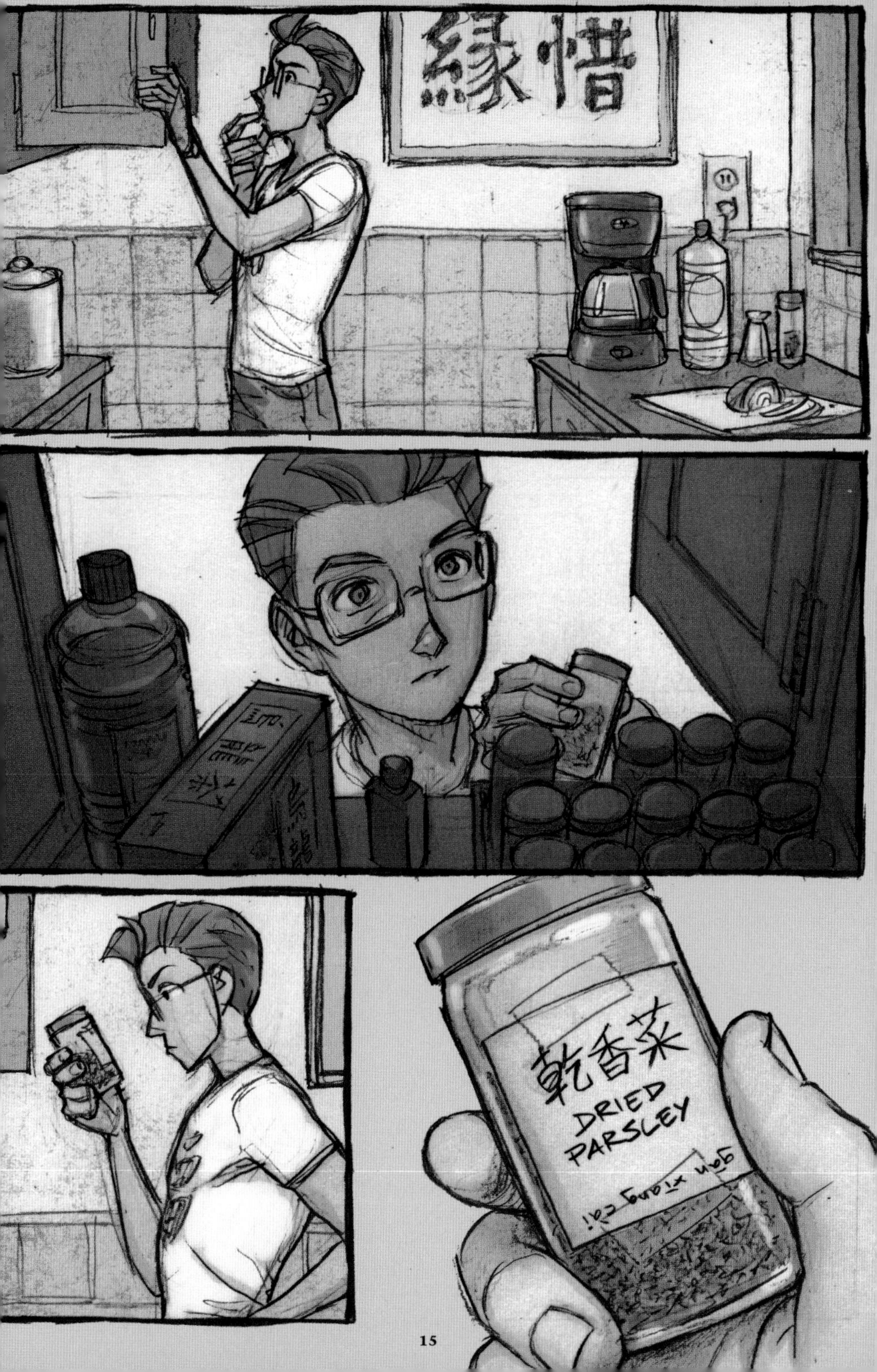

惜緣
乾香菜
DRIED PARSLEY
gan xiang cai!

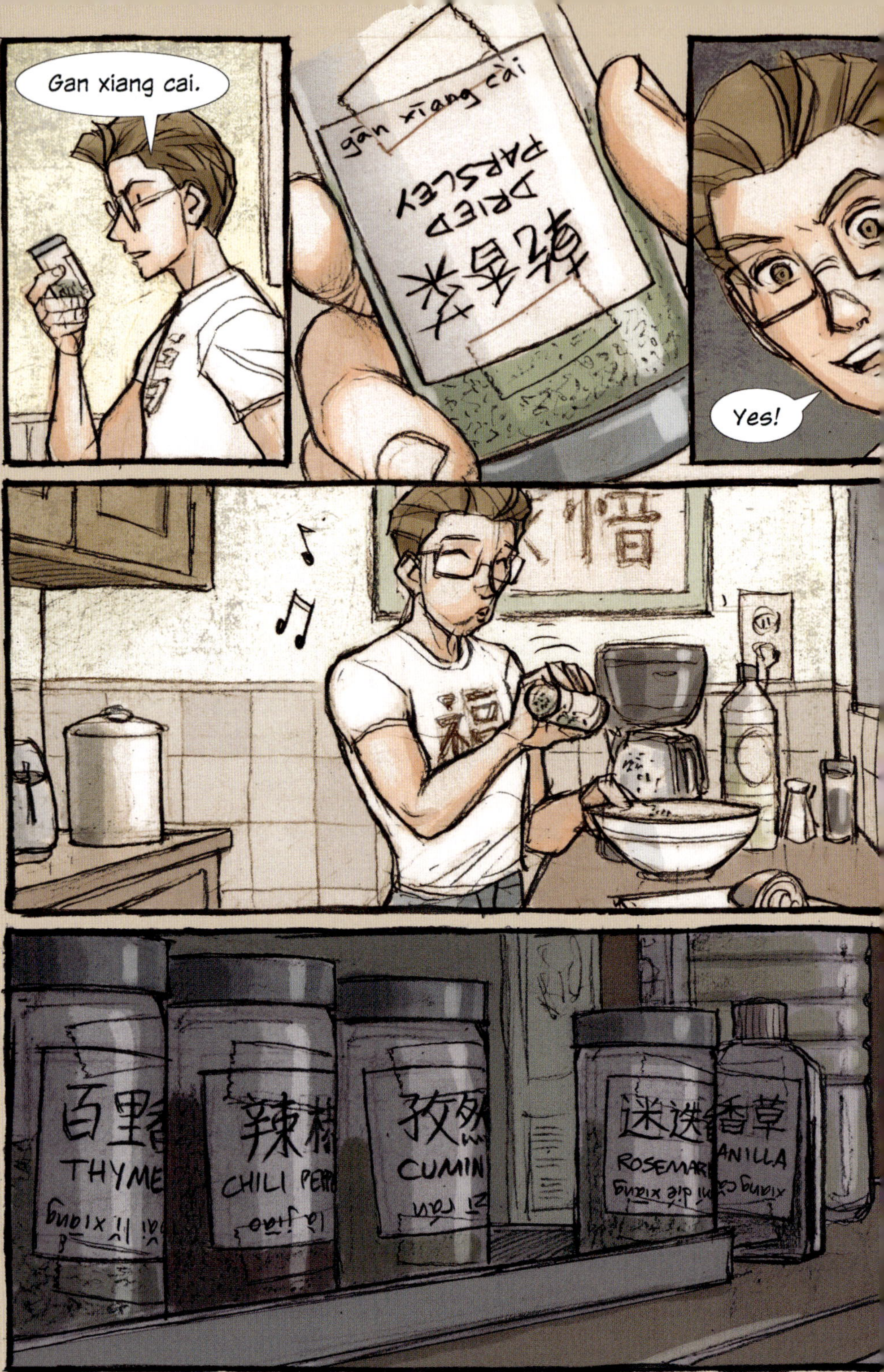
Gan xiang cai.
gān xiāng cài
DRIED PARSLEY
Yes!
百里香
THYME
孜然
CUMIN

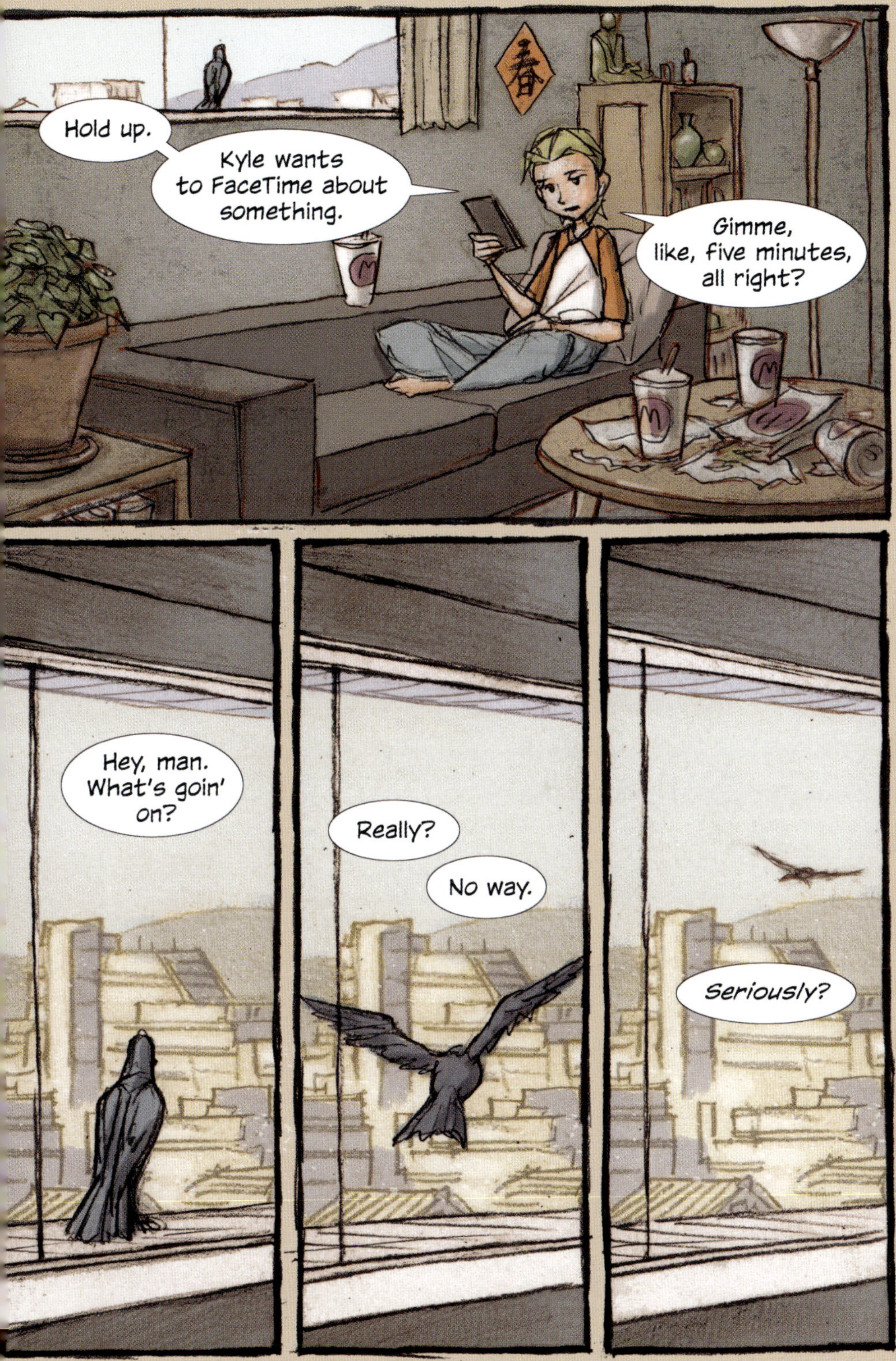
Hold up.
Kyle wants to FaceTime about something.
Gimme, like, five minutes, all right?
Hey, man. What's goin' on?
Really?
No way.
Seriously?

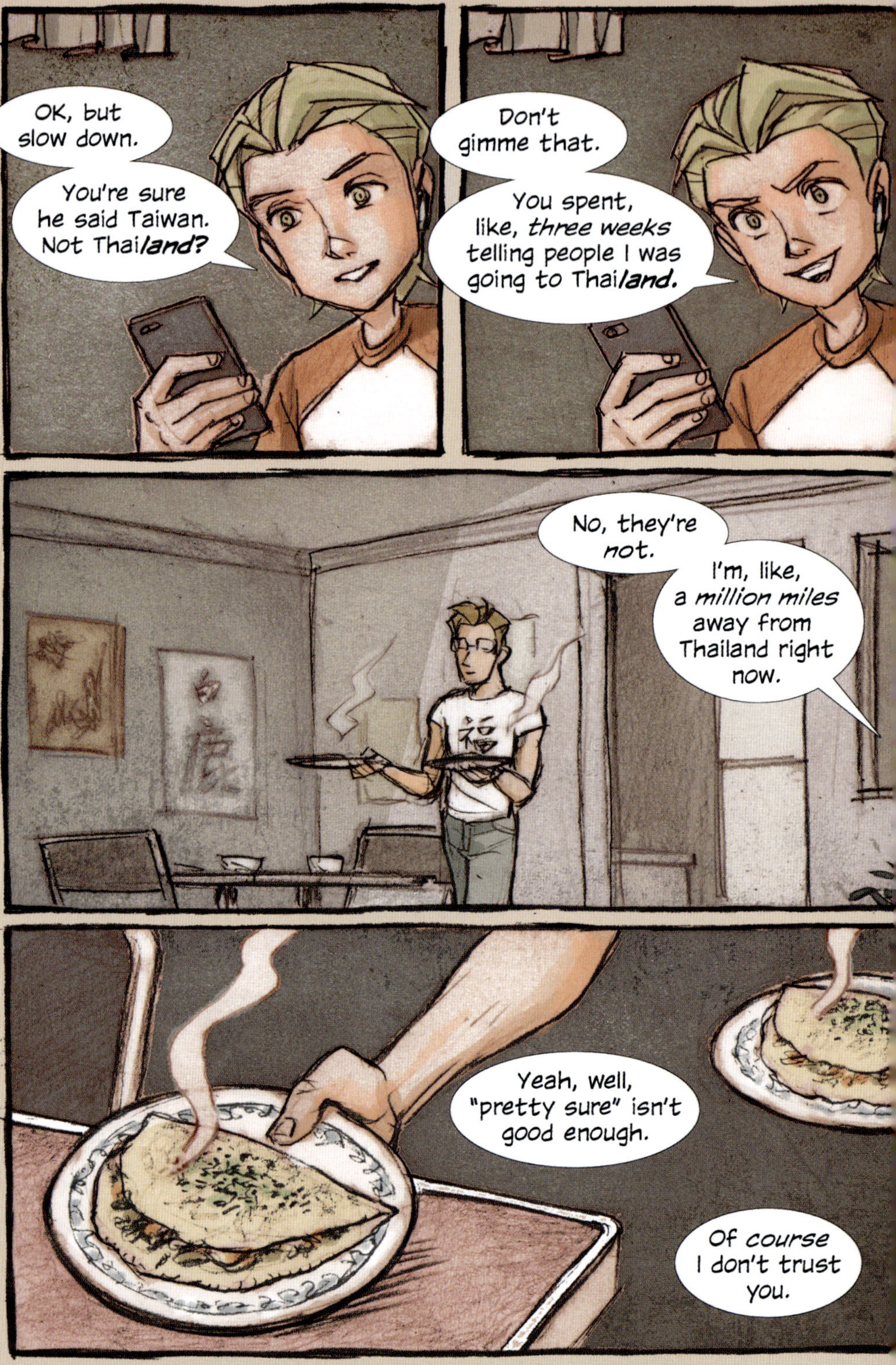
OK, but slow down.
You're sure he said Taiwan. Not Thai*land?*
Don't gimme that.
You spent, like, *three weeks* telling people I was going to Thai*land.*
No, they're *not.*
I'm, like, a *million miles* away from Thailand right now.
Yeah, well, "pretty sure" isn't good enough.
Of course I don't trust you.

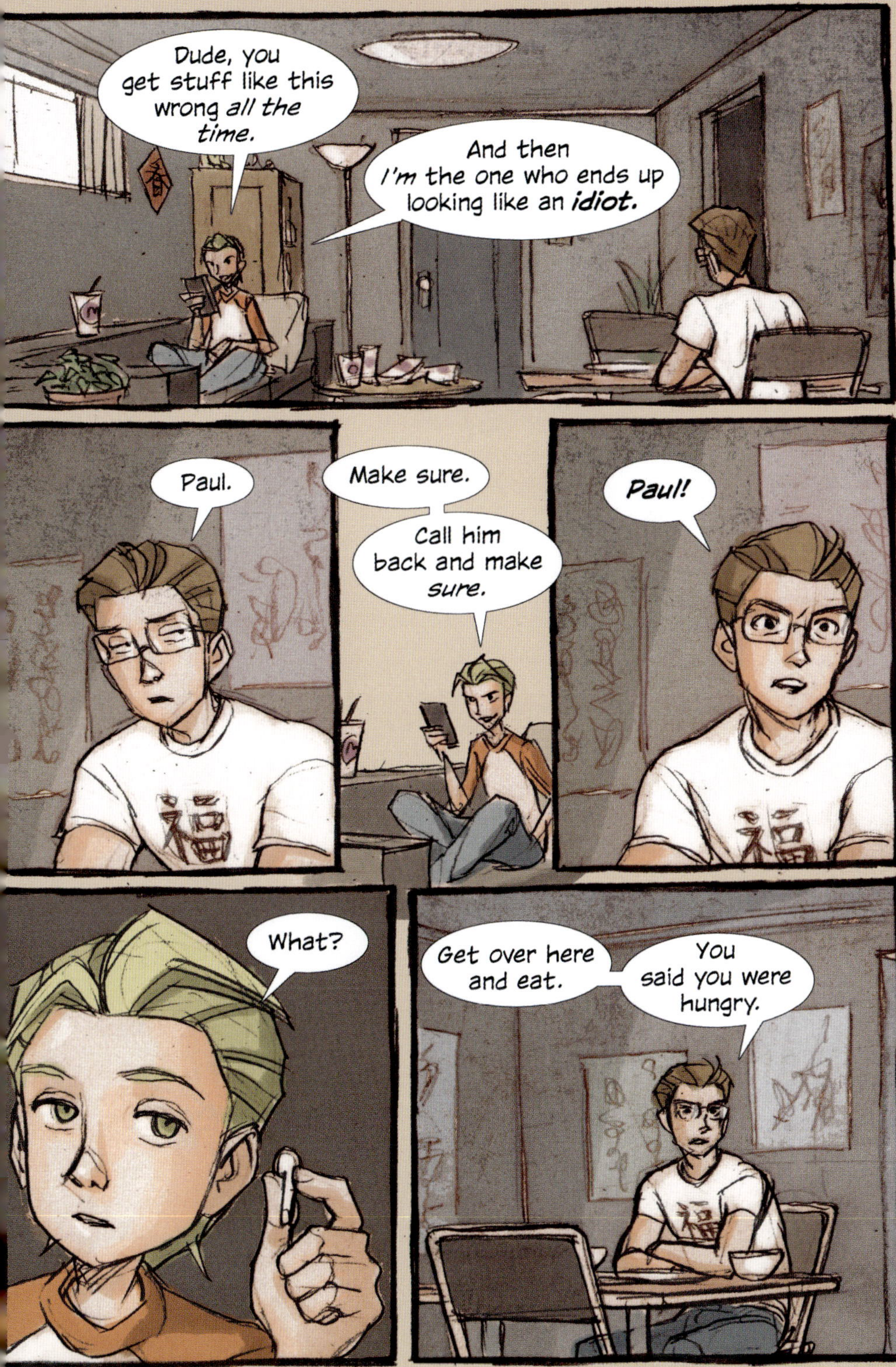
Dude, you get stuff like this wrong *all the time.*
And then *I'm* the one who ends up looking like an ***idiot.***
Paul.
Make sure.
Call him back and make *sure.*
Paul!
What?
Get over here and eat.
You said you were hungry.

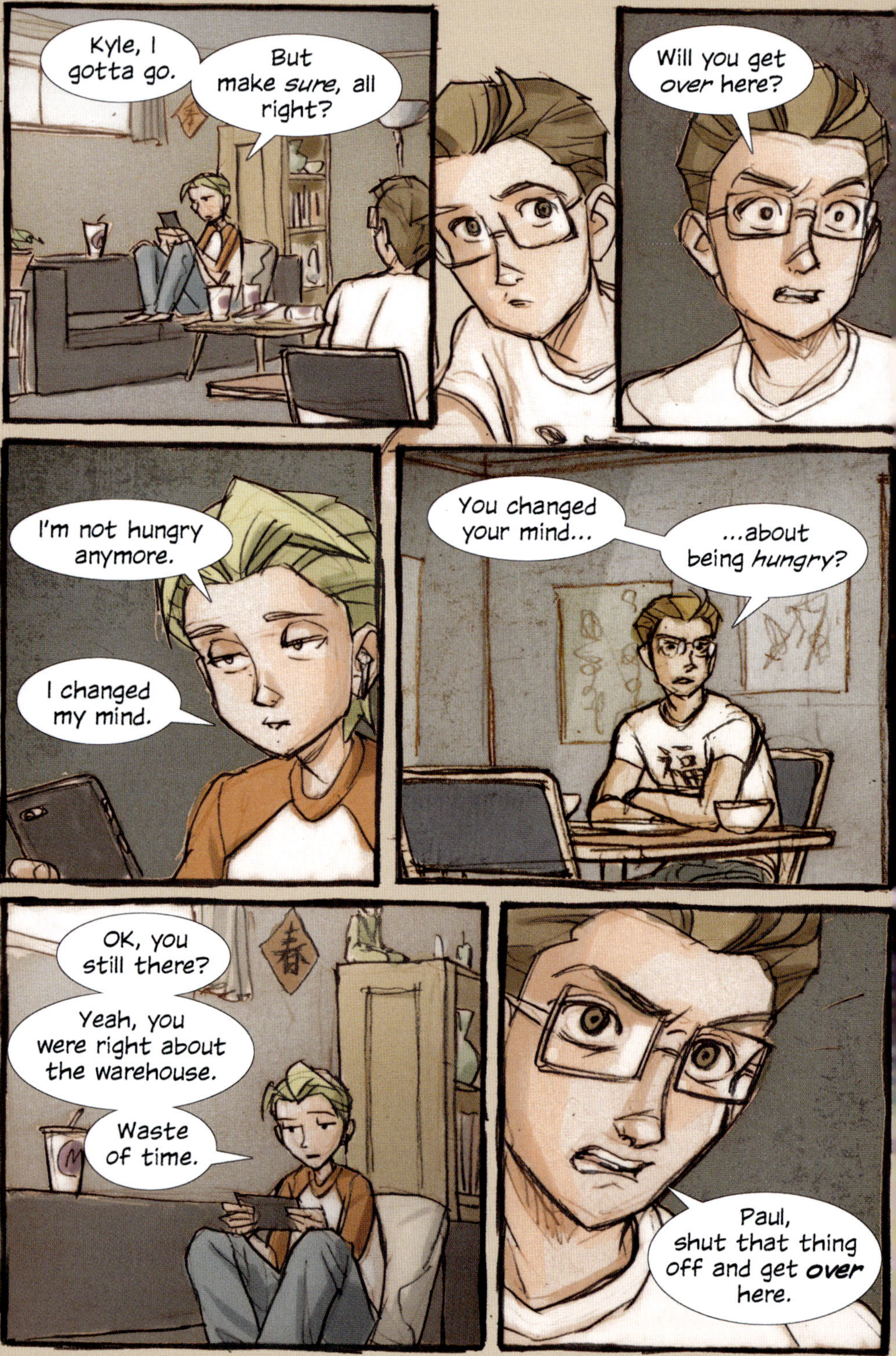
Kyle, I gotta go.
But make *sure*, all right?
Will you get *over* here?
I'm not hungry anymore.
I changed my mind.
You changed your mind...
...about being *hungry*?
OK, you still there?
Yeah, you were right about the warehouse.
Waste of time.
Paul, shut that thing off and get ***over*** here.

Dude, I gotta go.
All right.
Later.
SIGH
You've been here four days.
Four days.
And you've stayed on that couch almost the entire time.
Mm-hm.

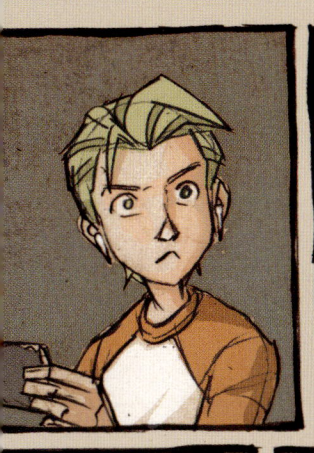

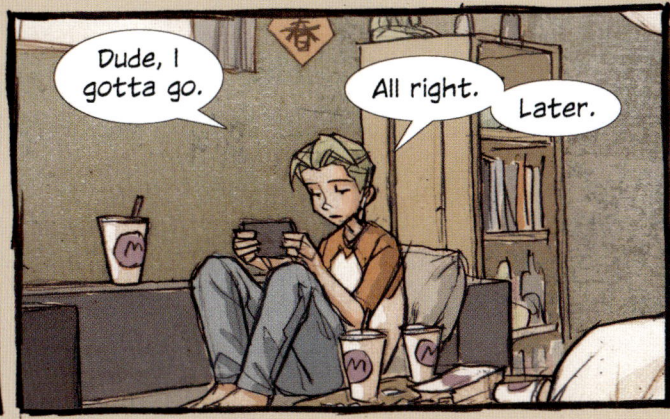

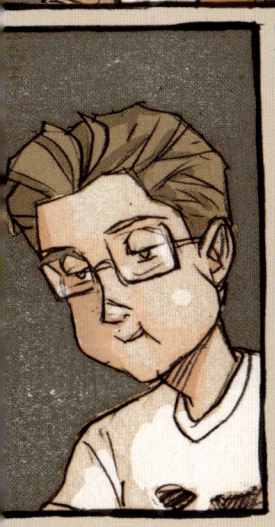

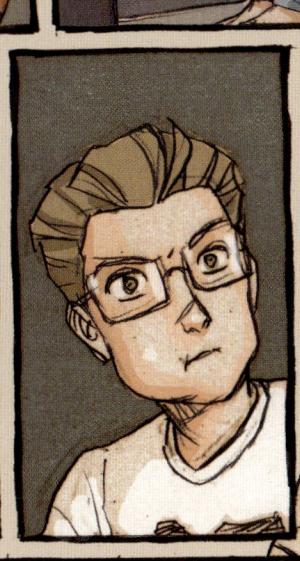

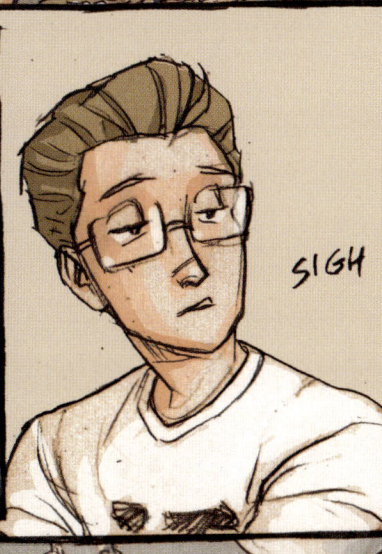

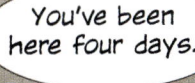

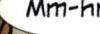

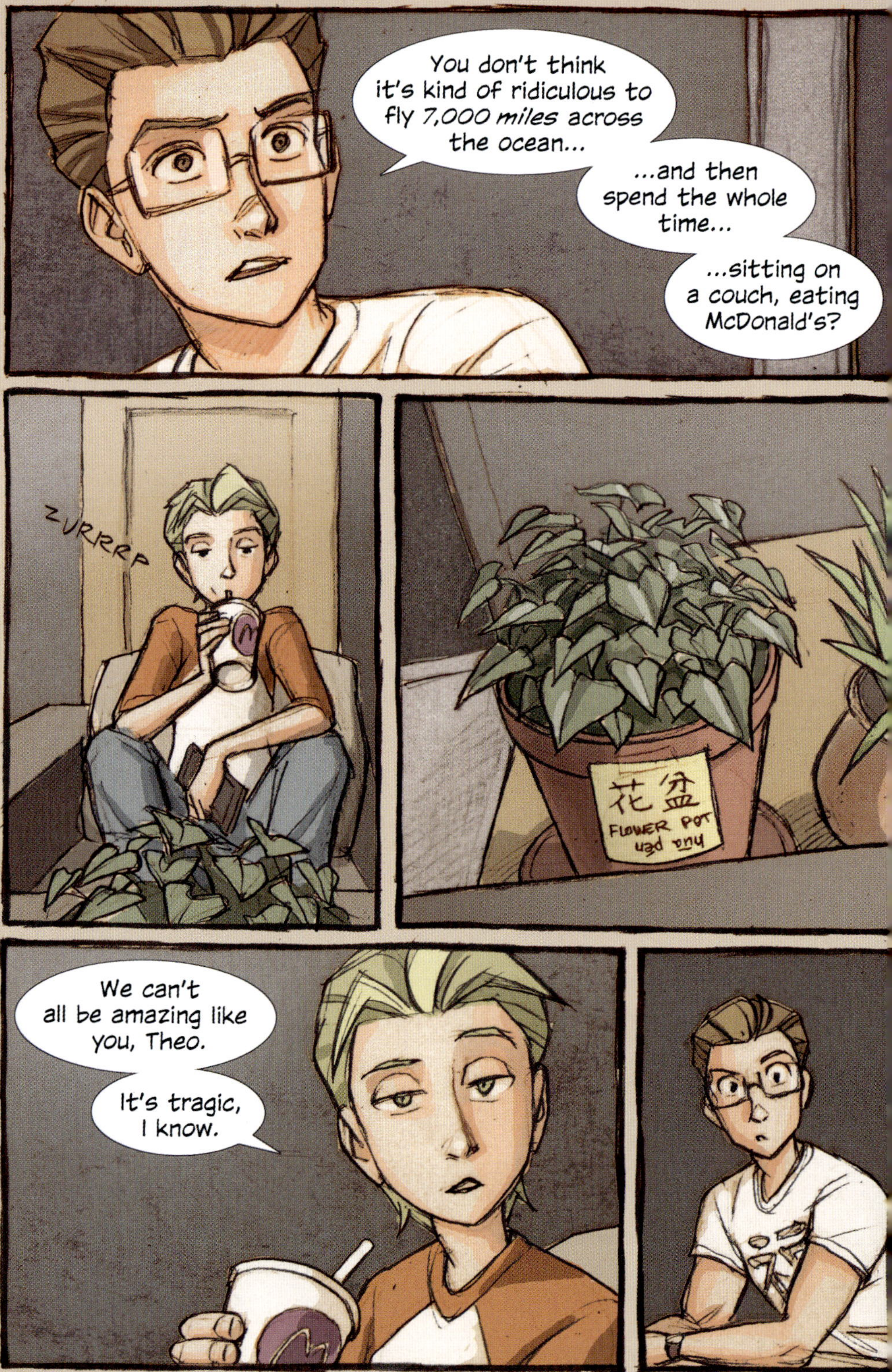
You don't think it's kind of ridiculous to fly *7,000 miles* across the ocean...
...and then spend the whole time...
...sitting on a couch, eating McDonald's?
ZURRRP
花盆
FLOWER POT
hua pen
We can't all be amazing like you, Theo.
It's tragic, I know.

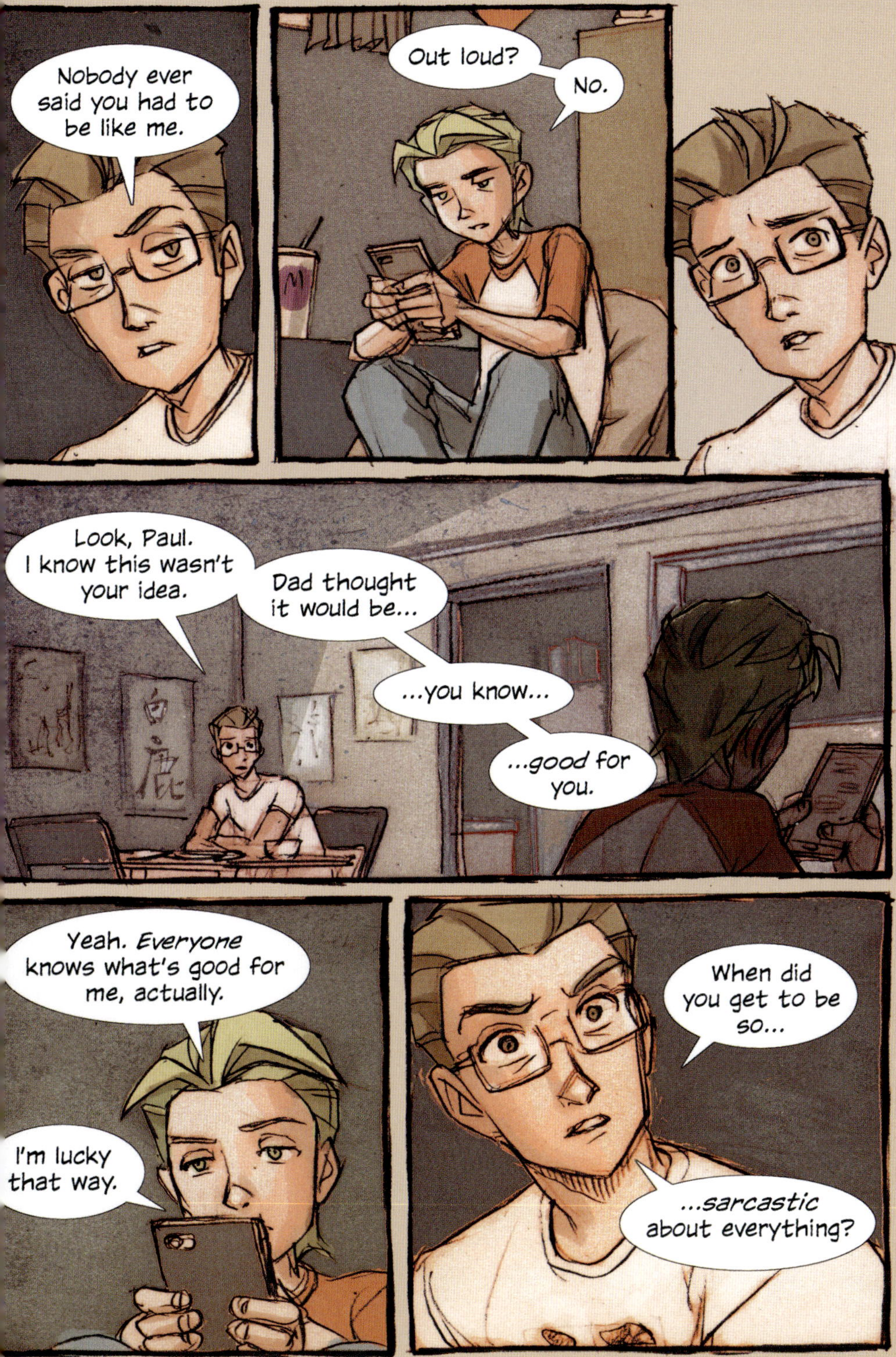
Nobody ever said you had to be like me.
Out loud?
No.
Look, Paul. I know this wasn't your idea.
Dad thought it would be...
...you know...
...good for you.
Yeah. *Everyone* knows what's good for me, actually.
I'm lucky that way.
When did you get to be so...
...*sarcastic* about everything?

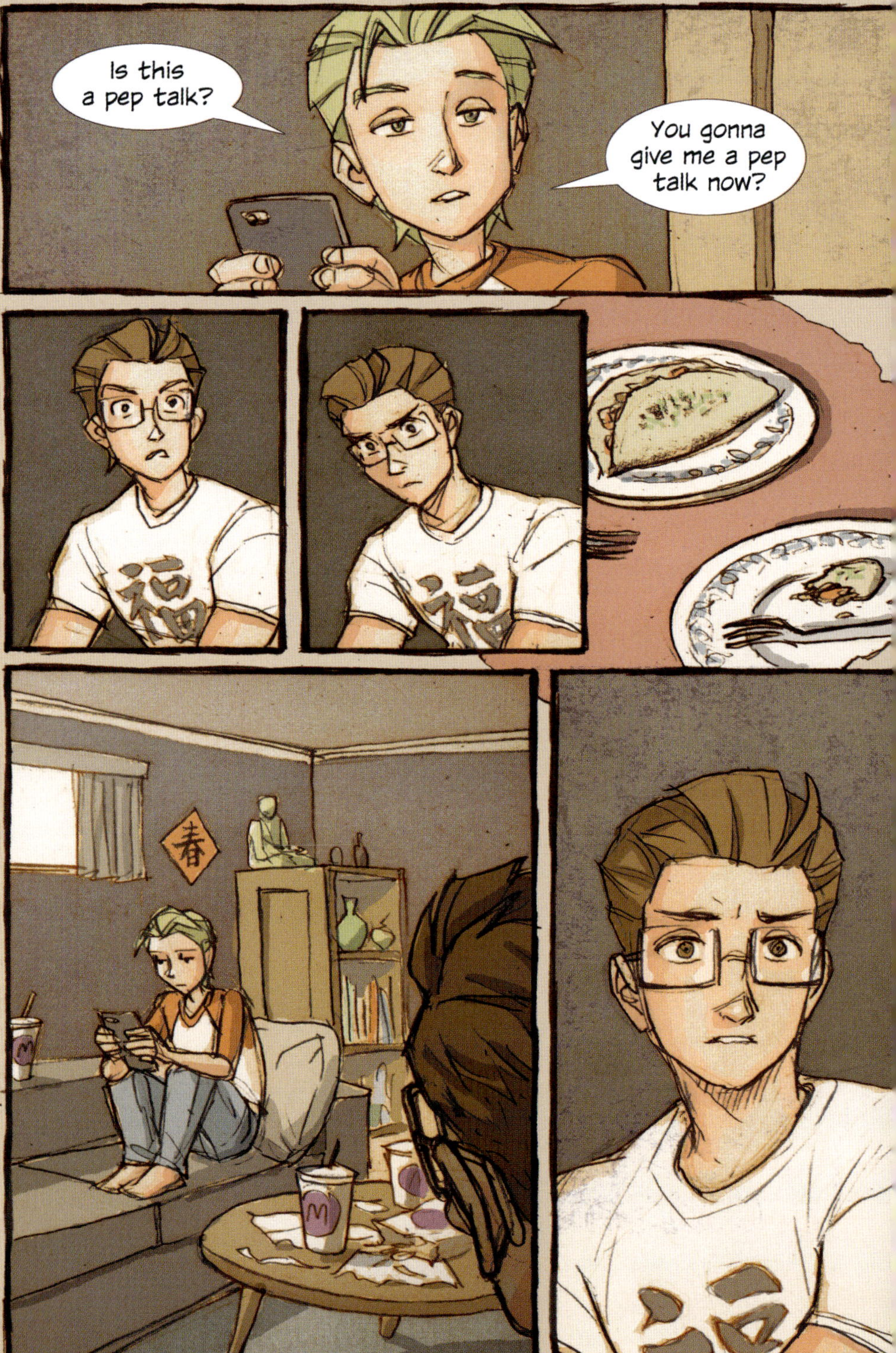
Is this a pep talk?
You gonna give me a pep talk now?
福
春
福

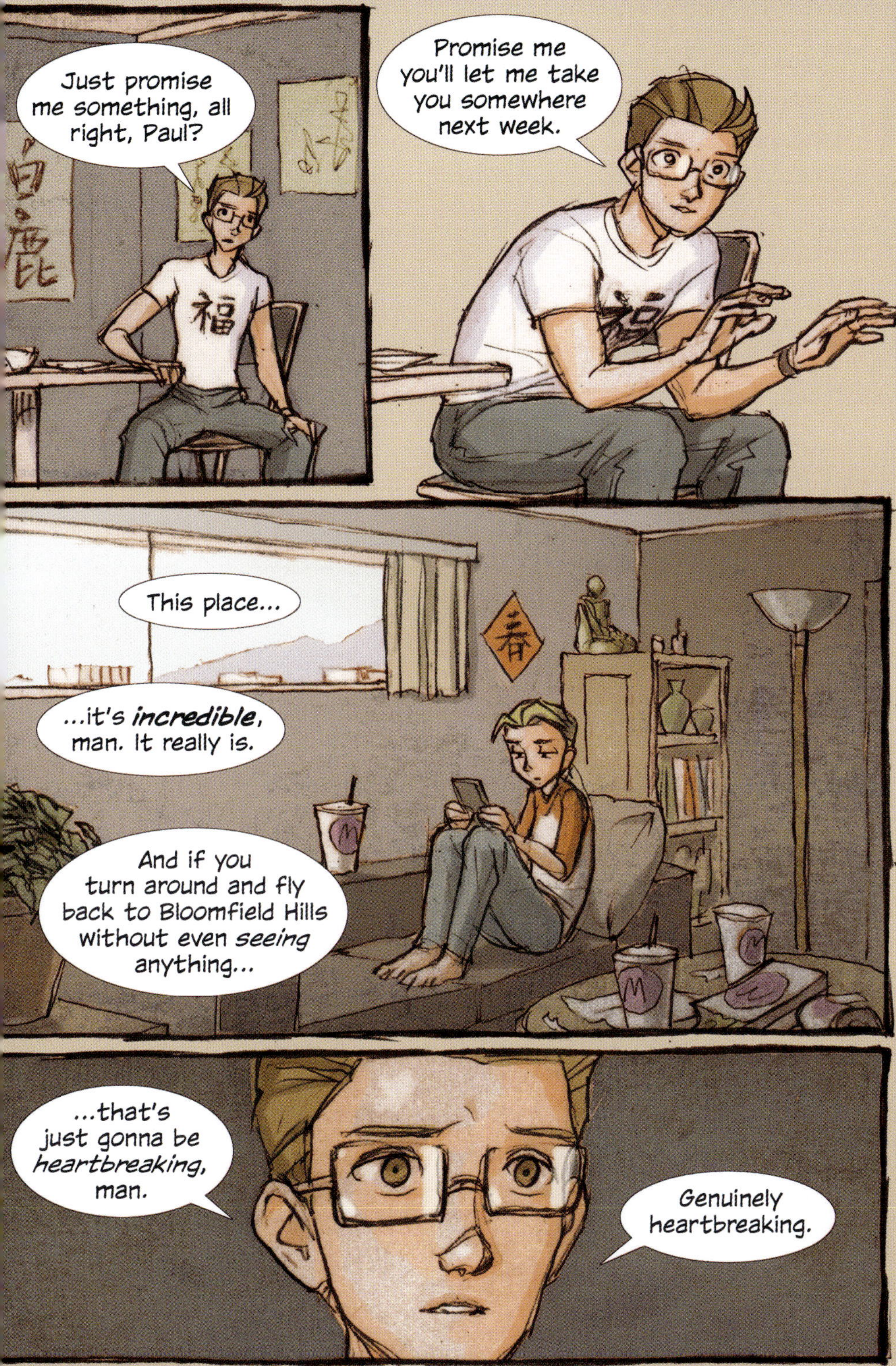
Just promise me something, all right, Paul?
Promise me you'll let me take you somewhere next week.
This place...
...it's *incredible*, man. It really is.
And if you turn around and fly back to Bloomfield Hills without even *seeing* anything...
...that's just gonna be *heartbreaking*, man.
Genuinely heartbreaking.

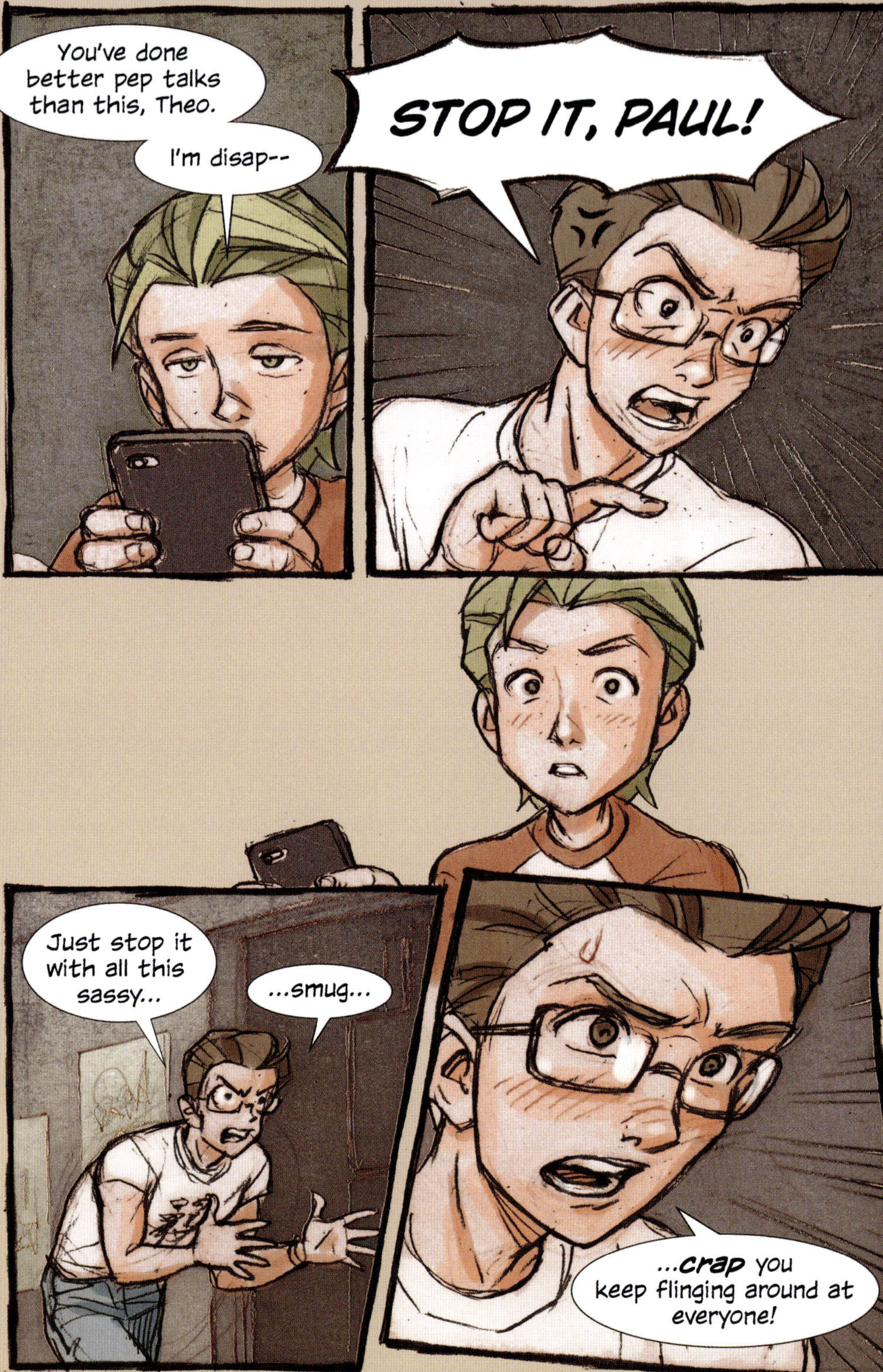
You've done better pep talks than this, Theo.
I'm disap--
STOP IT, PAUL!
Just stop it with all this sassy...
...smug...
...crap you keep flinging around at everyone!

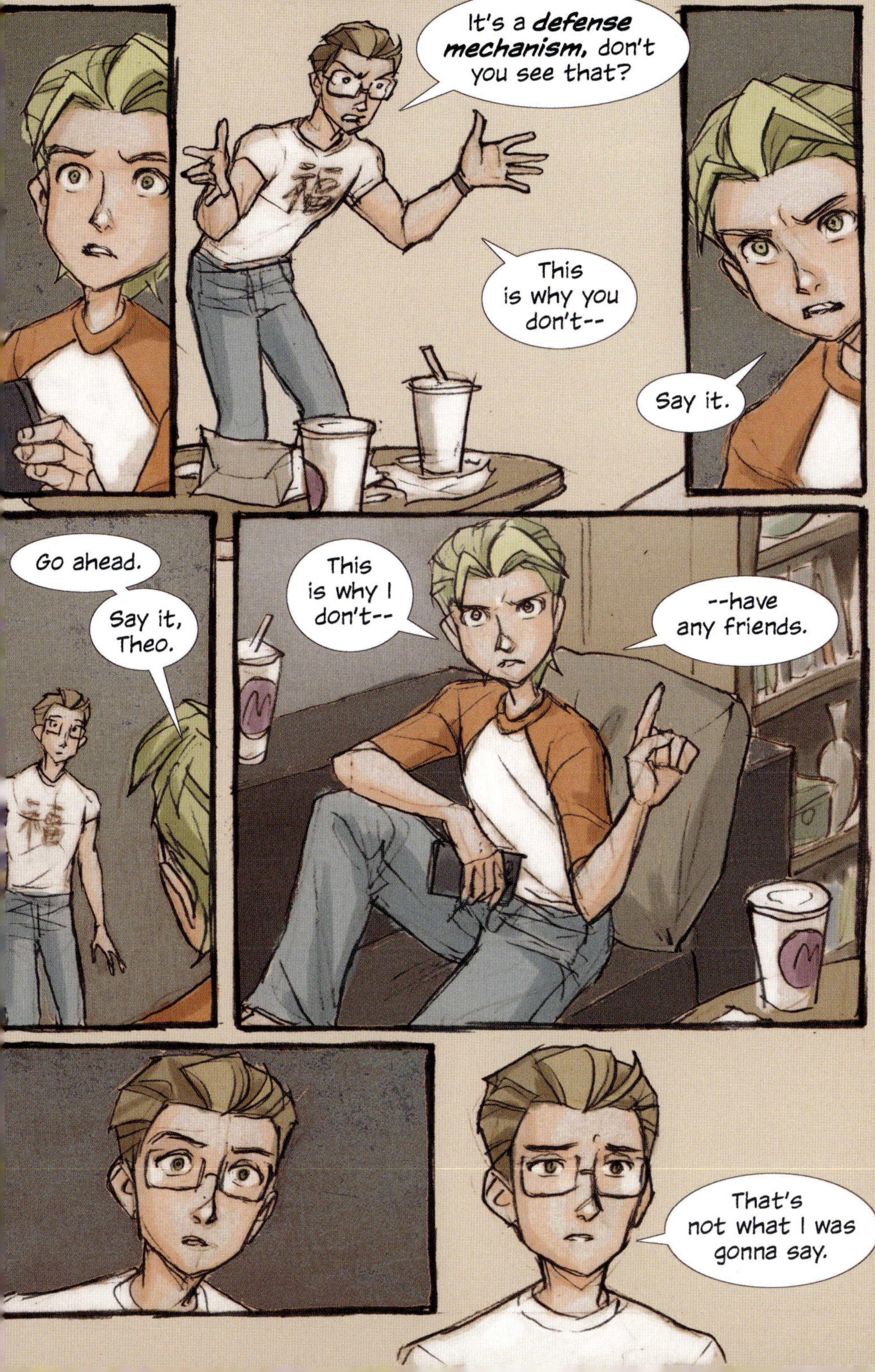
It's a **defense mechanism,** don't you see that?
This is why you don't--
Say it.
Go ahead.
Say it, Theo.
This is why I don't--
--have any friends.
That's not what I was gonna say.

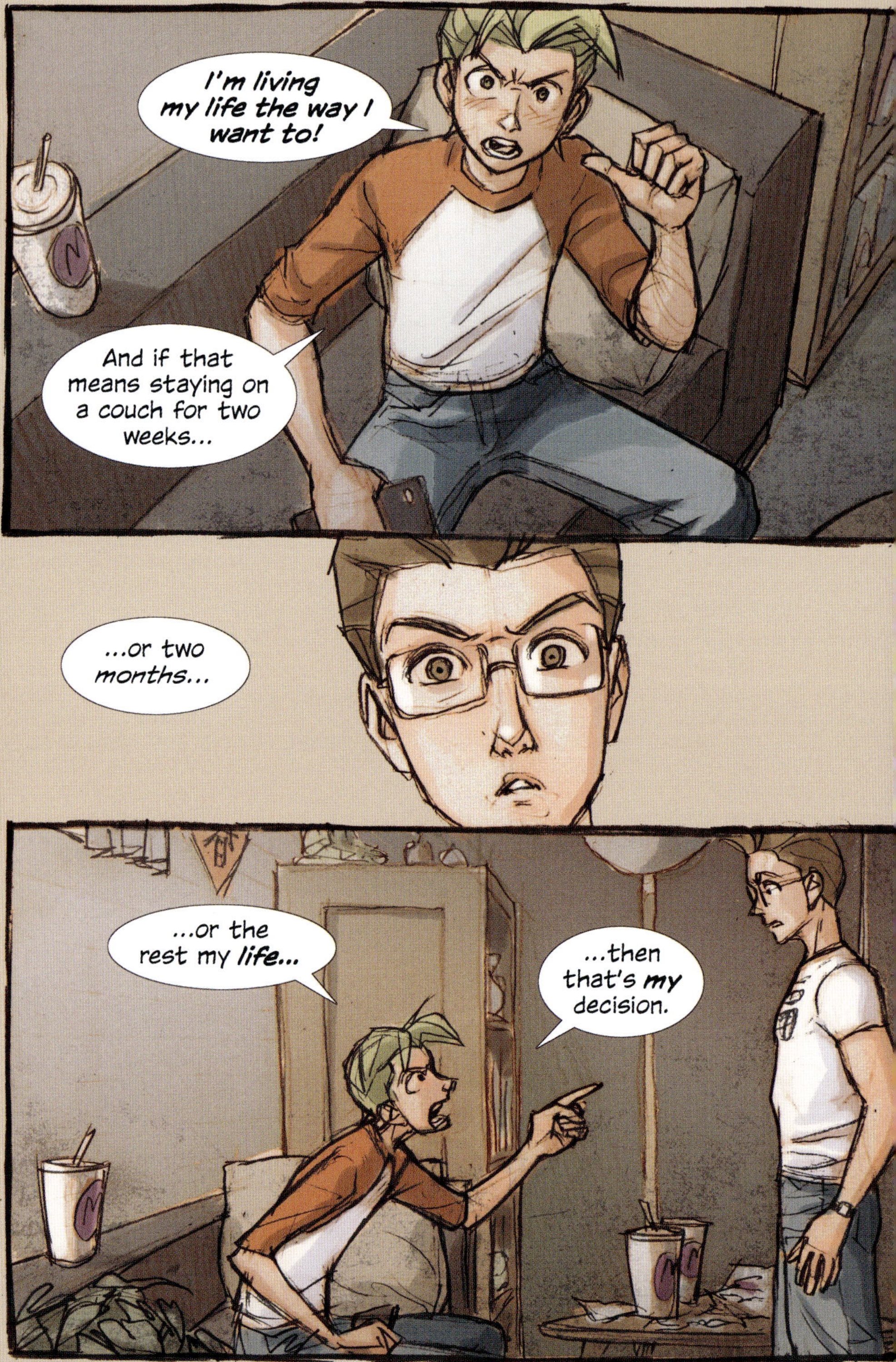
I'm living my life the way I want to!
And if that means staying on a couch for two weeks...
...or two *months*...
...or the rest my *life*...
...then that's *my* decision.

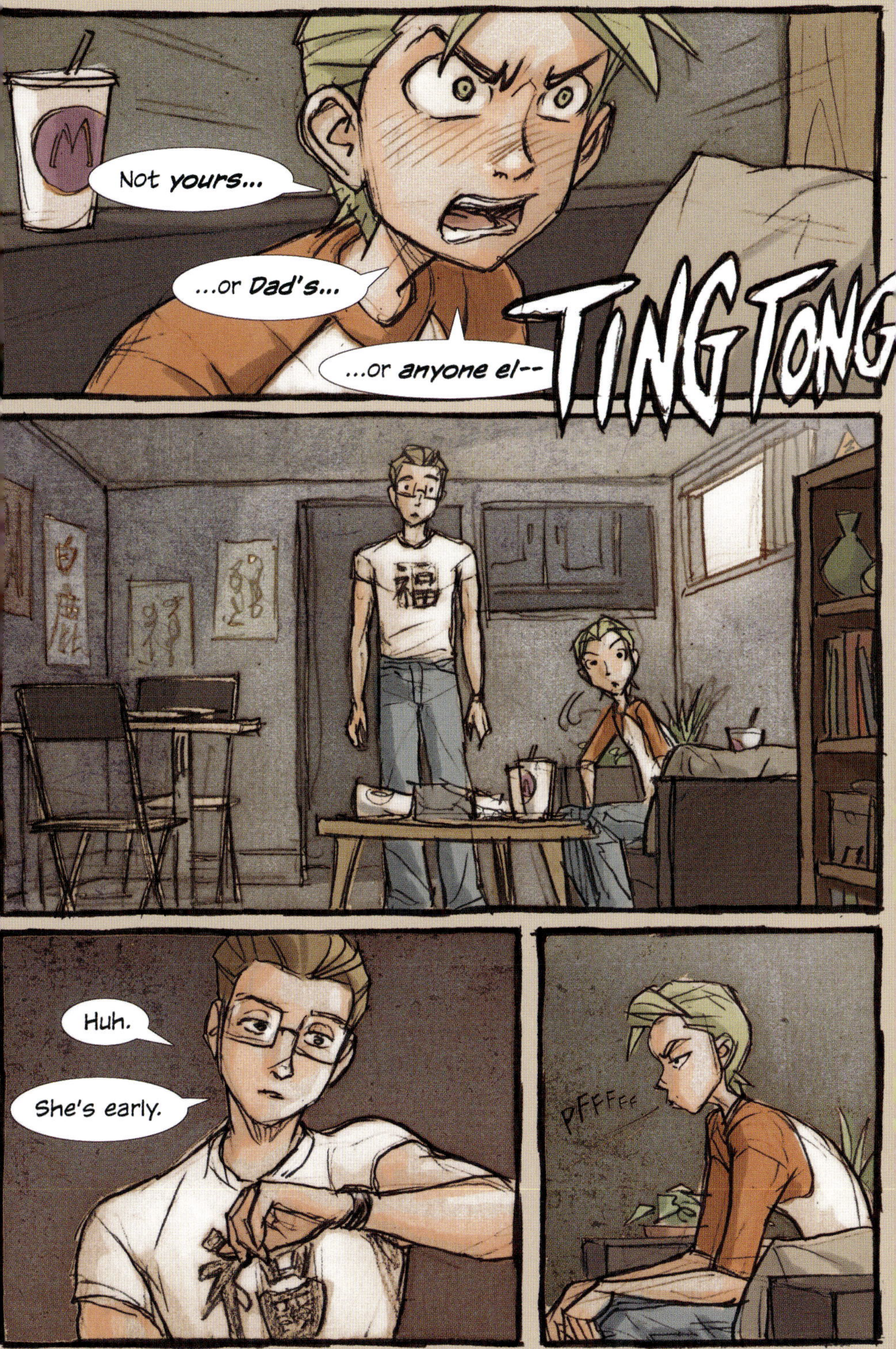
Not yours...
...or Dad's...
...or anyone el--
TING TONG
Huh.
She's early.
PFFFFF

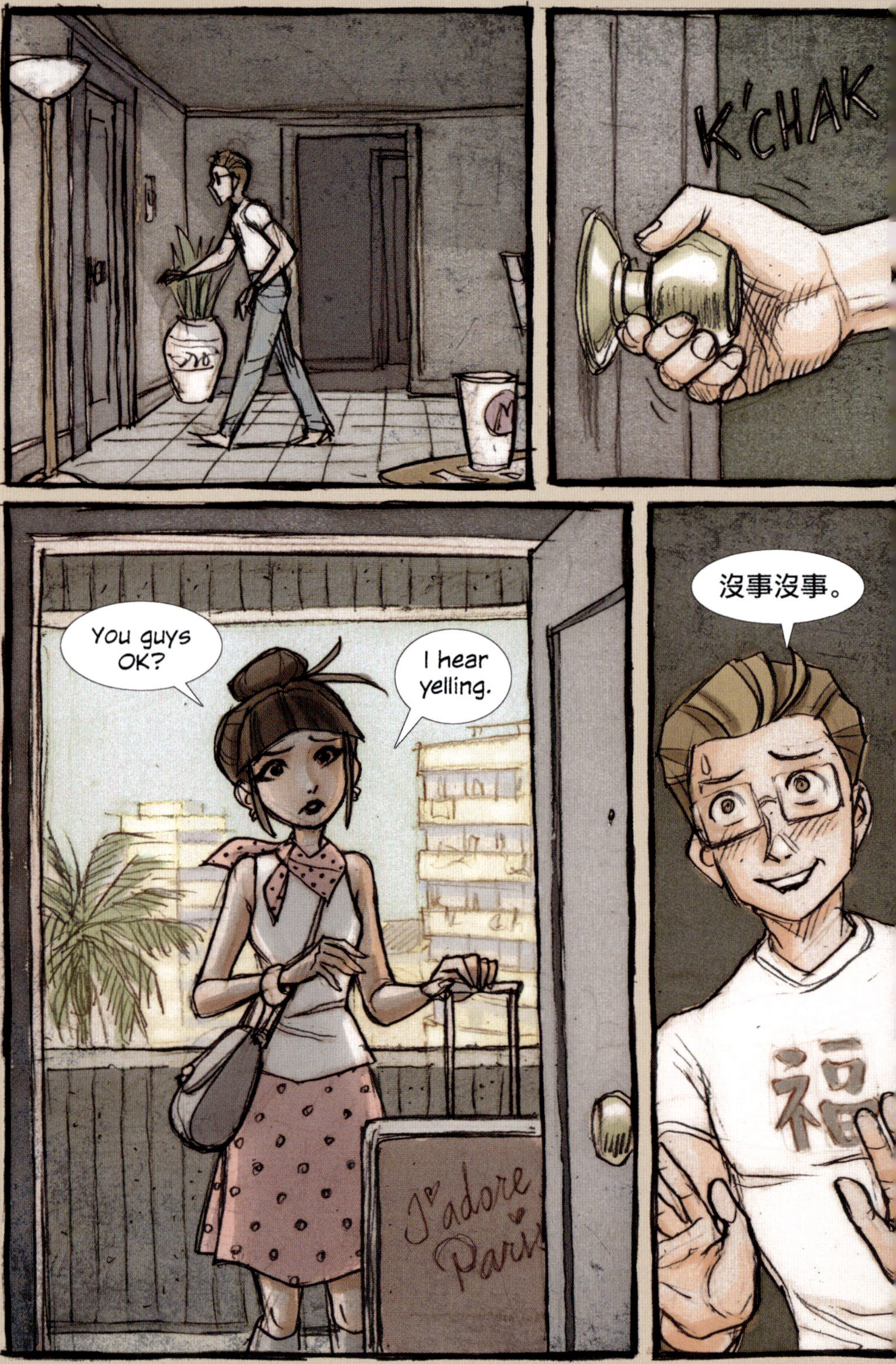
K'CHAK
You guys OK?
I hear yelling.
沒事沒事。
J'adore Paris

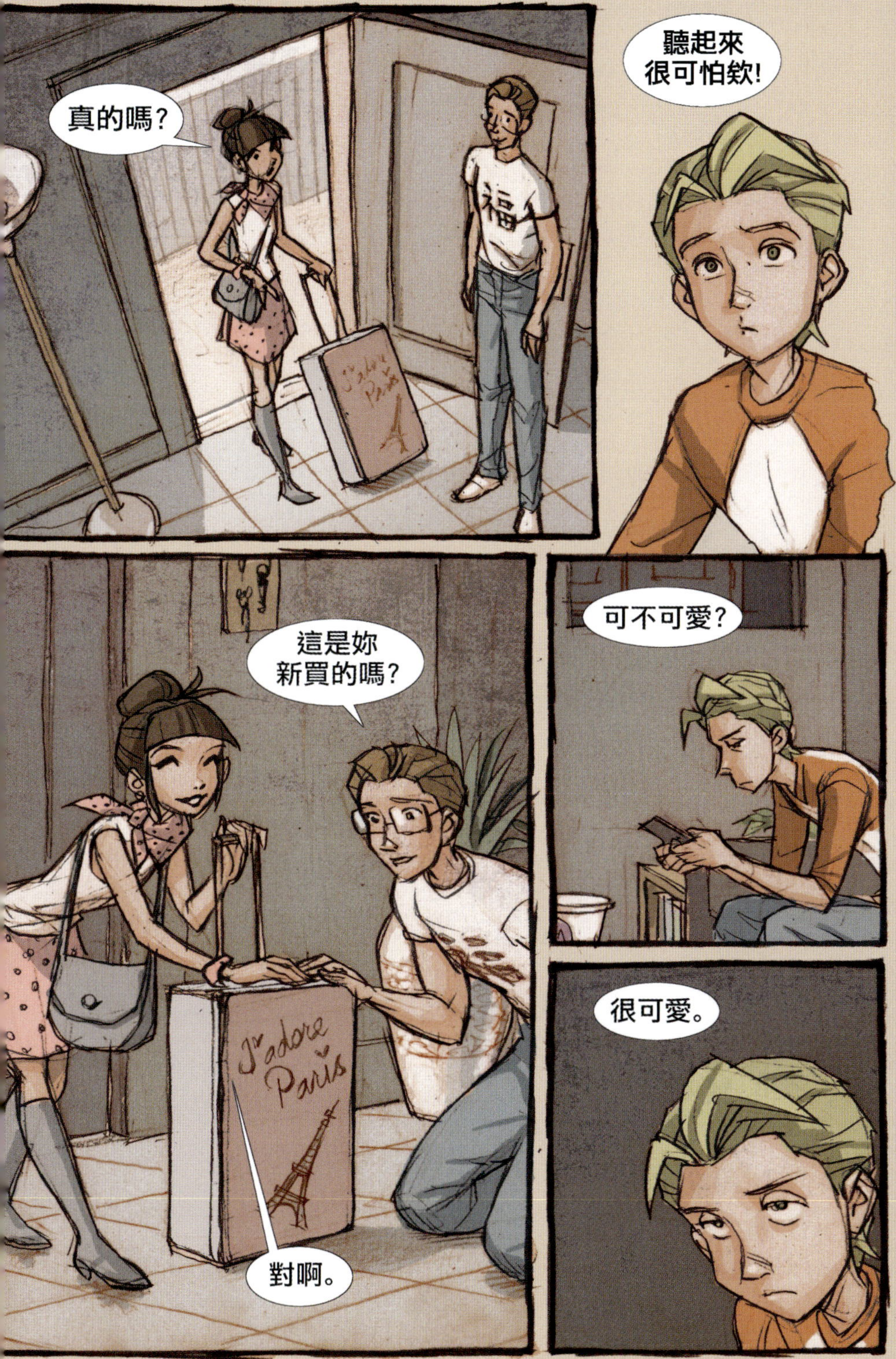
真的嗎?
聽起來
很可怕欸!
這是妳
新買的嗎?
對啊。
J'adore Paris
可不可愛?
很可愛。

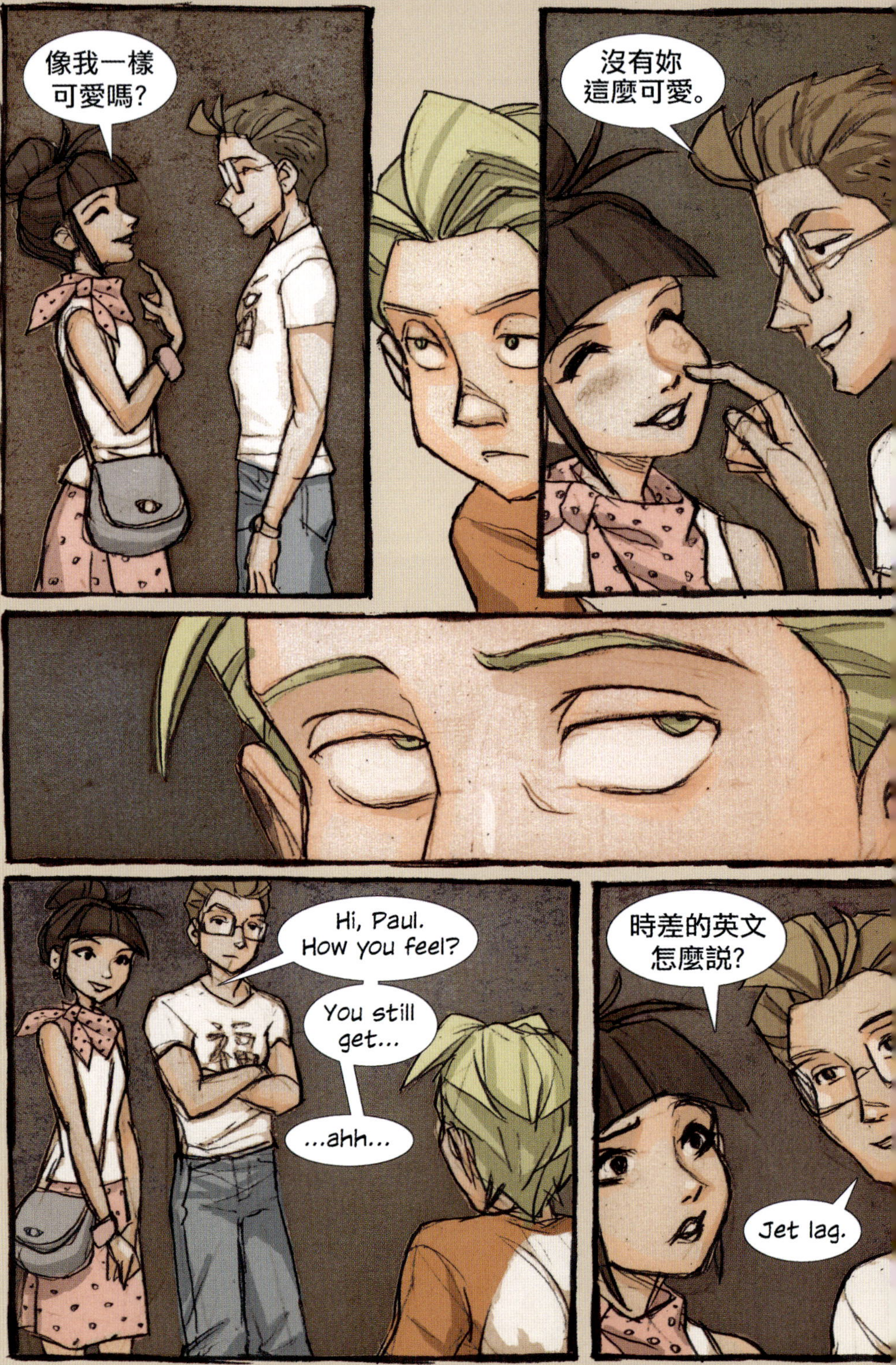
像我一樣
可愛嗎?
沒有妳
這麼可愛。
Hi, Paul.
How you feel?
You still
get...
...ahh...
時差的英文
怎麼說?
Jet lag.

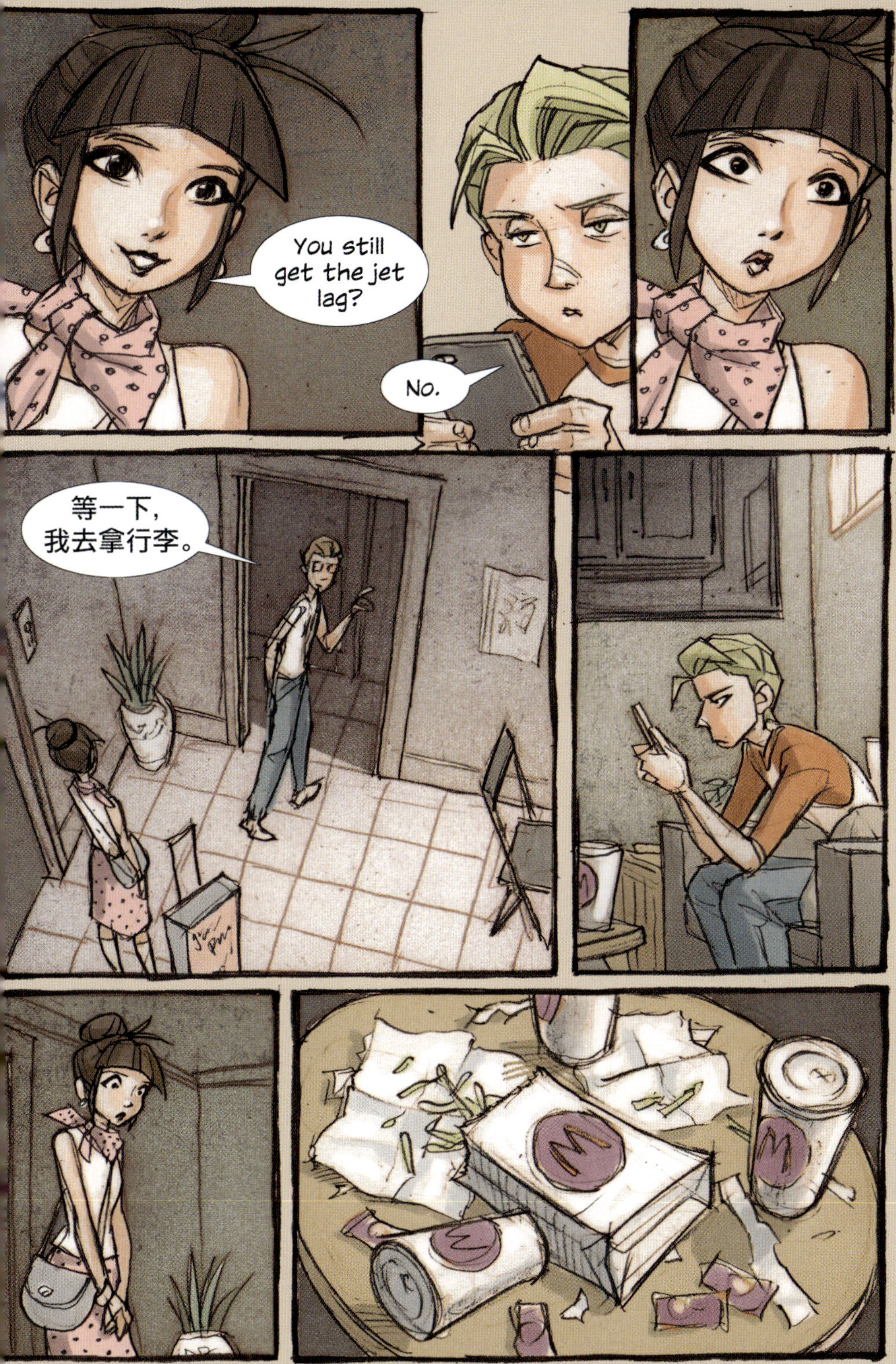
You still get the jet lag?
No.
等一下，我去拿行李。

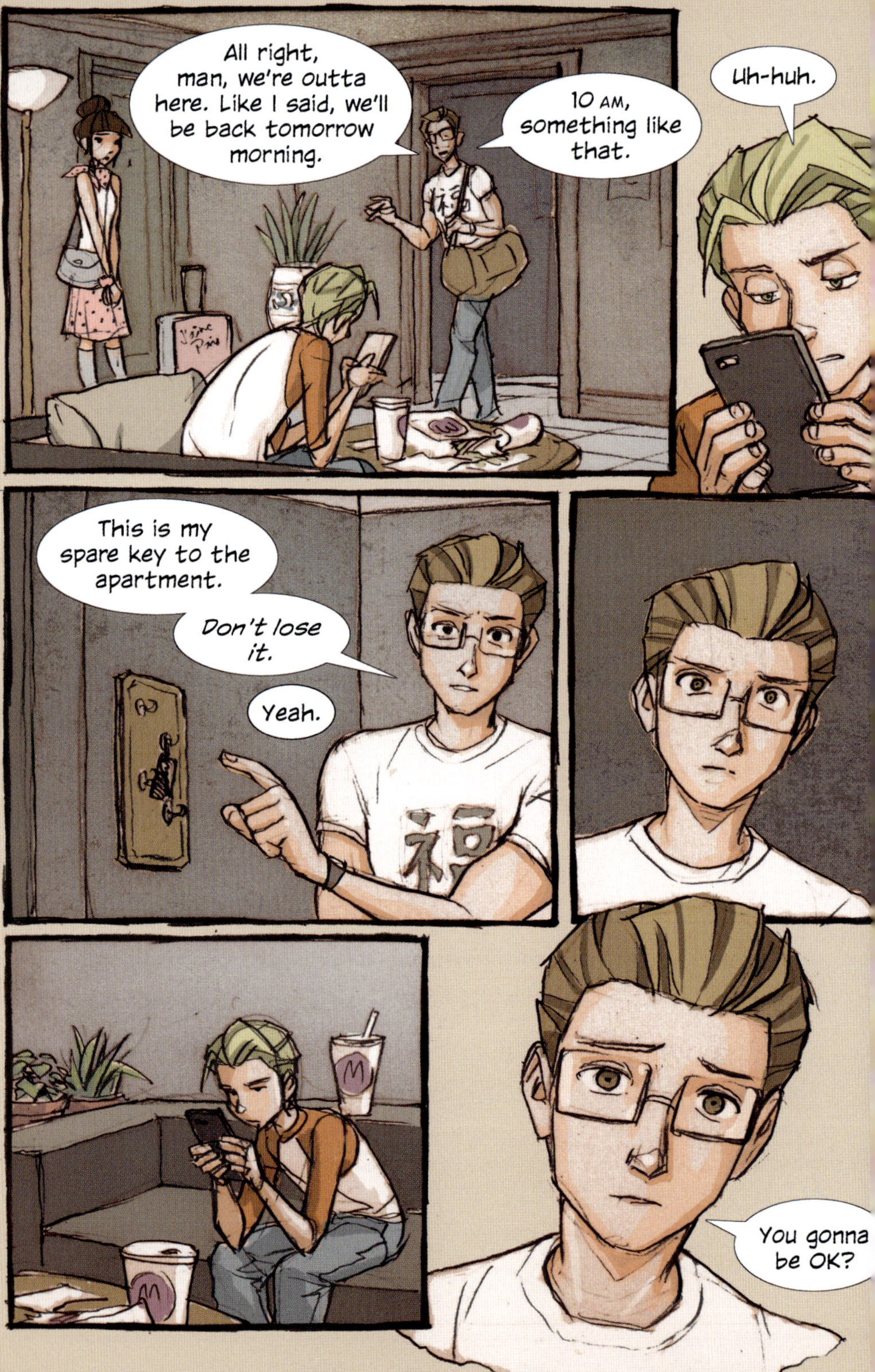
All right, man, we're outta here. Like I said, we'll be back tomorrow morning.
10 AM, something like that.
Uh-huh.
This is my spare key to the apartment.
Don't lose it.
Yeah.
You gonna be OK?

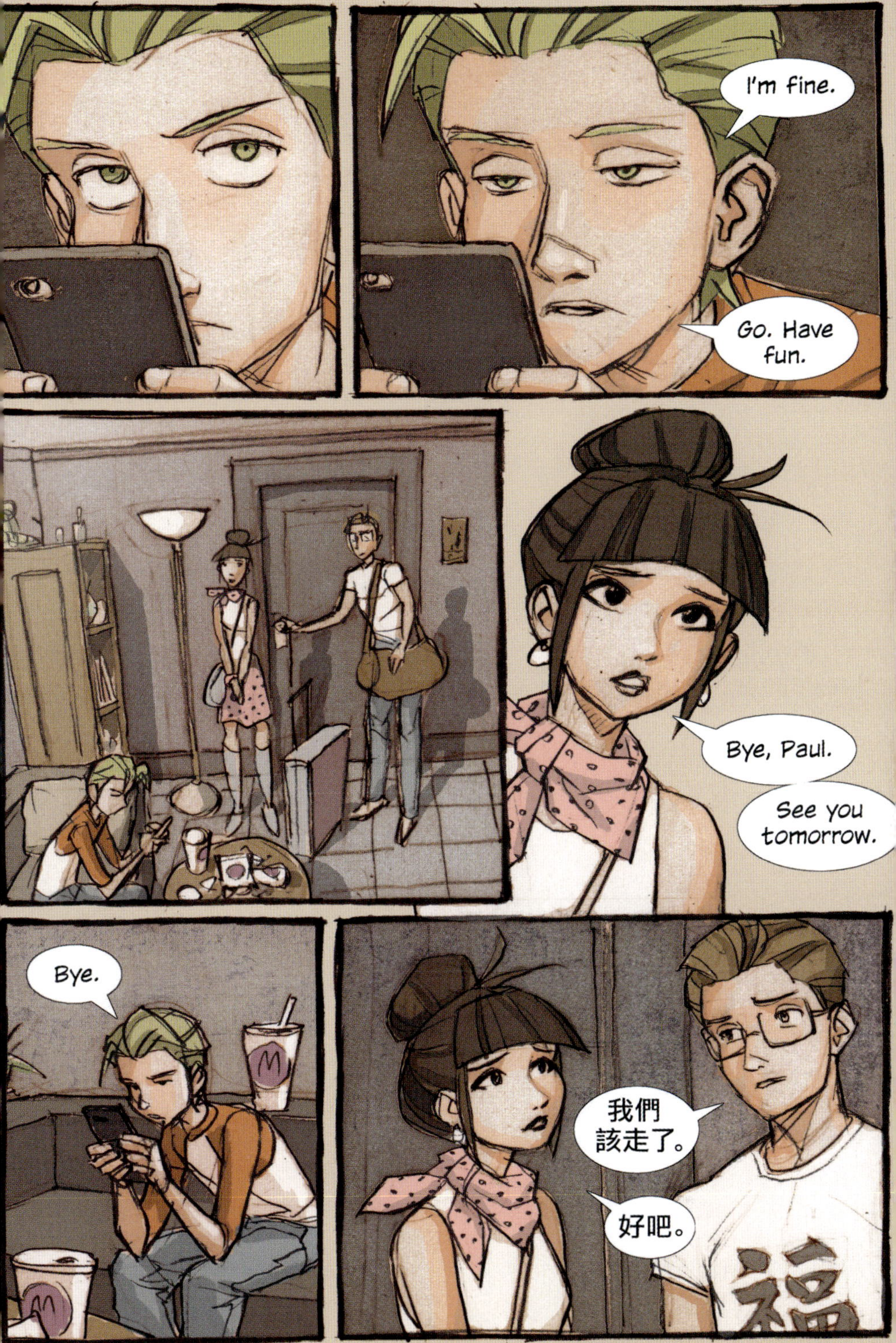
I'm fine.
Go. Have fun.
Bye, Paul.
See you tomorrow.
Bye.
我們該走了。
好吧。

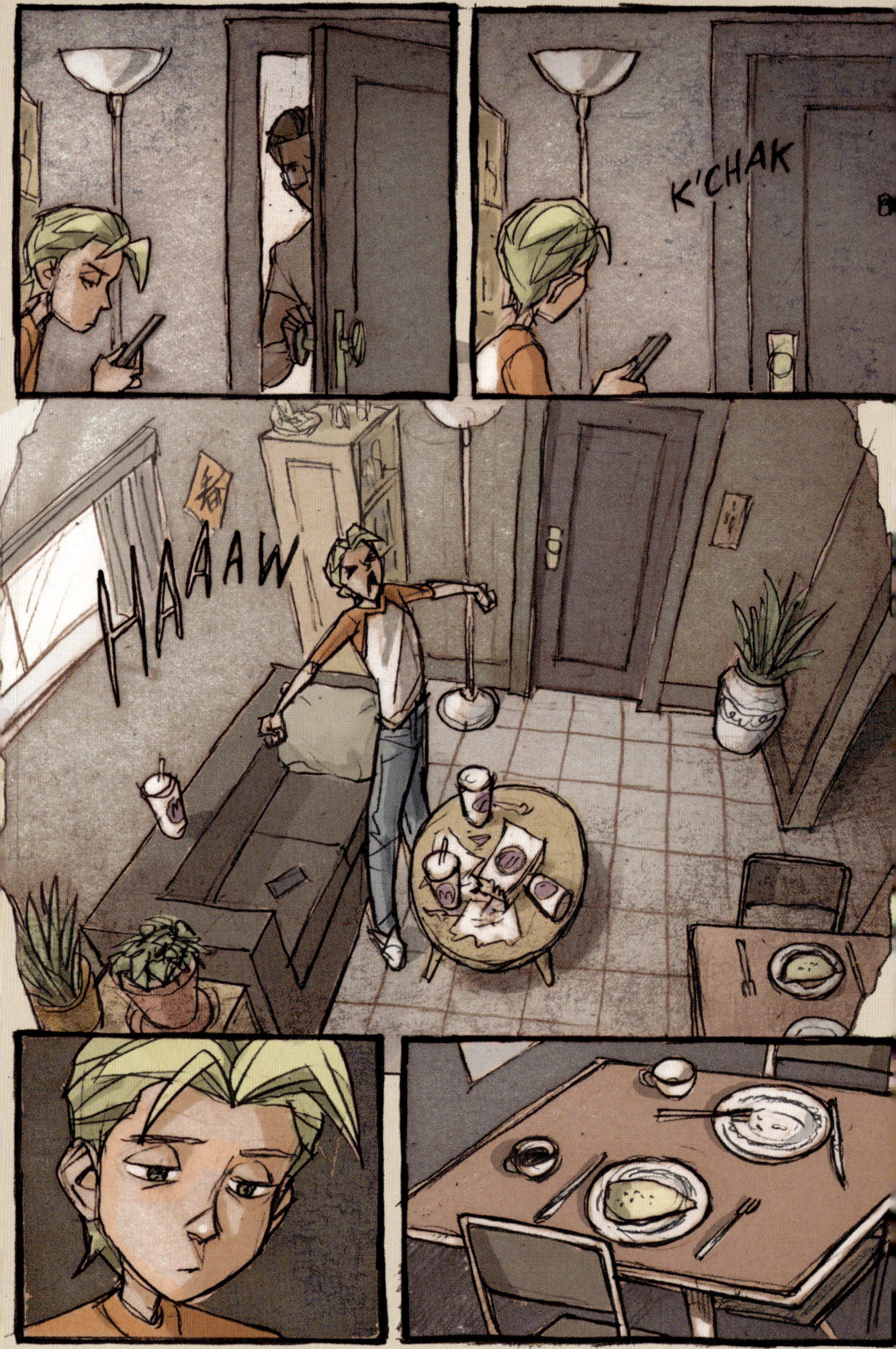
K'CHAK
HAAAW

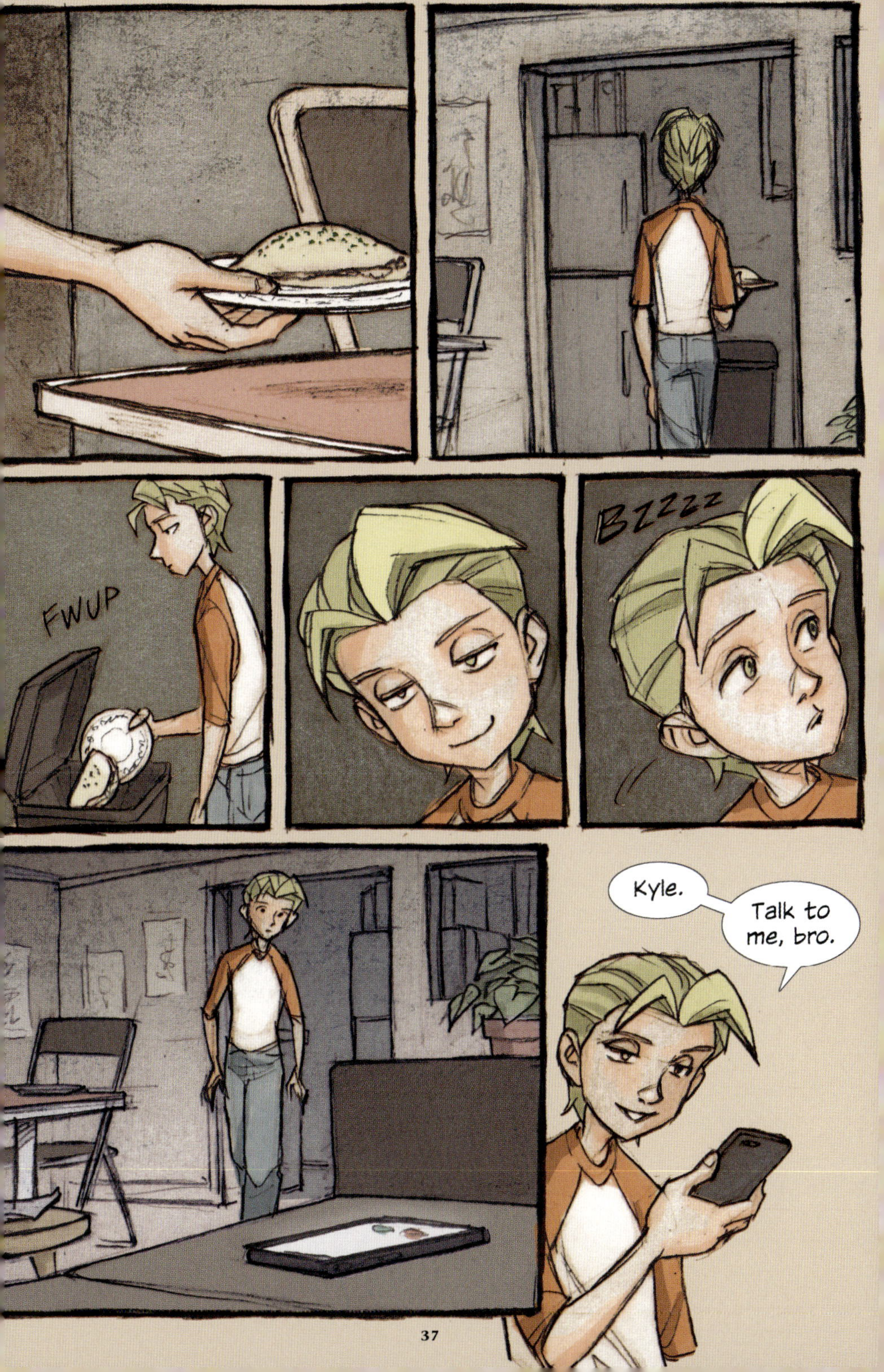
FWUP
BZZZZ
Kyle.
Talk to me, bro.

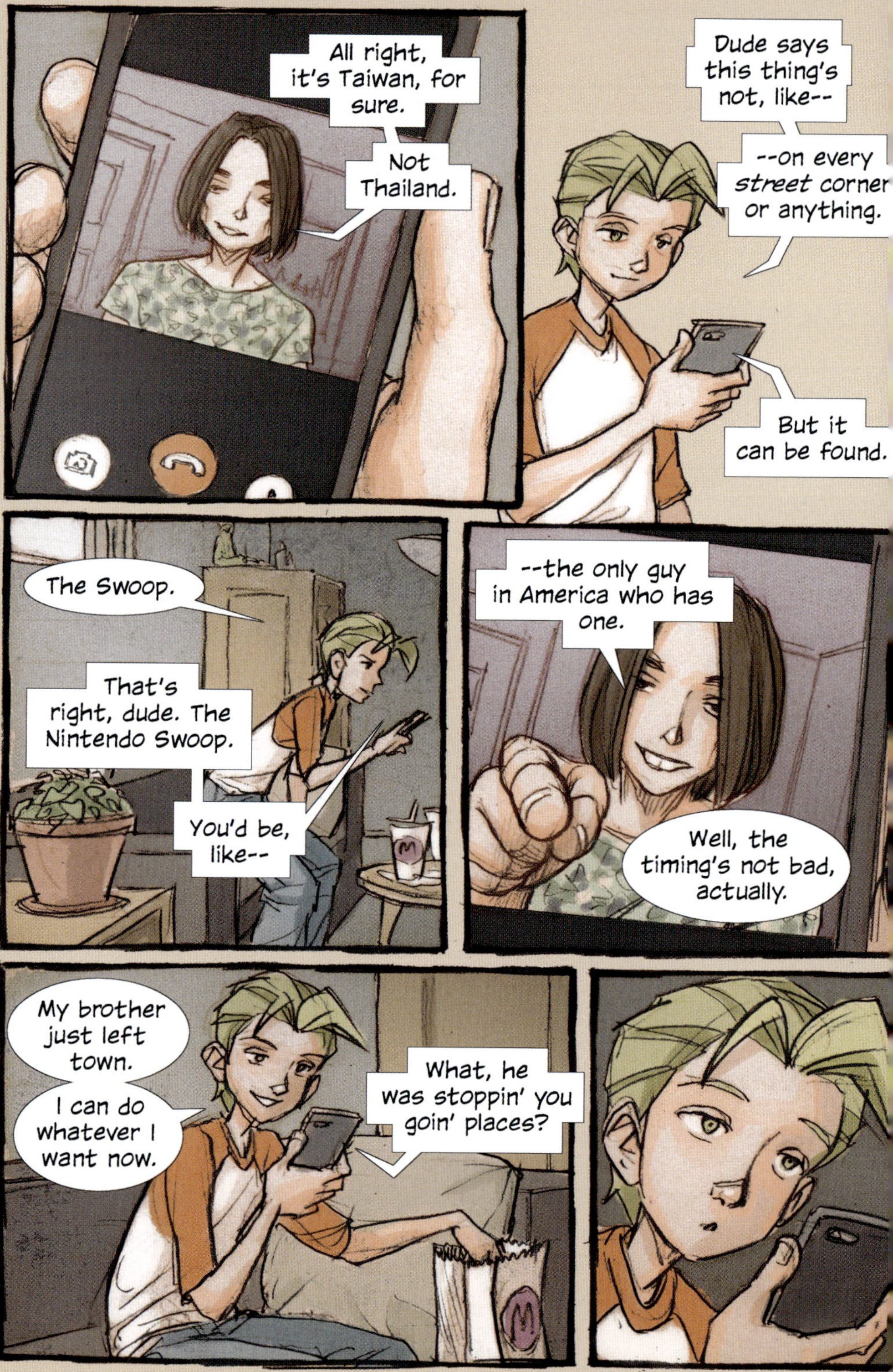

All right, it's Taiwan, for sure.
Not Thailand.
Dude says this thing's not, like--
--on every *street* corner or anything.
But it can be found.
The Swoop.
That's right, dude. The Nintendo Swoop.
You'd be, like--
--the only guy in America who has one.
Well, the timing's not bad, actually.
My brother just left town.
I can do whatever I want now.
What, he was stoppin' you goin' places?

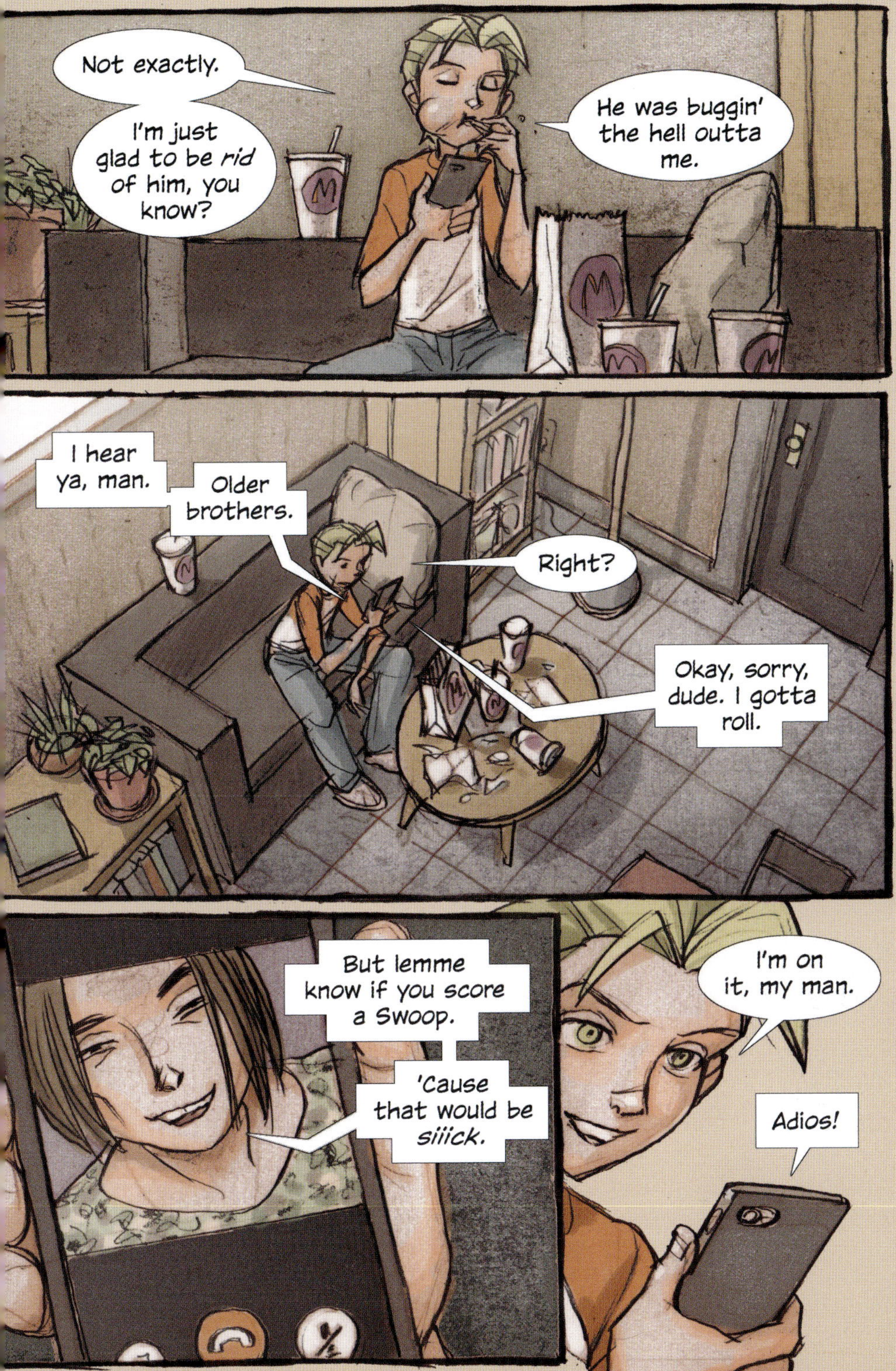
Not exactly.
I'm just glad to be *rid* of him, you know?
He was buggin' the hell outta me.
I hear ya, man.
Older brothers.
Right?
Okay, sorry, dude. I gotta roll.
But lemme know if you score a Swoop.
'Cause that would be *siiick*.
I'm on it, my man.
Adios!

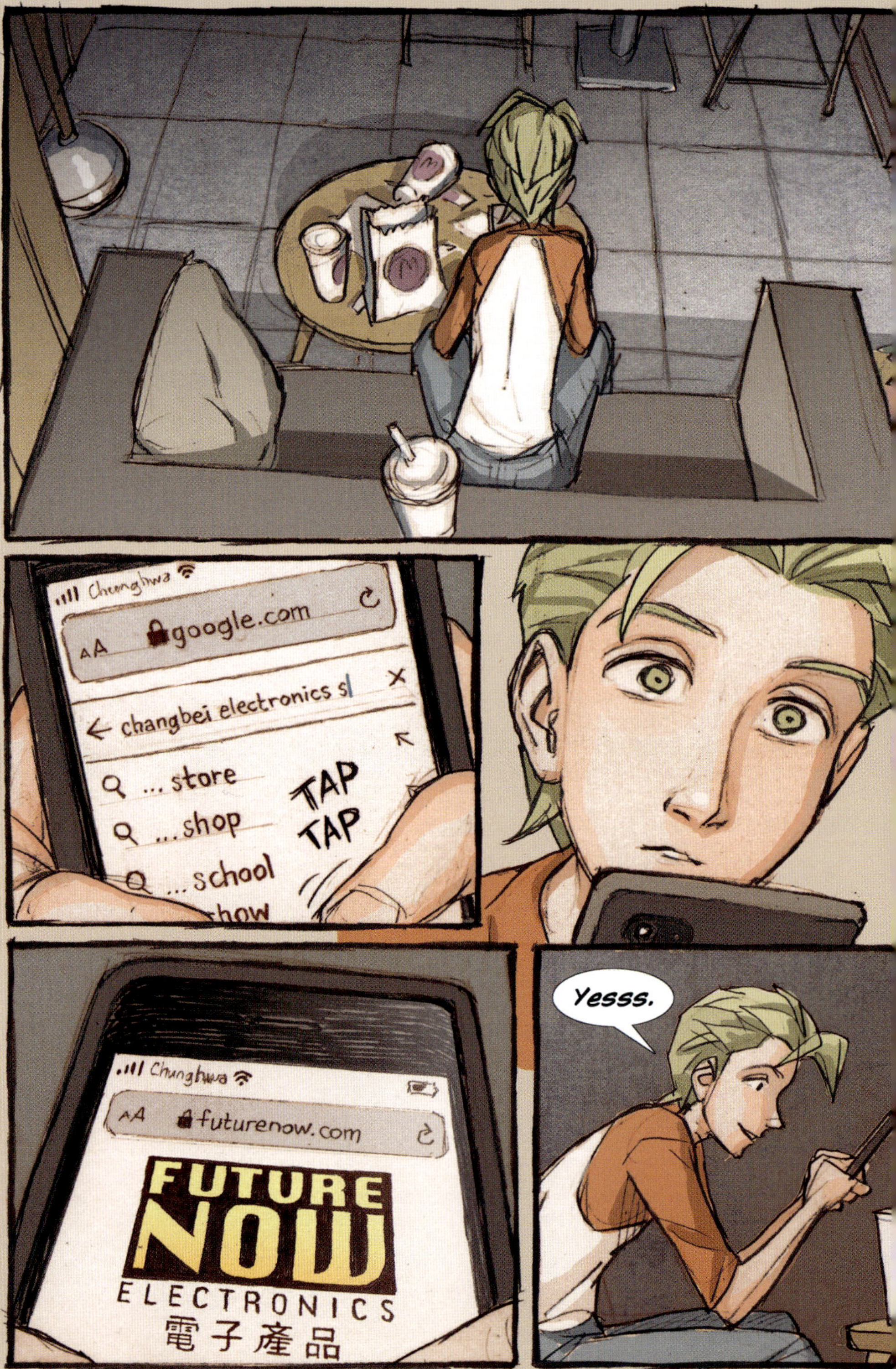
Chunghwa
google.com
changbei electronics s
... store
... shop
... school
TAP
TAP
Chunghwa
futurenow.com
FUTURE NOW
ELECTRONICS
電子產品
Yesss.

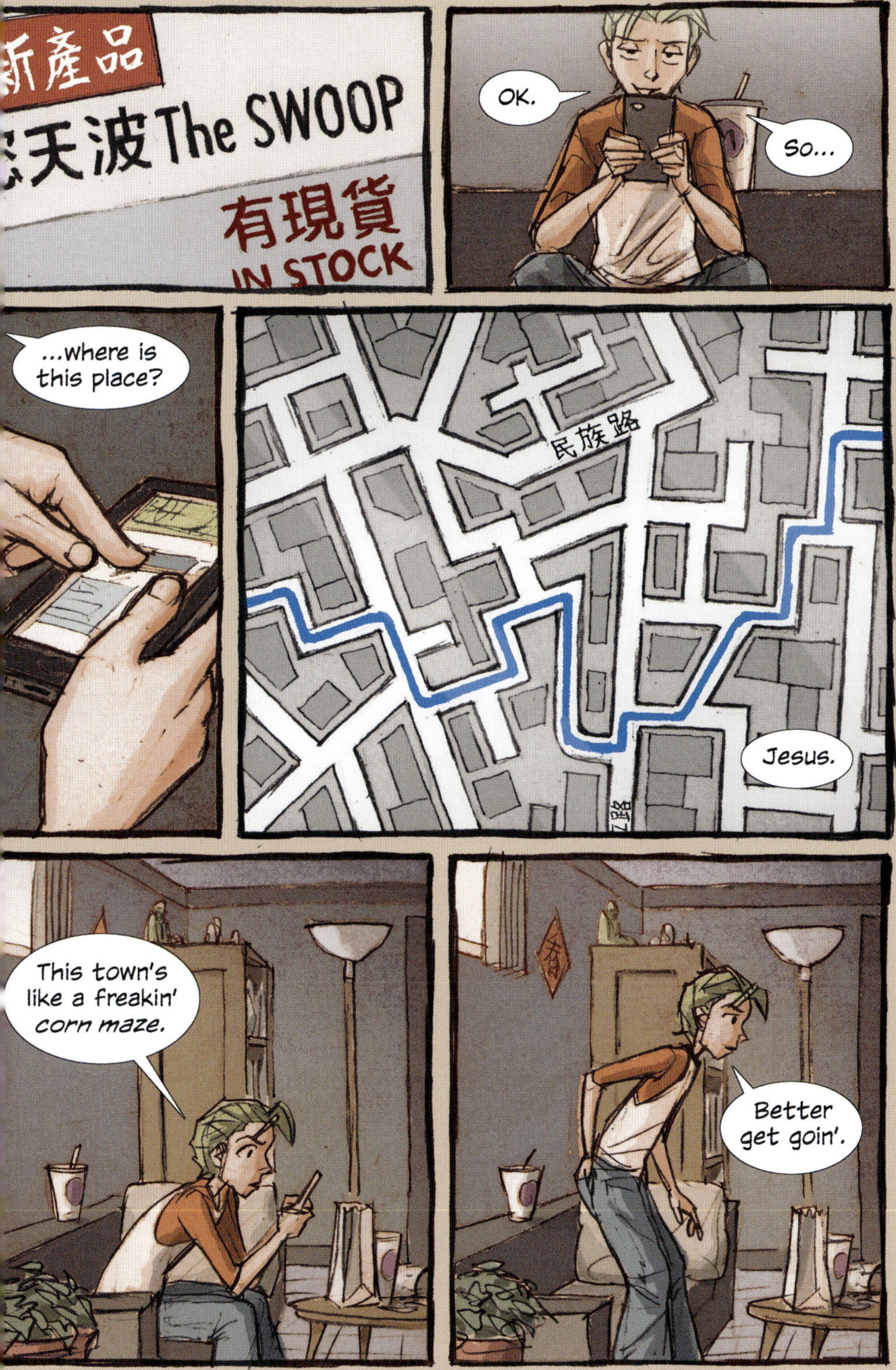

The SWOOP
有現貨
IN STOCK
OK.
So...
...where is this place?
民族路
Jesus.
This town's like a freakin' corn maze.
Better get goin'.

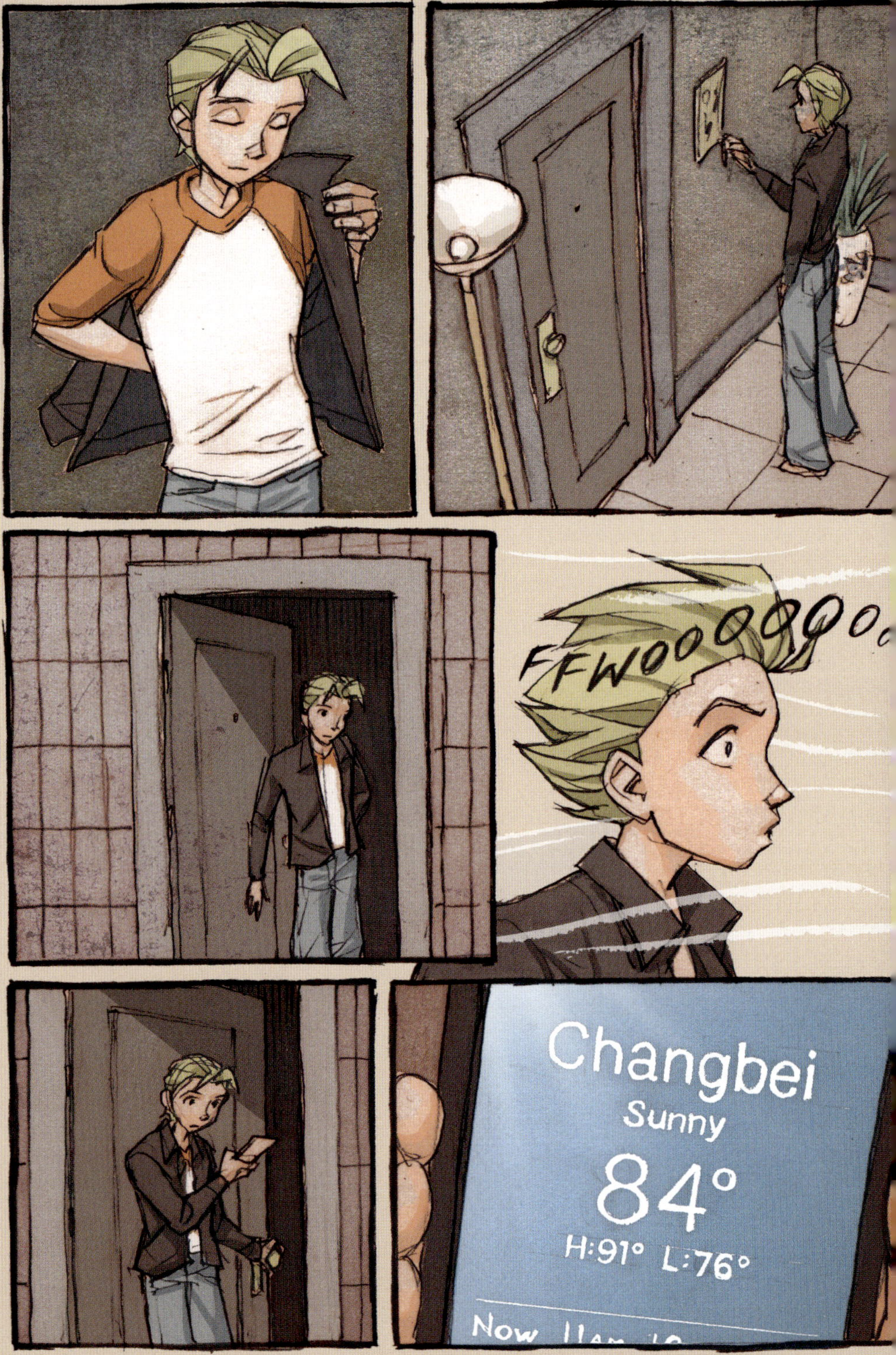
FFWOOOOOOO
Changbei
Sunny
84°
H:91° L:76°

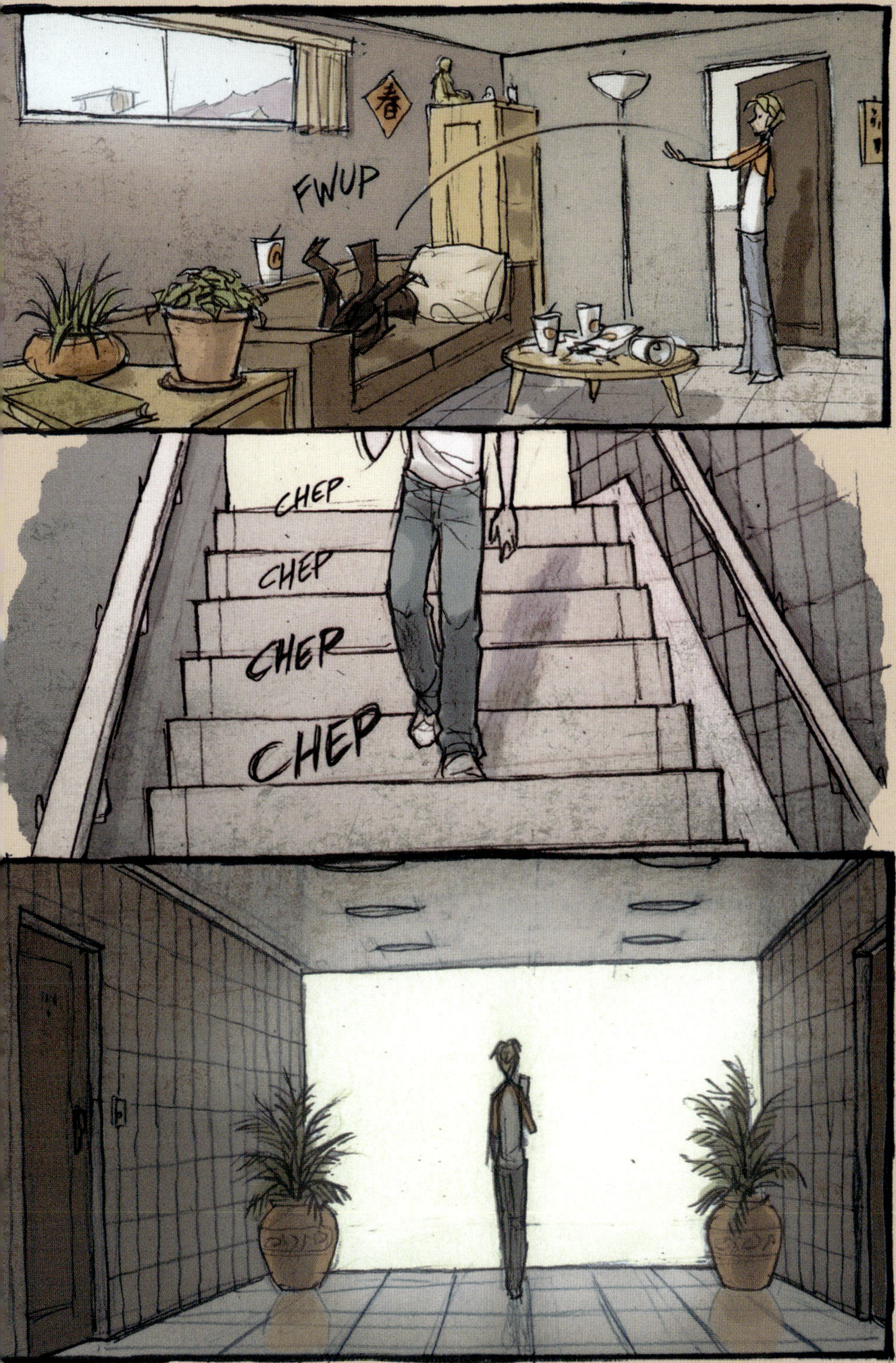
春
FWUP
CHEP
CHEP
CHEP
CHEP

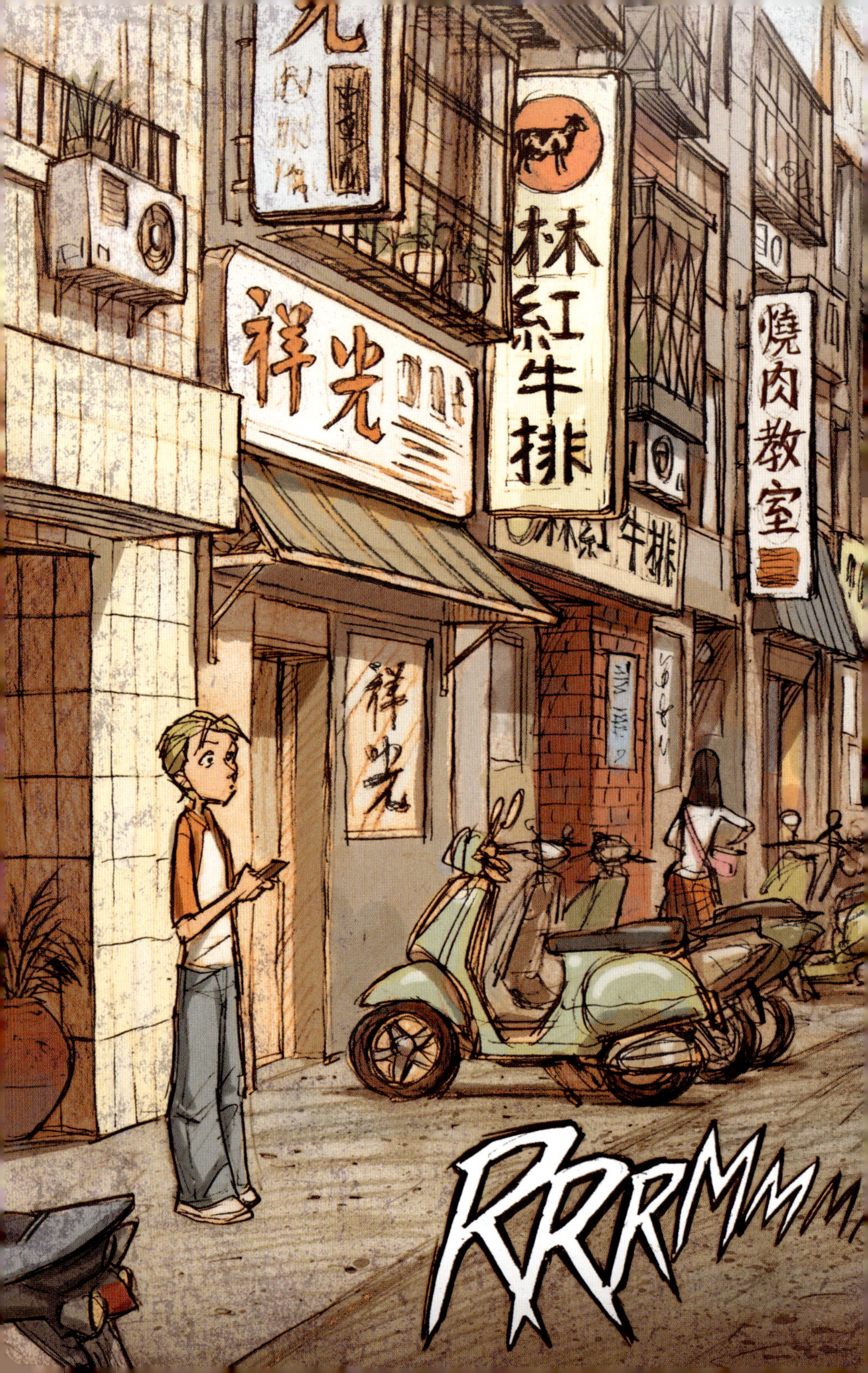
祥光
林紅牛排
燒肉教室
林紅牛排
祥光
RRRMMM...

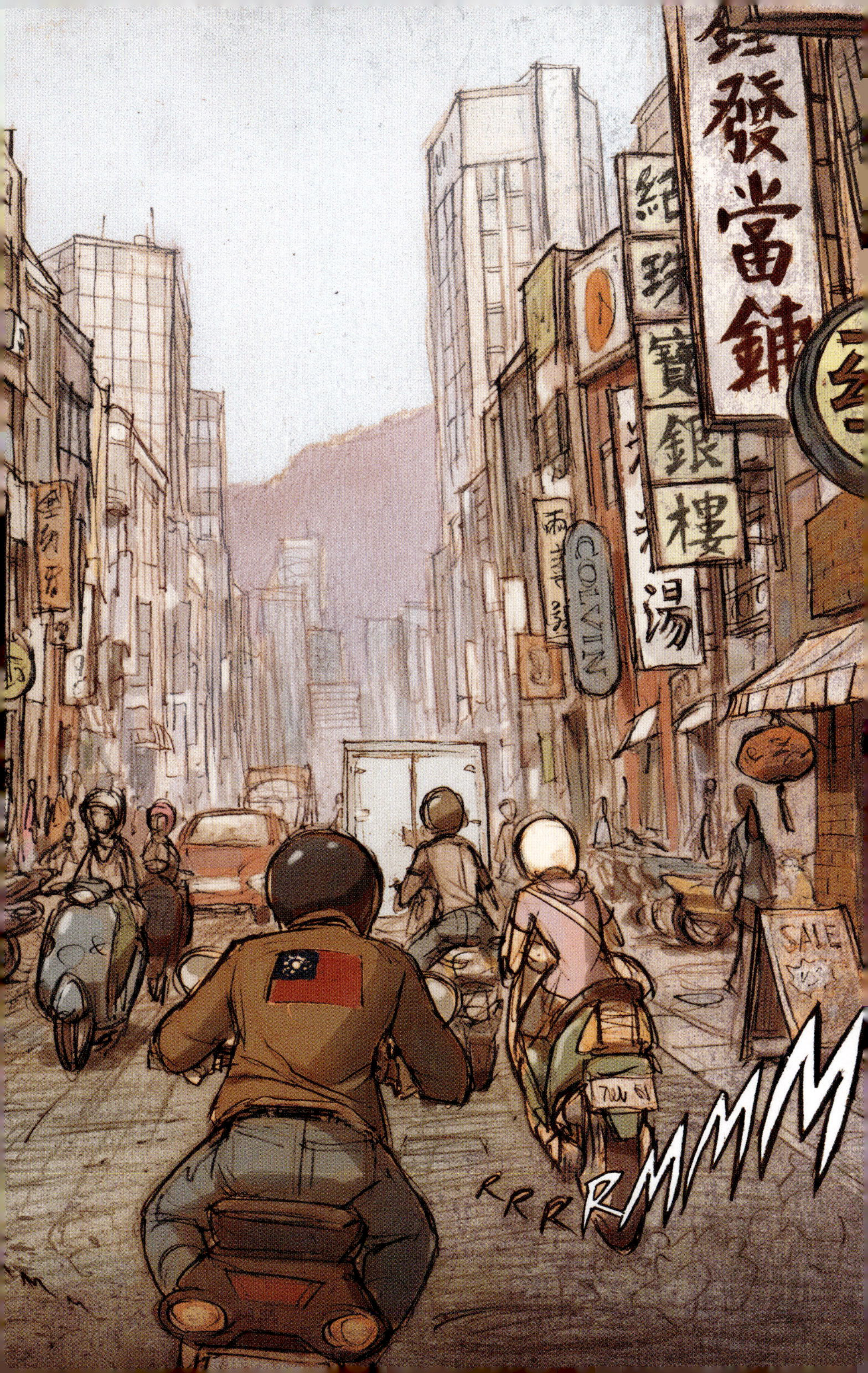
發當鋪
紀珠寶銀樓
COLVIN
SALE
RRRRMMMM

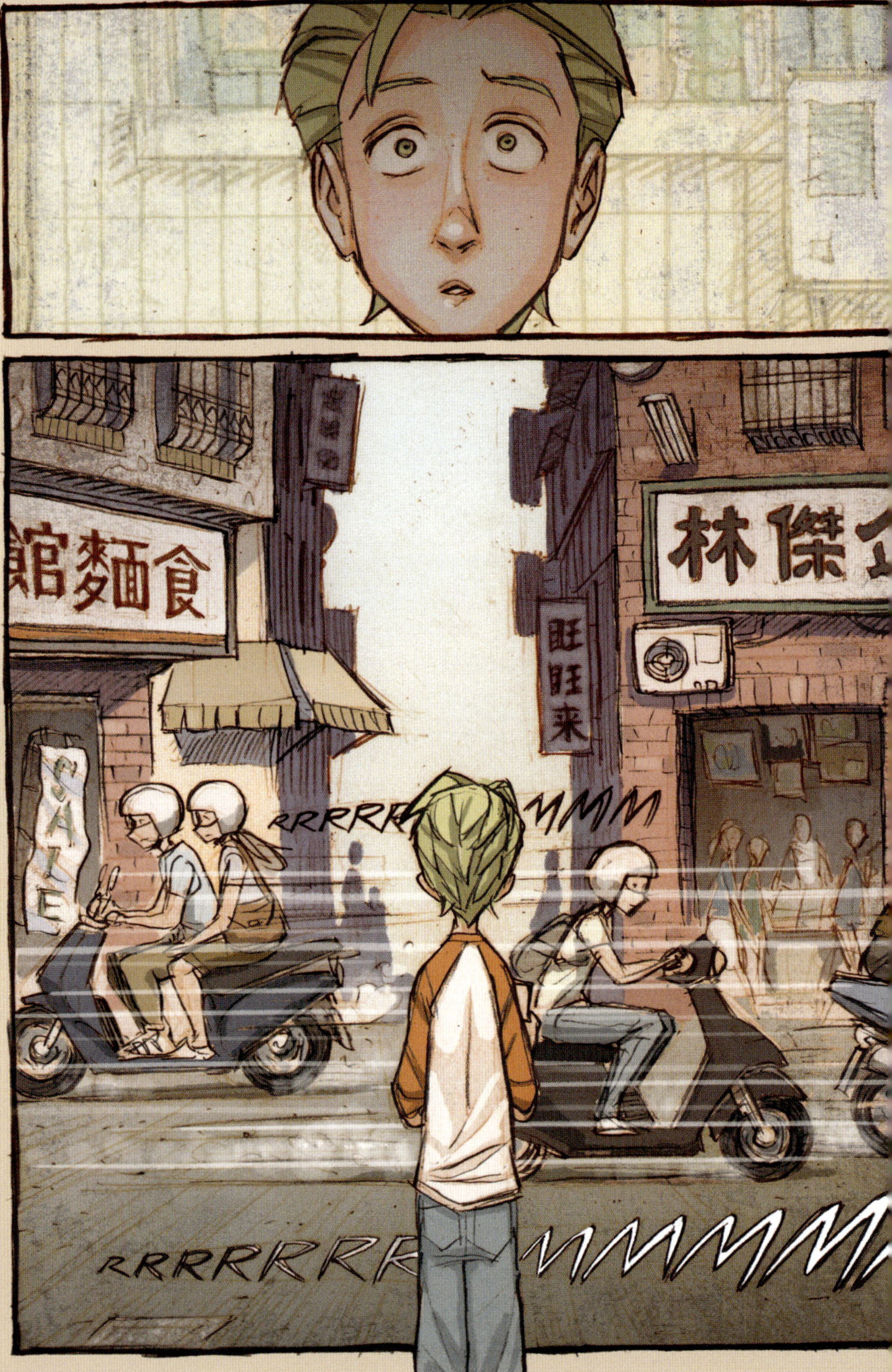

食麵館
林傑
旺旺来
SALE
RRRRRMMMM
RRRRRRRRMMMMM

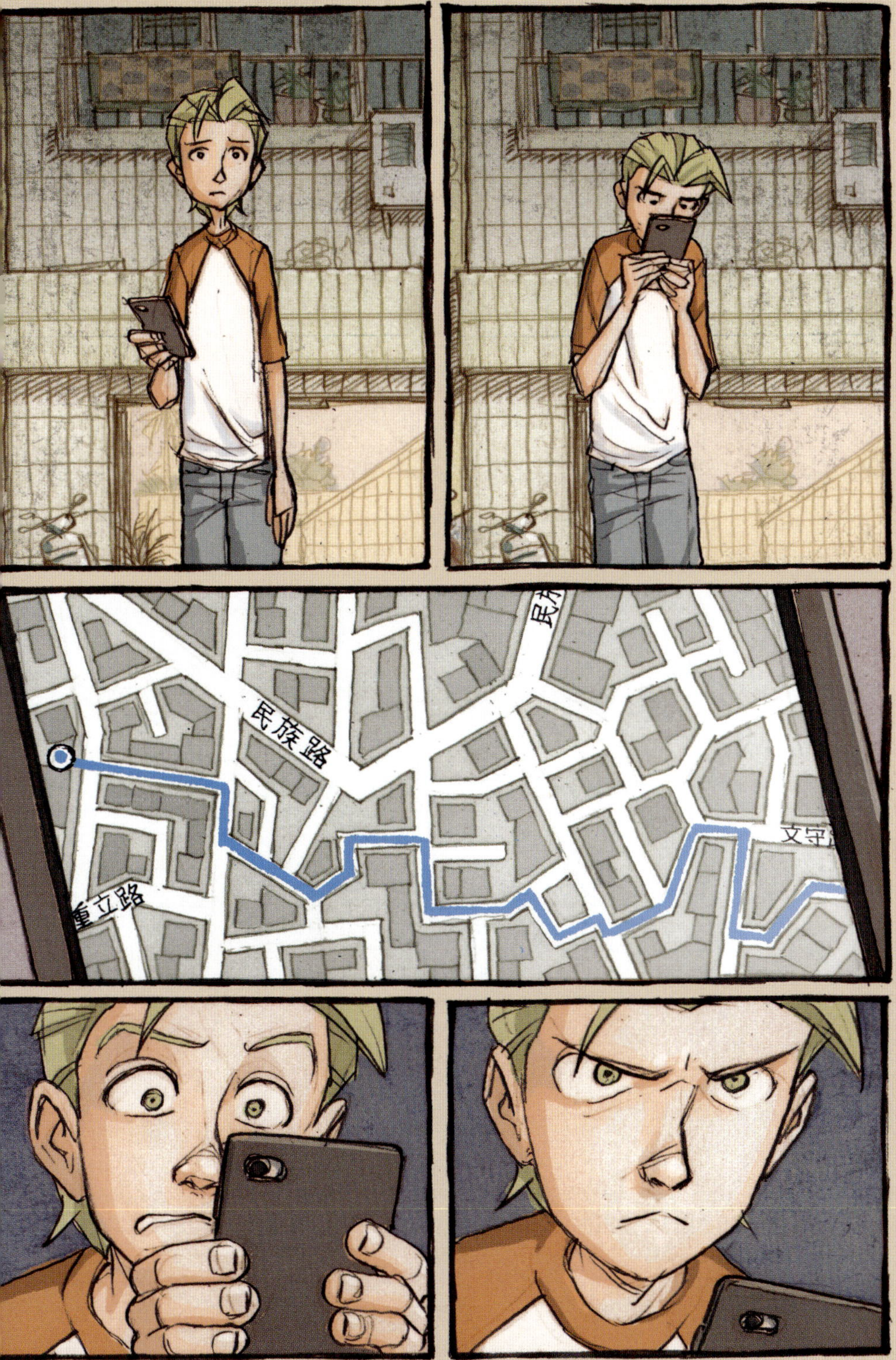
民族路

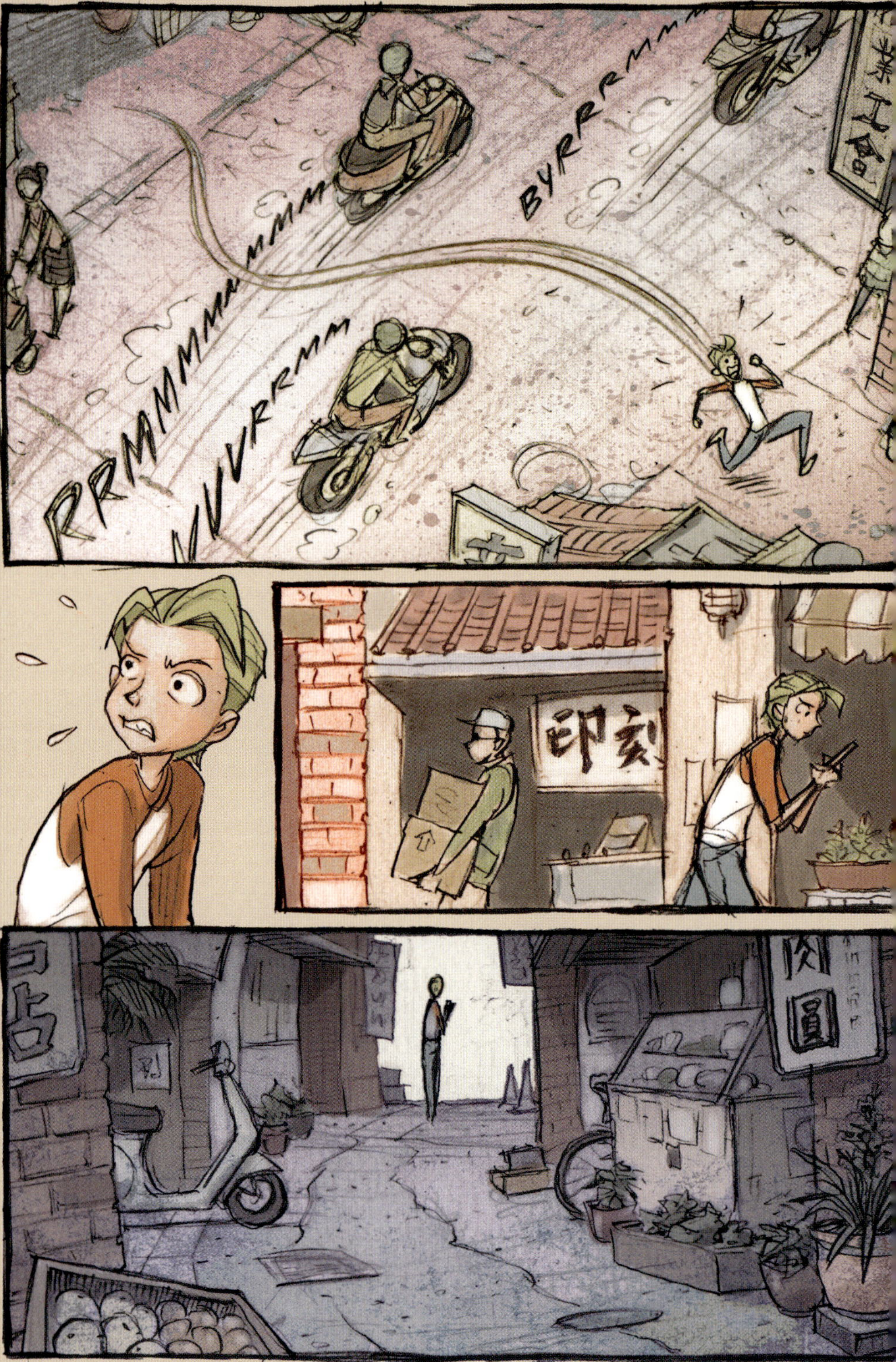

RRMMMMMMMMMMMM
VVVRRMM
BYRRRMM
印刻

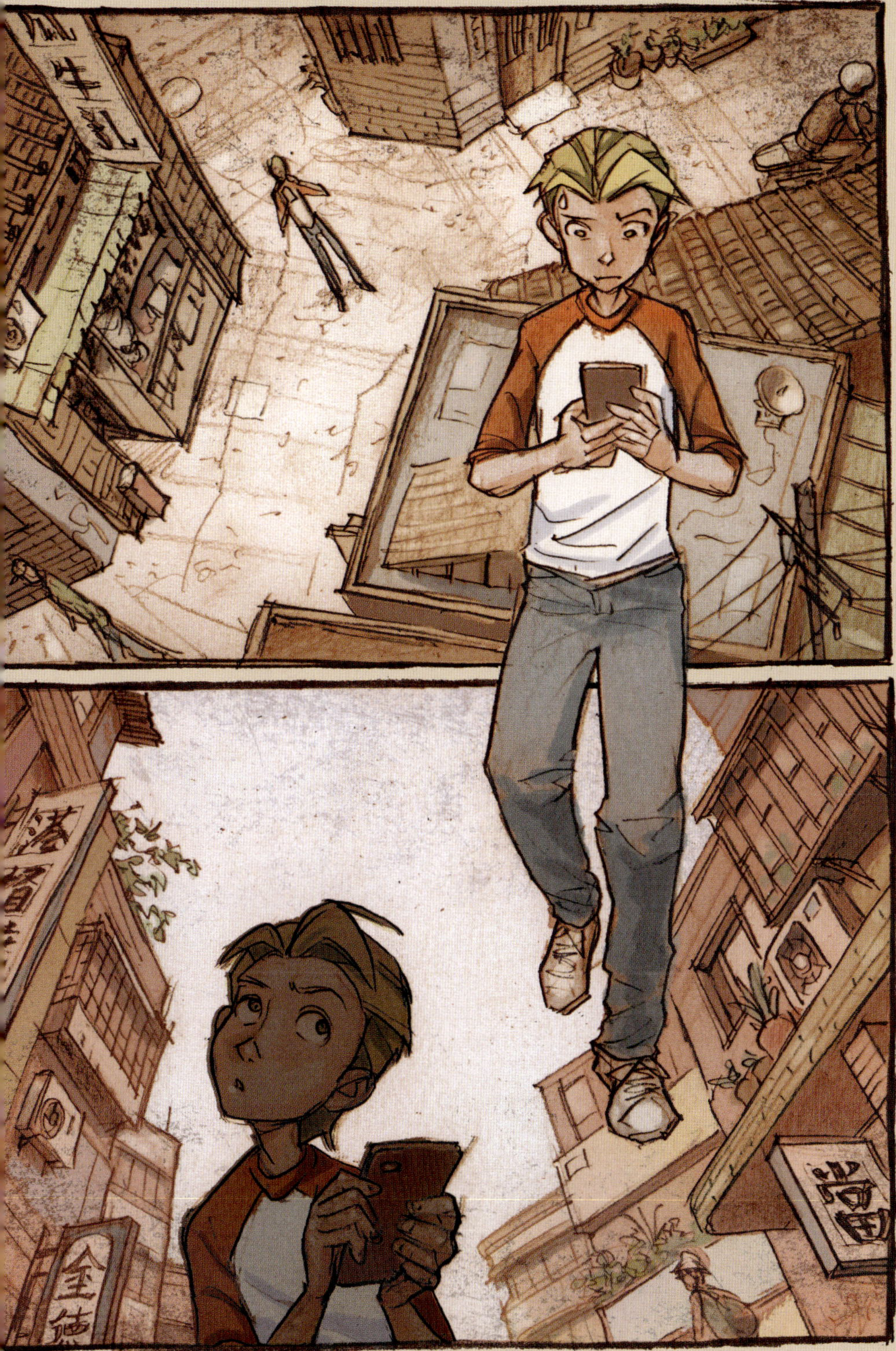

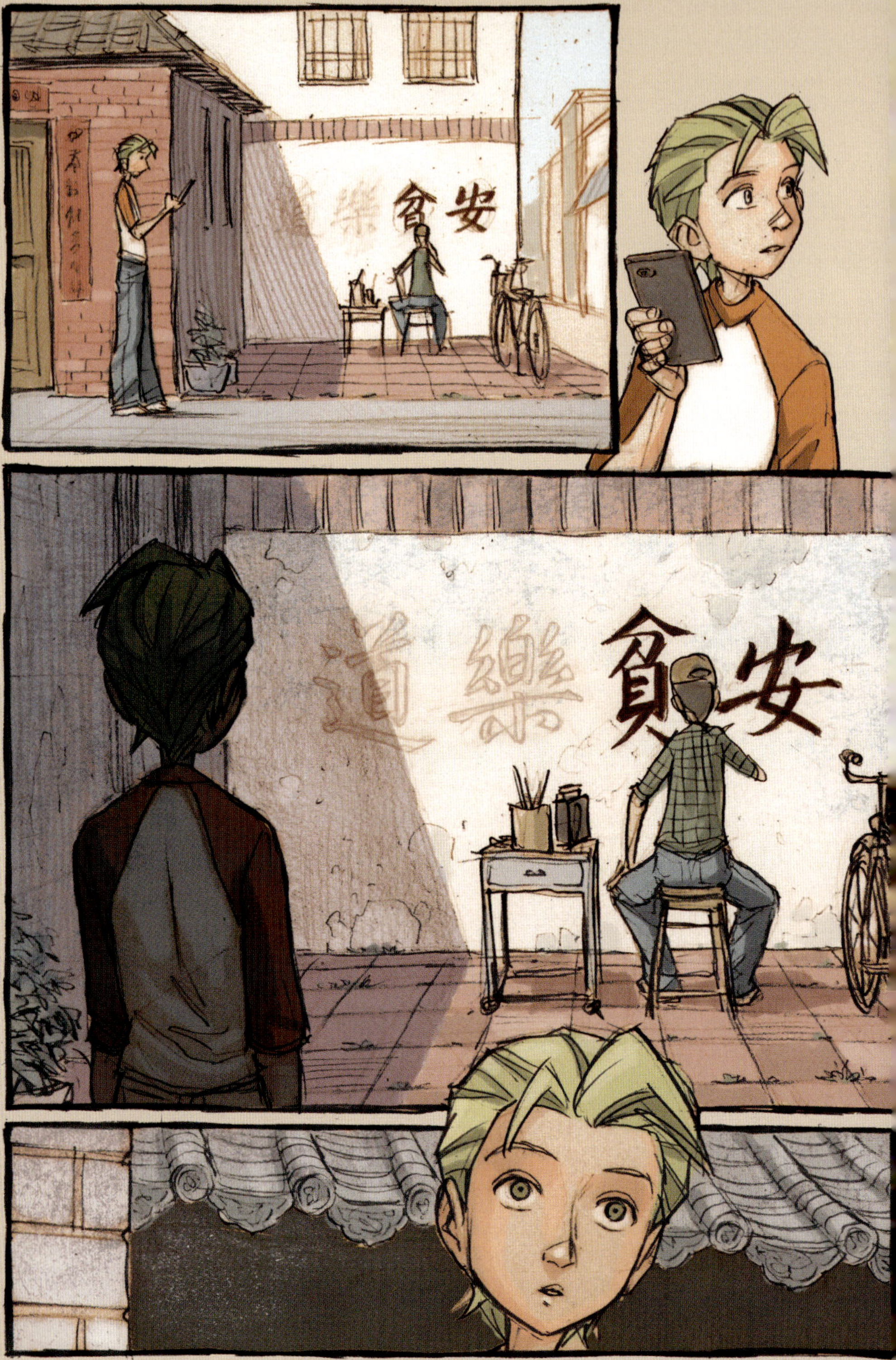
安貧樂道

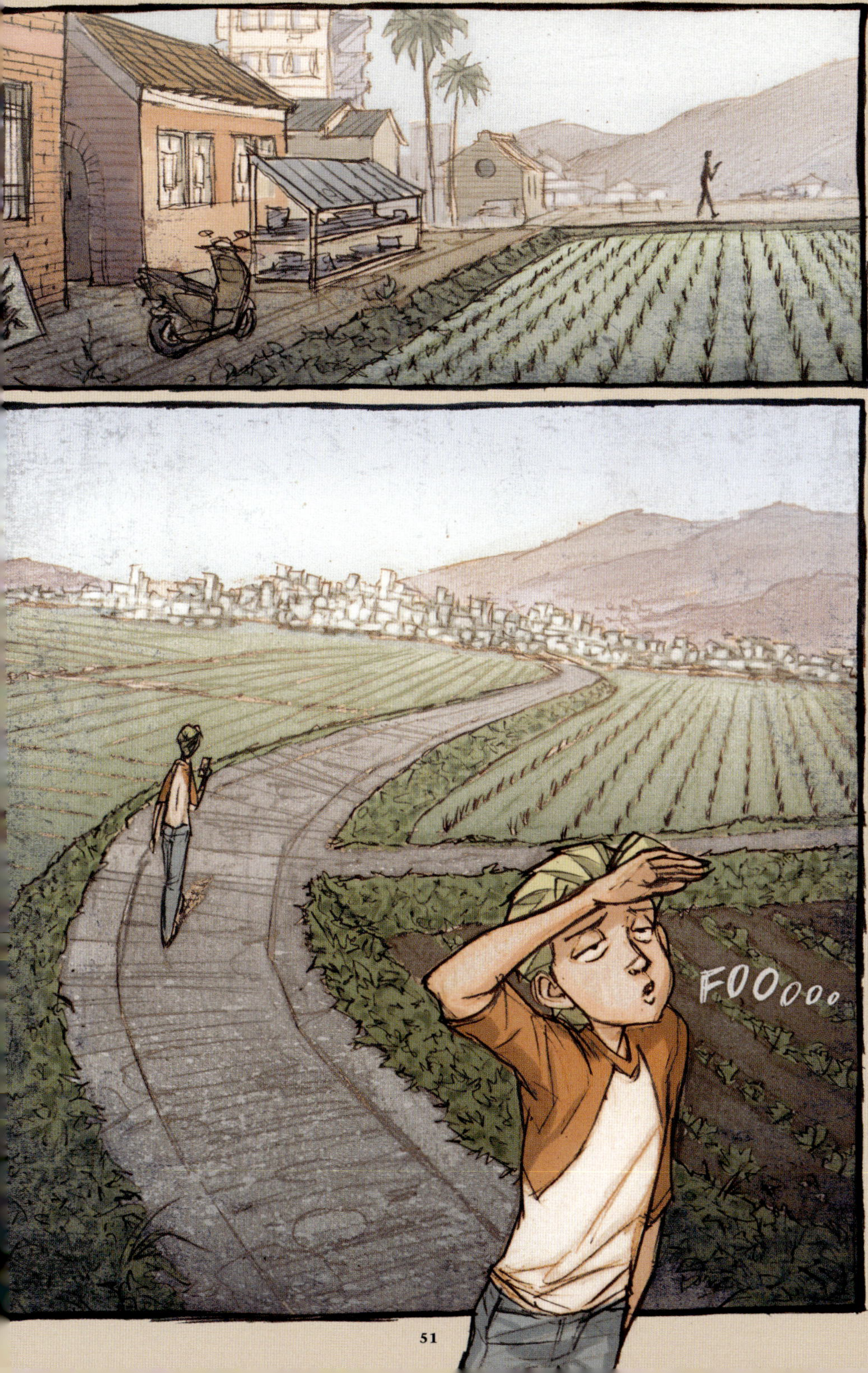
FOOooo

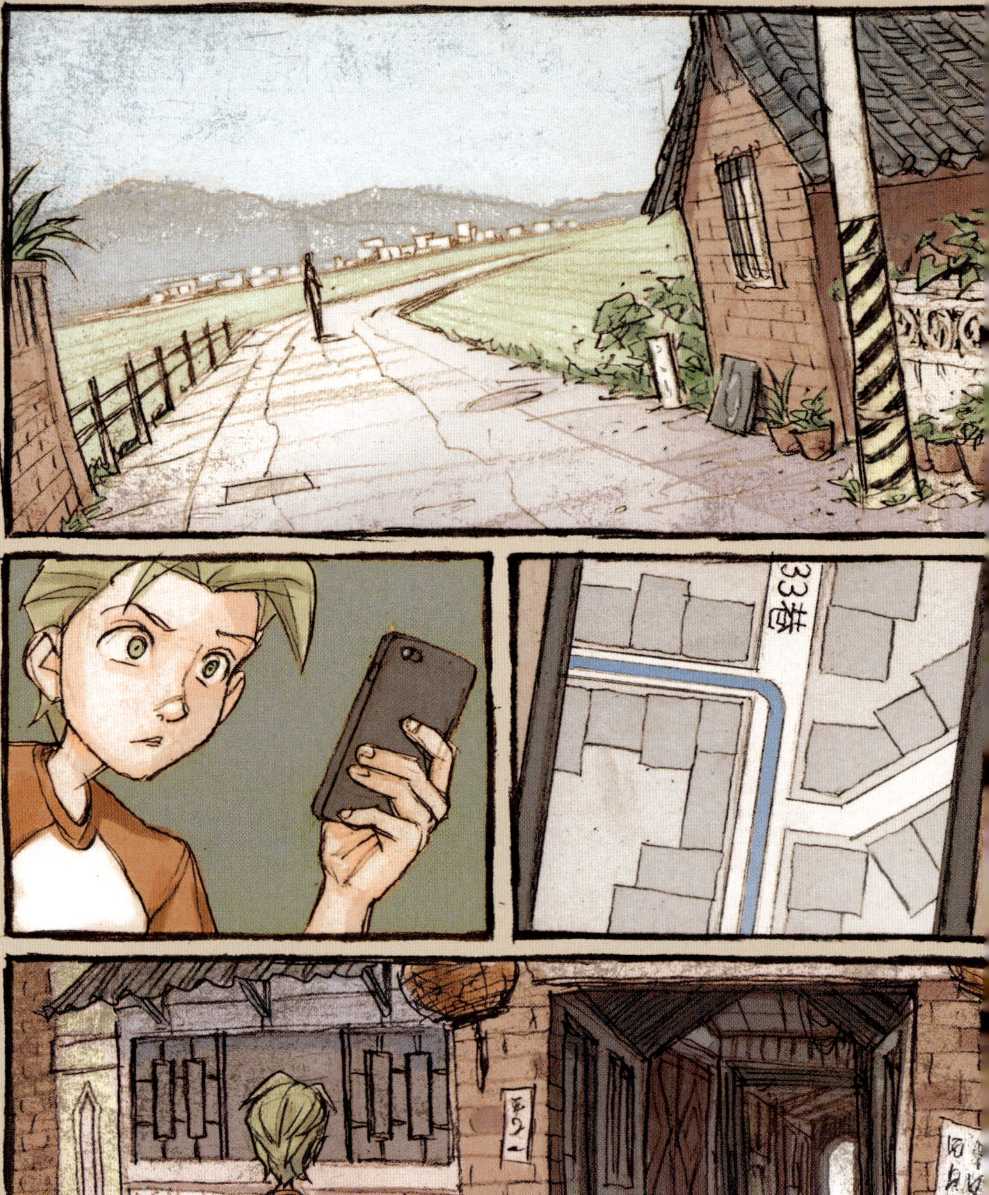
33巷

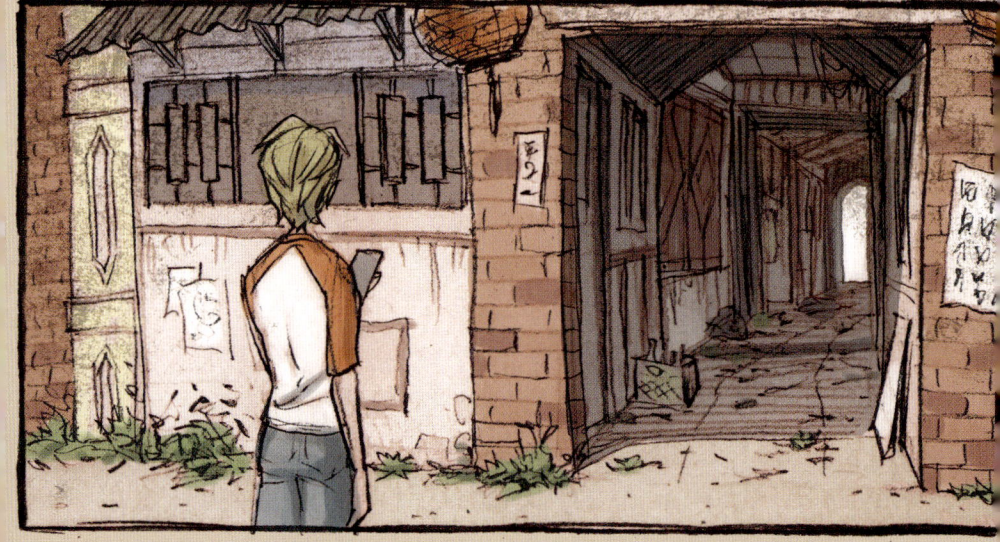

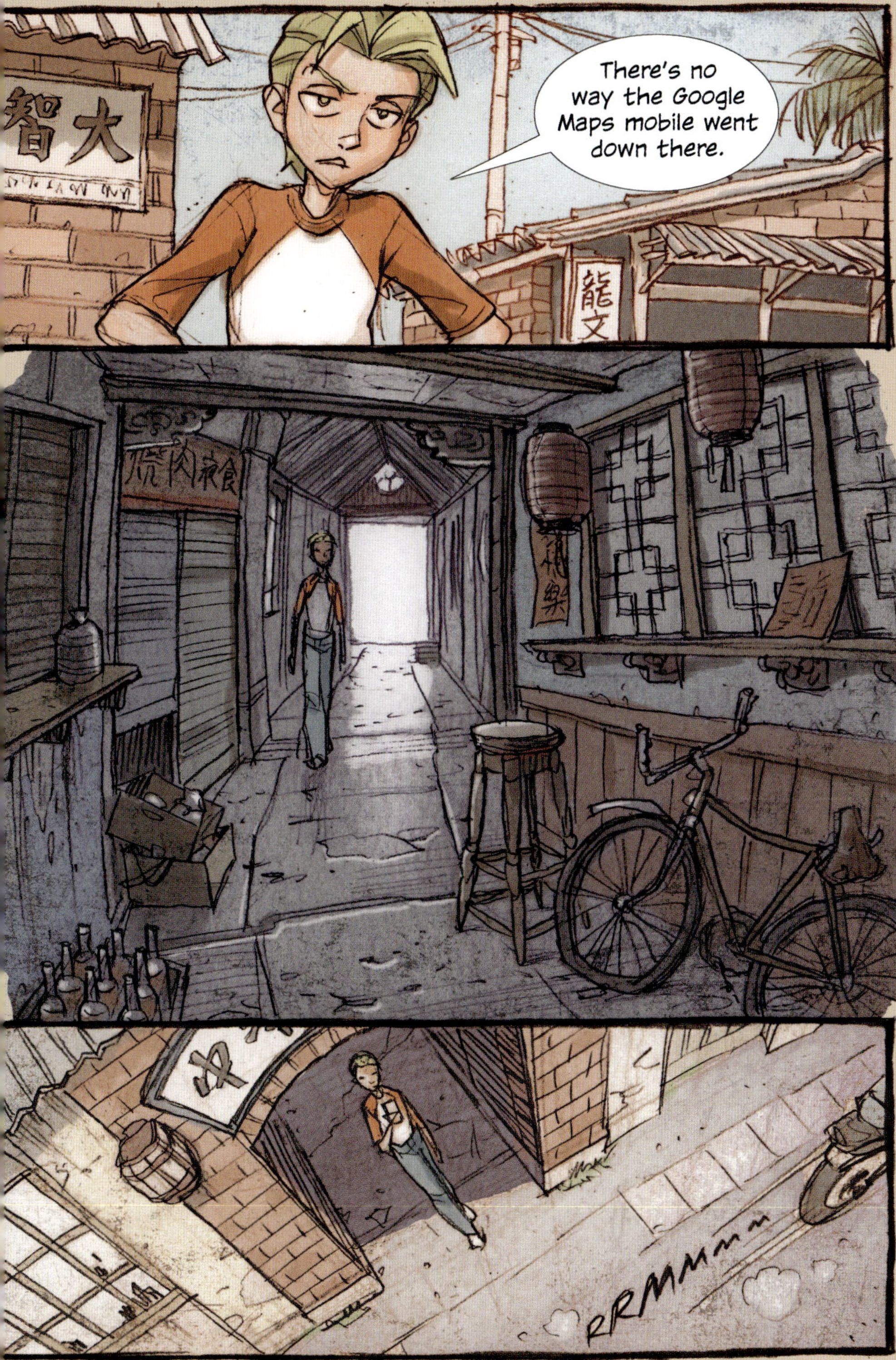
There's no way the Google Maps mobile went down there.
RRMMMmmm

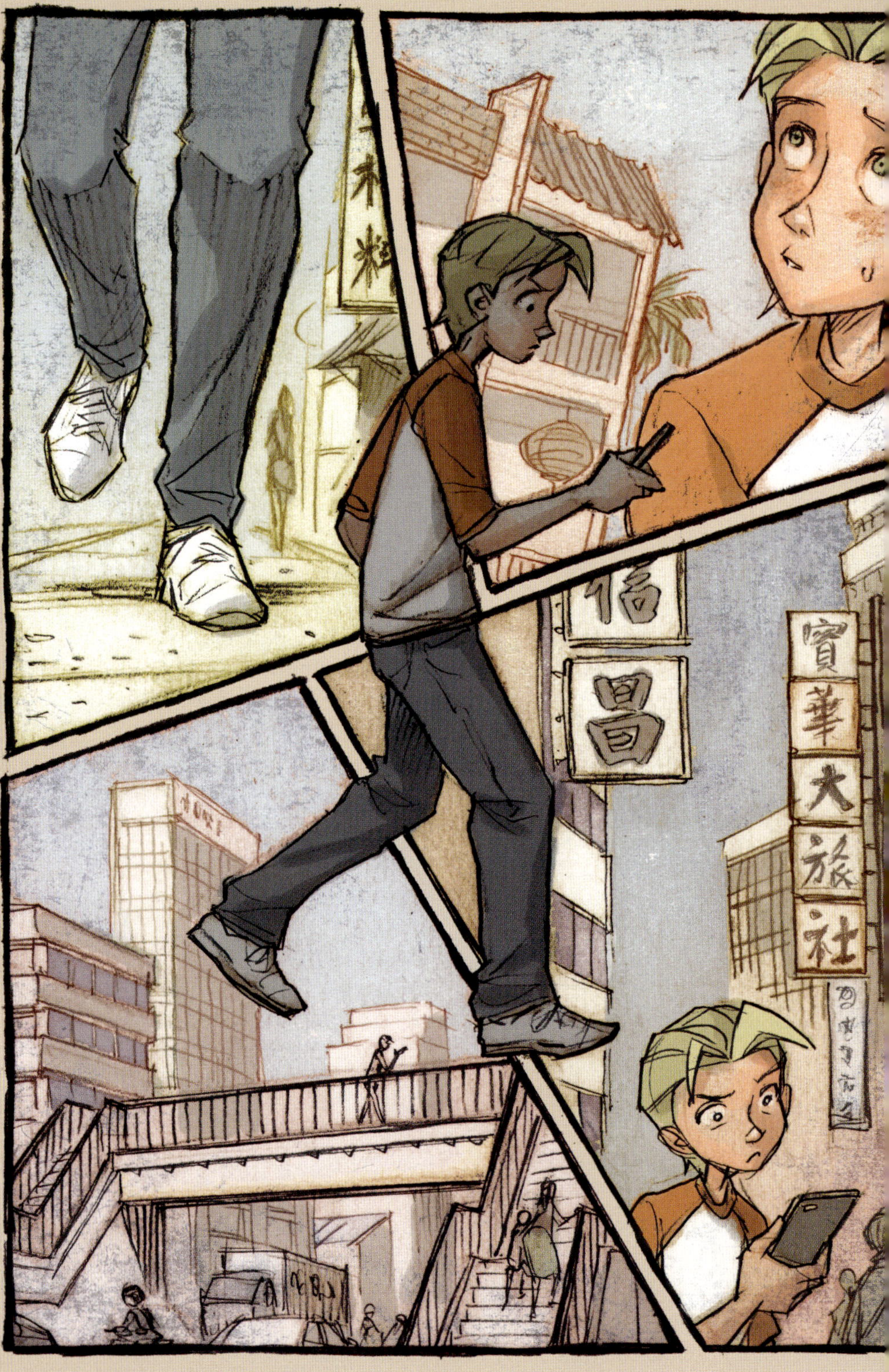
信
昌
賓華大旅社

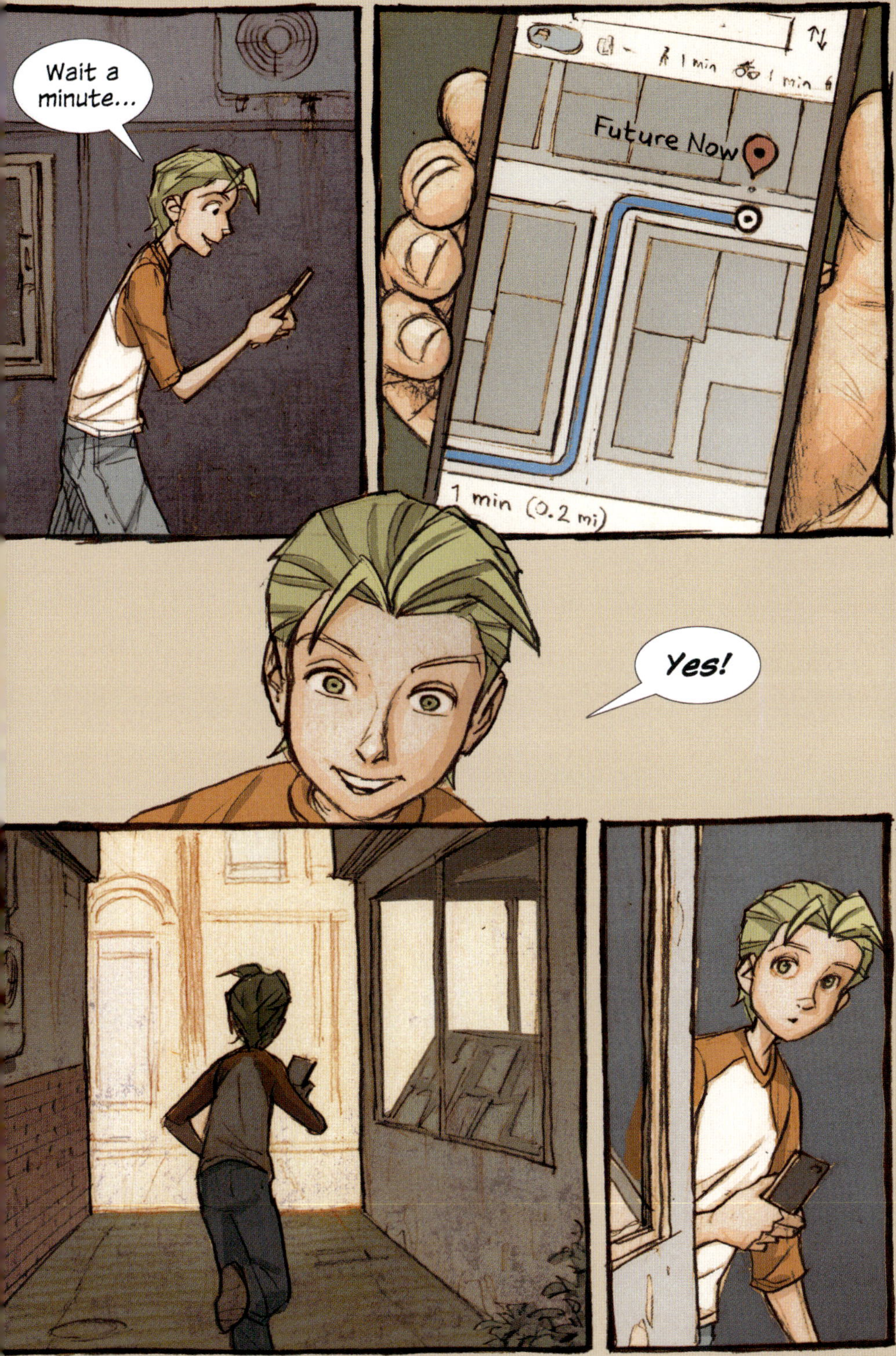
Wait a minute...
Future Now
1 min (0.2 mi)
Yes!

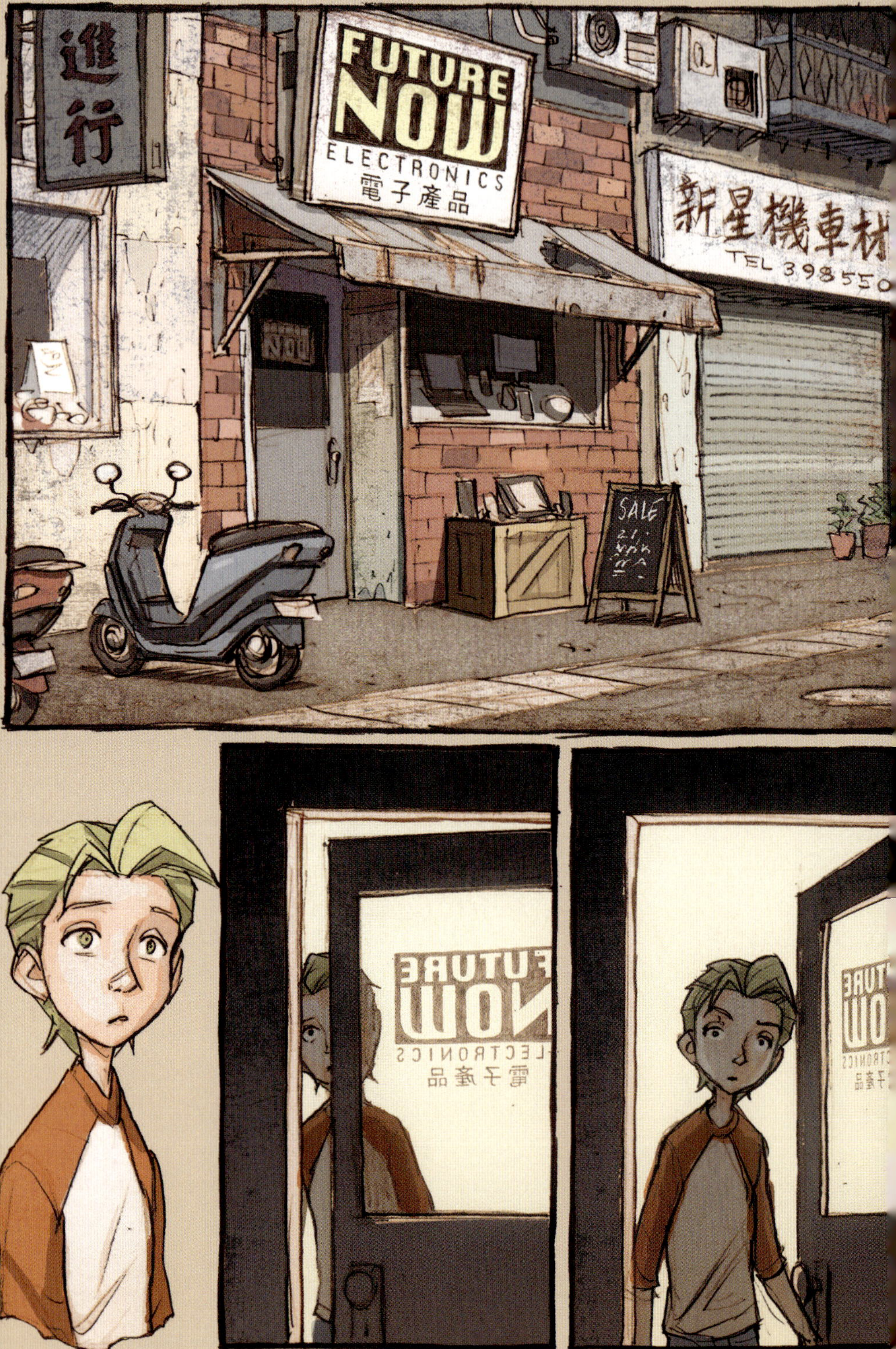

進行
FUTURE NOW
ELECTRONICS
電子產品
新星機車材
TEL 398550
NOW
SALE

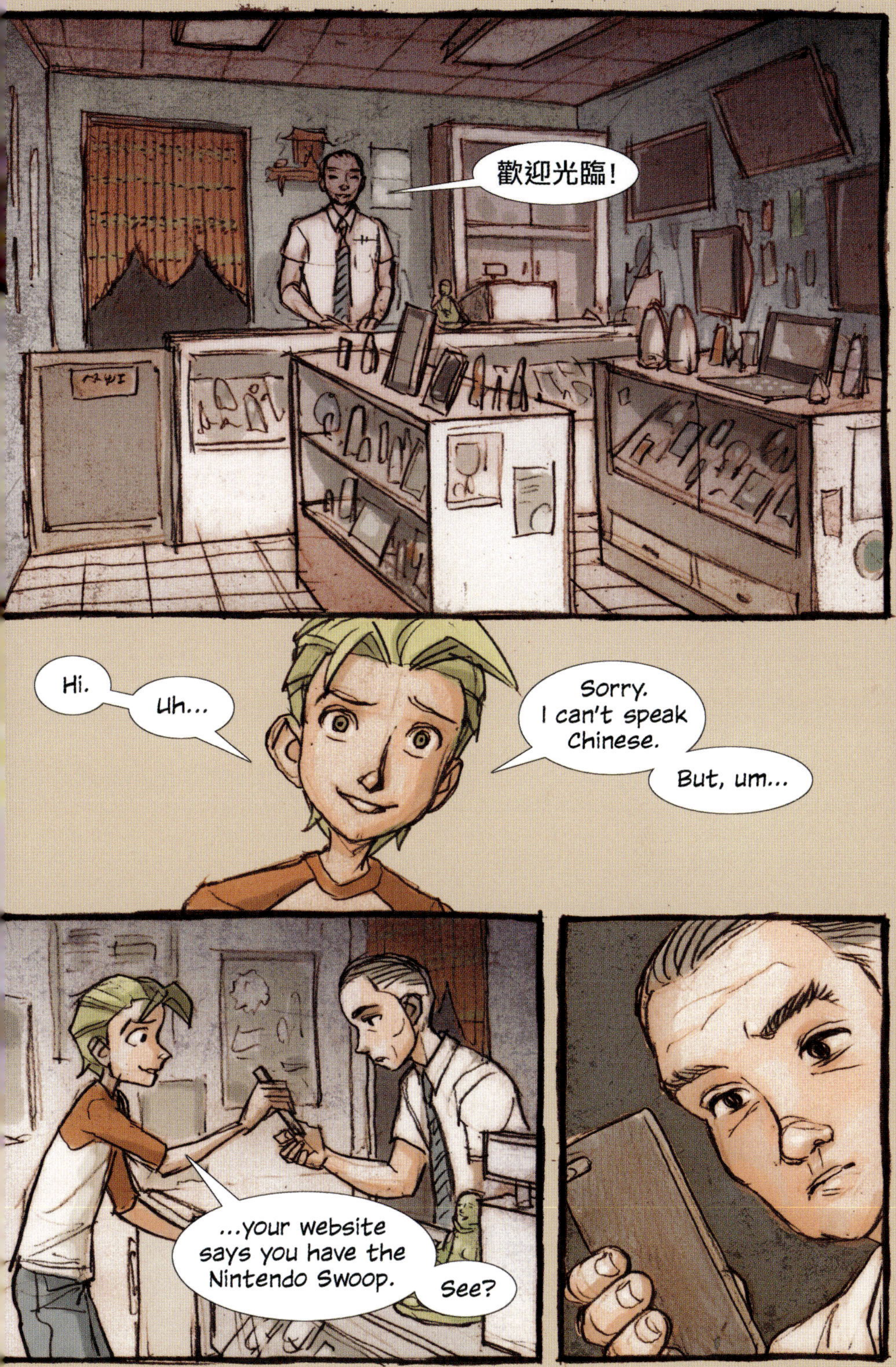

歡迎光臨!
Hi.
Uh...
Sorry. I can't speak Chinese.
But, um...
...your website says you have the Nintendo Swoop.
See?

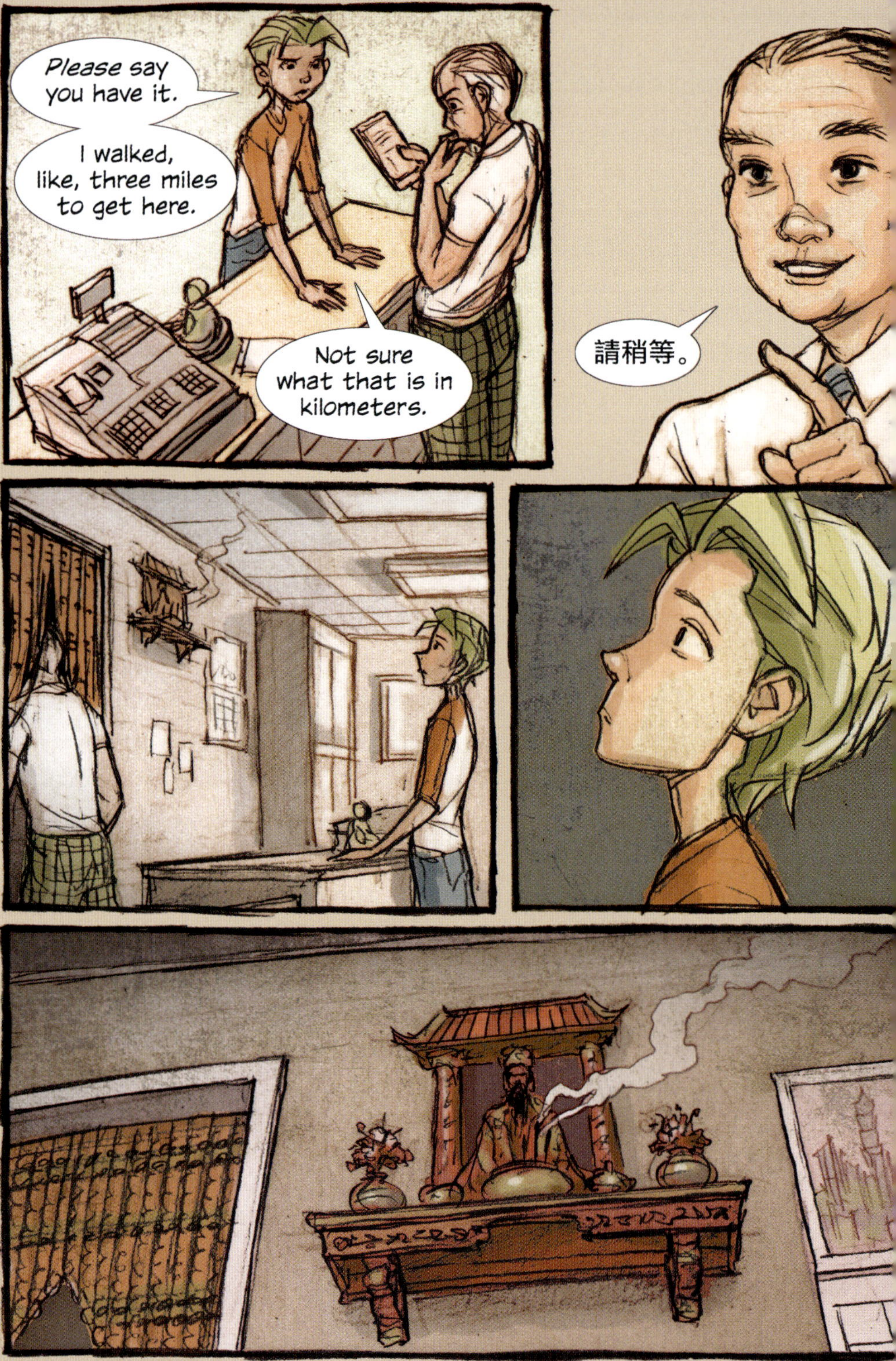
Please say you have it.
I walked, like, three miles to get here.
Not sure what that is in kilometers.
請稍等。

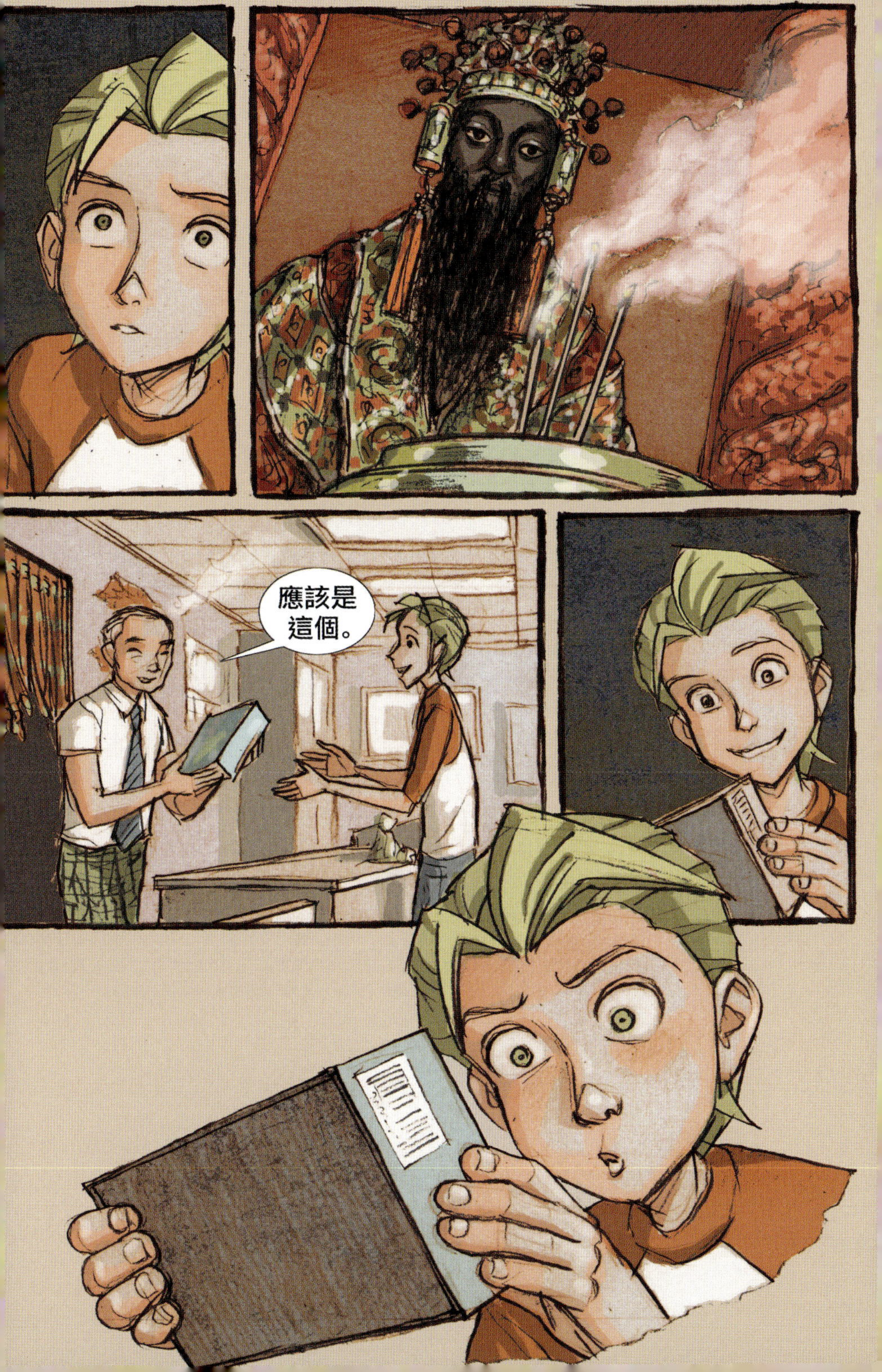
應該是這個。

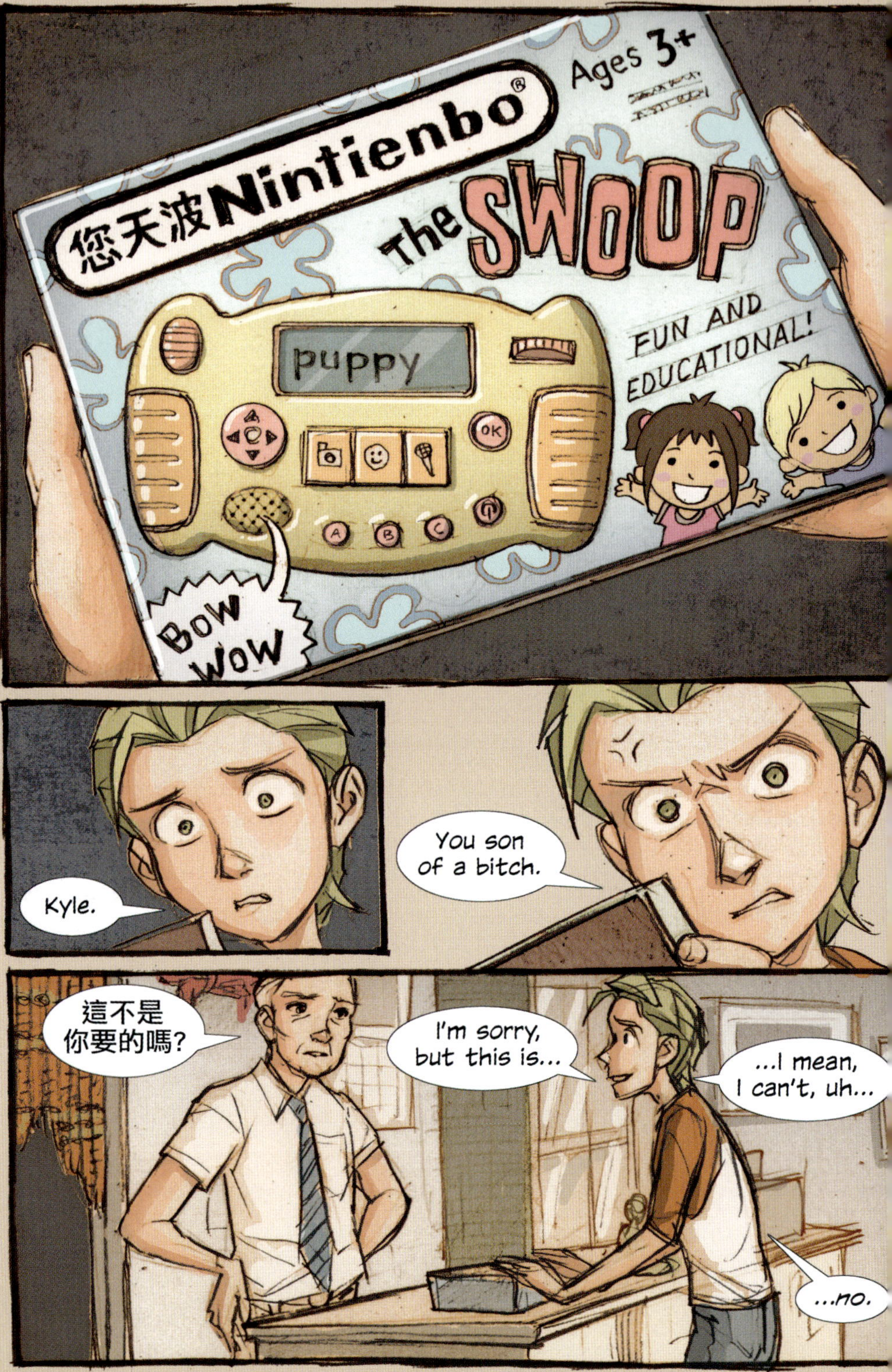
您天波 Nintienbo®
Ages 3+
the SWOOP
puppy
FUN AND EDUCATIONAL!
OK
A
B
C
BOW WOW
Kyle.
You son of a bitch.
這不是你要的嗎?
I'm sorry, but this is...
...I mean, I can't, uh...
...no.

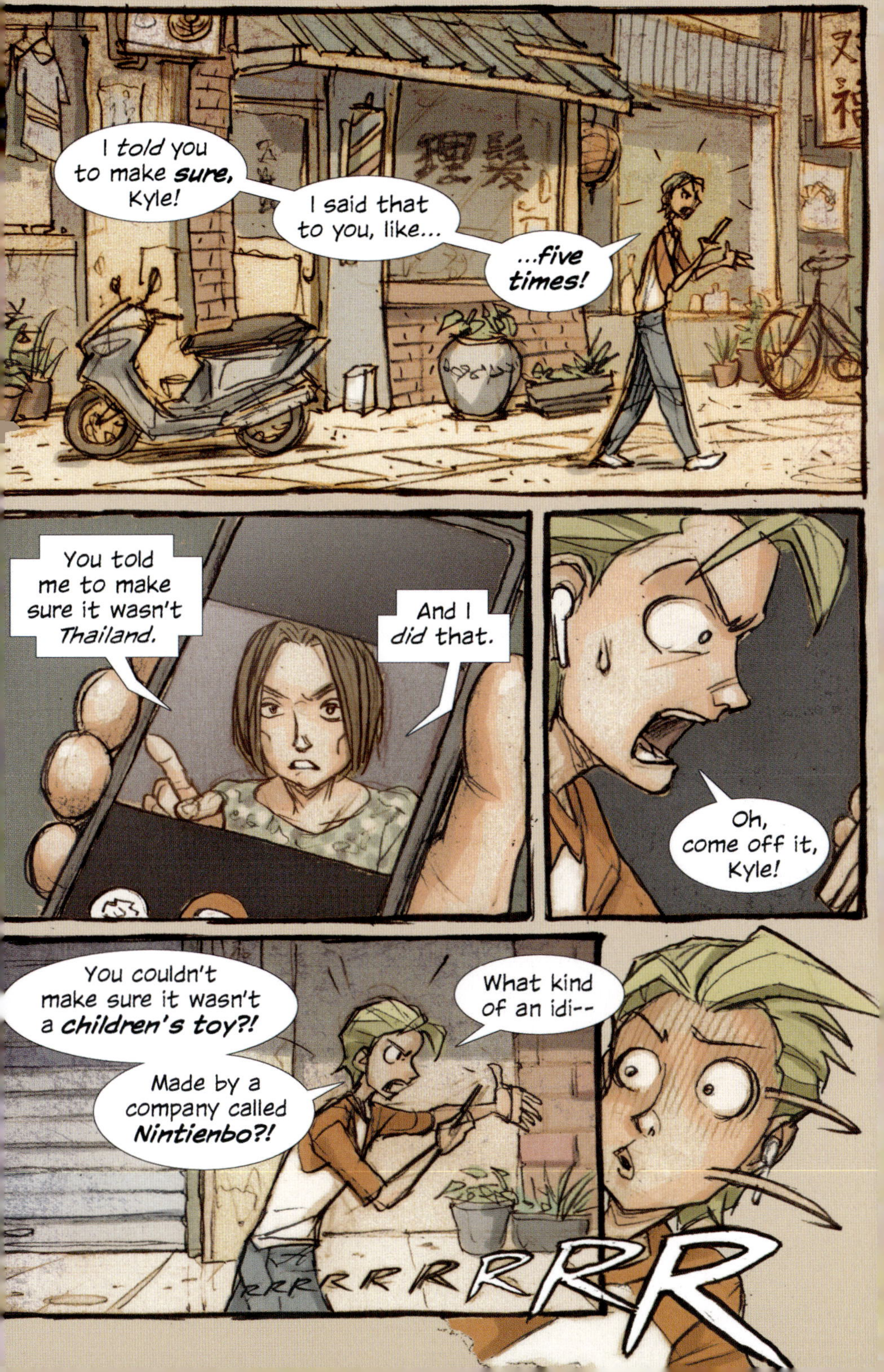
I told you to make sure, Kyle!
I said that to you, like...
...five times!
You told me to make sure it wasn't Thailand.
And I did that.
Oh, come off it, Kyle!
You couldn't make sure it wasn't a children's toy?!
Made by a company called Nintienbo?!
What kind of an idi--
RRRRRRRRRRR

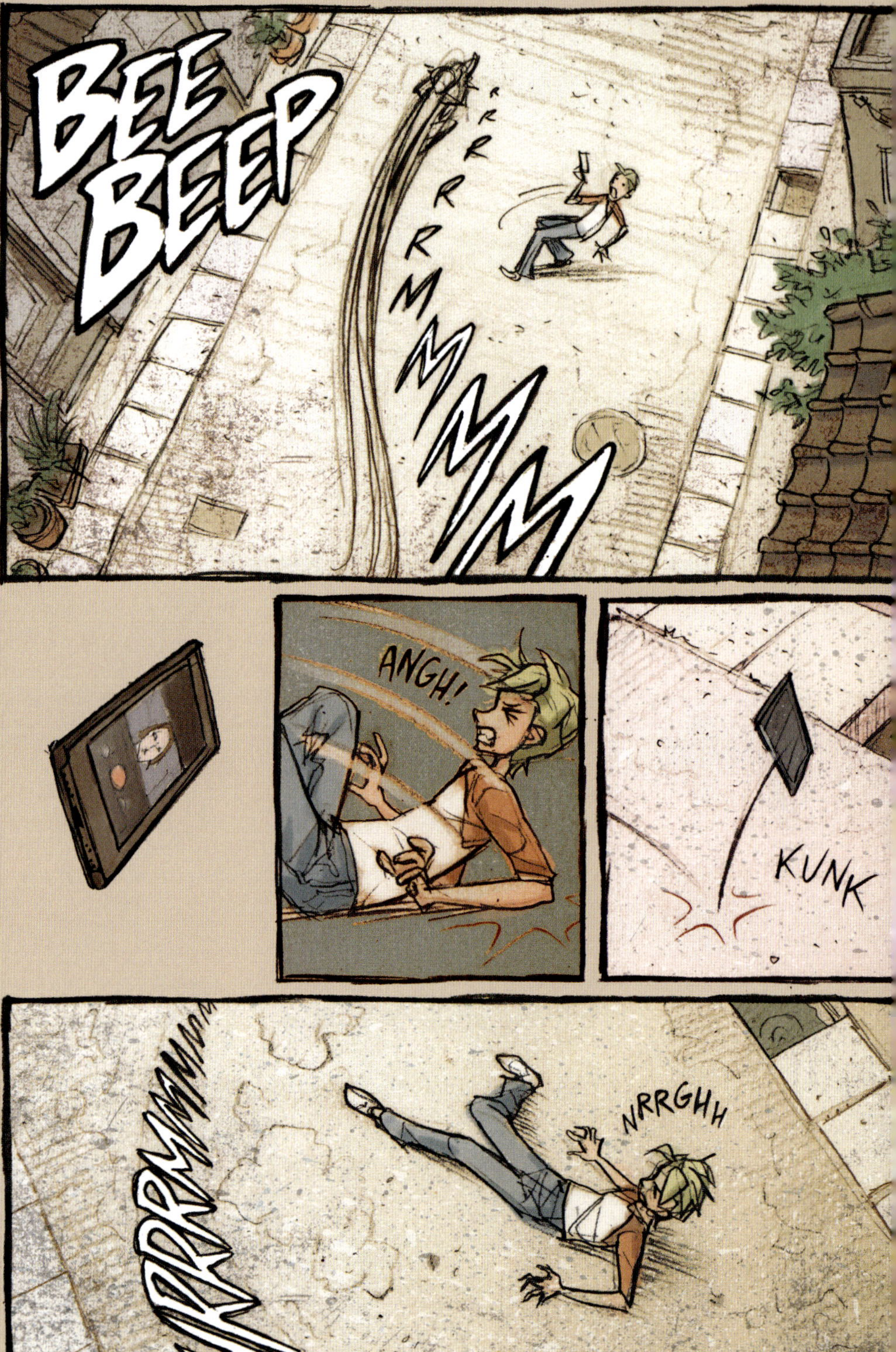
BEE BEEP
RRRRRMMMMM
ANGH!
KUNK
HARRRMMMMM
NRRGHH

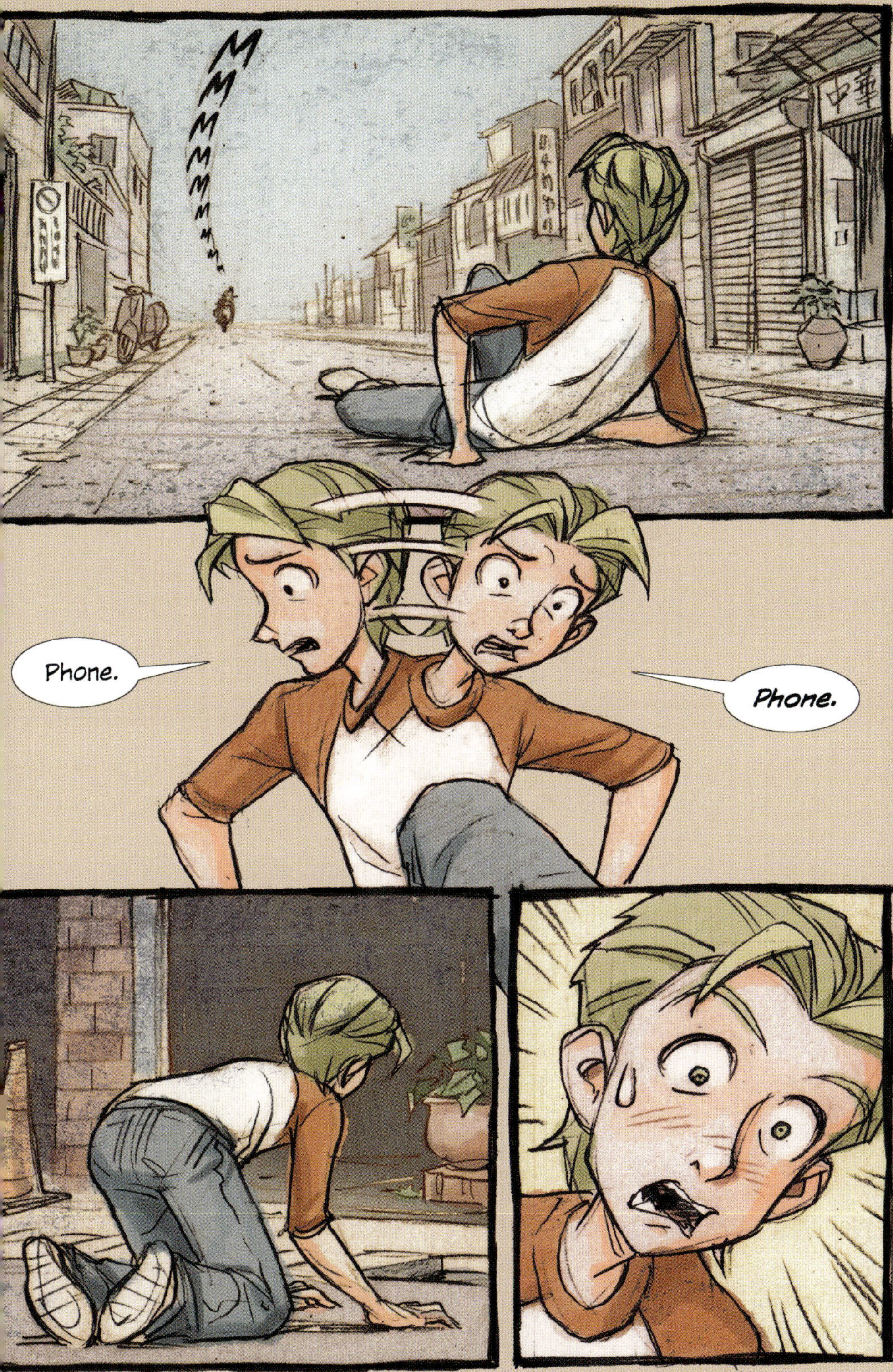
MMMMMMMMmmm
Phone.
Phone.

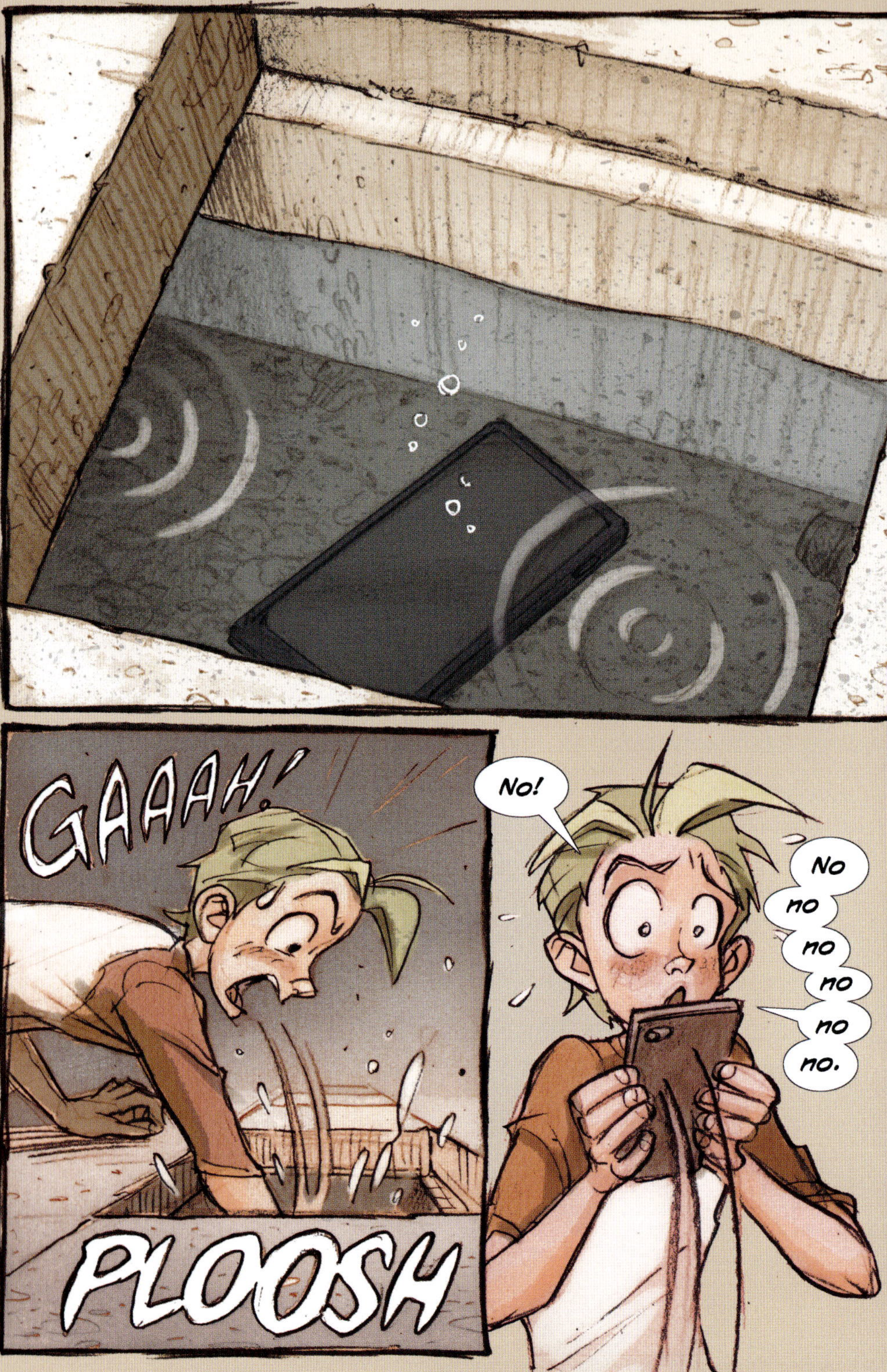
GAAAH!
No!
PLOOSH
No
no
no
no
no
no.

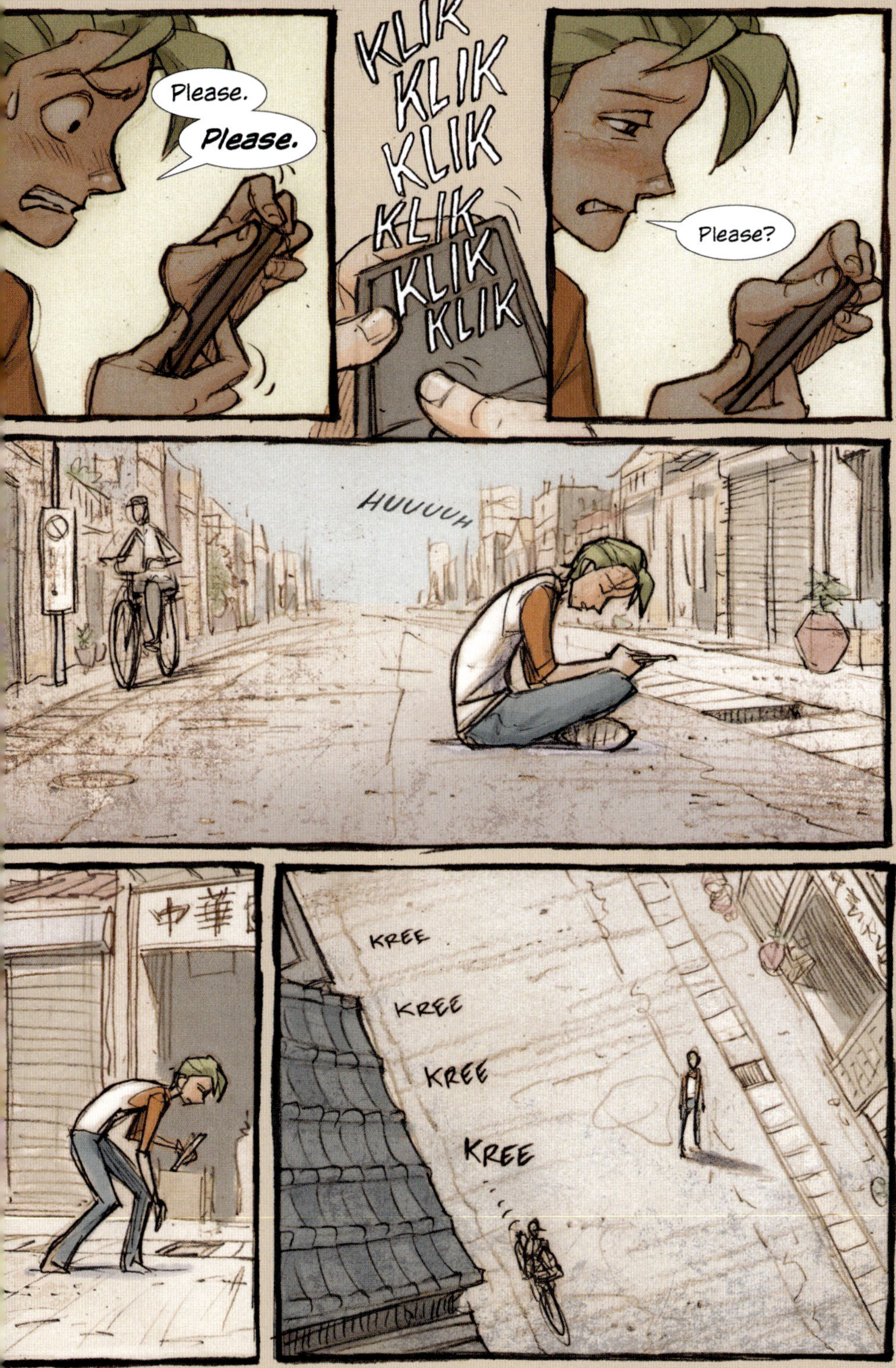
Please.
Please.
KLIK
KLIK
KLIK
KLIK
KLIK
KLIK
Please?
HUUUUH
中華
KREE
KREE
KREE
KREE

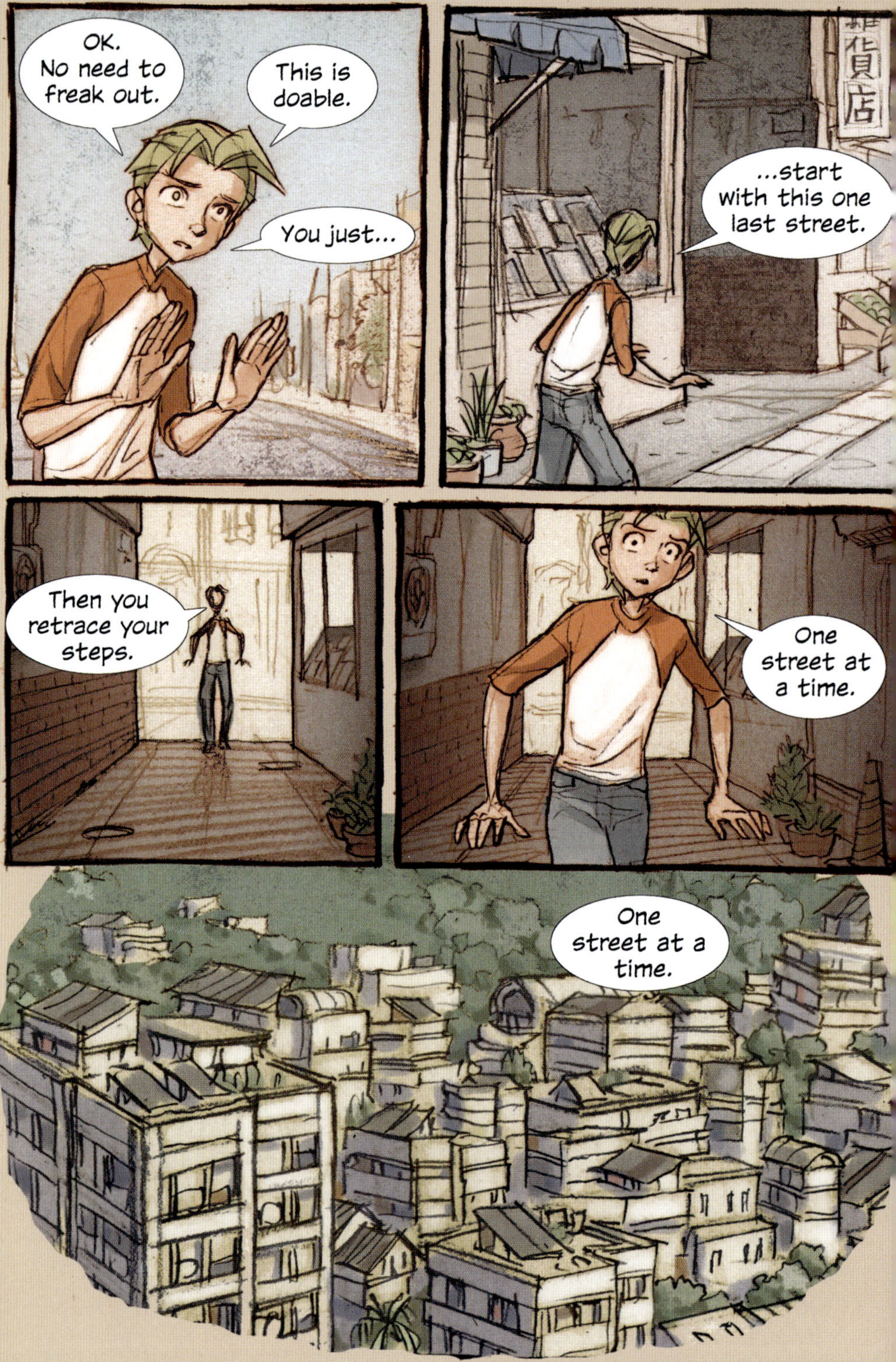
OK. No need to freak out.
This is doable.
You just...
貨店
...start with this one last street.
Then you retrace your steps.
One street at a time.
One street at a time.

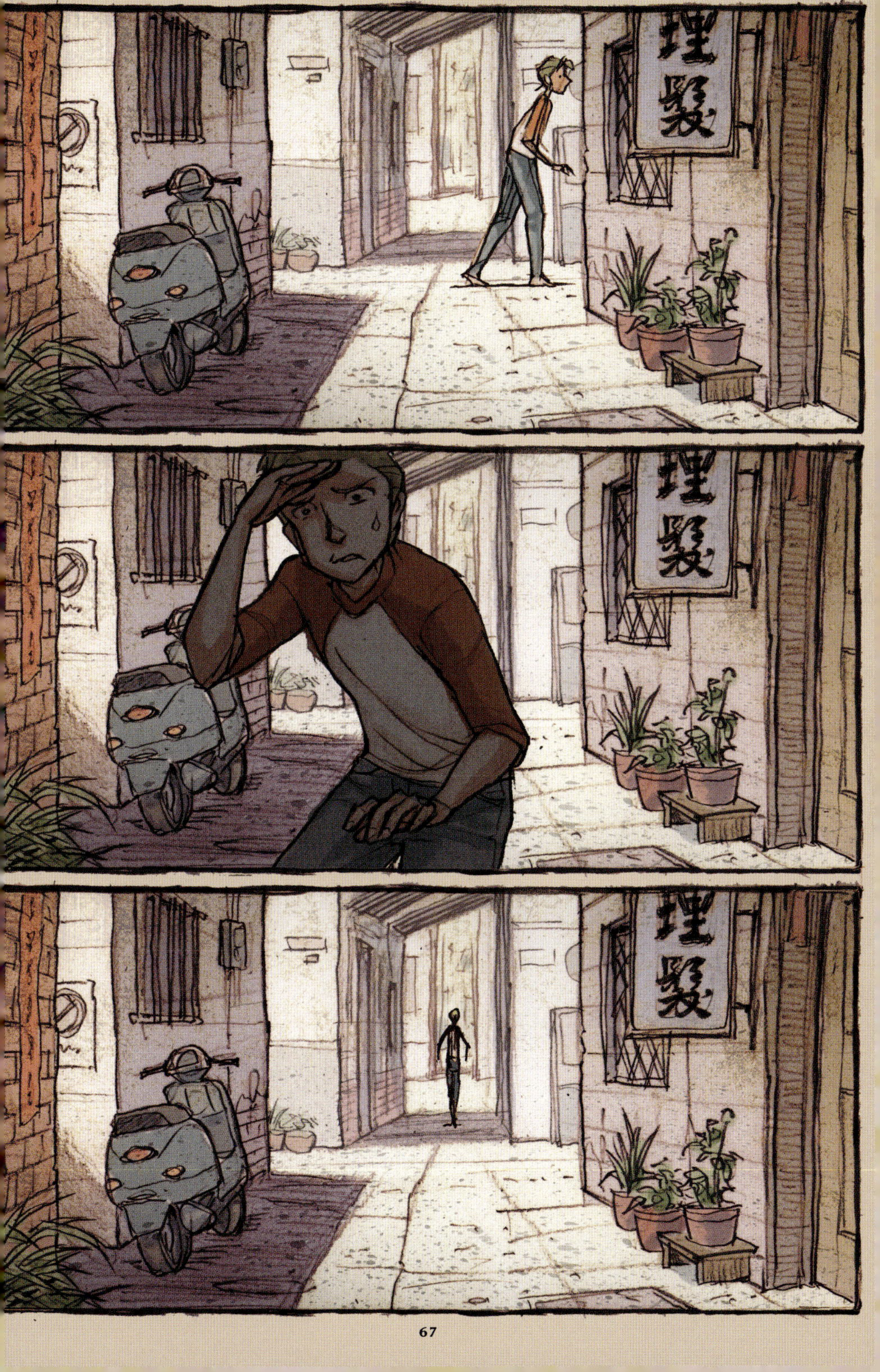
理髮
理髮
理髮

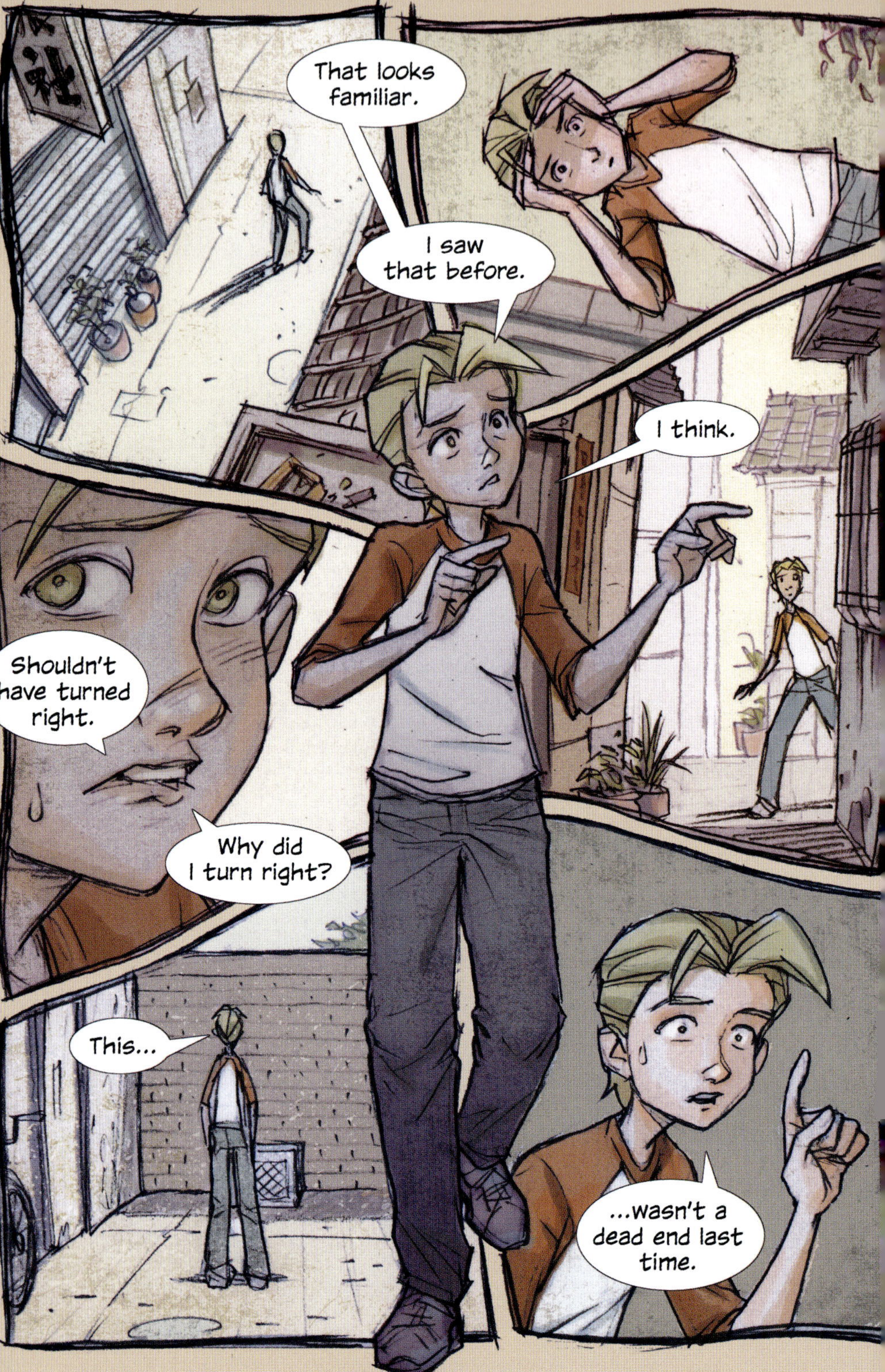

That looks familiar.
I saw that before.
I think.
Shouldn't have turned right.
Why did I turn right?
This...
...wasn't a dead end last time.

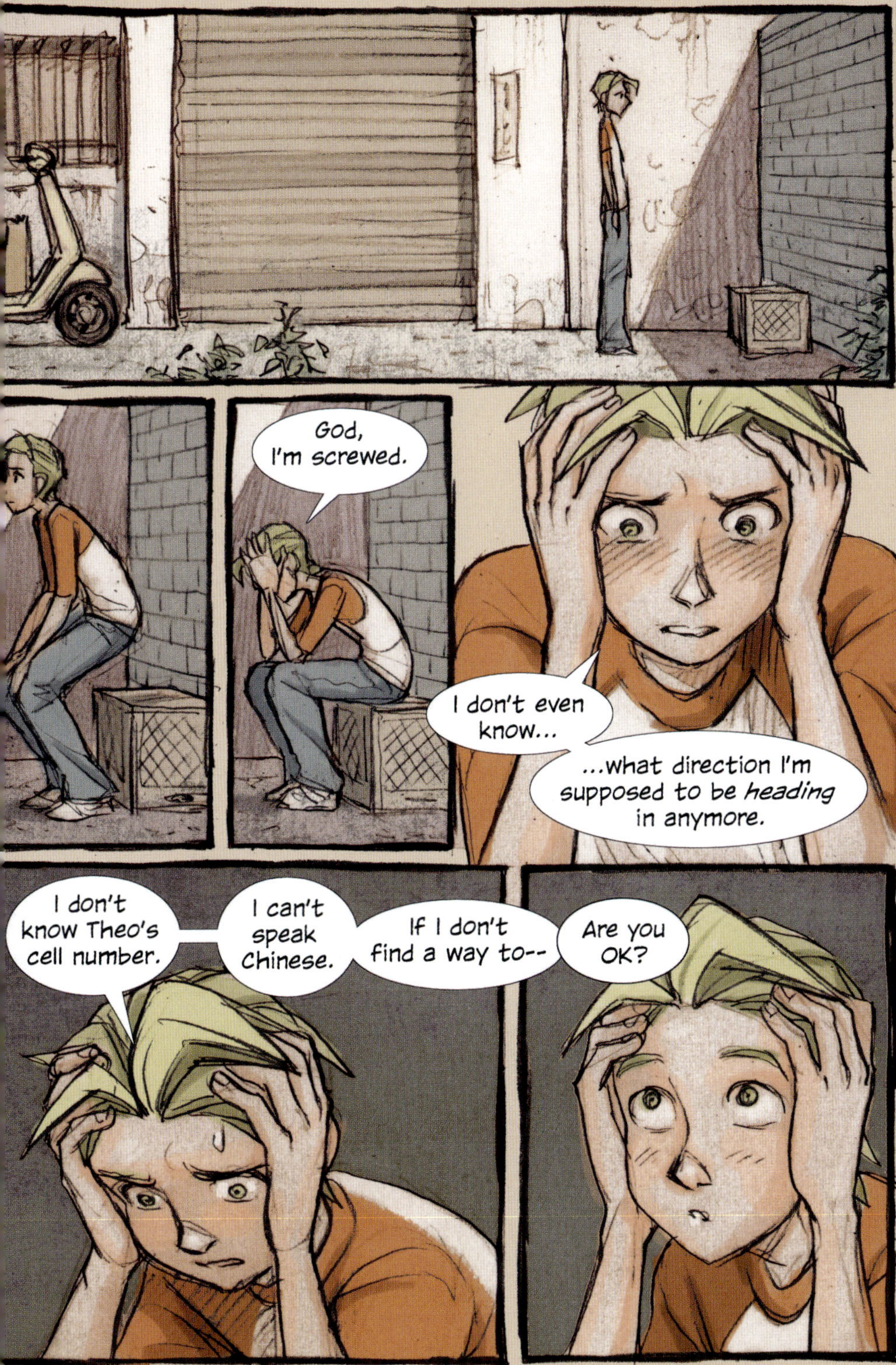

God, I'm screwed.
I don't even know...
...what direction I'm supposed to be *heading* in anymore.
I don't know Theo's cell number.
I can't speak Chinese.
If I don't find a way to--
Are you OK?

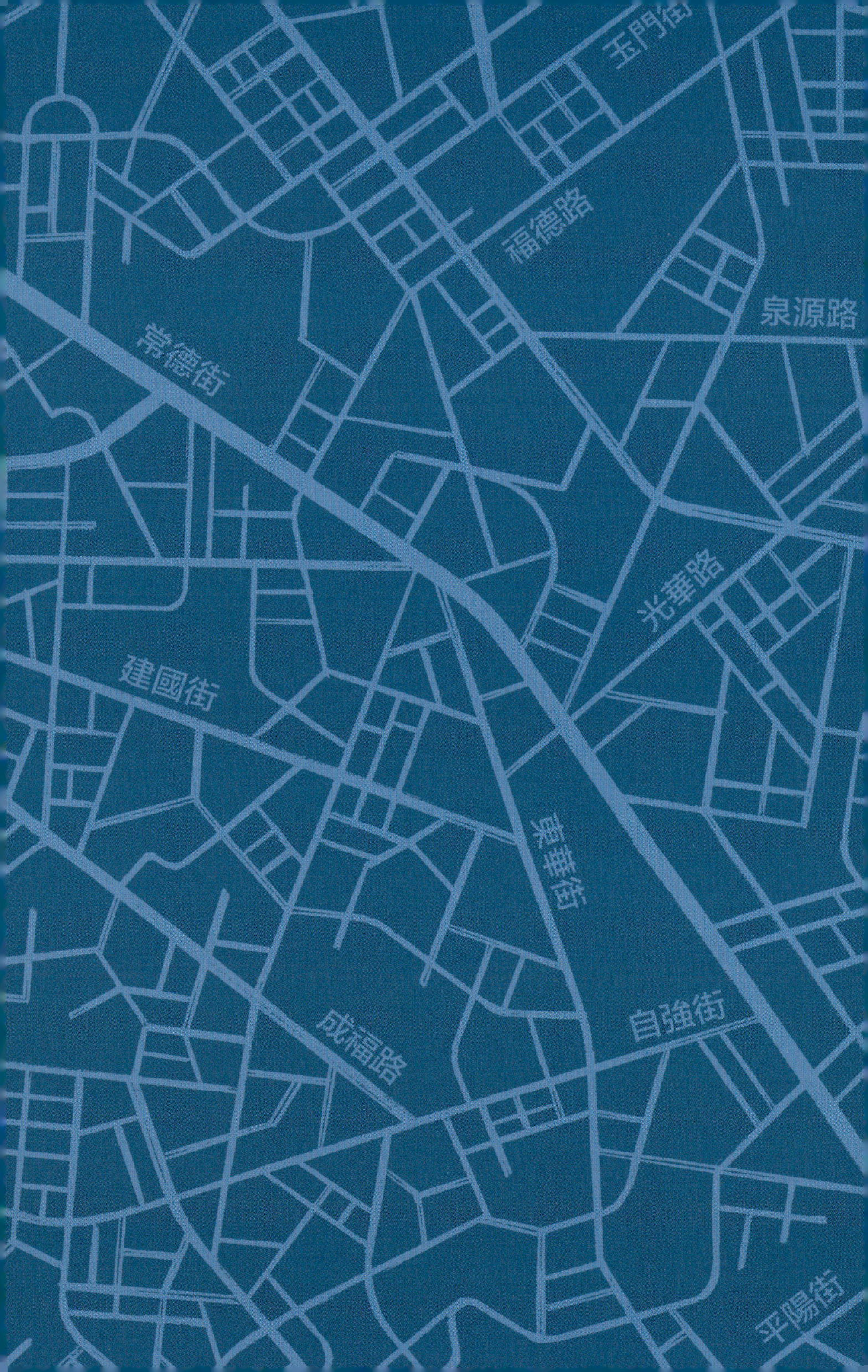
玉門街
福德路
泉源路
常德街
光華路
建國街
東華街
自強街
成福路
平陽街

CHAPTER 2

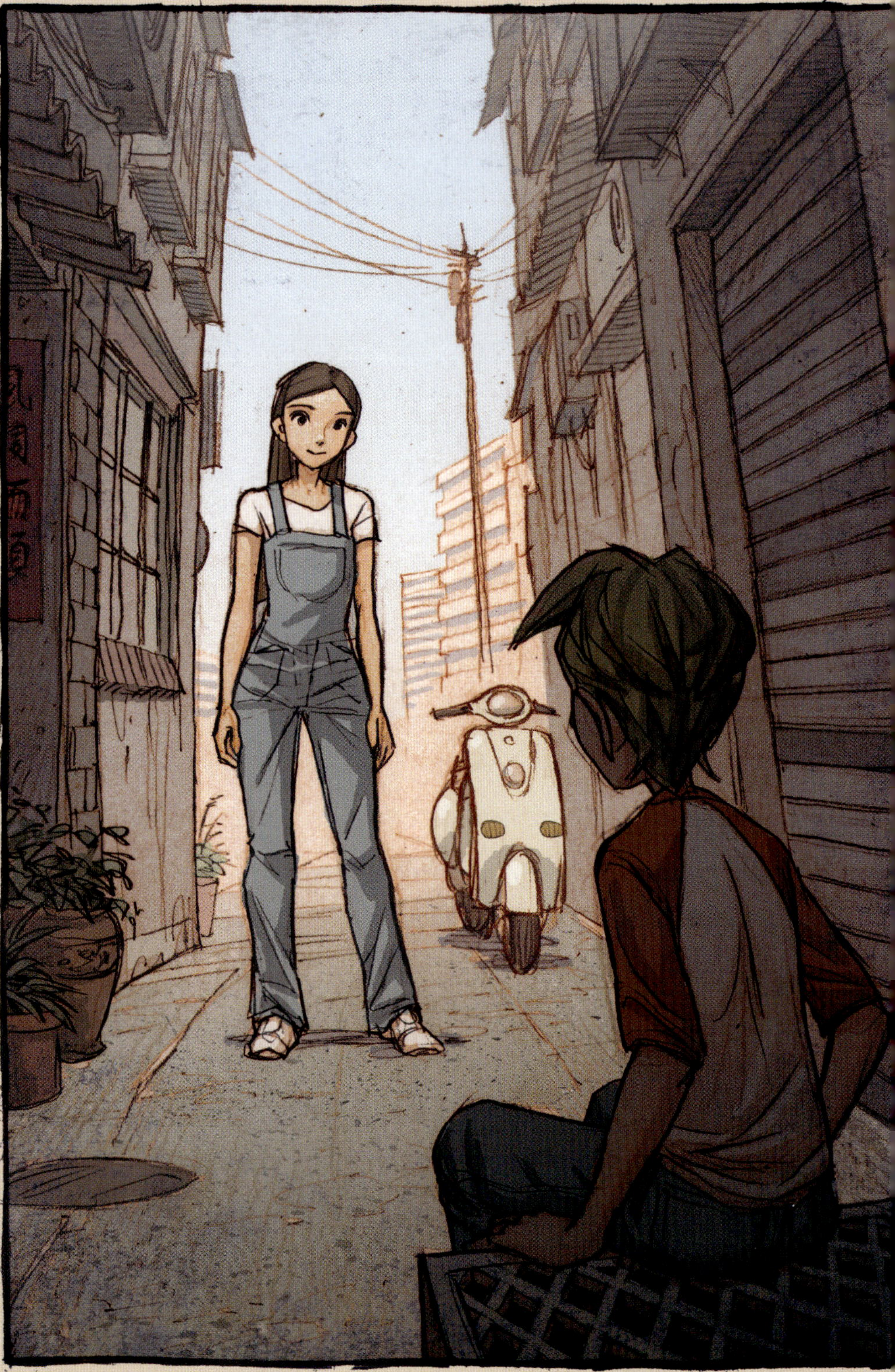

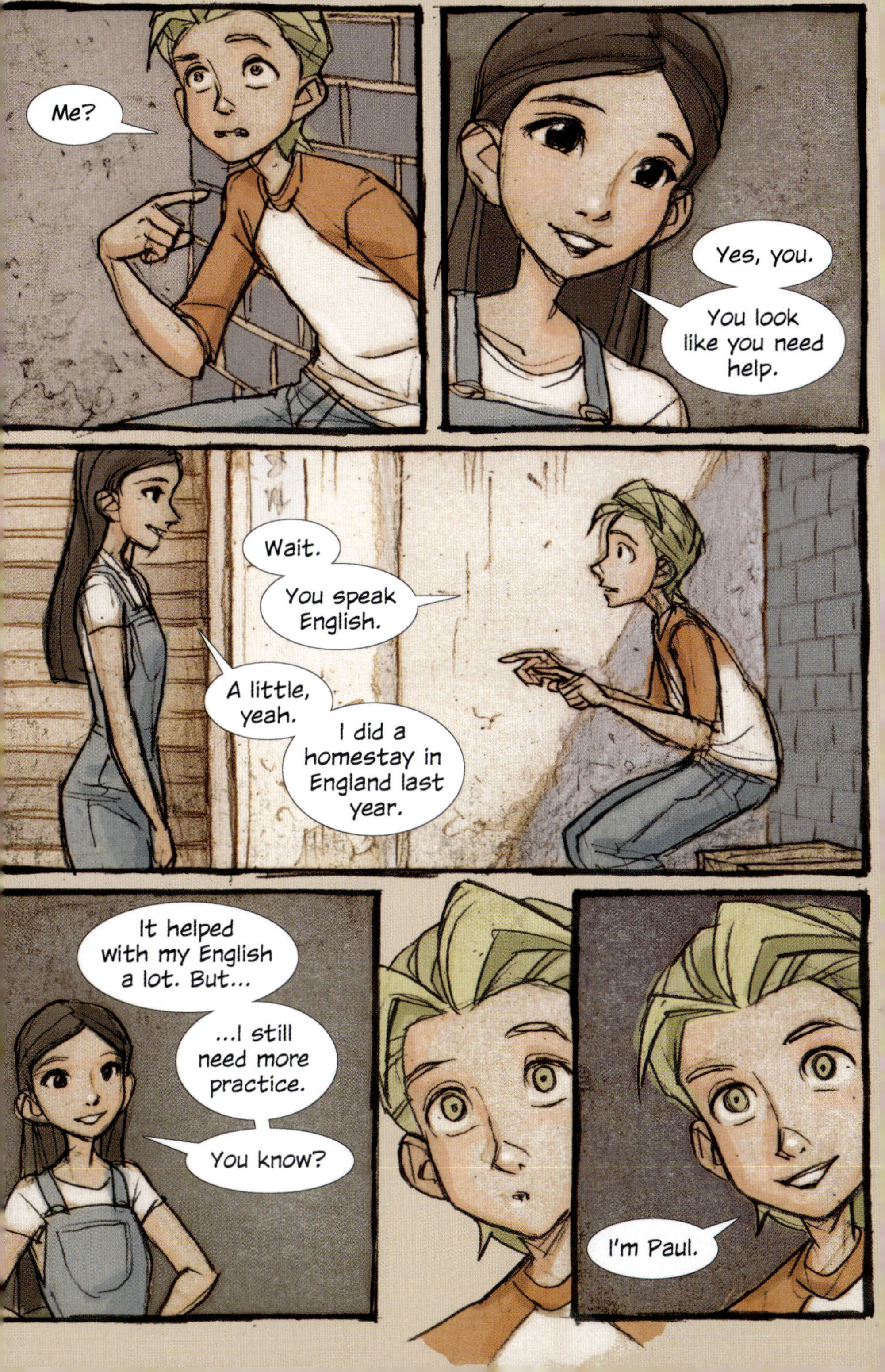
Me?
Yes, you.
You look like you need help.
Wait.
You speak English.
A little, yeah.
I did a homestay in England last year.
It helped with my English a lot. But...
...I still need more practice.
You know?
I'm Paul.

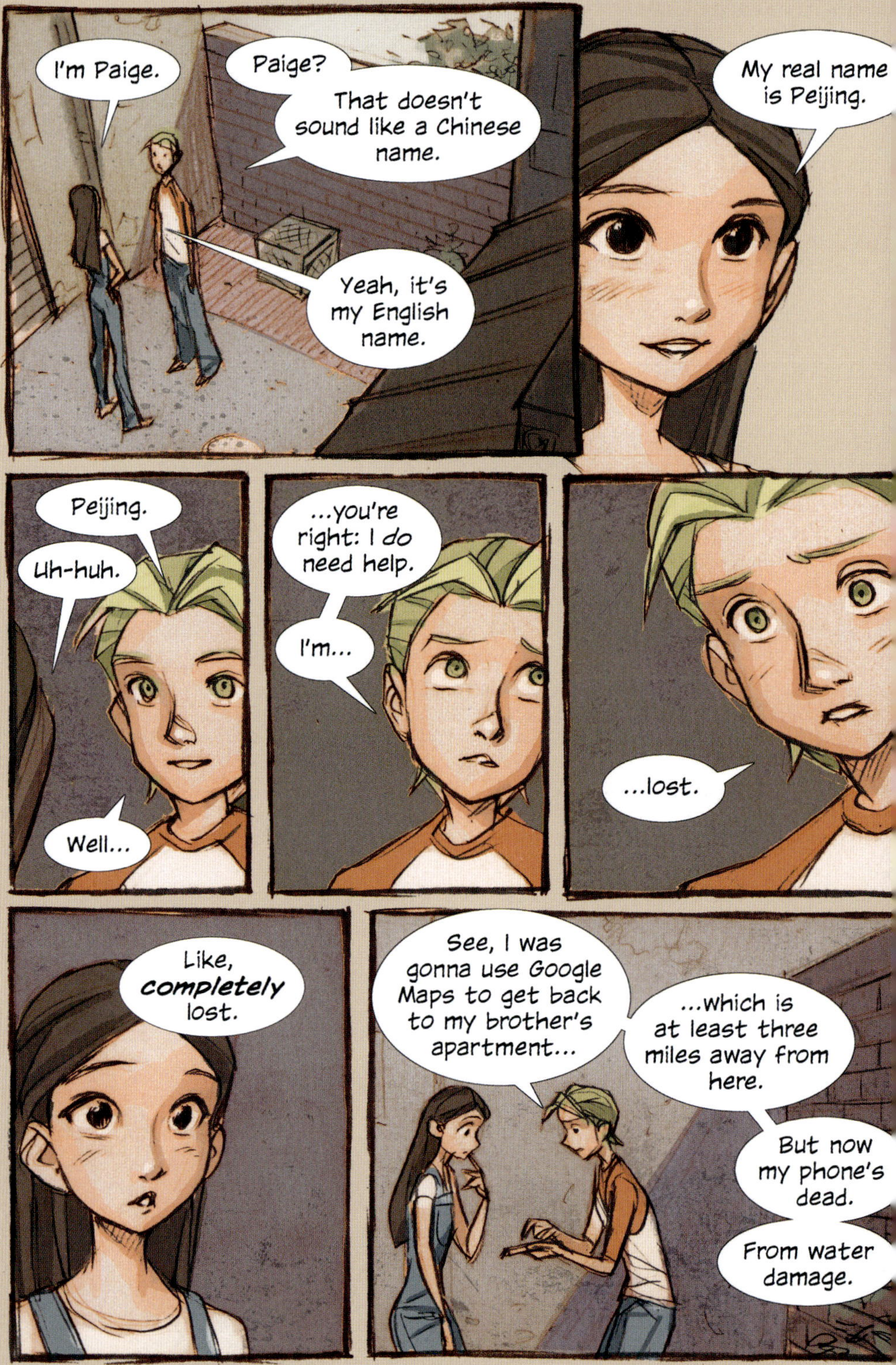
I'm Paige.
Paige?
That doesn't sound like a Chinese name.
Yeah, it's my English name.
My real name is Peijing.
Peijing.
Uh-huh.
Well...
...you're right: I *do* need help.
I'm...
...lost.
Like, ***completely*** lost.
See, I was gonna use Google Maps to get back to my brother's apartment...
...which is at least three miles away from here.
But now my phone's dead.
From water damage.

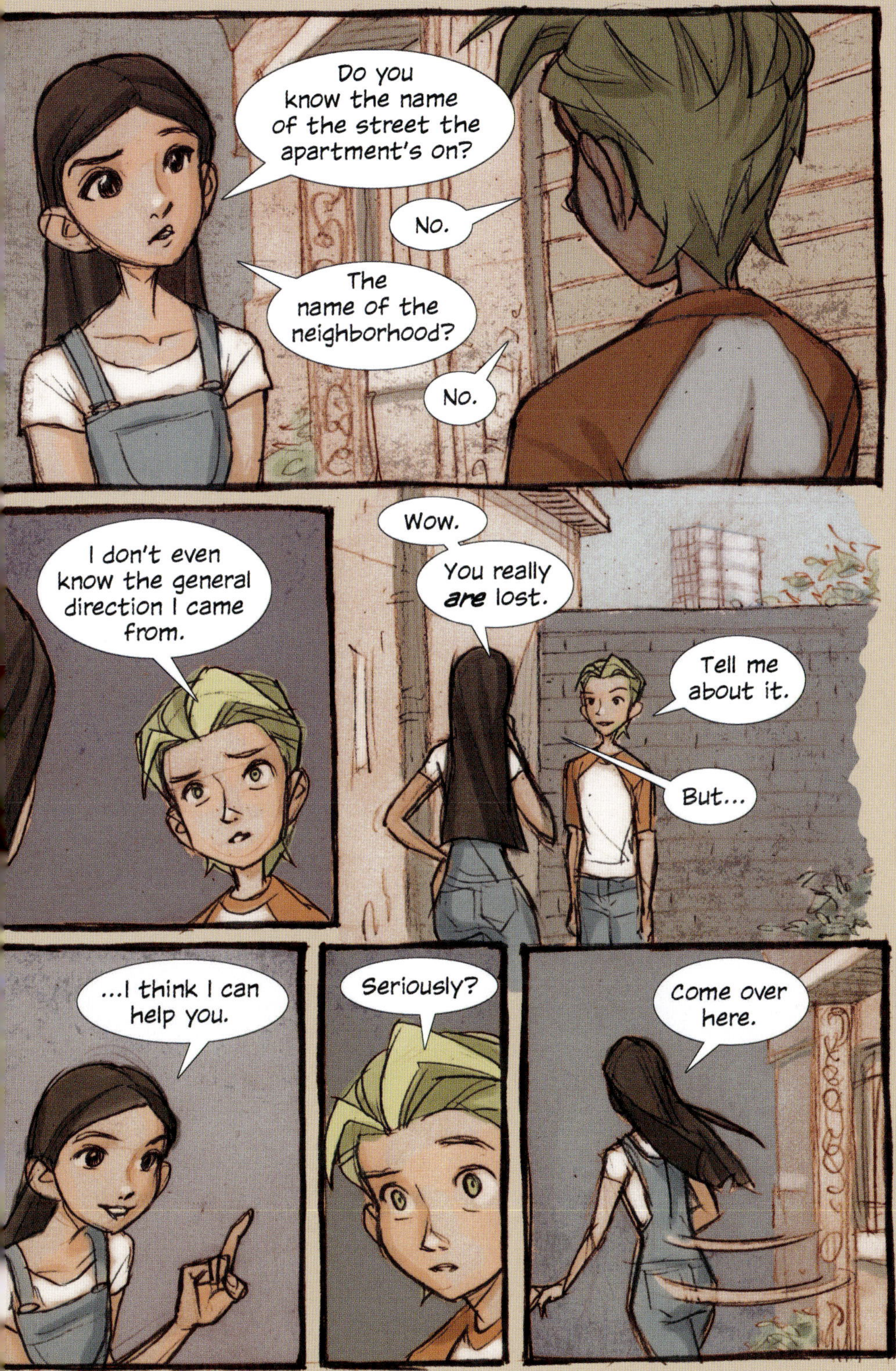
Do you know the name of the street the apartment's on?
No.
The name of the neighborhood?
No.
I don't even know the general direction I came from.
Wow.
You really *are* lost.
Tell me about it.
But...
...I think I can help you.
Seriously?
Come over here.

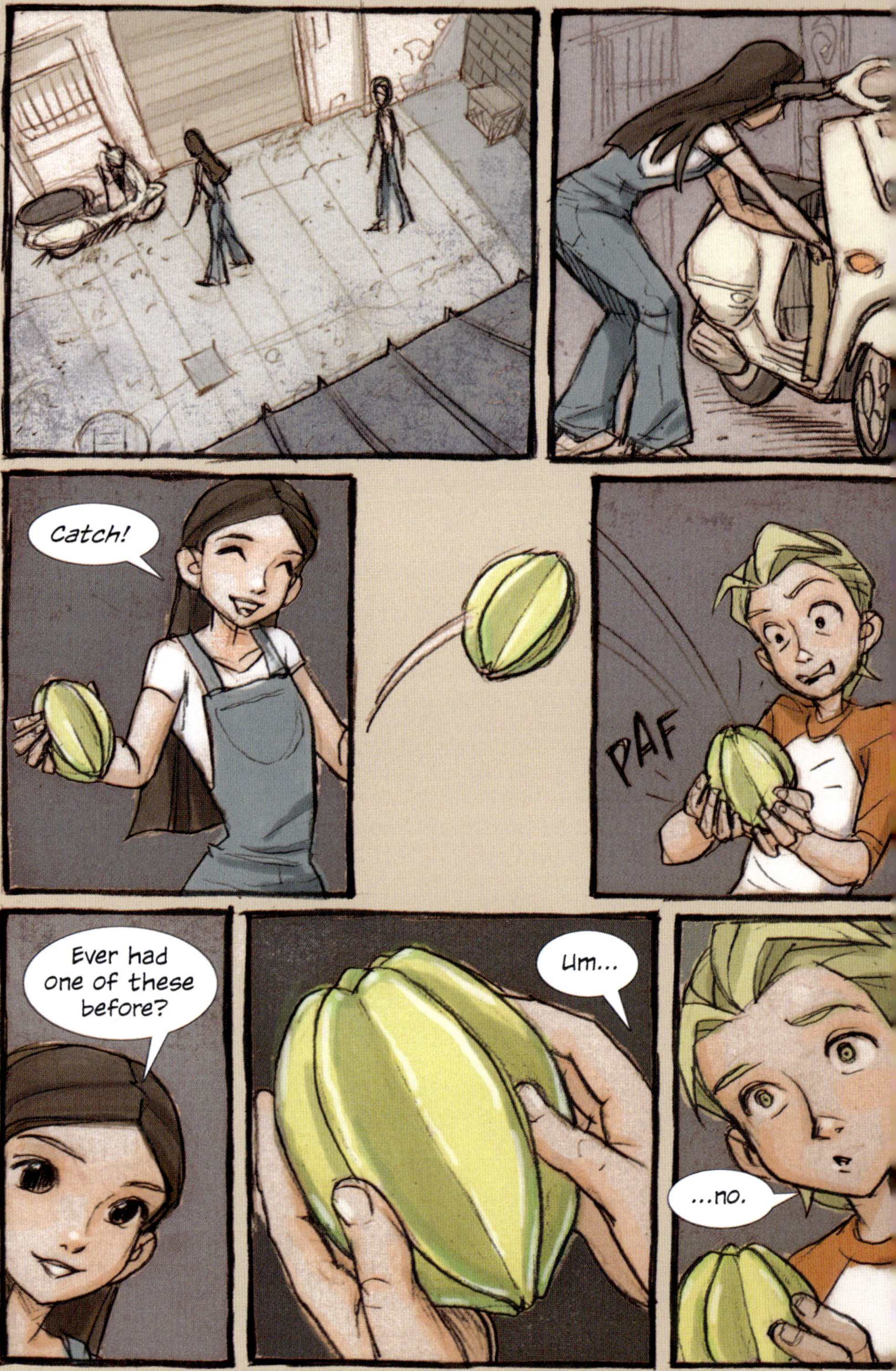
Catch!
PAF
Ever had one of these before?
Um...
...no.

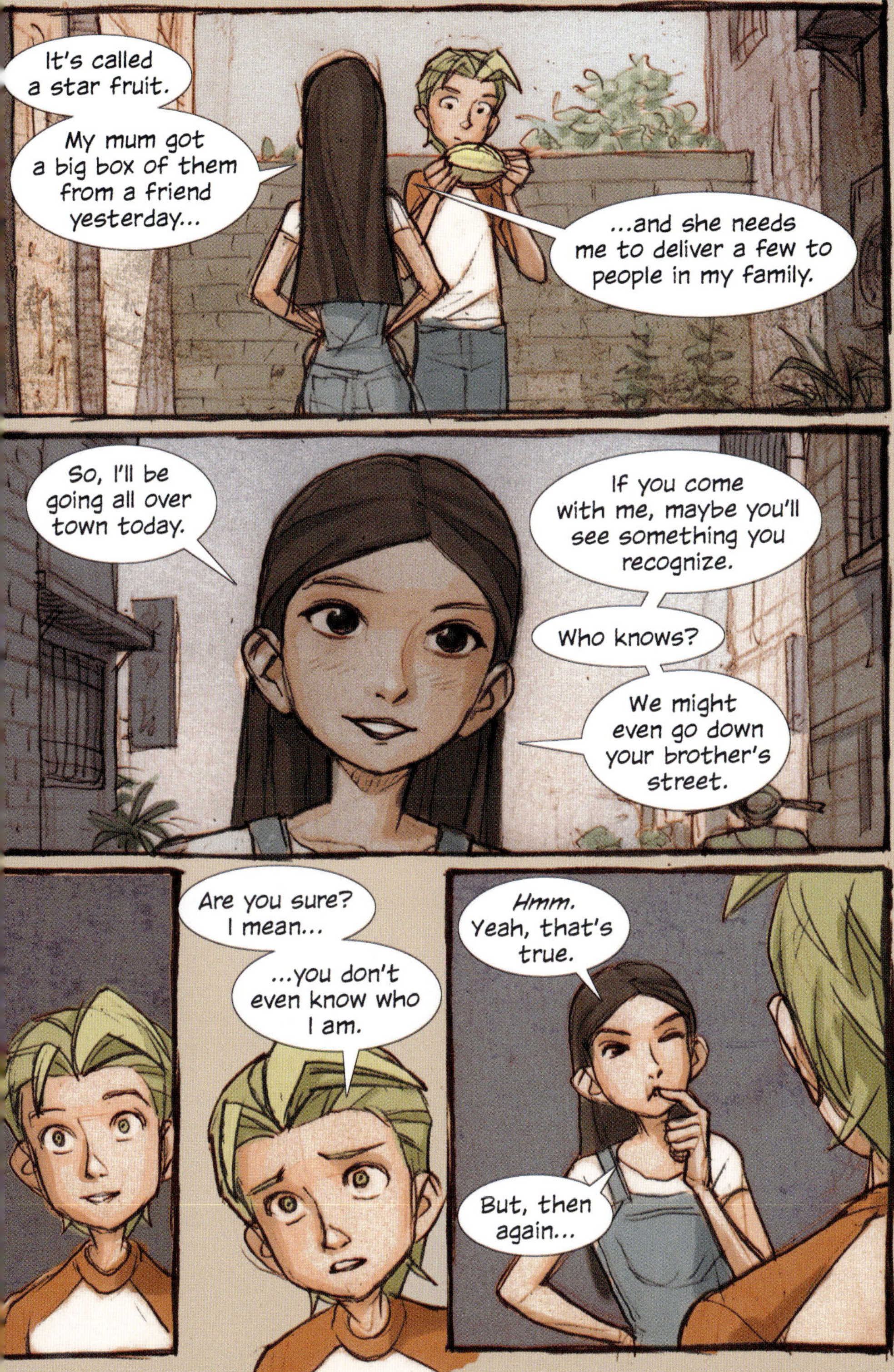
It's called a star fruit.
My mum got a big box of them from a friend yesterday...
...and she needs me to deliver a few to people in my family.
So, I'll be going all over town today.
If you come with me, maybe you'll see something you recognize.
Who knows?
We might even go down your brother's street.
Are you sure? I mean...
...you don't even know who I am.
Hmm. Yeah, that's true.
But, then again...

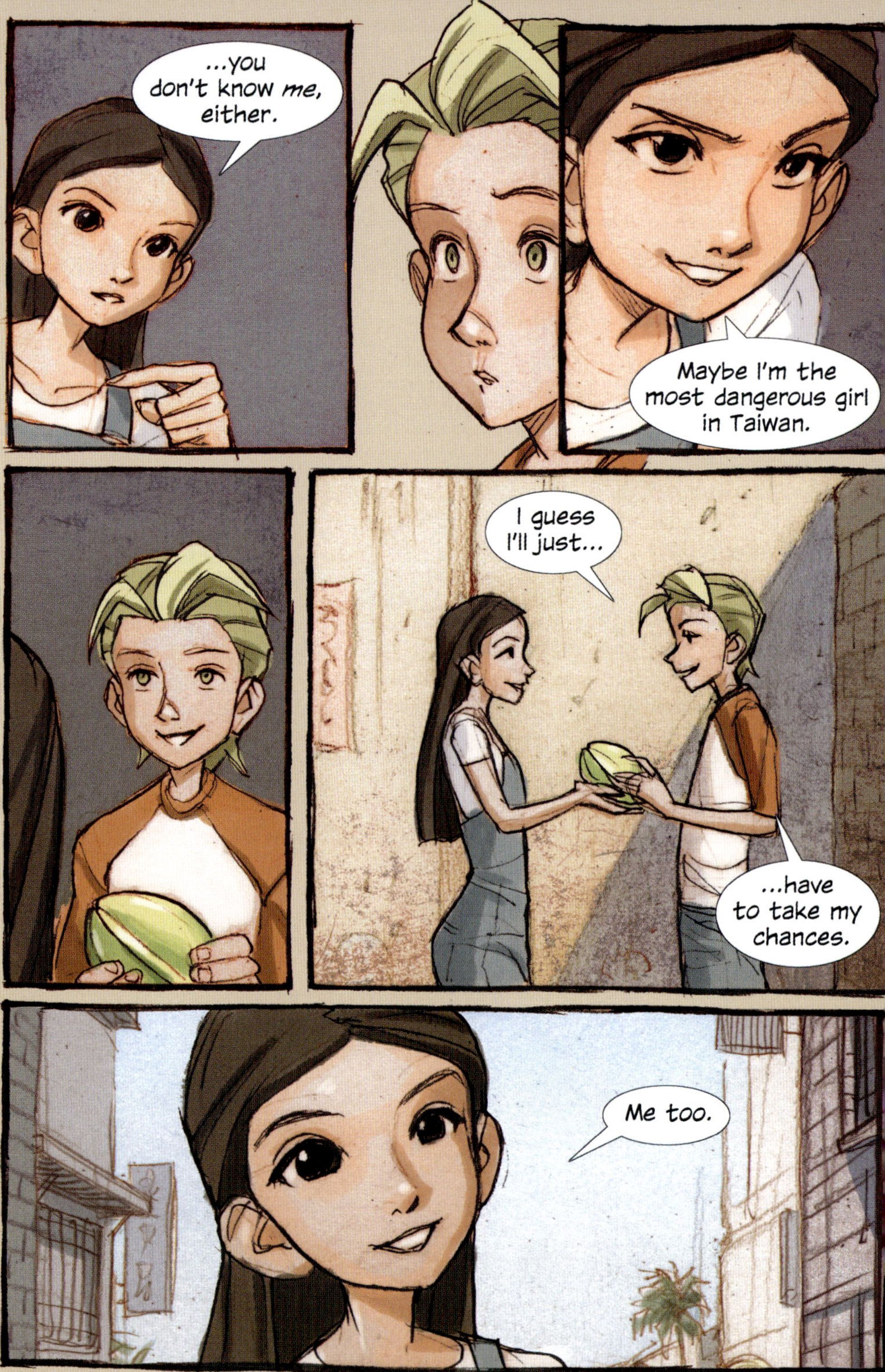
...you don't know *me*, either.
Maybe I'm the most dangerous girl in Taiwan.
I guess I'll just...
...have to take my chances.
Me too.

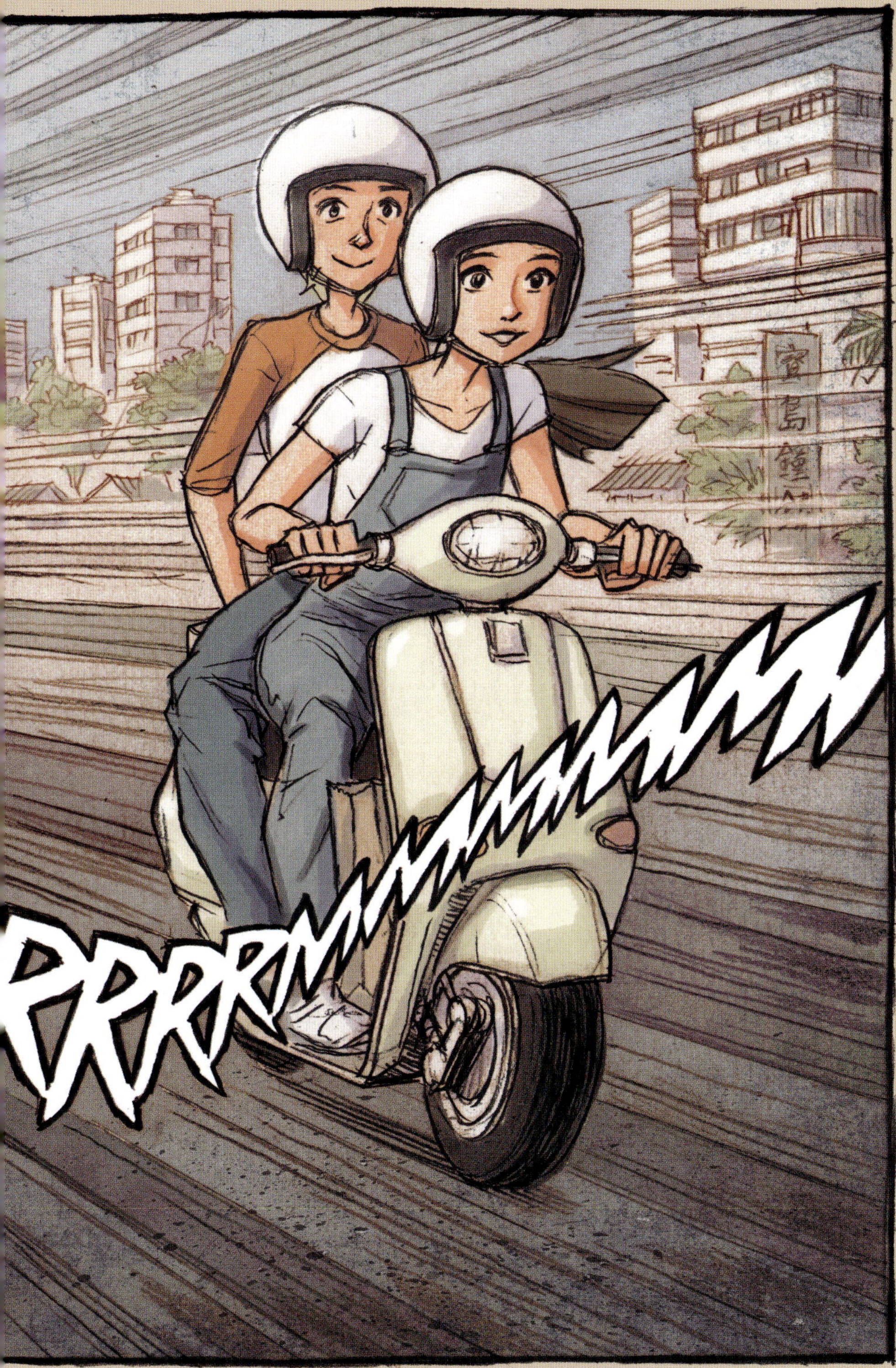
PRRRMMMMMMMMMM

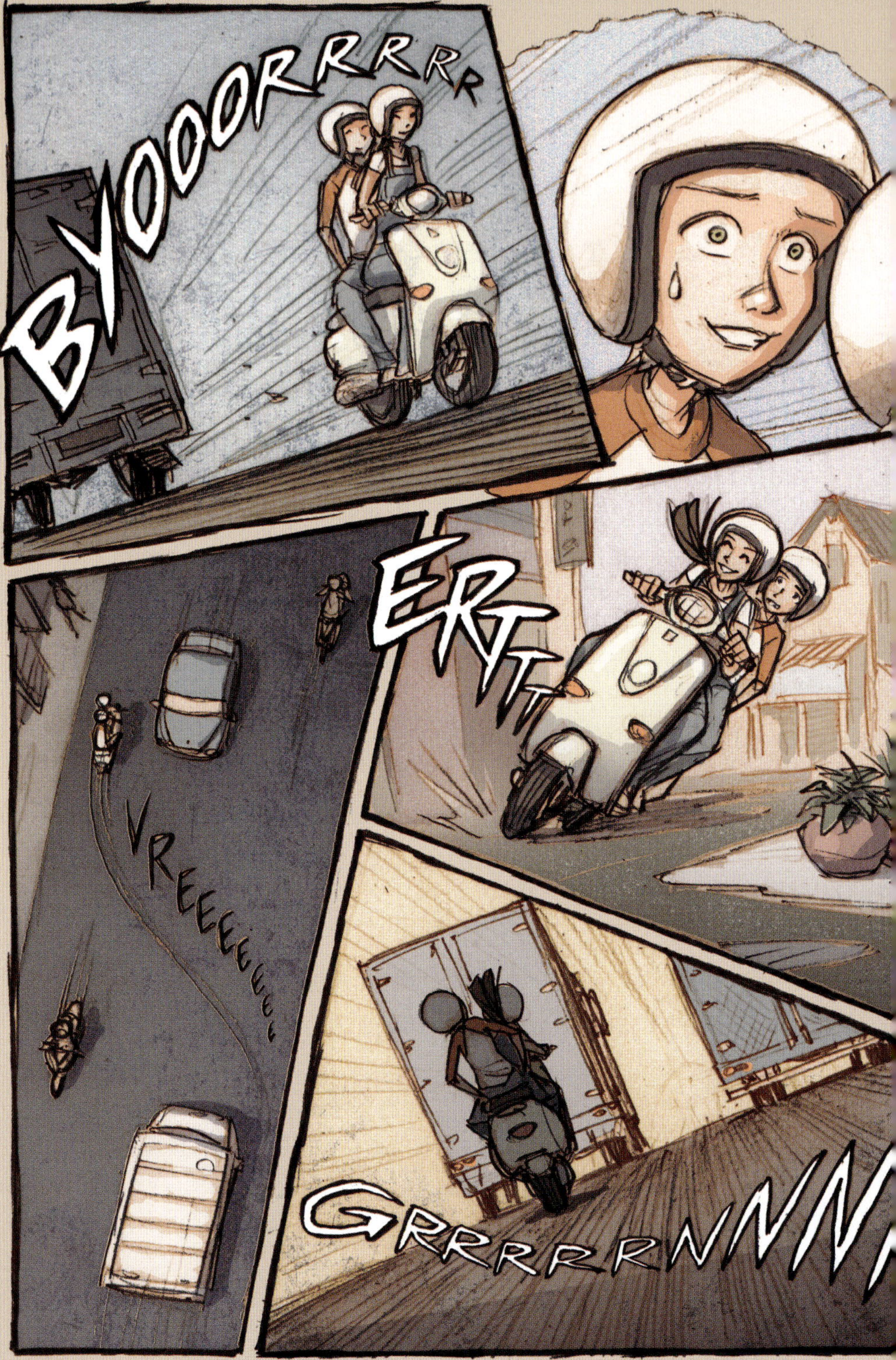
BYOOORRRRR
ERTTT
VREEEEEEE
GRRRRRRNNNN

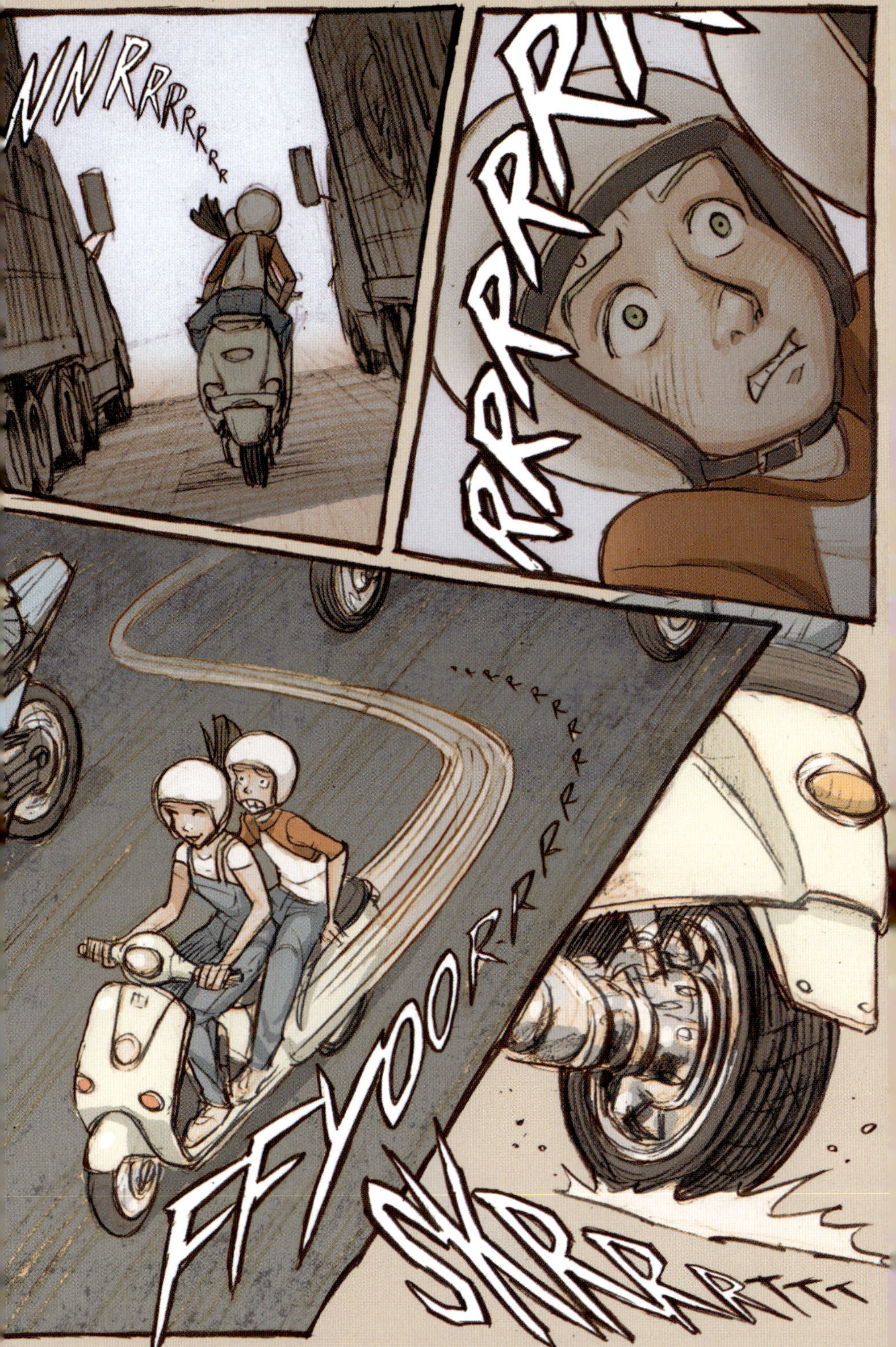
NNRRRRRRRR
RRRRRRT!
FFYOOR-RRRRRRRRR
SKRRRRTTT

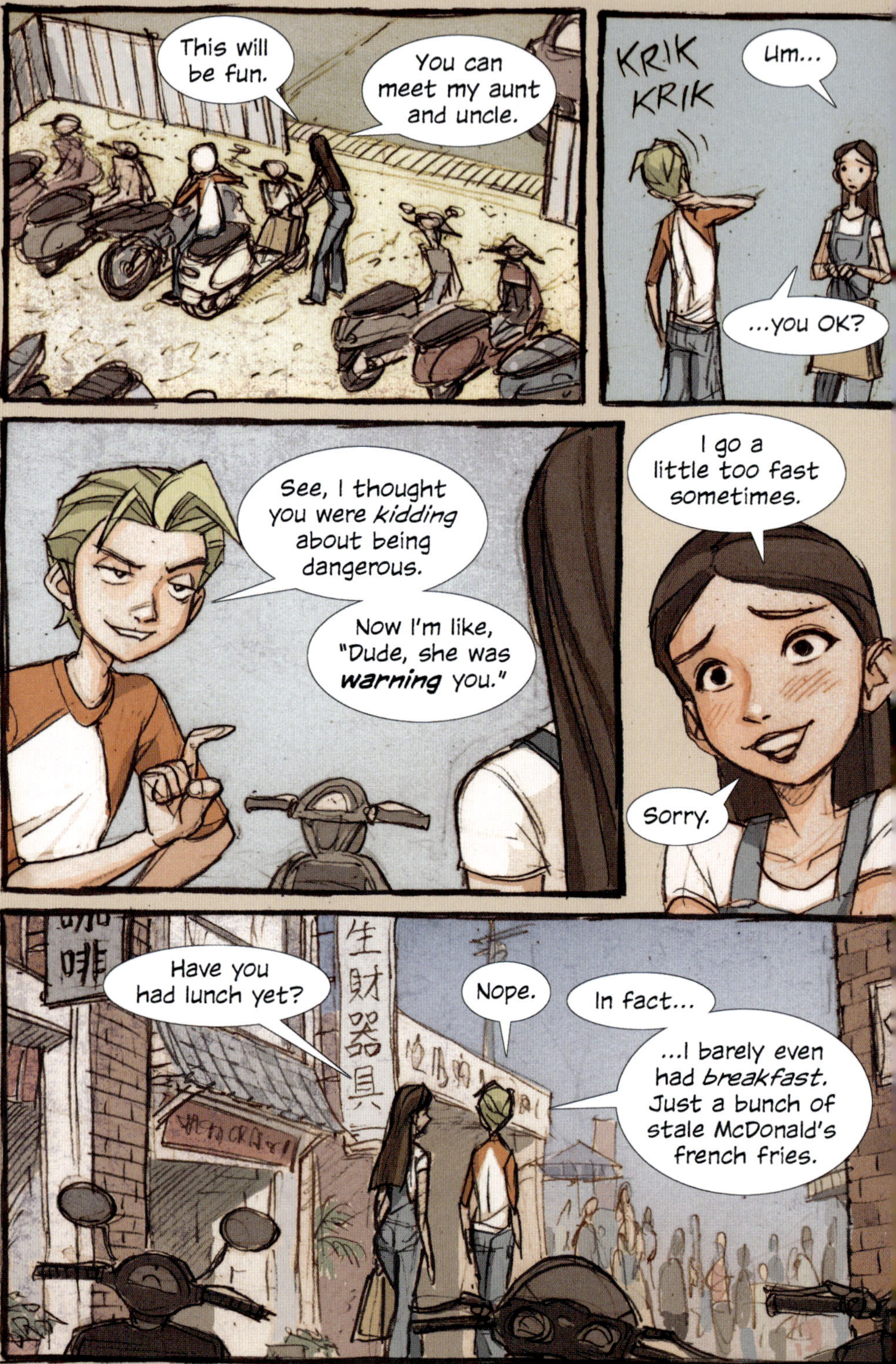
This will be fun.
You can meet my aunt and uncle.
KRIK KRIK
Um...
...you OK?
See, I thought you were *kidding* about being dangerous.
Now I'm like, "Dude, she was ***warning*** you."
I go a little too fast sometimes.
Sorry.
生財器具
Have you had lunch yet?
Nope.
In fact...
...I barely even had *breakfast.* Just a bunch of stale McDonald's french fries.

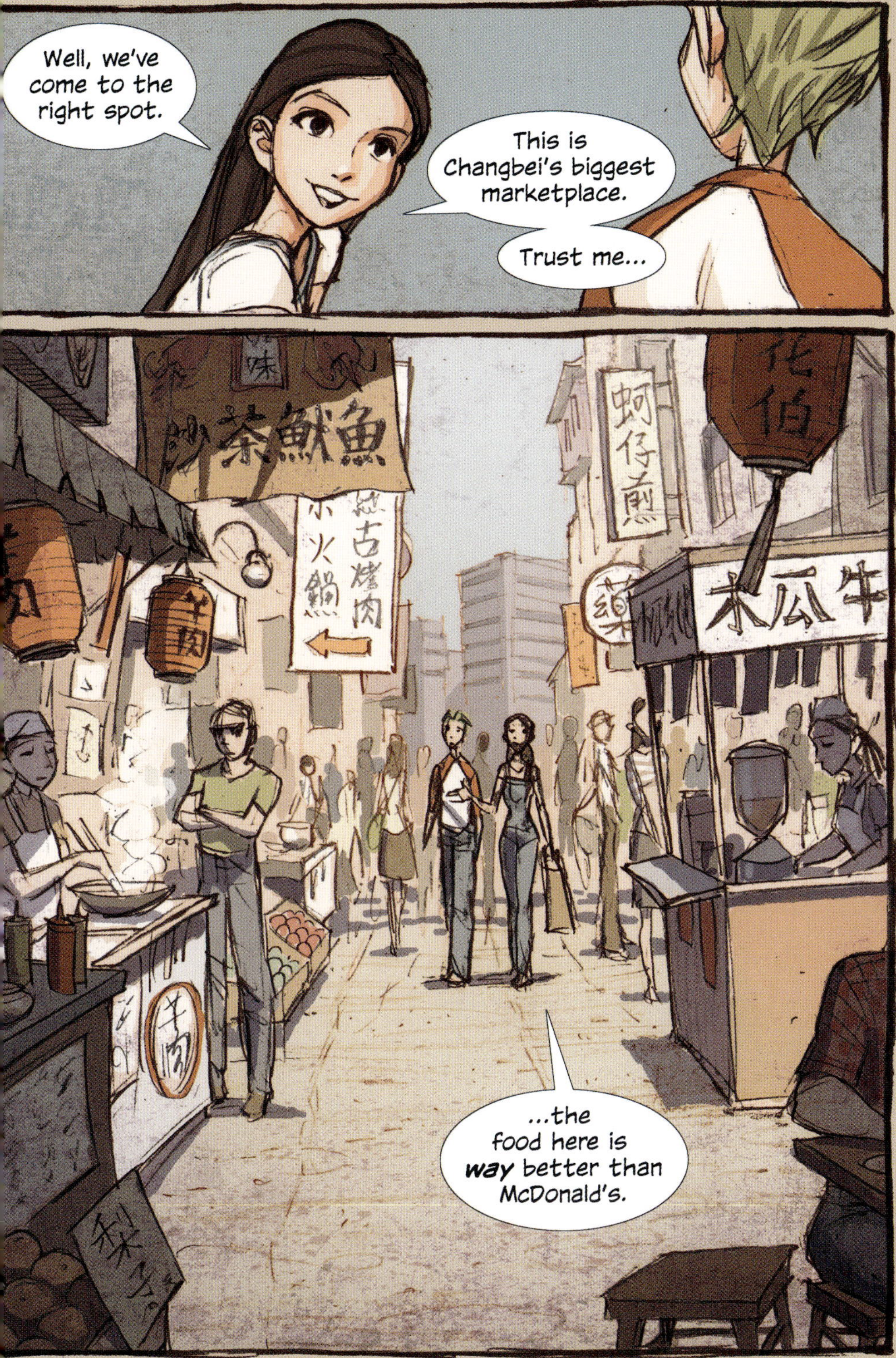
Well, we've come to the right spot.
This is Changbei's biggest marketplace.
Trust me...
沙茶魷魚
蚵仔煎
小火鍋
木瓜牛
...the food here is **way** better than McDonald's.

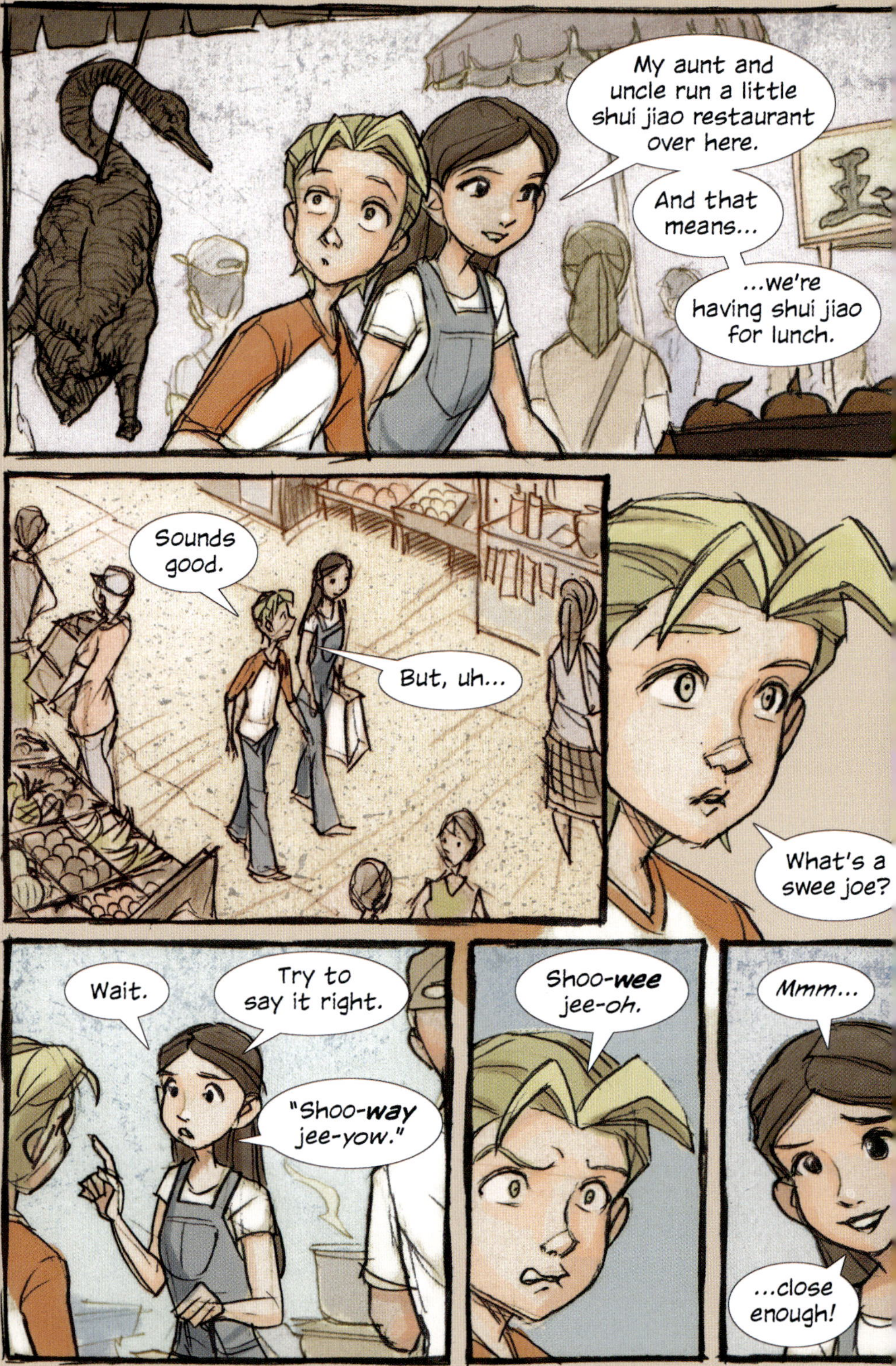
My aunt and uncle run a little shui jiao restaurant over here.
And that means...
...we're having shui jiao for lunch.
Sounds good.
But, uh...
What's a swee joe?
Wait.
Try to say it right.
"Shoo-**way** jee-yow."
Shoo-**wee** jee-oh.
Mmm...
...close enough!

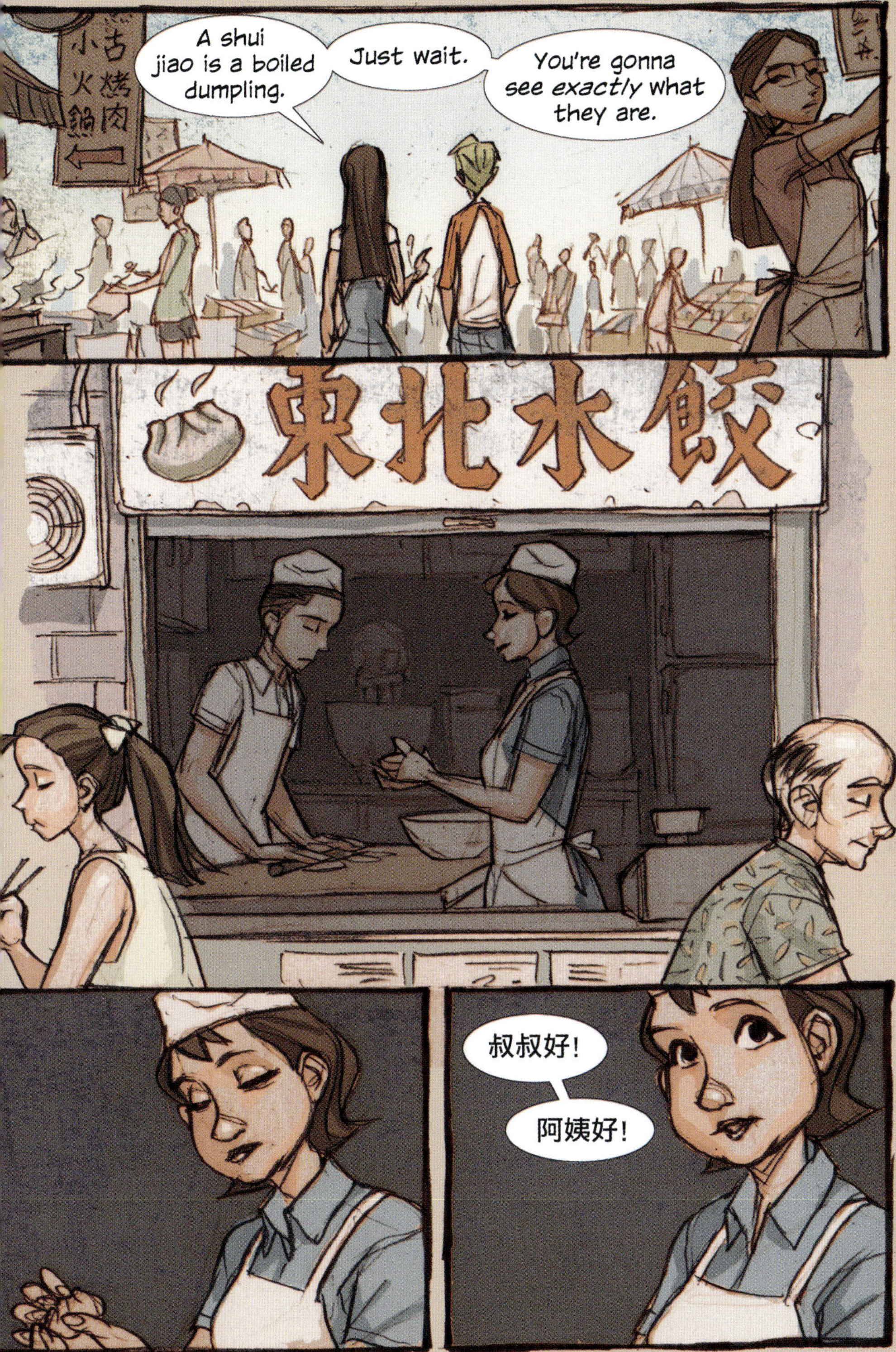

A shui jiao is a boiled dumpling.
Just wait.
You're gonna see *exactly* what they are.
東北水餃
叔叔好!
阿姨好!

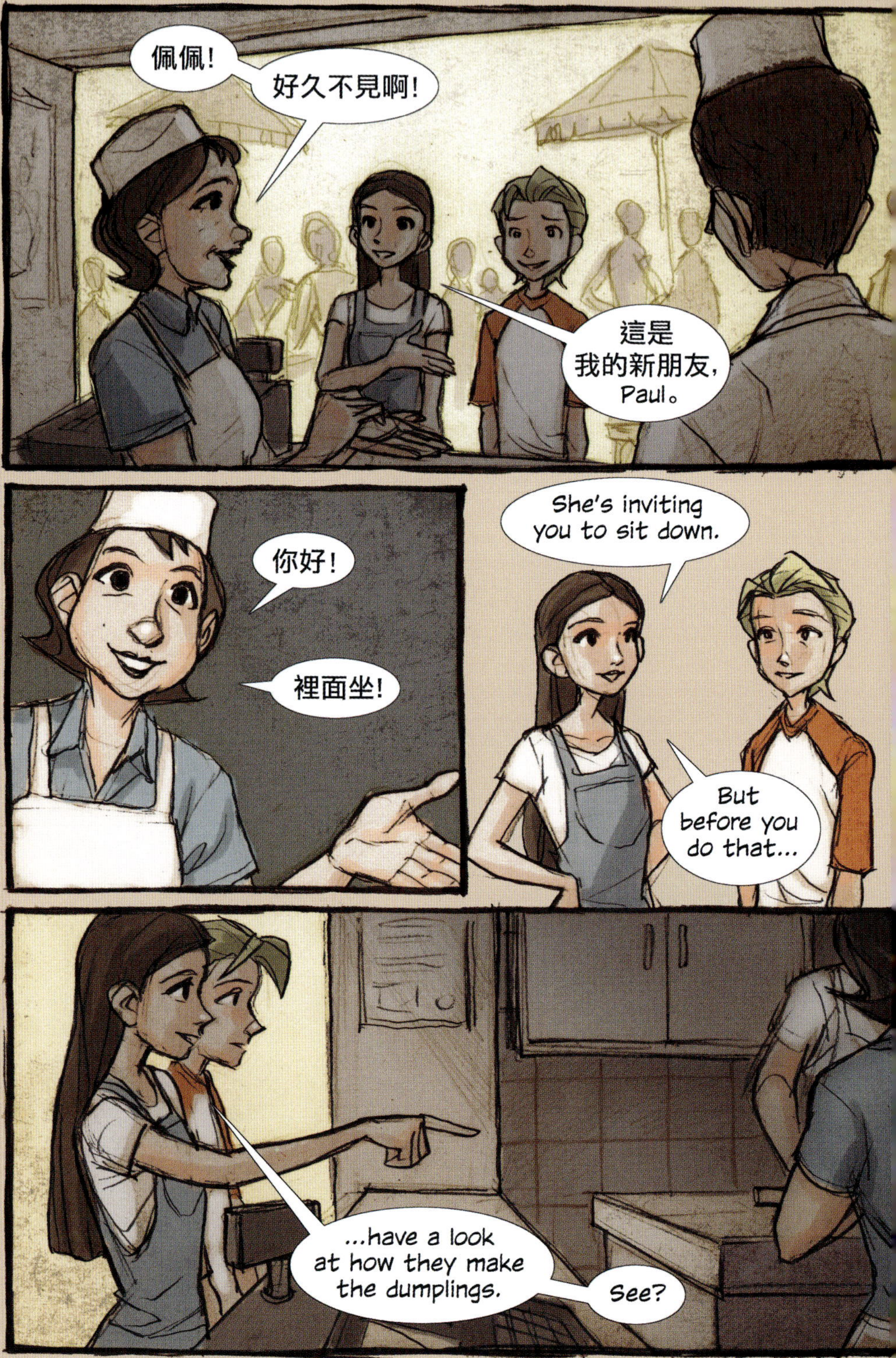
佩佩!
好久不見啊!
這是我的新朋友,Paul。
你好!
裡面坐!
She's inviting you to sit down.
But before you do that...
...have a look at how they make the dumplings.
See?

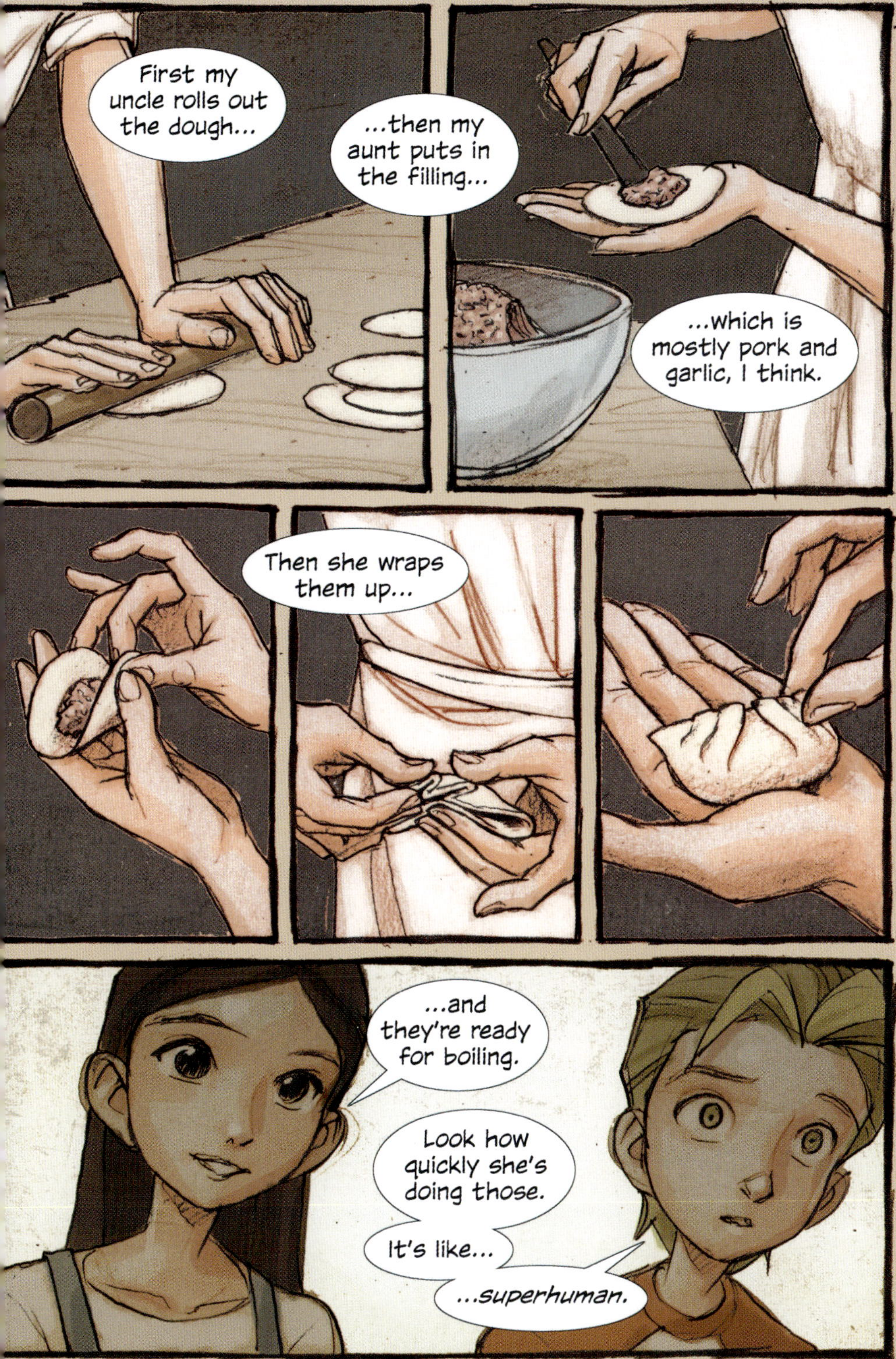
First my uncle rolls out the dough...
...then my aunt puts in the filling...
...which is mostly pork and garlic, I think.
Then she wraps them up...
...and they're ready for boiling.
Look how quickly she's doing those.
It's like...
...superhuman.

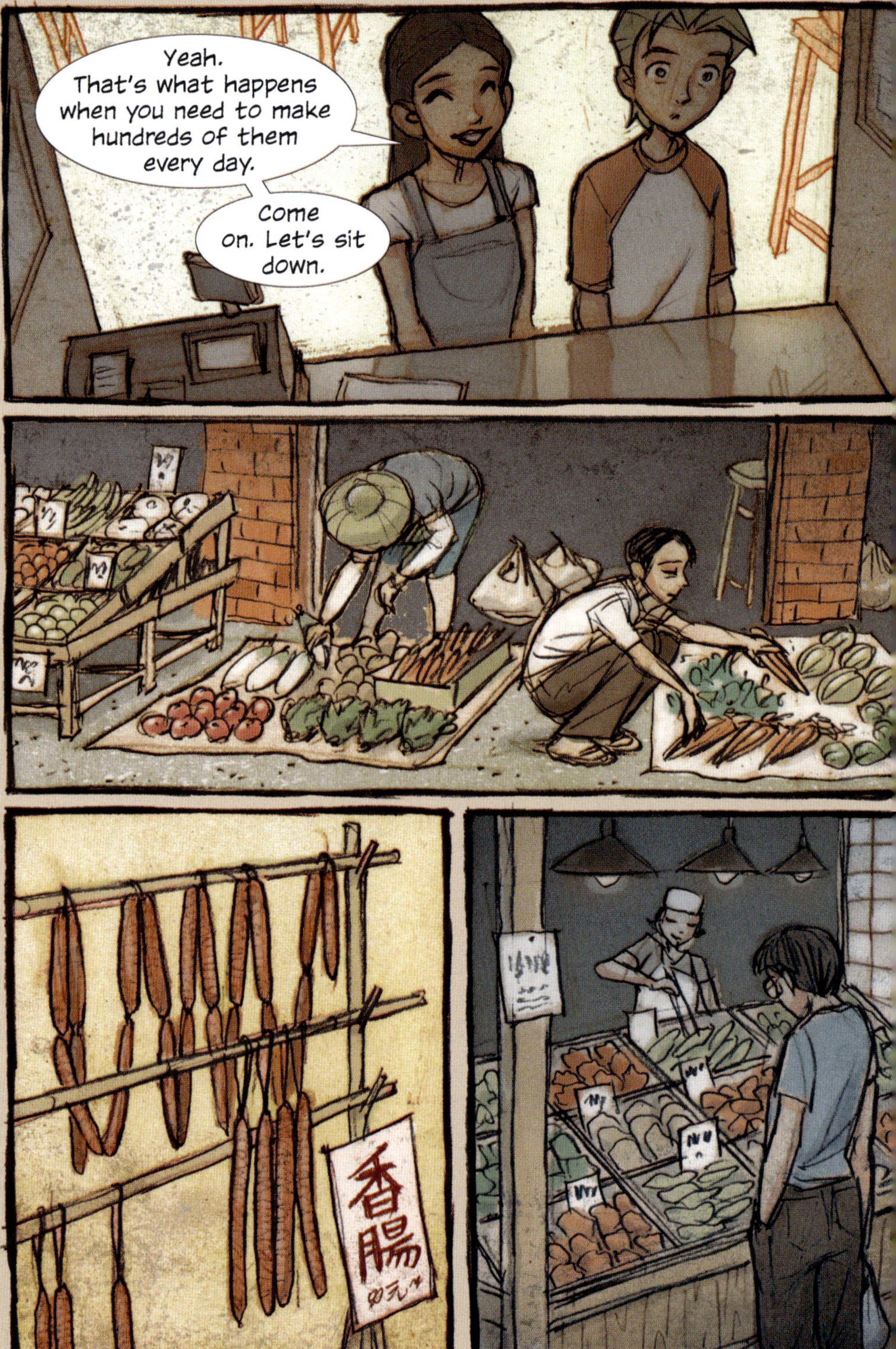
Yeah. That's what happens when you need to make hundreds of them every day.
Come on. Let's sit down.
香腸

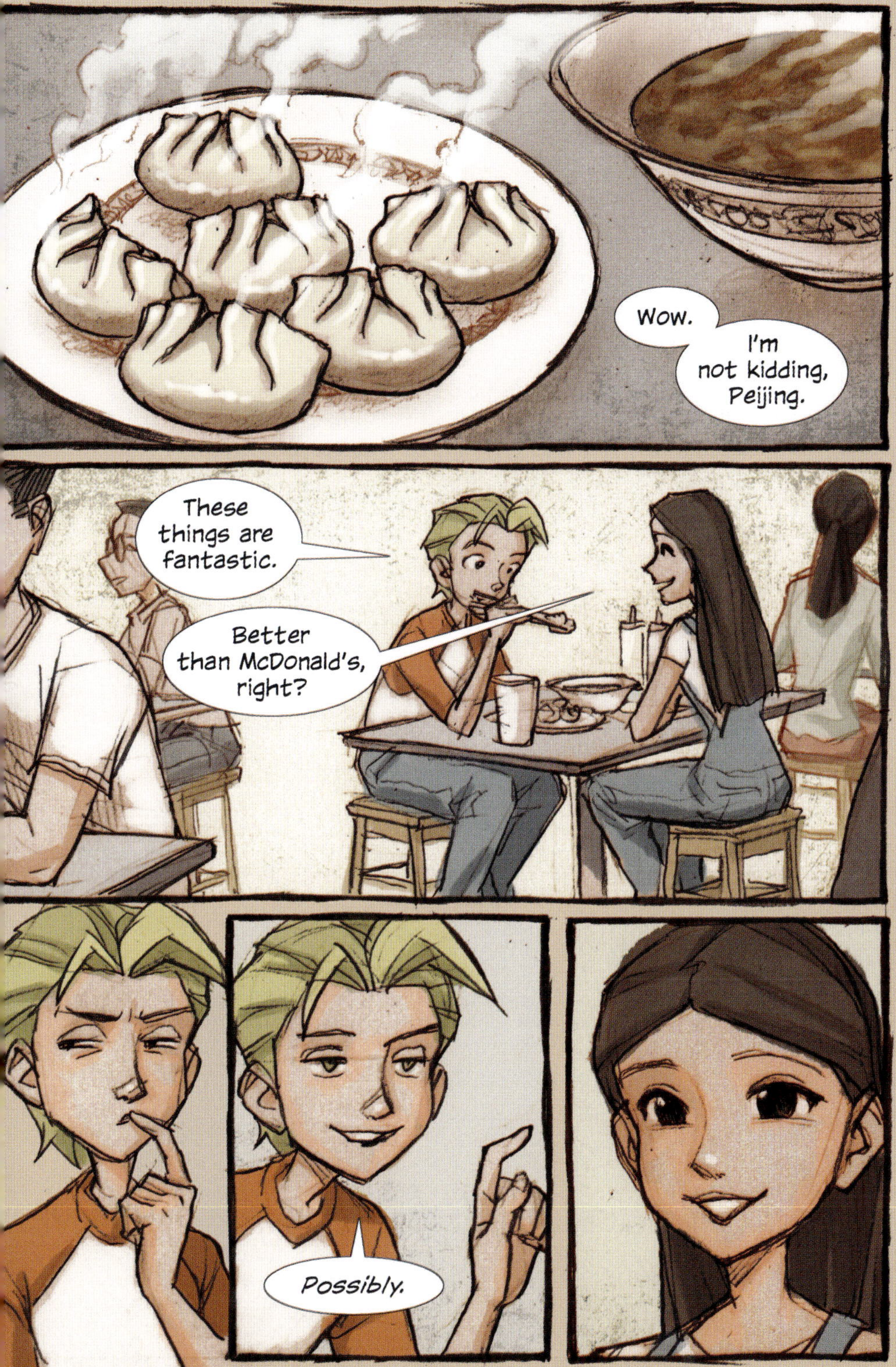
Wow.
I'm not kidding, Peijing.
These things are fantastic.
Better than McDonald's, right?
Possibly.

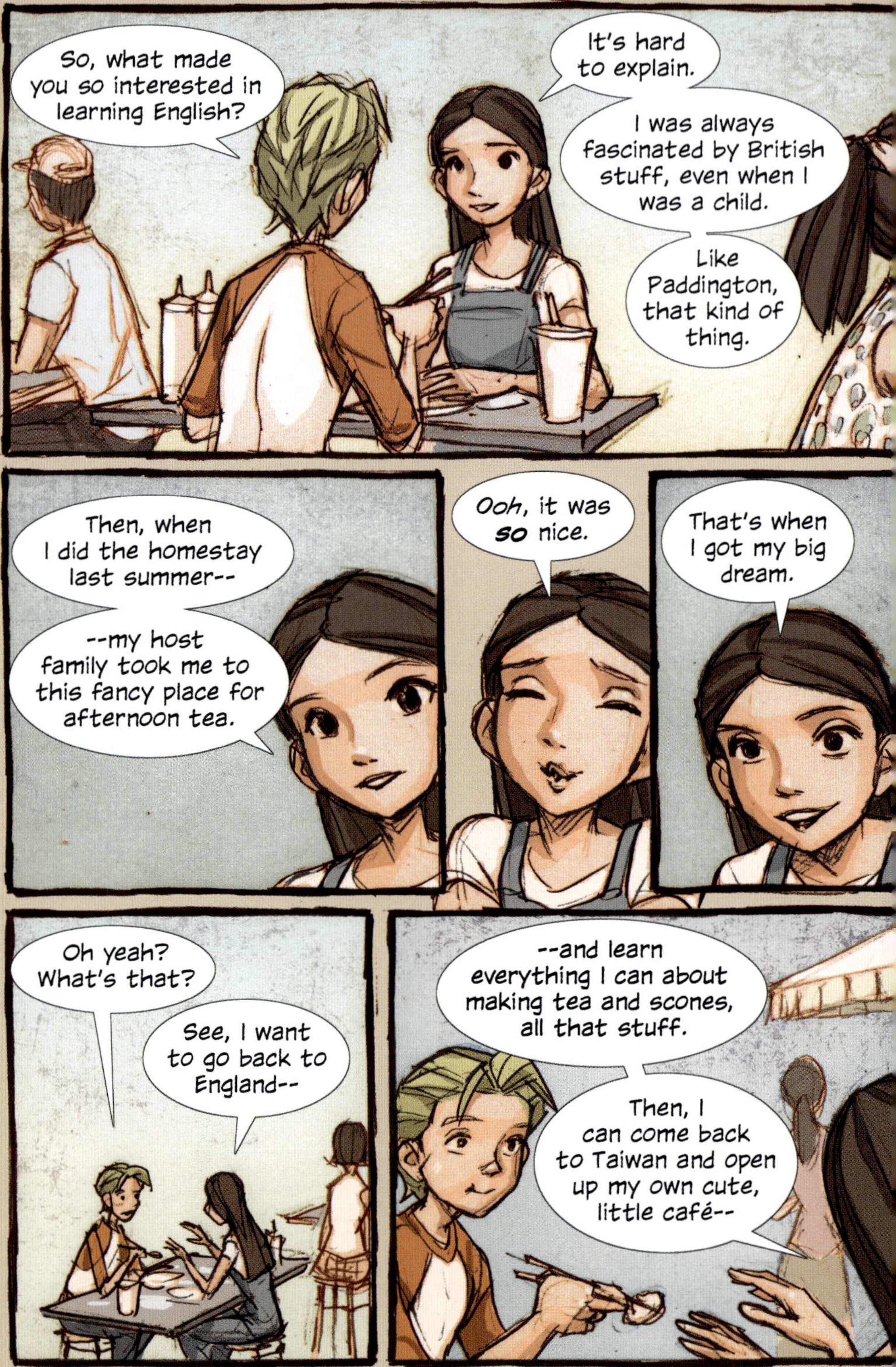
So, what made you so interested in learning English?
It's hard to explain.
I was always fascinated by British stuff, even when I was a child.
Like Paddington, that kind of thing.
Then, when I did the homestay last summer--
--my host family took me to this fancy place for afternoon tea.
Ooh, it was ***so*** nice.
That's when I got my big dream.
Oh yeah? What's that?
See, I want to go back to England--
--and learn everything I can about making tea and scones, all that stuff.
Then, I can come back to Taiwan and open up my own cute, little café--

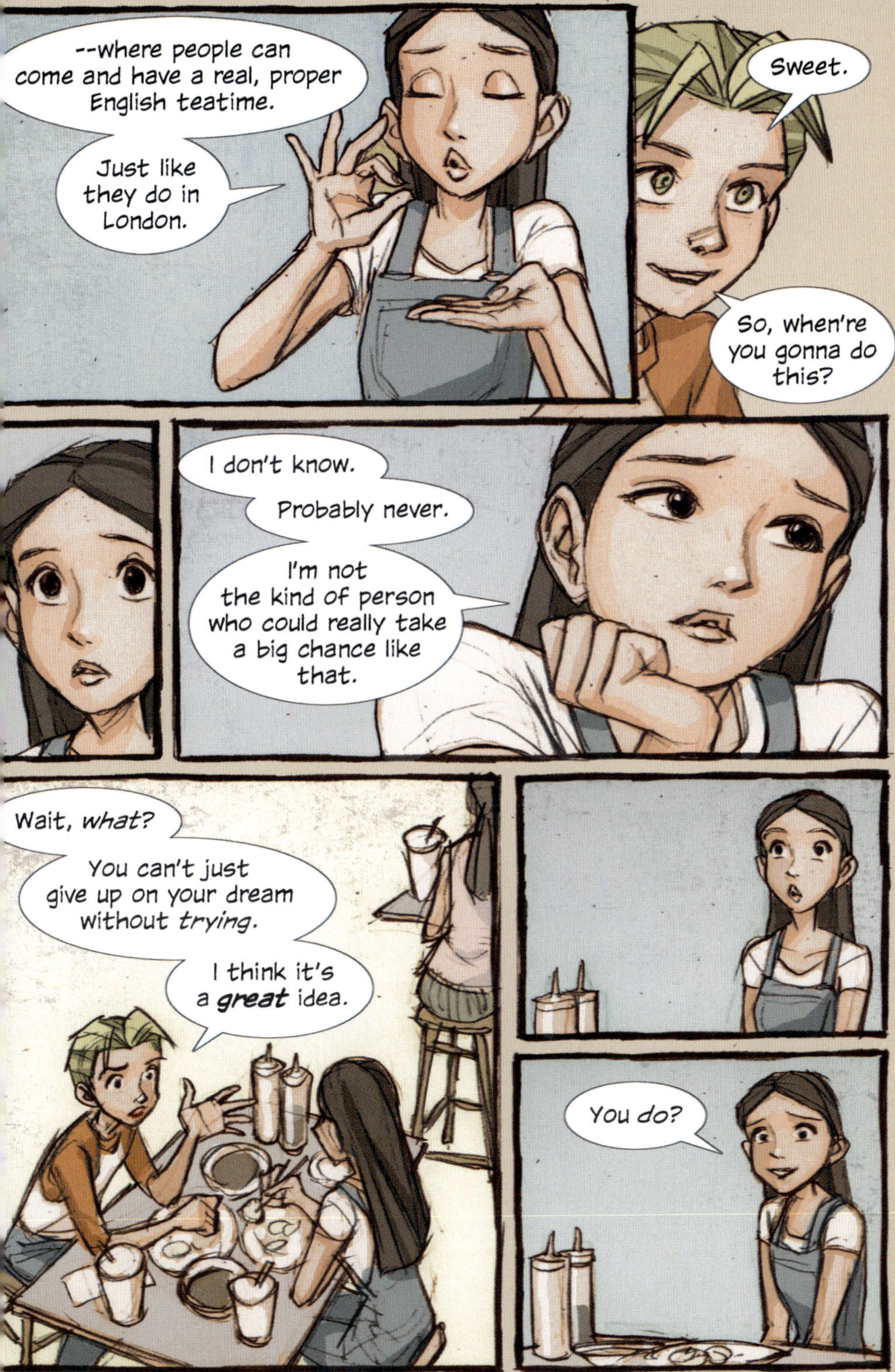
--where people can come and have a real, proper English teatime.
Just like they do in London.
Sweet.
So, when're you gonna do this?
I don't know.
Probably never.
I'm not the kind of person who could really take a big chance like that.
Wait, *what?*
You can't just give up on your dream without *trying*.
I think it's a ***great*** idea.
You *do?*

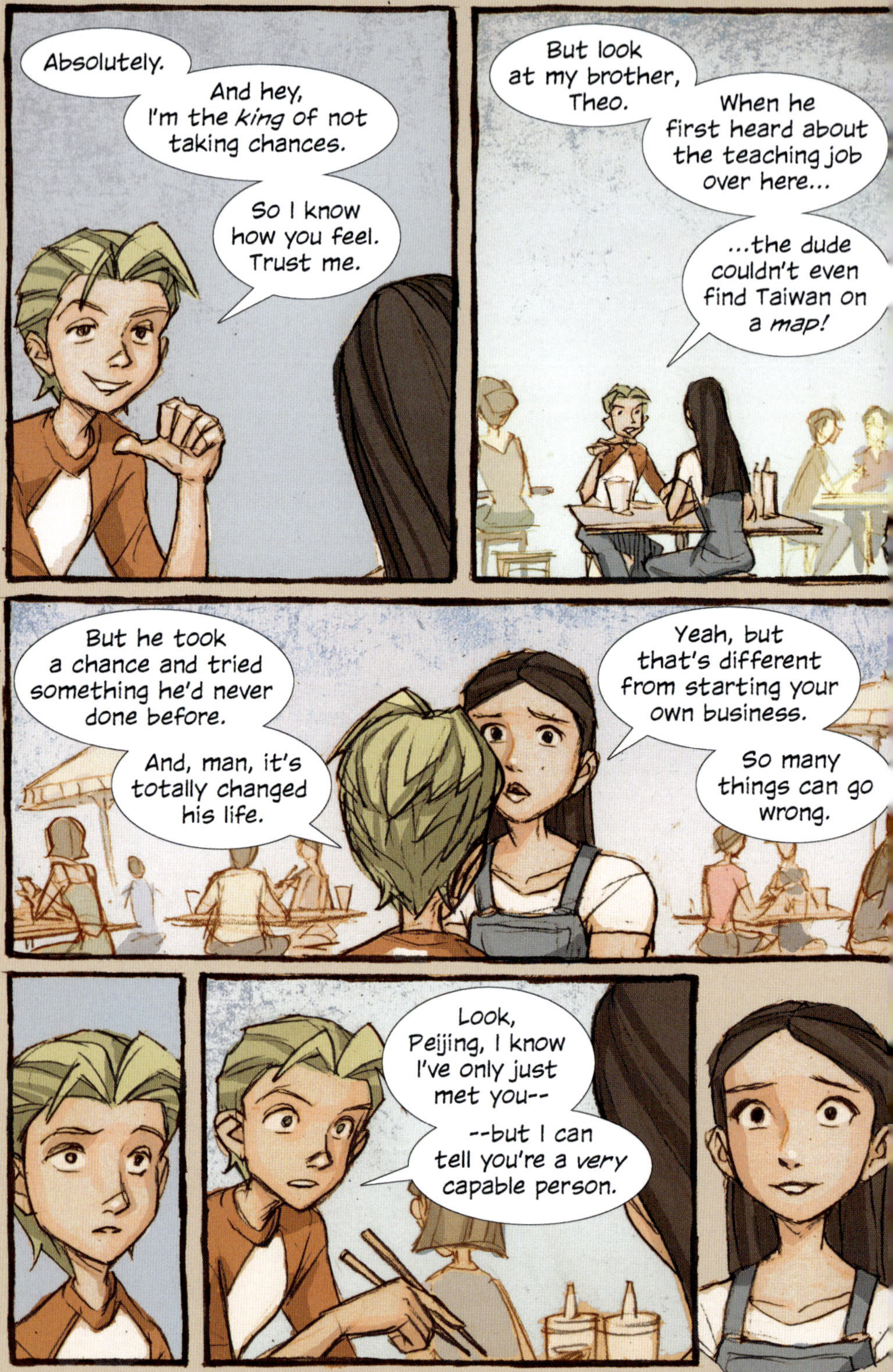
Absolutely.
And hey, I'm the *king* of not taking chances.
So I know how you feel. Trust me.
But look at my brother, Theo.
When he first heard about the teaching job over here...
...the dude couldn't even find Taiwan on a *map!*
But he took a chance and tried something he'd never done before.
And, man, it's totally changed his life.
Yeah, but that's different from starting your own business.
So many things can go wrong.
Look, Peijing, I know I've only just met you--
--but I can tell you're a *very* capable person.

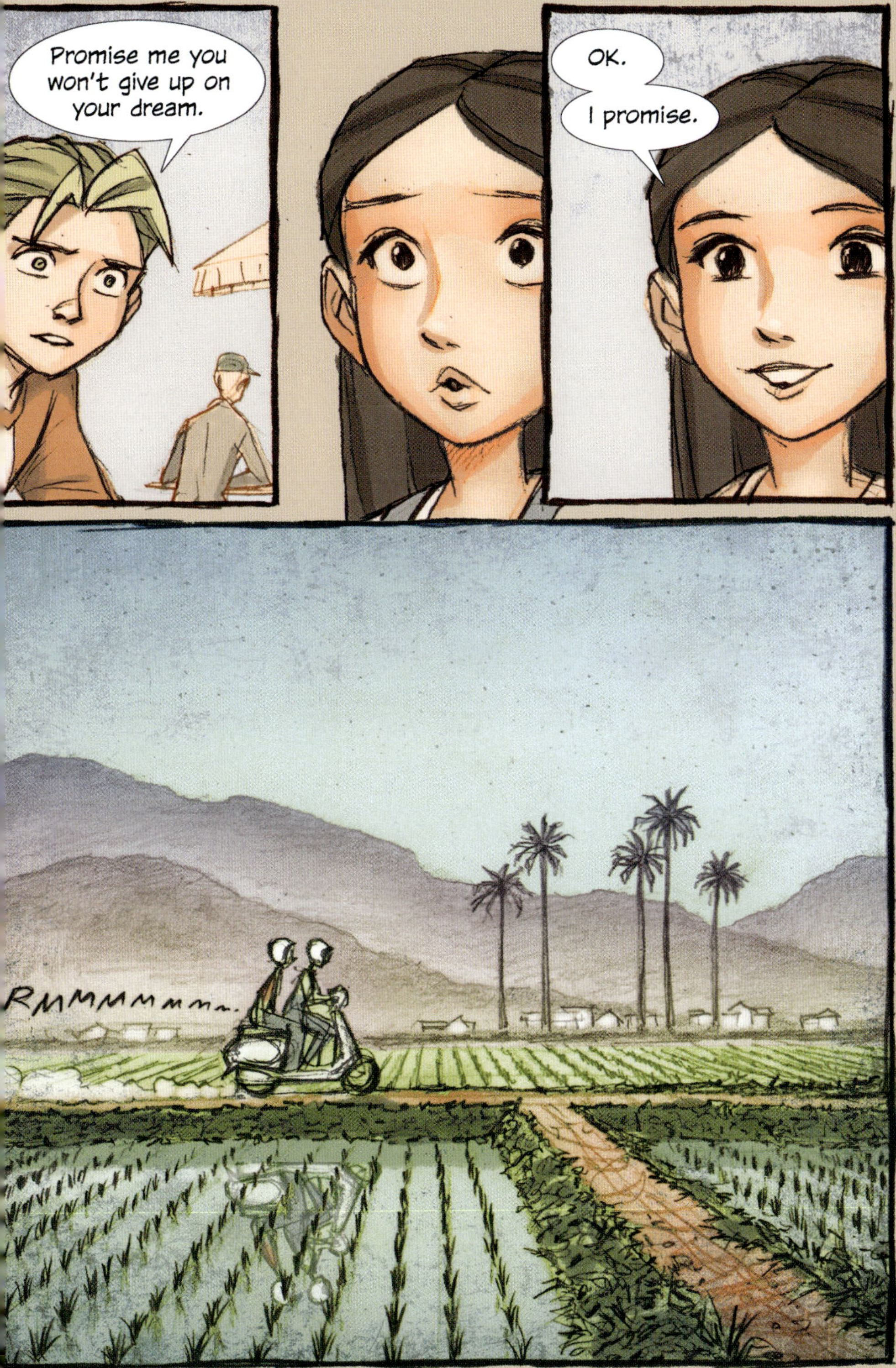
Promise me you won't give up on your dream.
OK.
I promise.
RMMMMMMM...

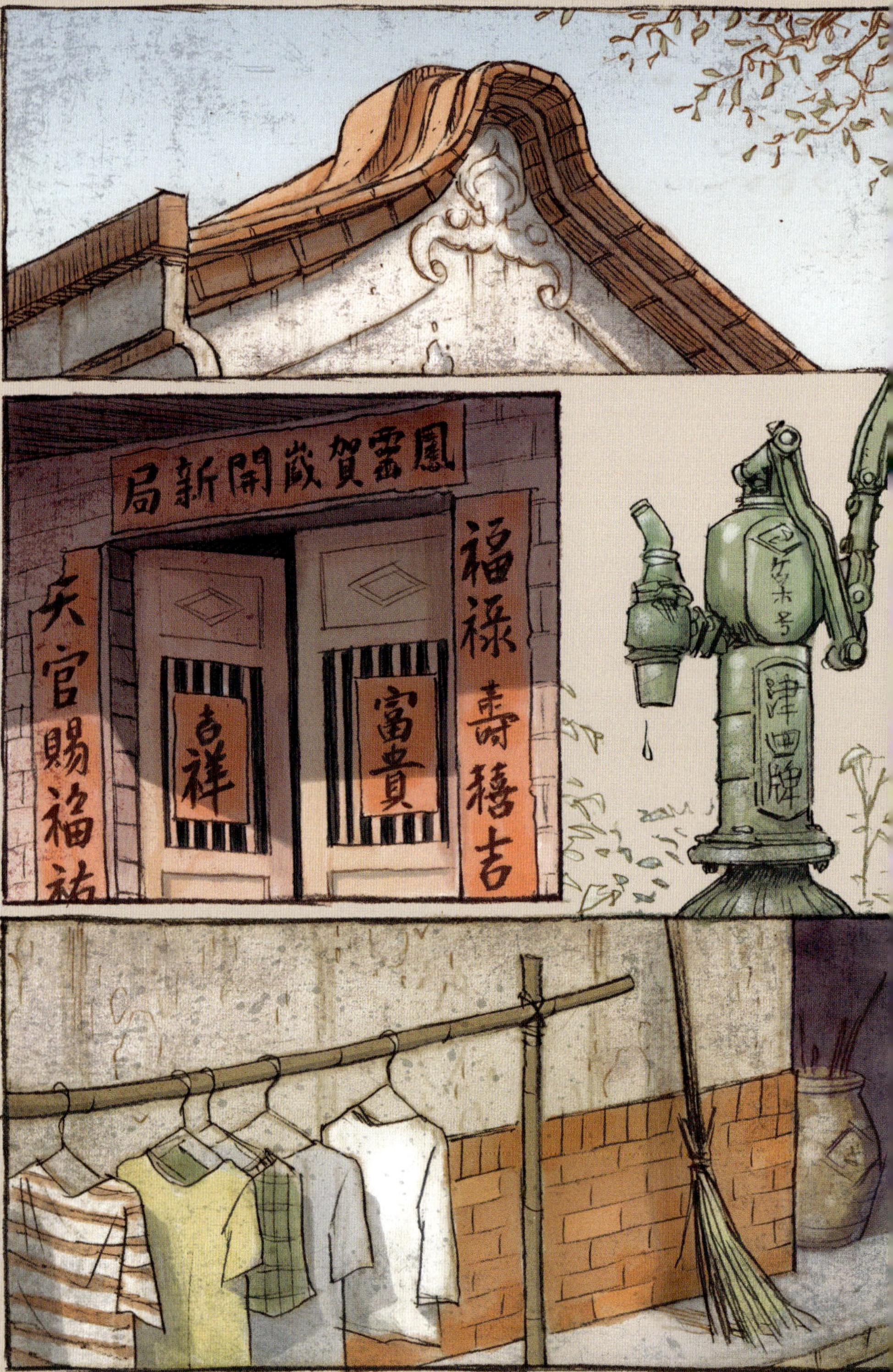
鳳霊賀歲開新局
天官賜福祐
福祿壽禧吉
吉祥
富貴

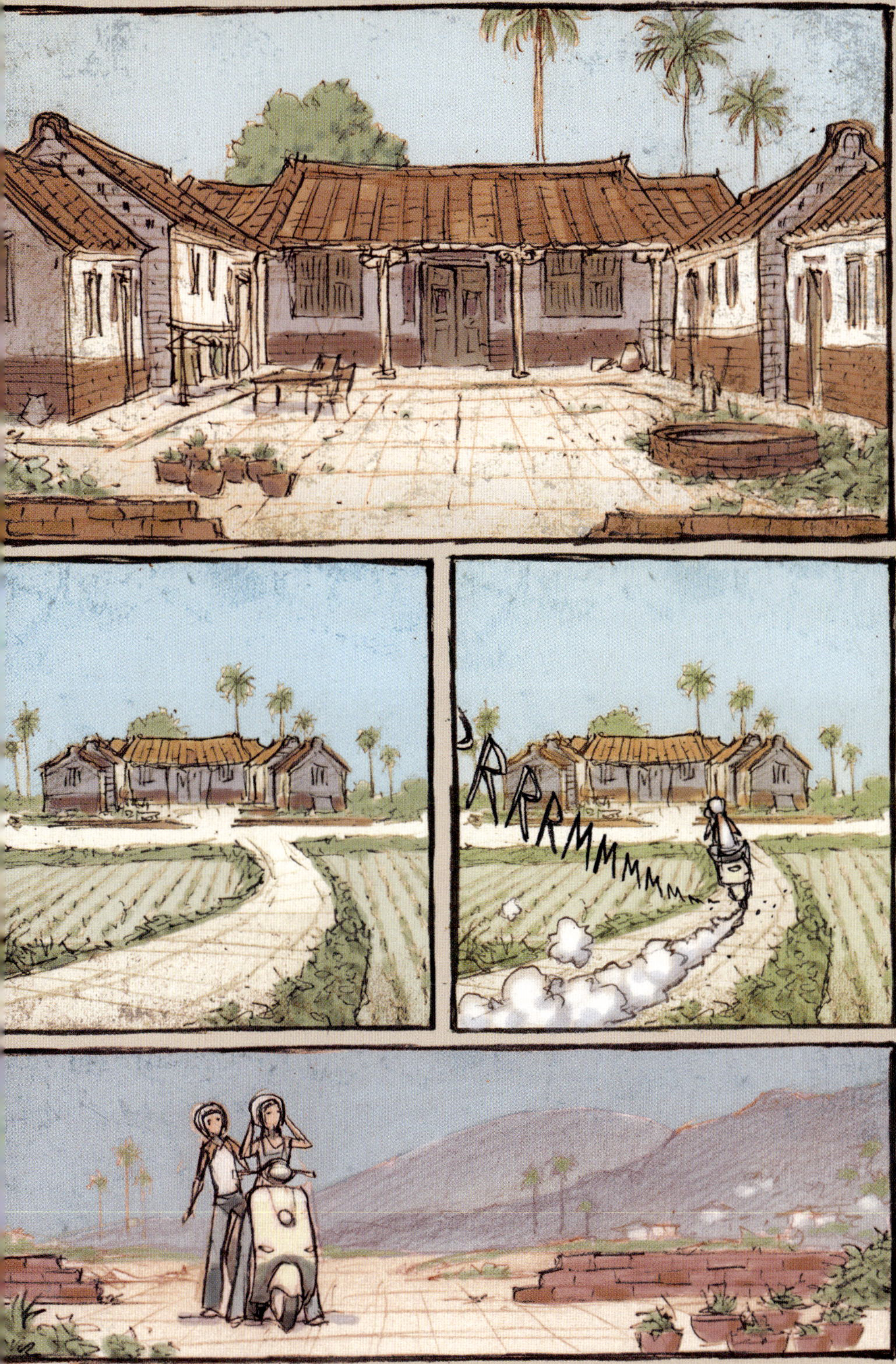

BRRRRMMMMMM

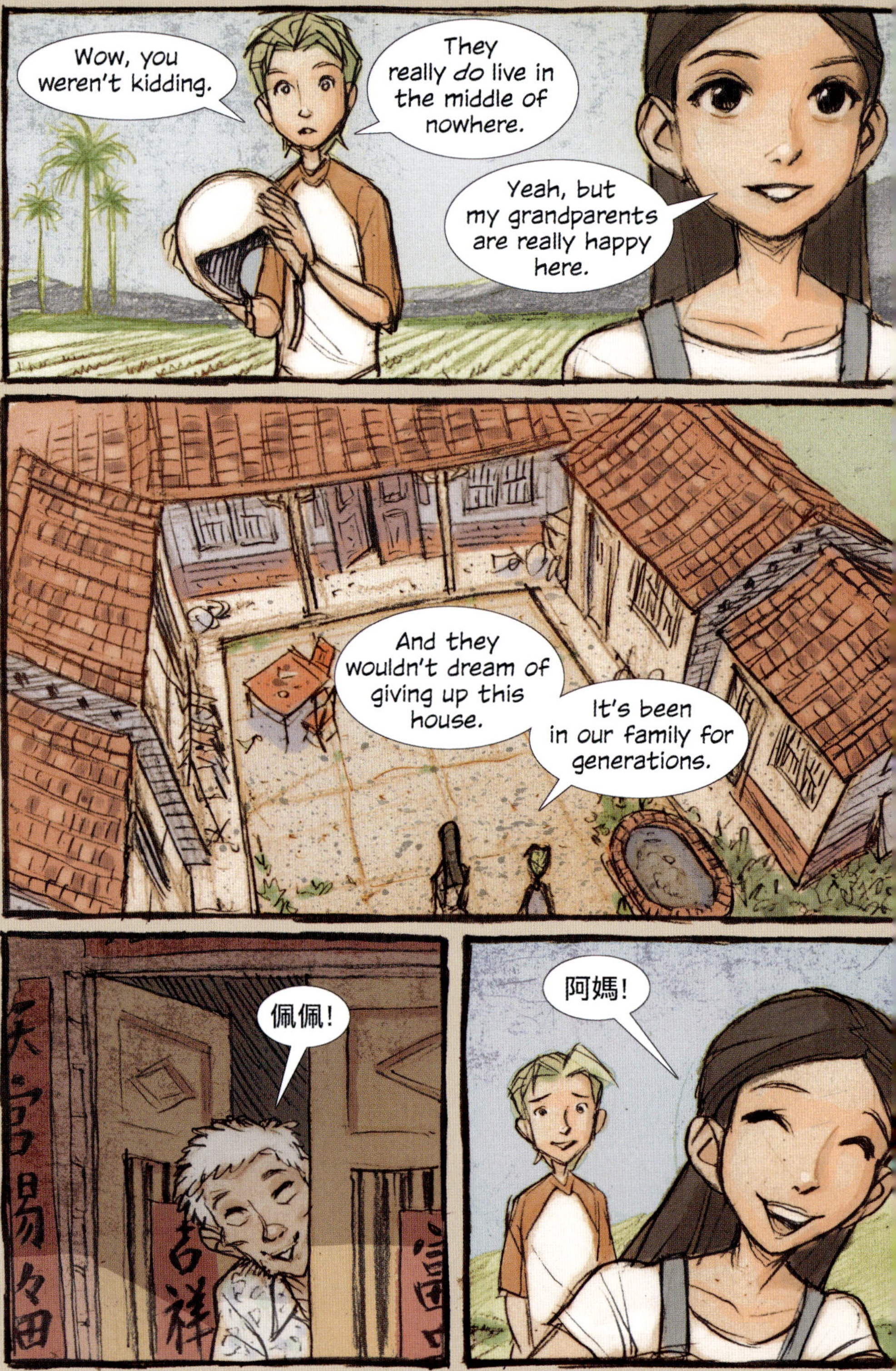
Wow, you weren't kidding.
They really *do* live in the middle of nowhere.
Yeah, but my grandparents are really happy here.
And they wouldn't dream of giving up this house.
It's been in our family for generations.
佩佩!
阿媽!

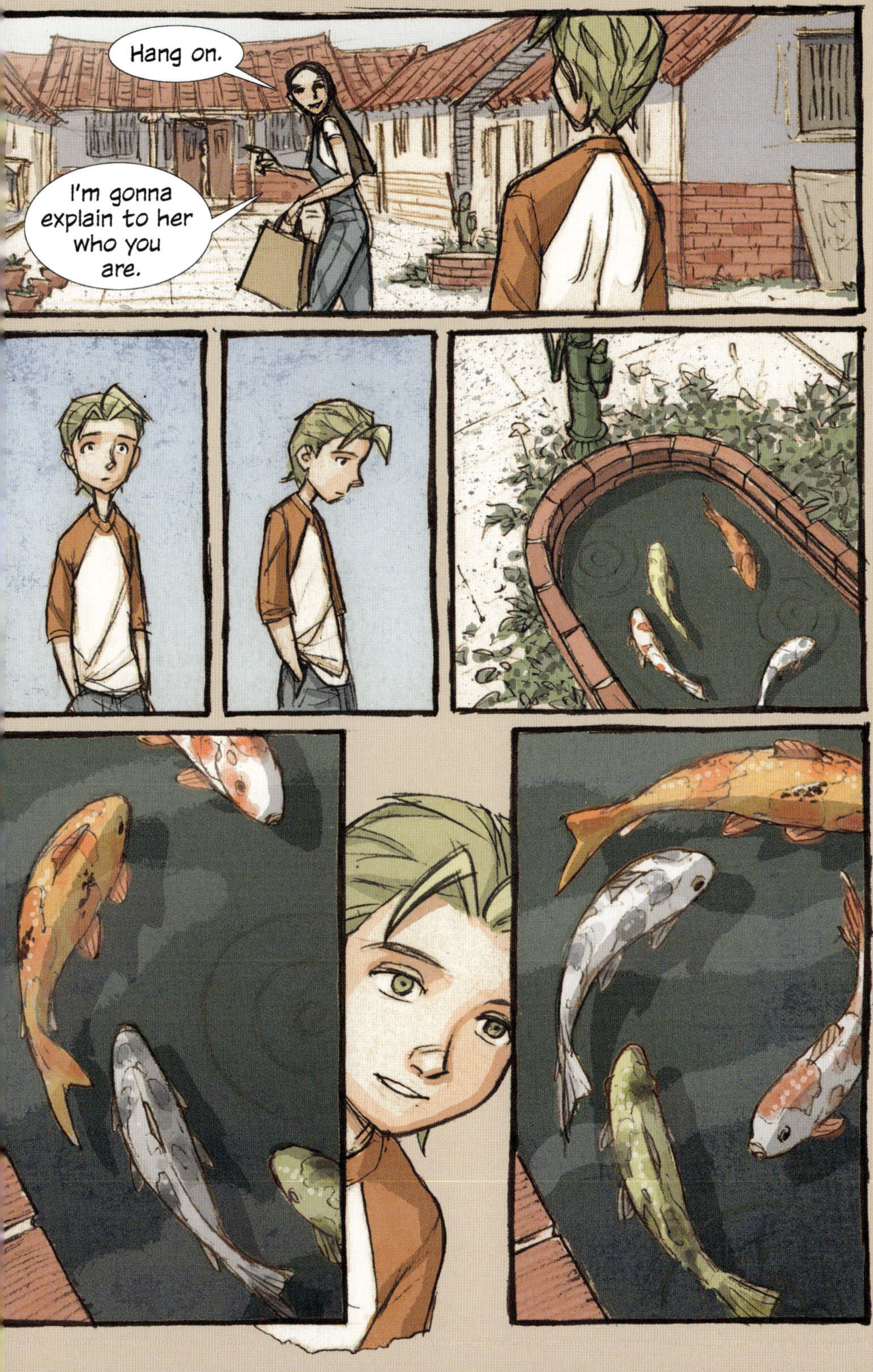
Hang on.
I'm gonna explain to her who you are.

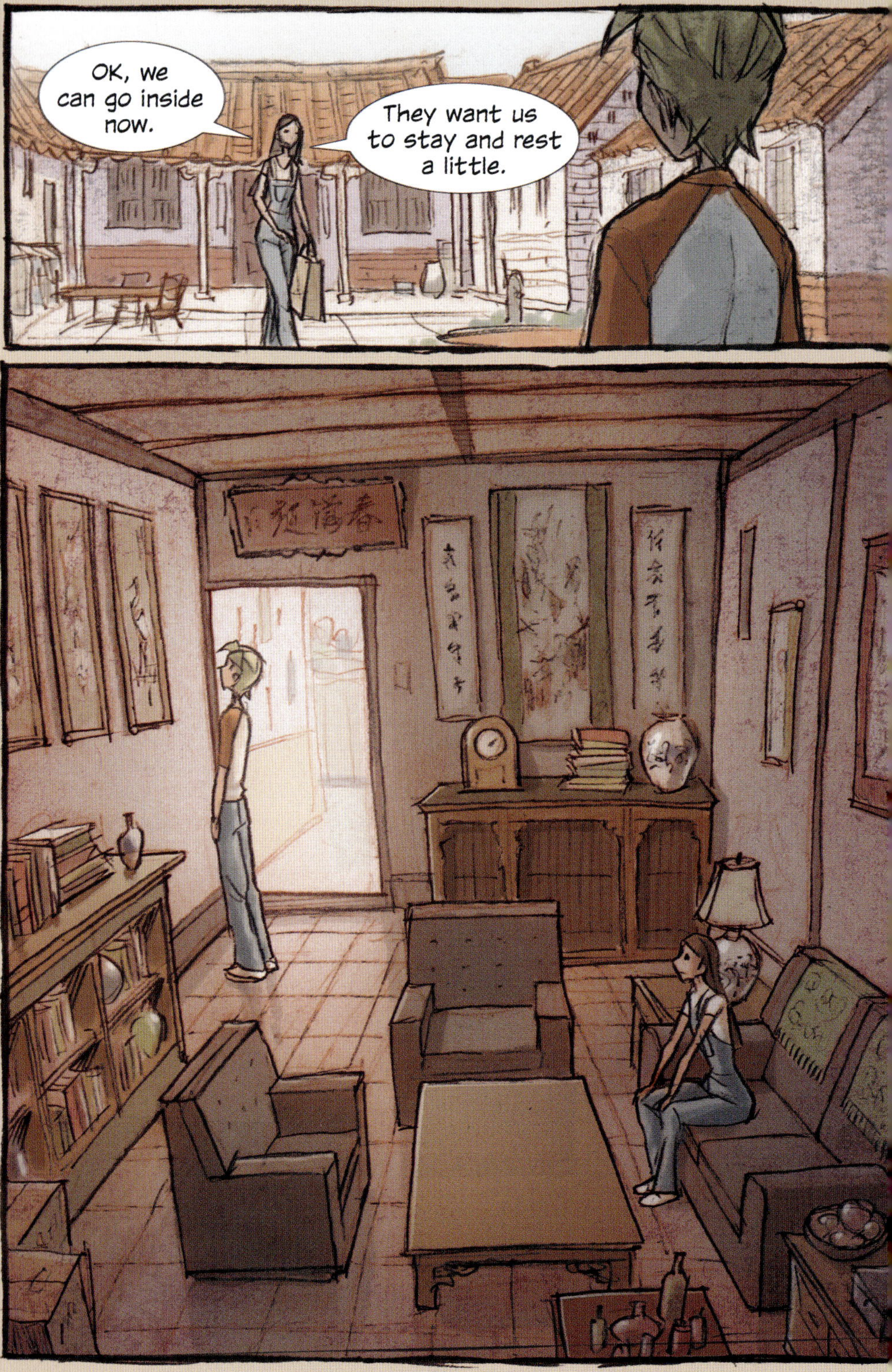
OK, we can go inside now.
They want us to stay and rest a little.

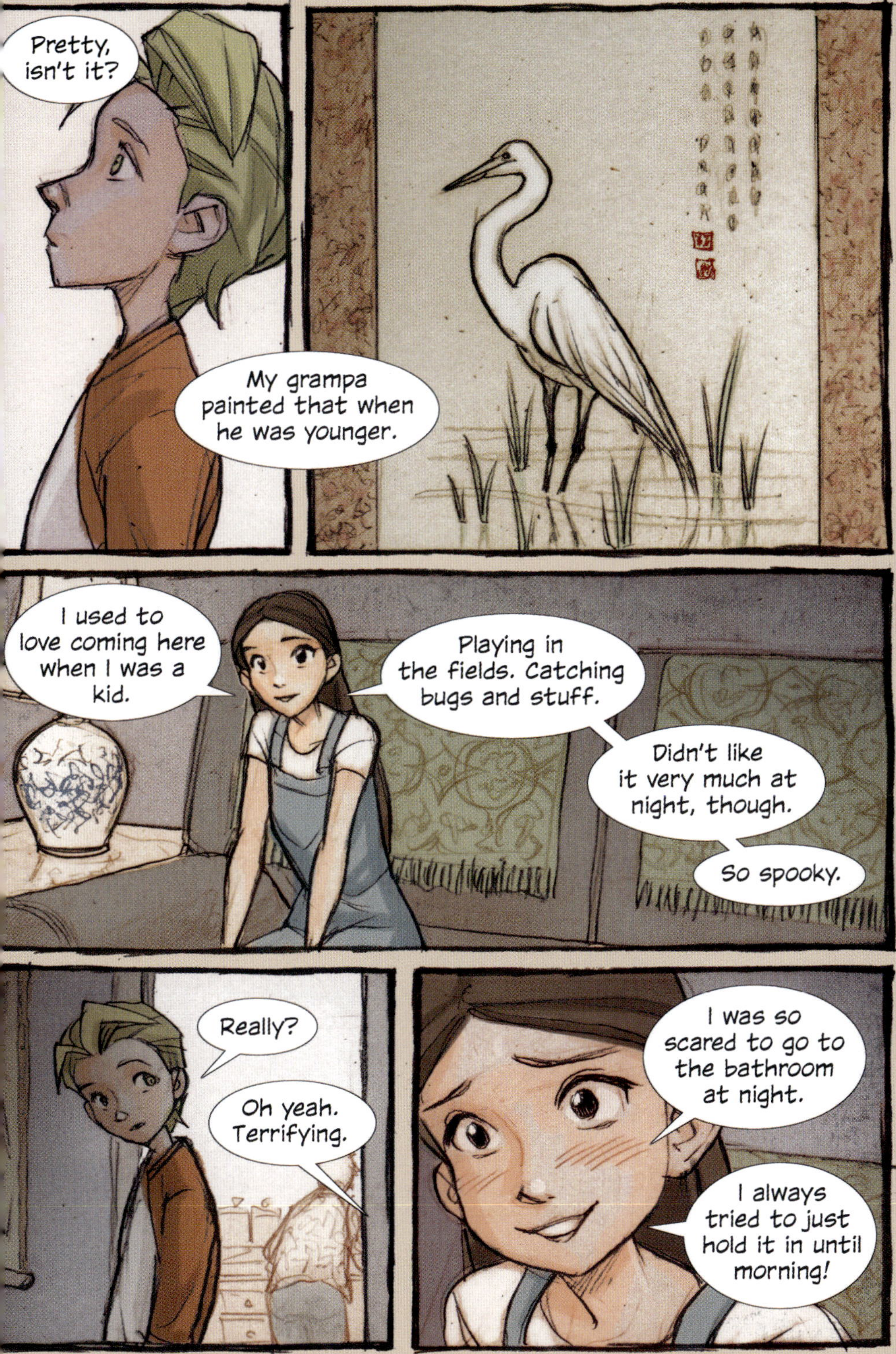
Pretty, isn't it?
My grampa painted that when he was younger.
I used to love coming here when I was a kid.
Playing in the fields. Catching bugs and stuff.
Didn't like it very much at night, though.
So spooky.
Really?
Oh yeah. Terrifying.
I was so scared to go to the bathroom at night.
I always tried to just hold it in until morning!

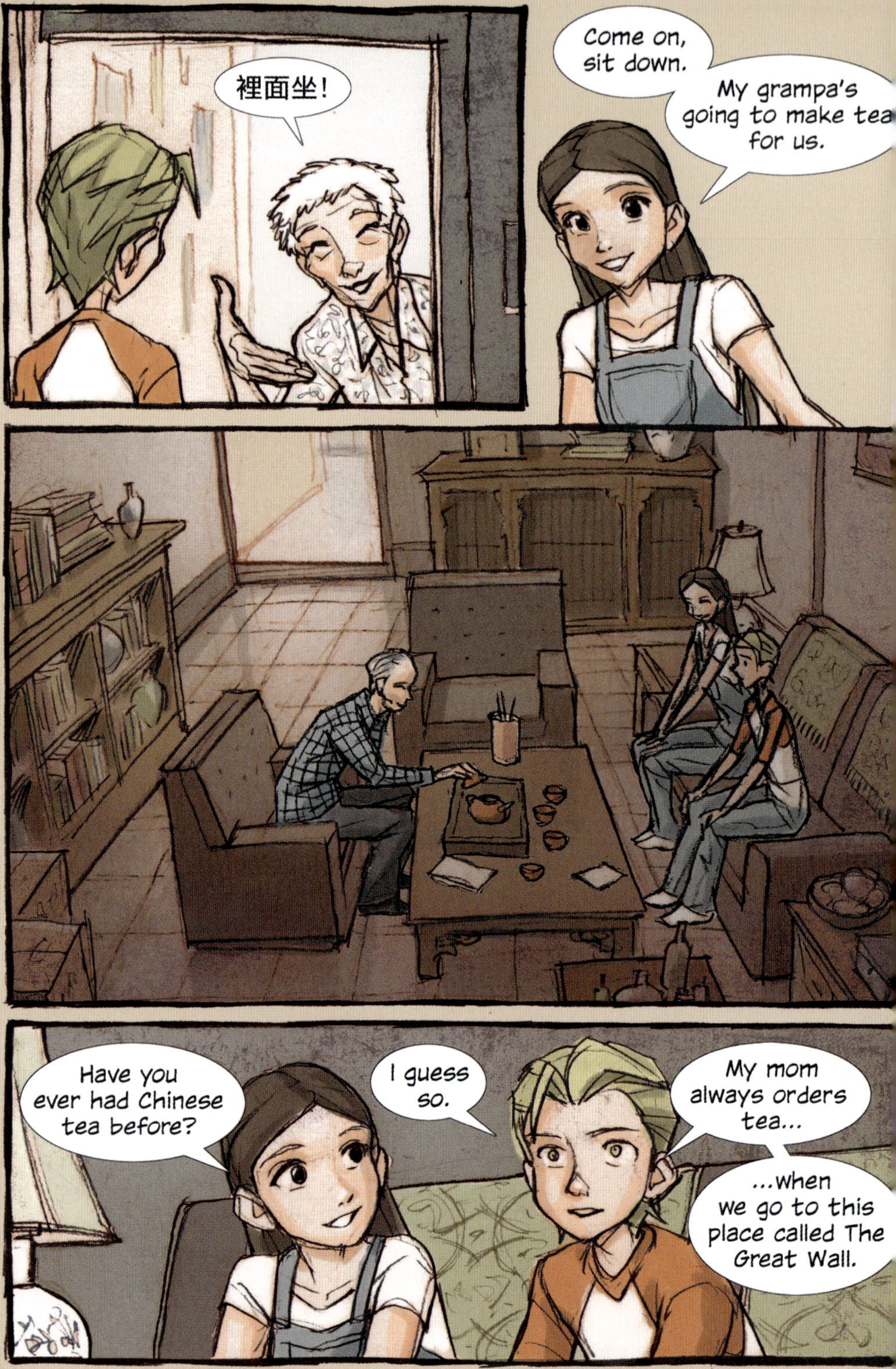

裡面坐!
Come on, sit down.
My grampa's going to make tea for us.
Have you ever had Chinese tea before?
I guess so.
My mom always orders tea...
...when we go to this place called The Great Wall.

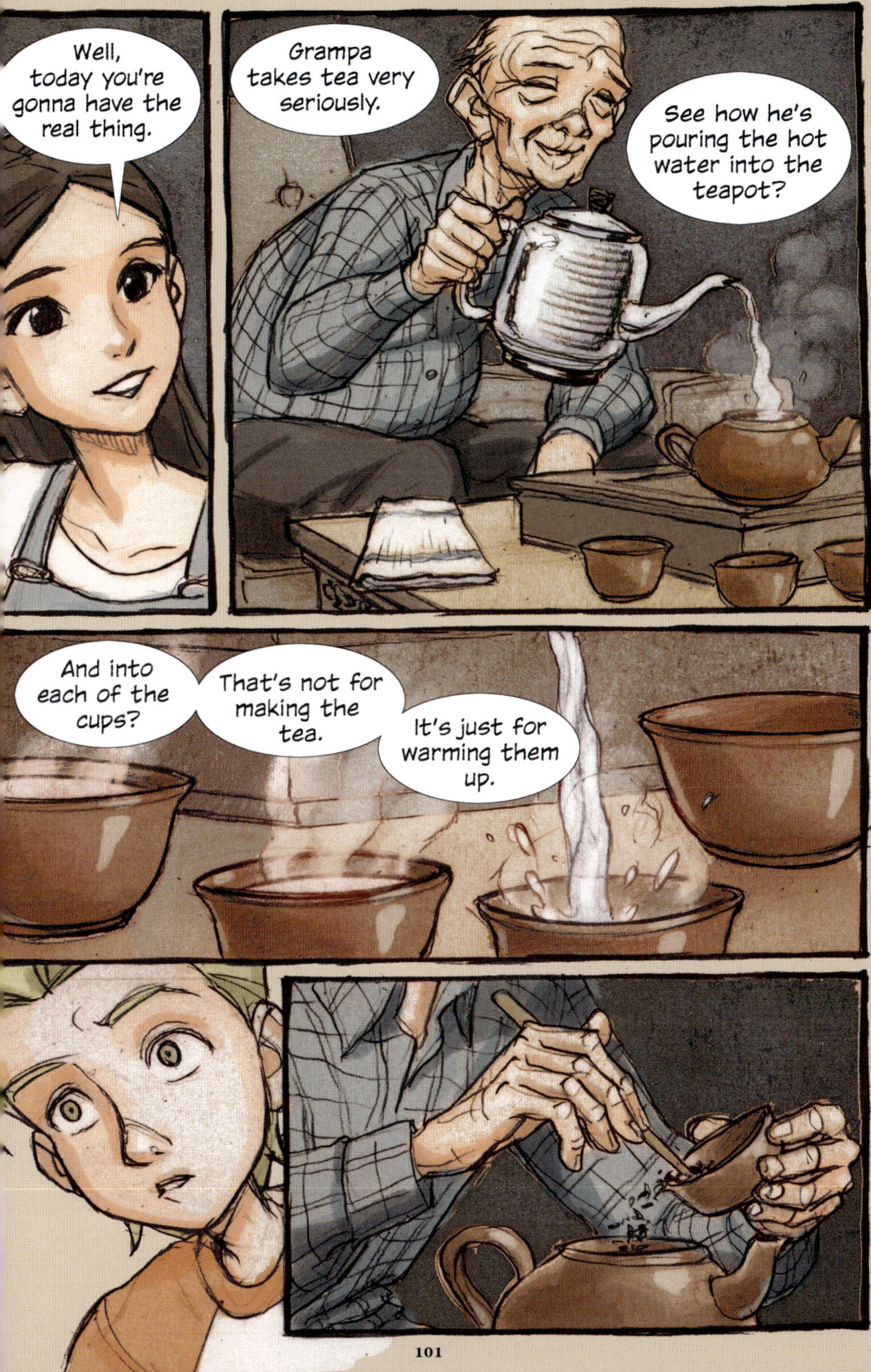
Well, today you're gonna have the real thing.
Grampa takes tea very seriously.
See how he's pouring the hot water into the teapot?
And into each of the cups?
That's not for making the tea.
It's just for warming them up.

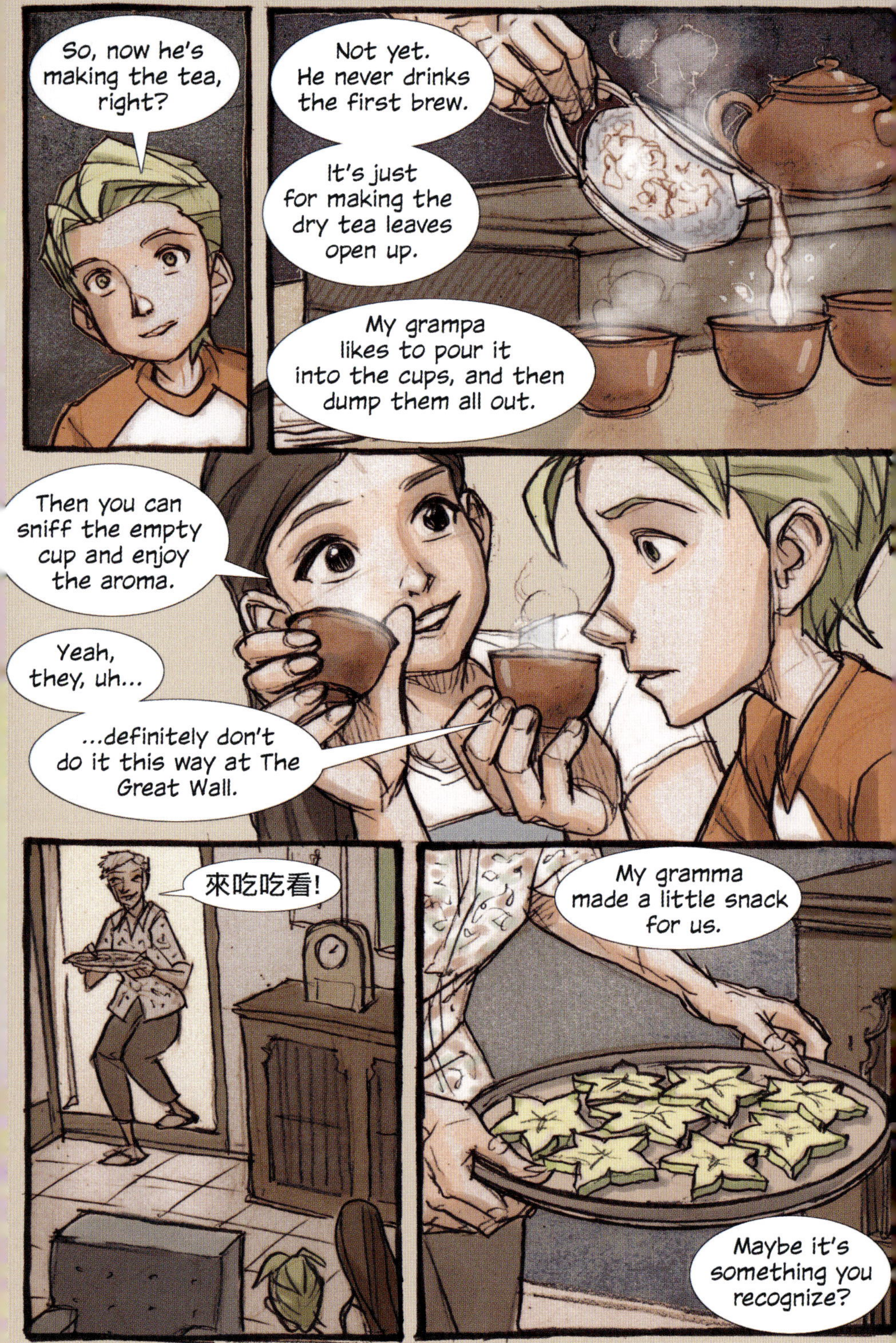
So, now he's making the tea, right?
Not yet. He never drinks the first brew.
It's just for making the dry tea leaves open up.
My grampa likes to pour it into the cups, and then dump them all out.
Then you can sniff the empty cup and enjoy the aroma.
Yeah, they, uh...
...definitely don't do it this way at The Great Wall.
來吃吃看!
My gramma made a little snack for us.
Maybe it's something you recognize?

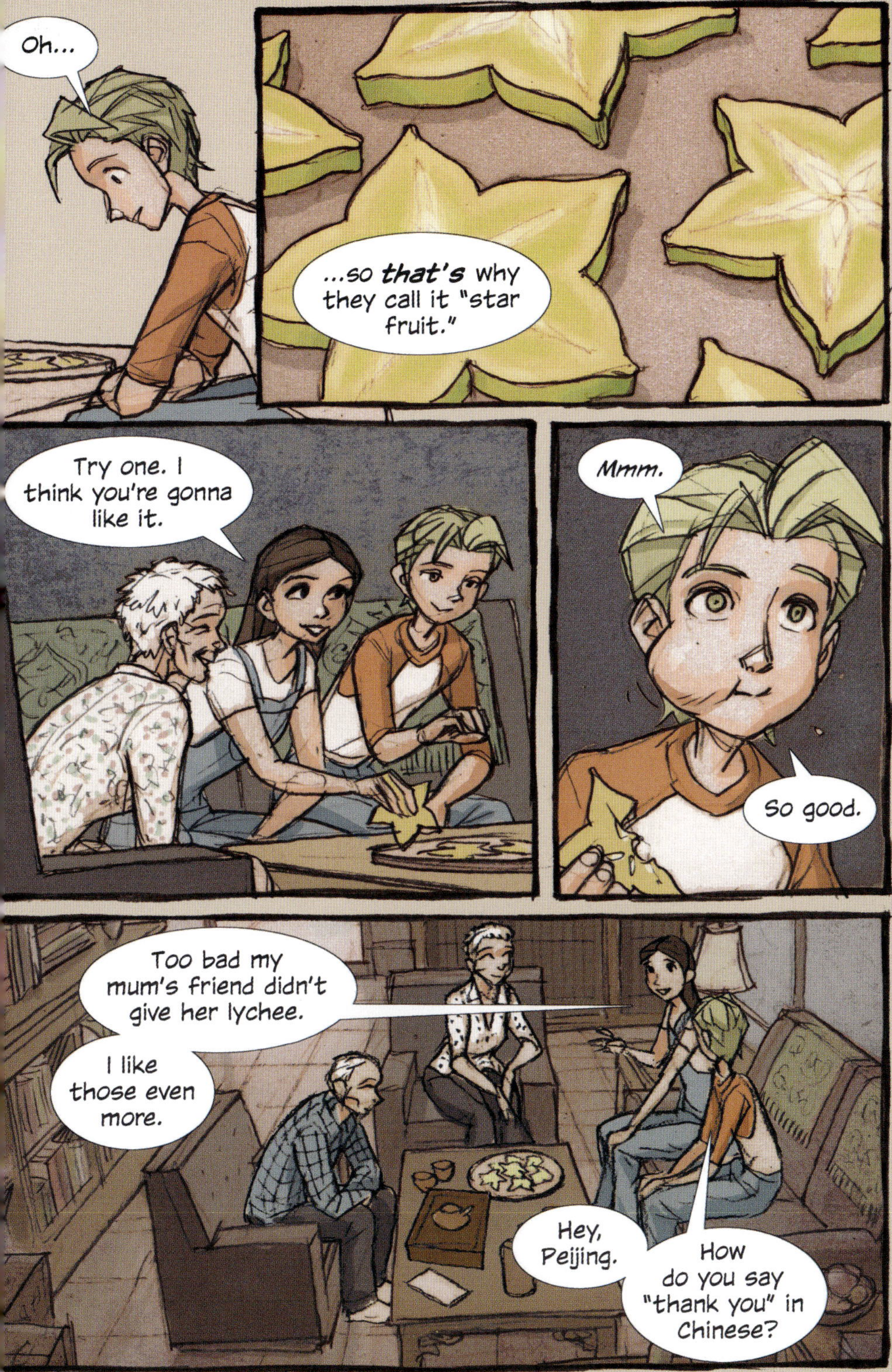
Oh...
...so *that's* why they call it "star fruit."
Try one. I think you're gonna like it.
Mmm.
So good.
Too bad my mum's friend didn't give her lychee.
I like those even more.
Hey, Peijing.
How do you say "thank you" in Chinese?

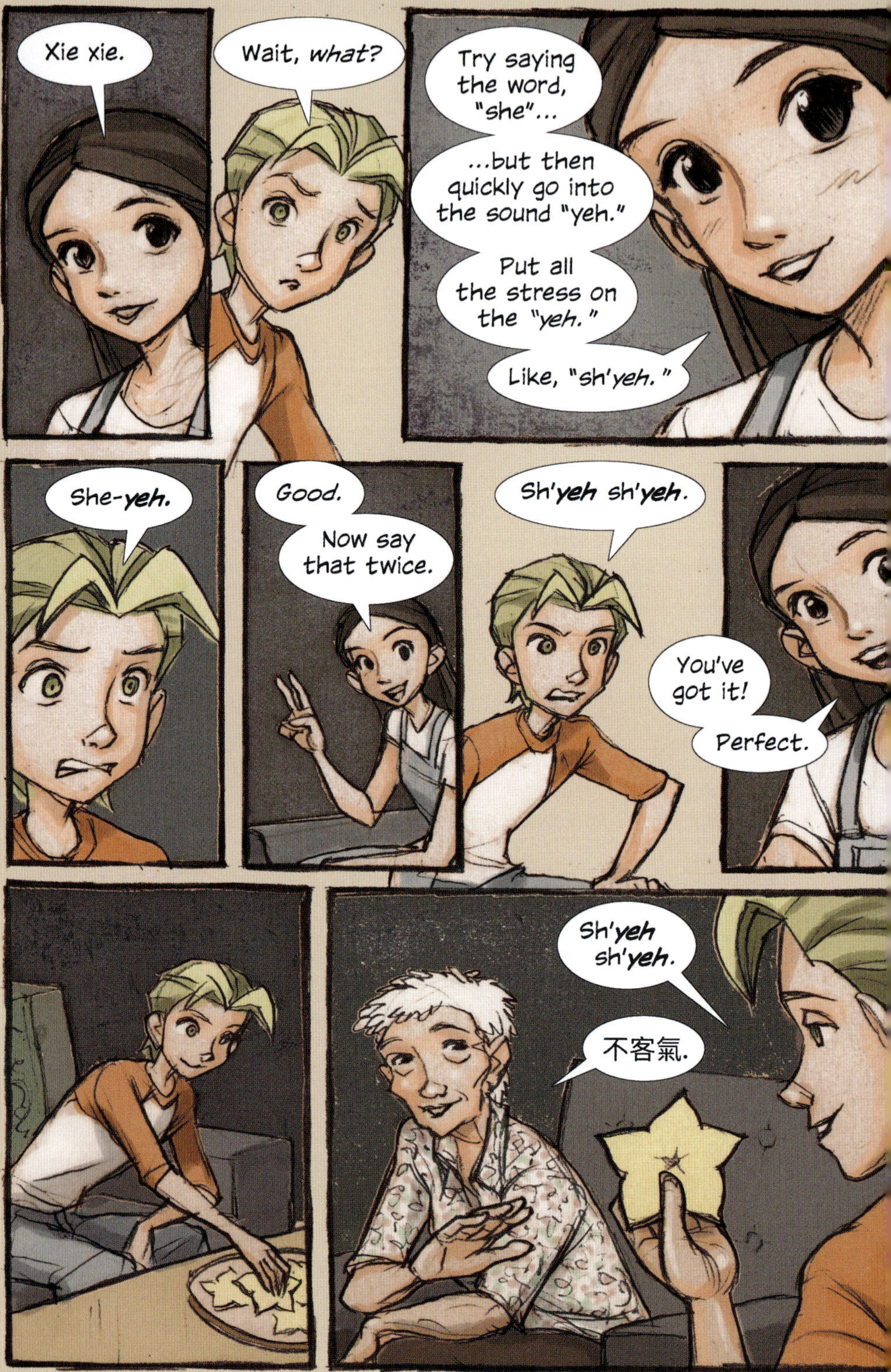
Xie xie.
Wait, *what?*
Try saying the word, "she"...
...but then quickly go into the sound "yeh."
Put all the stress on the "*yeh.*"
Like, "sh'*yeh.*"
She-**yeh.**
Good.
Now say that twice.
Sh'**yeh** sh'**yeh**.
You've got it!
Perfect.
Sh'**yeh** sh'**yeh**.
不客氣.

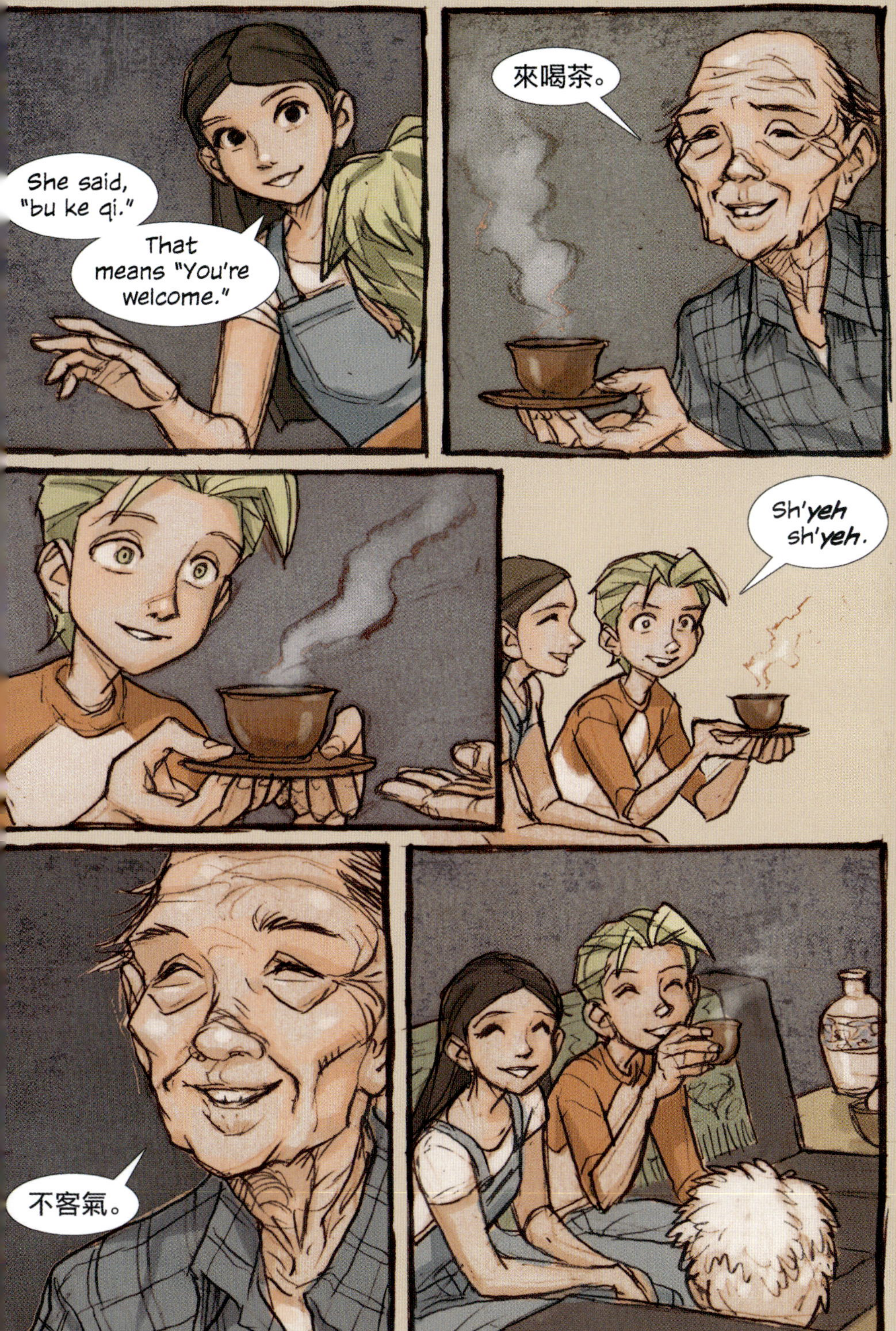
She said, "bu ke qi."
That means "You're welcome."
來喝茶。
Sh'yeh sh'yeh.
不客氣。

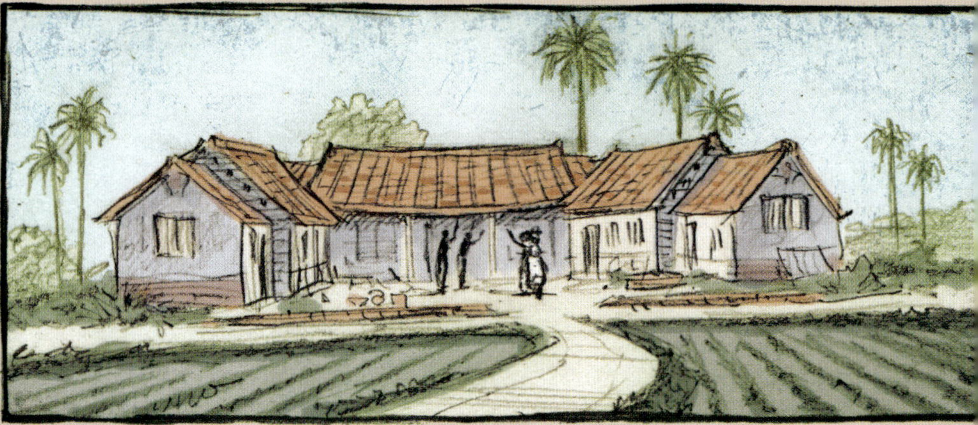

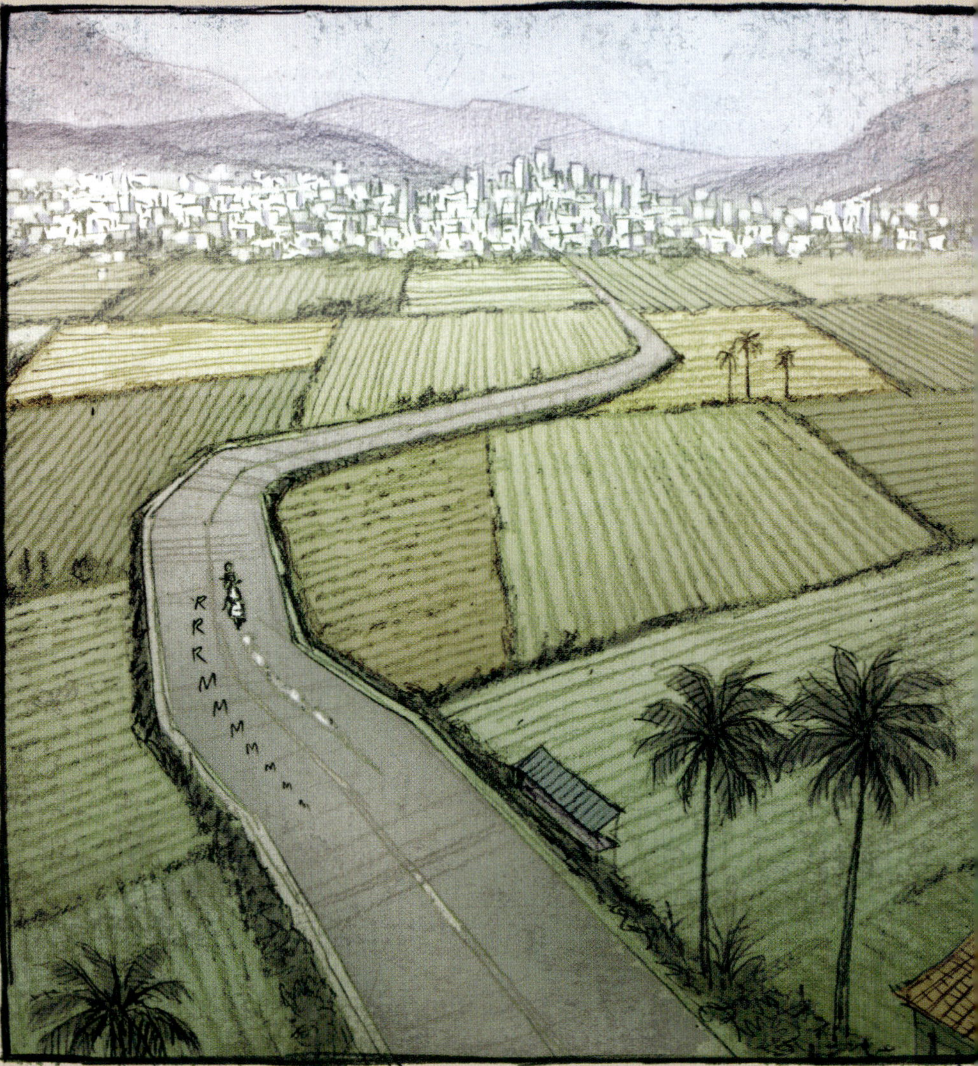
RRRMMMMmmm

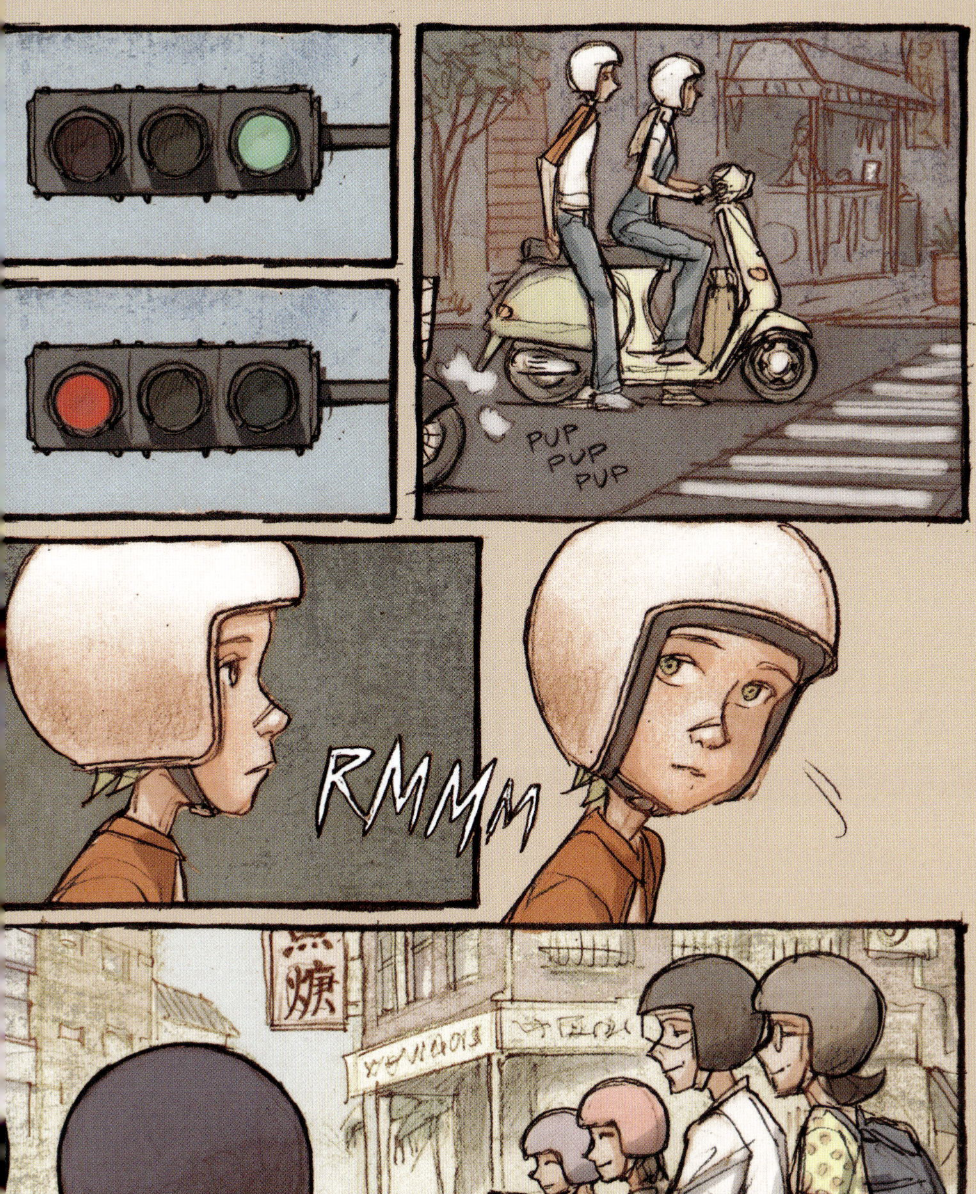
PUP
PUP
PUP
RMMM

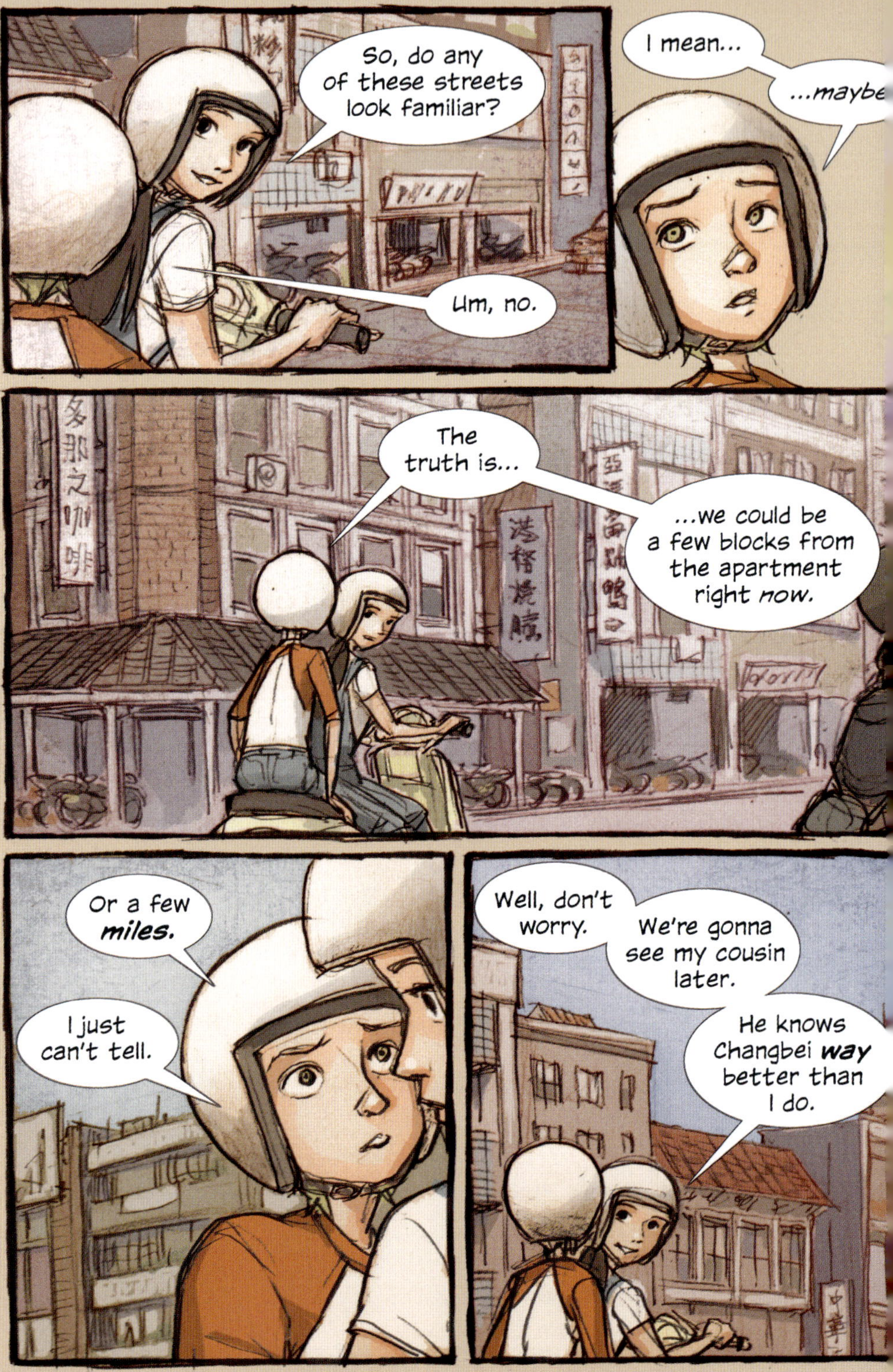
So, do any of these streets look familiar?
Um, no.
I mean...
...maybe
The truth is...
...we could be a few blocks from the apartment right *now.*
Or a few ***miles.***
I just can't tell.
Well, don't worry.
We're gonna see my cousin later.
He knows Changbei ***way*** better than I do.

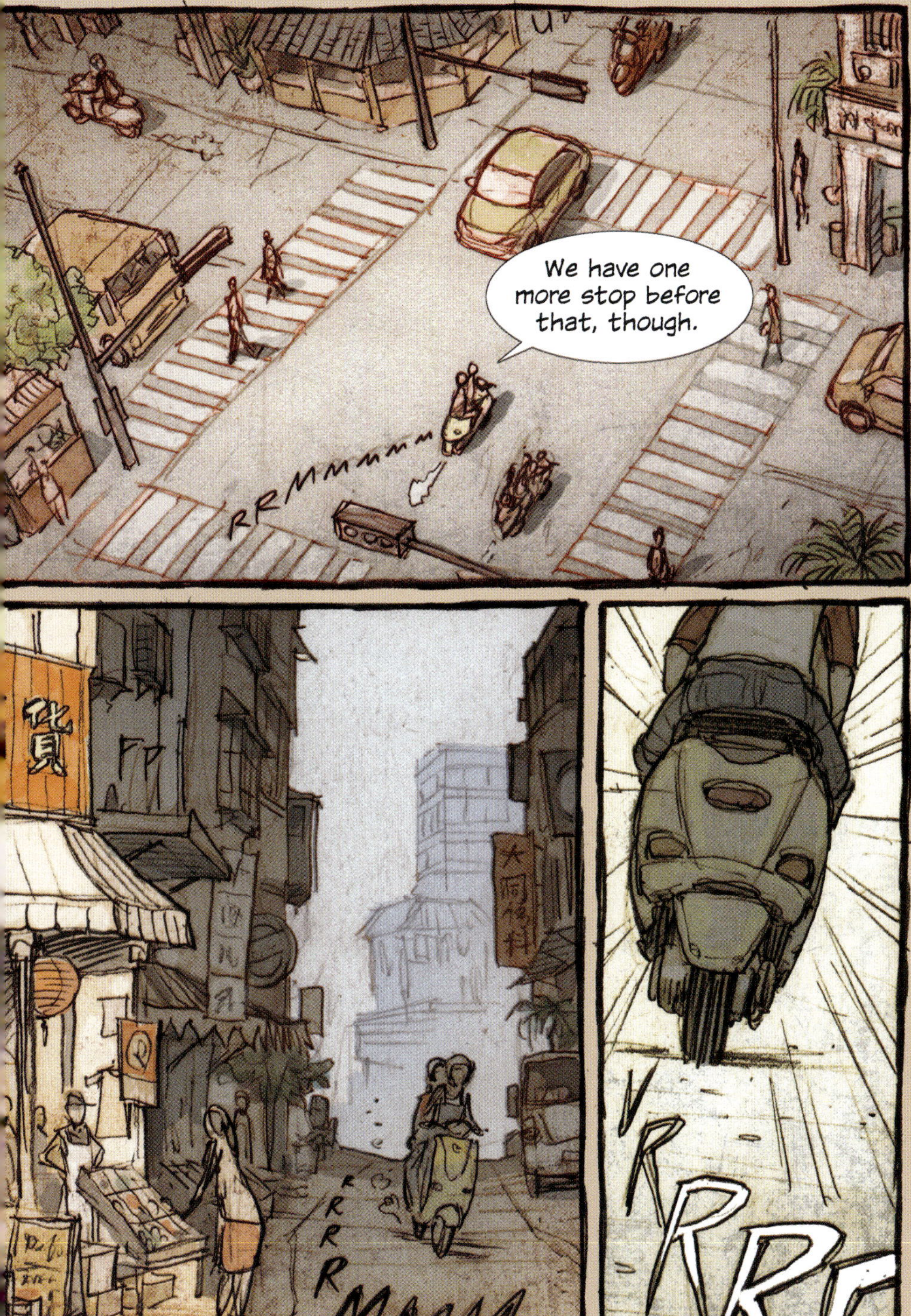
We have one more stop before that, though.
RRMMmmmm
RRRMMM
VRRRR

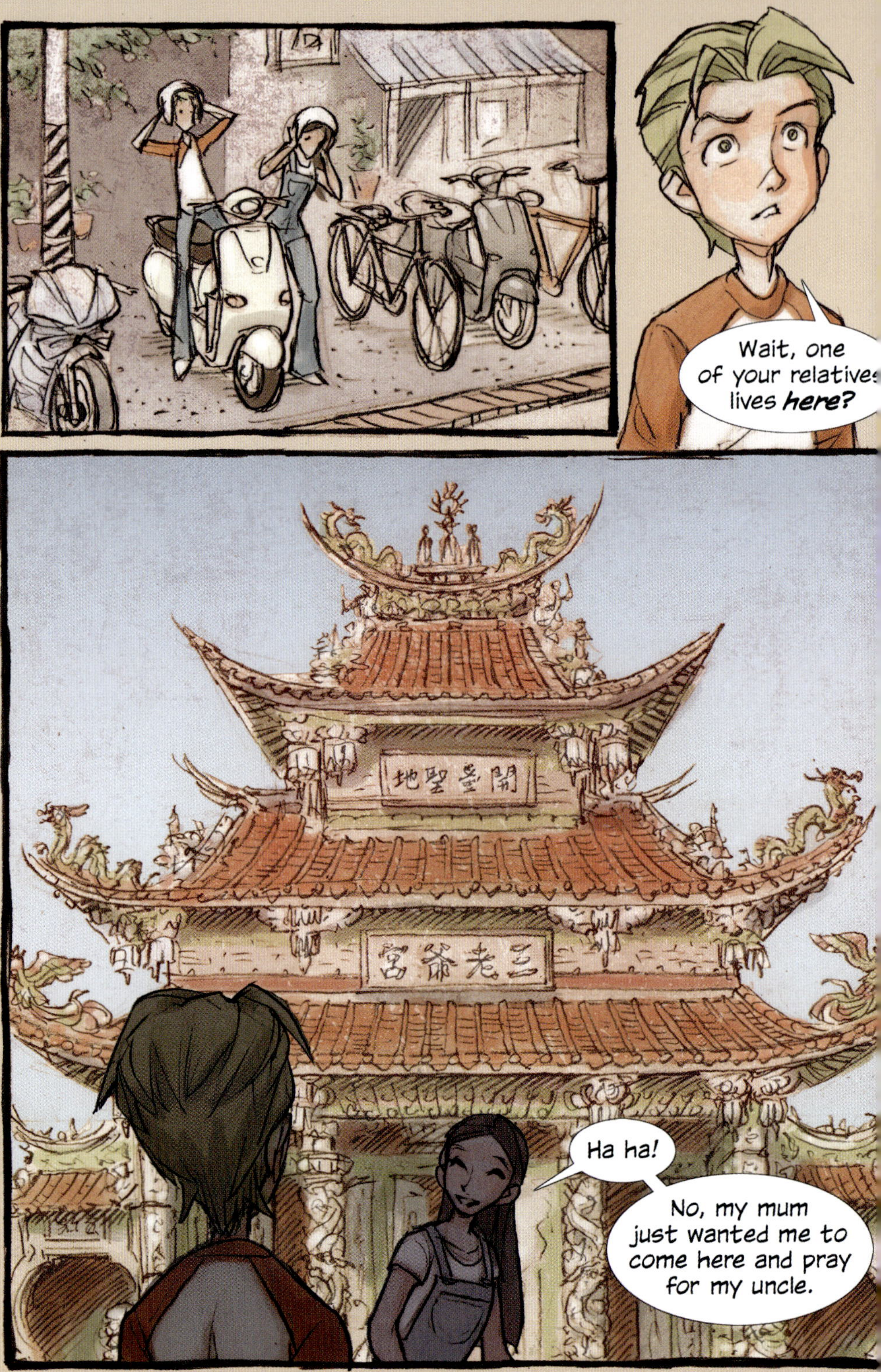
Wait, one of your relatives lives ***here?***
開臺聖地
三老爺宮
Ha ha!
No, my mum just wanted me to come here and pray for my uncle.

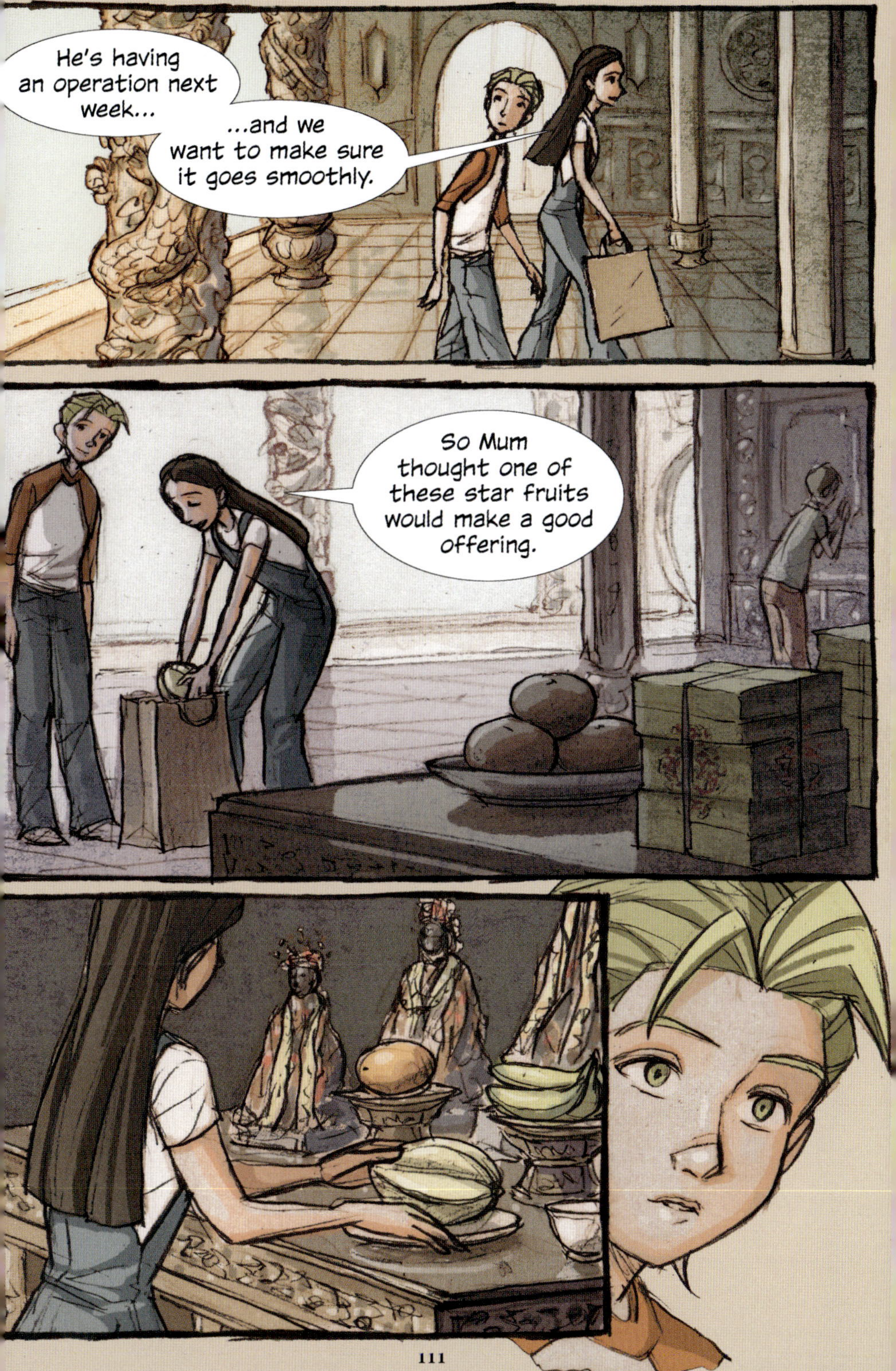
He's having an operation next week...
...and we want to make sure it goes smoothly.
So Mum thought one of these star fruits would make a good offering.

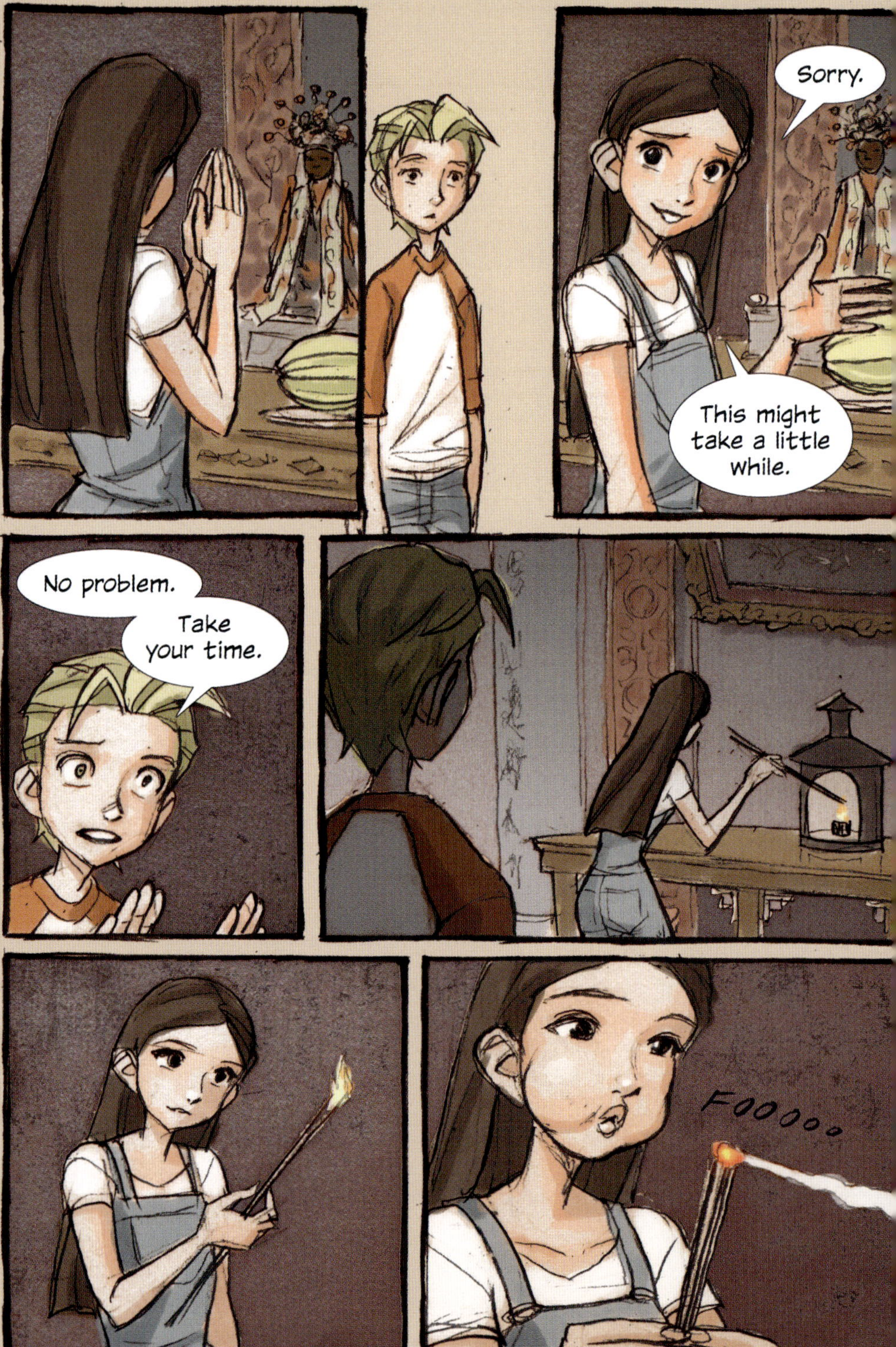
Sorry.
This might take a little while.
No problem.
Take your time.
FOOOOoo

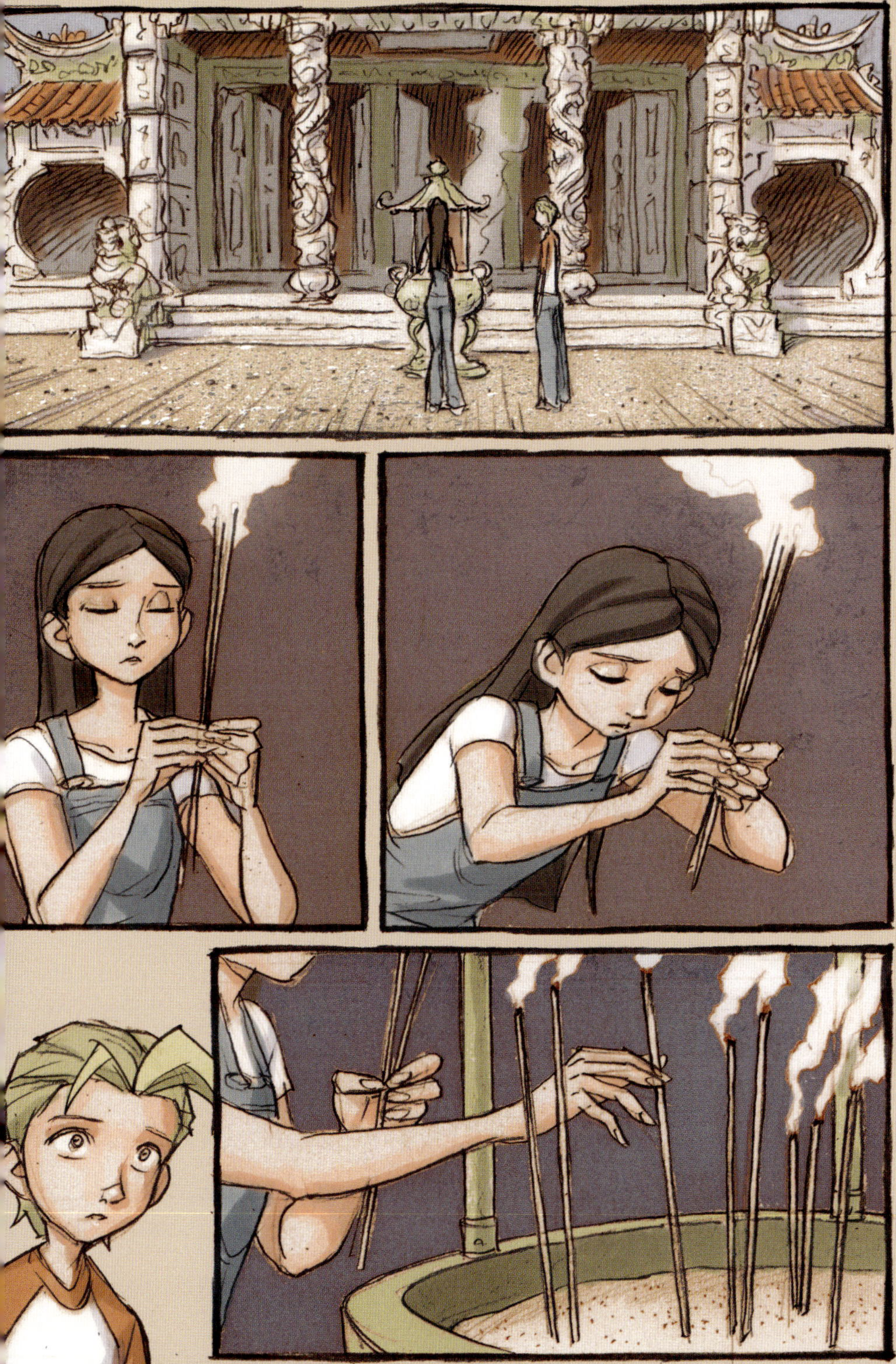

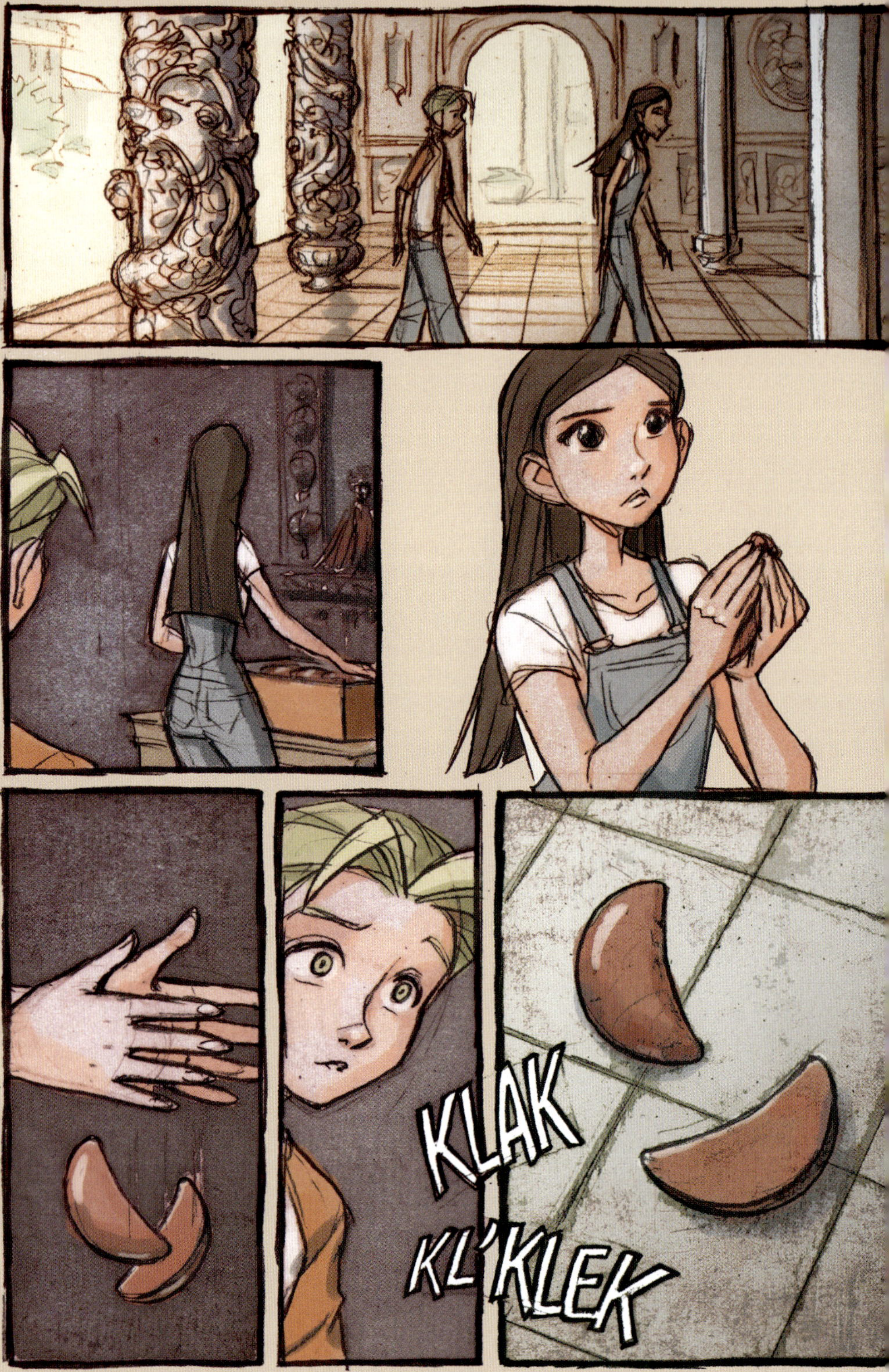
KLAK
KL'KLEK

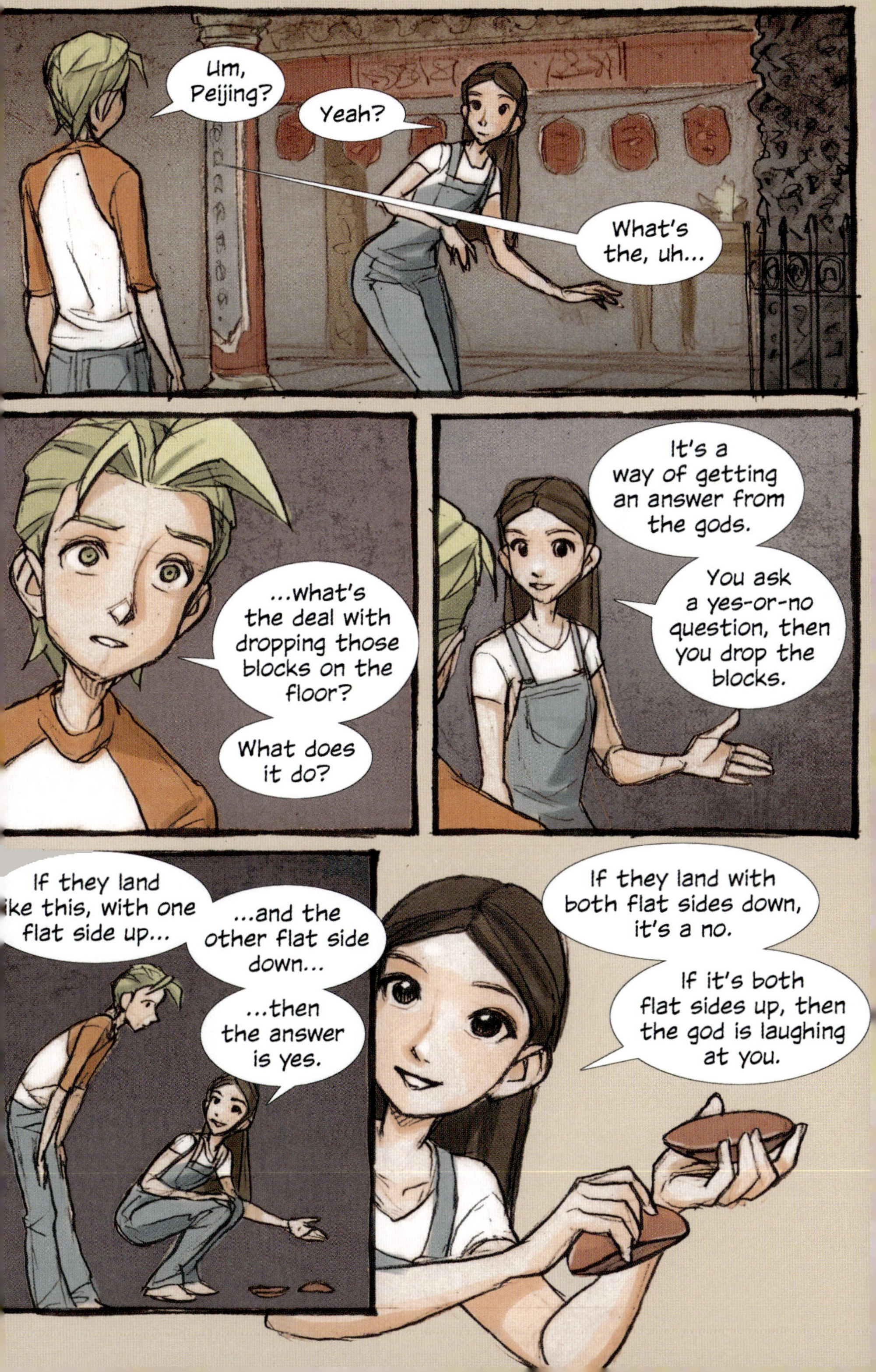
Um, Peijing?
Yeah?
What's the, uh...
...what's the deal with dropping those blocks on the floor?
What does it do?
It's a way of getting an answer from the gods.
You ask a yes-or-no question, then you drop the blocks.
If they land like this, with one flat side up...
...and the other flat side down...
...then the answer is yes.
If they land with both flat sides down, it's a no.
If it's both flat sides up, then the god is laughing at you.

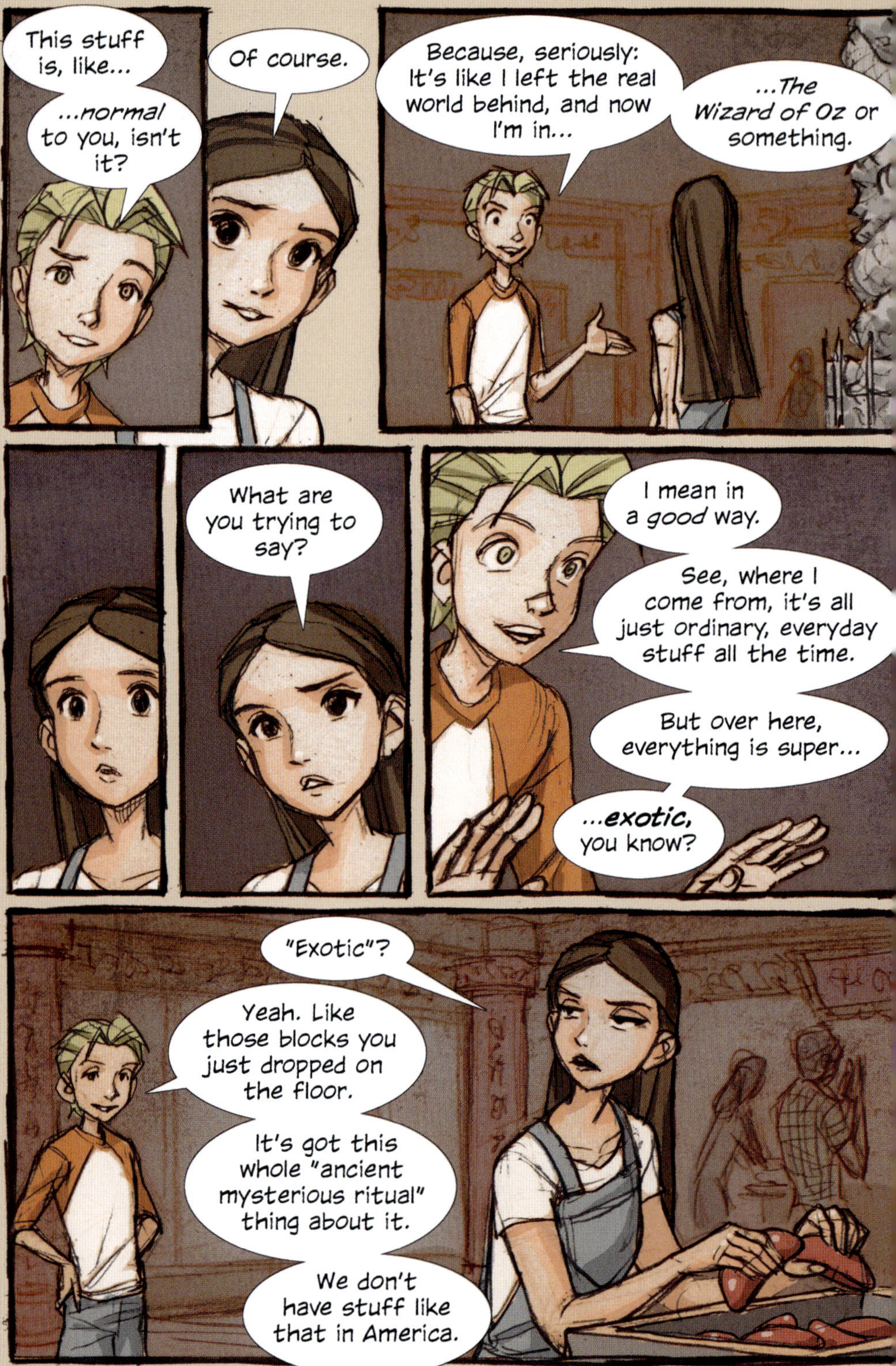
This stuff is, like...
...*normal* to you, isn't it?
Of course.
Because, seriously: It's like I left the real world behind, and now I'm in...
...*The Wizard of Oz* or something.
What are you trying to say?
I mean in a *good* way.
See, where I come from, it's all just ordinary, everyday stuff all the time.
But over here, everything is super...
...***exotic,*** you know?
"Exotic"?
Yeah. Like those blocks you just dropped on the floor.
It's got this whole "ancient mysterious ritual" thing about it.
We don't have stuff like that in America.

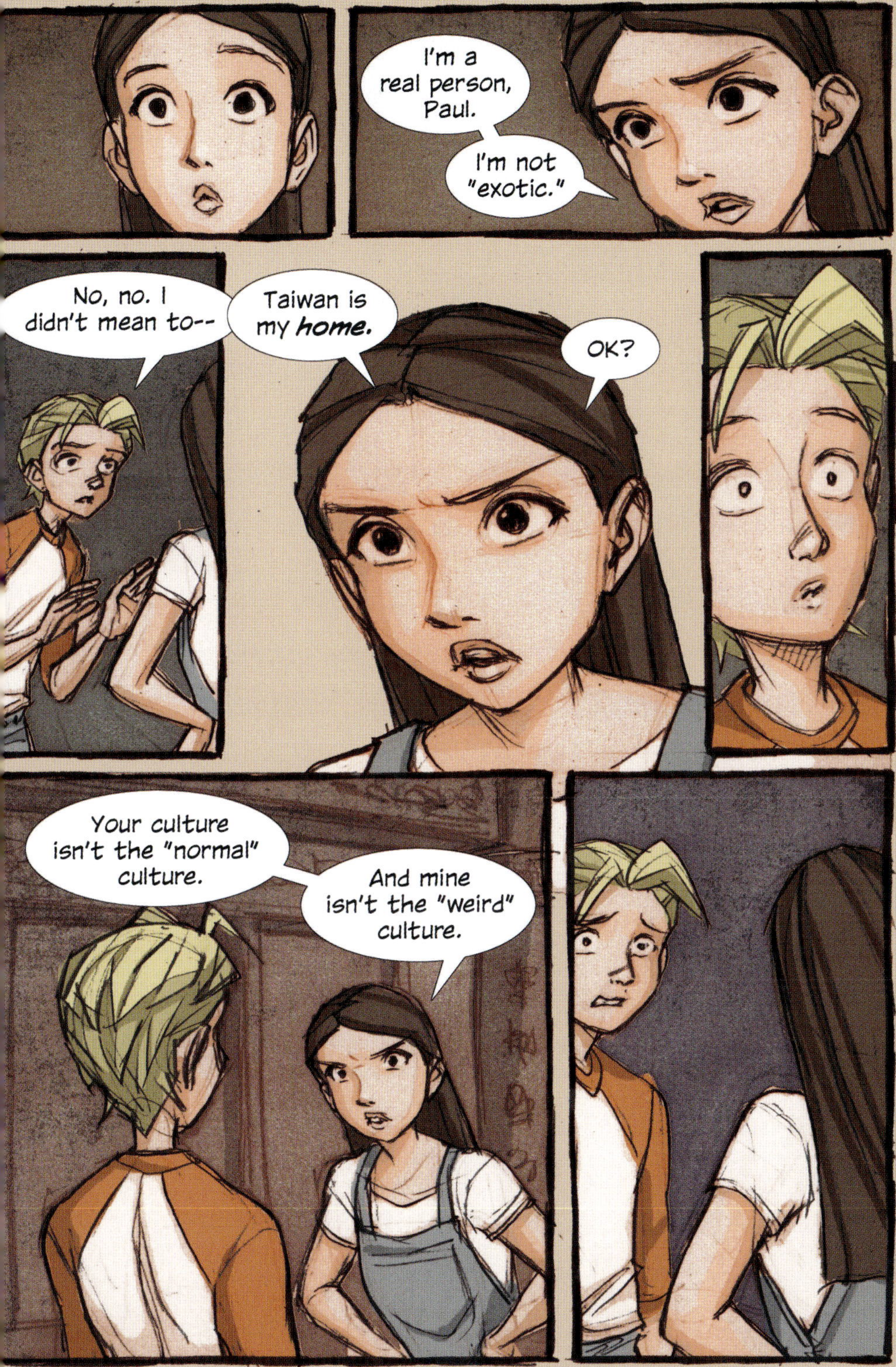
I'm a real person, Paul.
I'm not "exotic."
No, no. I didn't mean to--
Taiwan is my **home.**
OK?
Your culture isn't the "normal" culture.
And mine isn't the "weird" culture.

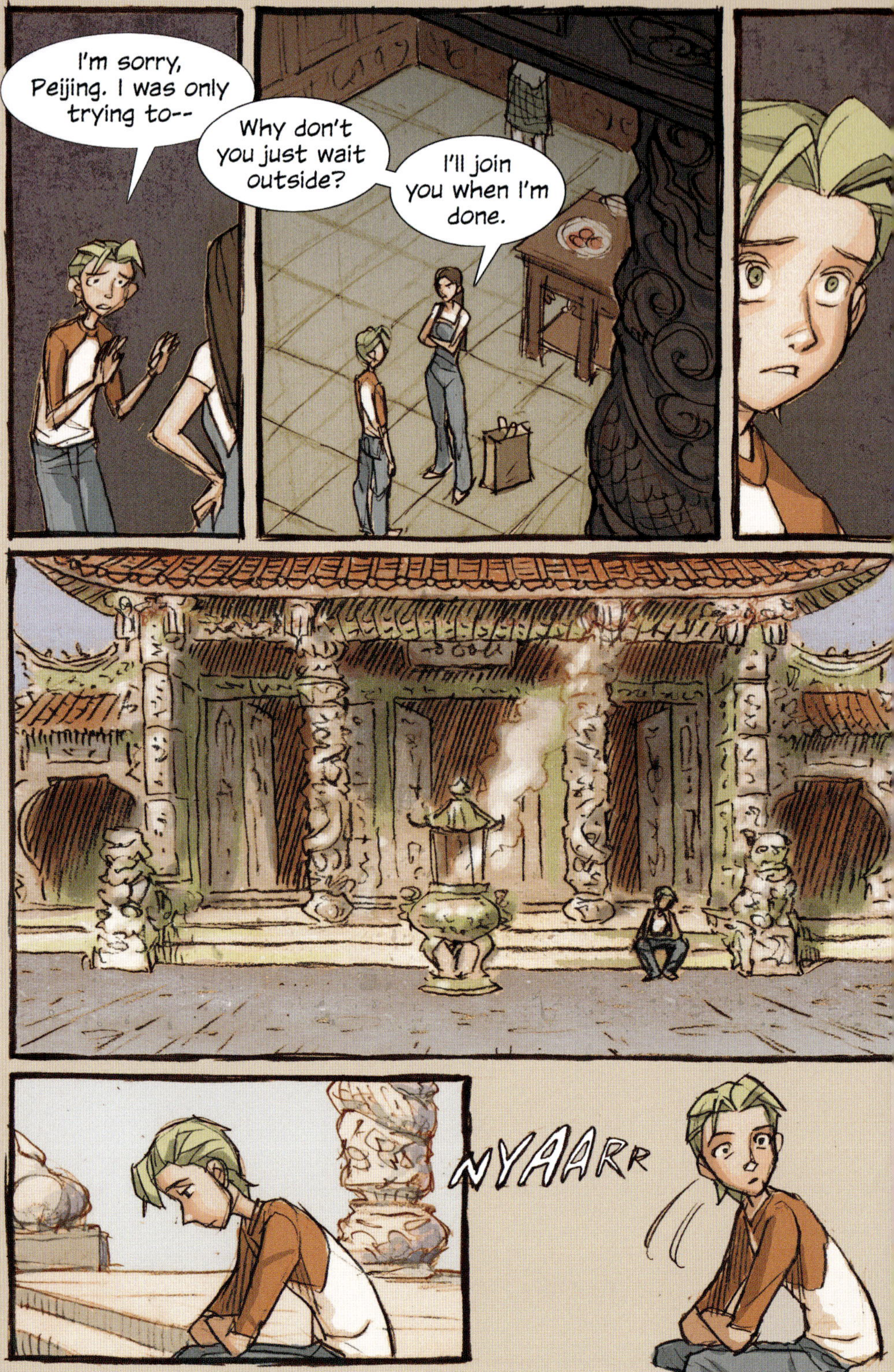

I'm sorry, Peijing. I was only trying to--
Why don't you just wait outside?
I'll join you when I'm done.
NYAARR

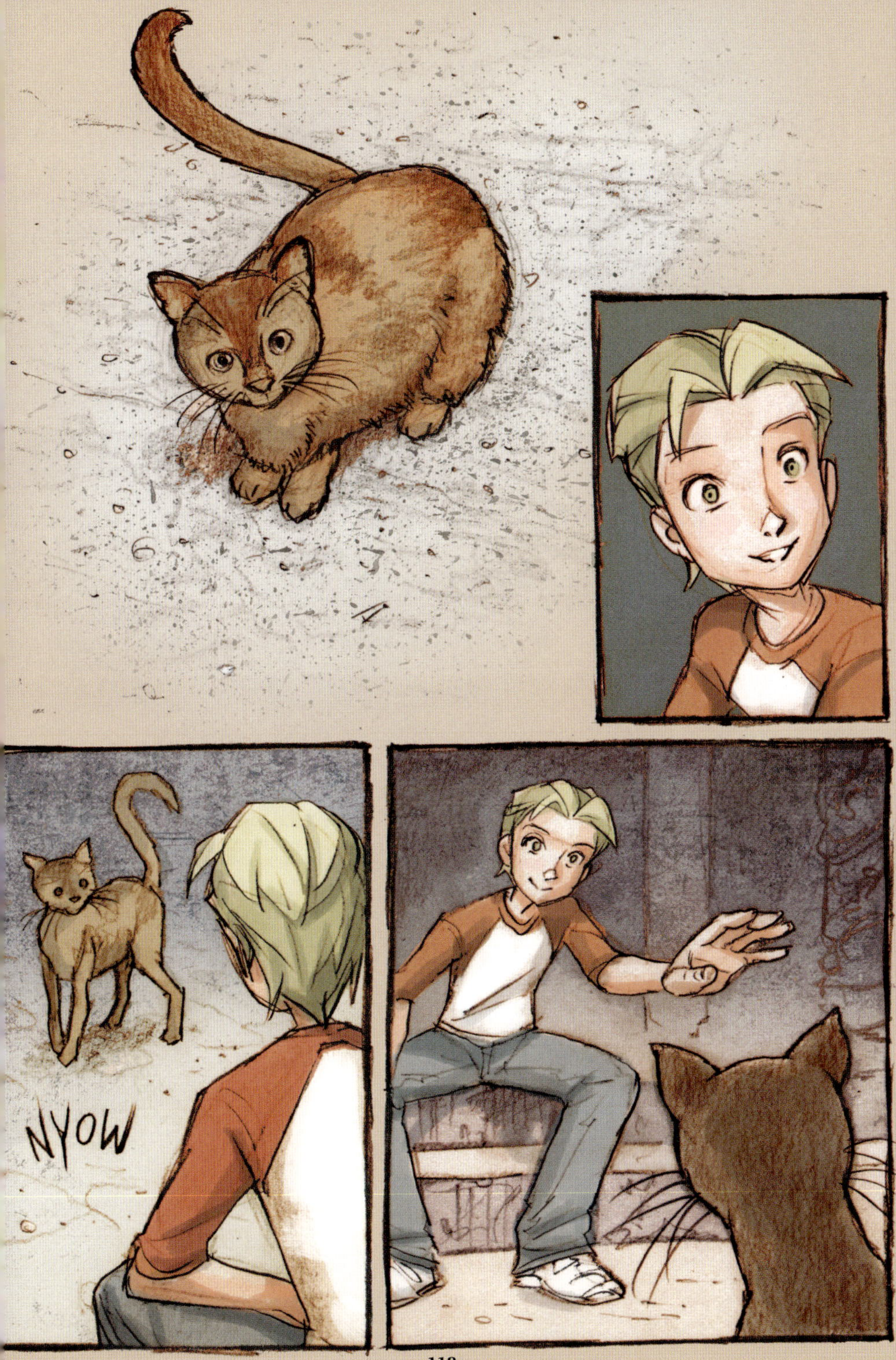
NYOW

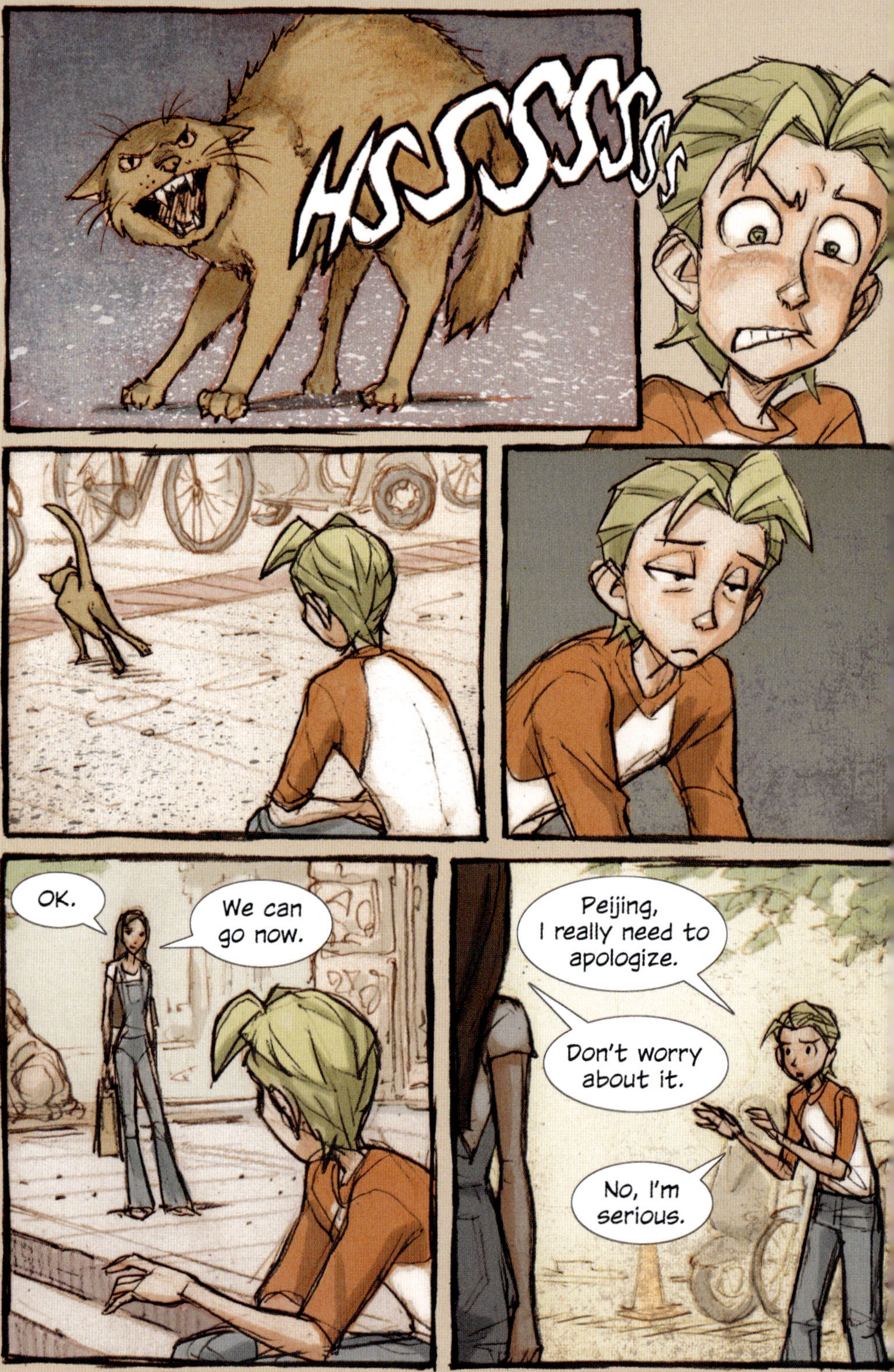
HSSSSSSSS
OK.
We can go now.
Peijing, I really need to apologize.
Don't worry about it.
No, I'm serious.

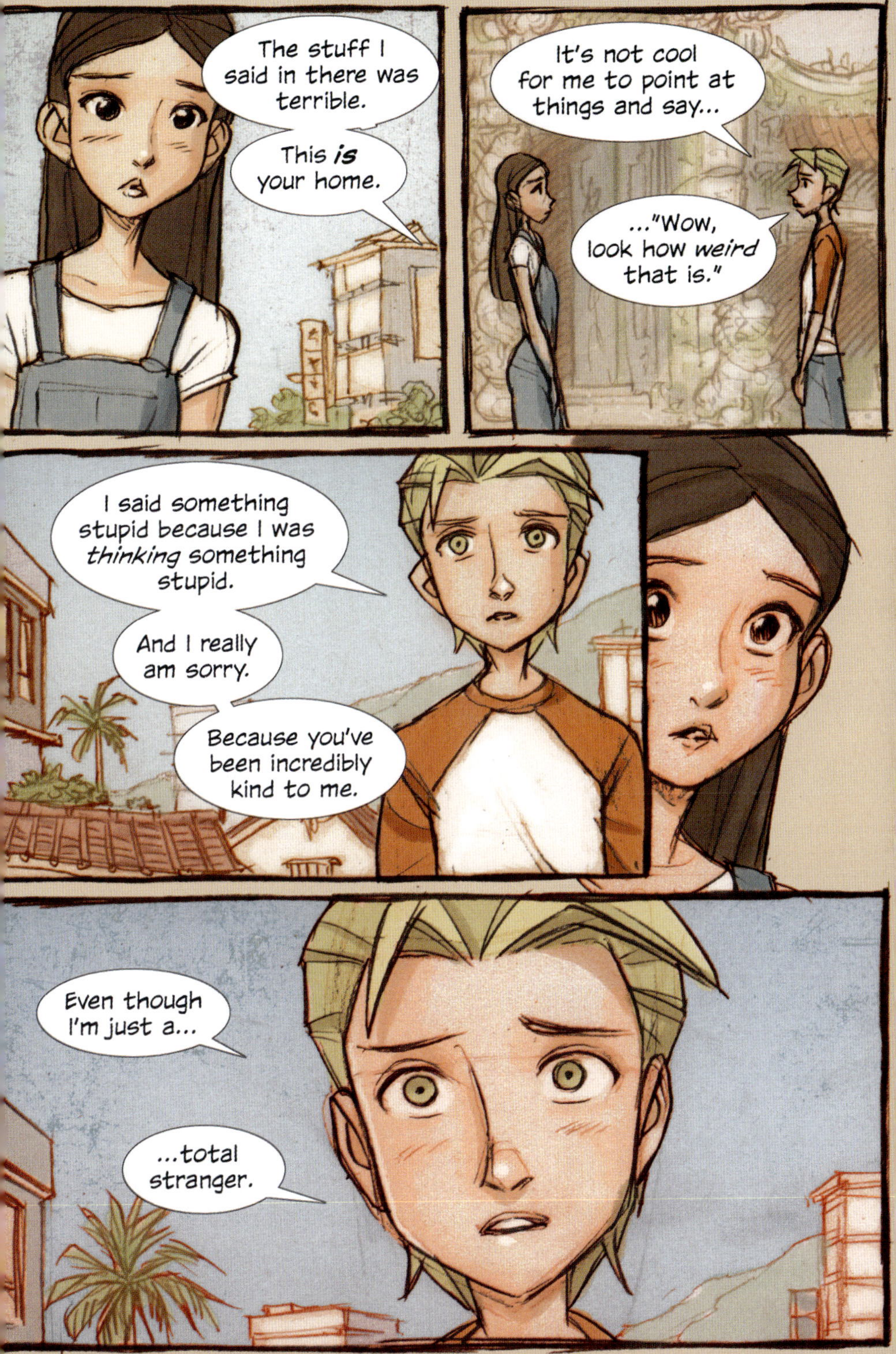
The stuff I said in there was terrible.
This *is* your home.
It's not cool for me to point at things and say...
..."Wow, look how *weird* that is."
I said something stupid because I was *thinking* something stupid.
And I really am sorry.
Because you've been incredibly kind to me.
Even though I'm just a...
...total stranger.

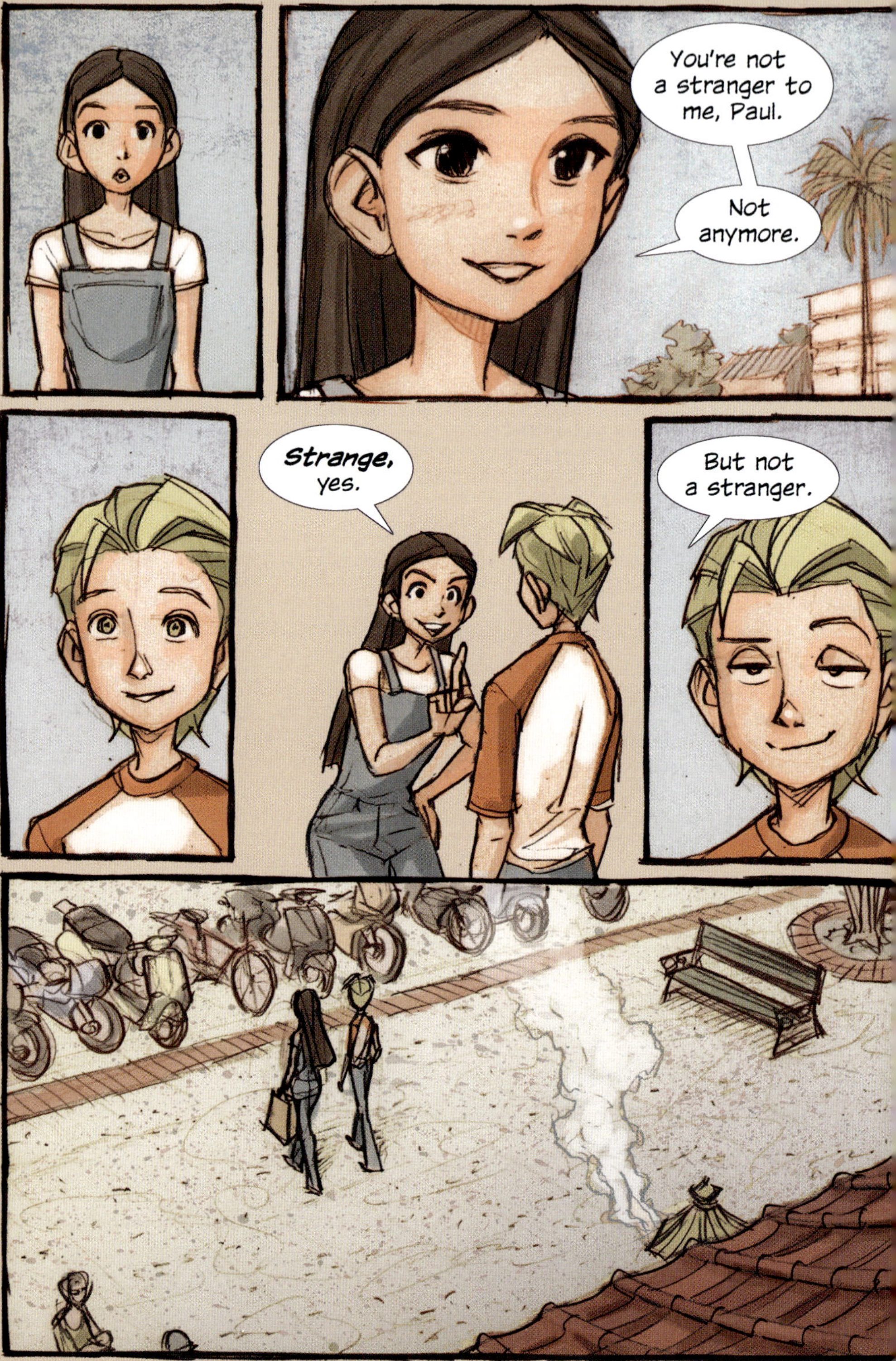

You're not a stranger to me, Paul.
Not anymore.
Strange, yes.
But not a stranger.

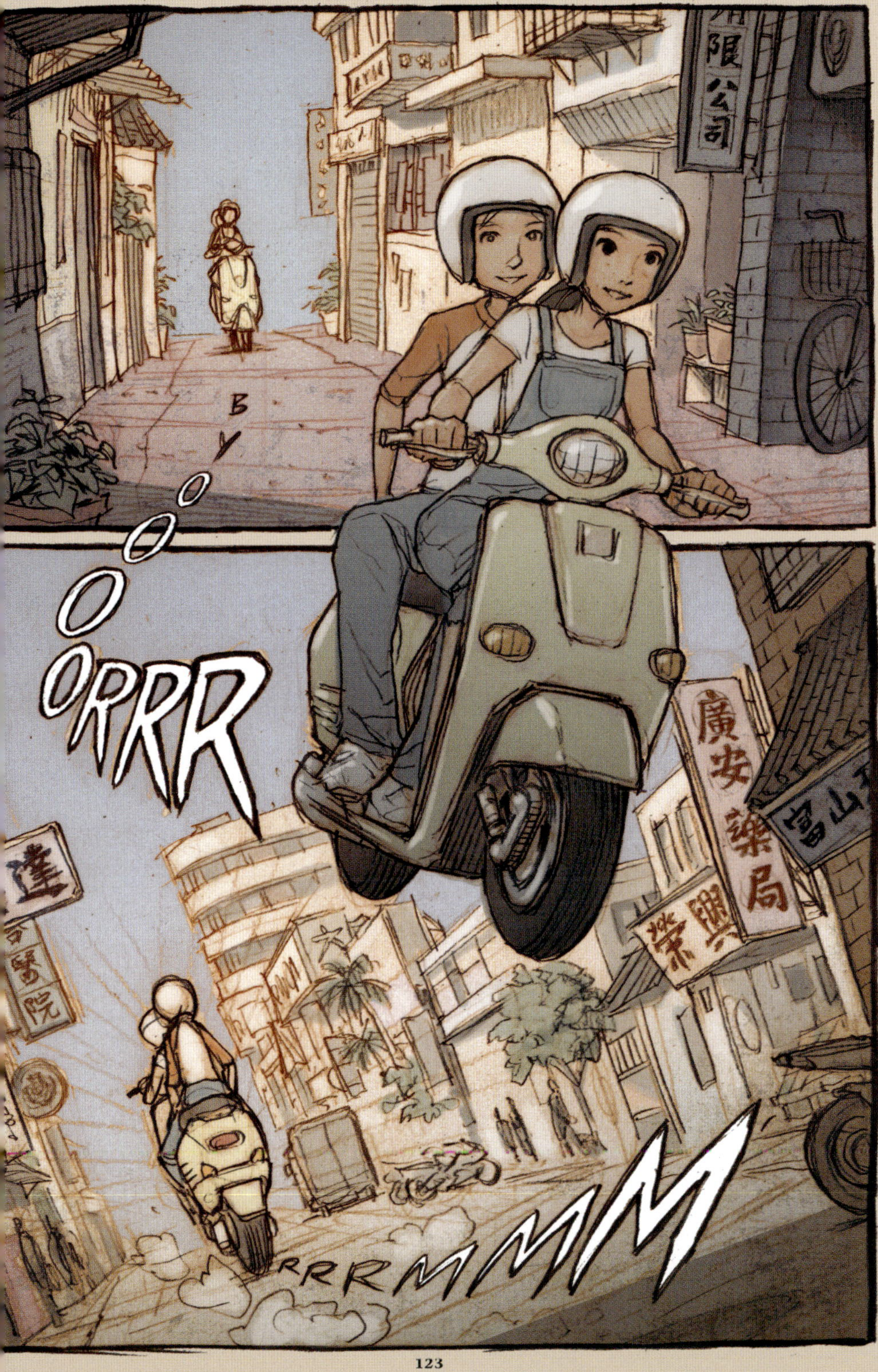
BYOOOORRR
RRRMMMM
廣安藥局

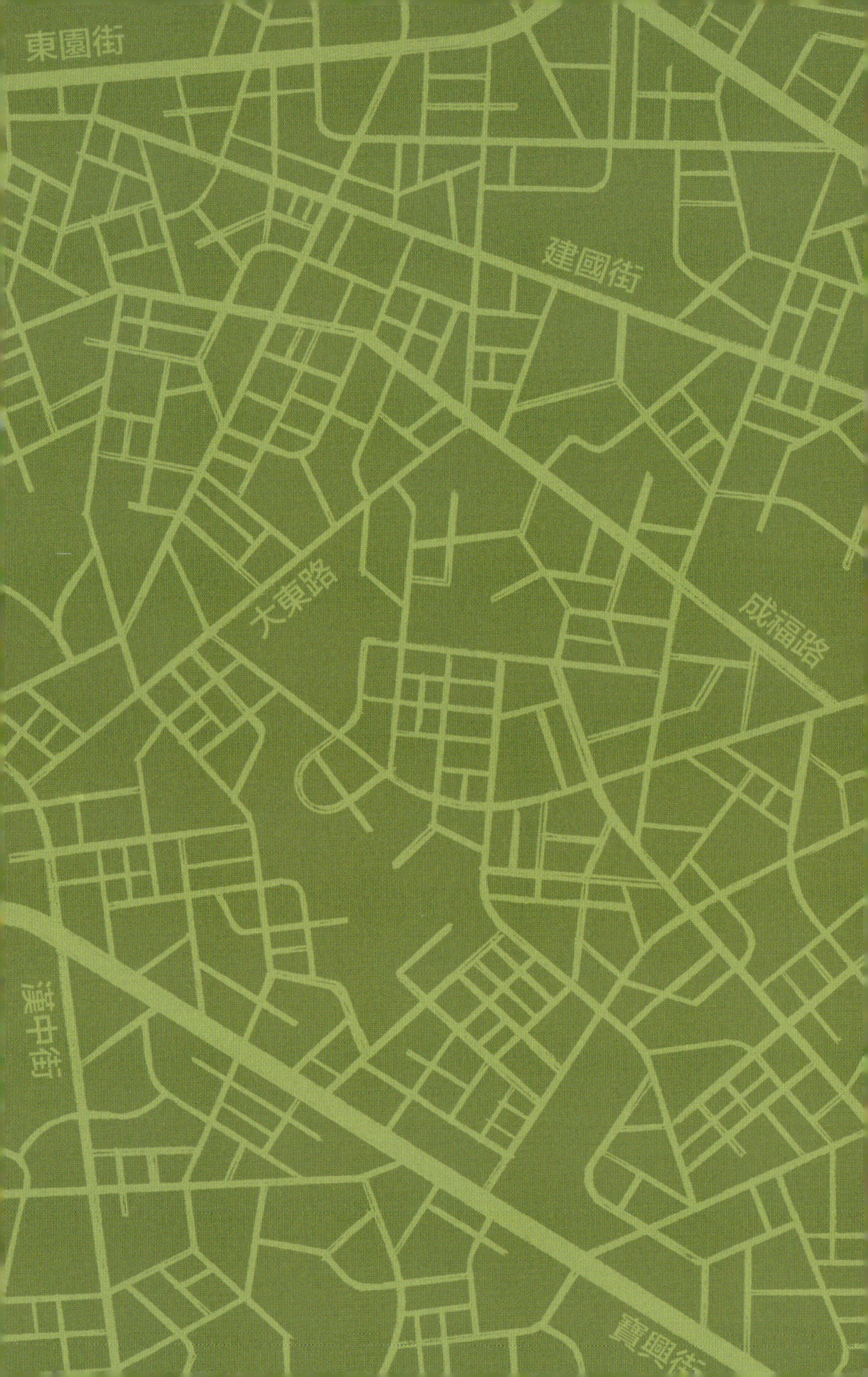
東園街
建國街
大東路
成福路
漢中街
寶興街

CHAPTER 3

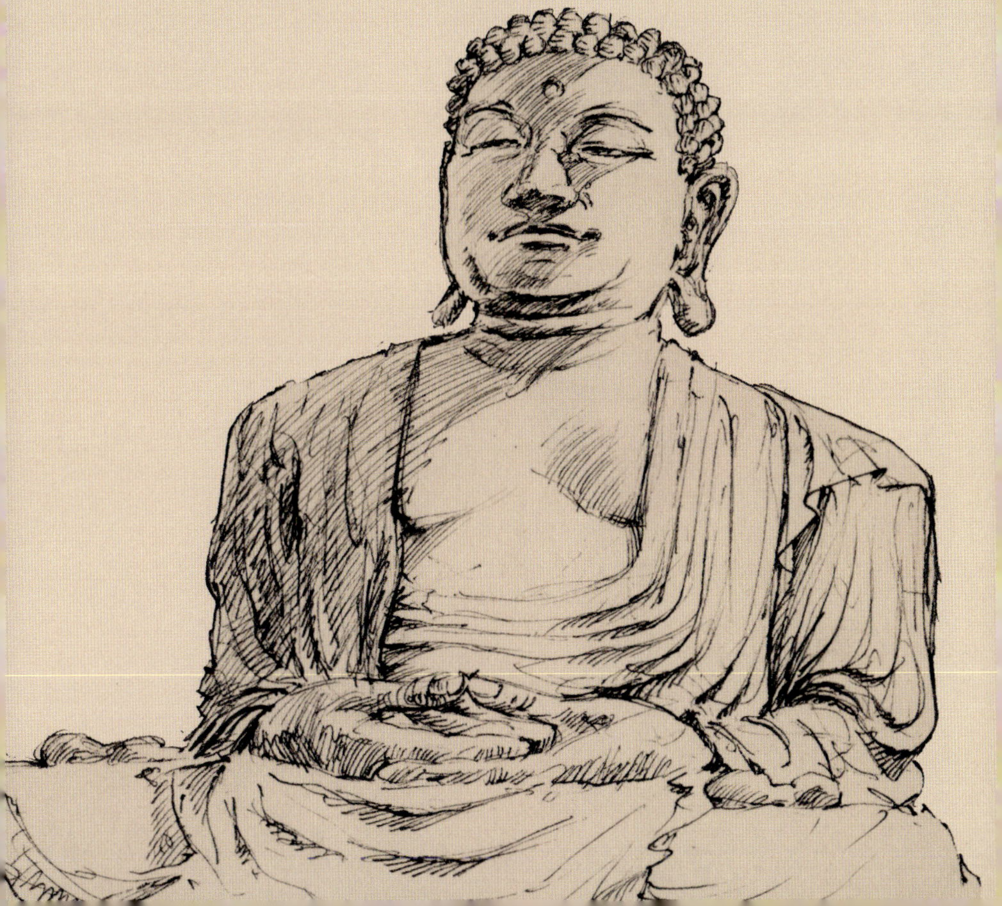

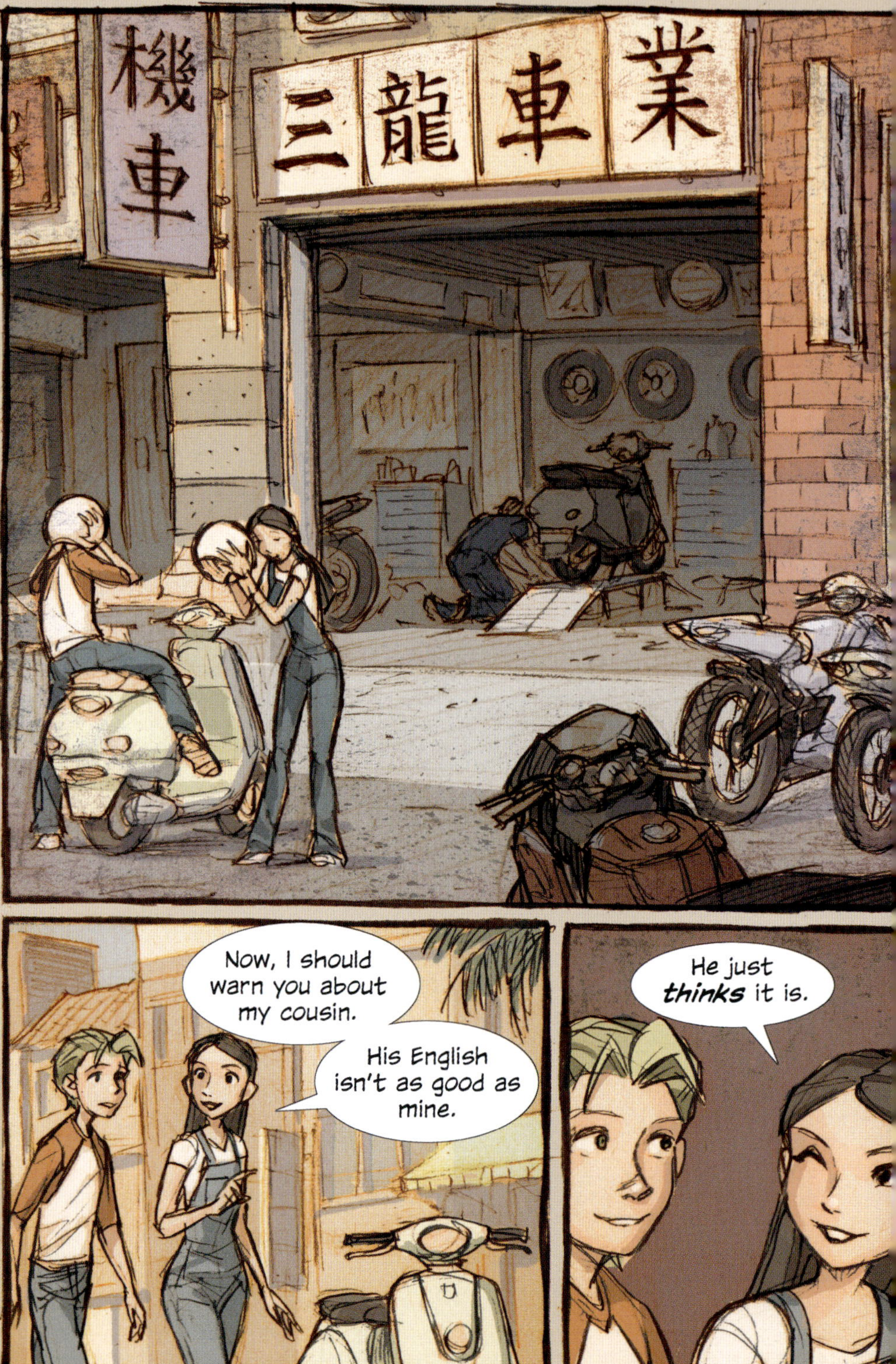
機車
三龍車業
Now, I should warn you about my cousin.
His English isn't as good as mine.
He just *thinks* it is.

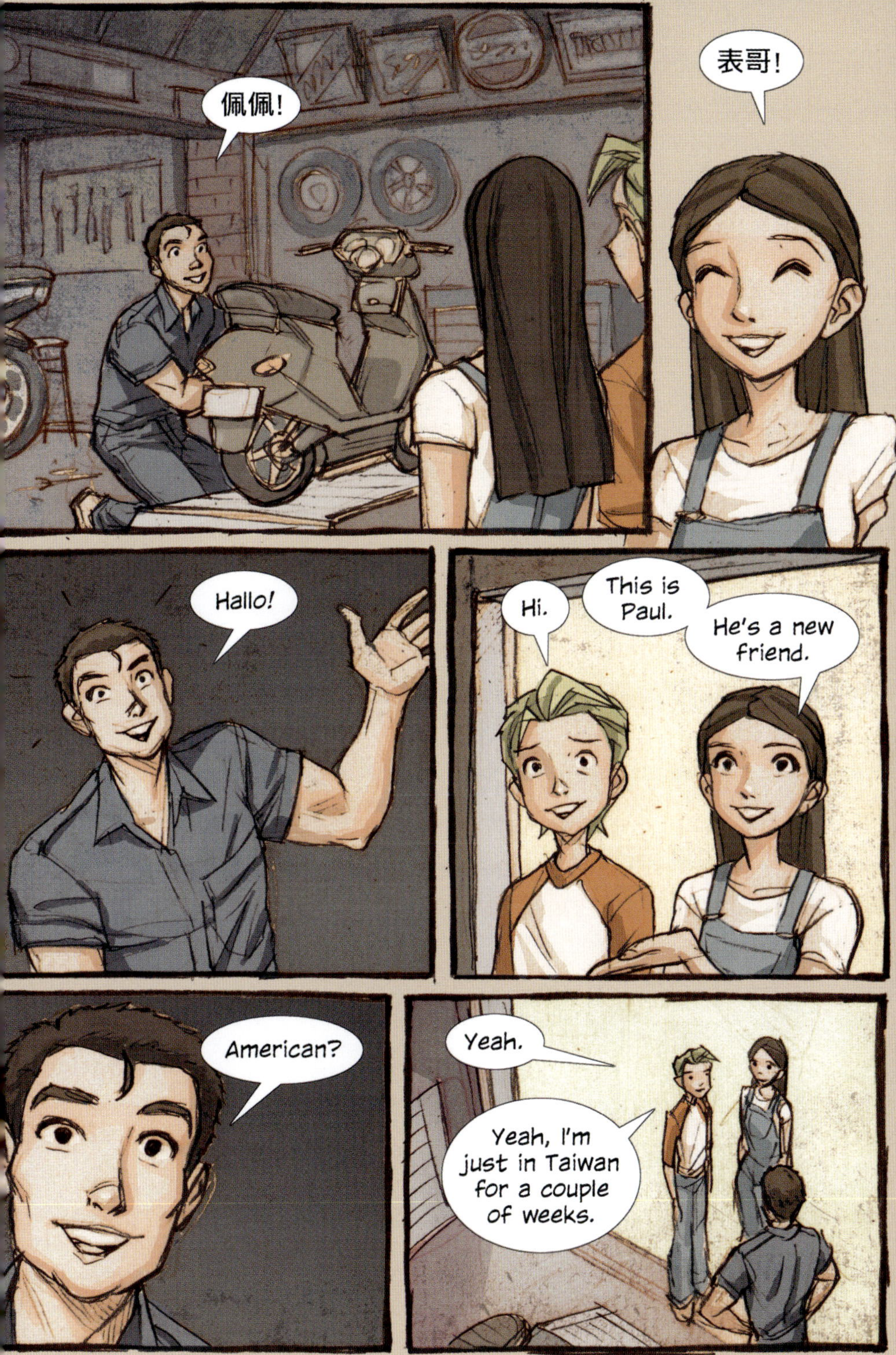
佩佩!
表哥!
Hallo!
Hi.
This is Paul.
He's a new friend.
American?
Yeah.
Yeah, I'm just in Taiwan for a couple of weeks.

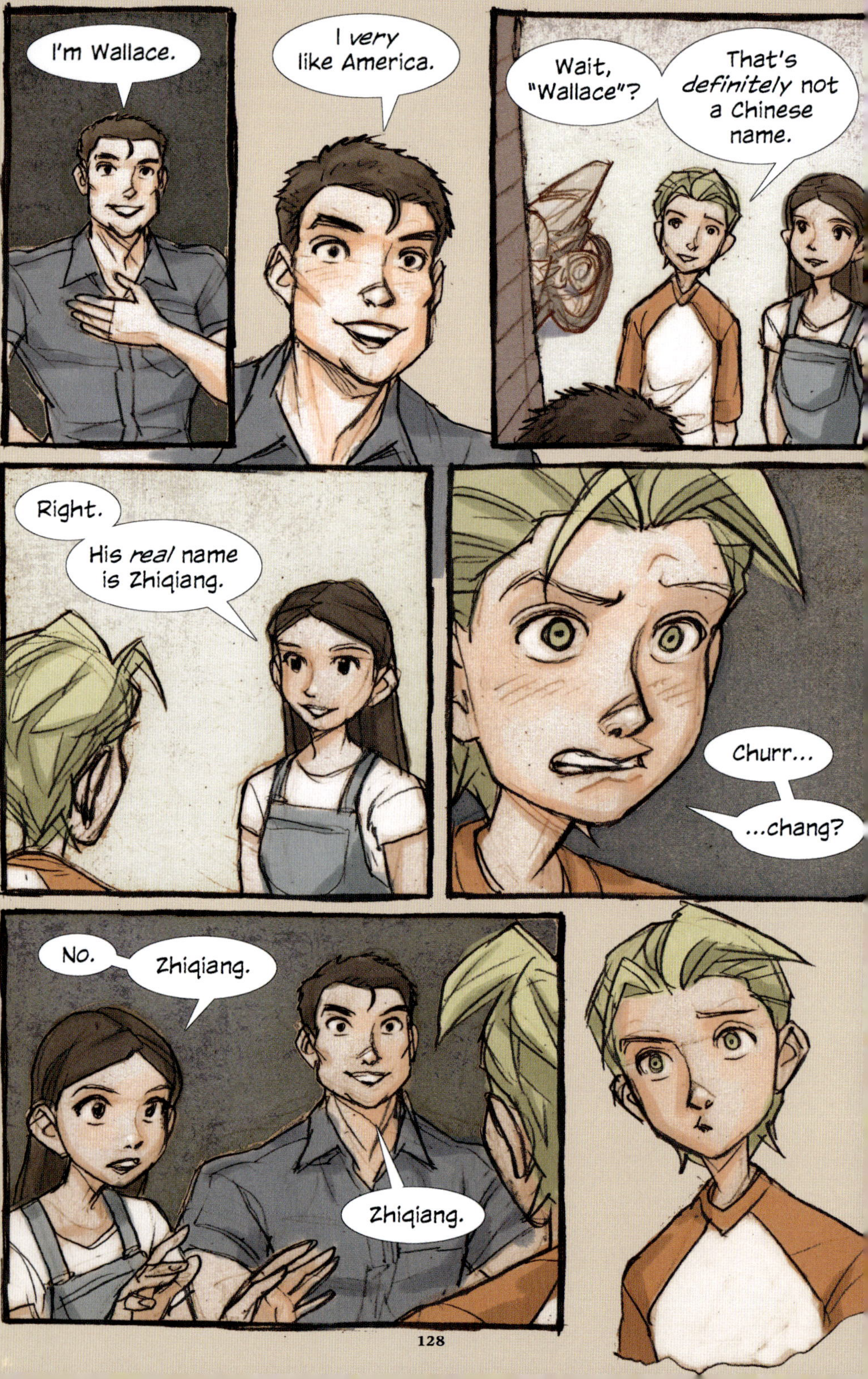
I'm Wallace.
I *very* like America.
Wait, "Wallace"?
That's *definitely* not a Chinese name.
Right.
His *real* name is Zhiqiang.
Churr...
...chang?
No.
Zhiqiang.
Zhiqiang.

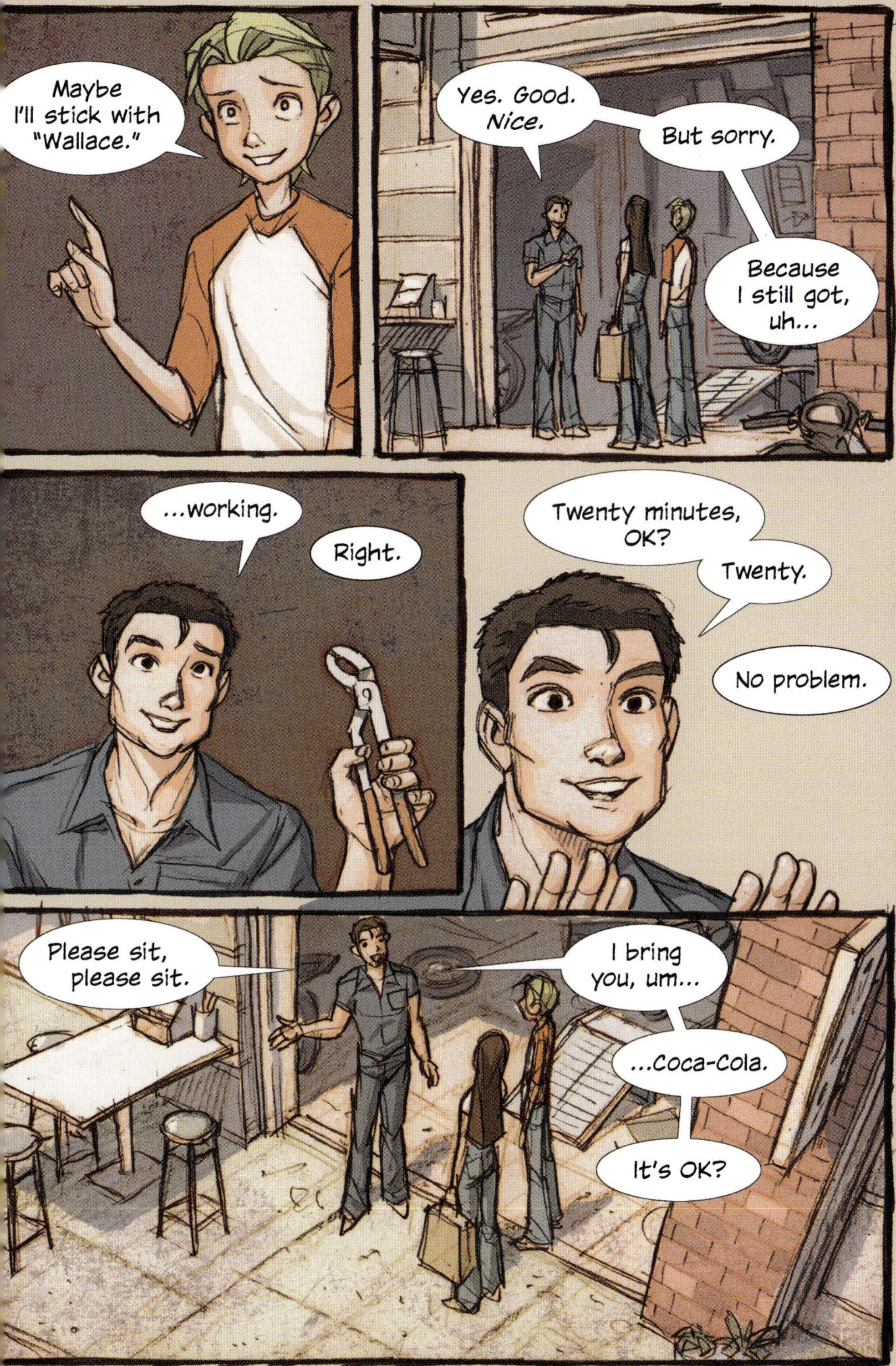
Maybe
I'll stick with
"Wallace."
Yes. Good.
Nice.
But sorry.
Because
I still got,
uh...
...working.
Right.
Twenty minutes,
OK?
Twenty.
No problem.
Please sit,
please sit.
I bring
you, um...
...Coca-Cola.
It's OK?

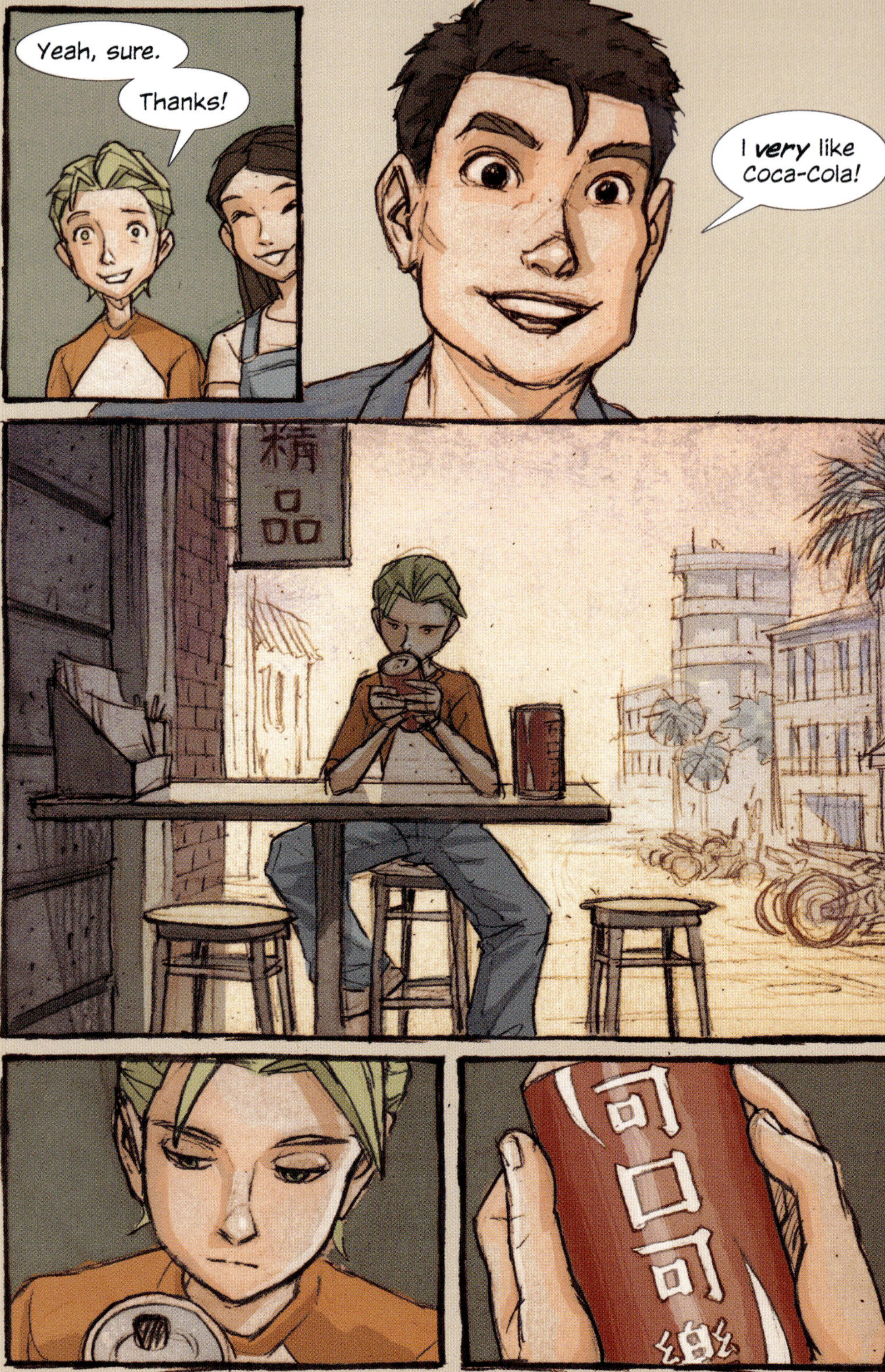
Yeah, sure.
Thanks!
I **very** like Coca-Cola!
精品
可口可樂

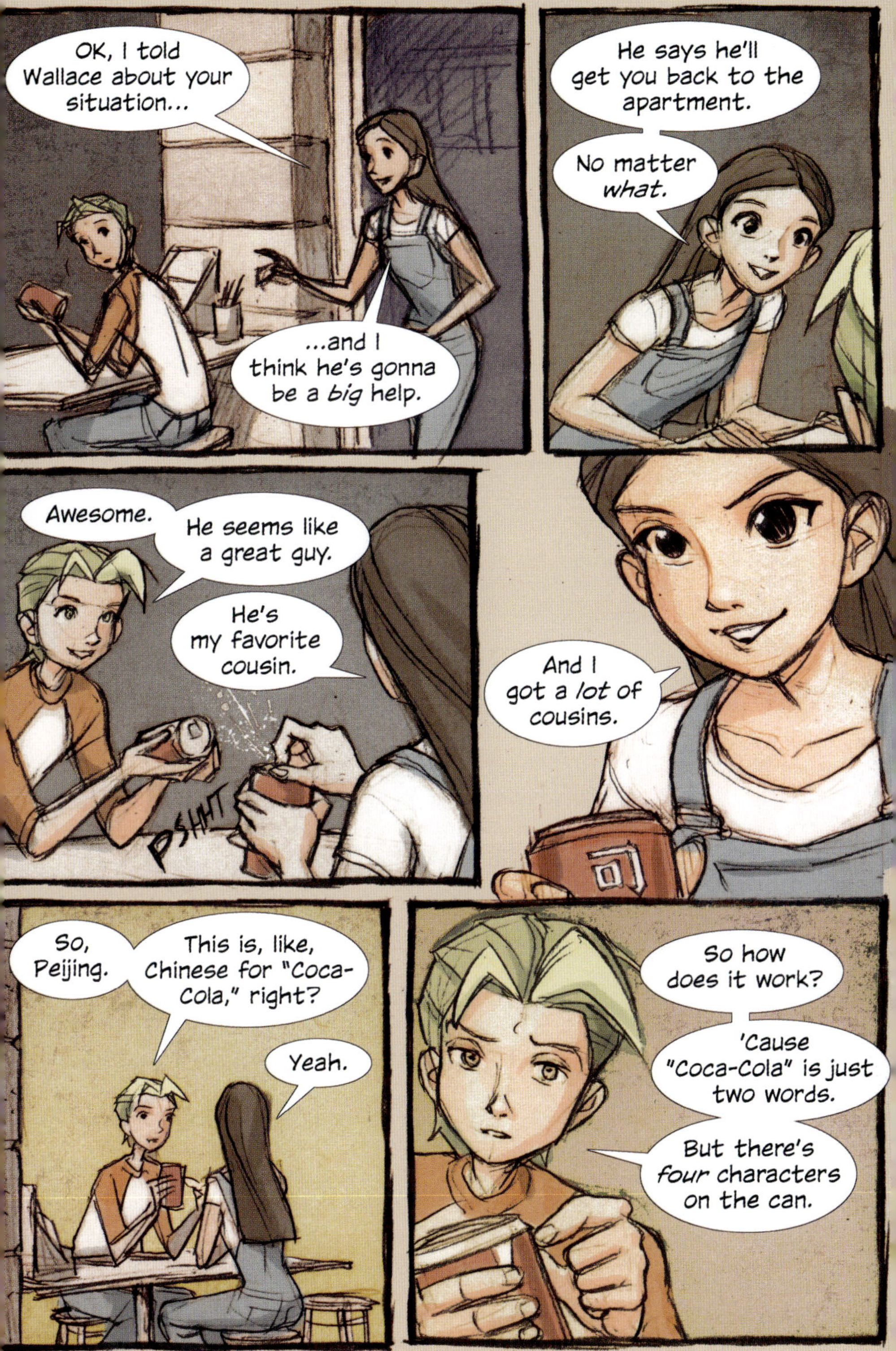
OK, I told Wallace about your situation...
...and I think he's gonna be a *big* help.
He says he'll get you back to the apartment.
No matter *what*.
Awesome.
He seems like a great guy.
He's my favorite cousin.
PSHHT
And I got a *lot* of cousins.
So, Peijing.
This is, like, Chinese for "Coca-Cola," right?
Yeah.
So how does it work?
'Cause "Coca-Cola" is just two words.
But there's *four* characters on the can.

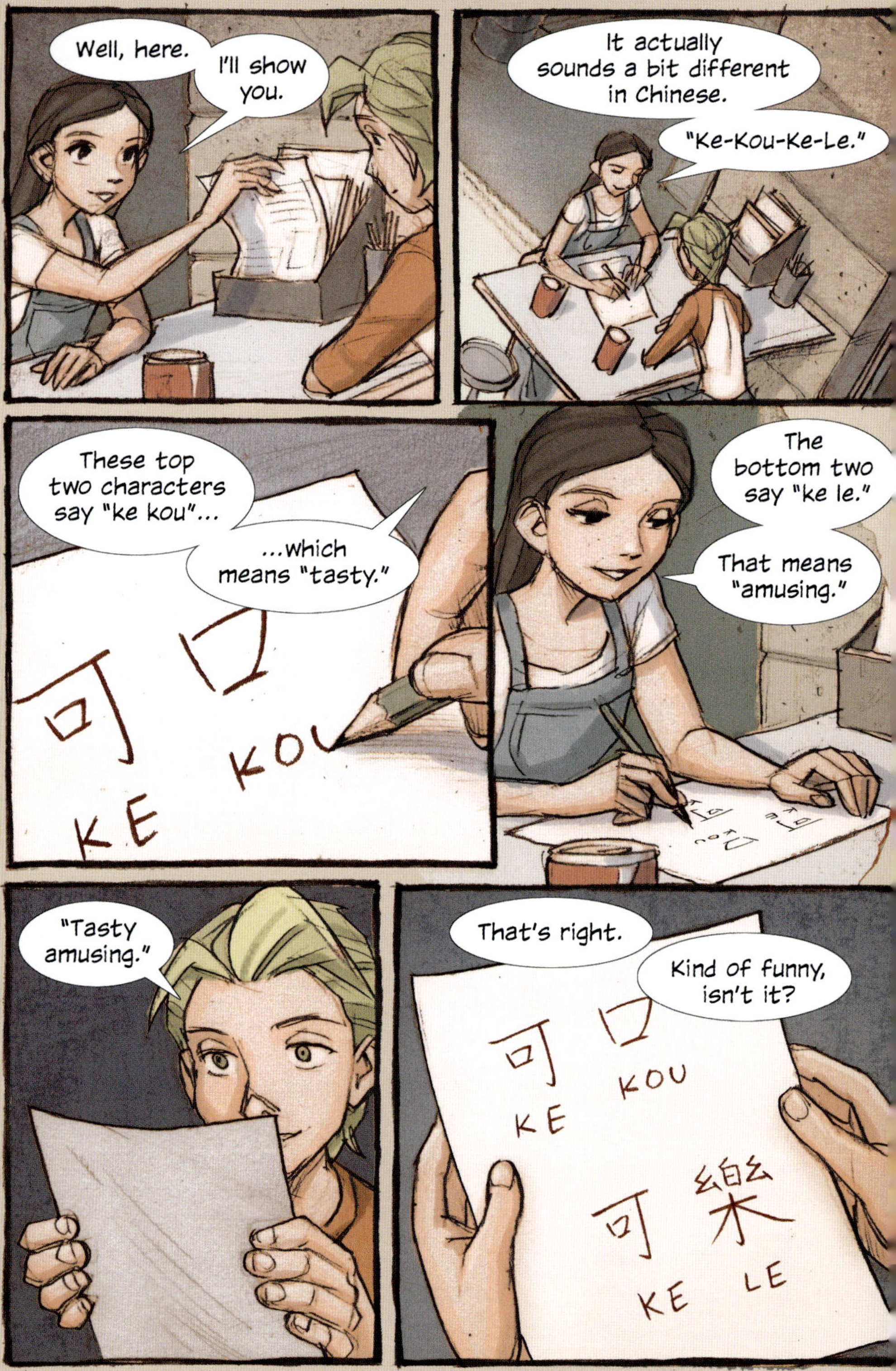
Well, here.
I'll show you.
It actually sounds a bit different in Chinese.
"Ke-Kou-Ke-Le."
These top two characters say "ke kou"...
...which means "tasty."
可口
KE KOU
The bottom two say "ke le."
That means "amusing."
"Tasty amusing."
That's right.
Kind of funny, isn't it?
可口
KE KOU
可樂
KE LE

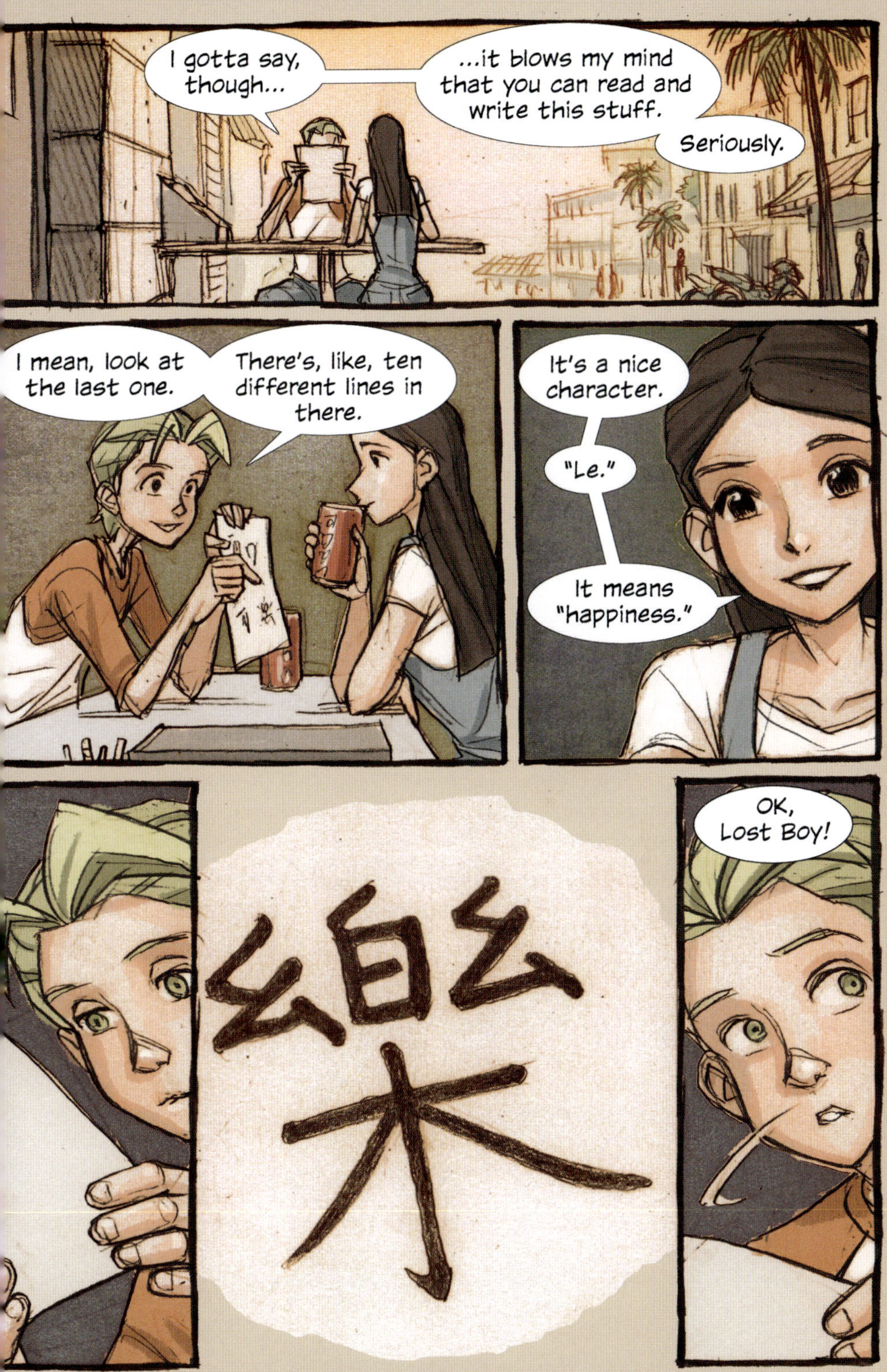
I gotta say, though...
...it blows my mind that you can read and write this stuff.
Seriously.
I mean, look at the last one.
There's, like, ten different lines in there.
It's a nice character.
"Le."
It means "happiness."
樂
OK, Lost Boy!

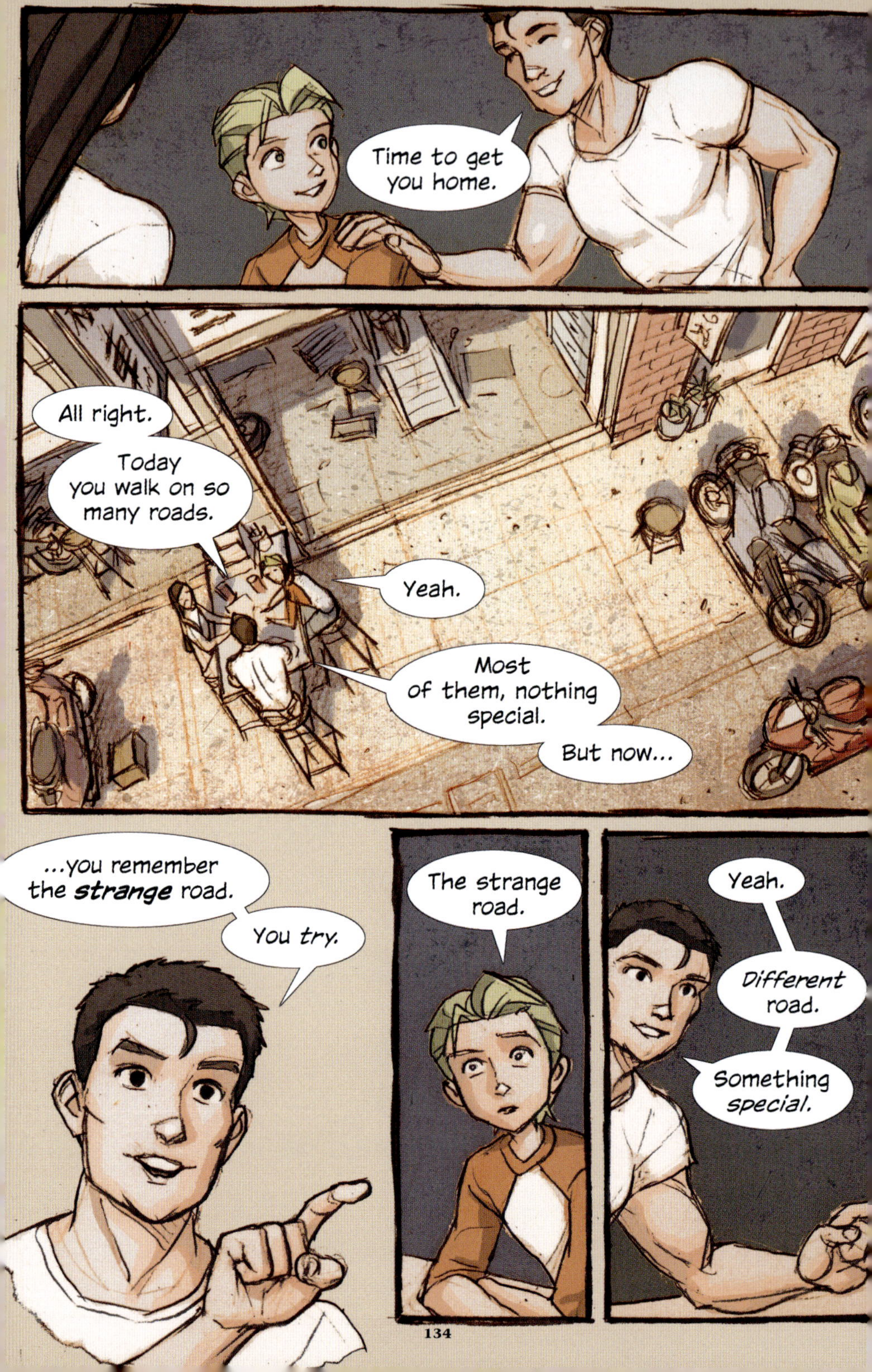
Time to get you home.
All right.
Today you walk on so many roads.
Yeah.
Most of them, nothing special.
But now...
...you remember the *strange* road.
You *try*.
The strange road.
Yeah.
Different road.
Something special.

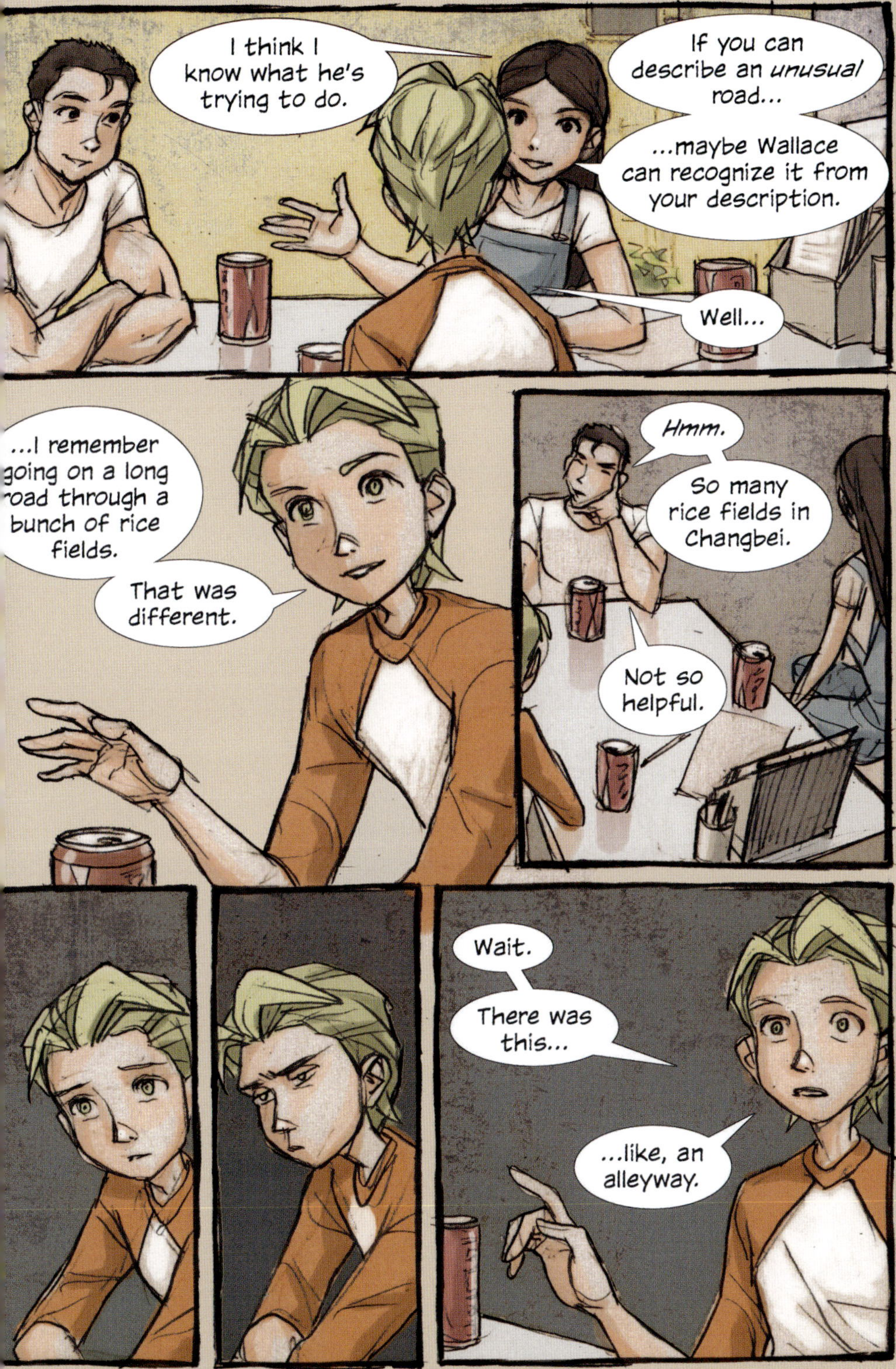

I think I know what he's trying to do.
If you can describe an *unusual* road...
...maybe Wallace can recognize it from your description.
Well...
...I remember going on a long road through a bunch of rice fields.
That was different.
Hmm.
So many rice fields in Changbei.
Not so helpful.
Wait.
There was this...
...like, an alleyway.

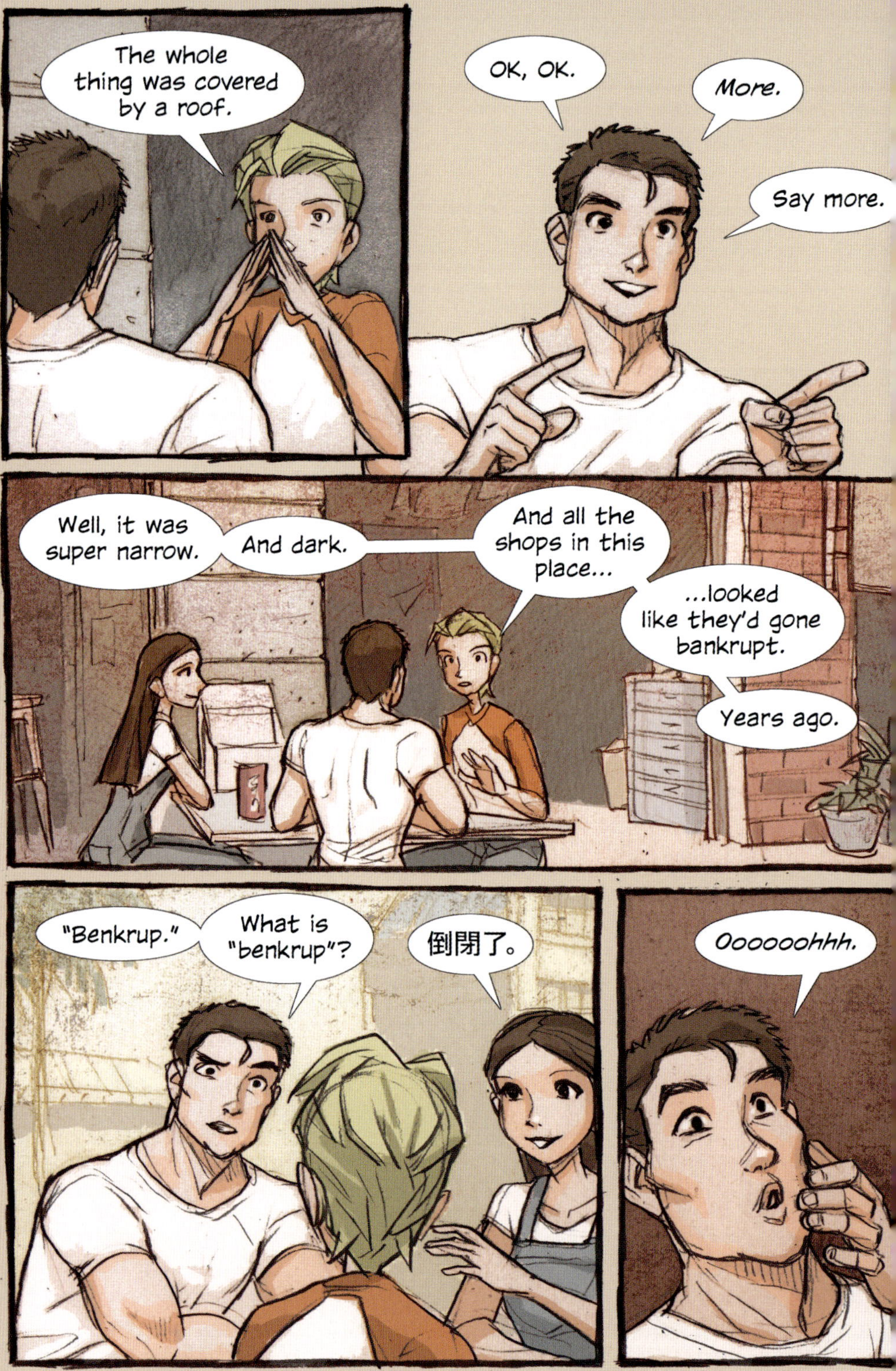
The whole thing was covered by a roof.
OK, OK.
More.
Say more.
Well, it was super narrow.
And dark.
And all the shops in this place...
...looked like they'd gone bankrupt.
Years ago.
"Benkrup."
What is "benkrup"?
倒閉了。
Oooooohhh.

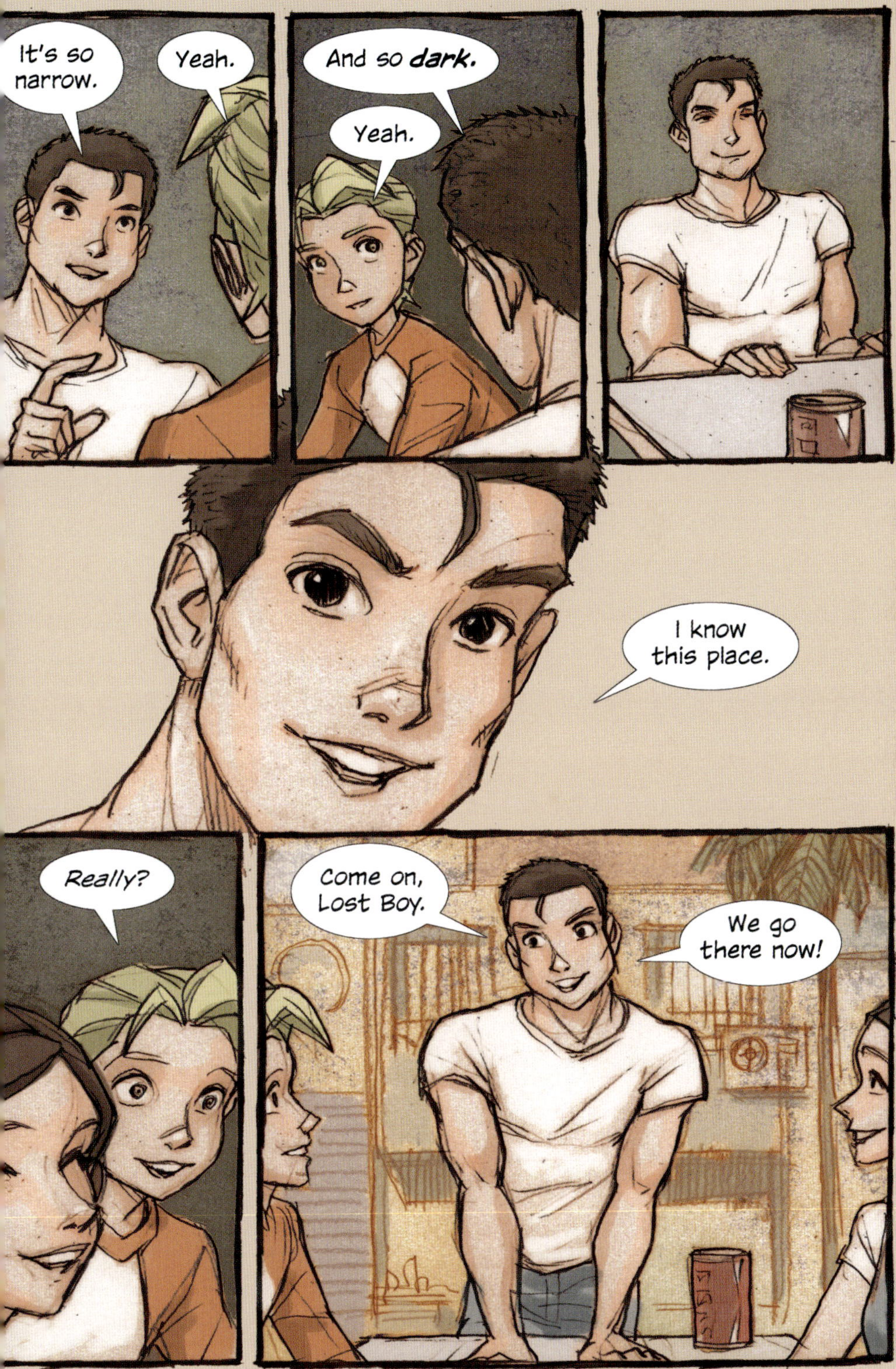
It's so narrow.
Yeah.
And so *dark.*
Yeah.
I know this place.
Really?
Come on, Lost Boy.
We go there now!

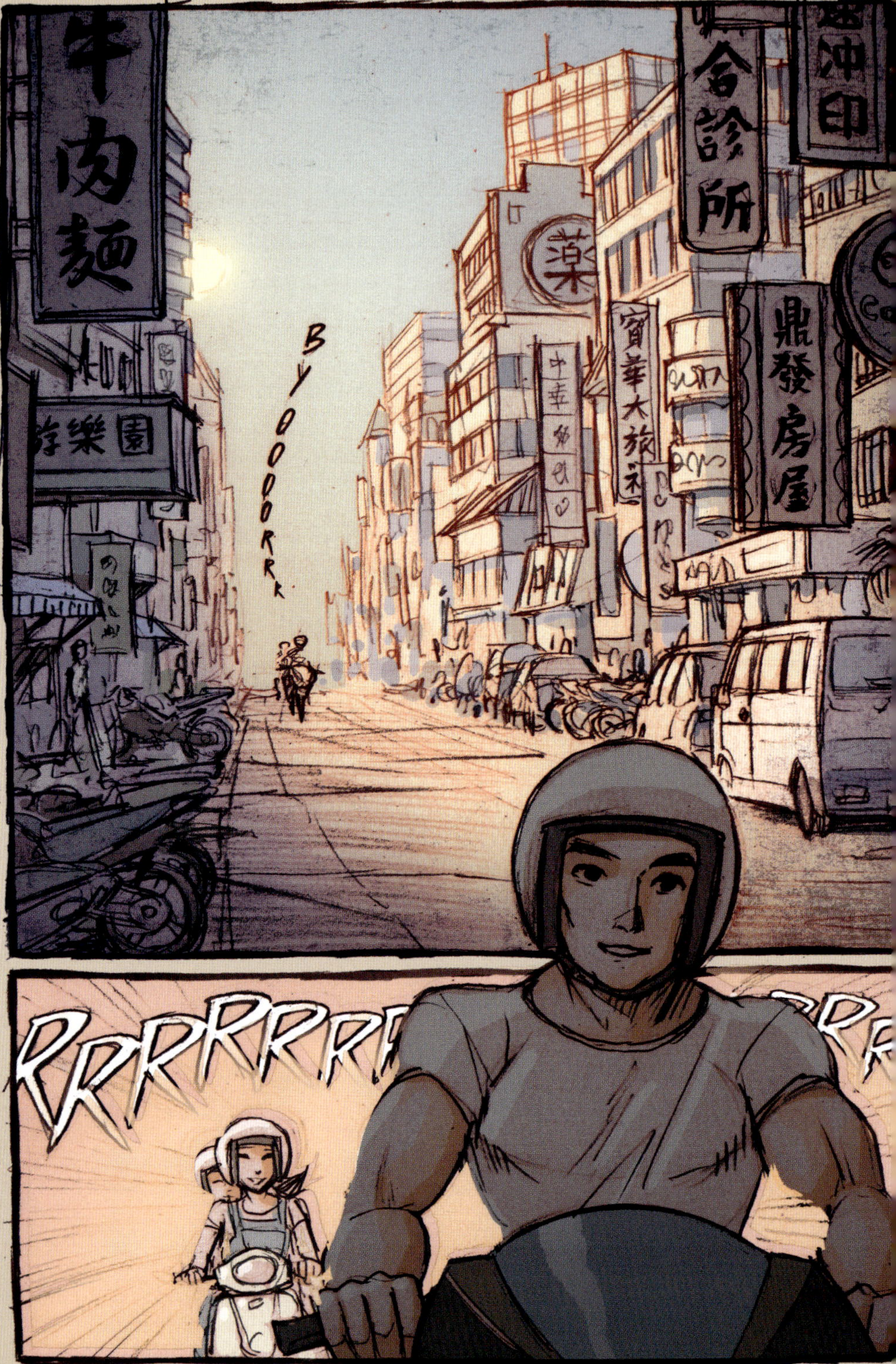
牛肉麵
合診所
沖印
藥
鼎發房屋
BYOOOORRK
RRRRRRRR
RRR

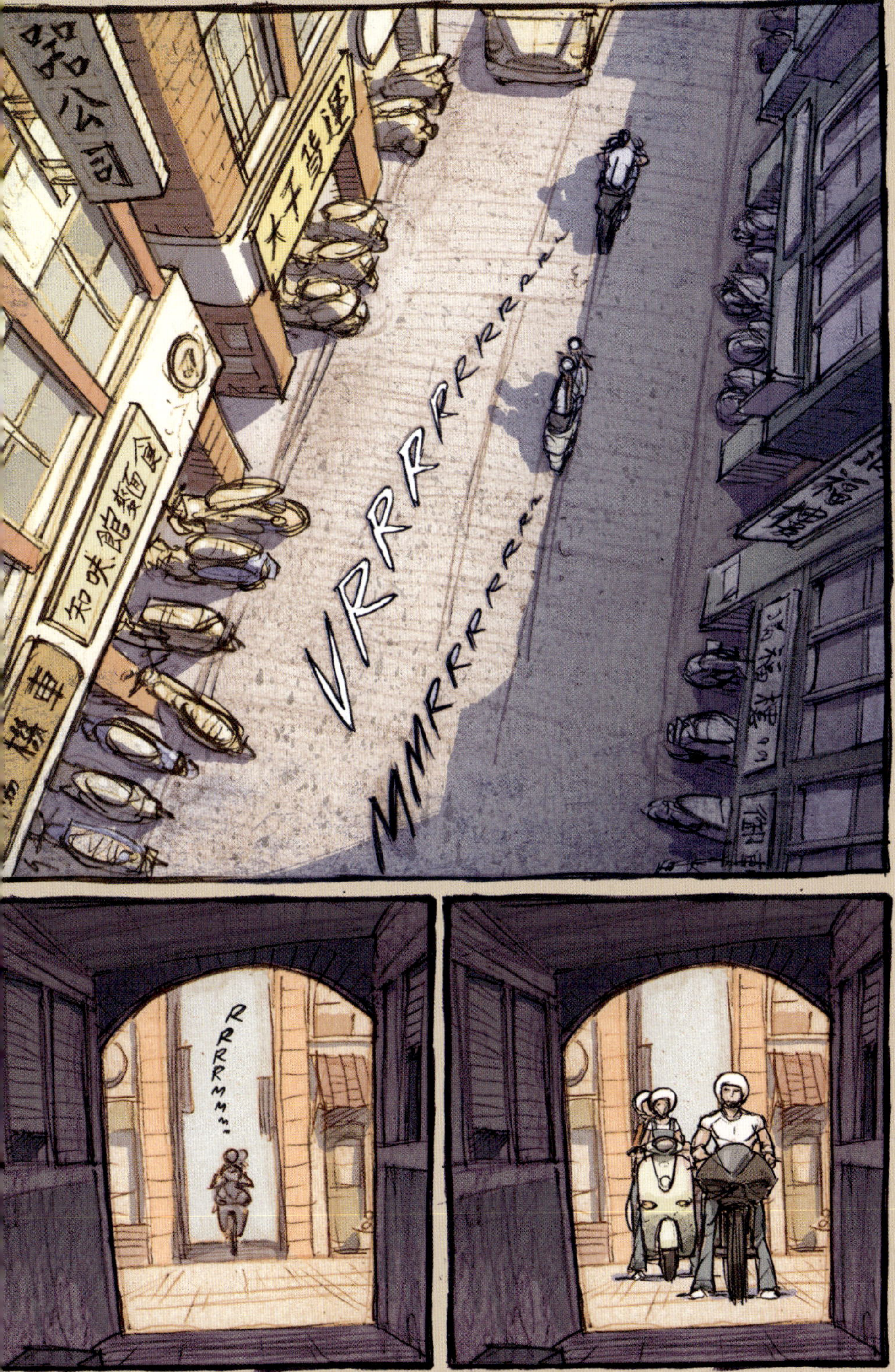
VRRRRRRRRRrrr
MMRRRRRRRrrr
RRRRMMm

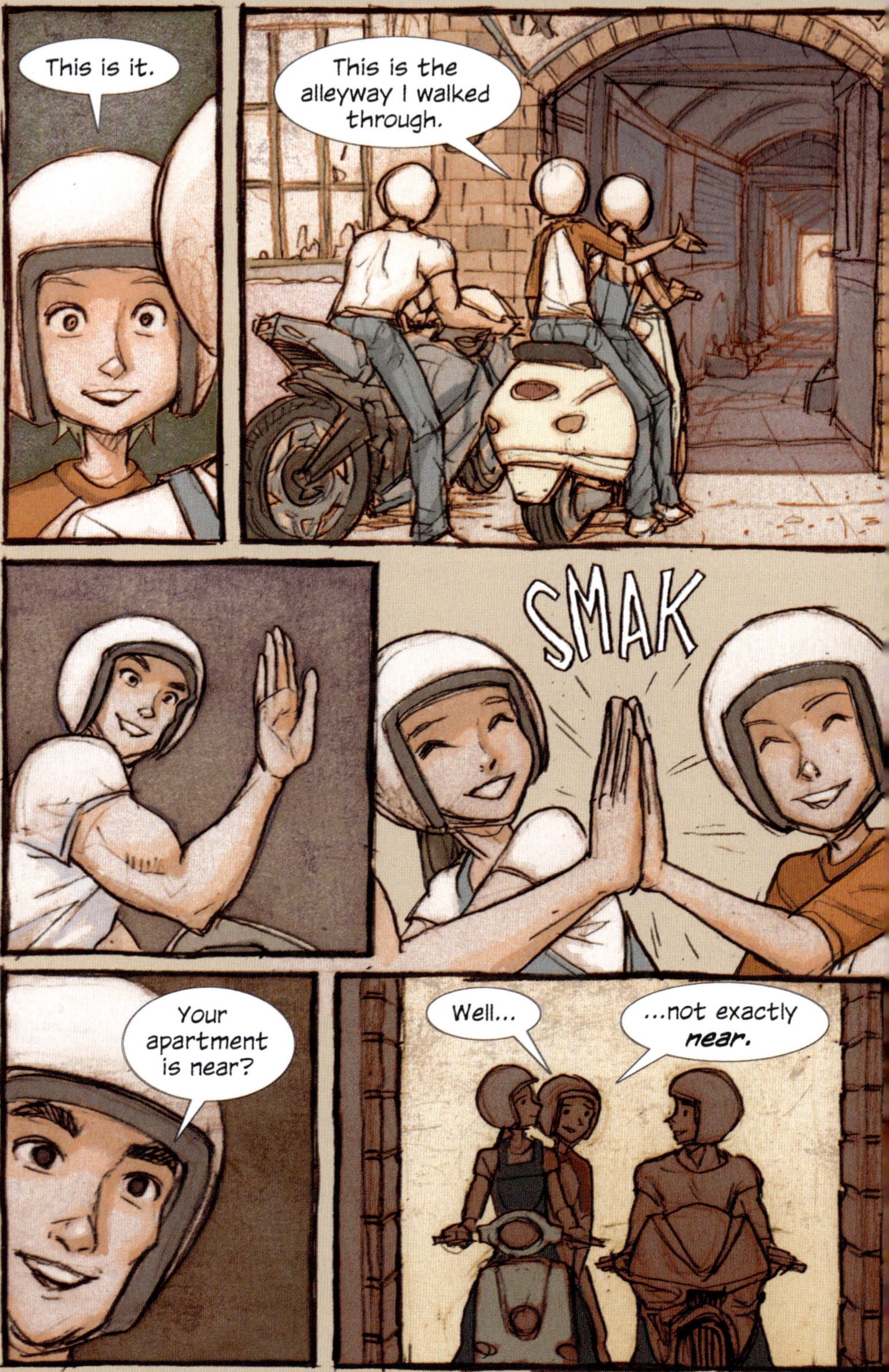
This is it.
This is the alleyway I walked through.
SMAK
Your apartment is near?
Well...
...not exactly *near*.

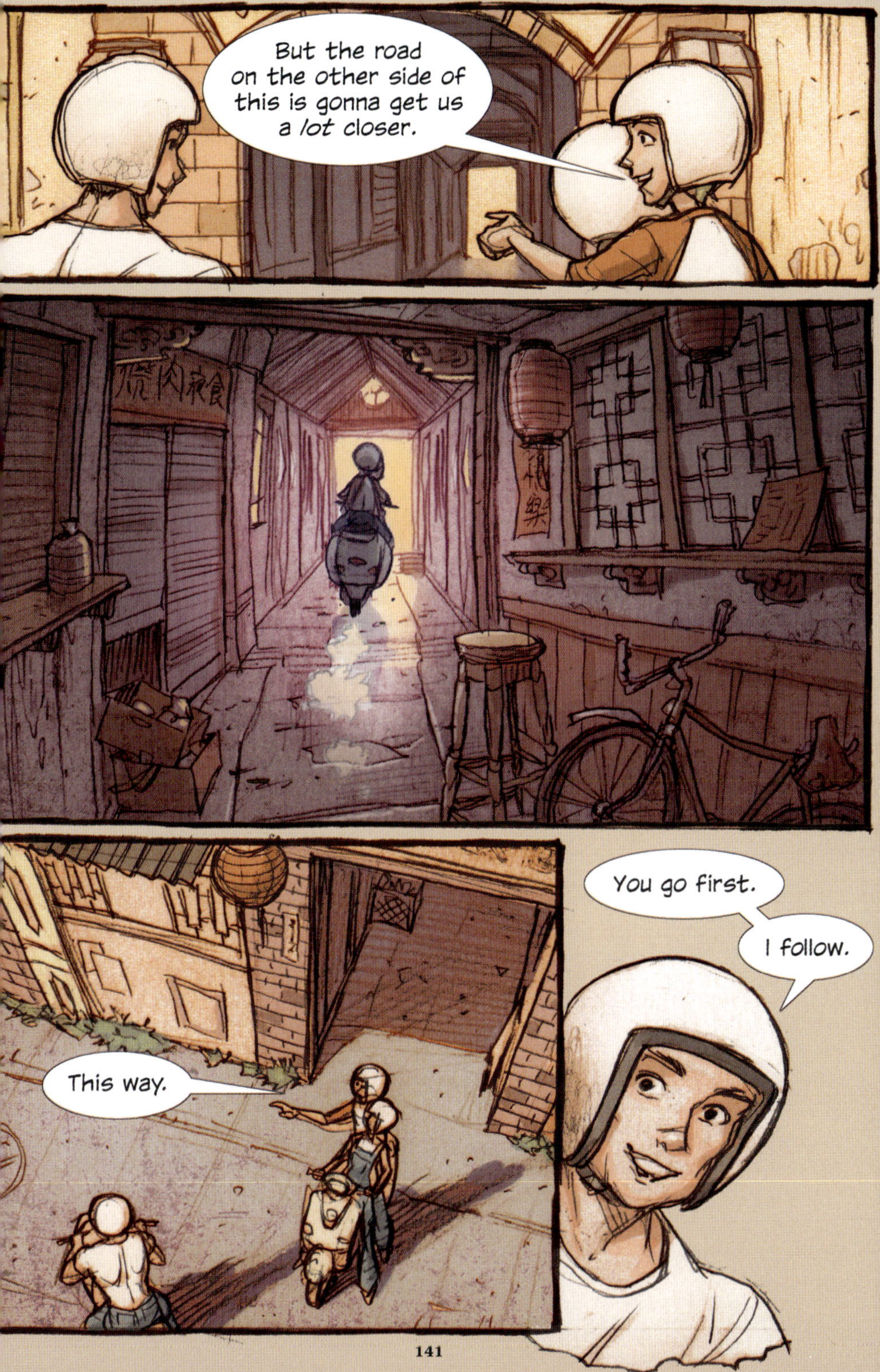
But the road on the other side of this is gonna get us a *lot* closer.
You go first.
I follow.
This way.

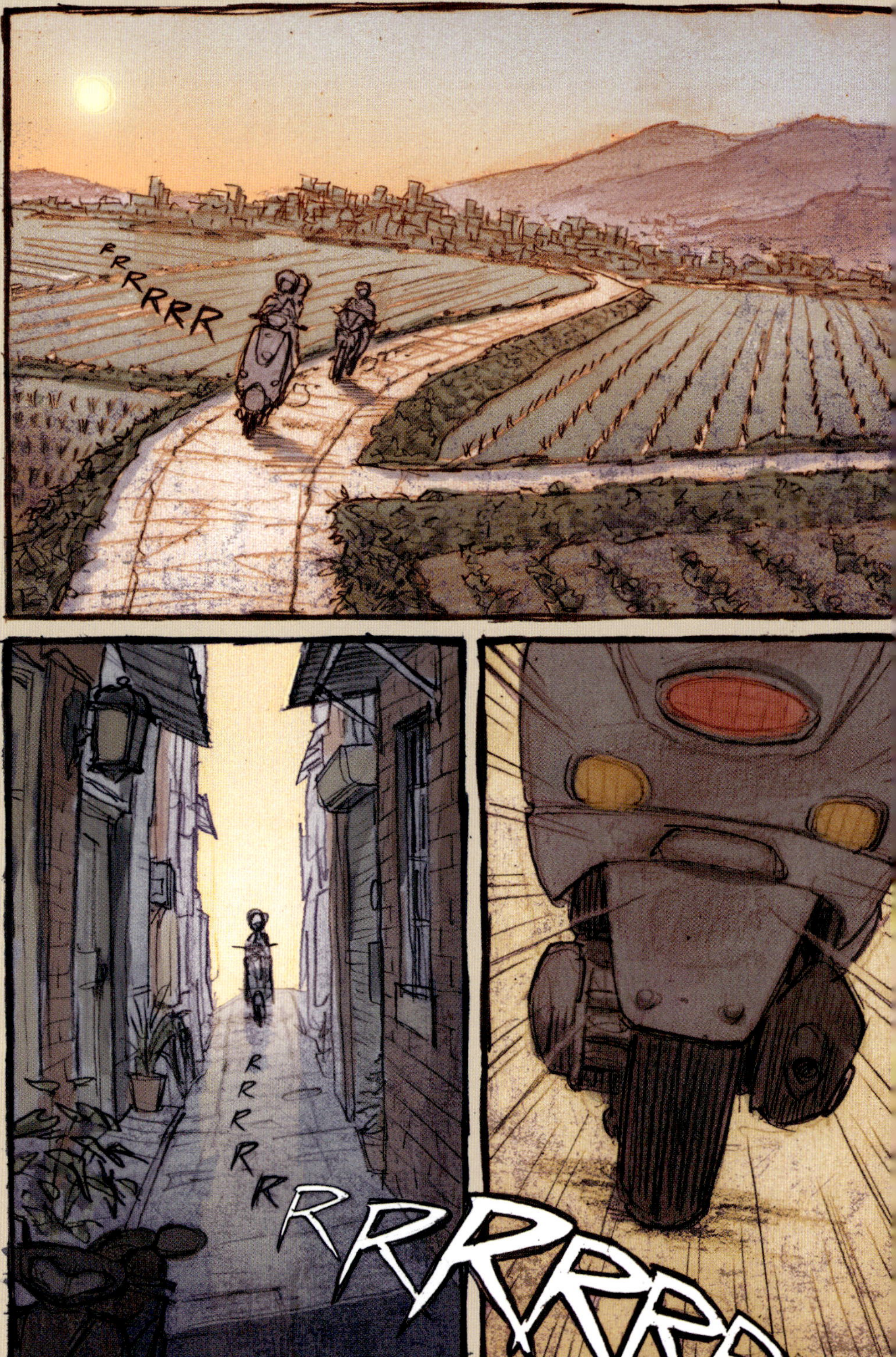
RRRRRR
RRRRRRRRRRD

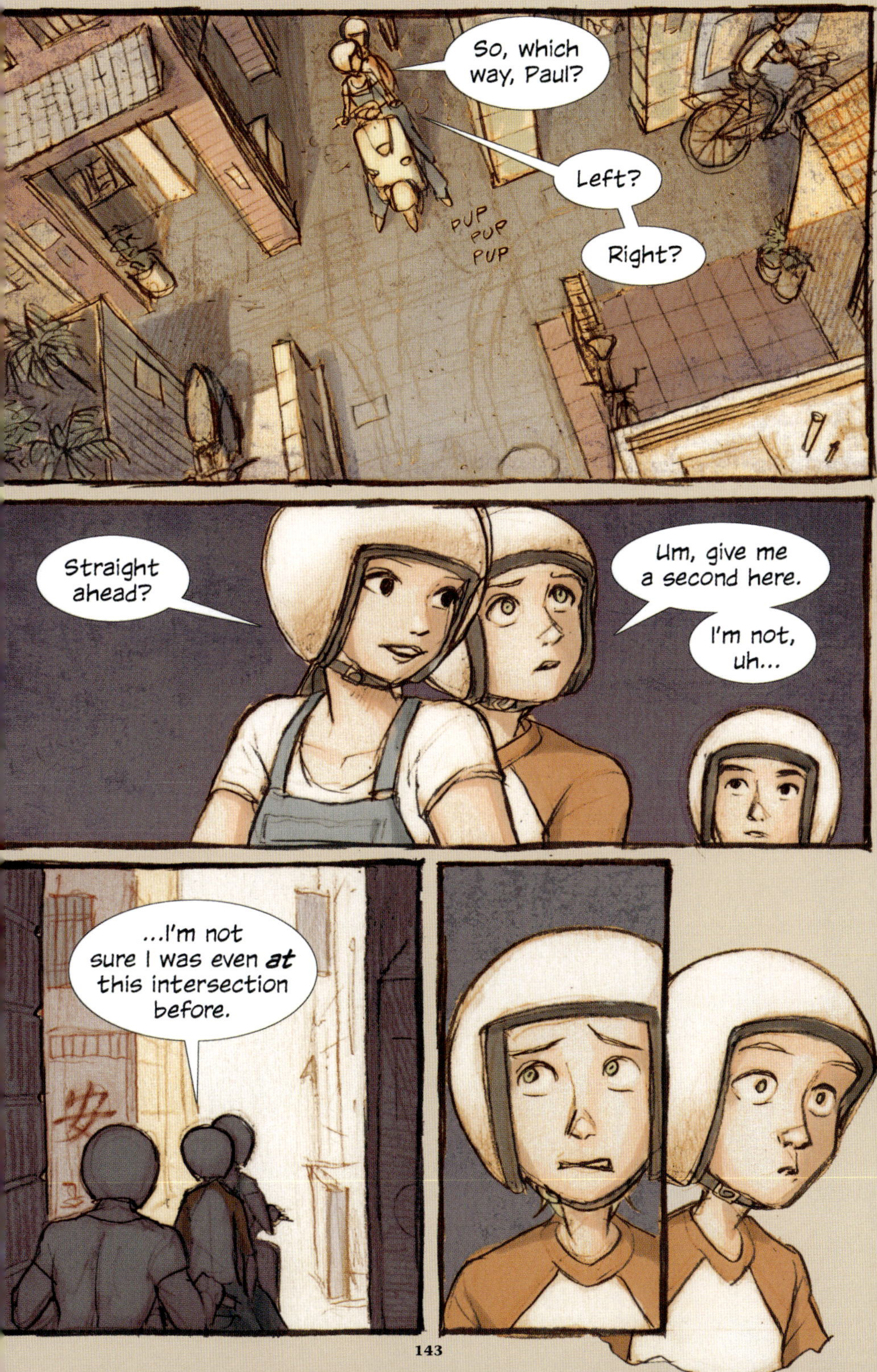
So, which way, Paul?
Left?
Right?
PUP PUP PUP
Straight ahead?
Um, give me a second here.
I'm not, uh...
...I'm not sure I was even **at** this intersection before.

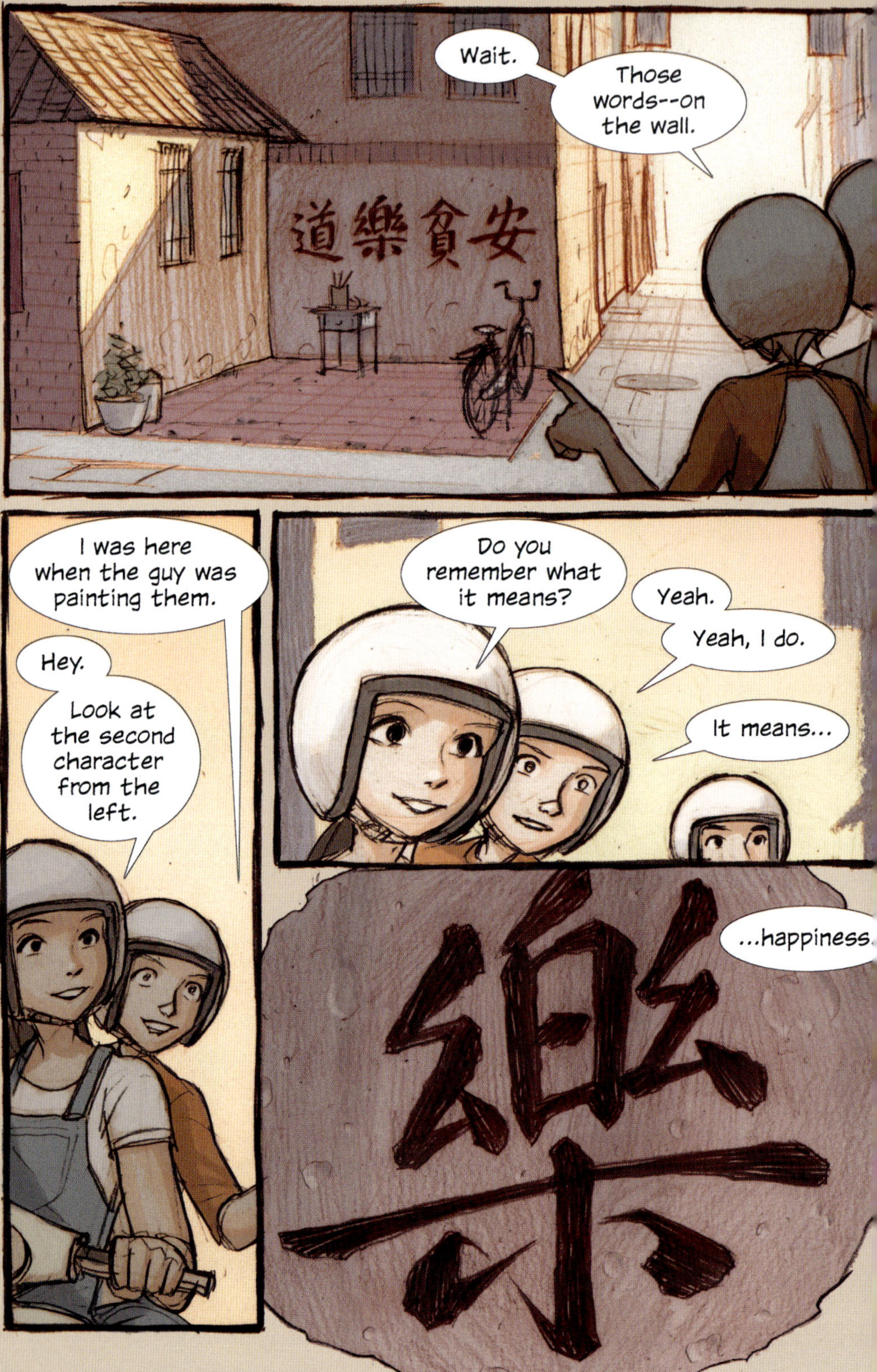
Wait.
Those words--on the wall.
道樂貧安
I was here when the guy was painting them.
Hey.
Look at the second character from the left.
Do you remember what it means?
Yeah.
Yeah, I do.
It means...
樂
...happiness.

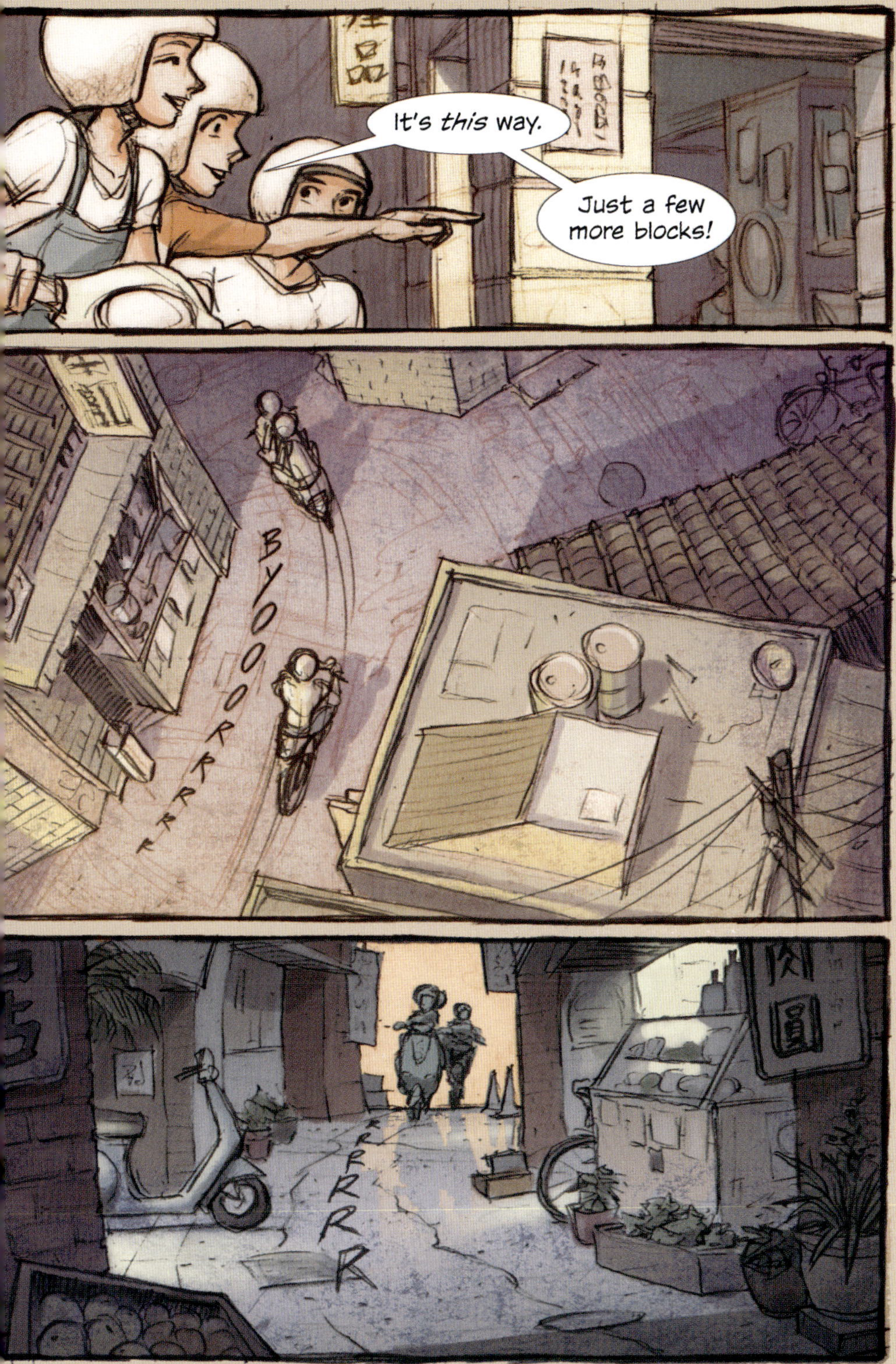
It's *this* way.
Just a few more blocks!
BYOOOORRRRRR
RRRRR

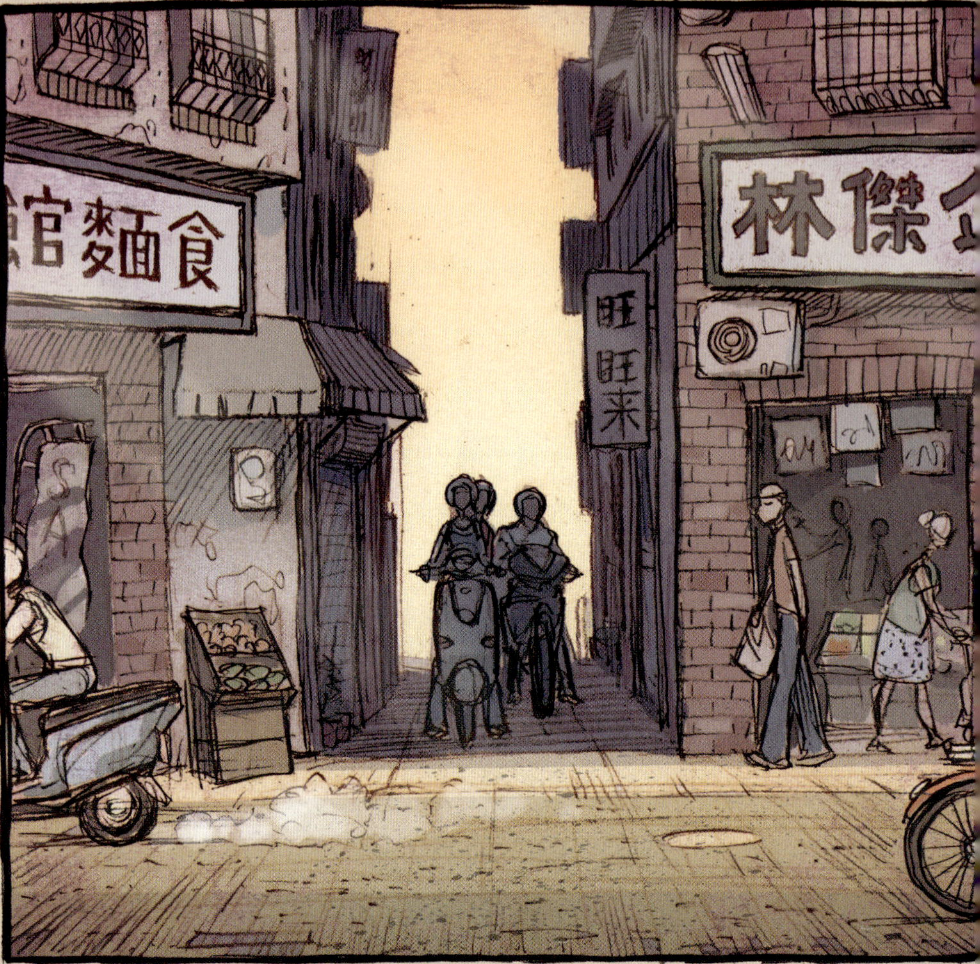
館官麵食
旺旺来
林傑

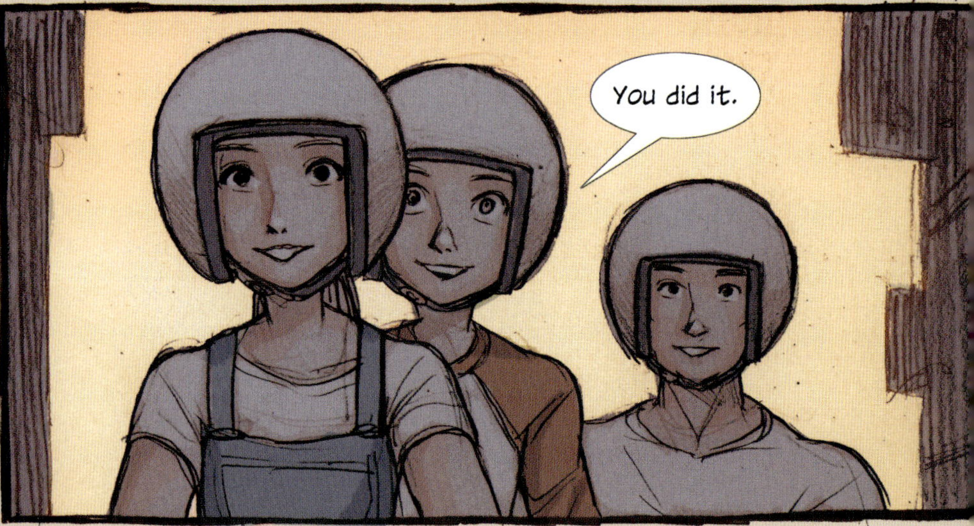
You did it.

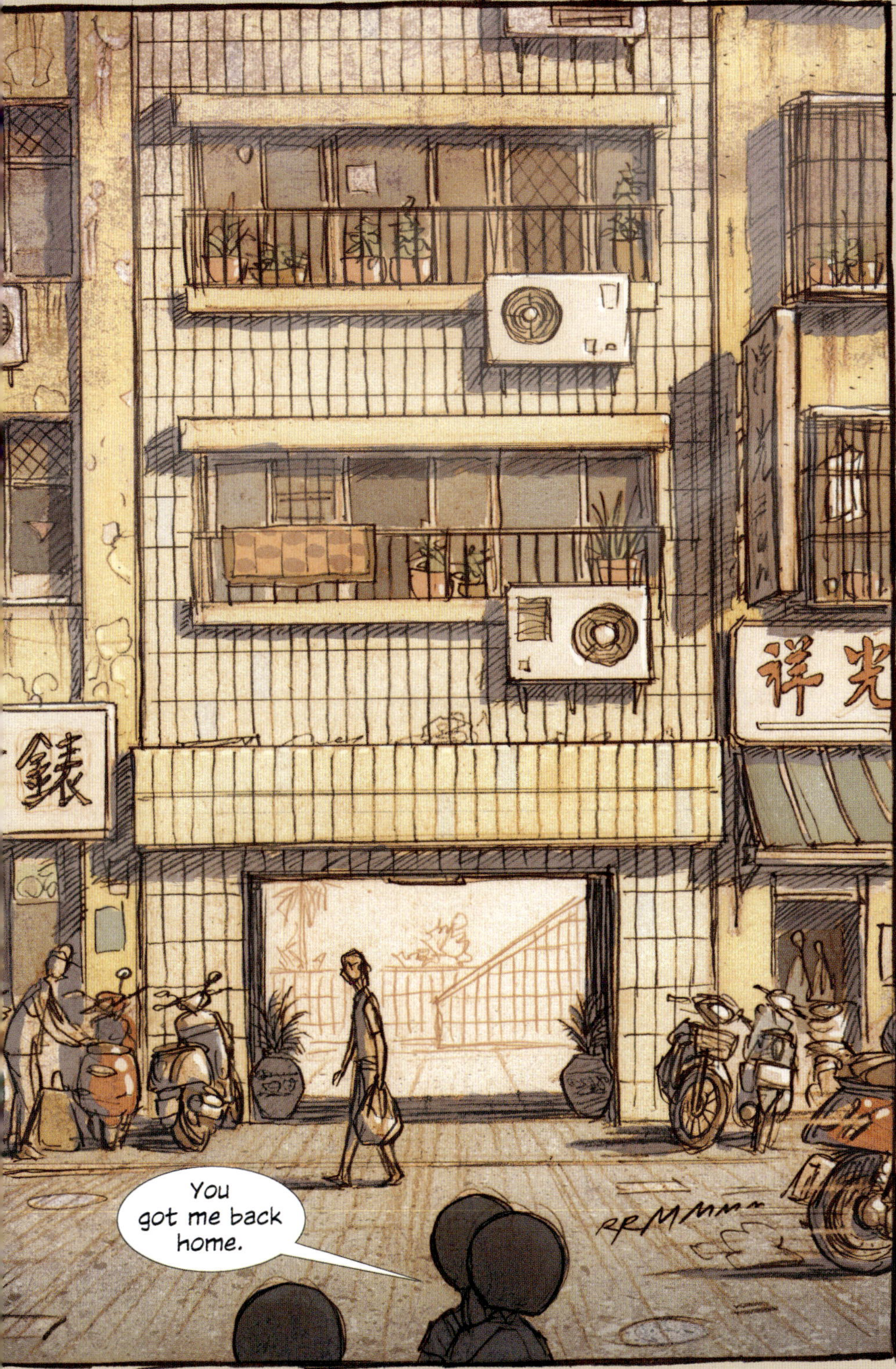
錶
祥光
You got me back home.
RRMMMM

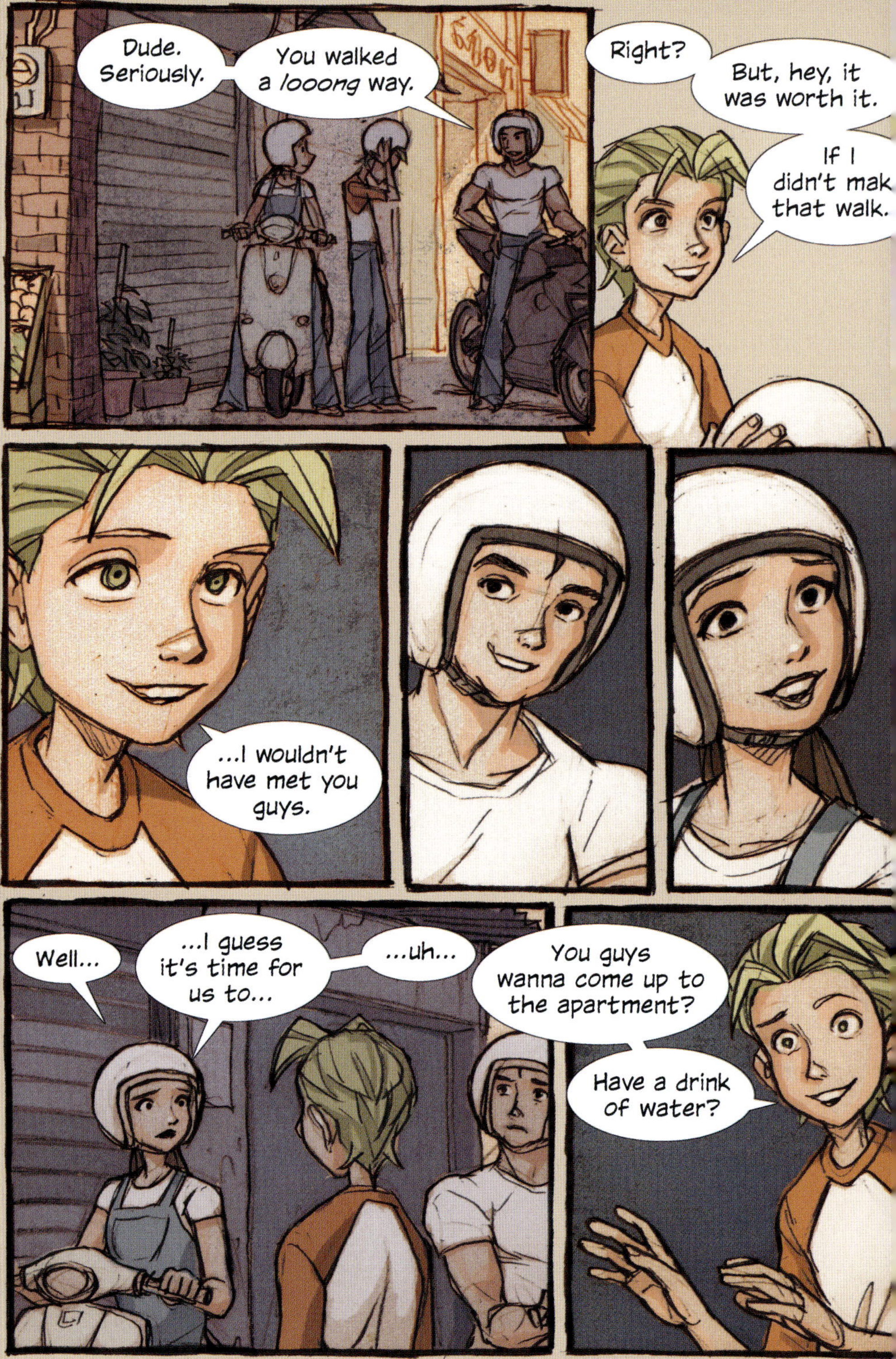
Dude. Seriously.
You walked a *looong* way.
Right?
But, hey, it was worth it.
If I didn't mak that walk.
...I wouldn't have met you guys.
Well...
...I guess it's time for us to...
...uh...
You guys wanna come up to the apartment?
Have a drink of water?

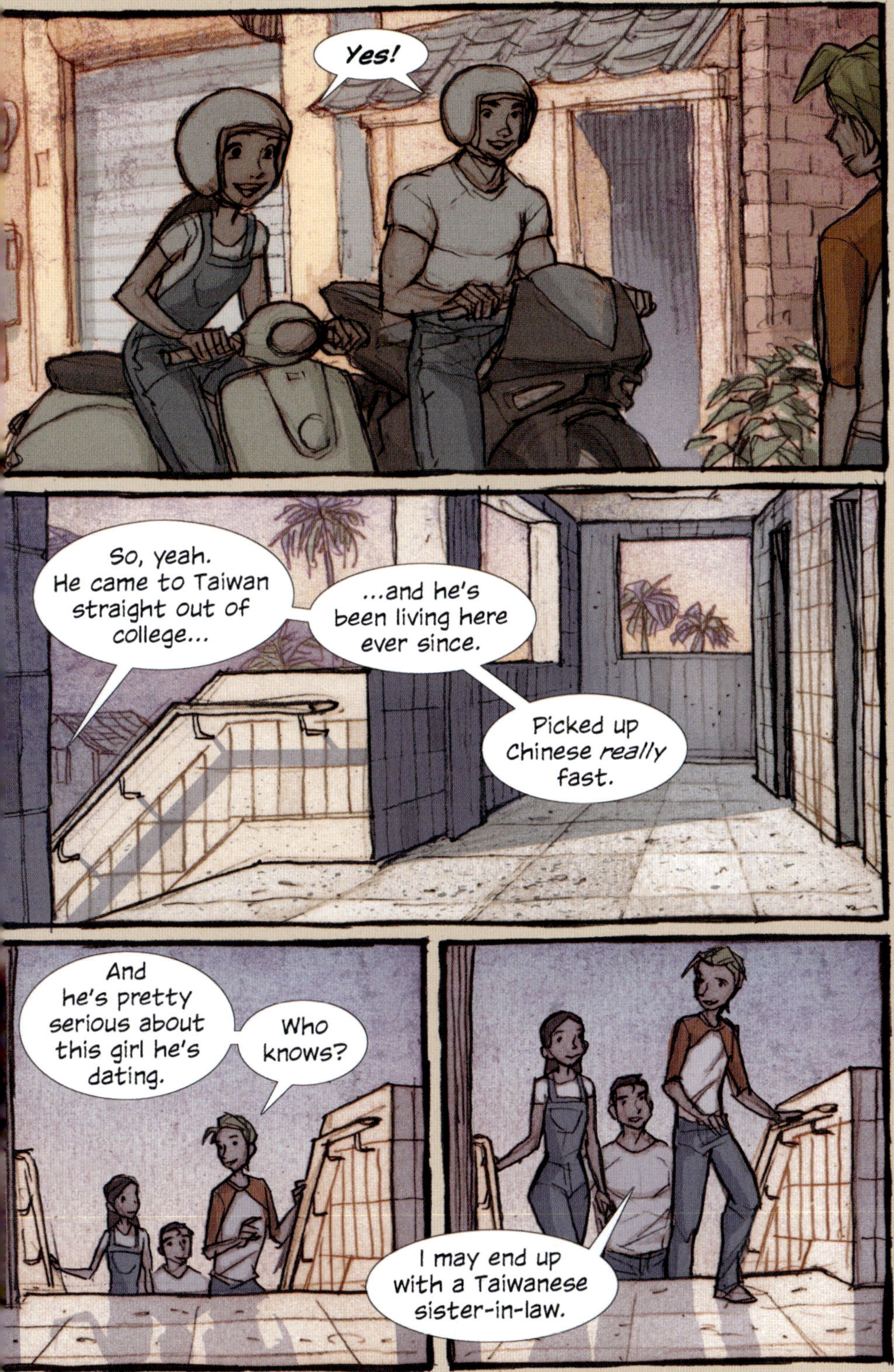
Yes!
So, yeah. He came to Taiwan straight out of college...
...and he's been living here ever since.
Picked up Chinese *really* fast.
And he's pretty serious about this girl he's dating.
Who knows?
I may end up with a Taiwanese sister-in-law.

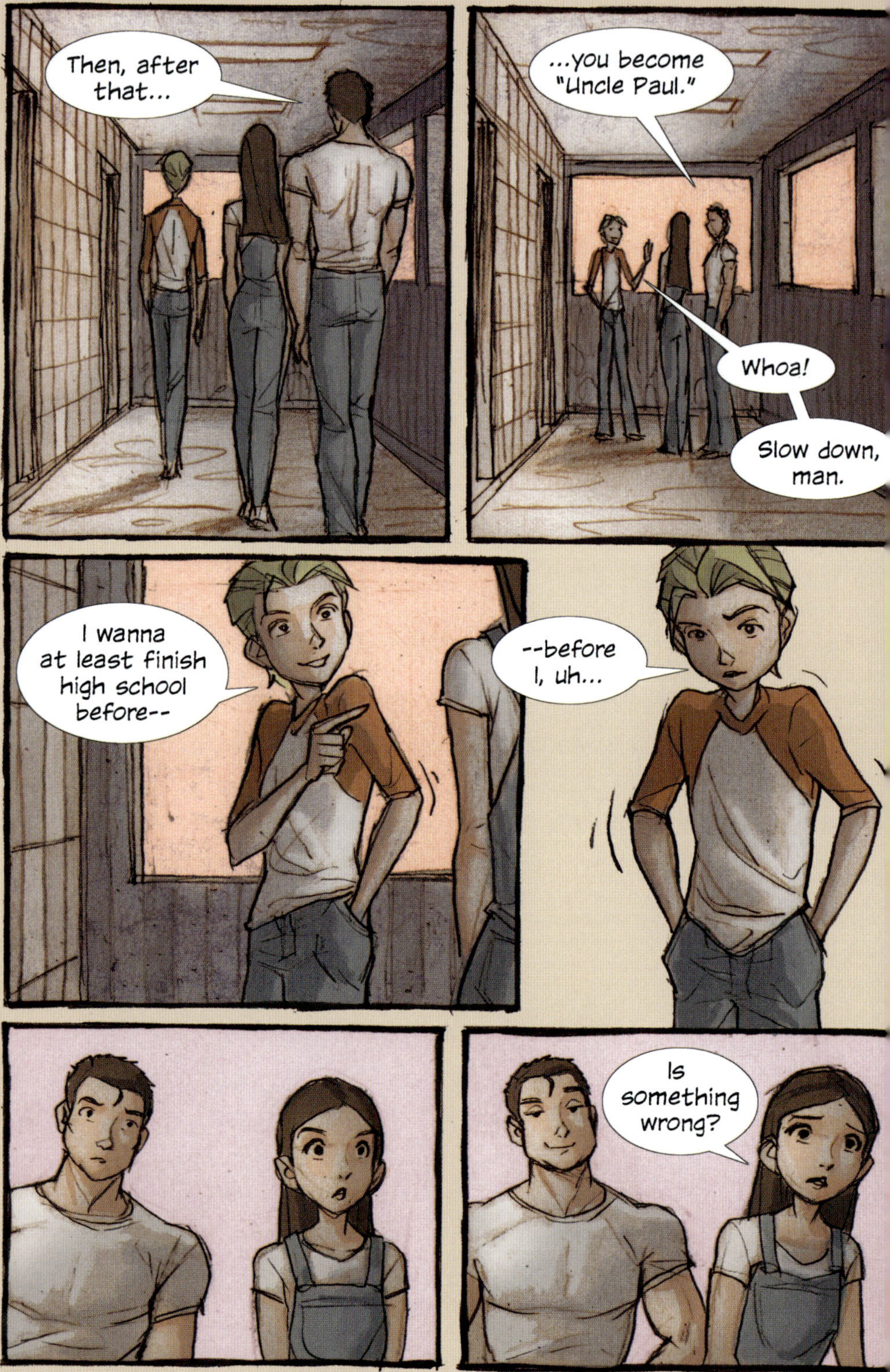
Then, after that...
...you become "Uncle Paul."
Whoa!
Slow down, man.
I wanna at least finish high school before--
--before I, uh...
Is something wrong?

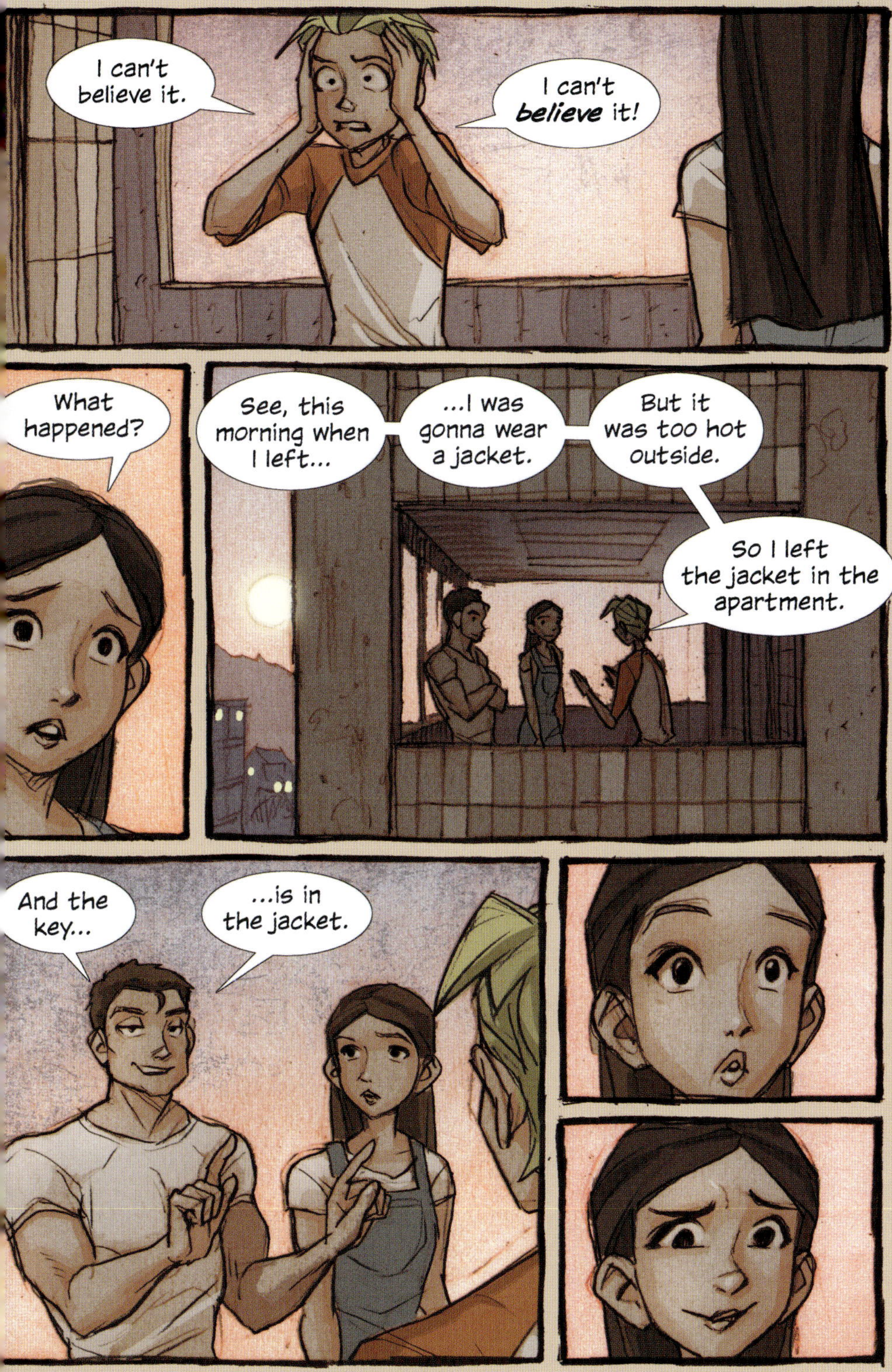
I can't believe it.
I can't *believe* it!
What happened?
See, this morning when I left...
...I was gonna wear a jacket.
But it was too hot outside.
So I left the jacket in the apartment.
And the key...
...is in the jacket.

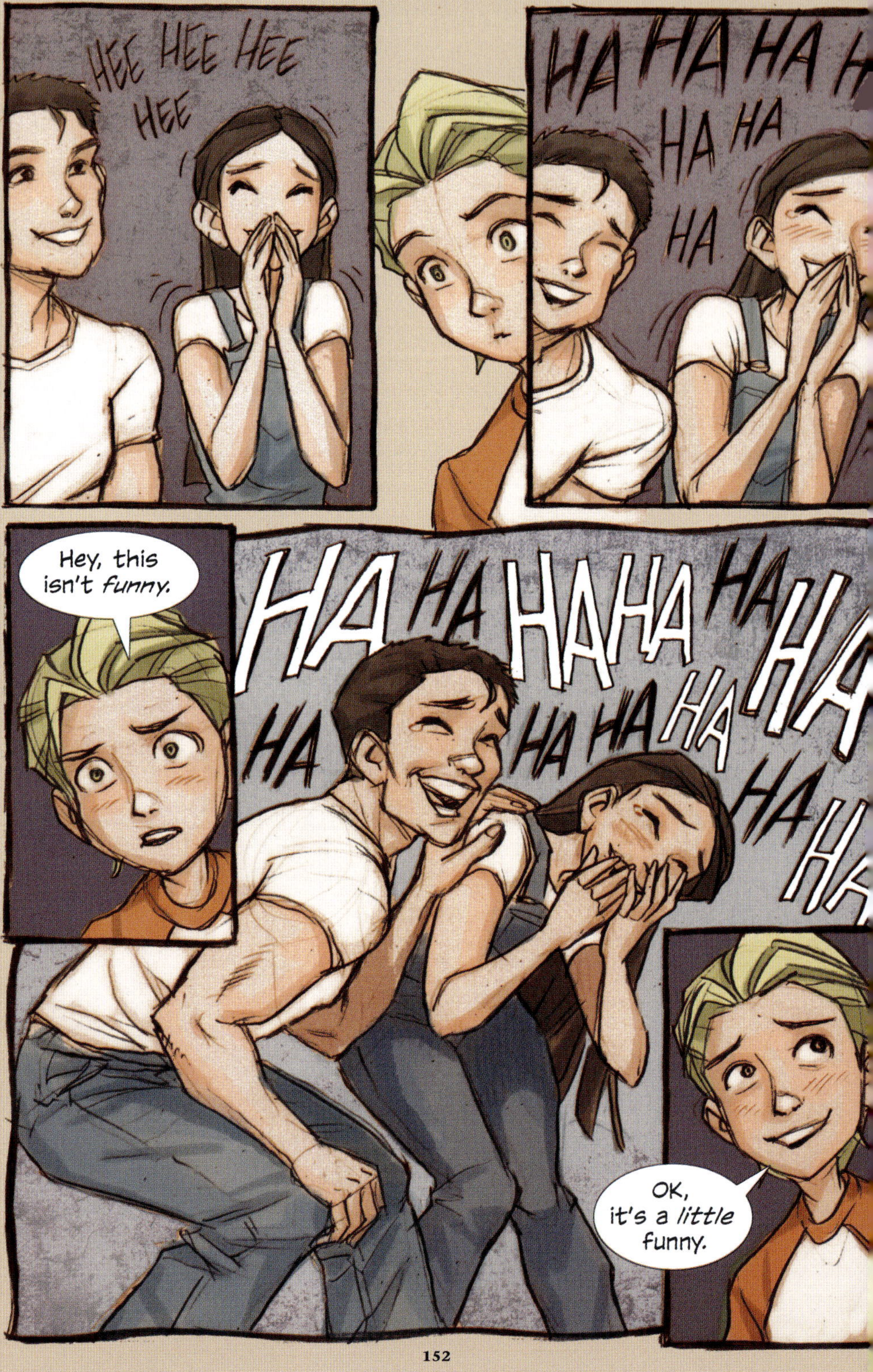
HEE HEE HEE
HEE
HA HA HA HA H
HA HA
HA
Hey, this isn't *funny*.
HA HA HAHA HA HA
HA
HA HA HA HA
HA
HA
OK, it's a *little* funny.

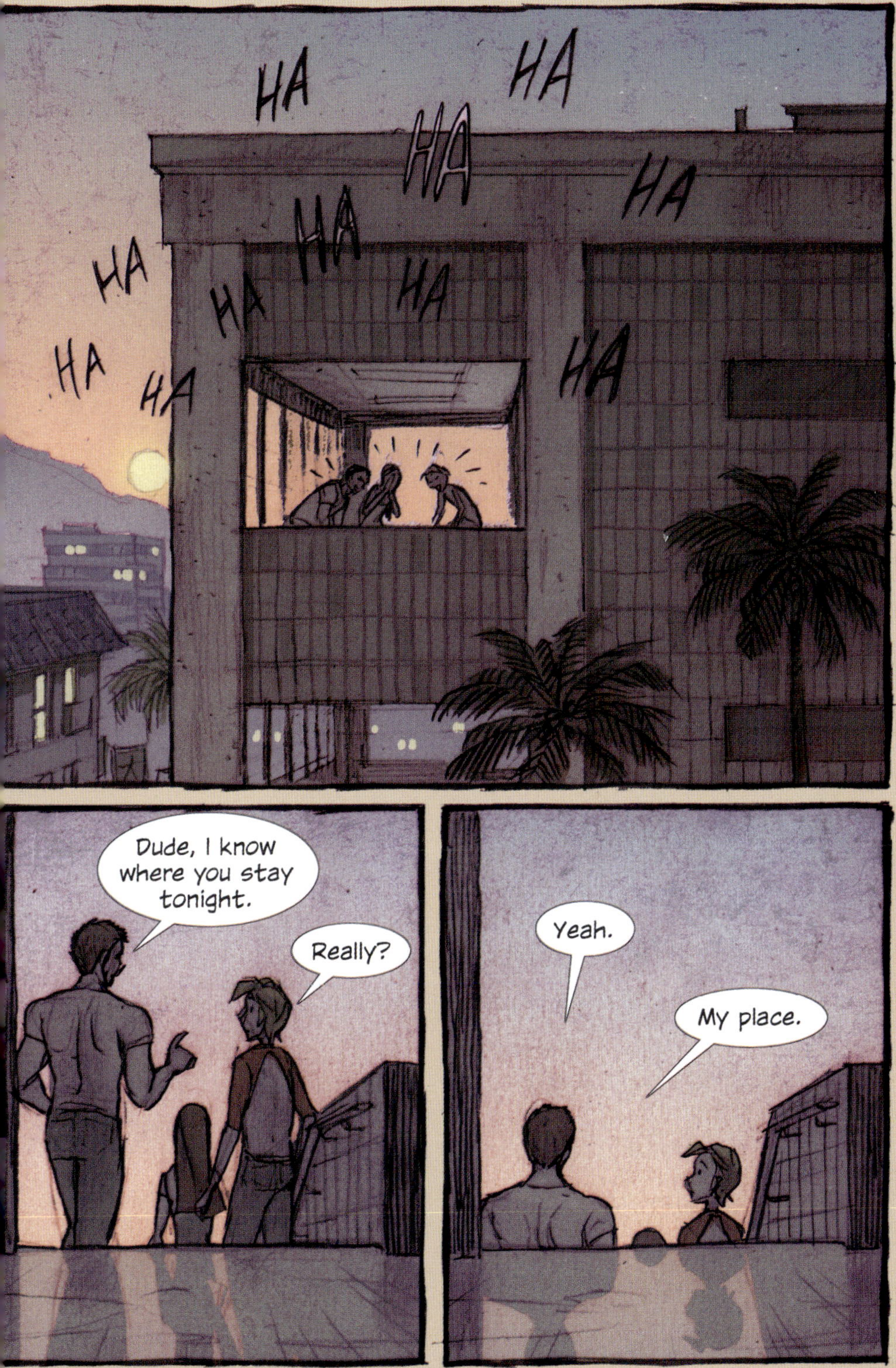
HA
HA
HA
HA
HA
HA
HA
HA
HA
HA
HA
Dude, I know where you stay tonight.
Really?
Yeah.
My place.

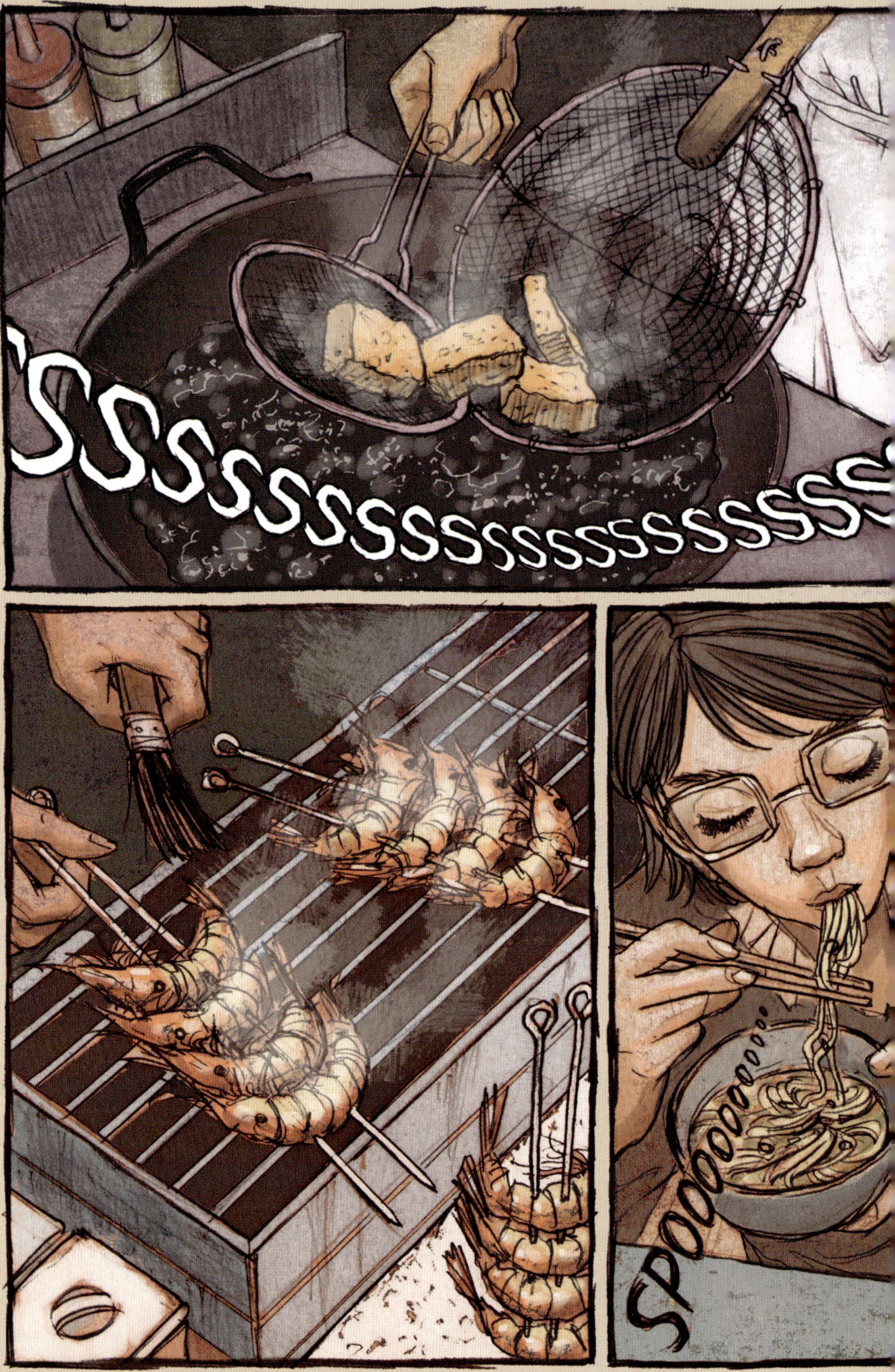
SSSSSSSSSSSSSSSSSSSS
SPOOOOOOOOOOO

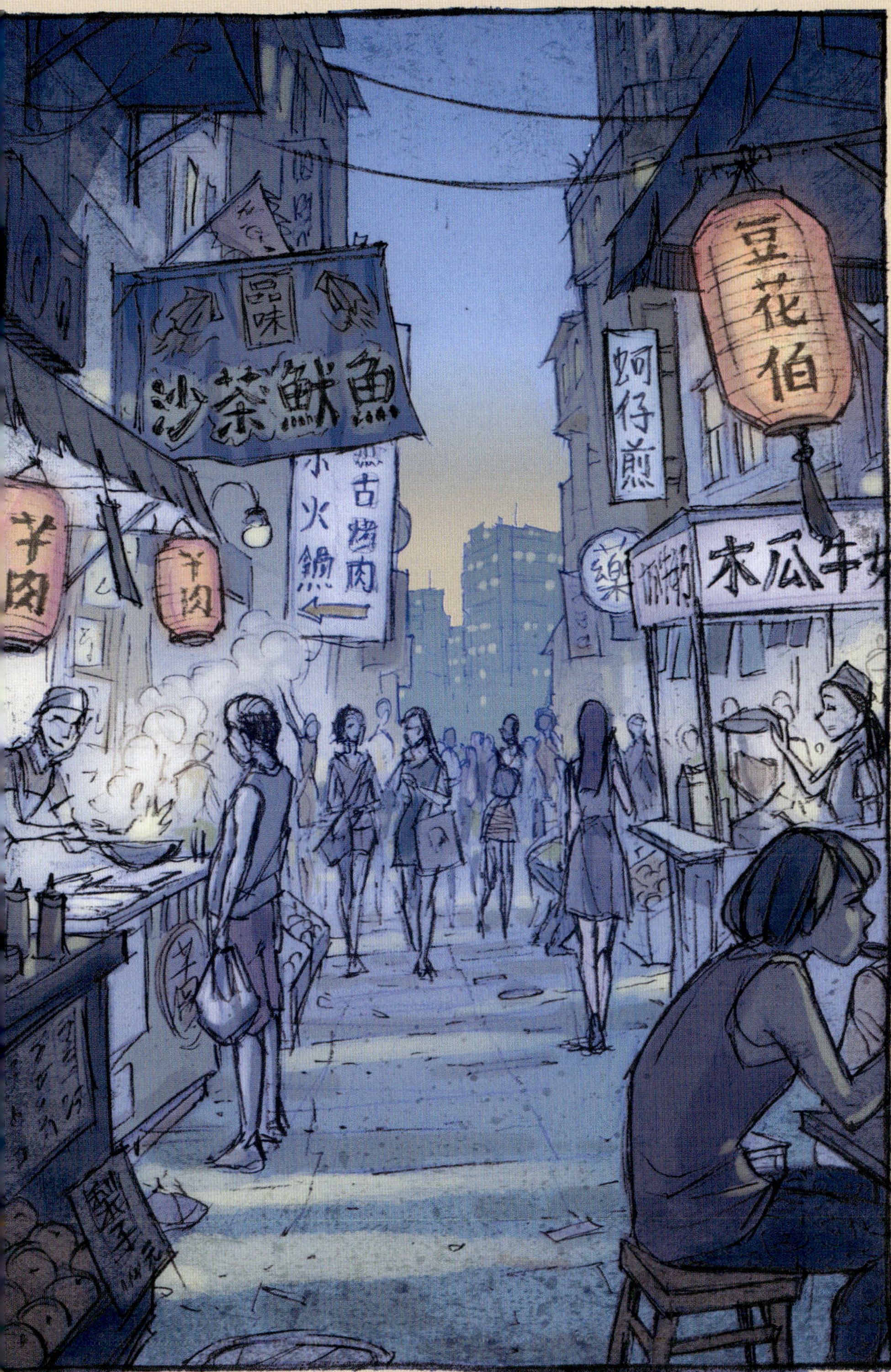
品味
沙茶魷魚
小火鍋
蚵仔煎
豆花伯
羊肉
羊肉

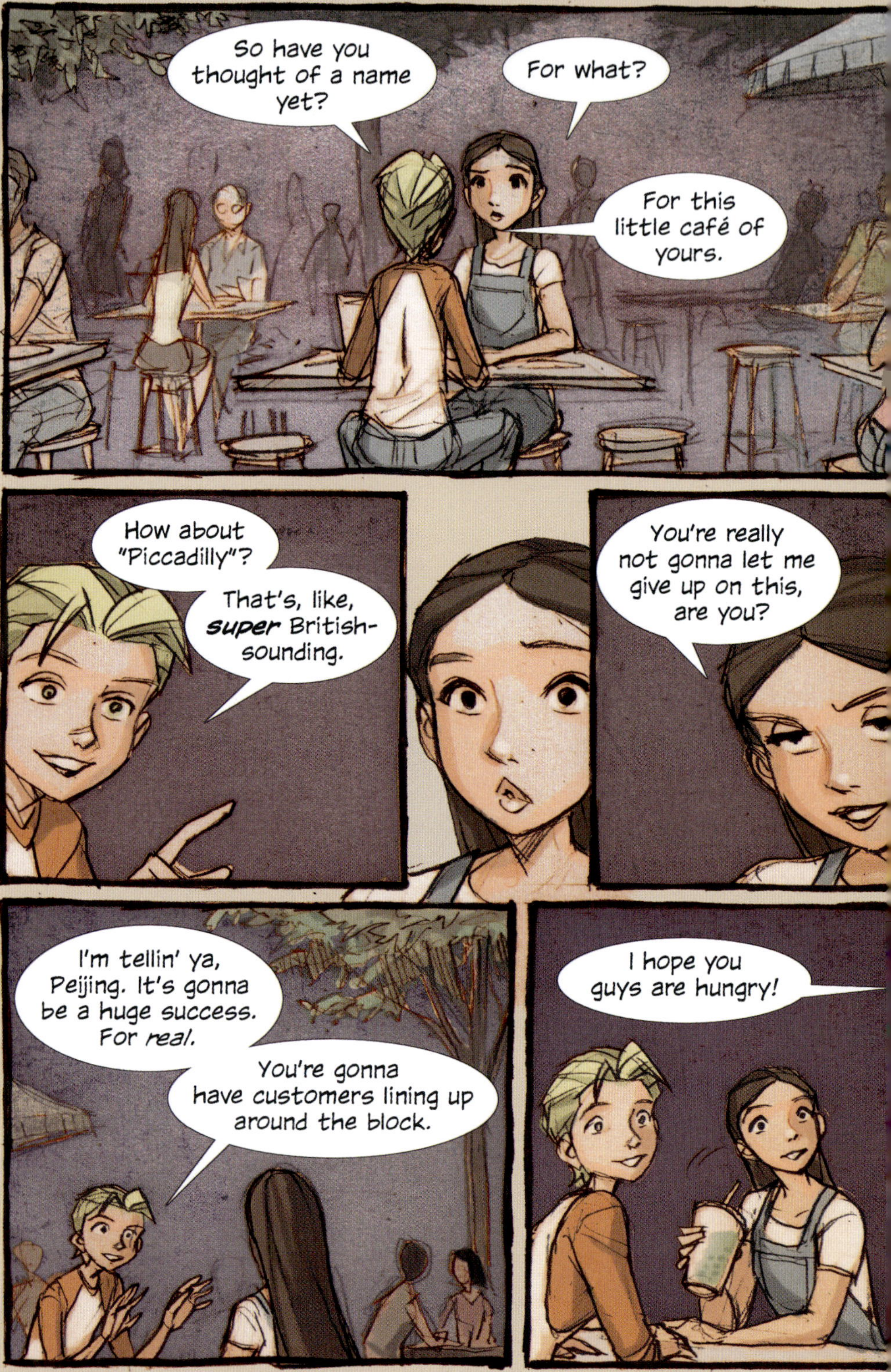
So have you thought of a name yet?
For what?
For this little café of yours.
How about "Piccadilly"?
That's, like, *super* British-sounding.
You're really not gonna let me give up on this, are you?
I'm tellin' ya, Peijing. It's gonna be a huge success. For *real*.
You're gonna have customers lining up around the block.
I hope you guys are hungry!

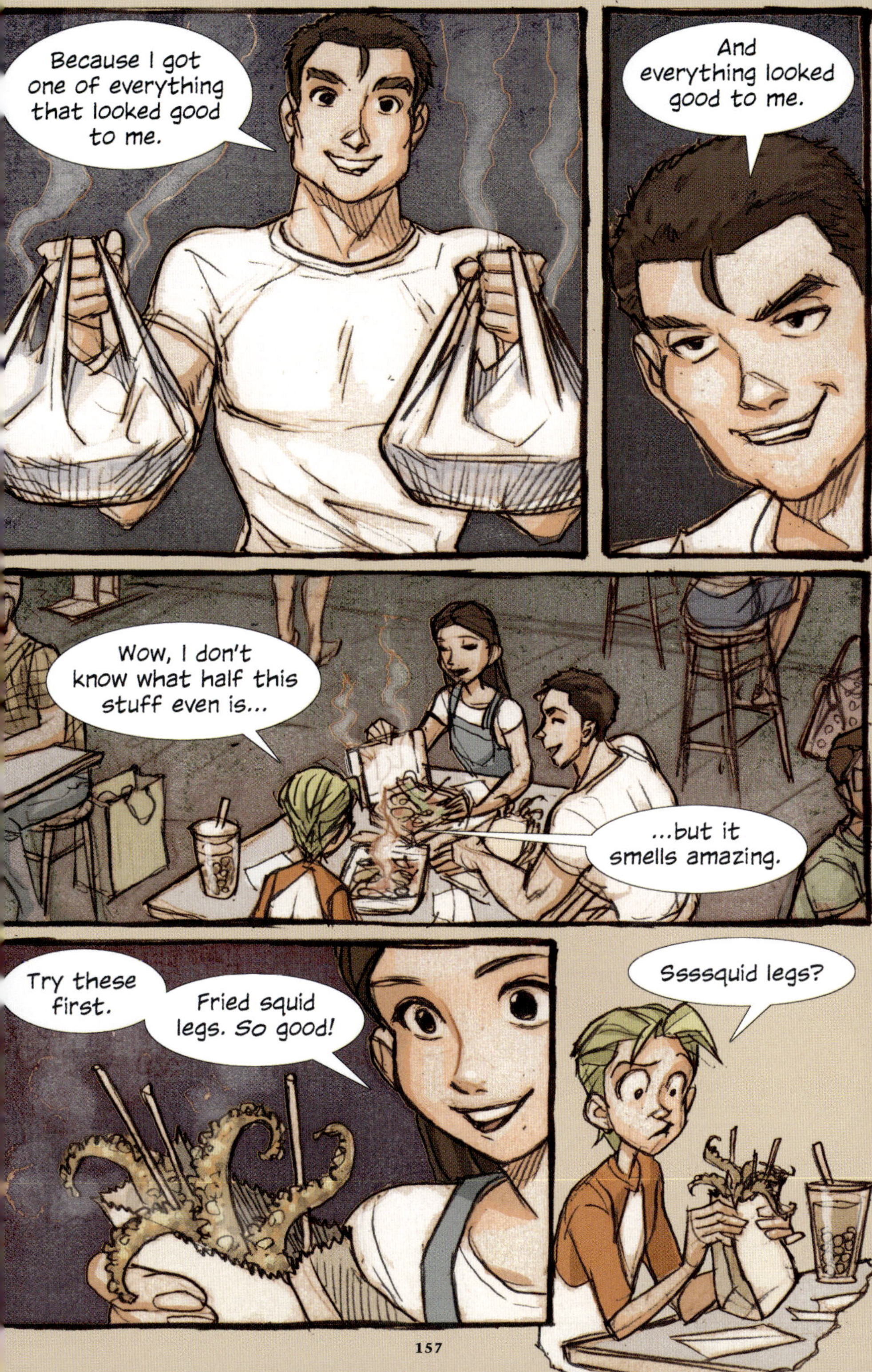
Because I got one of everything that looked good to me.
And everything looked good to me.
Wow, I don't know what half this stuff even is...
...but it smells amazing.
Try these first.
Fried squid legs. So good!
Ssssquid legs?

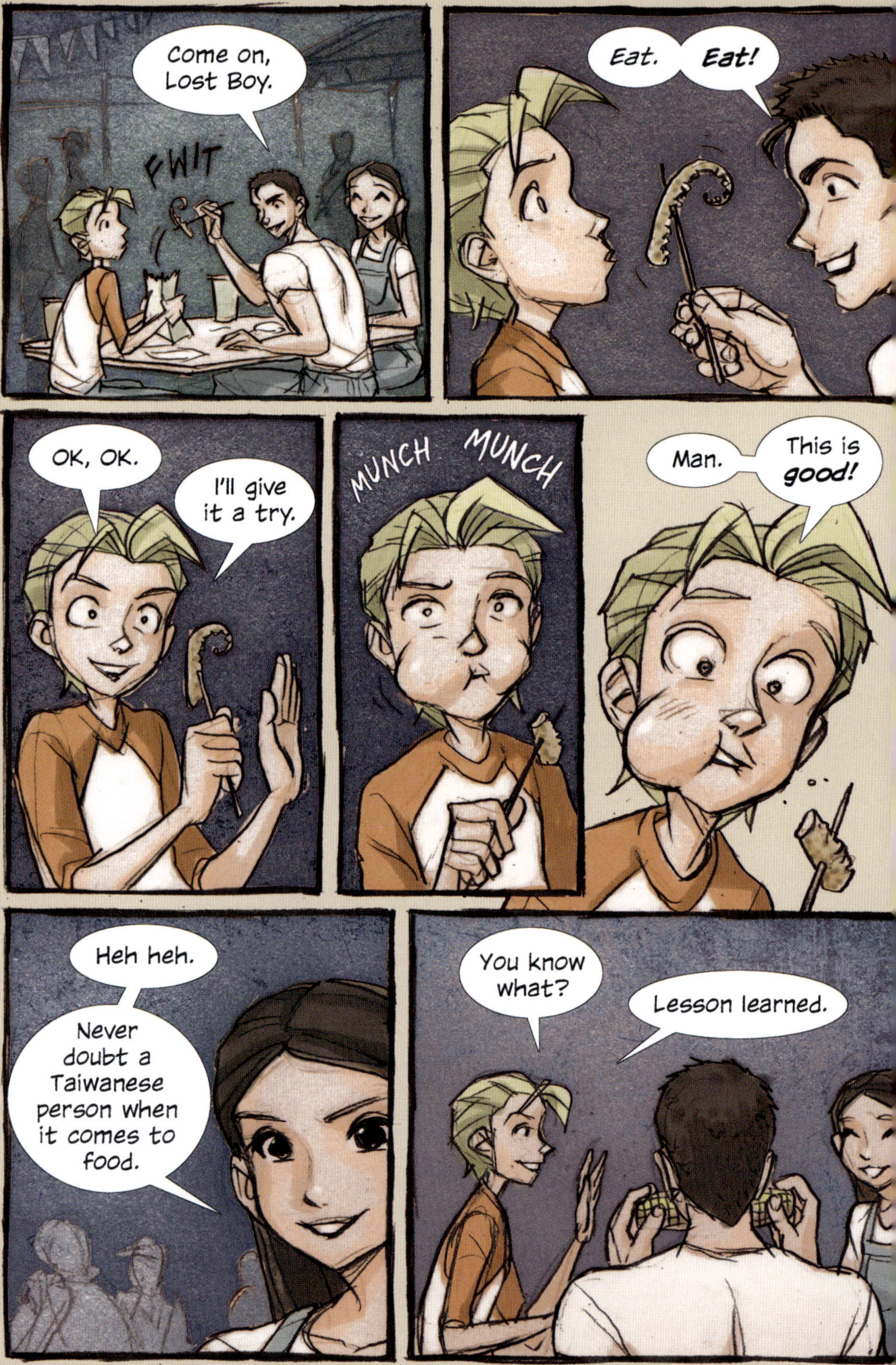
Come on, Lost Boy.
FWIT
Eat.
Eat!
OK, OK.
I'll give it a try.
MUNCH MUNCH
Man.
This is good!
Heh heh.
Never doubt a Taiwanese person when it comes to food.
You know what?
Lesson learned.

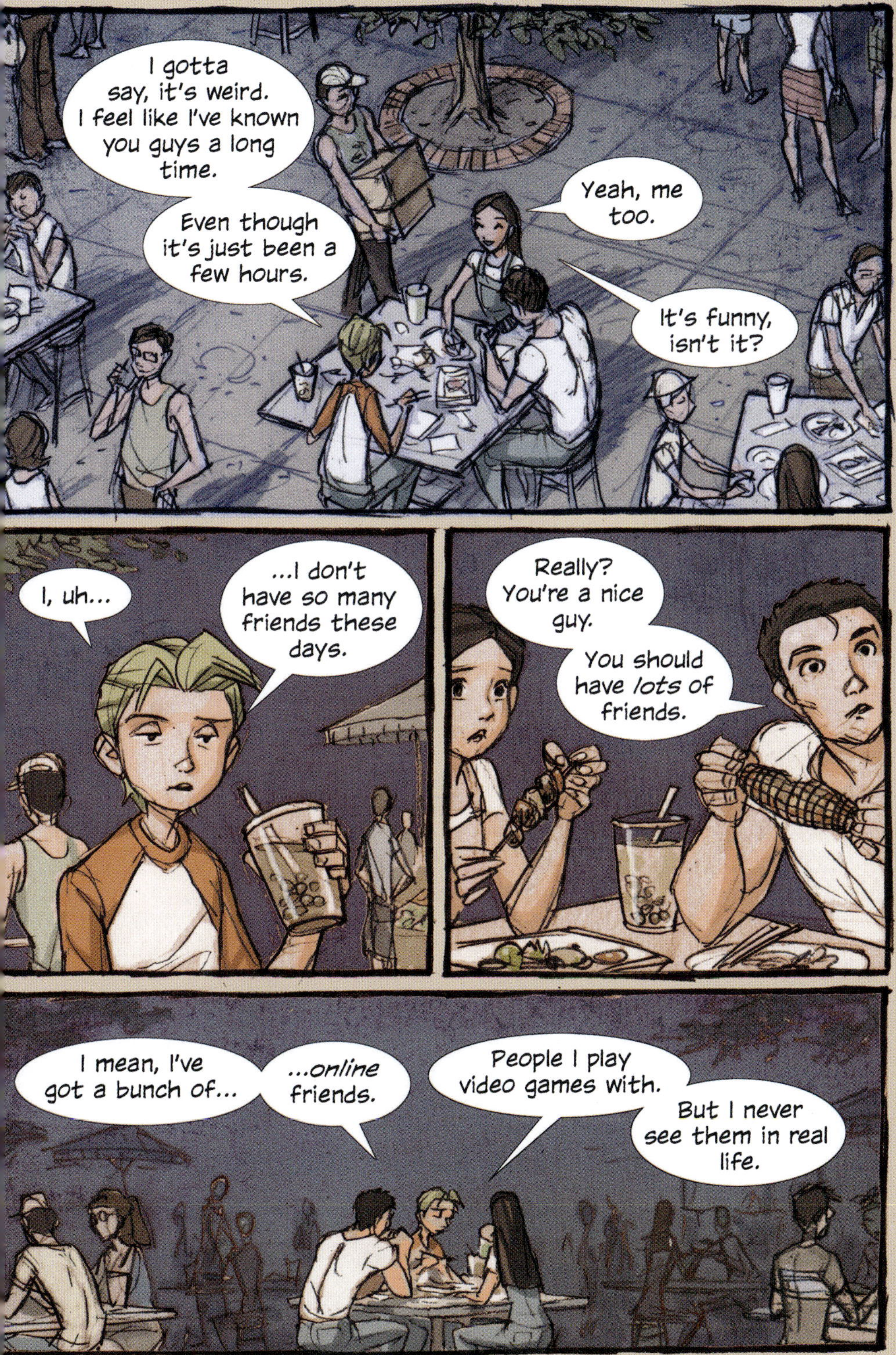
I gotta say, it's weird. I feel like I've known you guys a long time.
Even though it's just been a few hours.
Yeah, me too.
It's funny, isn't it?
I, uh...
...I don't have so many friends these days.
Really? You're a nice guy.
You should have *lots* of friends.
I mean, I've got a bunch of...
...*online* friends.
People I play video games with.
But I never see them in real life.

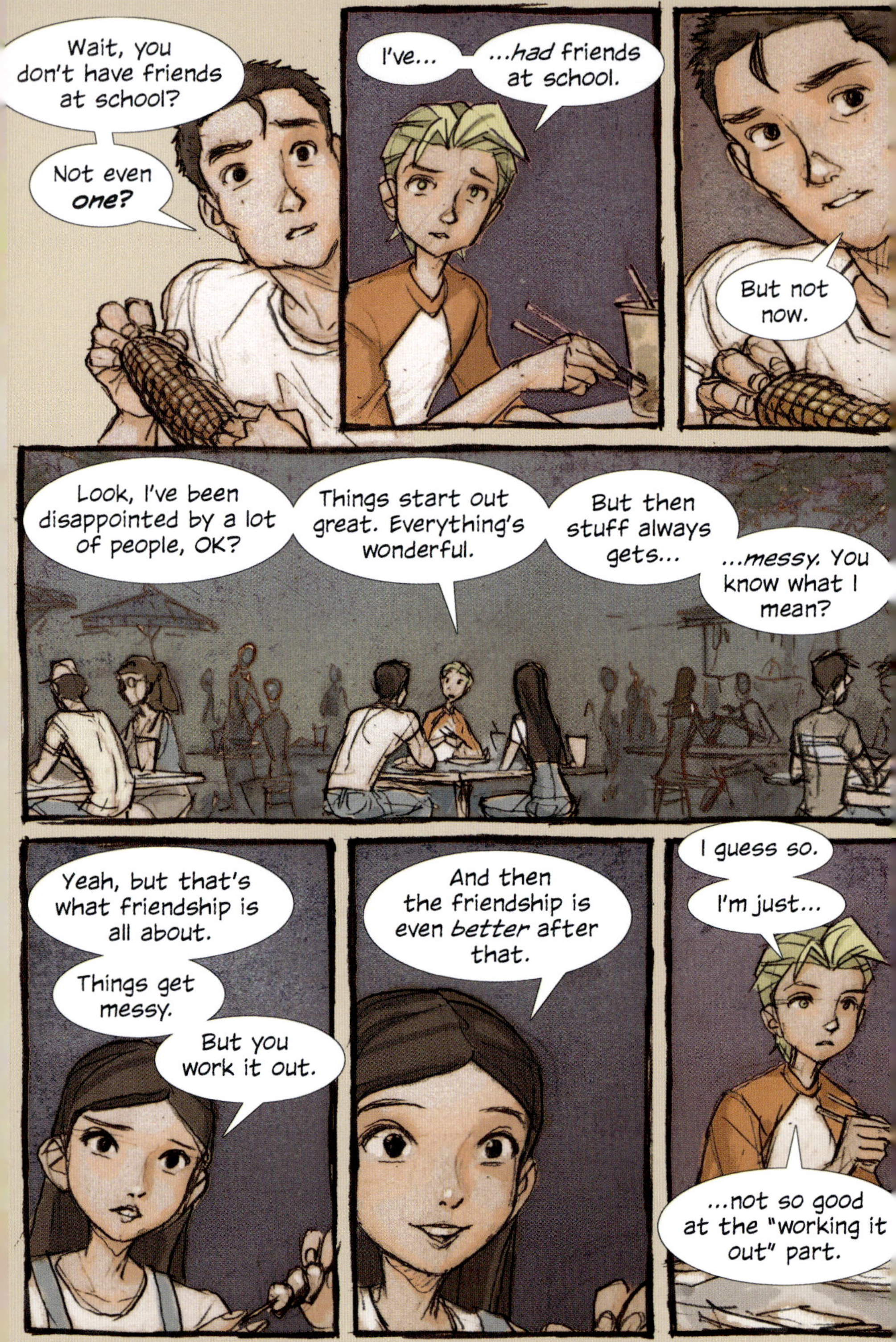
Wait, you don't have friends at school?
Not even *one?*
I've...
...*had* friends at school.
But not now.
Look, I've been disappointed by a lot of people, OK?
Things start out great. Everything's wonderful.
But then stuff always gets...
...*messy.* You know what I mean?
Yeah, but that's what friendship is all about.
Things get messy.
But you work it out.
And then the friendship is even *better* after that.
I guess so.
I'm just...
...not so good at the "working it out" part.

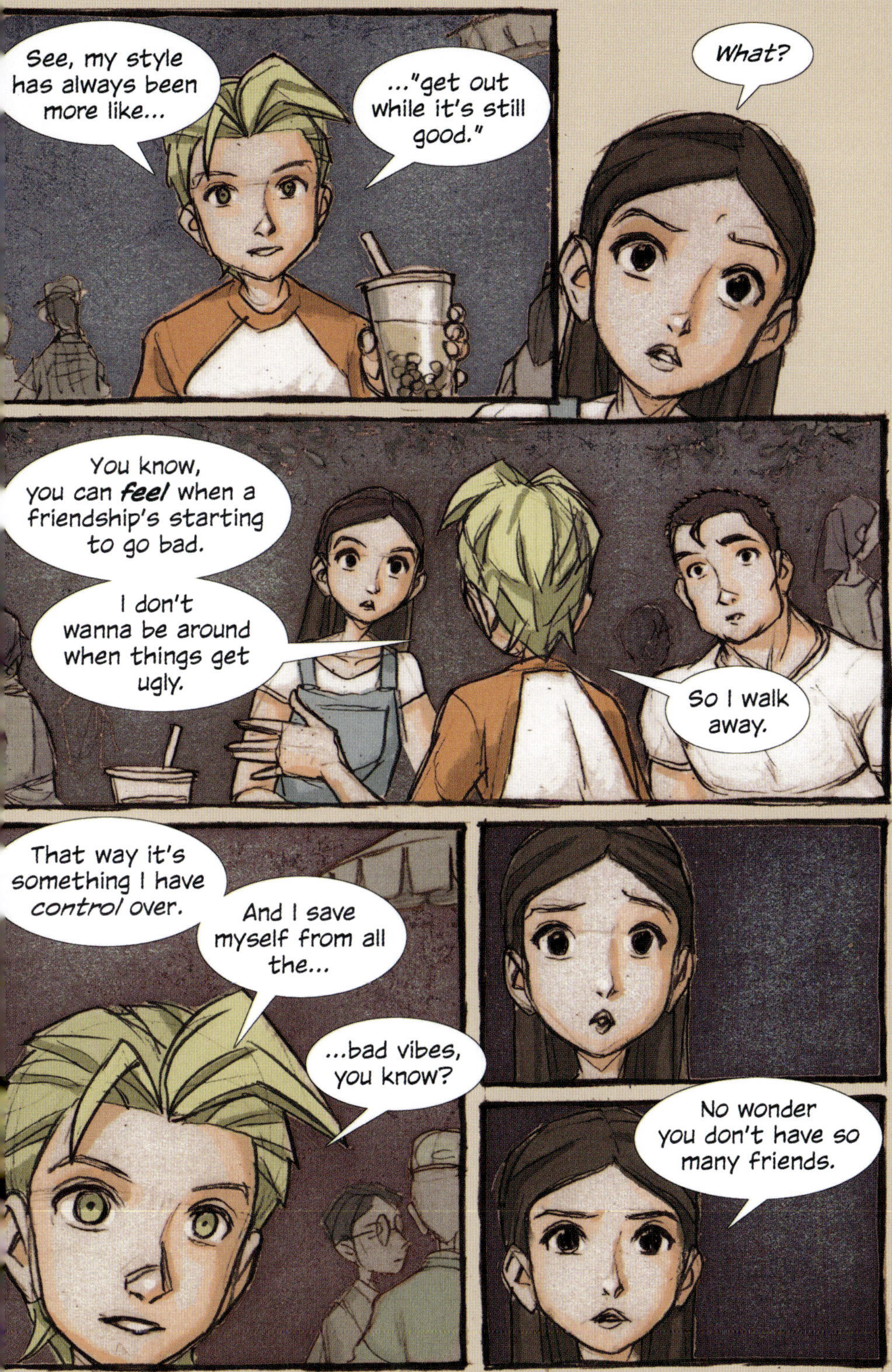

See, my style has always been more like...
..."get out while it's still good."
What?
You know, you can *feel* when a friendship's starting to go bad.
I don't wanna be around when things get ugly.
So I walk away.
That way it's something I have *control* over.
And I save myself from all the...
...bad vibes, you know?
No wonder you don't have so many friends.

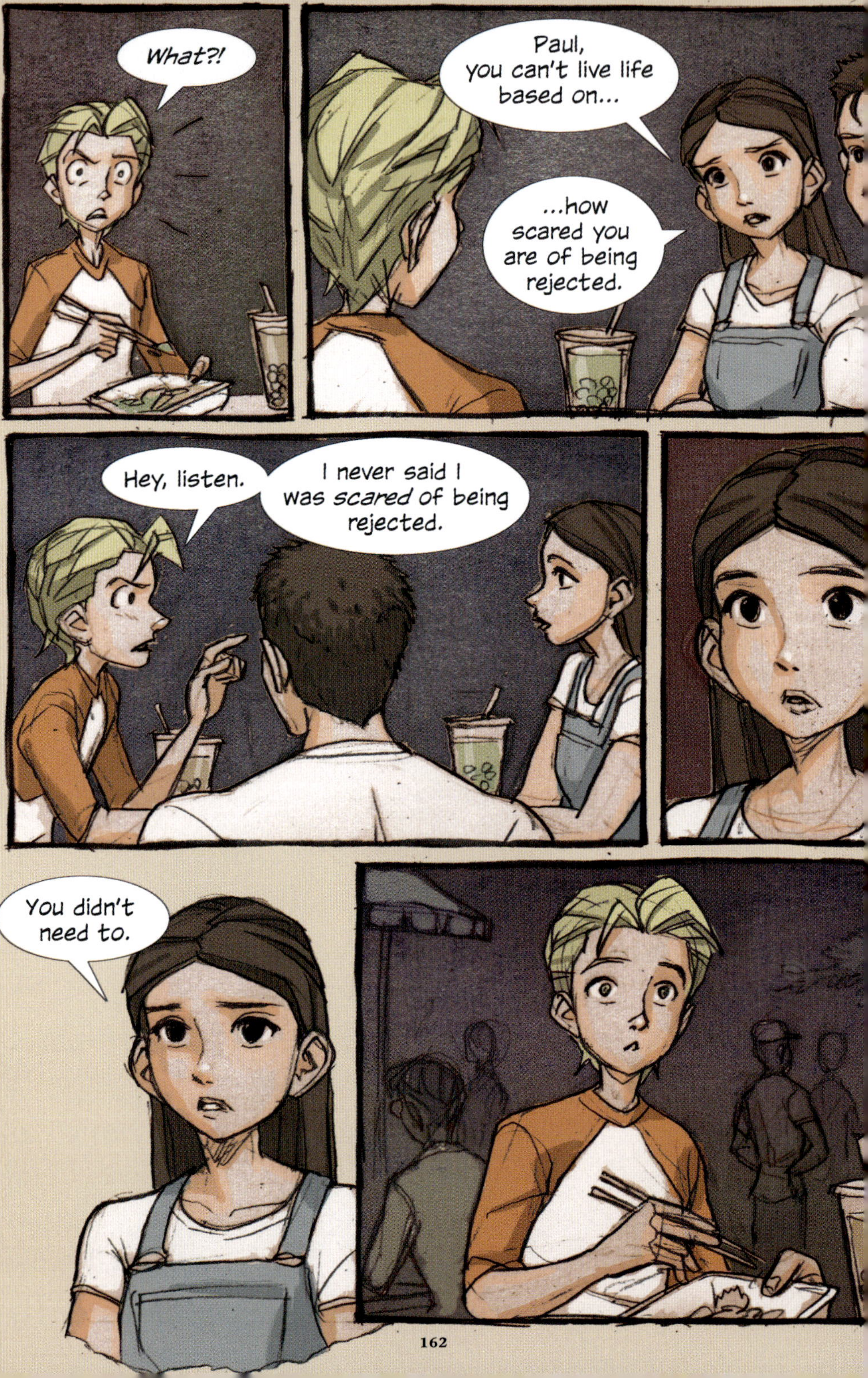
What?!
Paul, you can't live life based on...
...how scared you are of being rejected.
Hey, listen.
I never said I was *scared* of being rejected.
You didn't need to.

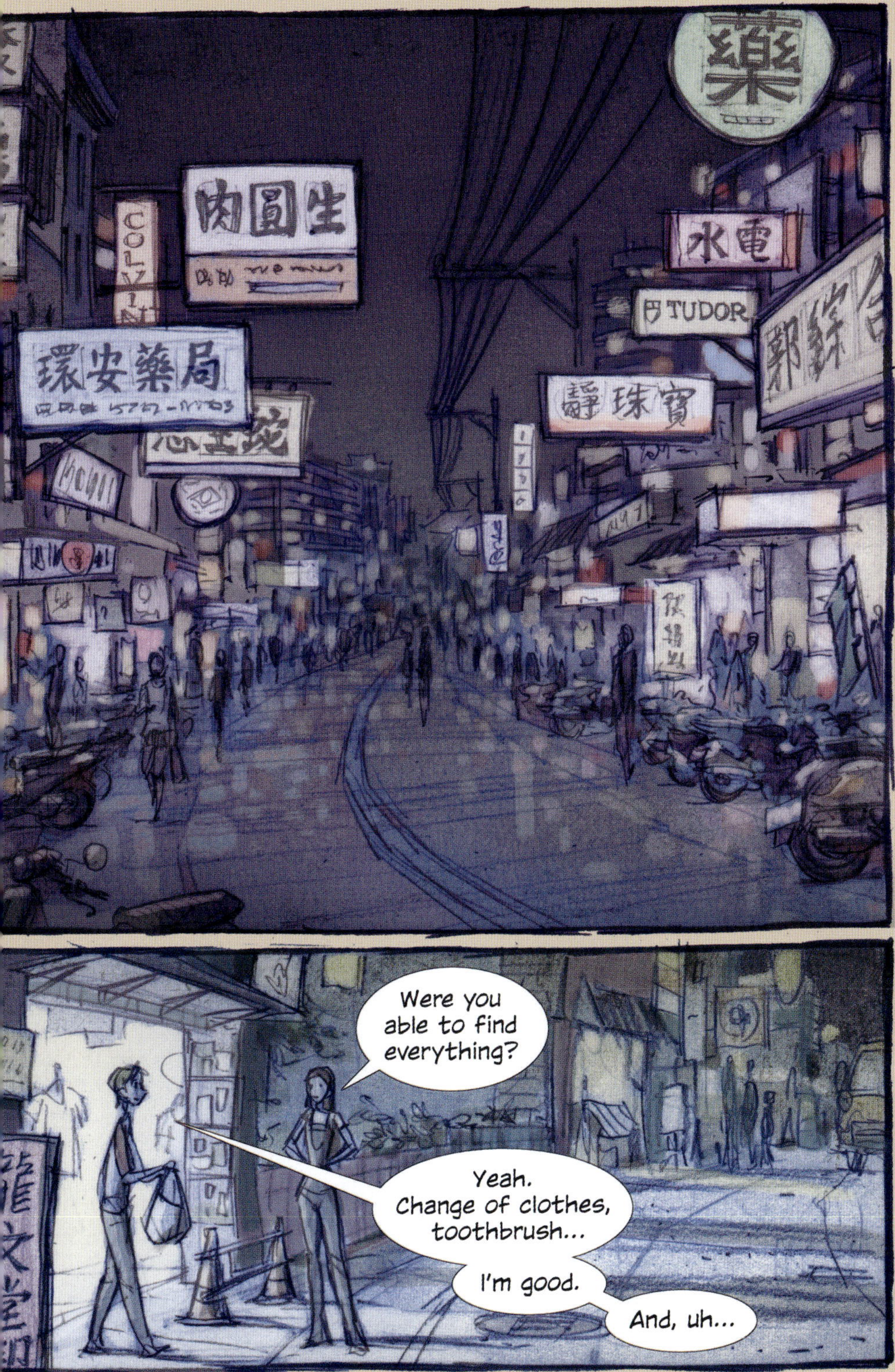
藥
肉圓生
水電
TUDOR
環安藥局
Were you able to find everything?
Yeah. Change of clothes, toothbrush...
I'm good.
And, uh...

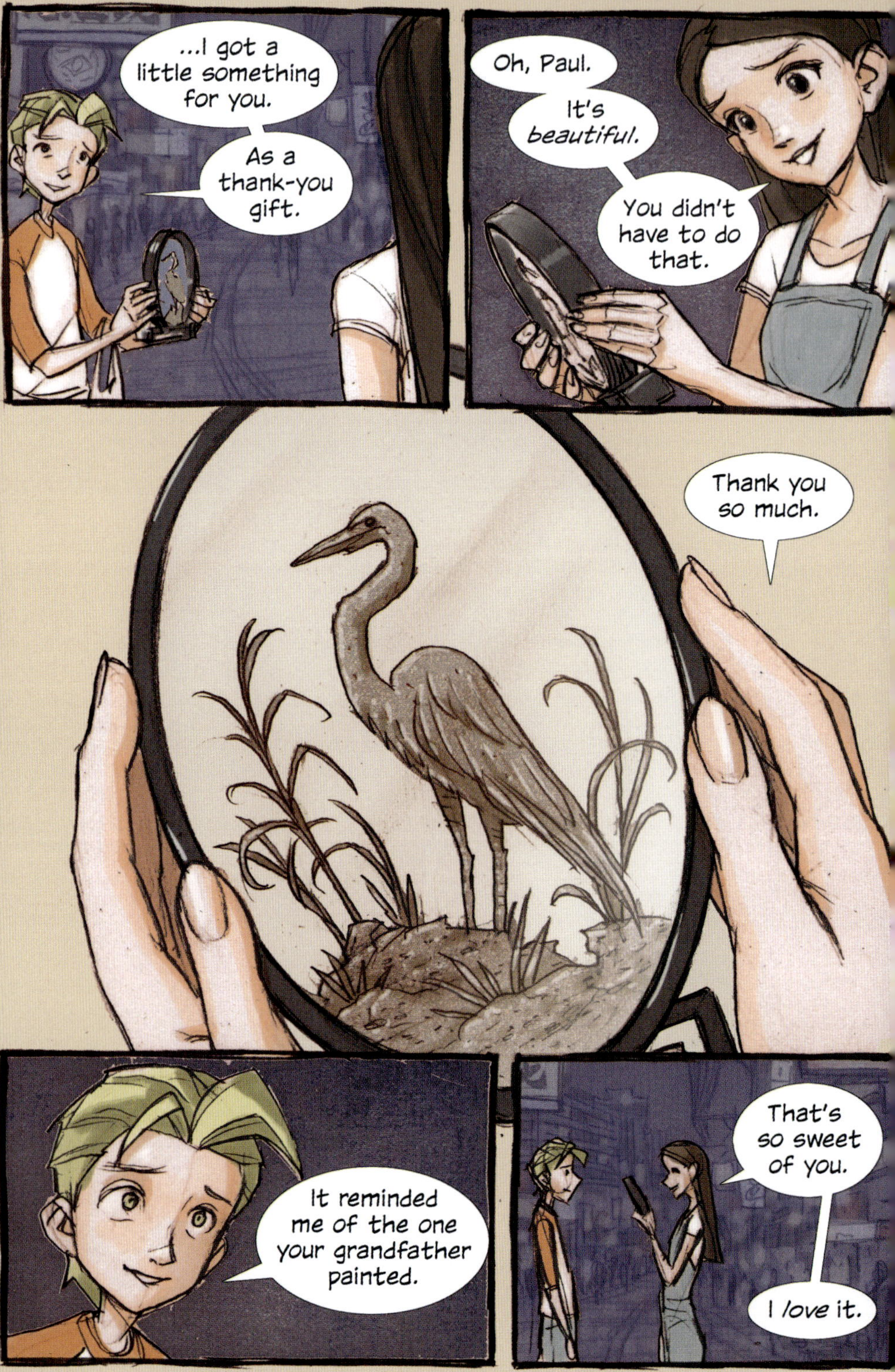
...I got a little something for you.
As a thank-you gift.
Oh, Paul.
It's *beautiful*.
You didn't have to do that.
Thank you so much.
It reminded me of the one your grandfather painted.
That's so sweet of you.
I *love* it.

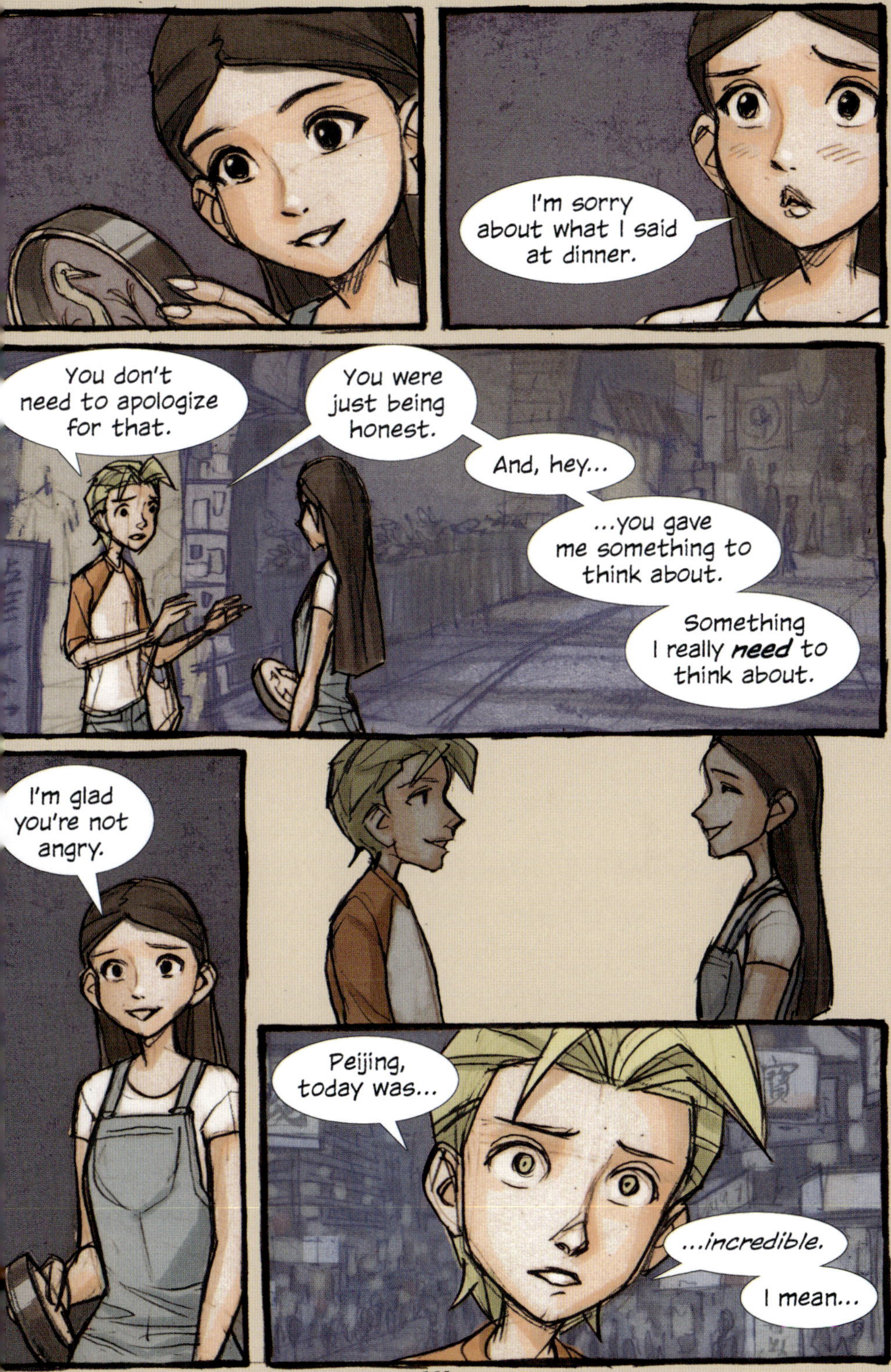
I'm sorry about what I said at dinner.
You don't need to apologize for that.
You were just being honest.
And, hey...
...you gave me something to think about.
Something I really *need* to think about.
I'm glad you're not angry.
Peijing, today was...
...incredible.
I mean...

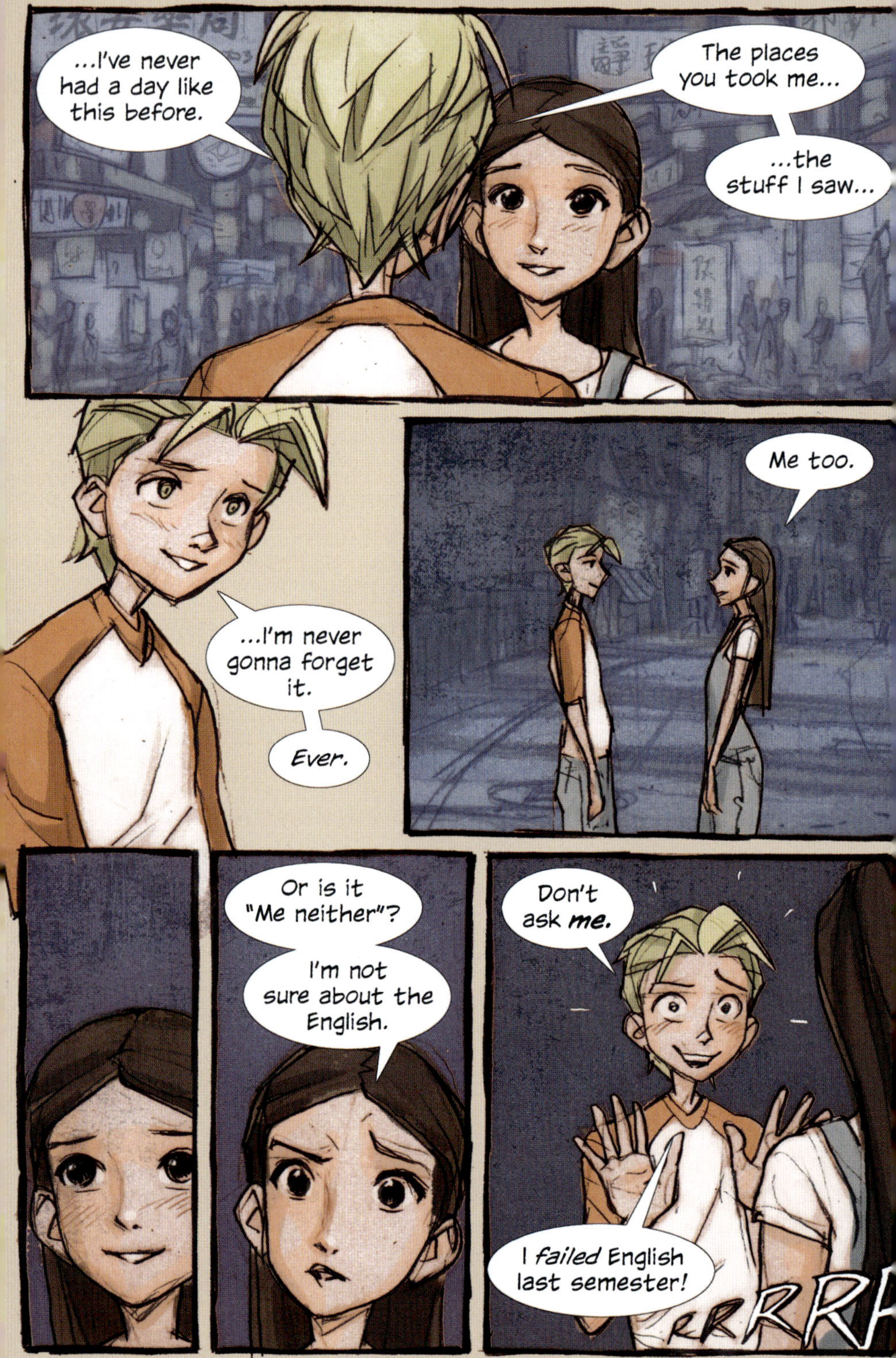
...I've never had a day like this before.
The places you took me...
...the stuff I saw...
...I'm never gonna forget it.
Ever.
Me too.
Or is it "Me neither"?
I'm not sure about the English.
Don't ask **me.**
I *failed* English last semester!
RRRRR

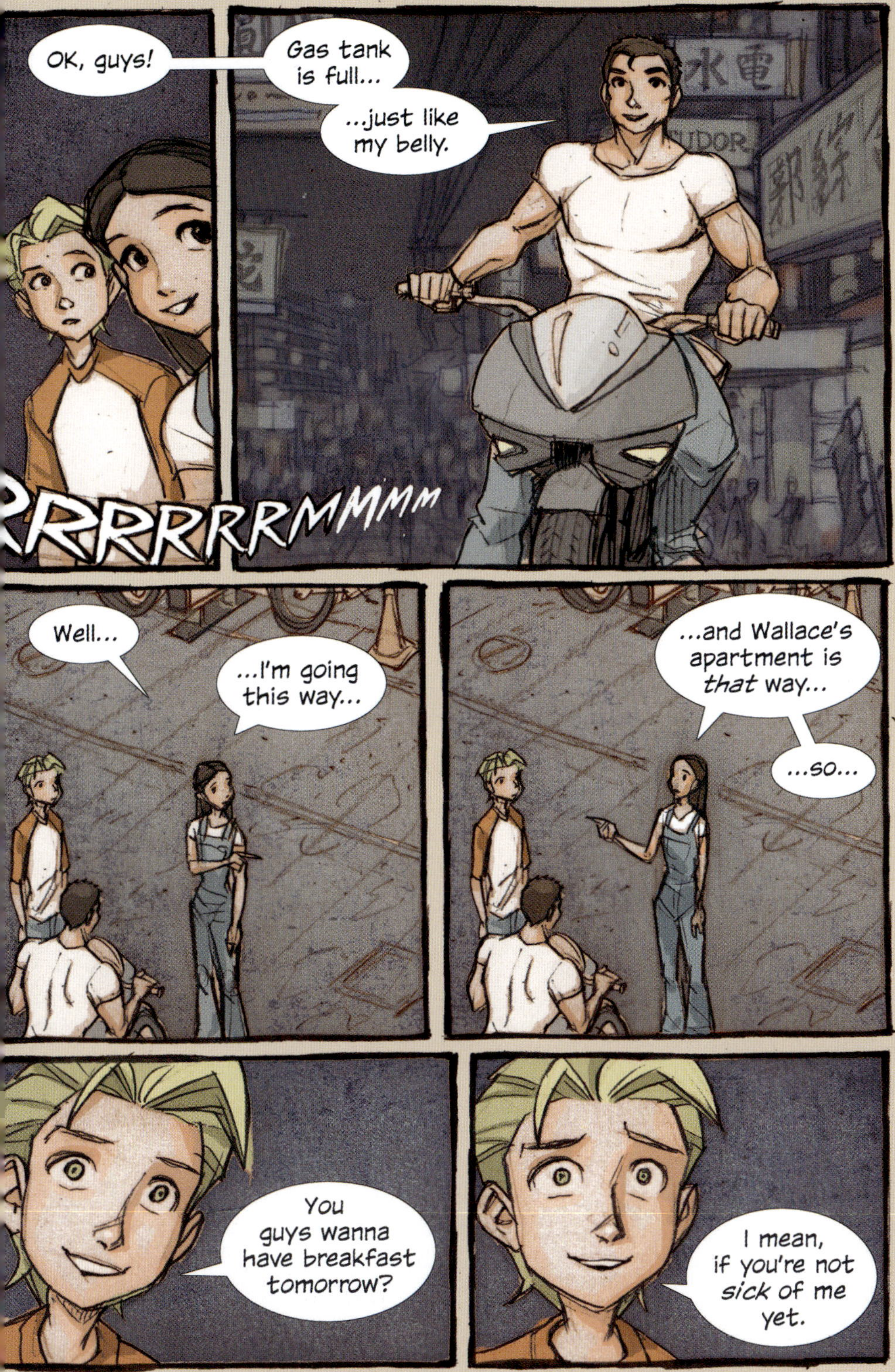
OK, guys!
Gas tank is full...
...just like my belly.
RRRRRRRMMMM
Well...
...I'm going this way...
...and Wallace's apartment is *that* way...
...so...
You guys wanna have breakfast tomorrow?
I mean, if you're not *sick* of me yet.

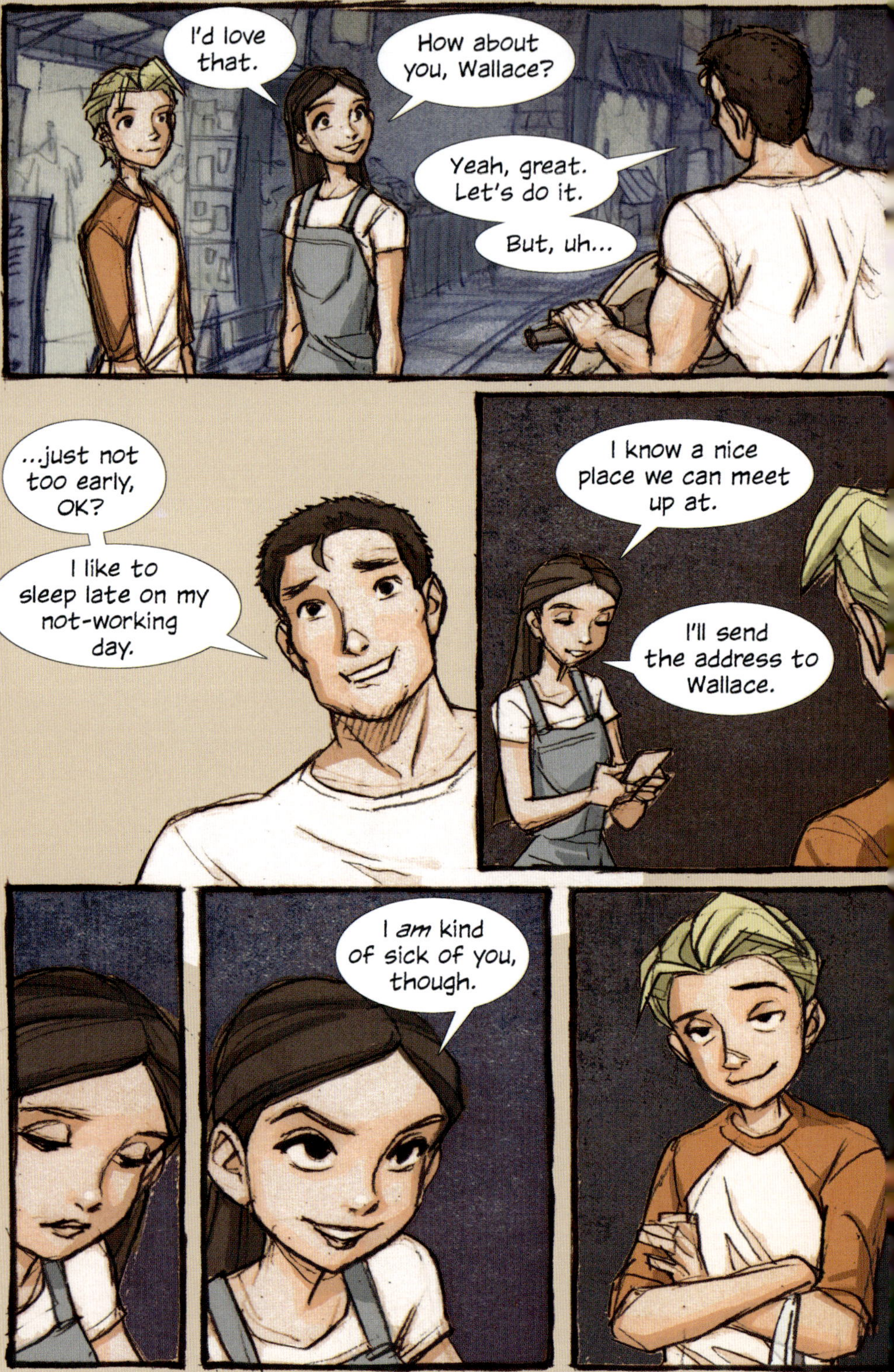
I'd love that.
How about you, Wallace?
Yeah, great. Let's do it.
But, uh...
...just not too early, OK?
I like to sleep late on my not-working day.
I know a nice place we can meet up at.
I'll send the address to Wallace.
I *am* kind of sick of you, though.

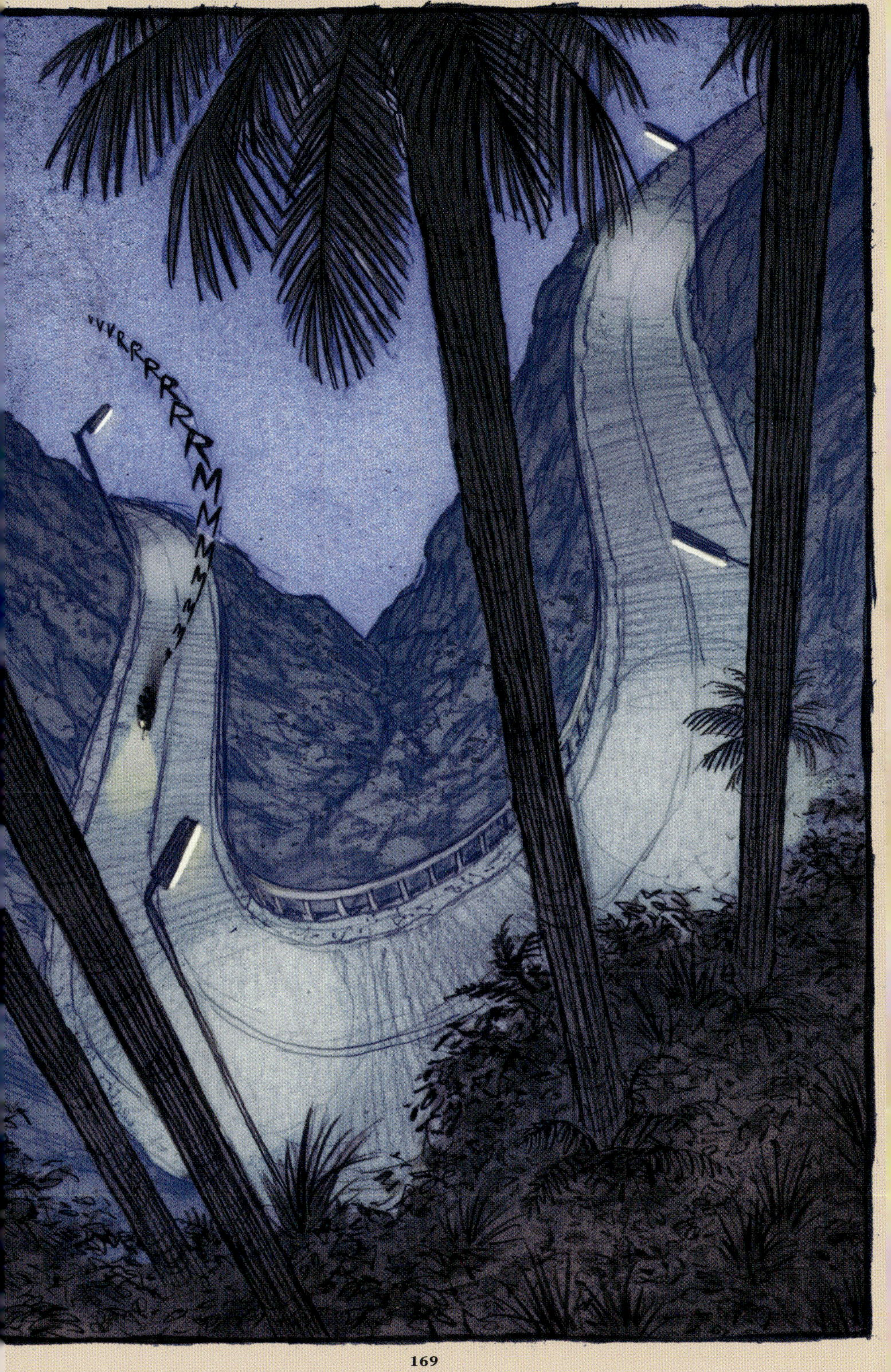
VVVRRRRRRRMMMMMMMMM

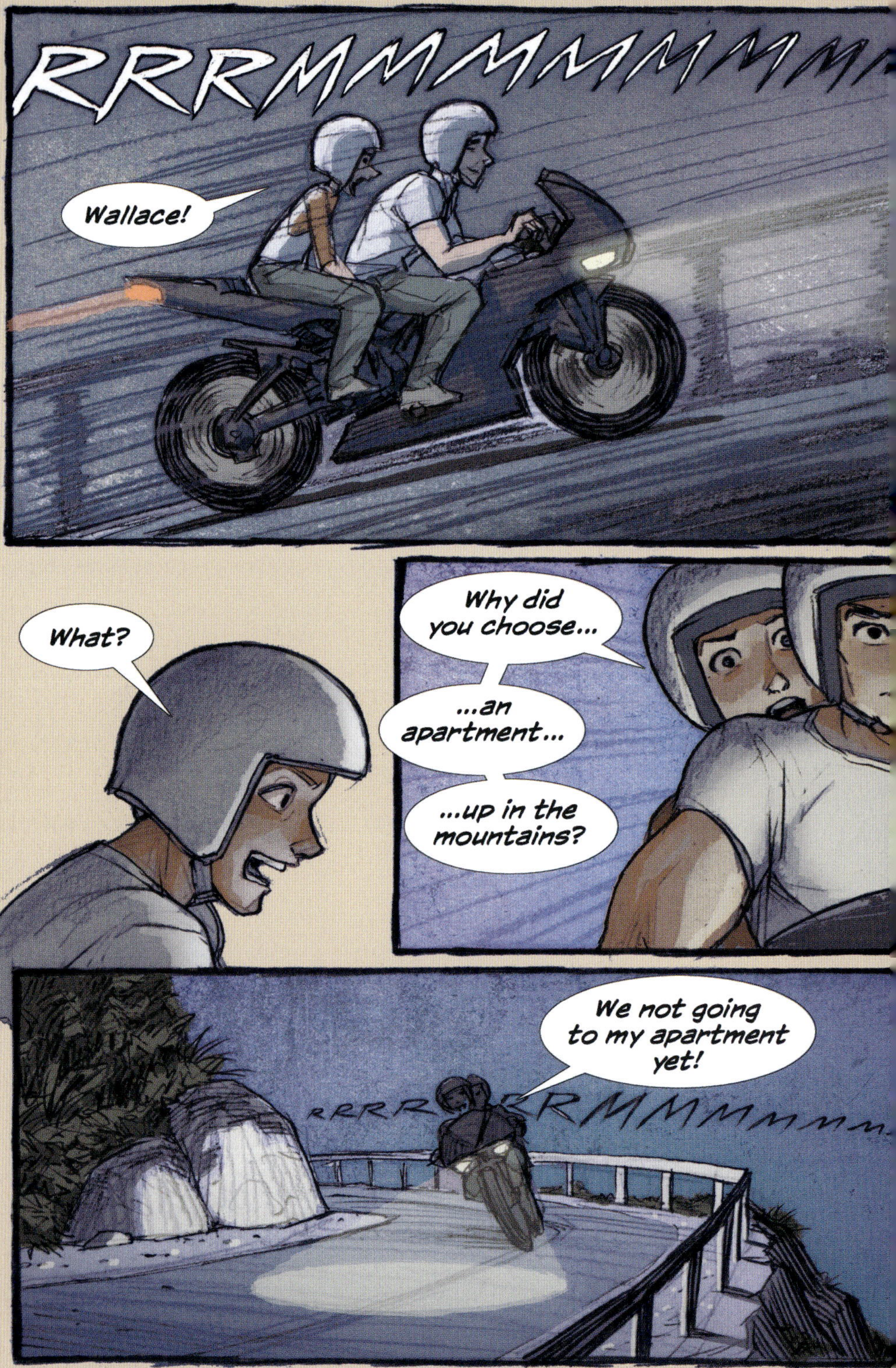
RRRMMMMMMMM
Wallace!
What?
Why did you choose...
...an apartment...
...up in the mountains?
We not going to my apartment yet!
RRRRRRRMMMMMMM

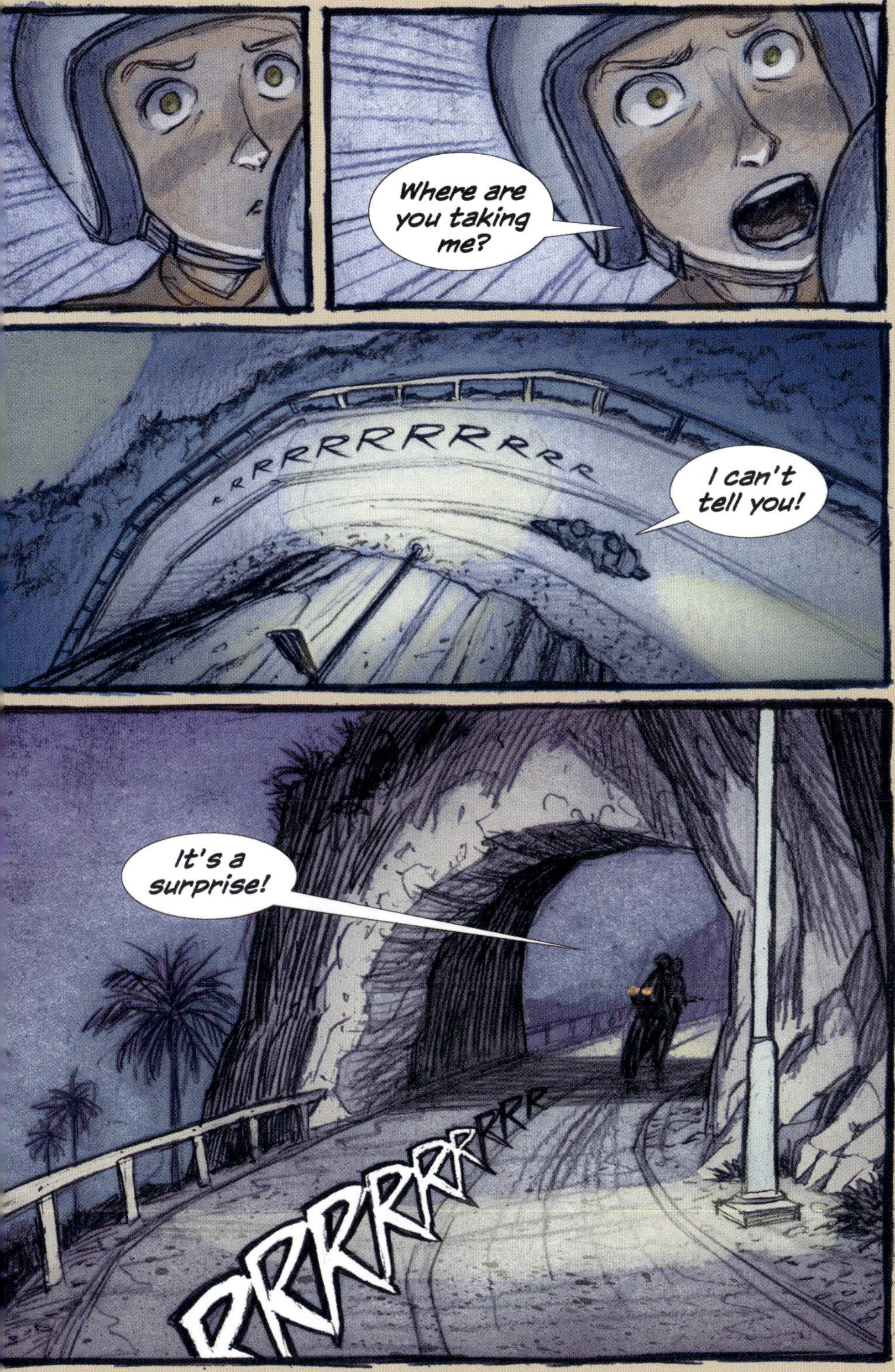
Where are you taking me?
rRRRRRRRRRrrr
I can't tell you!
It's a surprise!
RRRRRRRRRR

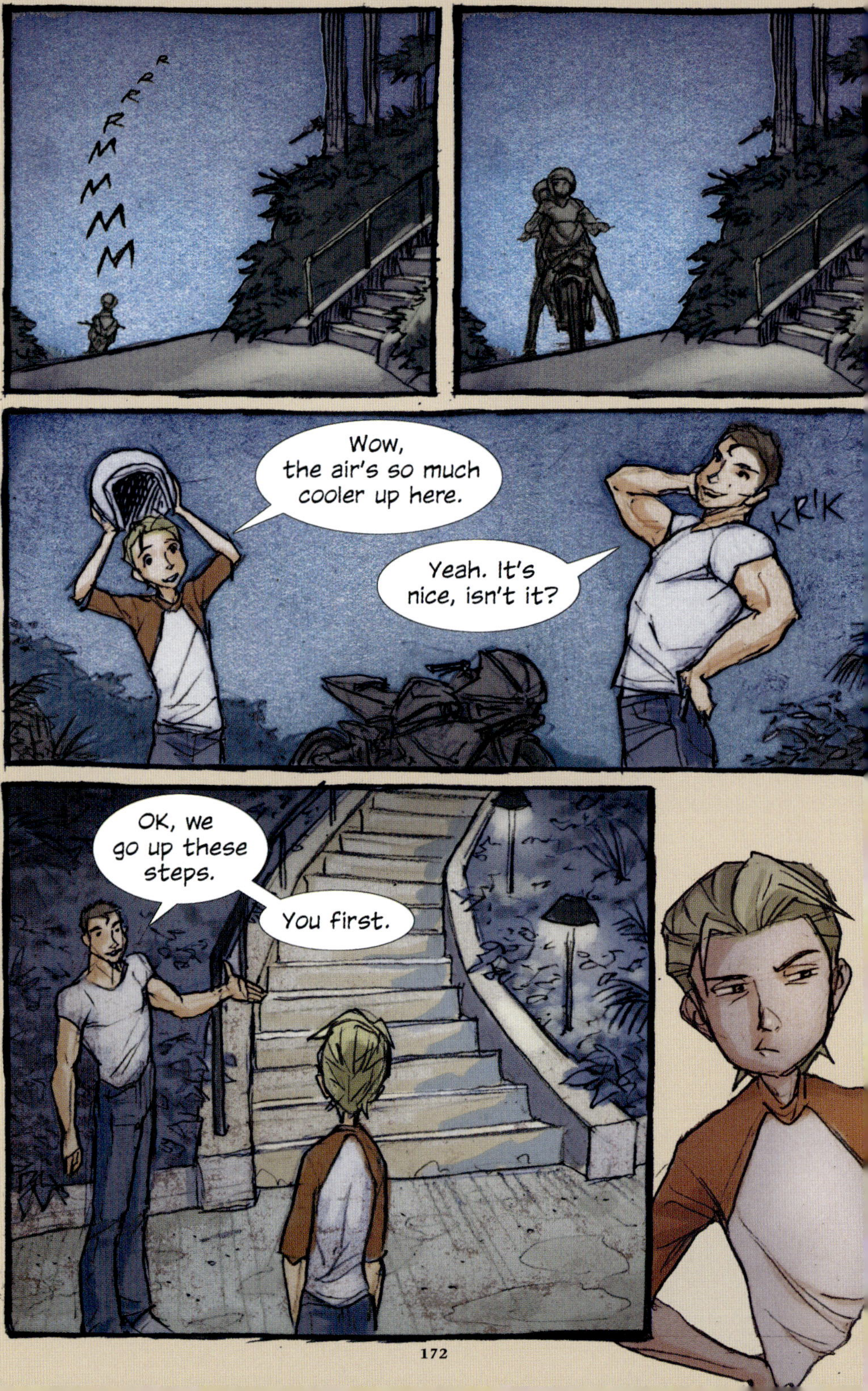
RRRMMMMM
Wow, the air's so much cooler up here.
Yeah. It's nice, isn't it?
KR'K
OK, we go up these steps.
You first.

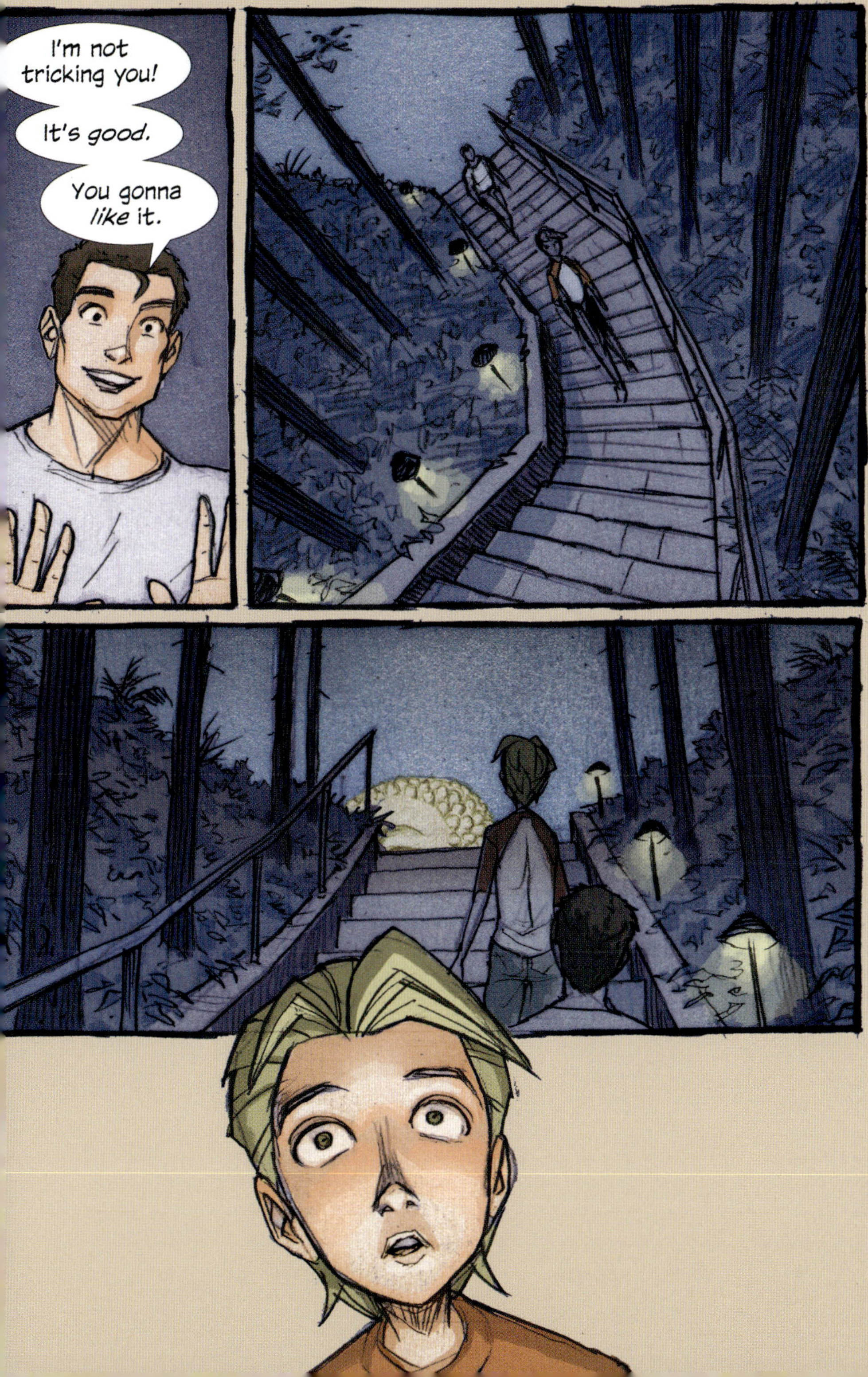
I'm not tricking you!
It's *good.*
You gonna *like* it.

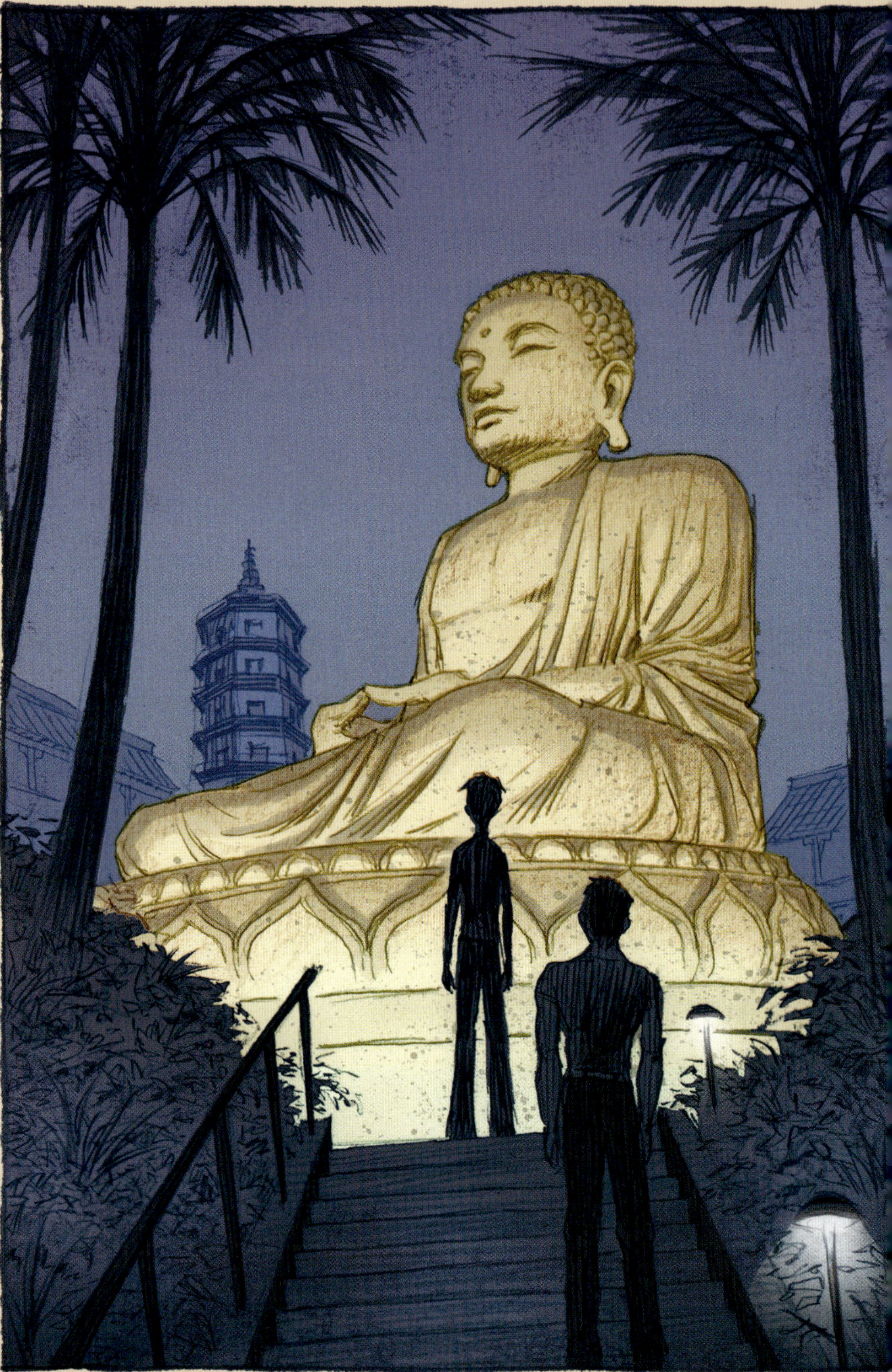

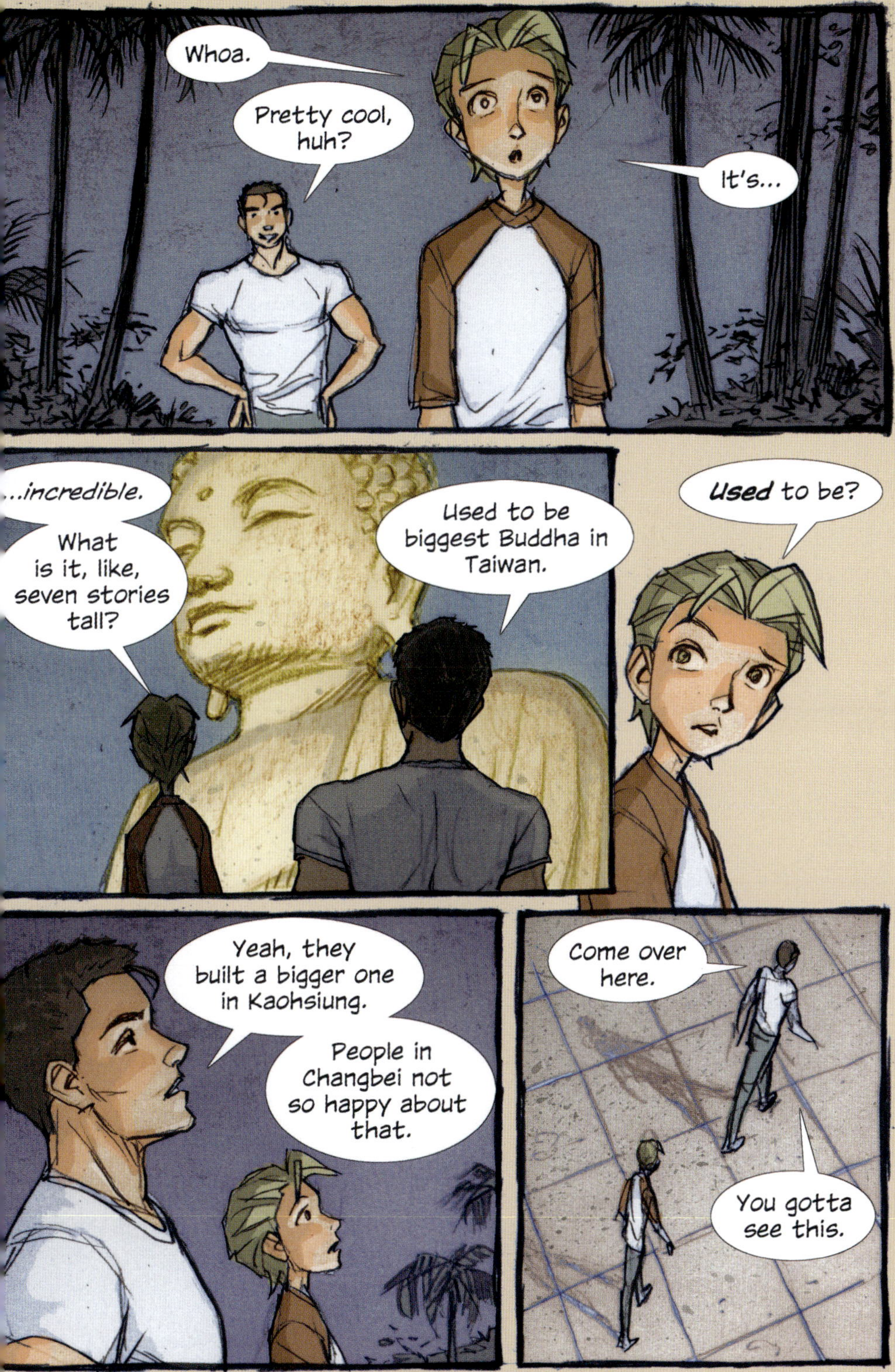
Whoa.
Pretty cool, huh?
It's...
...incredible.
What is it, like, seven stories tall?
Used to be biggest Buddha in Taiwan.
Used to be?
Yeah, they built a bigger one in Kaohsiung.
People in Changbei not so happy about that.
Come over here.
You gotta see this.

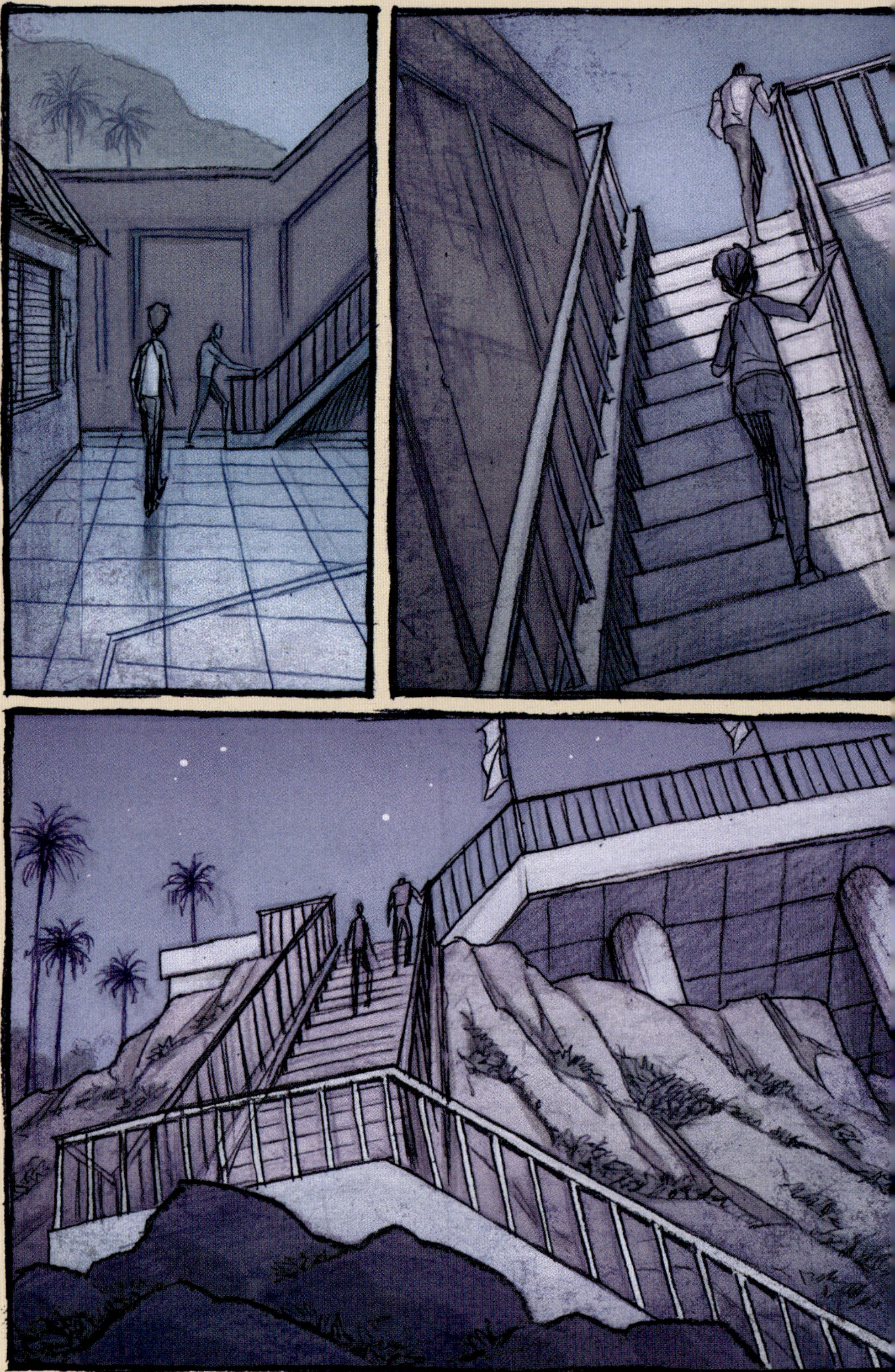

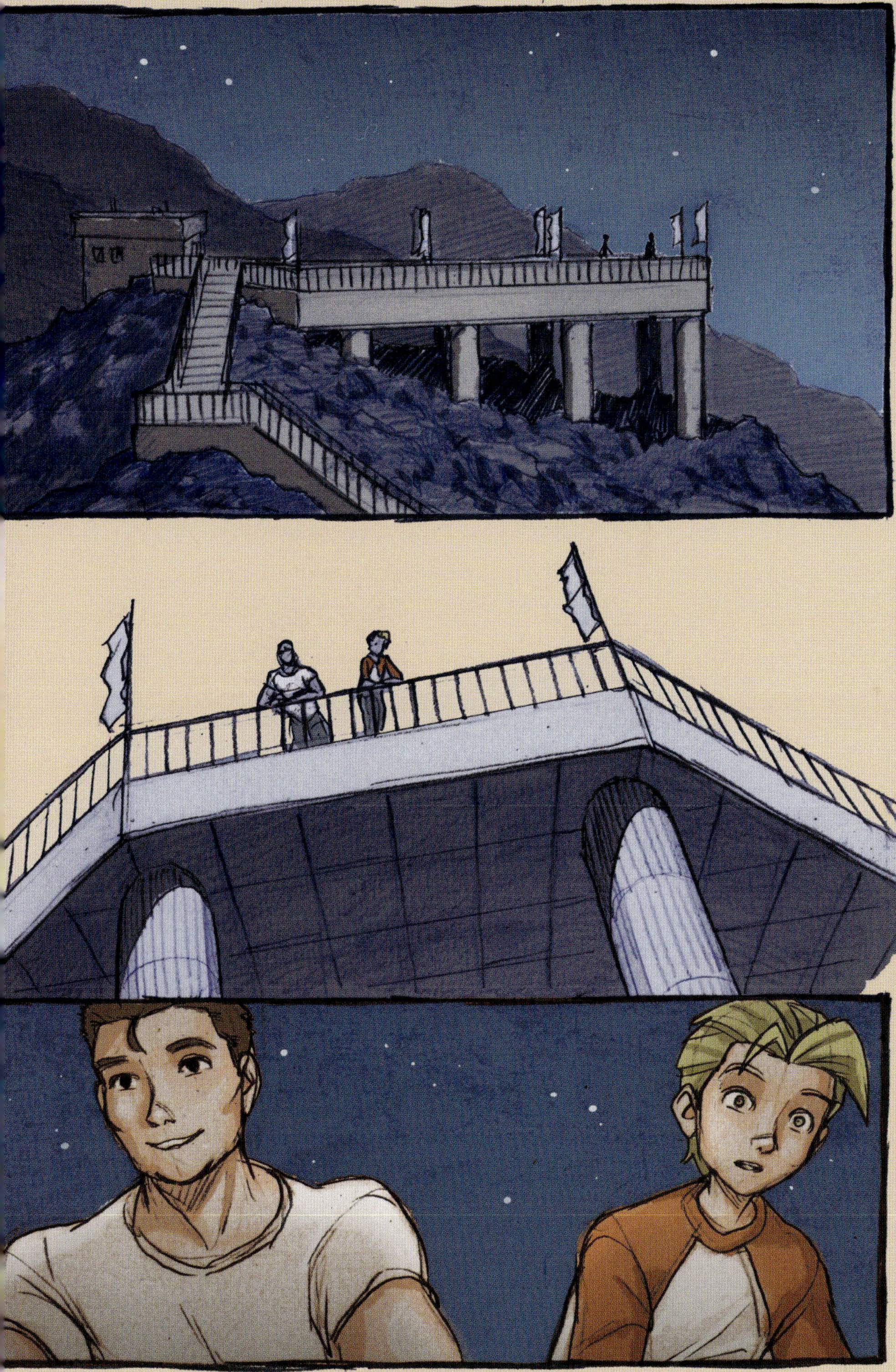

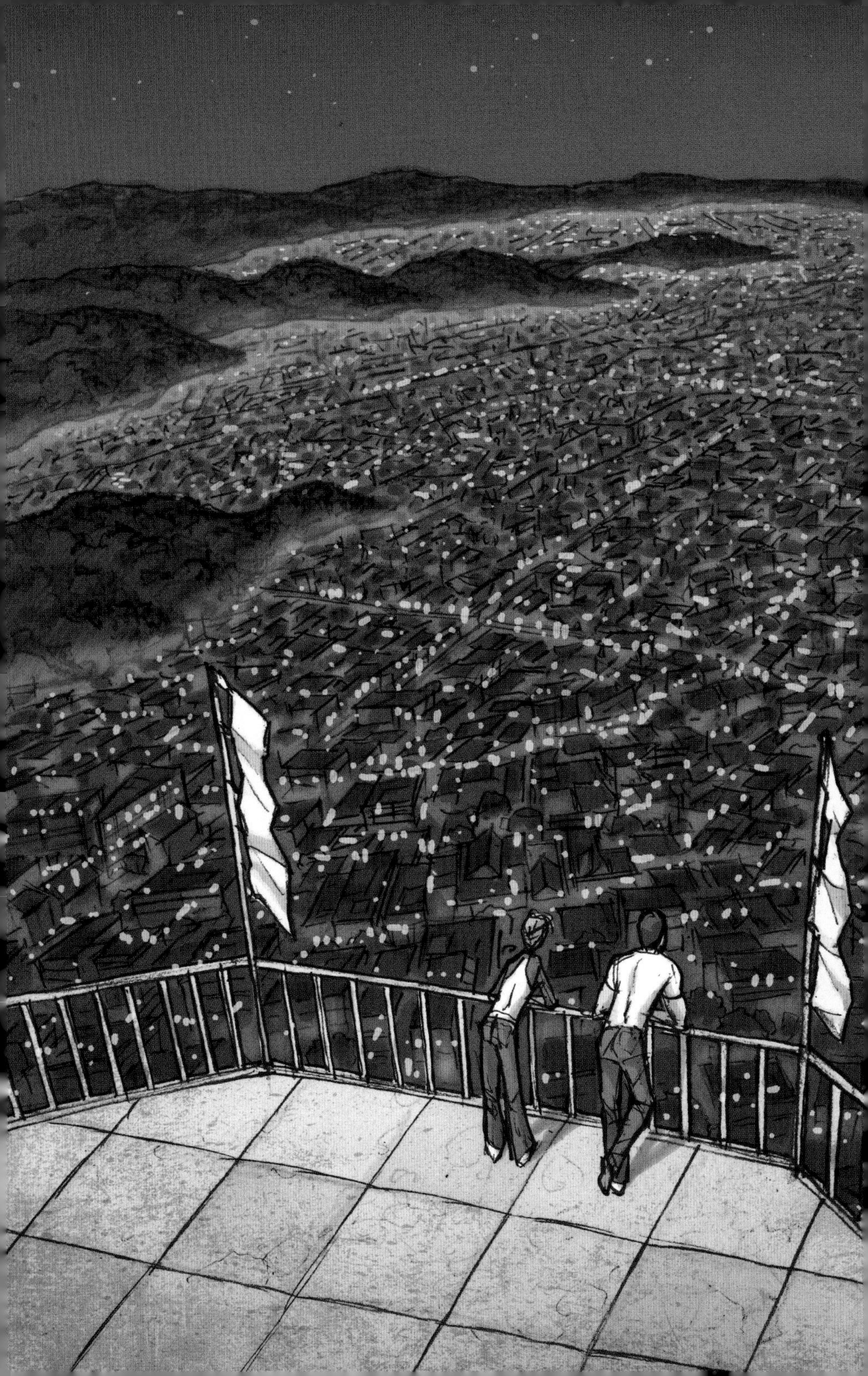

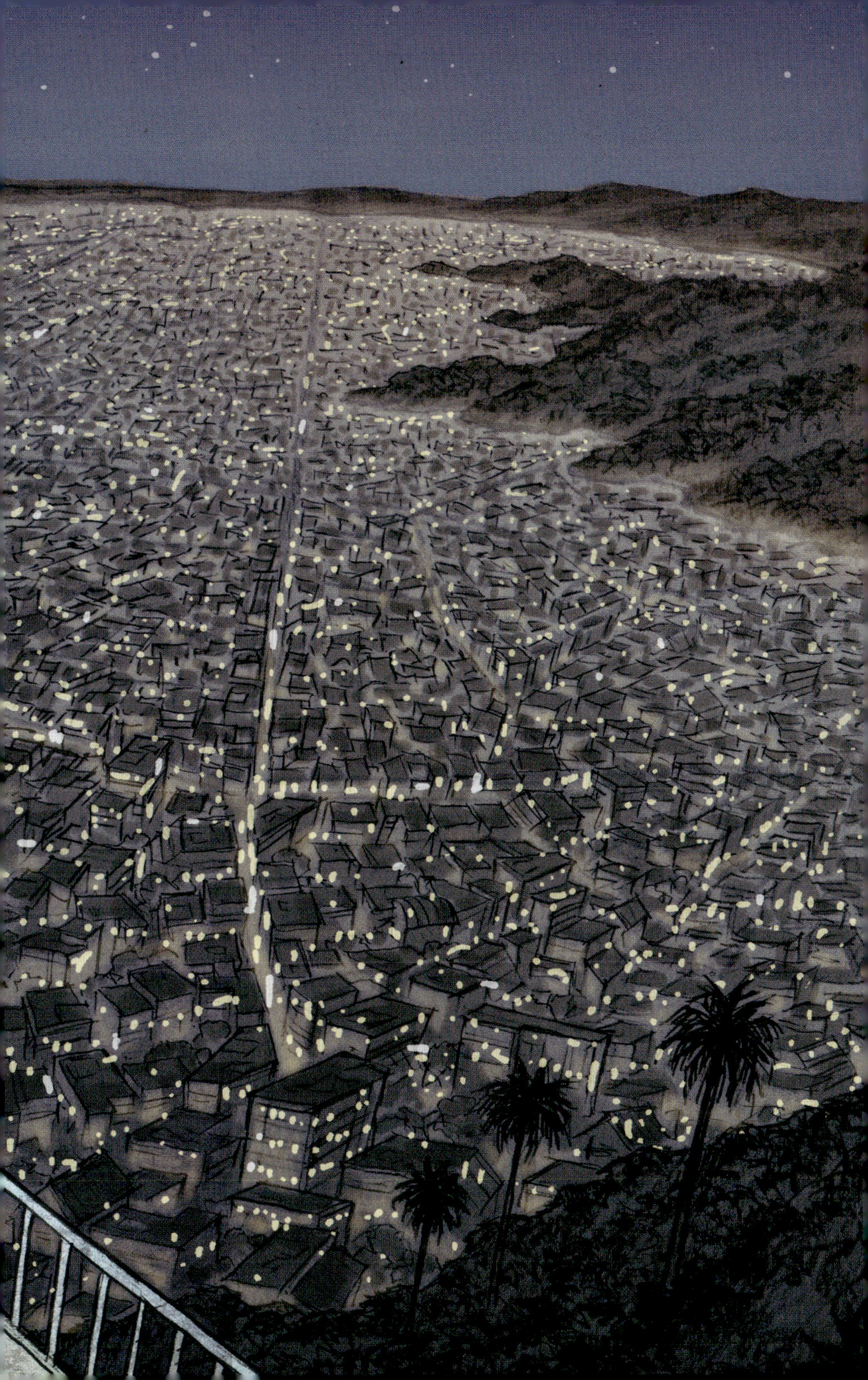

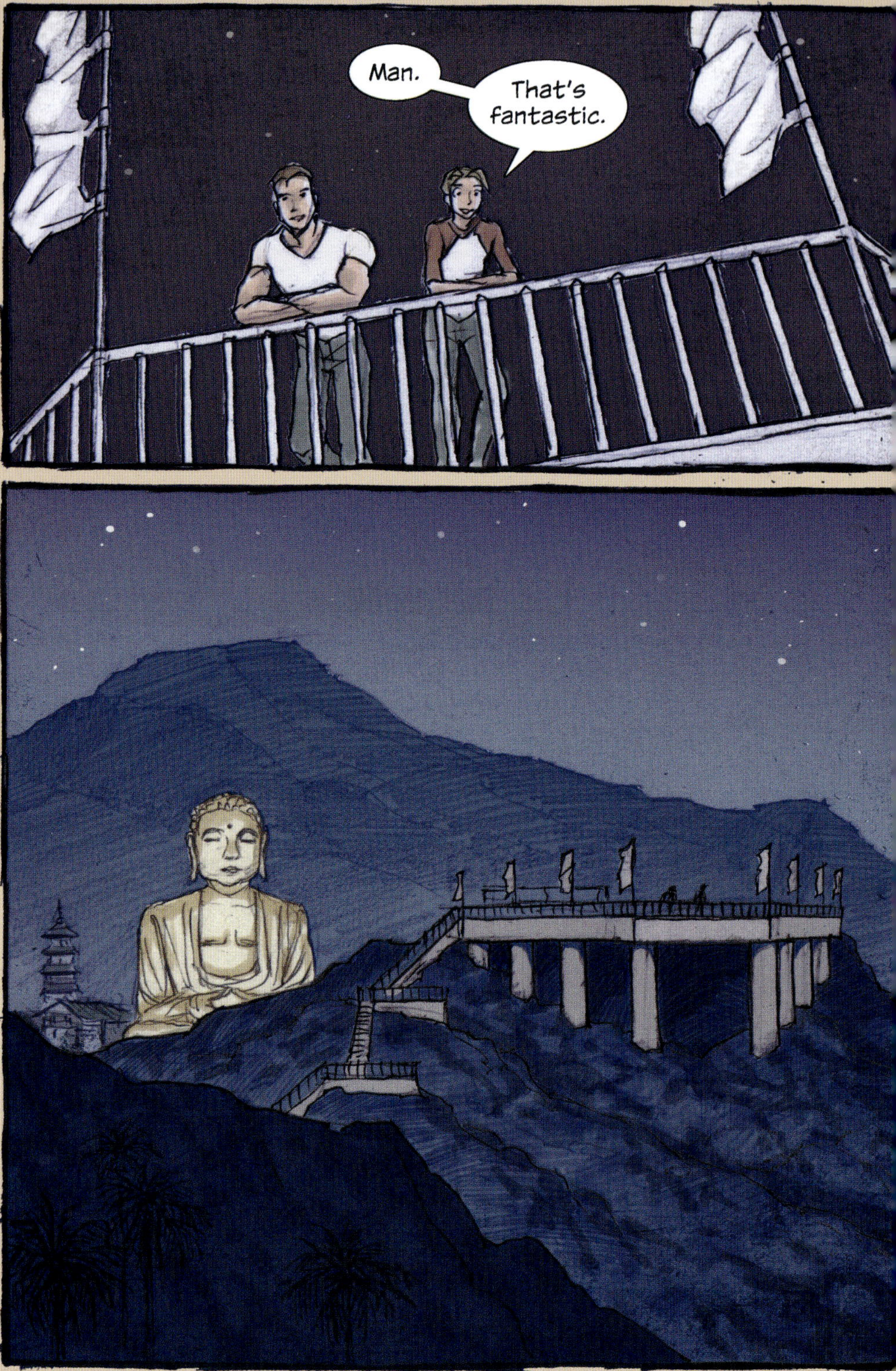
Man.
That's fantastic.

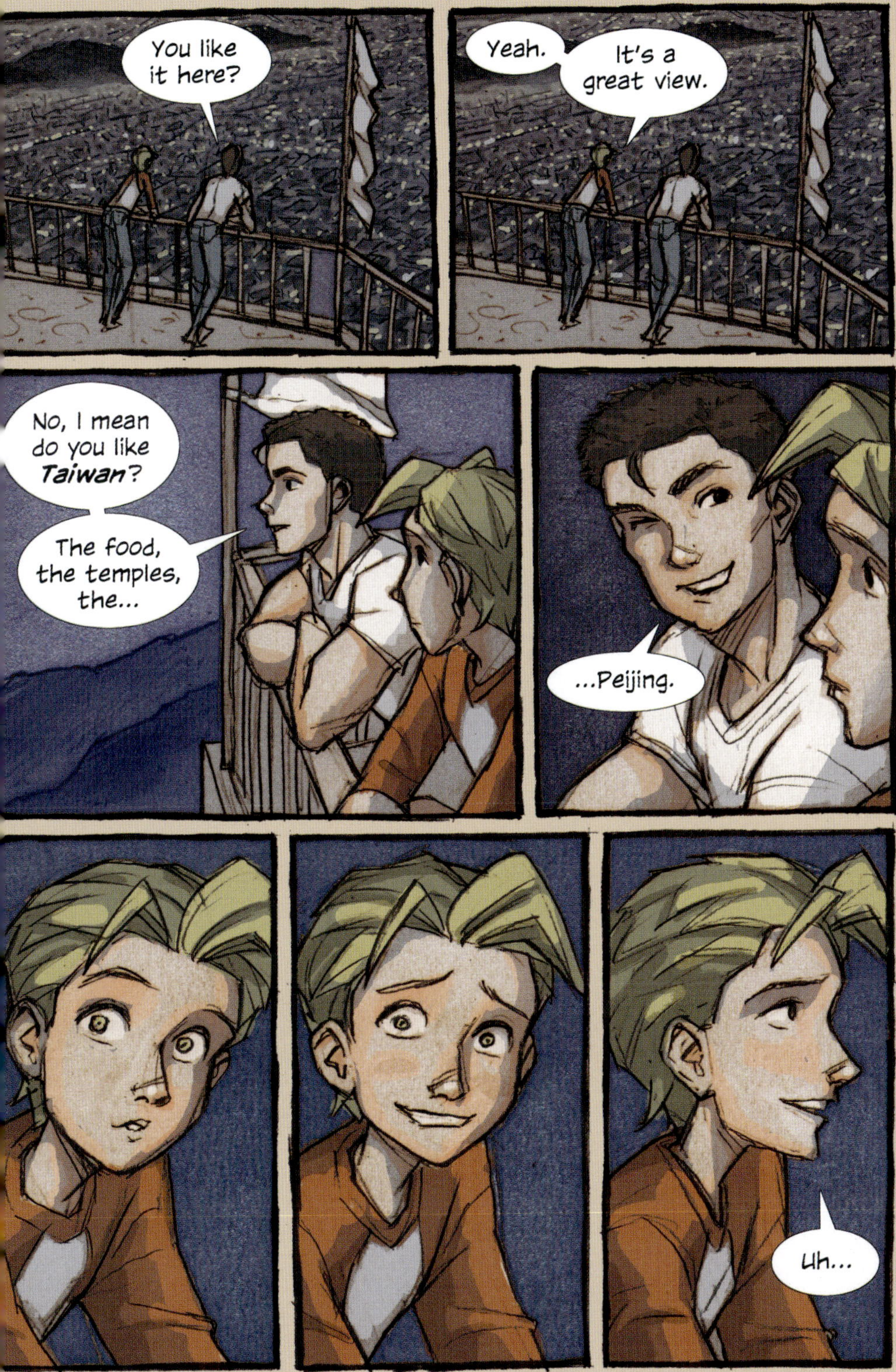
You like it here?
Yeah.
It's a great view.
No, I mean do you like *Taiwan*?
The food, the temples, the...
...Peijing.
Uh...

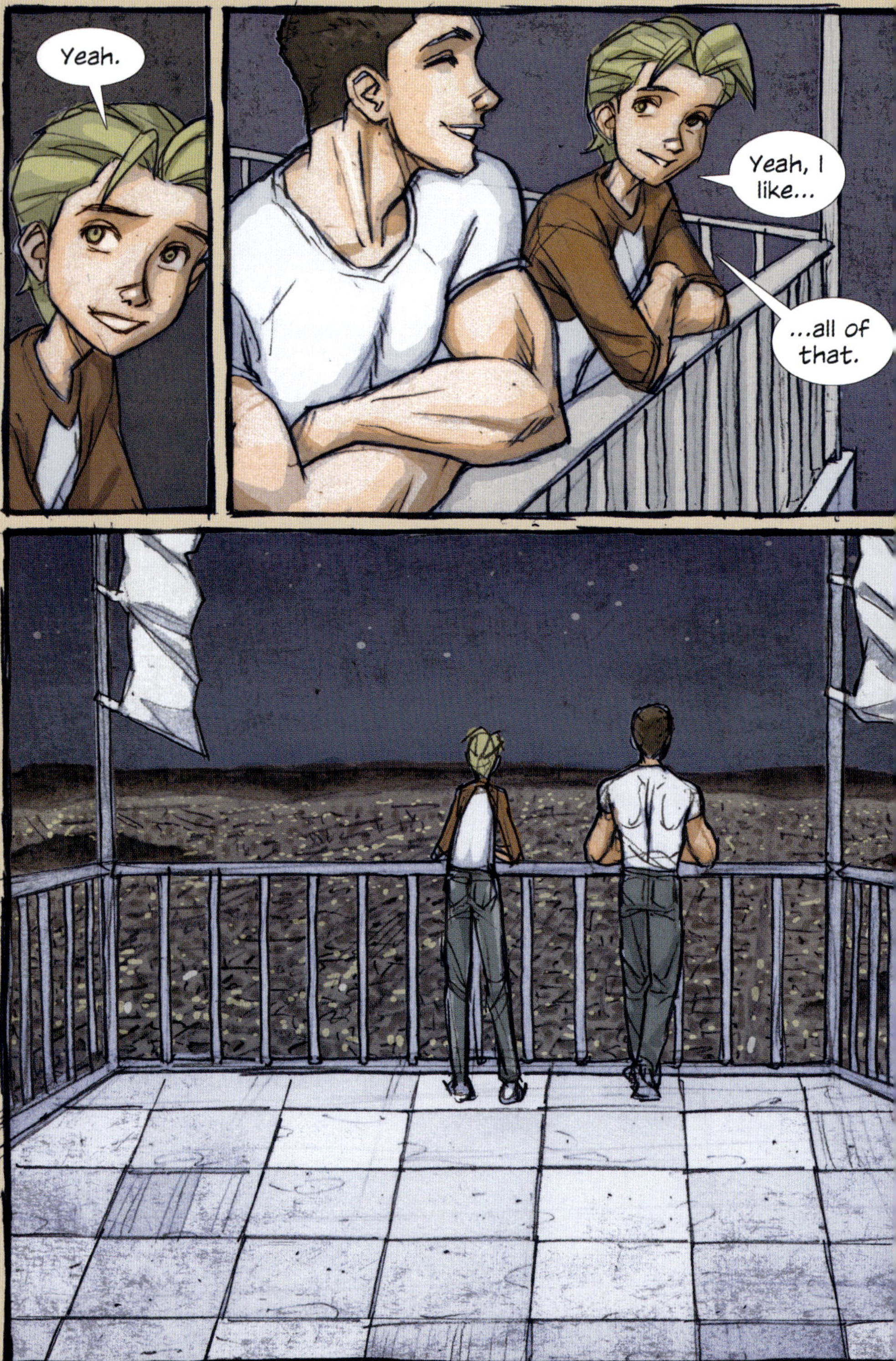
Yeah.
Yeah, I like...
...all of that.

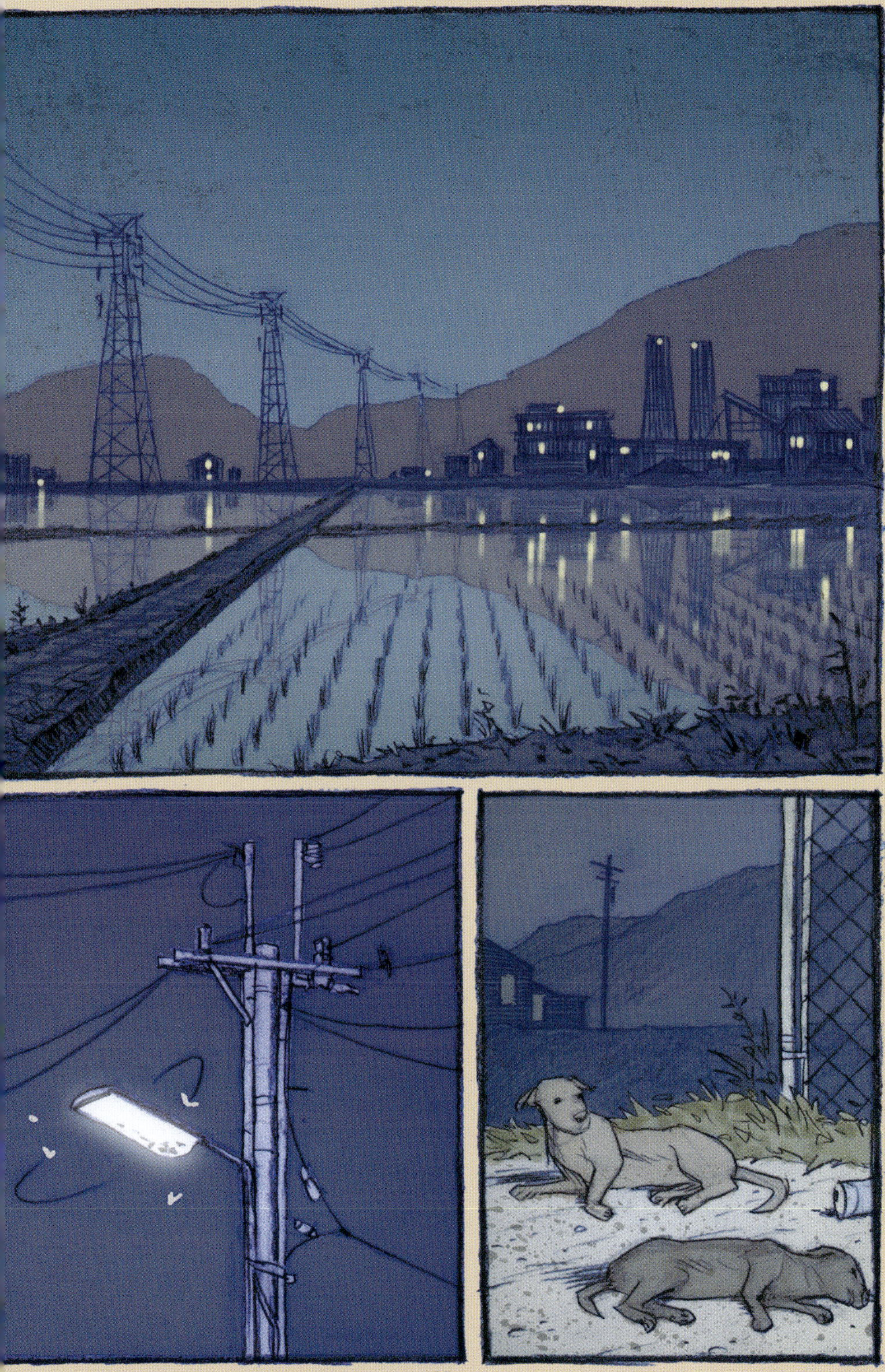

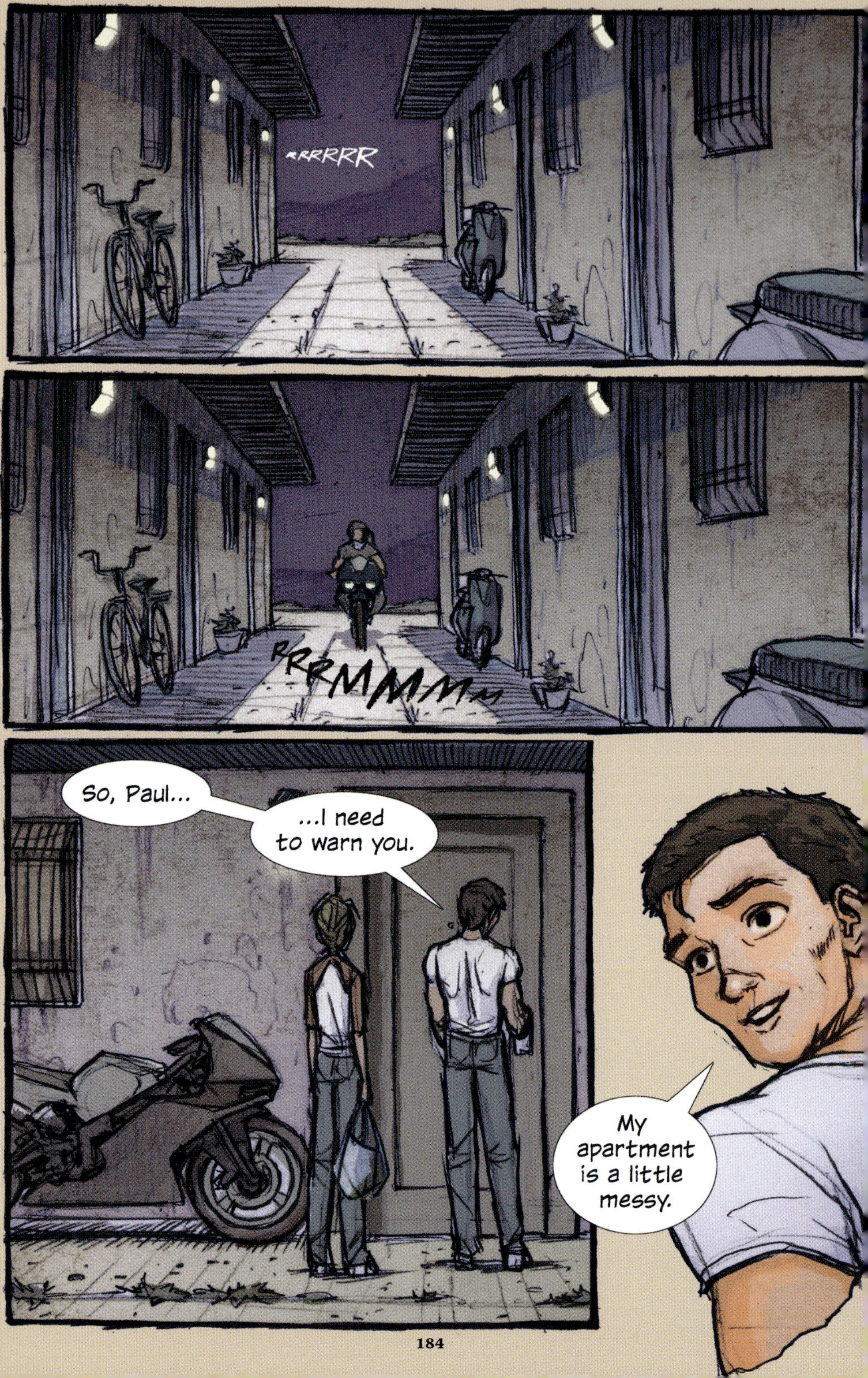
RRRRRR
RRRMMMMM
So, Paul...
...I need to warn you.
My apartment is a little messy.

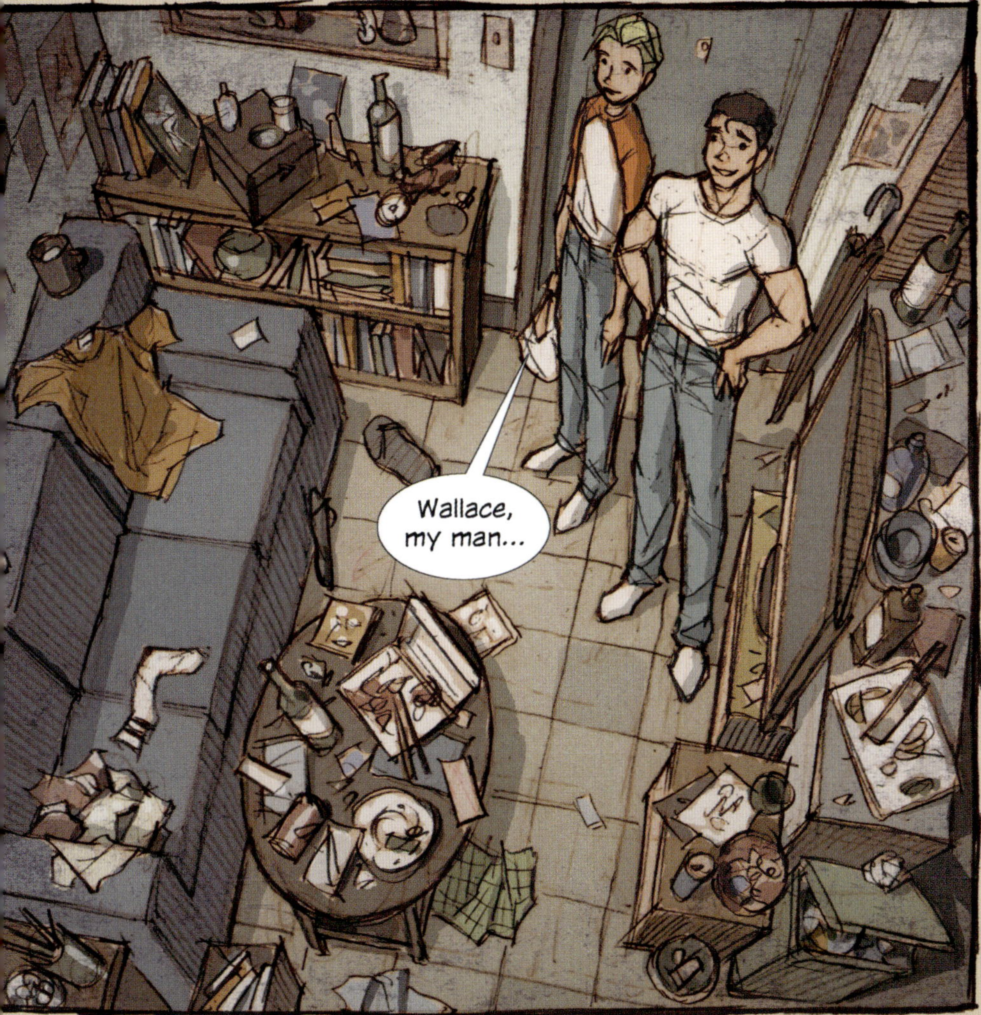
Wallace, my man...

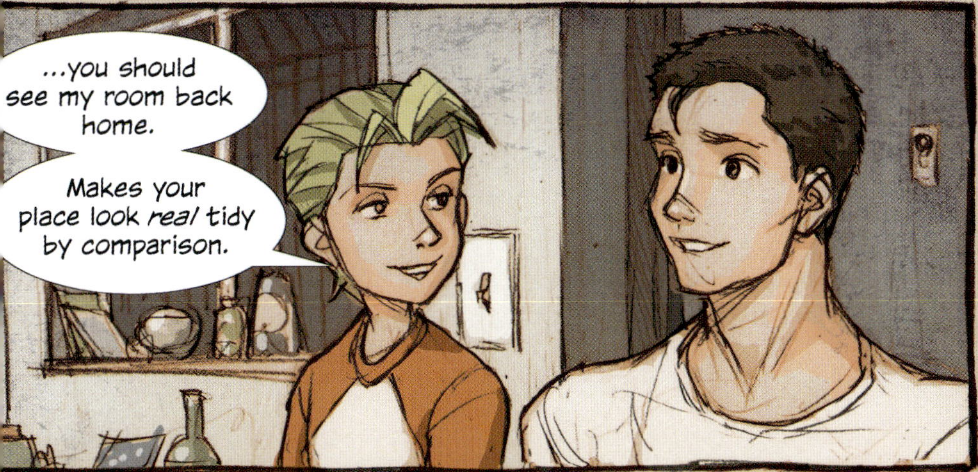
...you should see my room back home.
Makes your place look *real* tidy by comparison.

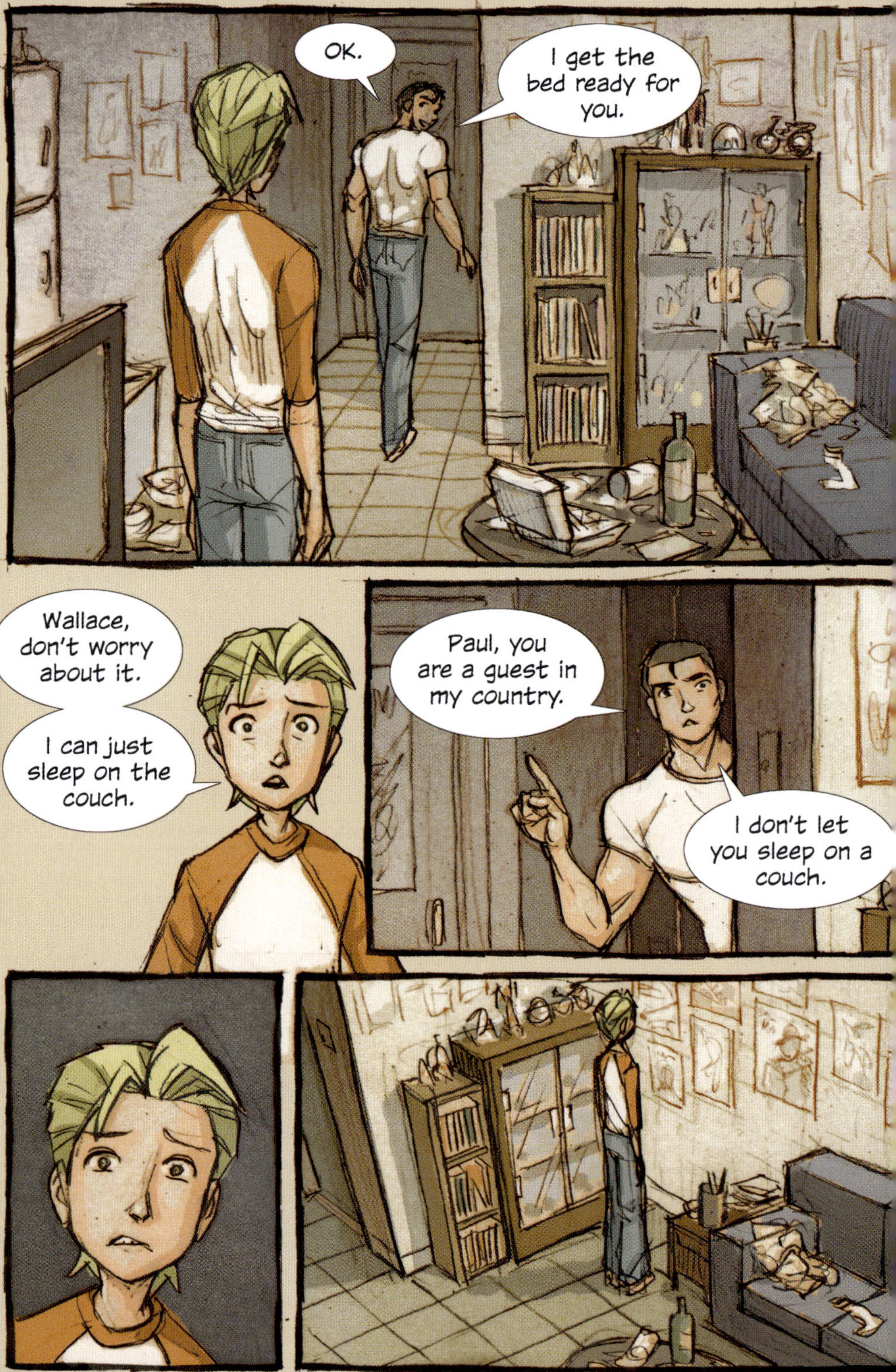
OK.
I get the bed ready for you.
Wallace, don't worry about it.
I can just sleep on the couch.
Paul, you are a guest in my country.
I don't let you sleep on a couch.

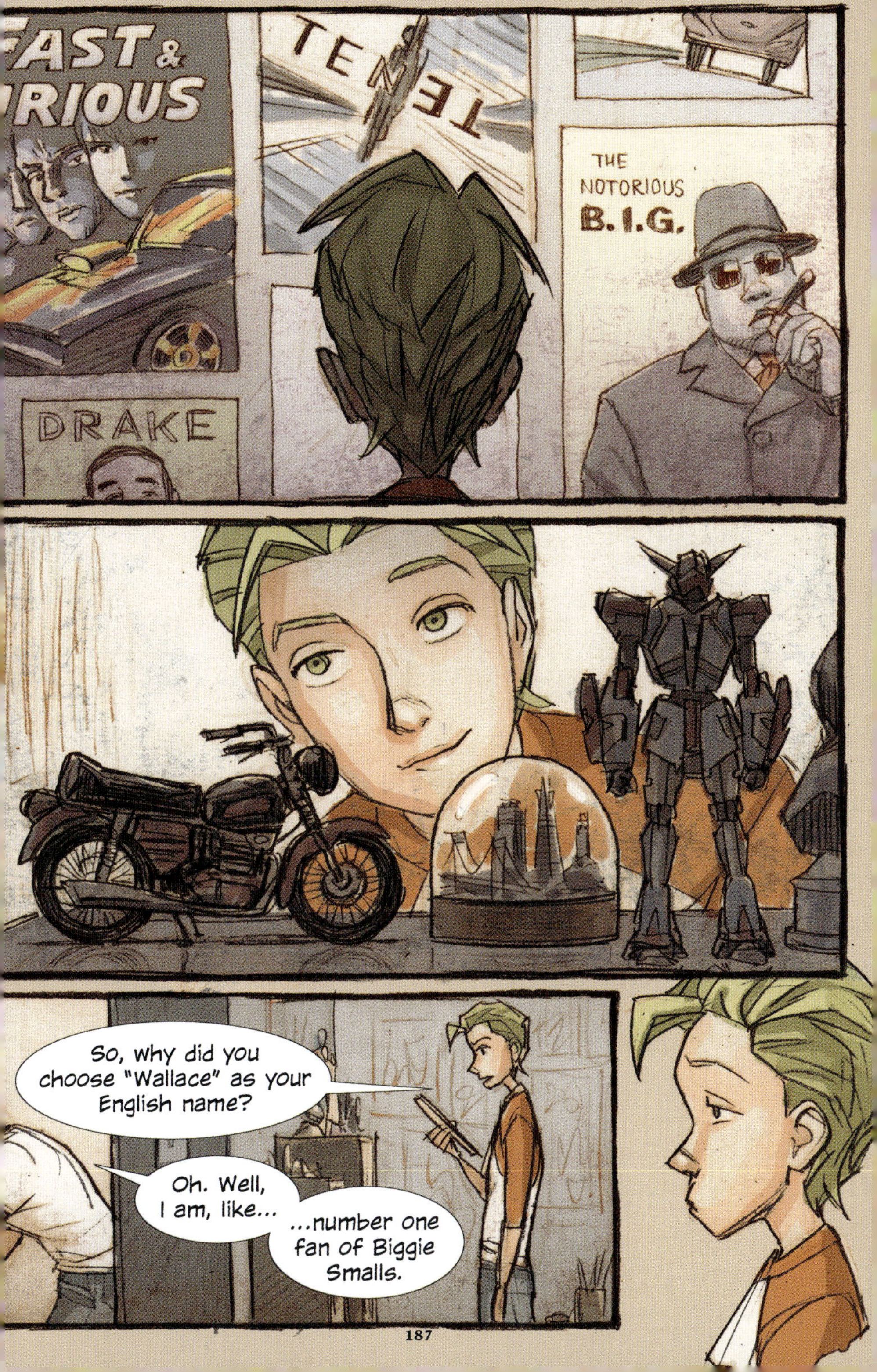
FAST &
RIOUS
TENET
THE NOTORIOUS B.I.G.
DRAKE
So, why did you choose "Wallace" as your English name?
Oh. Well, I am, like...
...number one fan of Biggie Smalls.

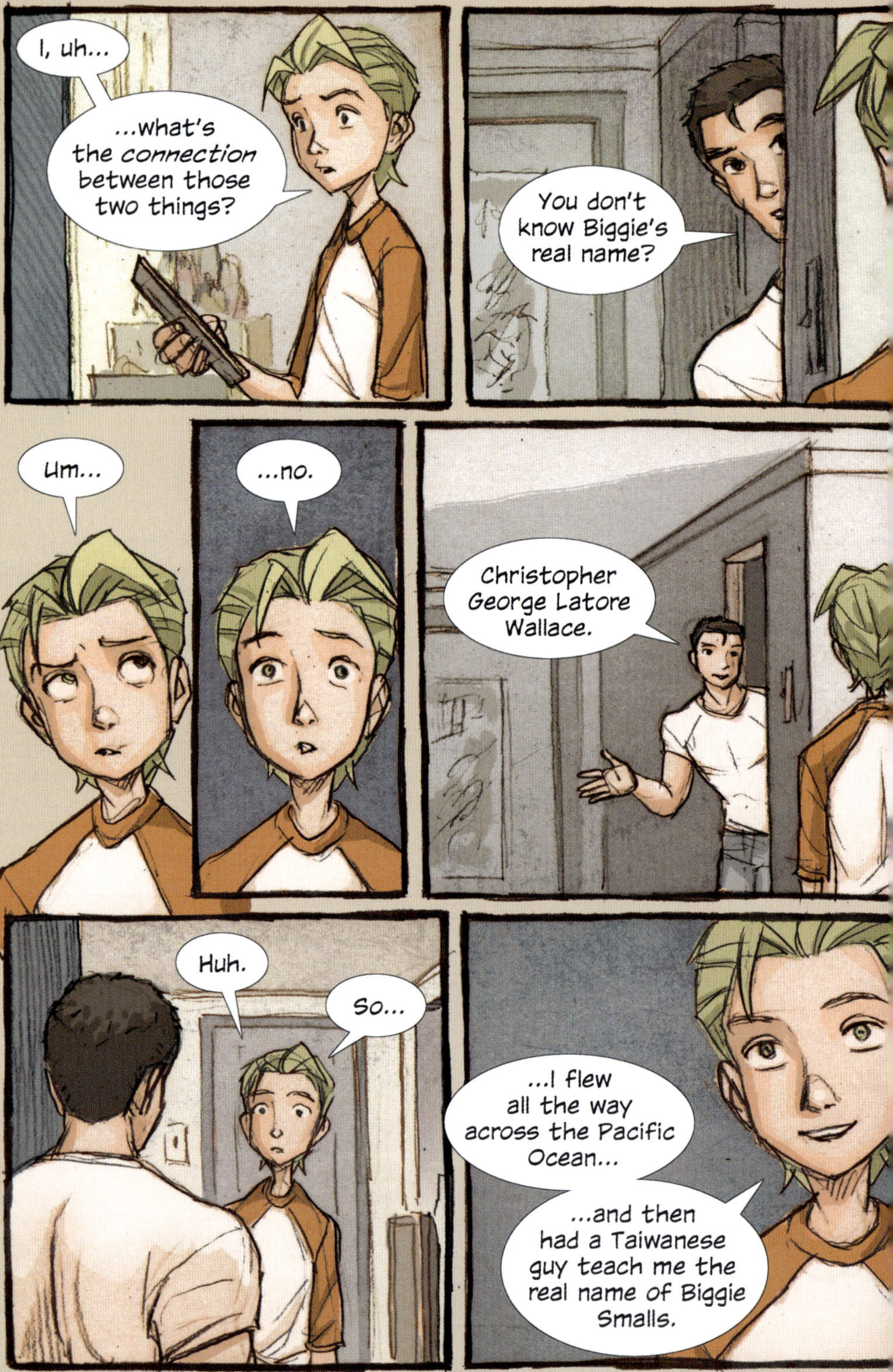
I, uh...
...what's the *connection* between those two things?
You don't know Biggie's real name?
Um...
...no.
Christopher George Latore Wallace.
Huh.
So...
...I flew all the way across the Pacific Ocean...
...and then had a Taiwanese guy teach me the real name of Biggie Smalls.

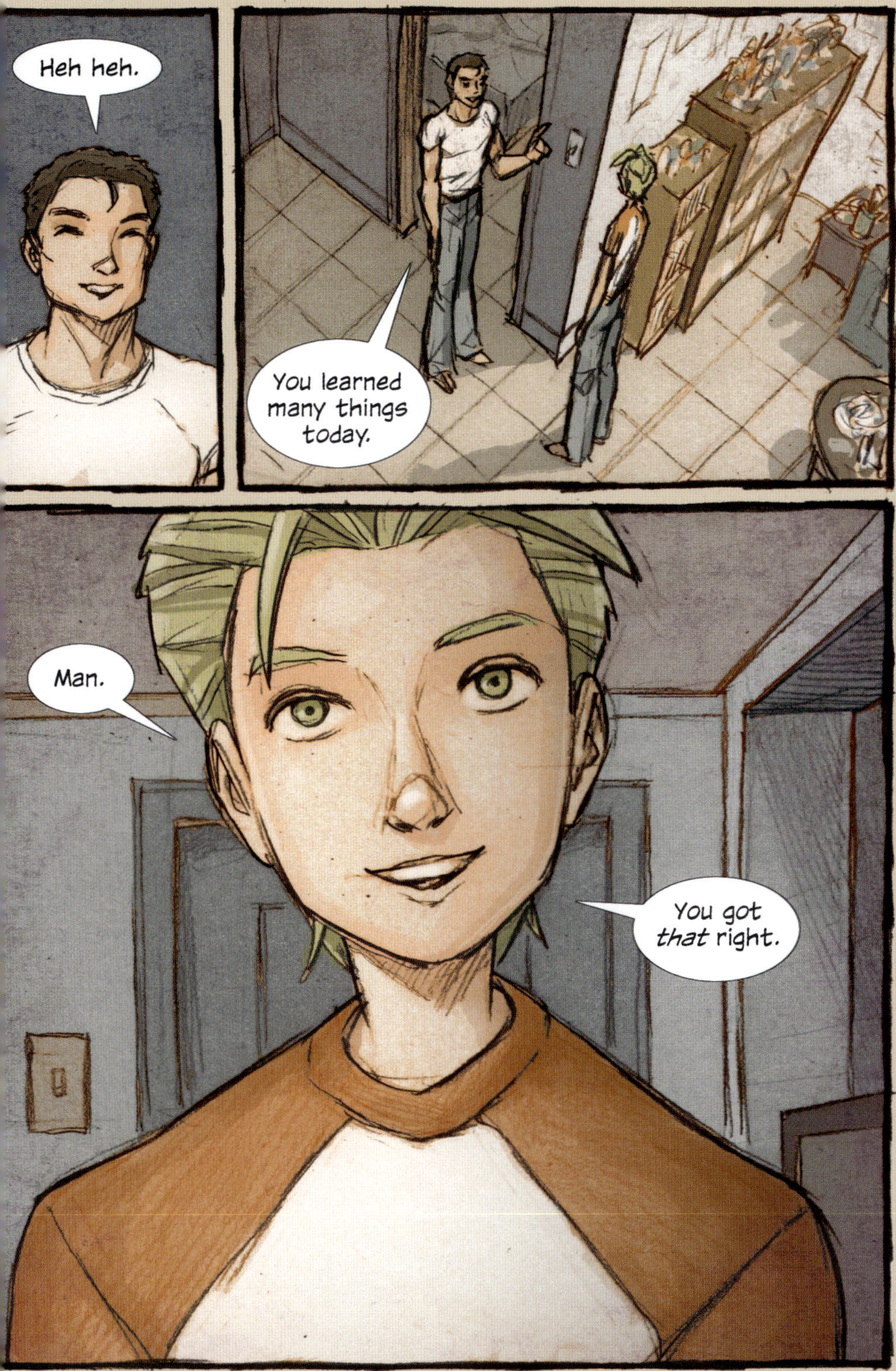
Heh heh.
You learned many things today.
Man.
You got *that* right.

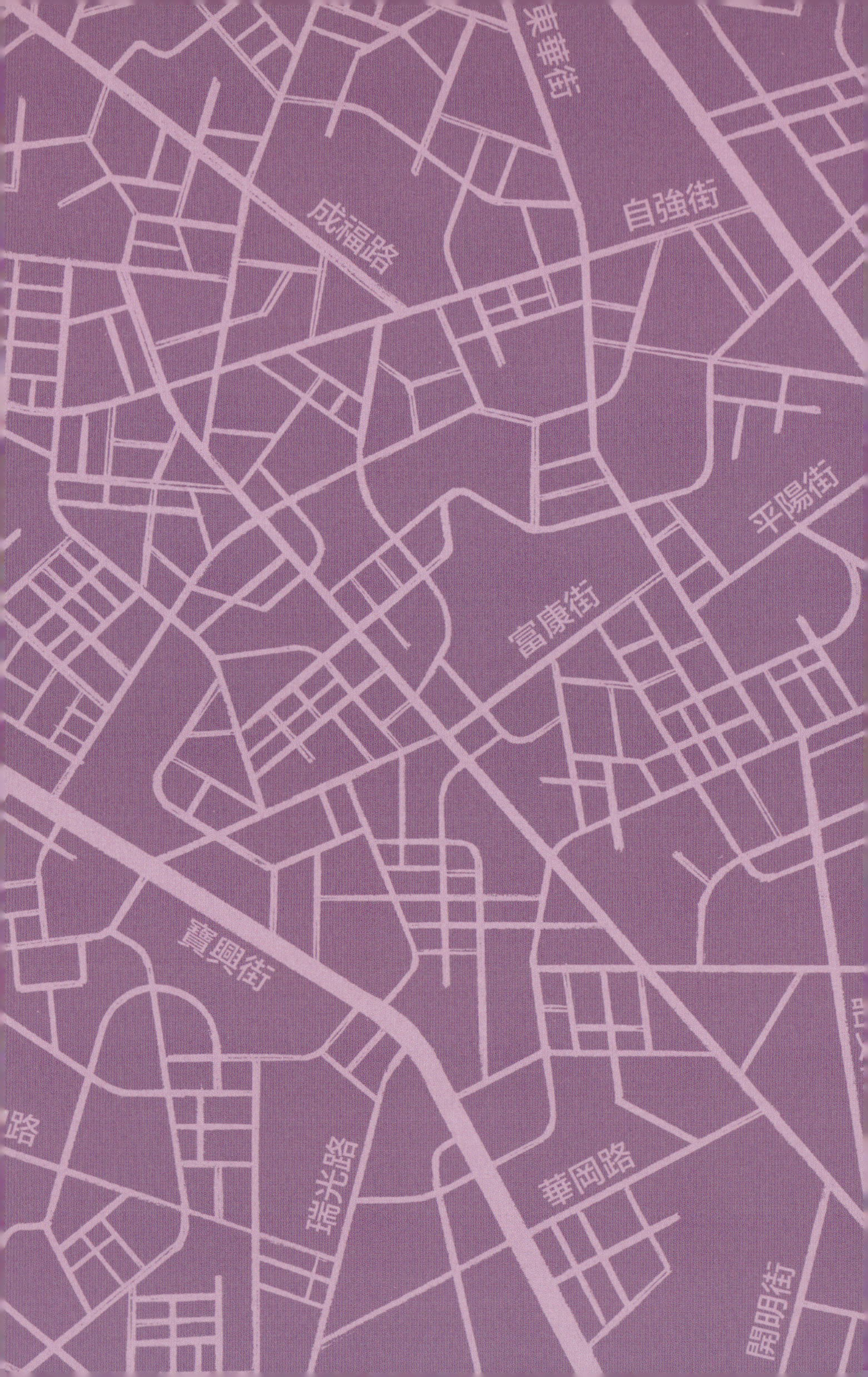
東華街
成福路
自強街
平陽街
富康街
寶興街
瑞光路
華岡路
開明街

CHAPTER 4

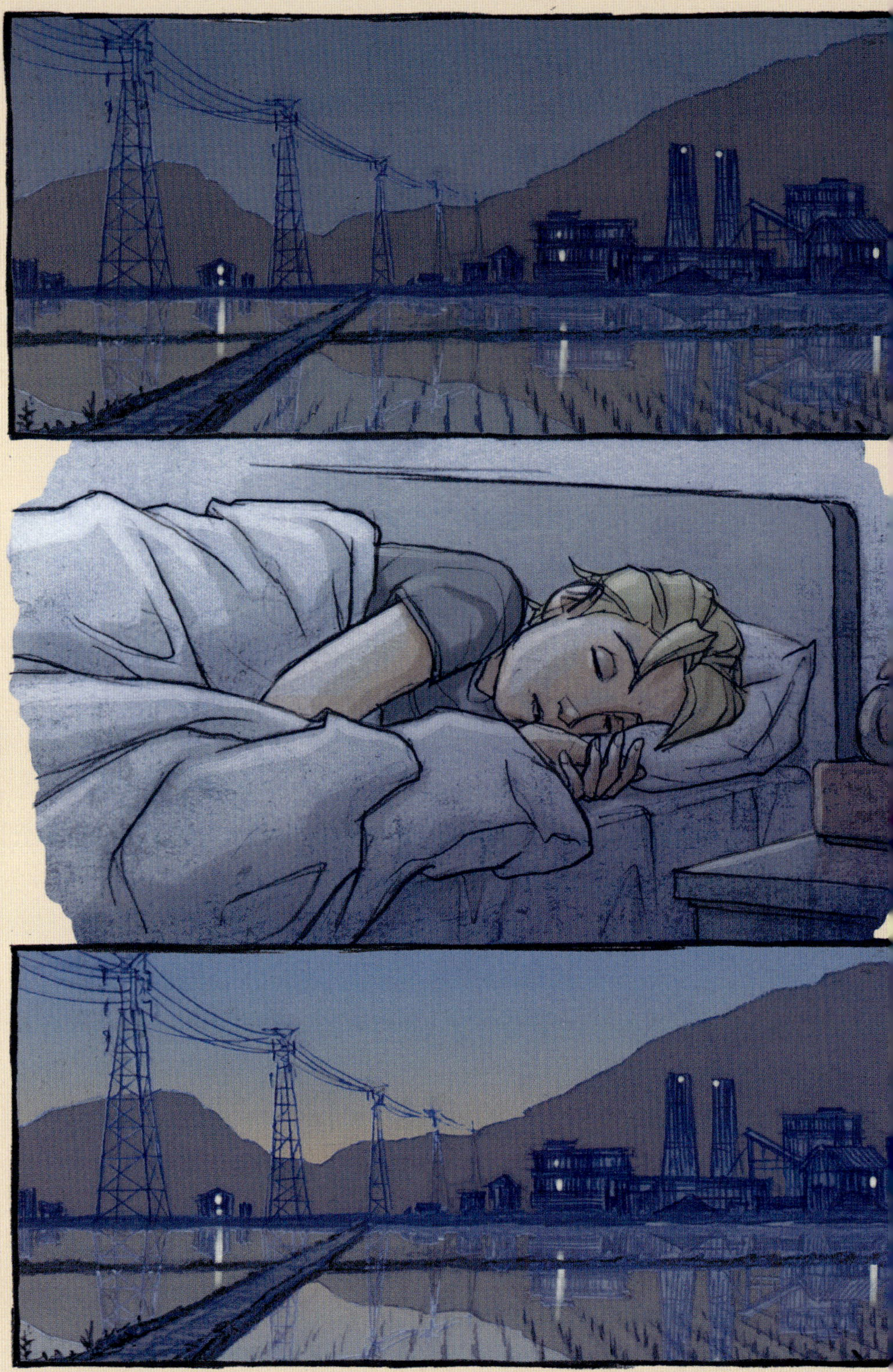

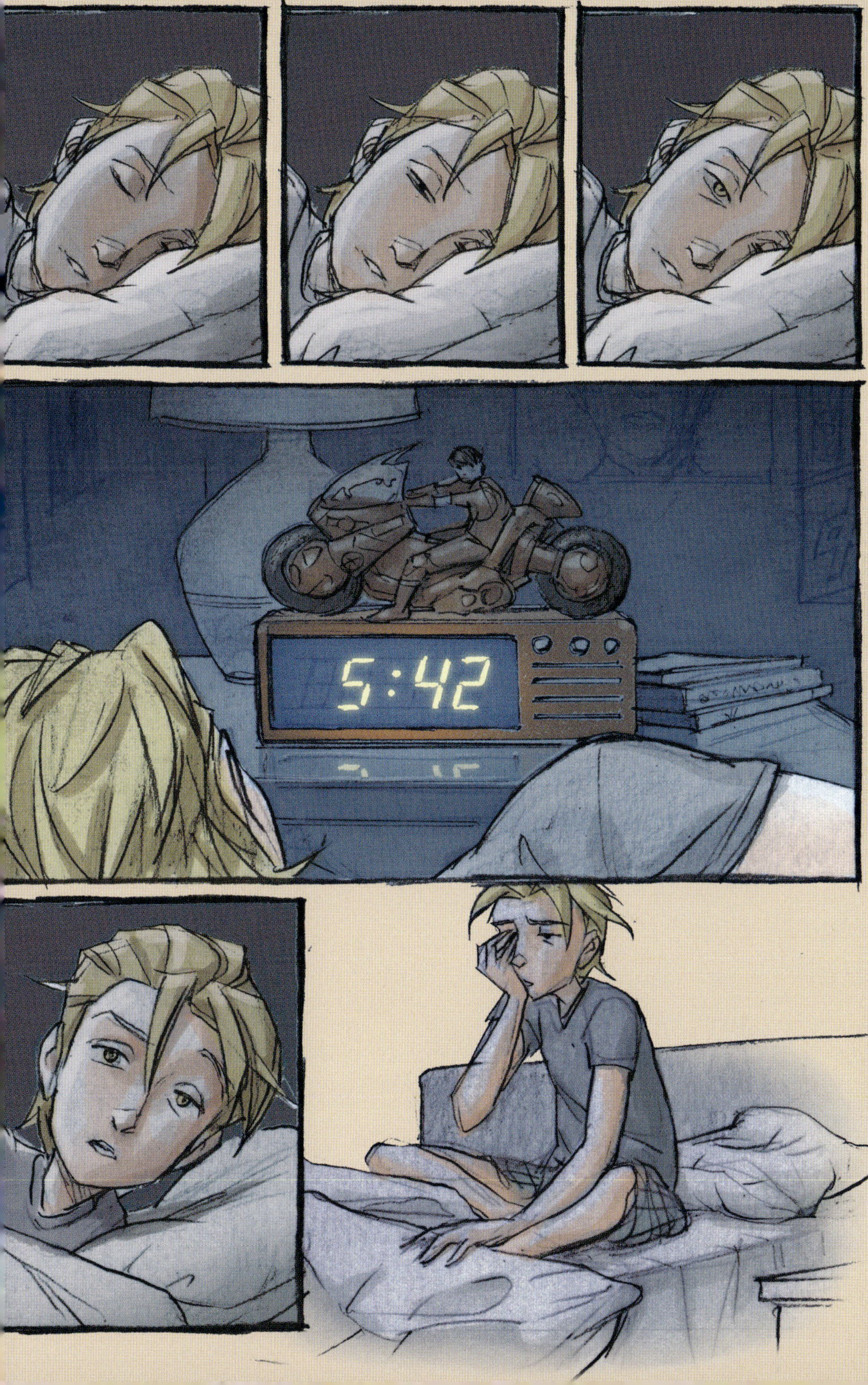
5:42

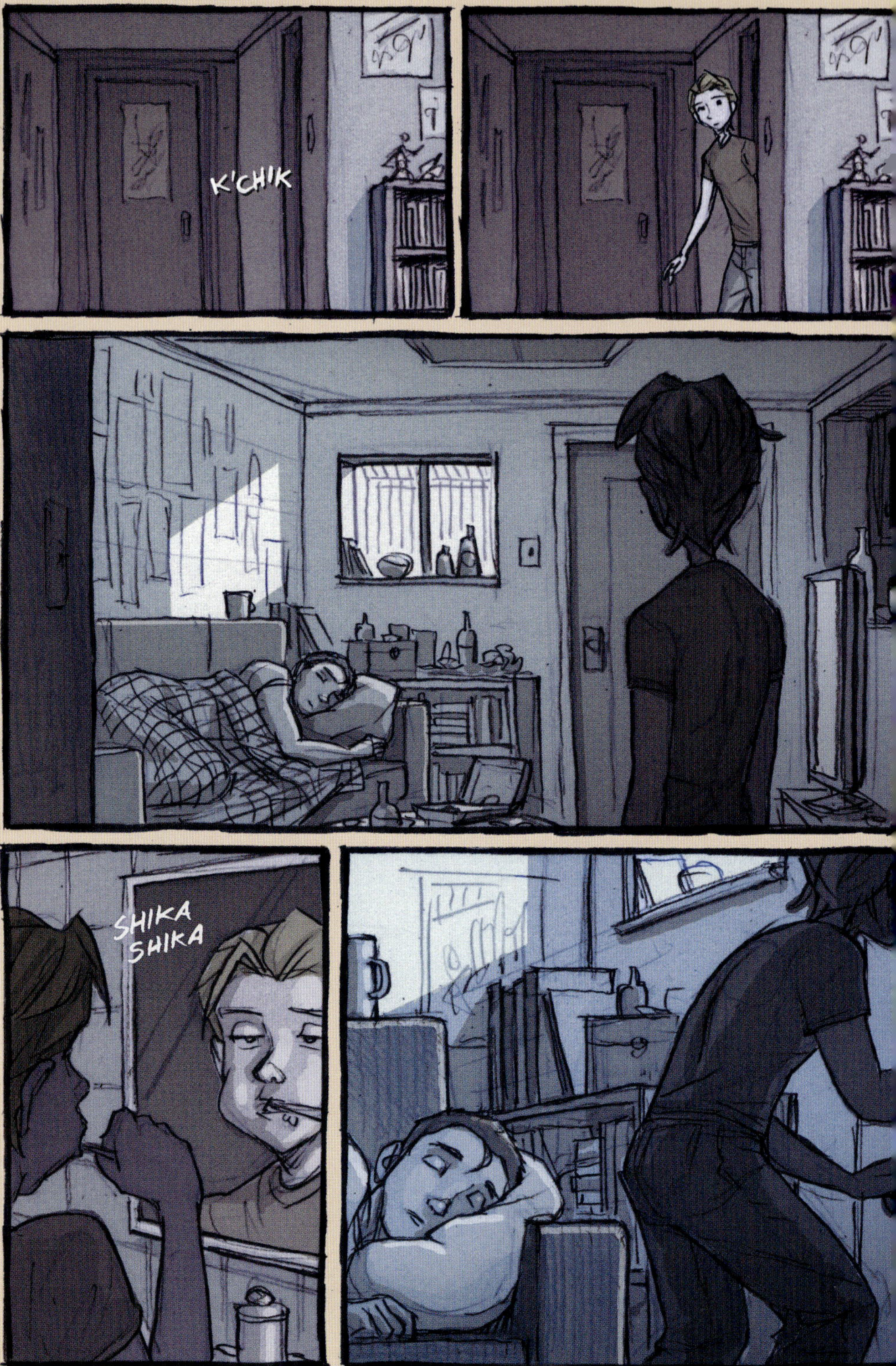
K'CHIK
SHIKA
SHIKA

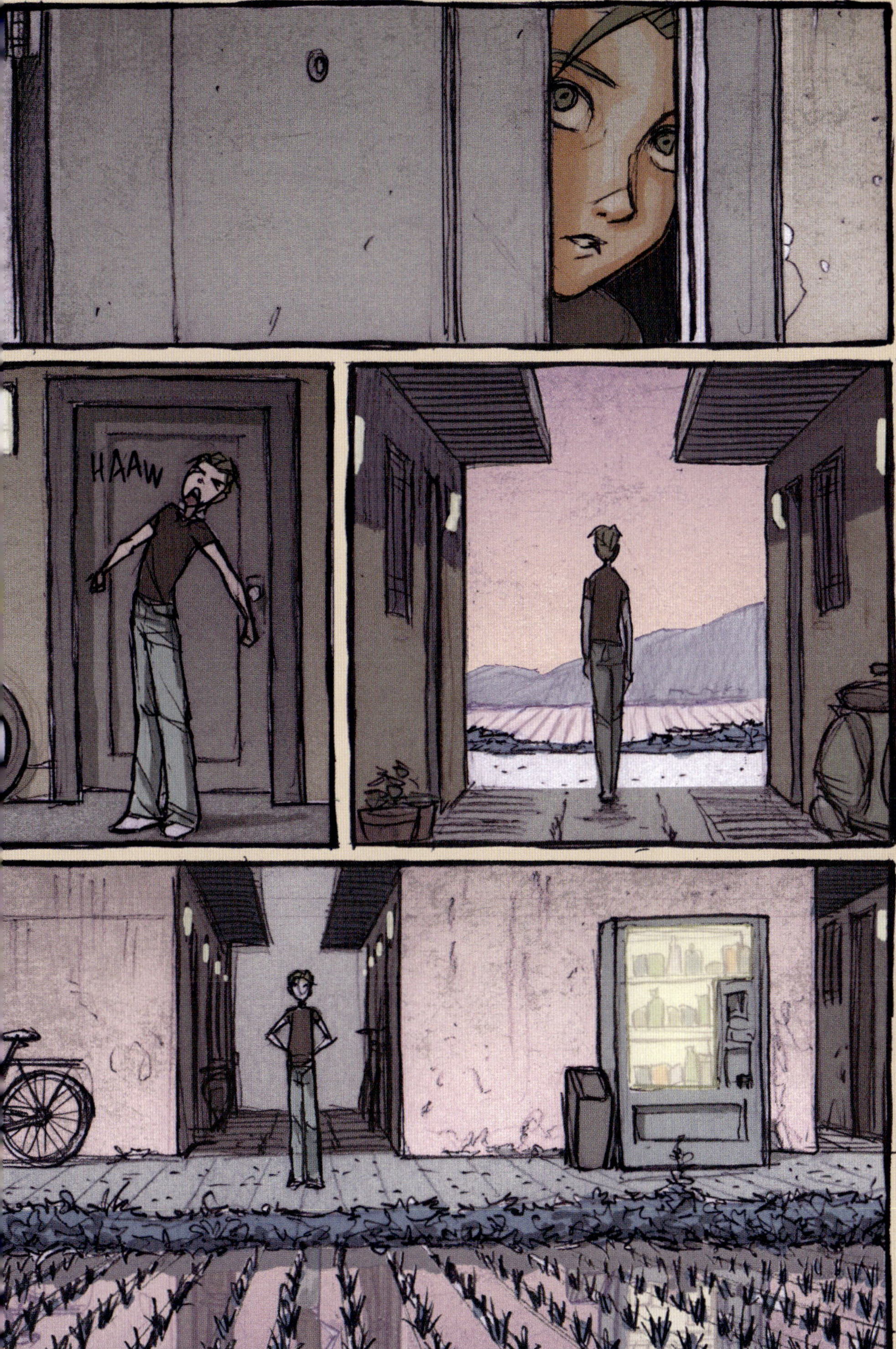
HAAW

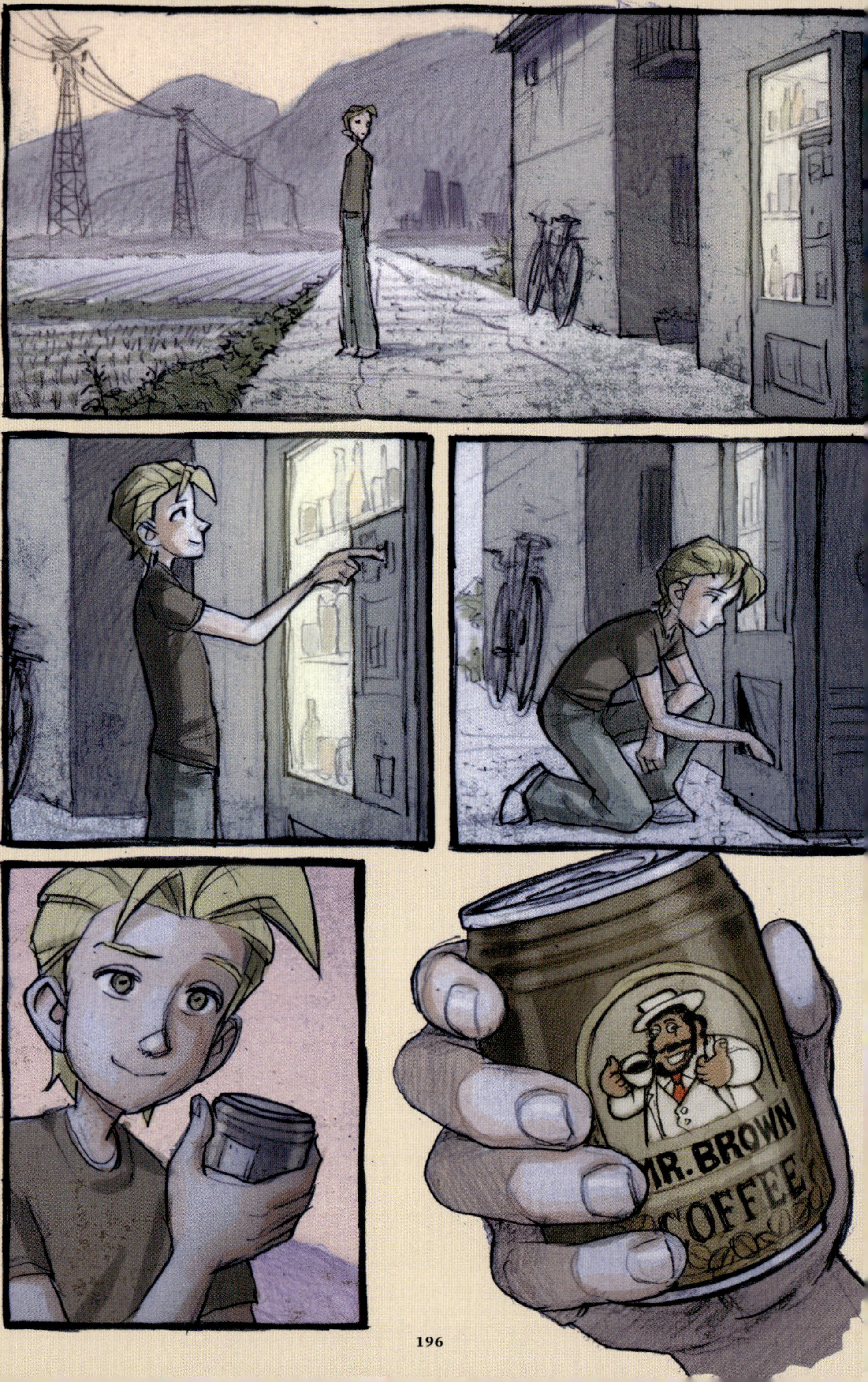
MR. BROWN
COFFEE

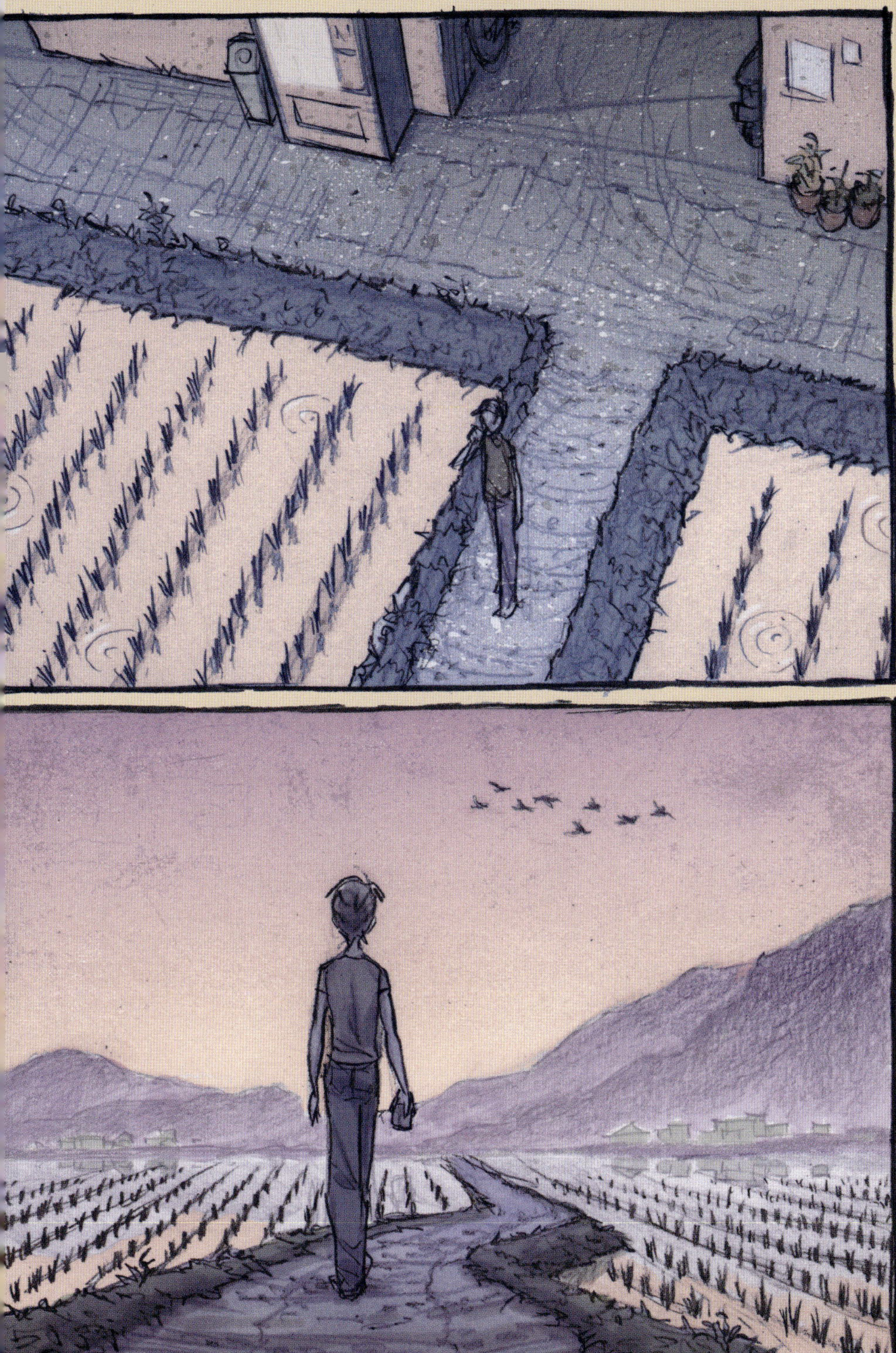

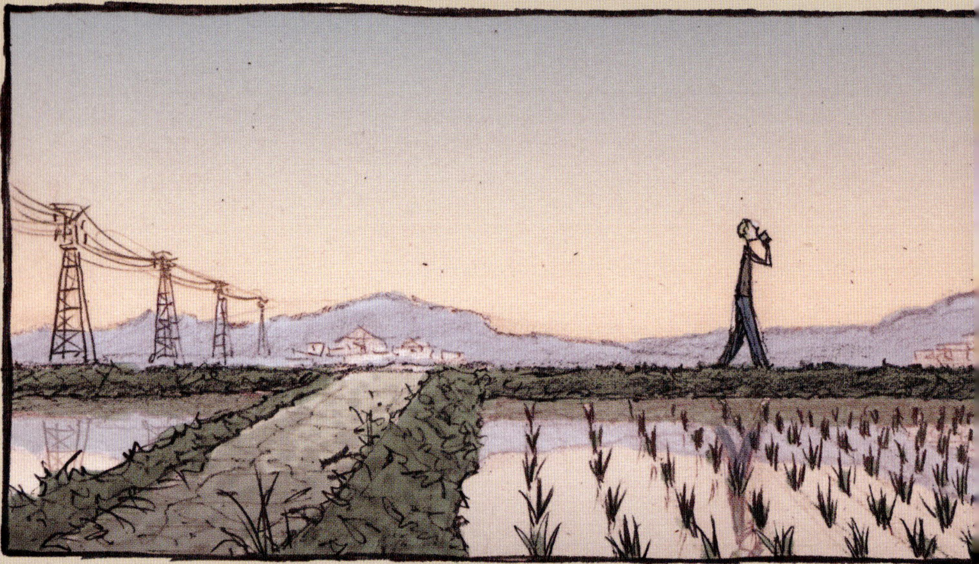

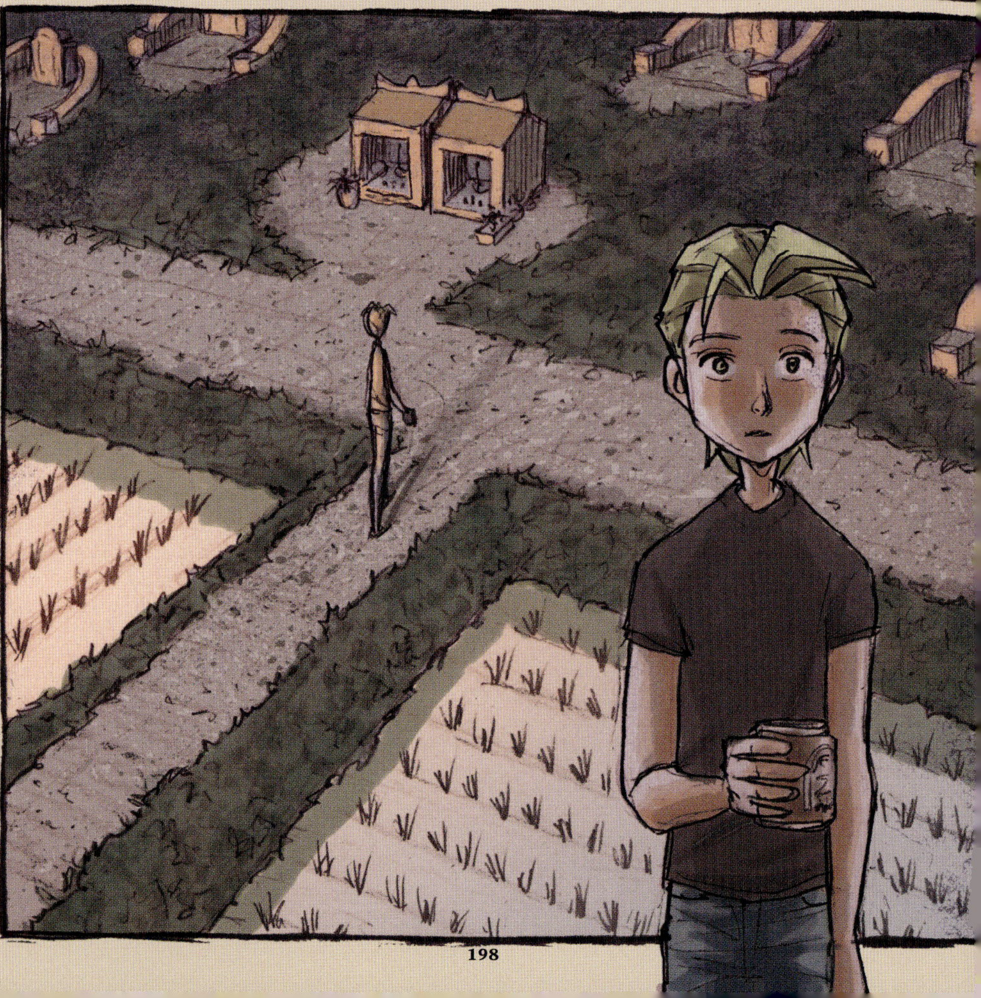

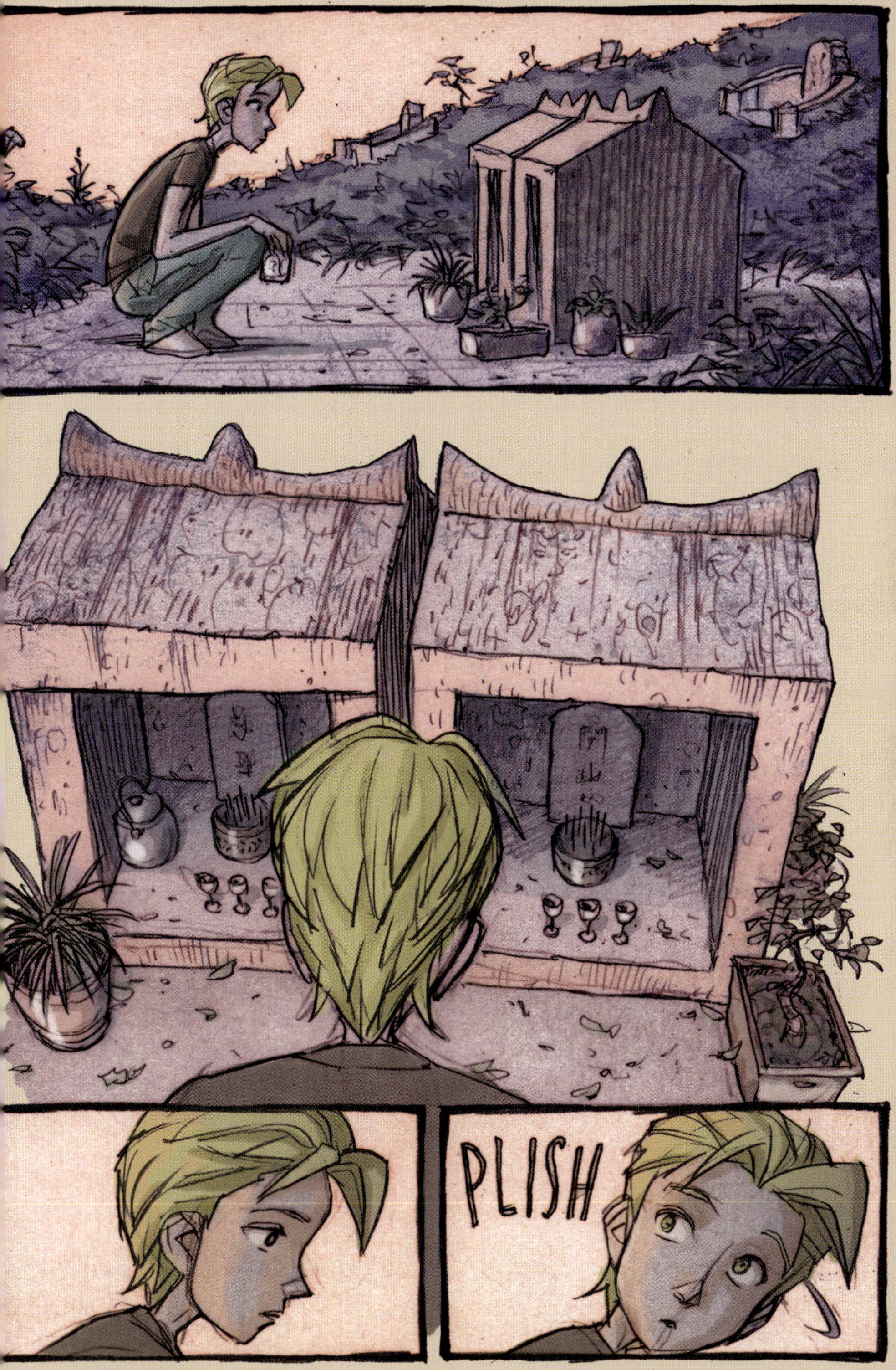
PLISH

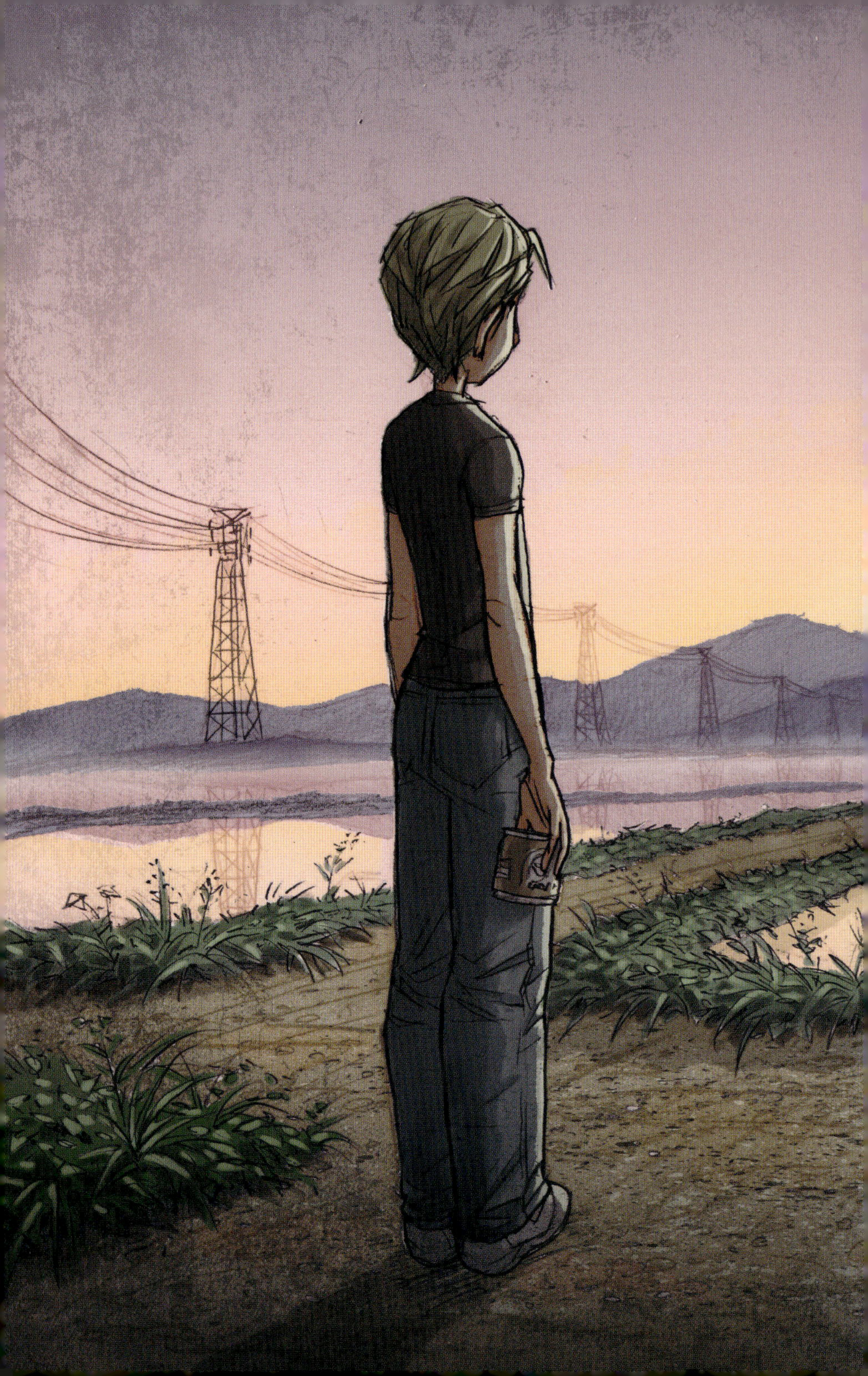

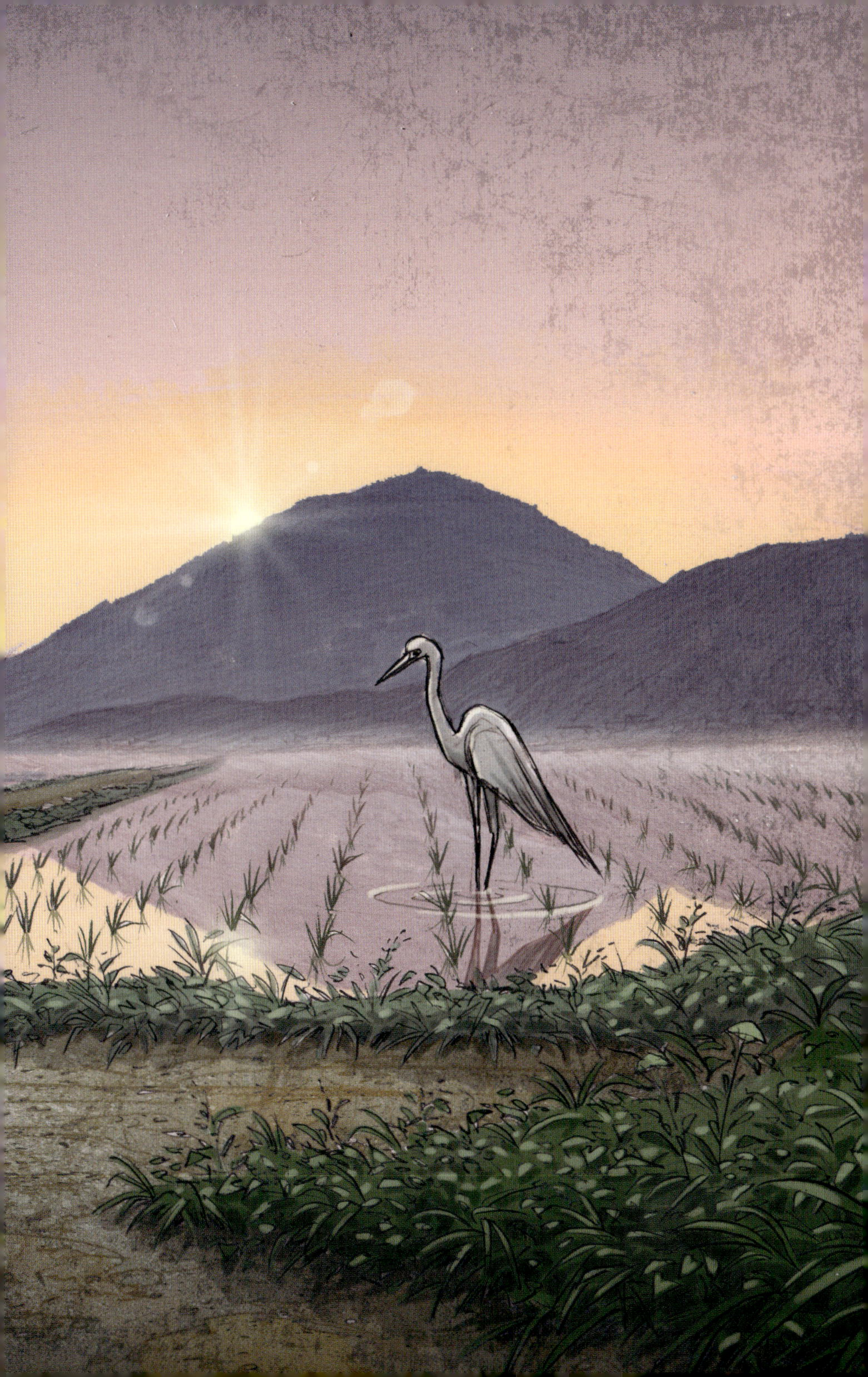

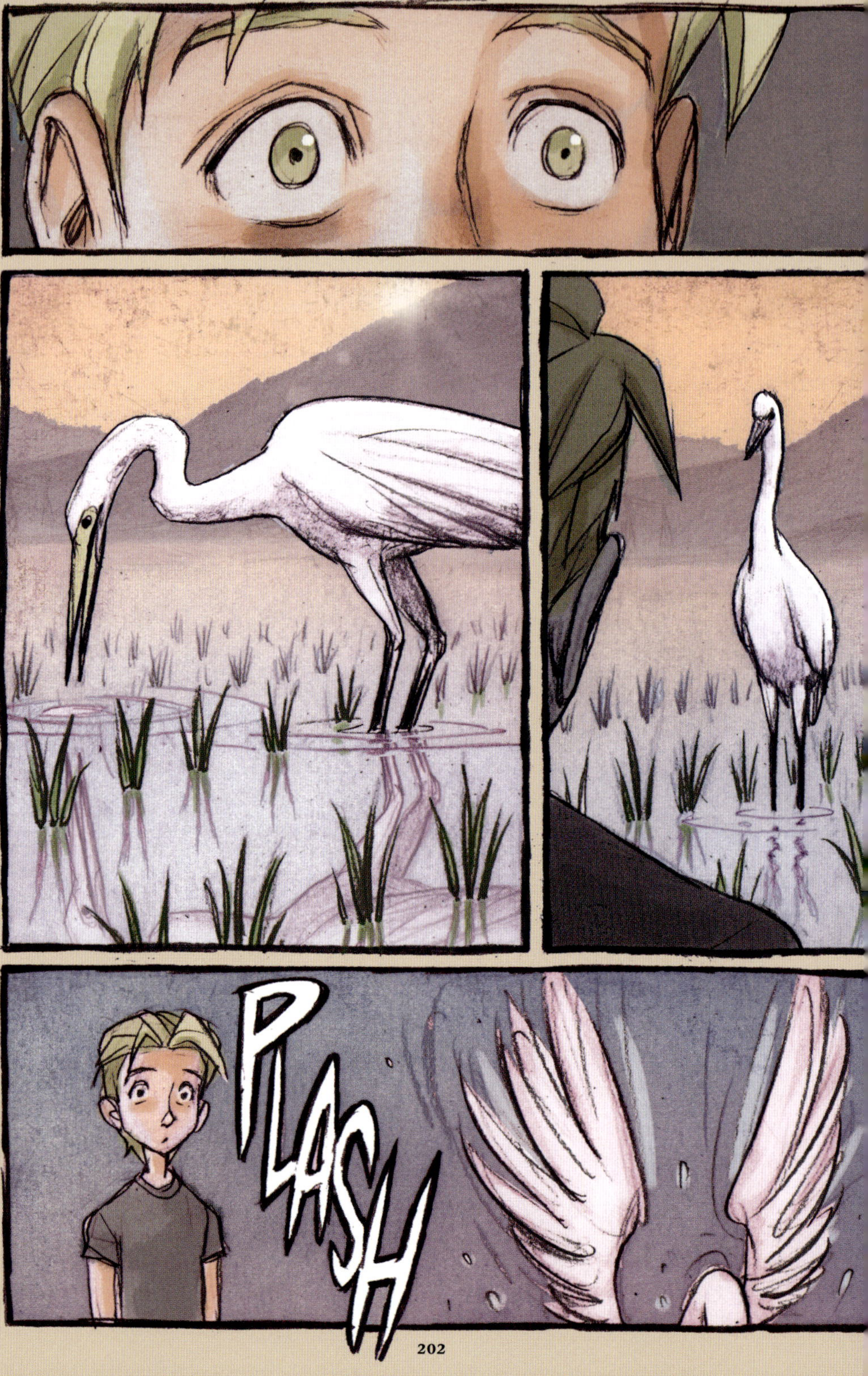
PLASH

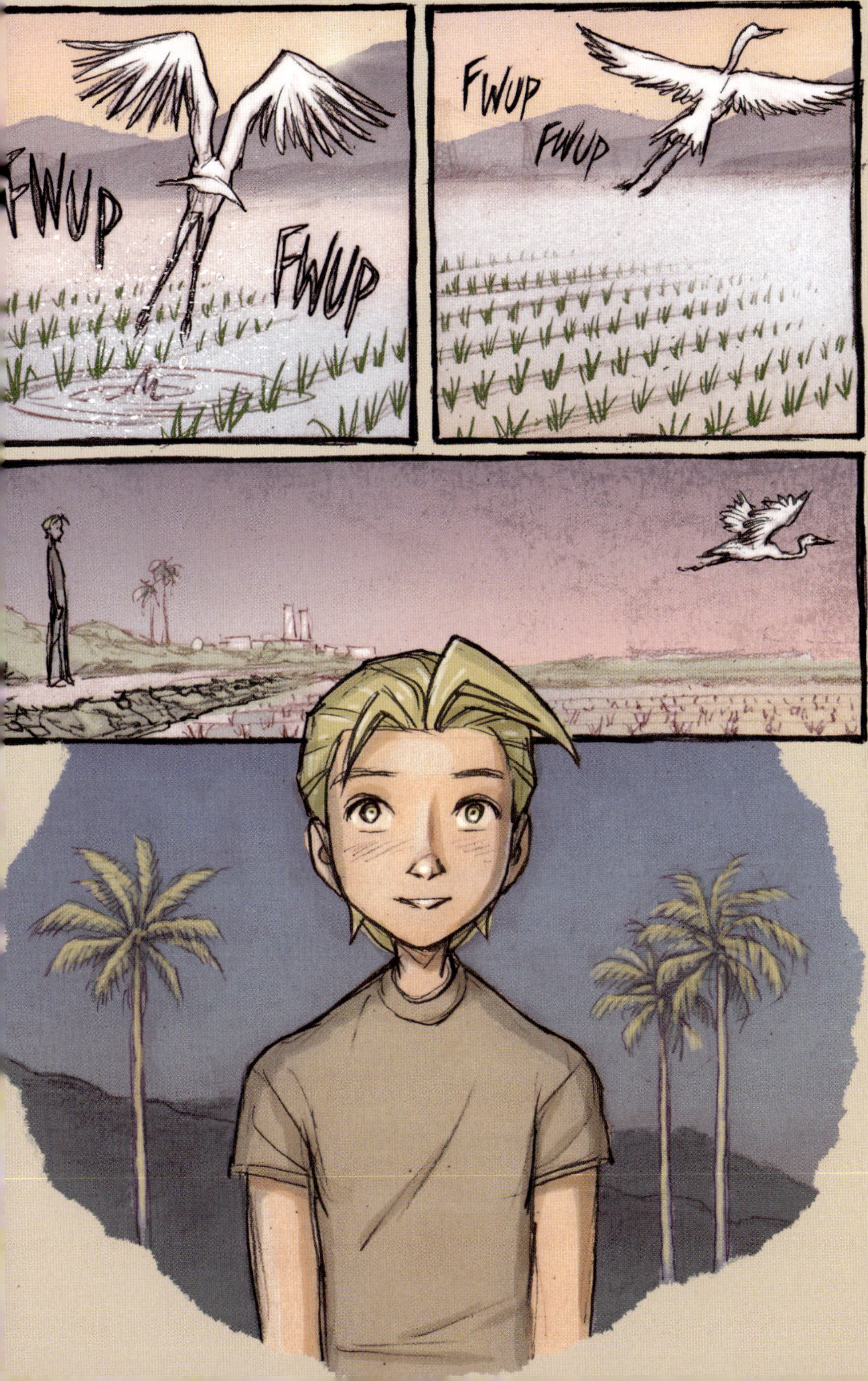
FWUP
FWUP
FWUP
FWUP

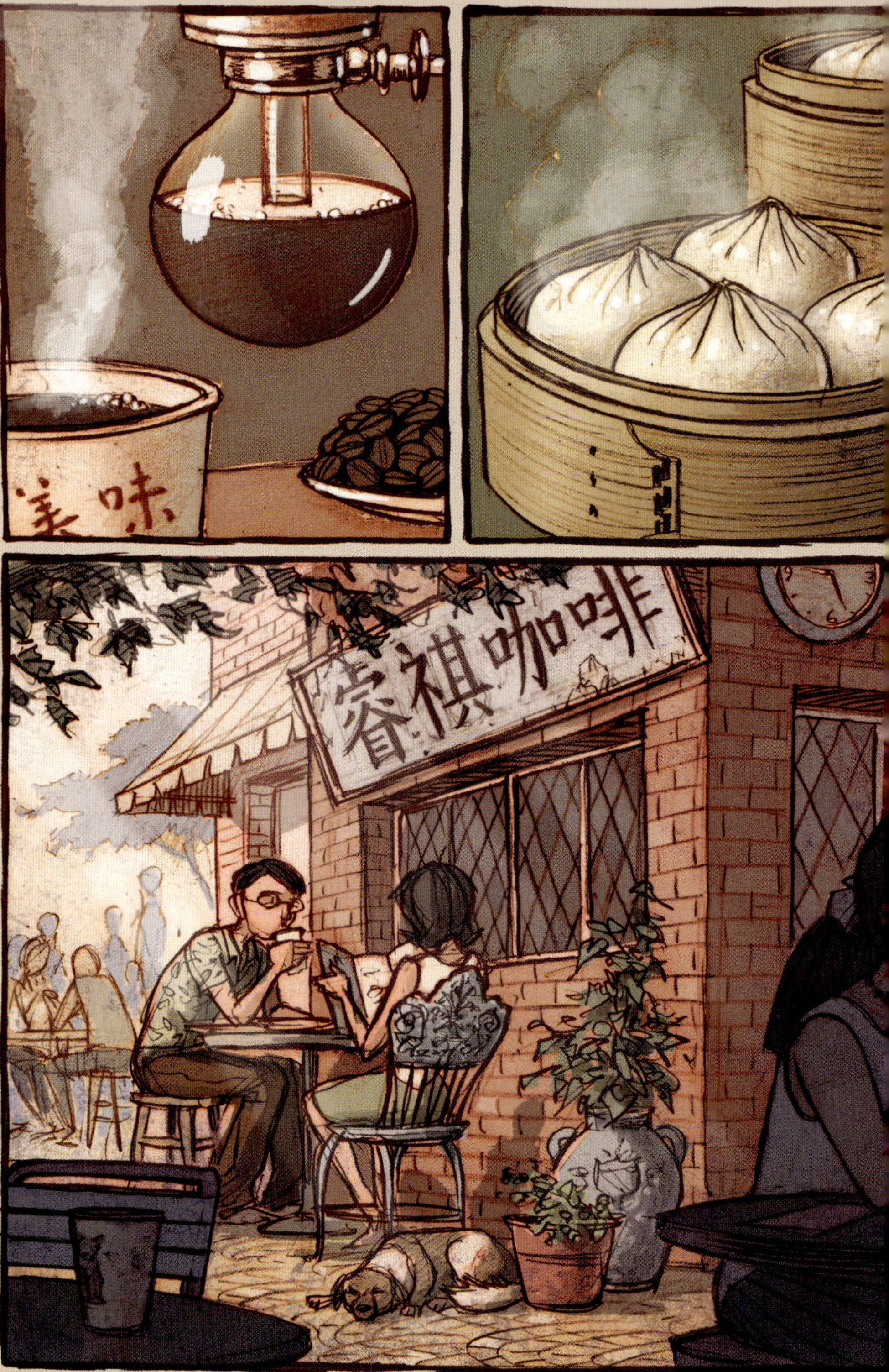
美味
睿祺咖啡

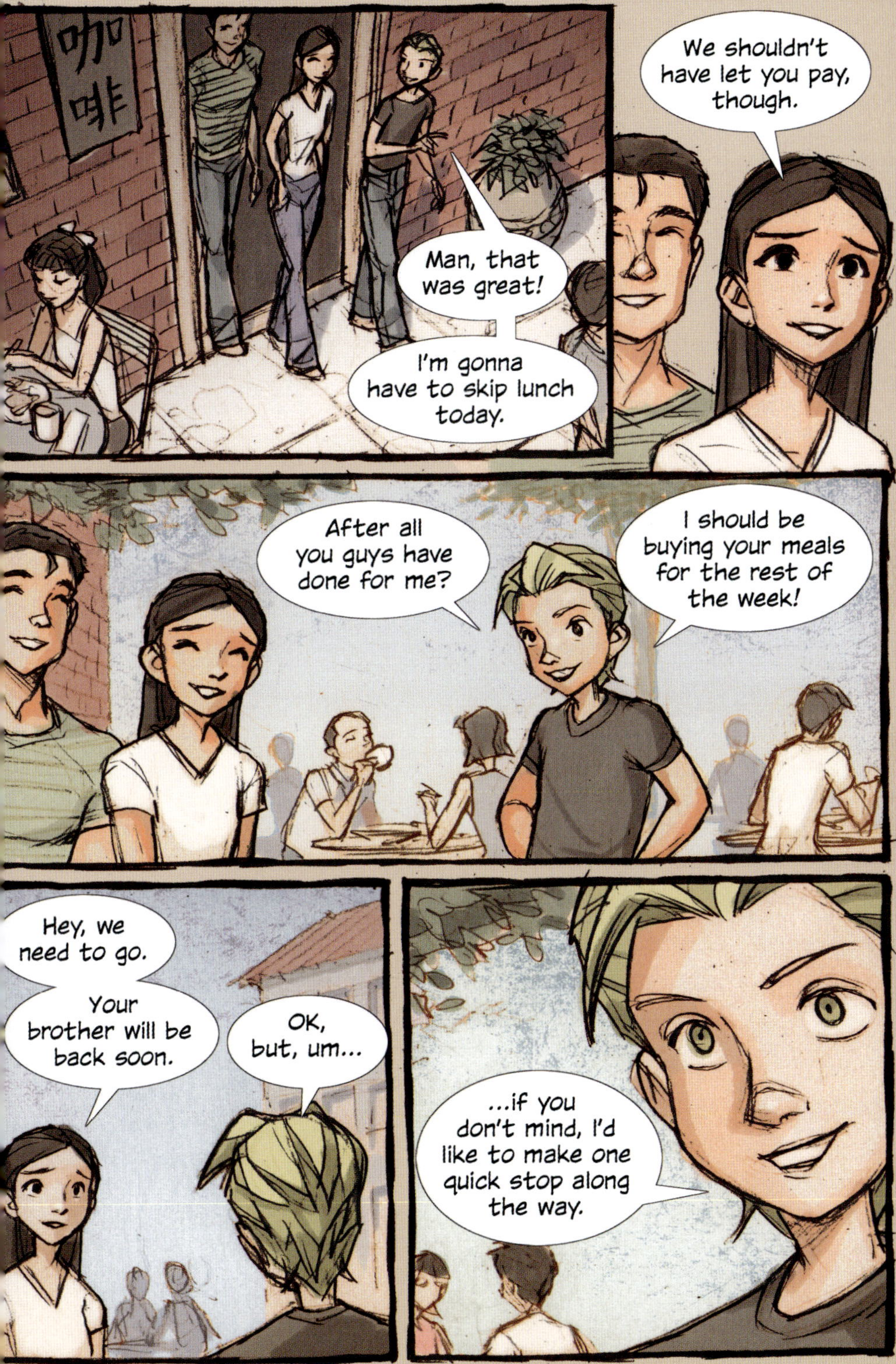
咖啡
Man, that was great!
I'm gonna have to skip lunch today.
We shouldn't have let you pay, though.
After all you guys have done for me?
I should be buying your meals for the rest of the week!
Hey, we need to go.
Your brother will be back soon.
OK, but, um...
...if you don't mind, I'd like to make one quick stop along the way.

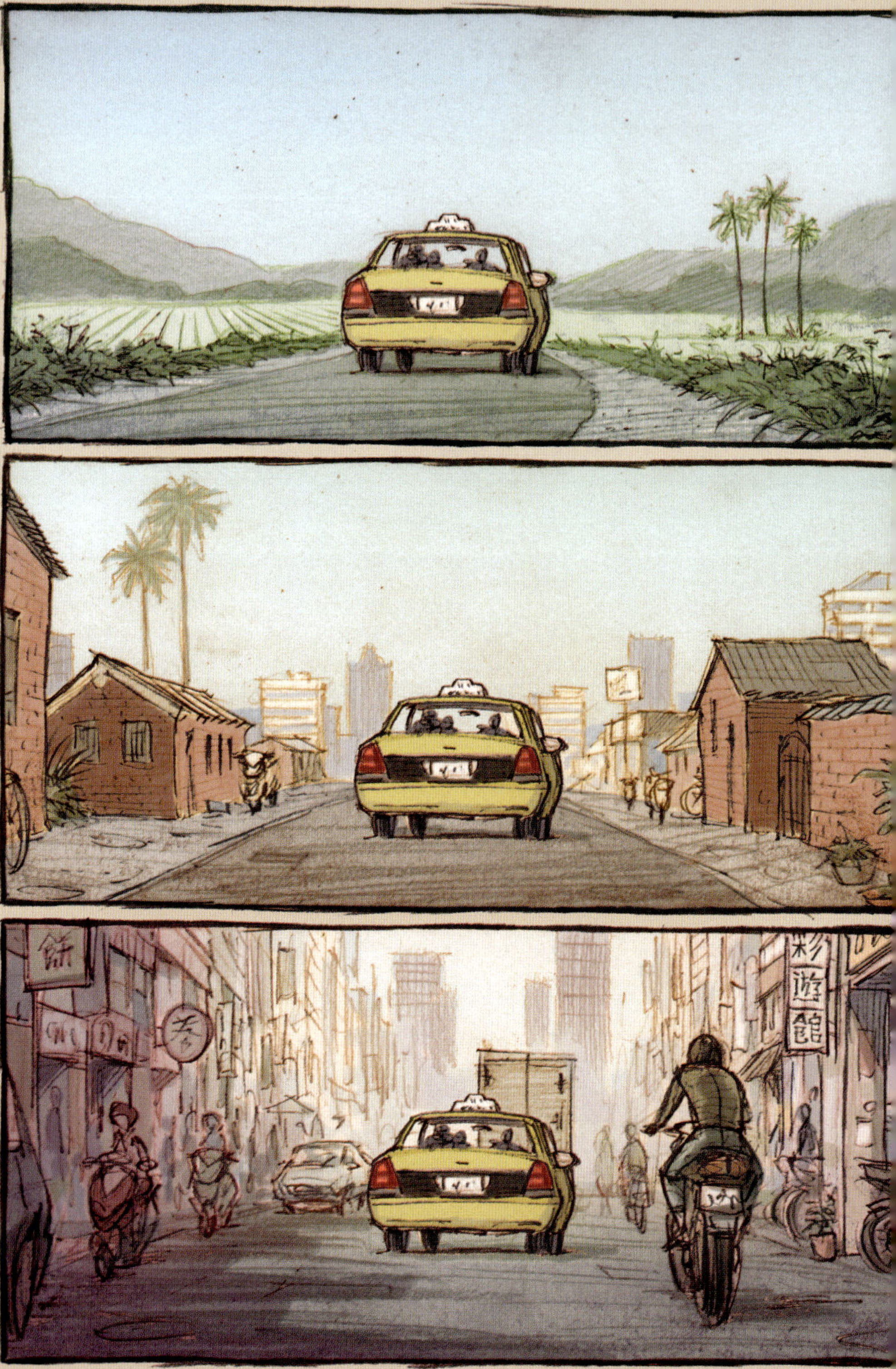
餅
彩遊館

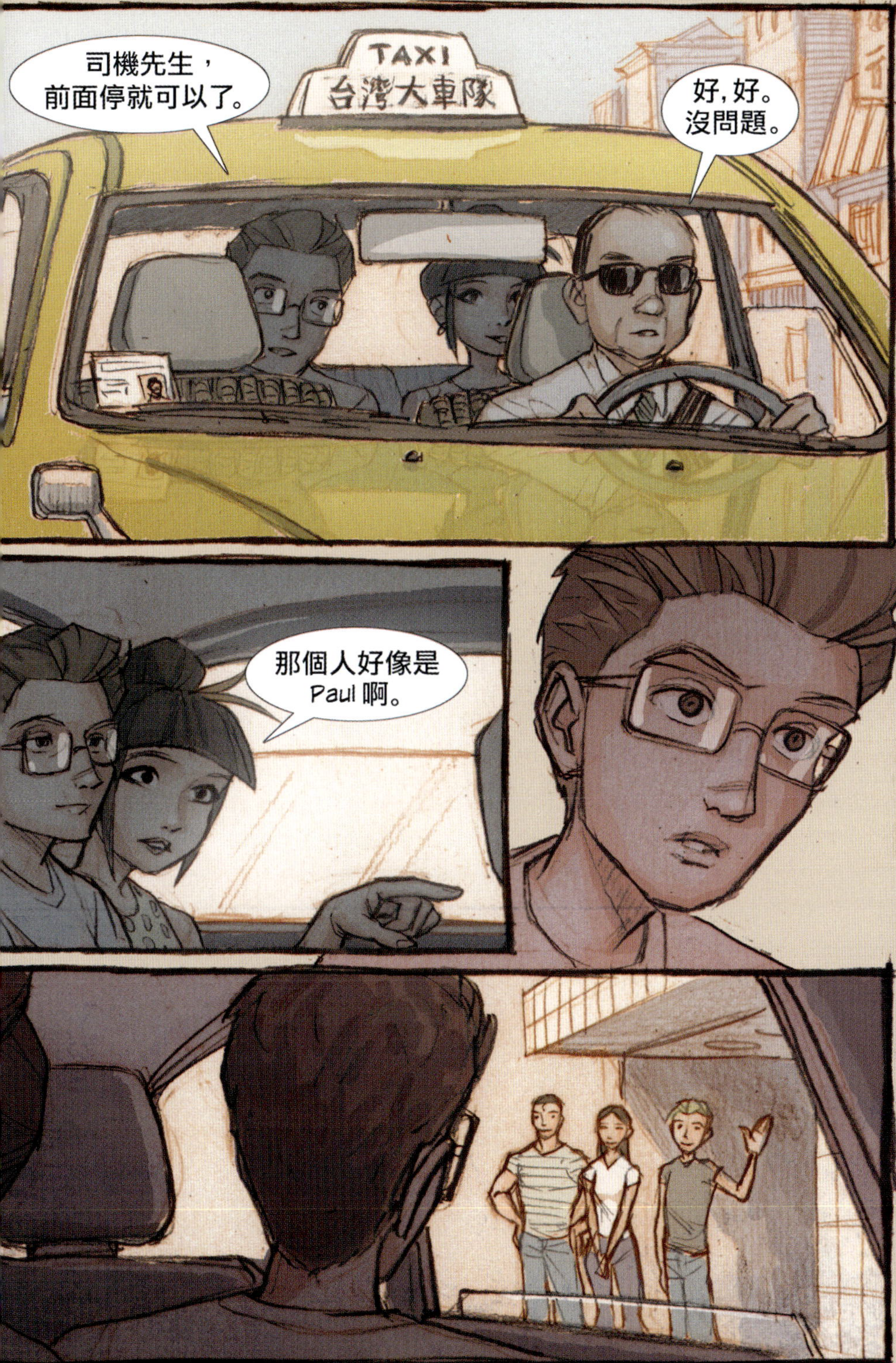
TAXI
台灣大車隊
司機先生，
前面停就可以了。
好, 好。
沒問題。
那個人好像是
Paul 啊。

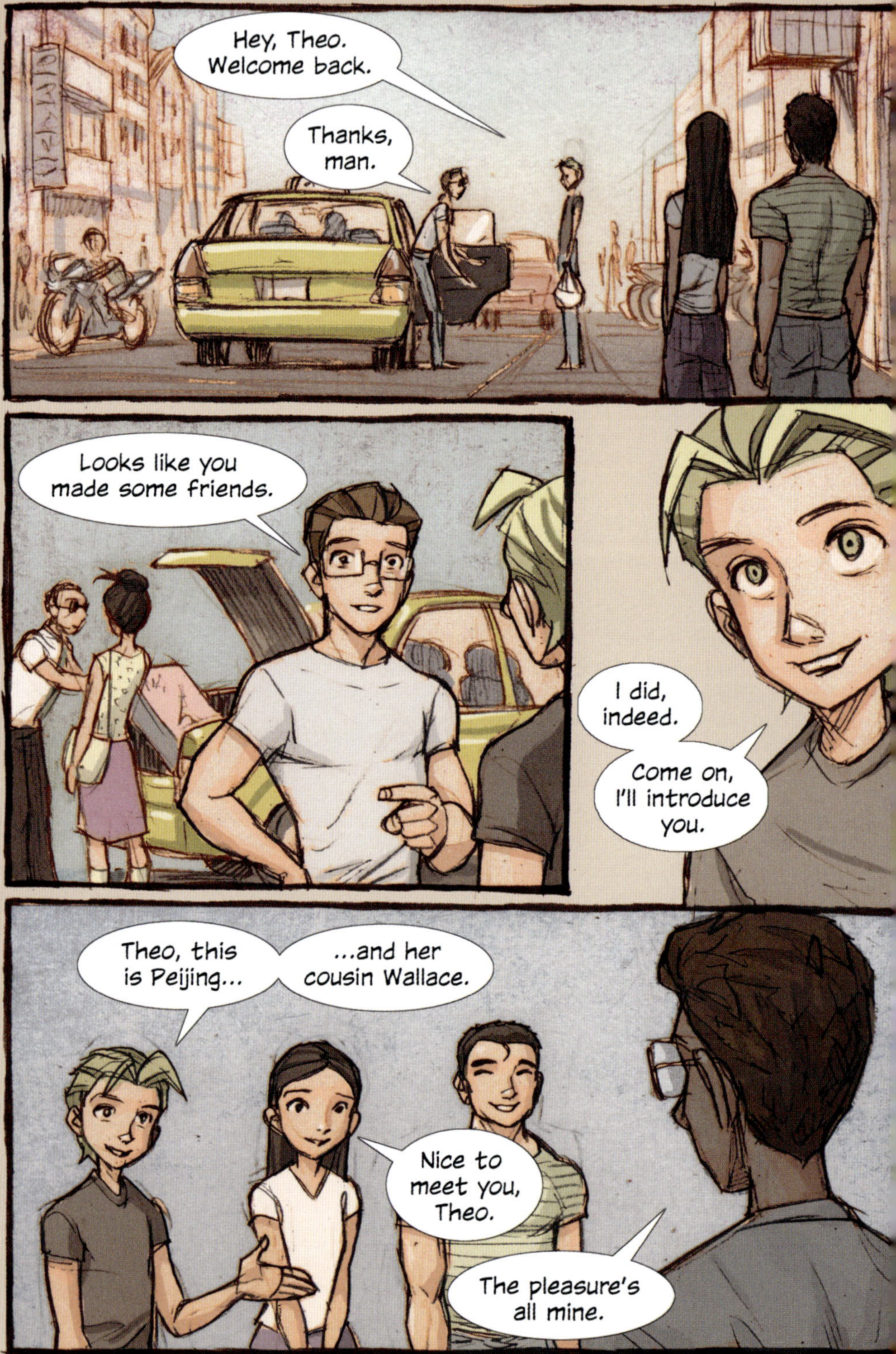
Hey, Theo. Welcome back.
Thanks, man.
Looks like you made some friends.
I did, indeed.
Come on, I'll introduce you.
Theo, this is Peijing...
...and her cousin Wallace.
Nice to meet you, Theo.
The pleasure's all mine.

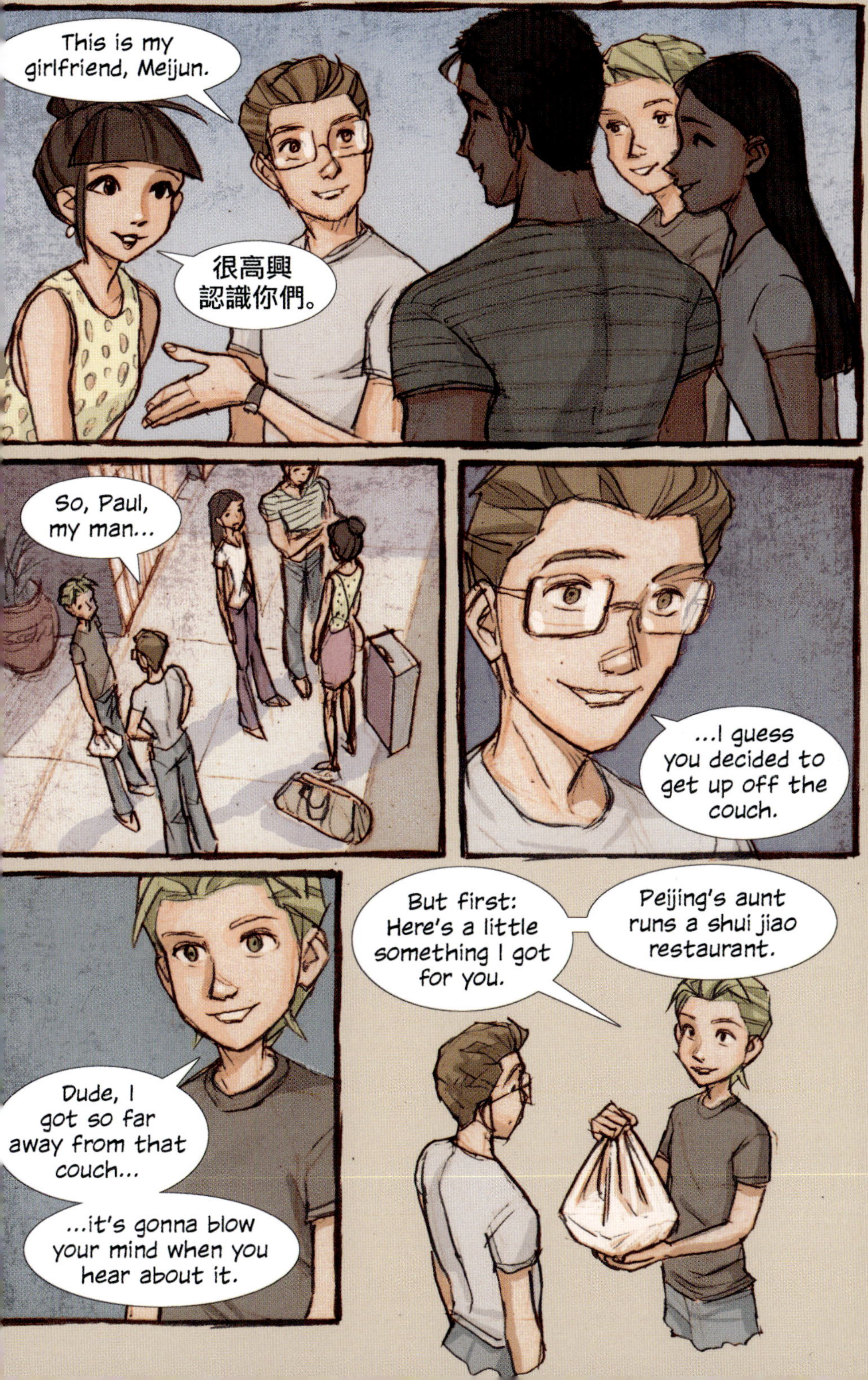

This is my girlfriend, Meijun.
很高興認識你們。
So, Paul, my man...
...I guess you decided to get up off the couch.
Dude, I got so far away from that couch...
...it's gonna blow your mind when you hear about it.
But first: Here's a little something I got for you.
Peijing's aunt runs a shui jiao restaurant.

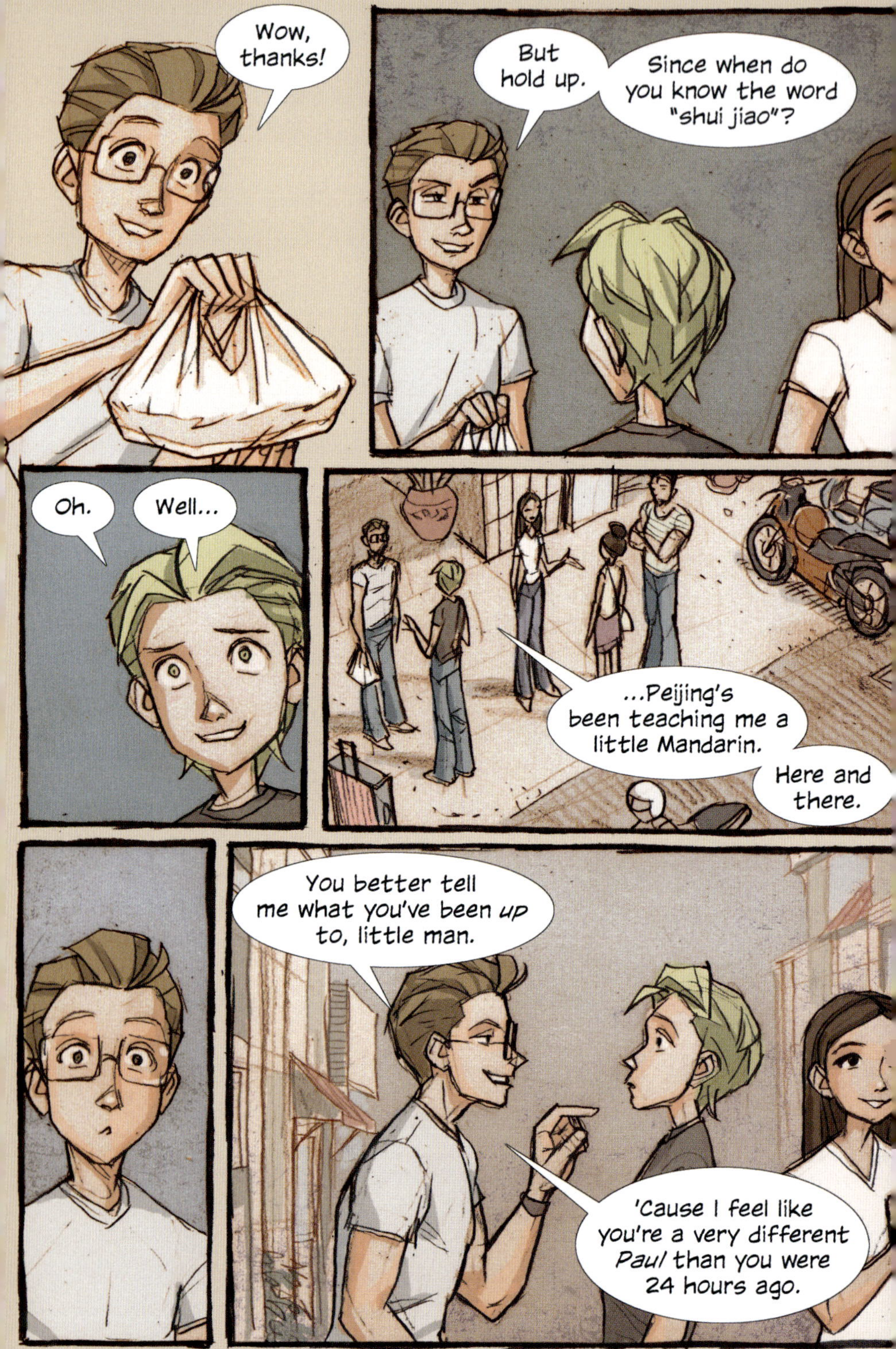
Wow, thanks!
But hold up.
Since when do you know the word "shui jiao"?
Oh.
Well...
...Peijing's been teaching me a little Mandarin.
Here and there.
You better tell me what you've been *up* to, little man.
'Cause I feel like you're a very different *Paul* than you were 24 hours ago.

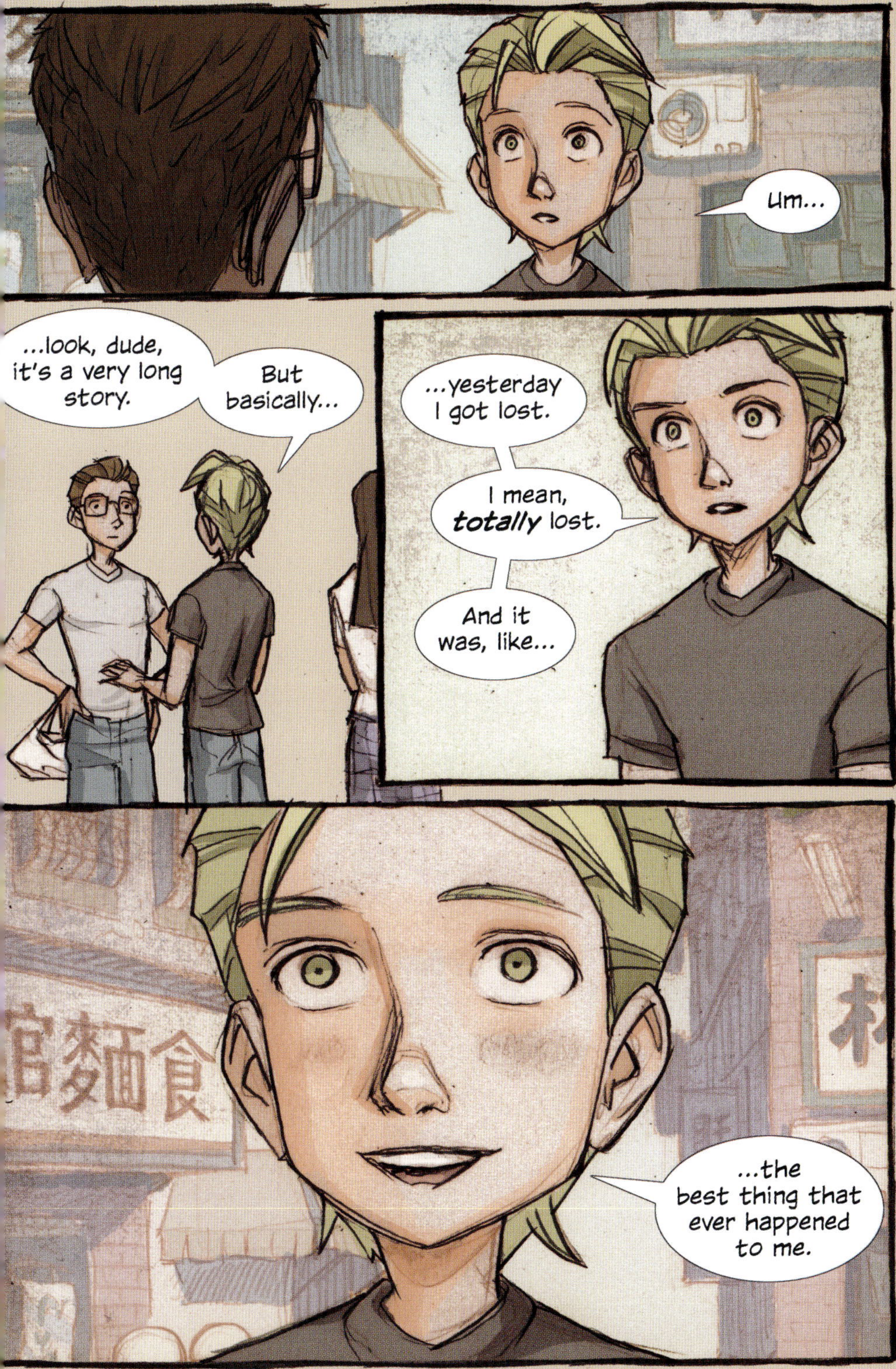
Um...
...look, dude, it's a very long story.
But basically...
...yesterday I got lost.
I mean, *totally* lost.
And it was, like...
...the best thing that ever happened to me.

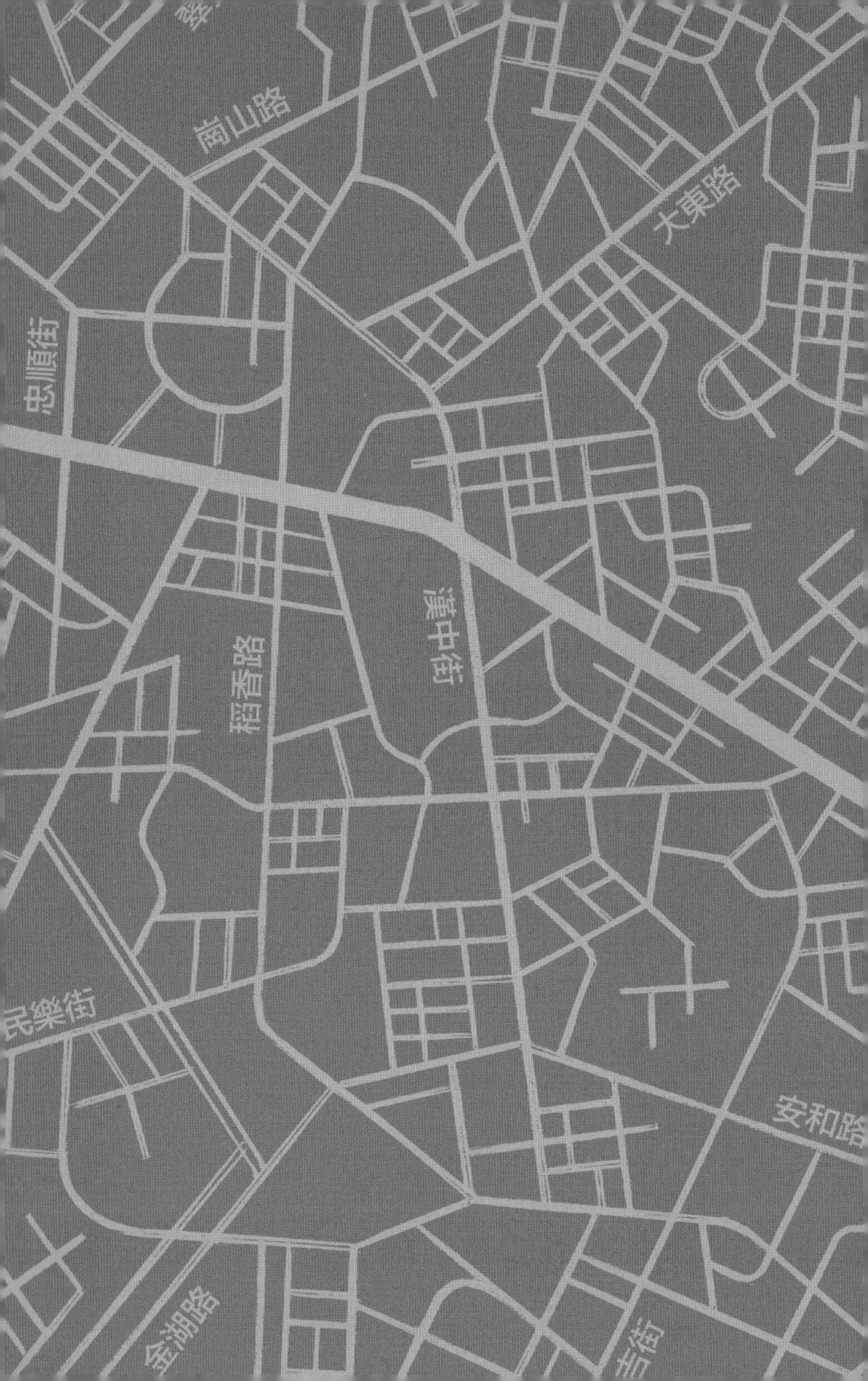
崗山路
大東路
忠順街
稻香路
漢中街
民樂街
安和路
金湖路

CHAPTER 5

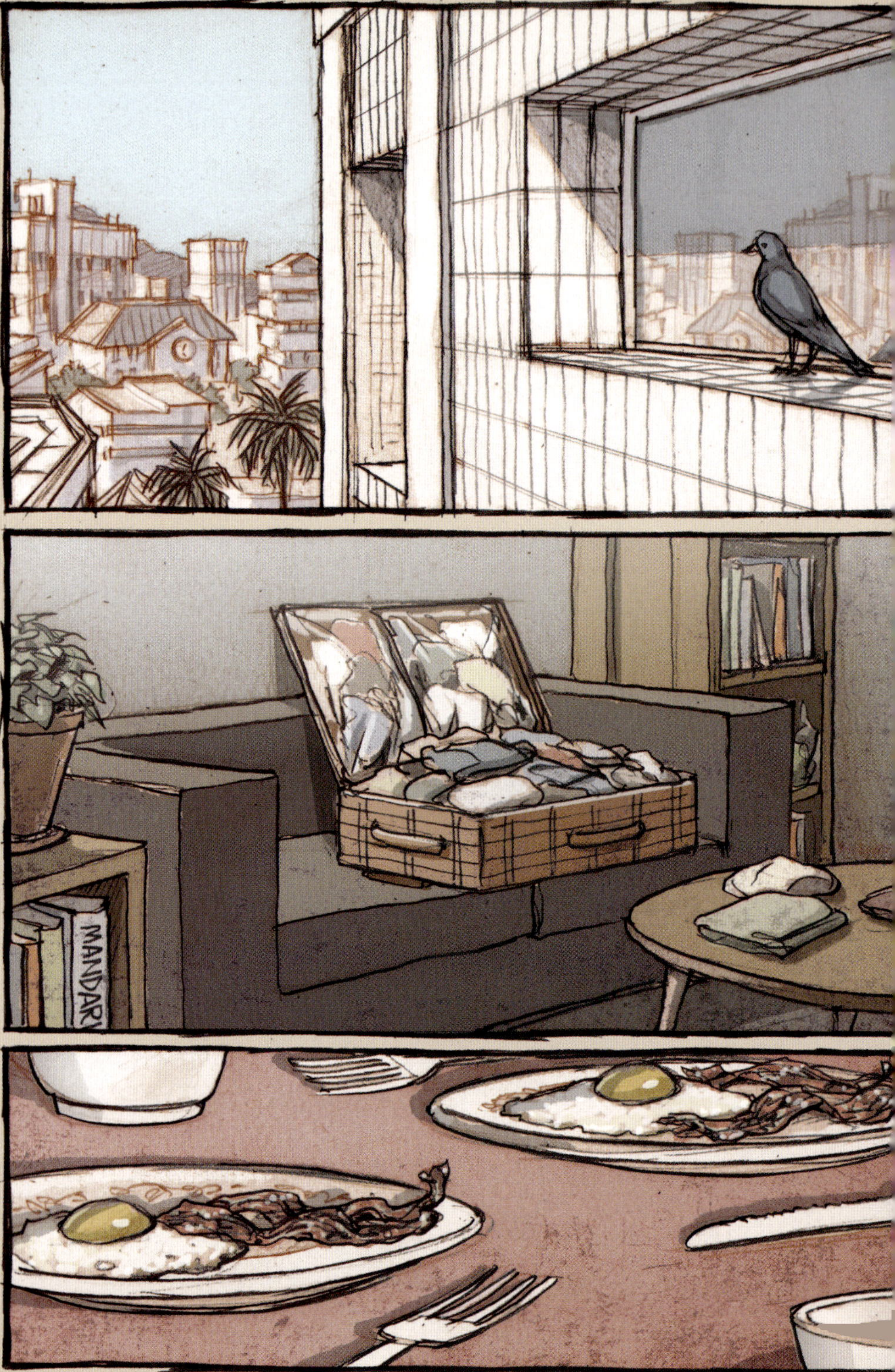

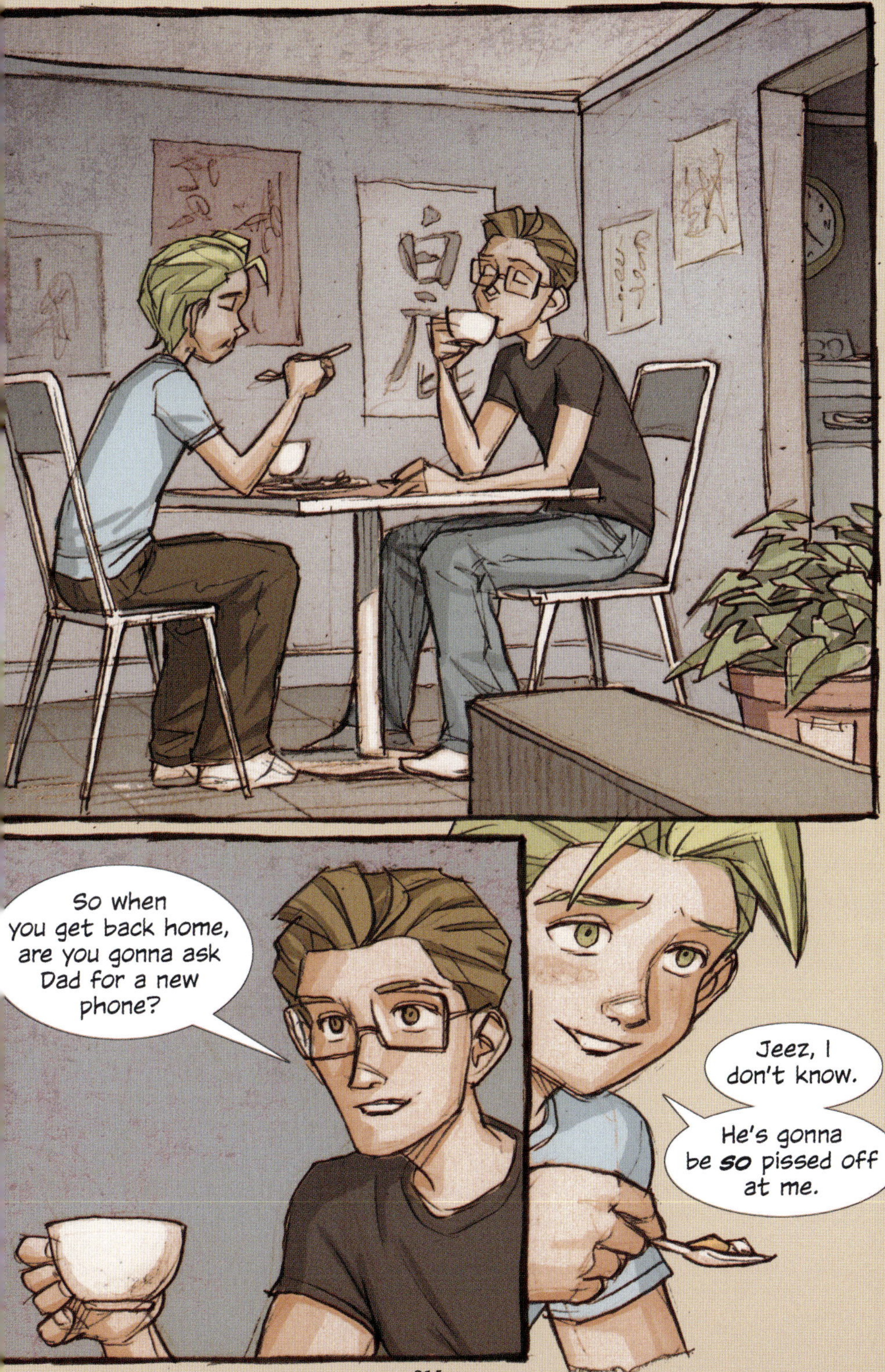
So when you get back home, are you gonna ask Dad for a new phone?
Jeez, I don't know.
He's gonna be *so* pissed off at me.

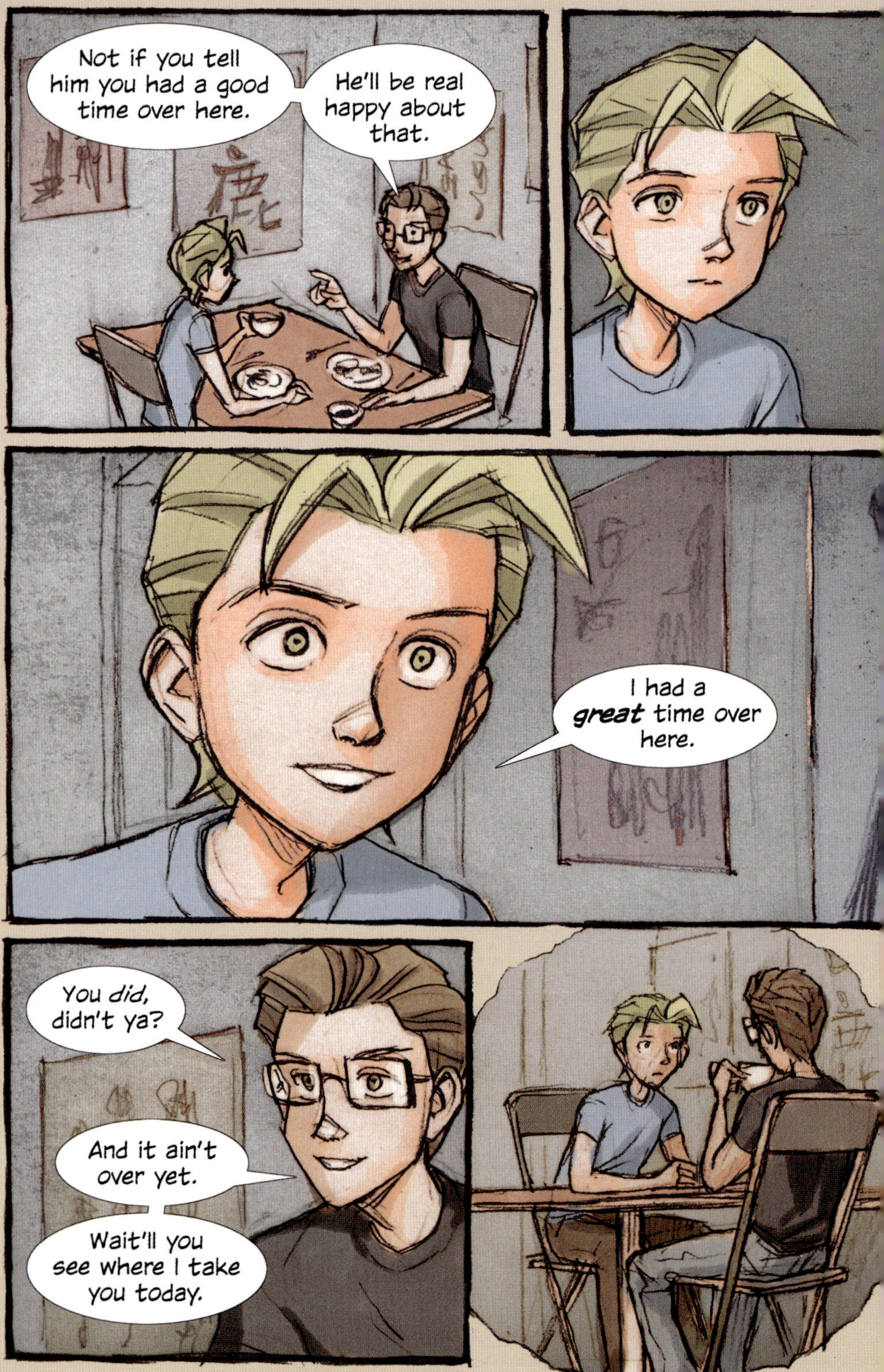
Not if you tell him you had a good time over here.
He'll be real happy about that.
I had a *great* time over here.
You *did,* didn't ya?
And it ain't over yet.
Wait'll you see where I take you today.

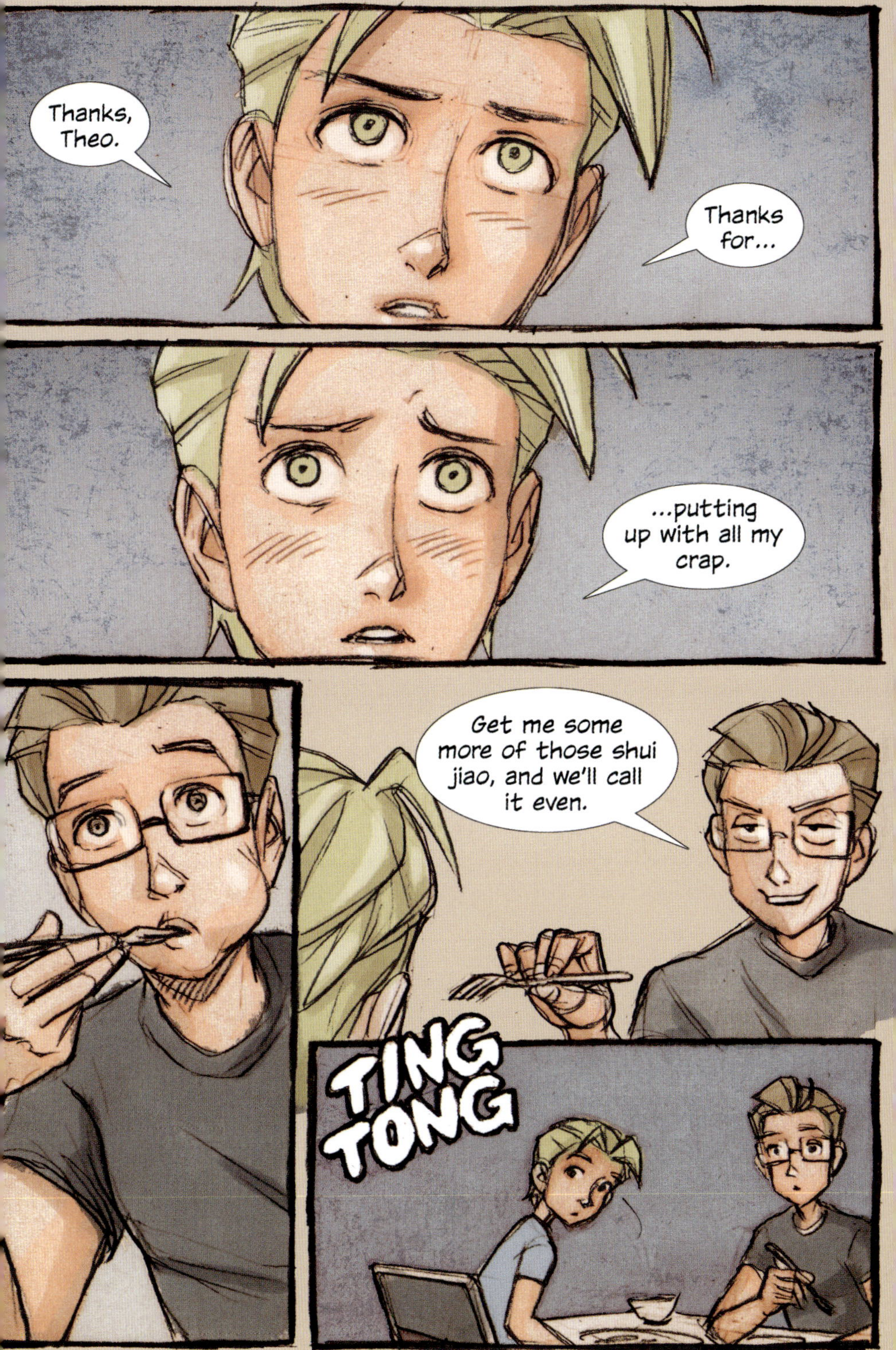

Thanks, Theo.
Thanks for...
...putting up with all my crap.
Get me some more of those shui jiao, and we'll call it even.
TING TONG

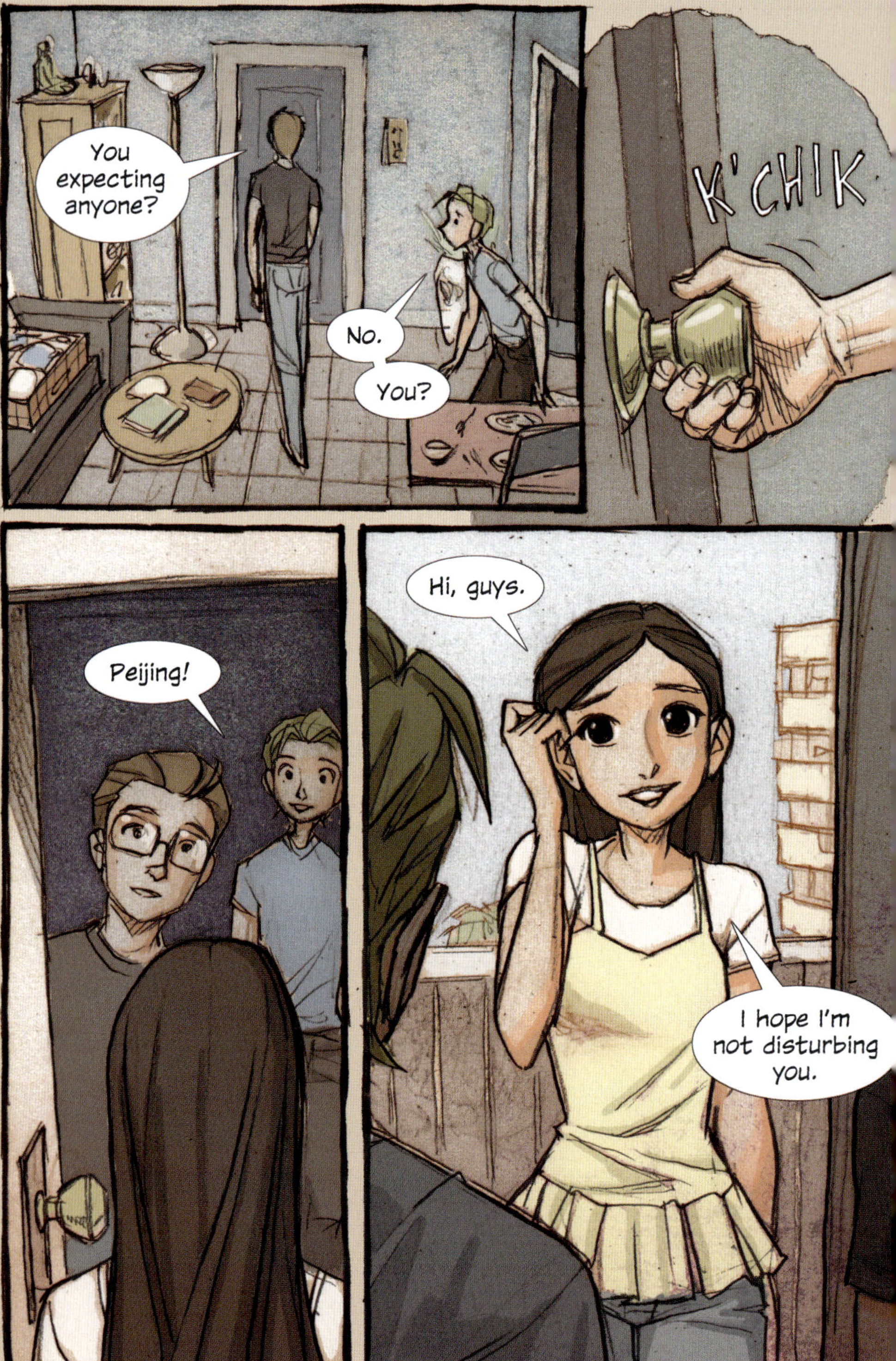
You expecting anyone?
No.
You?
K'CHIK
Peijing!
Hi, guys.
I hope I'm not disturbing you.

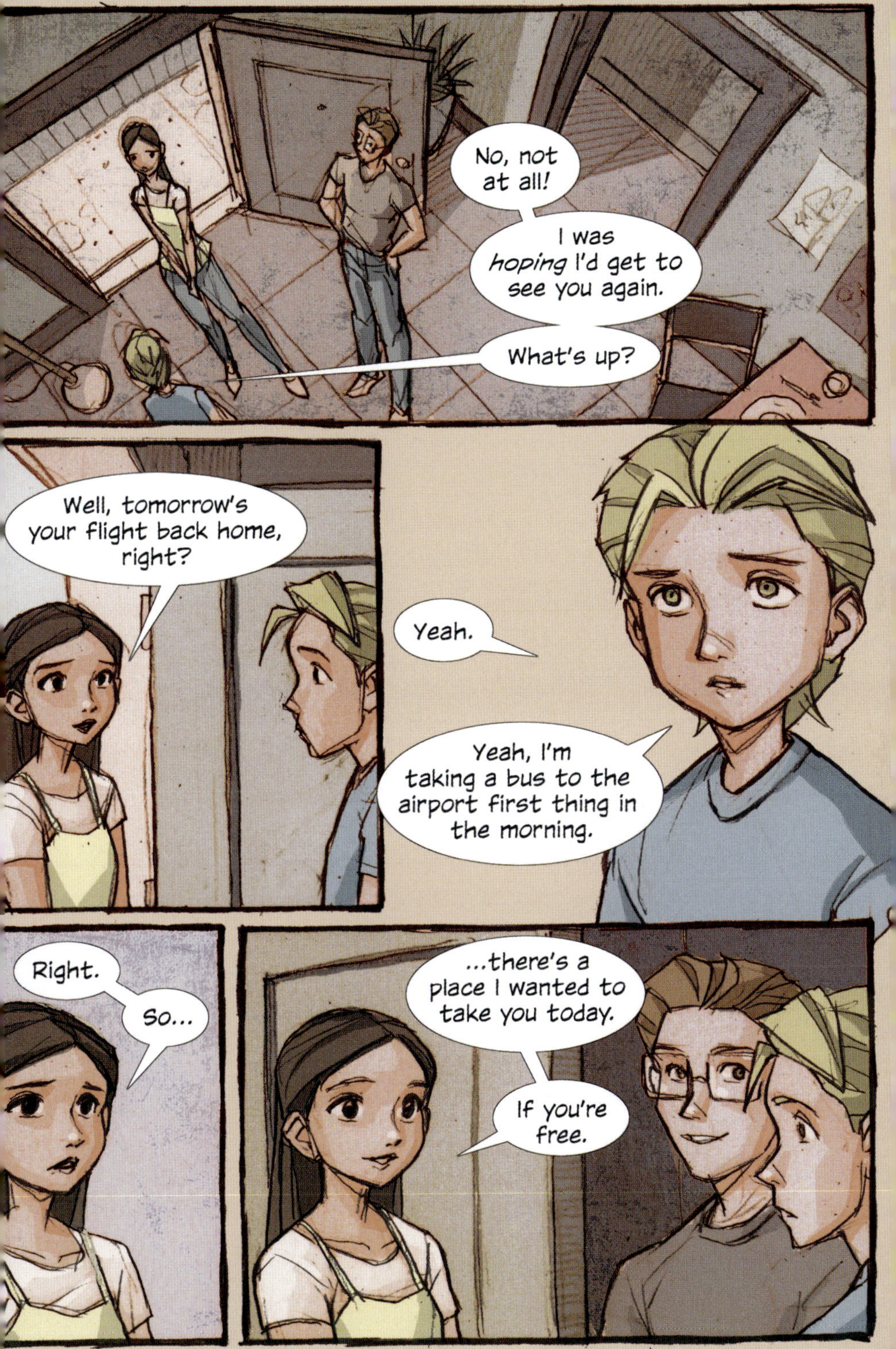
No, not at all!
I was *hoping* I'd get to see you again.
What's up?
Well, tomorrow's your flight back home, right?
Yeah.
Yeah, I'm taking a bus to the airport first thing in the morning.
Right.
So...
...there's a place I wanted to take you today.
If you're free.

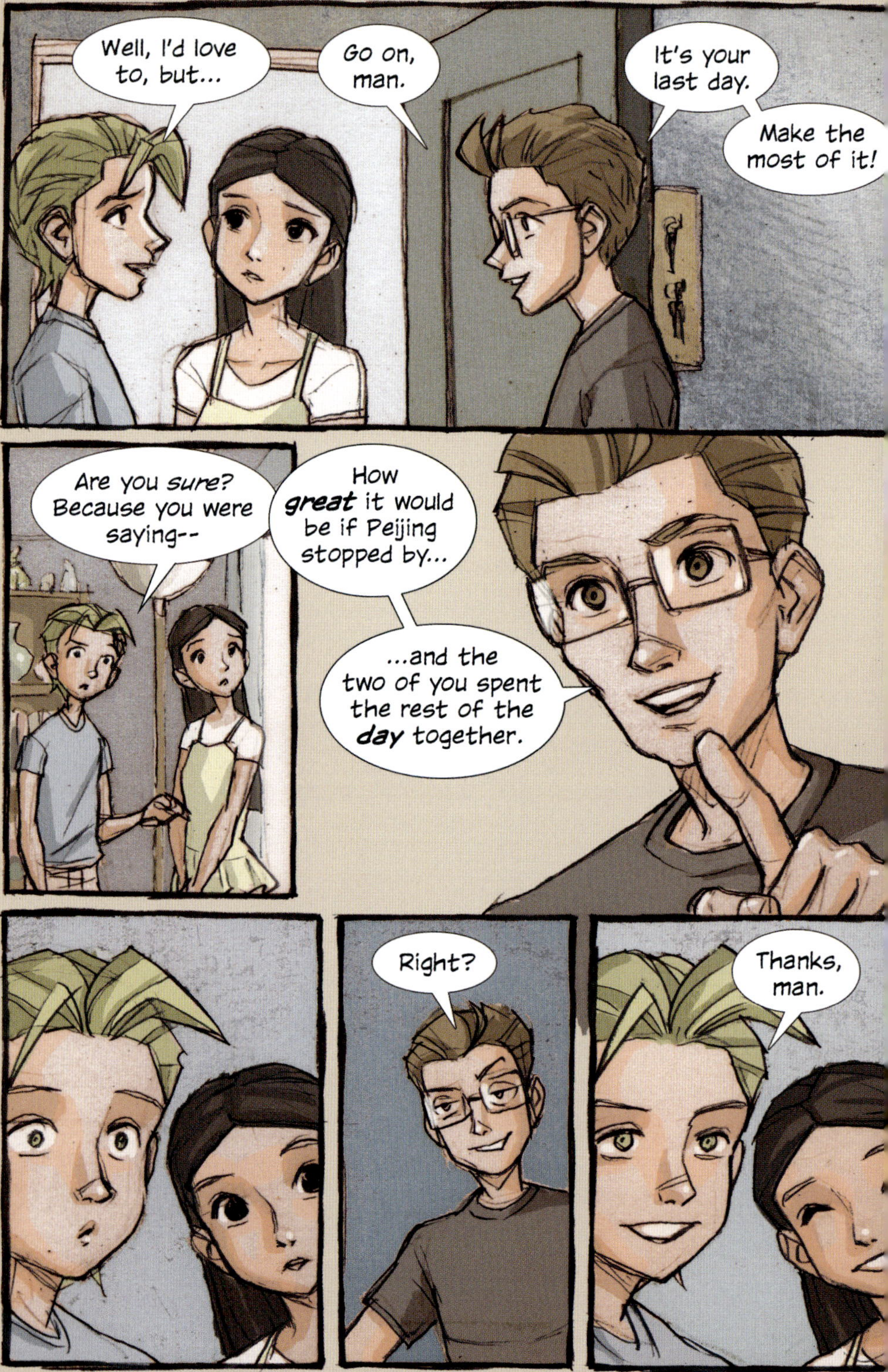
Well, I'd love to, but...
Go on, man.
It's your last day.
Make the most of it!
Are you *sure*? Because you were saying--
How ***great*** it would be if Peijing stopped by...
...and the two of you spent the rest of the ***day*** together.
Right?
Thanks, man.

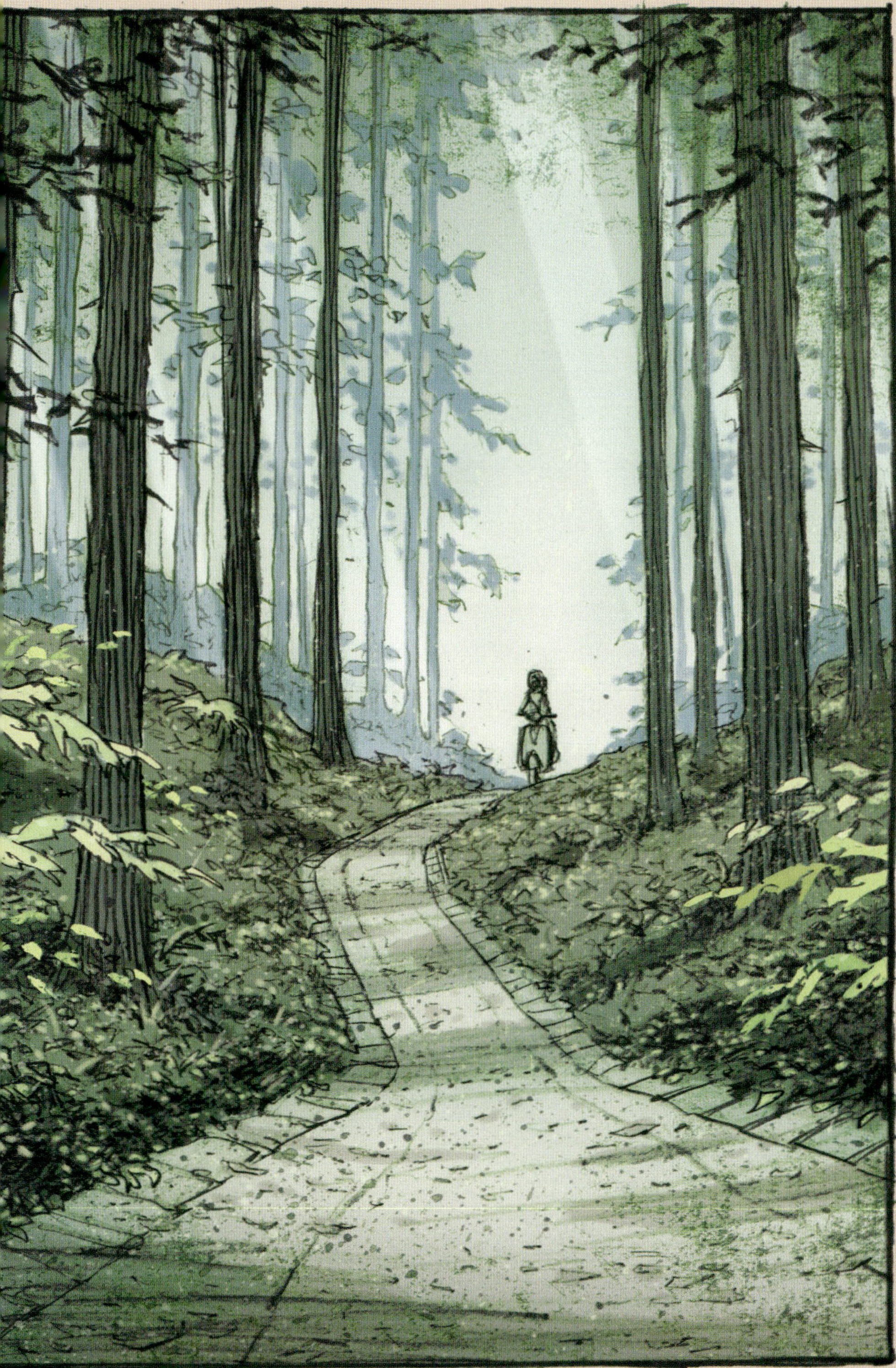

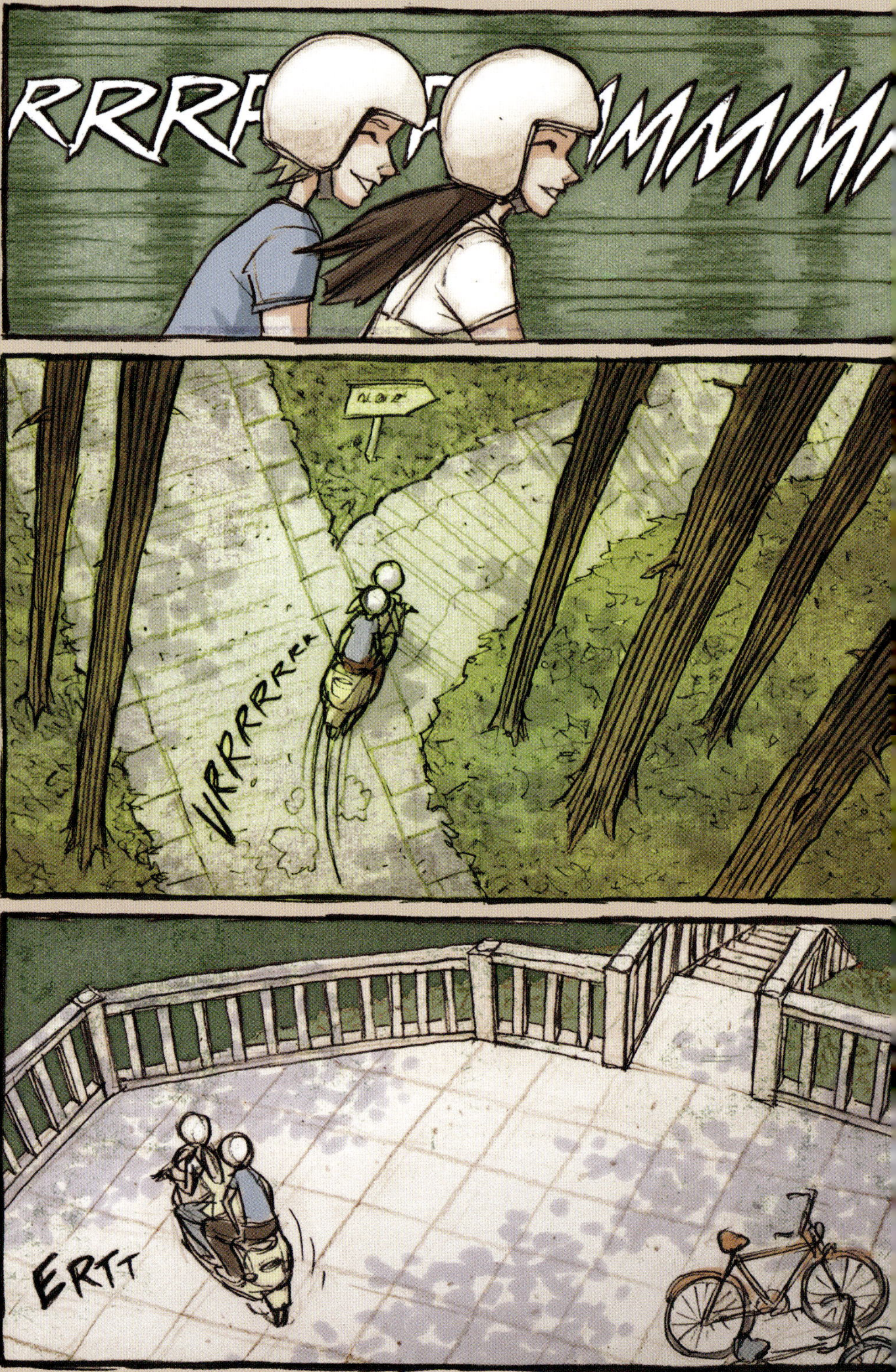
RRR
MMMM
VRRRRRRRR
ERTT

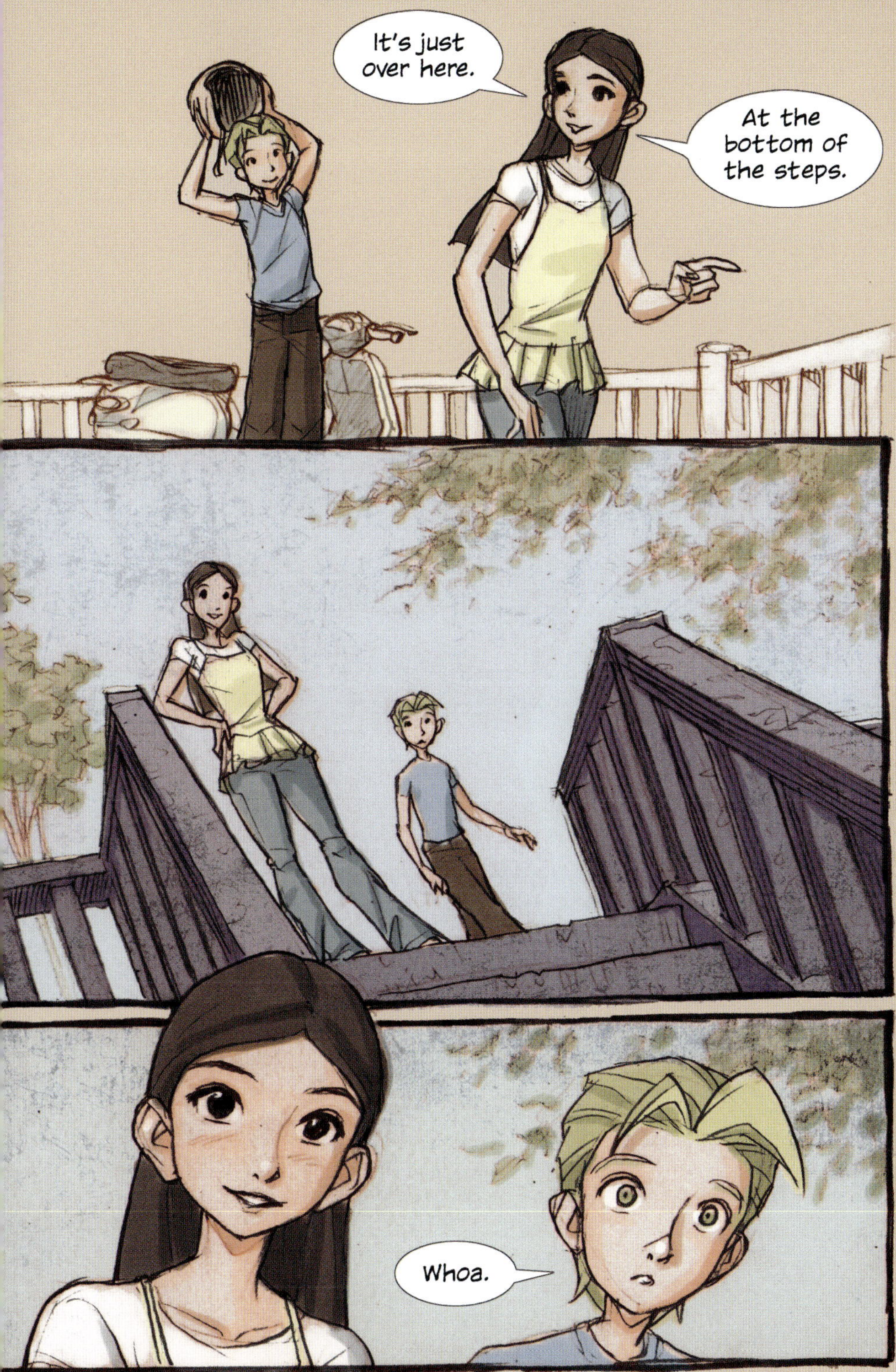
It's just over here.
At the bottom of the steps.
Whoa.

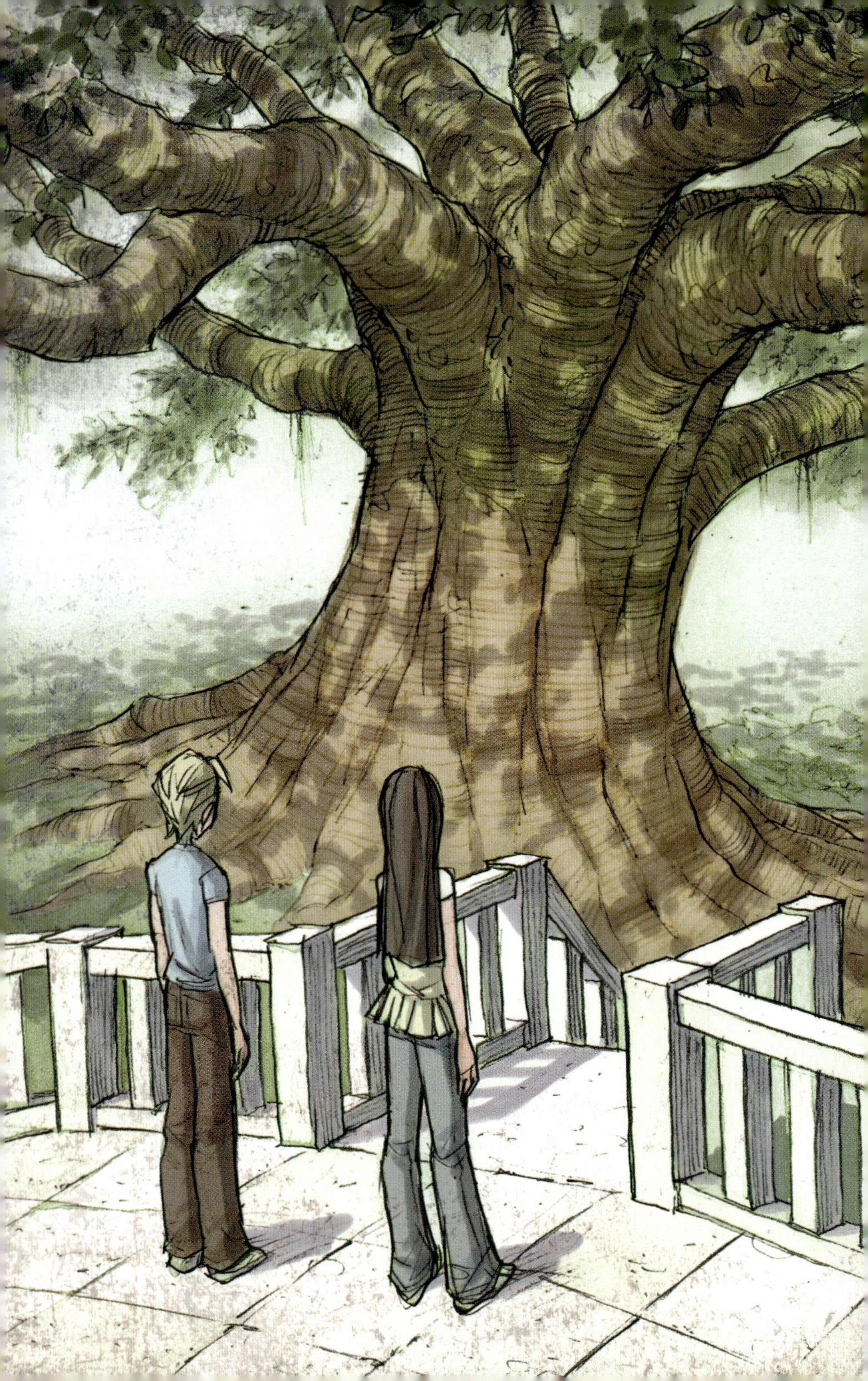

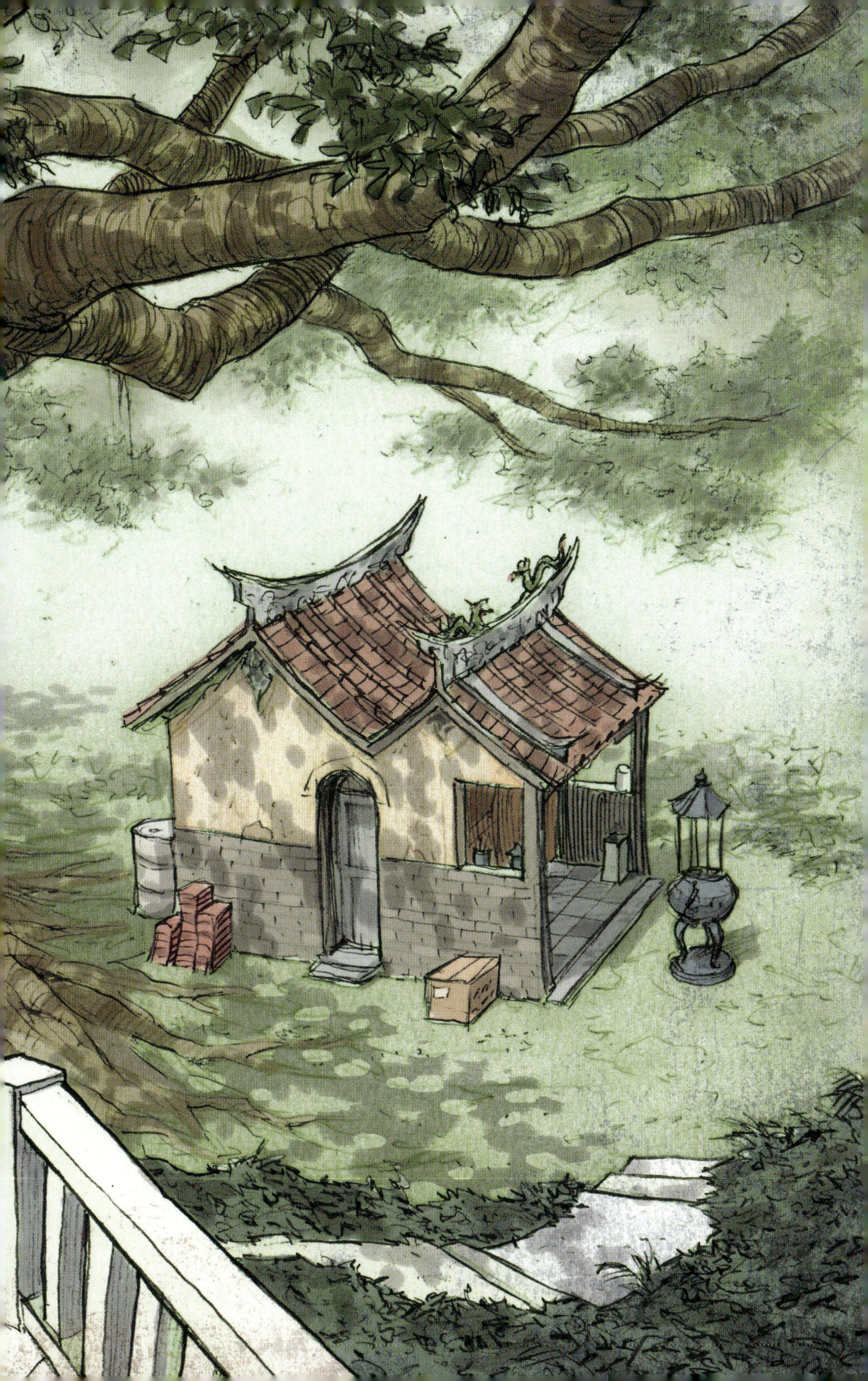

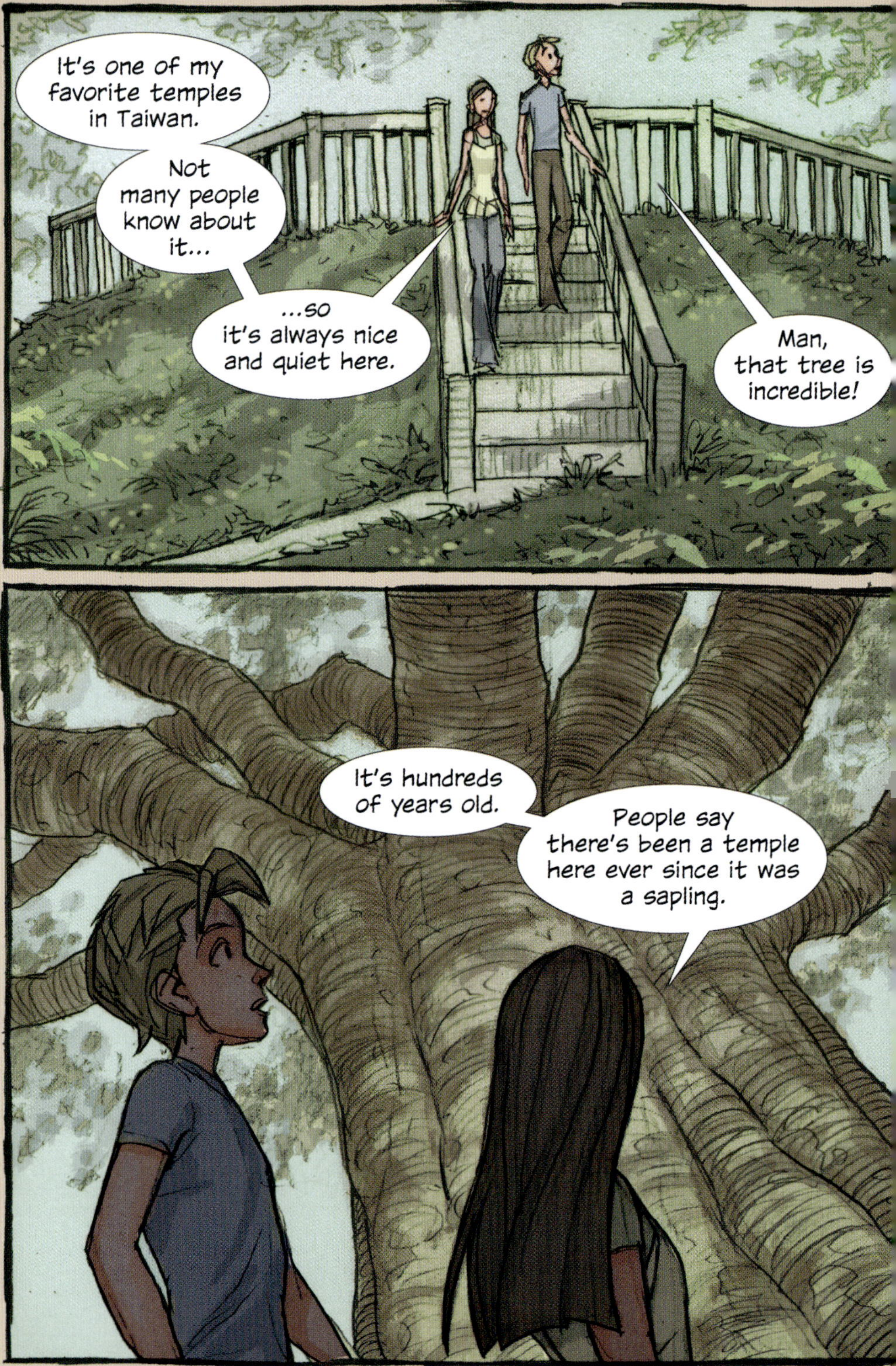
It's one of my favorite temples in Taiwan.
Not many people know about it...
...so it's always nice and quiet here.
Man, that tree is incredible!
It's hundreds of years old.
People say there's been a temple here ever since it was a sapling.

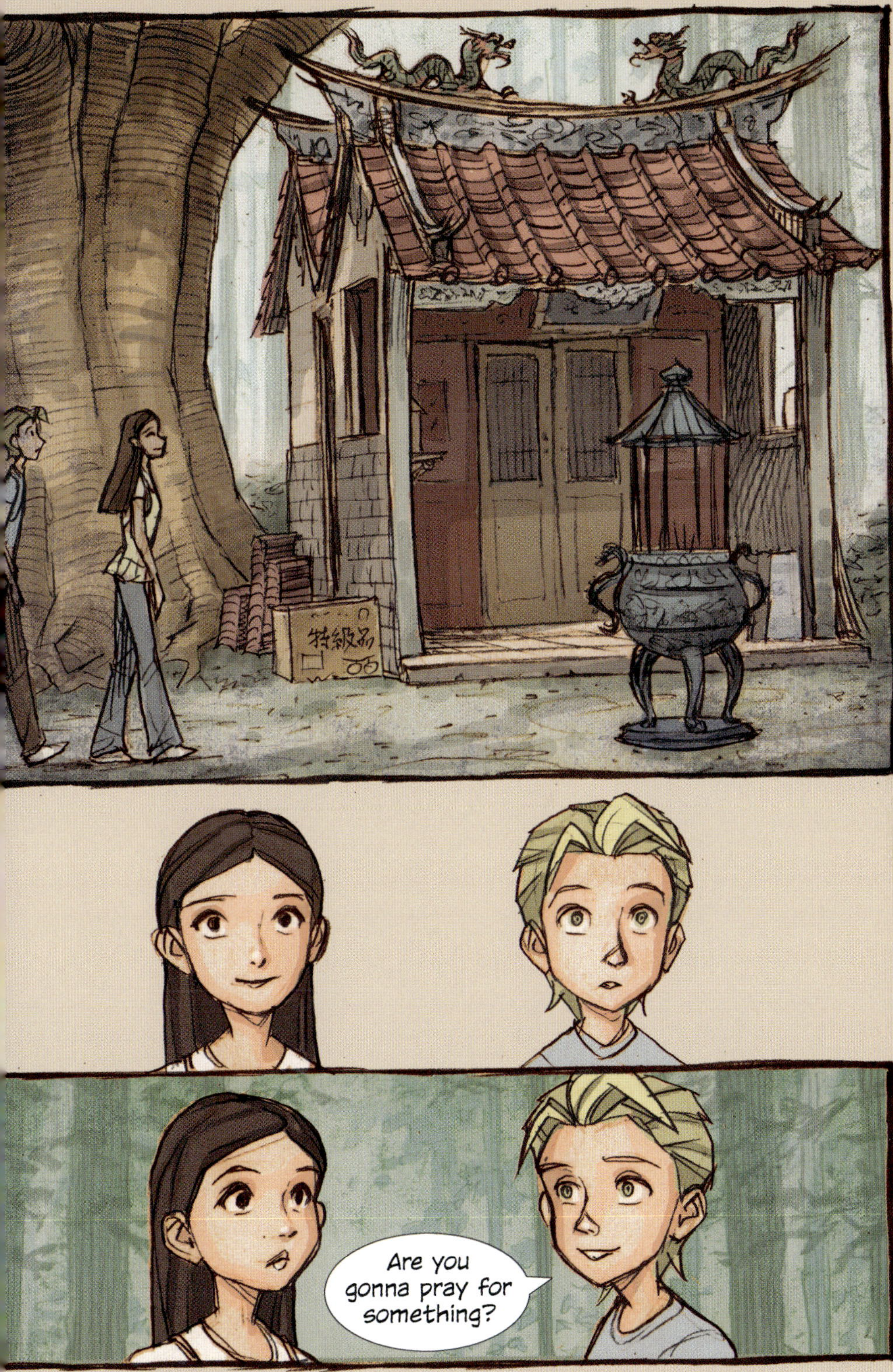
特級品
Are you gonna pray for something?

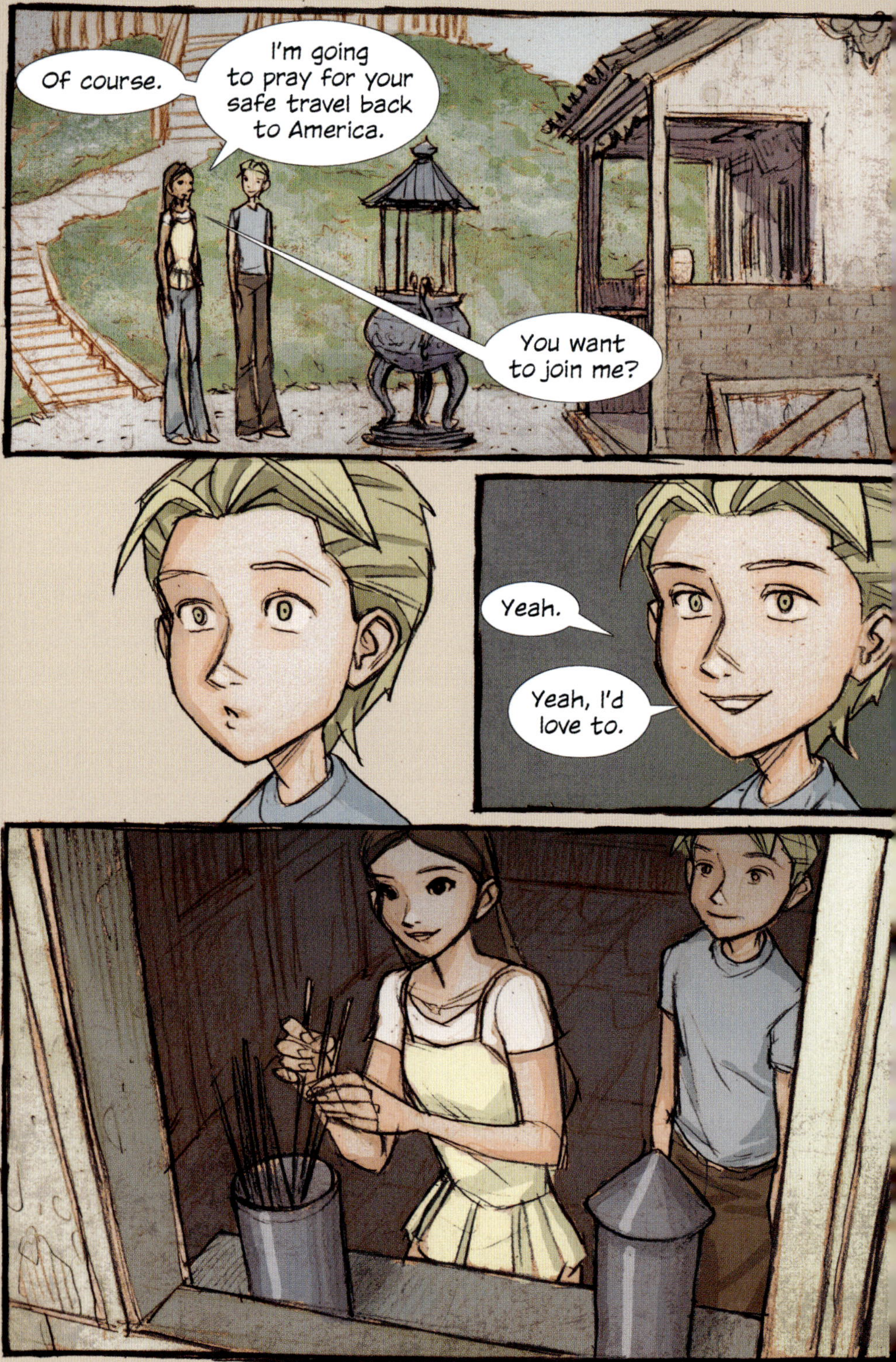
Of course.
I'm going to pray for your safe travel back to America.
You want to join me?
Yeah.
Yeah, I'd love to.

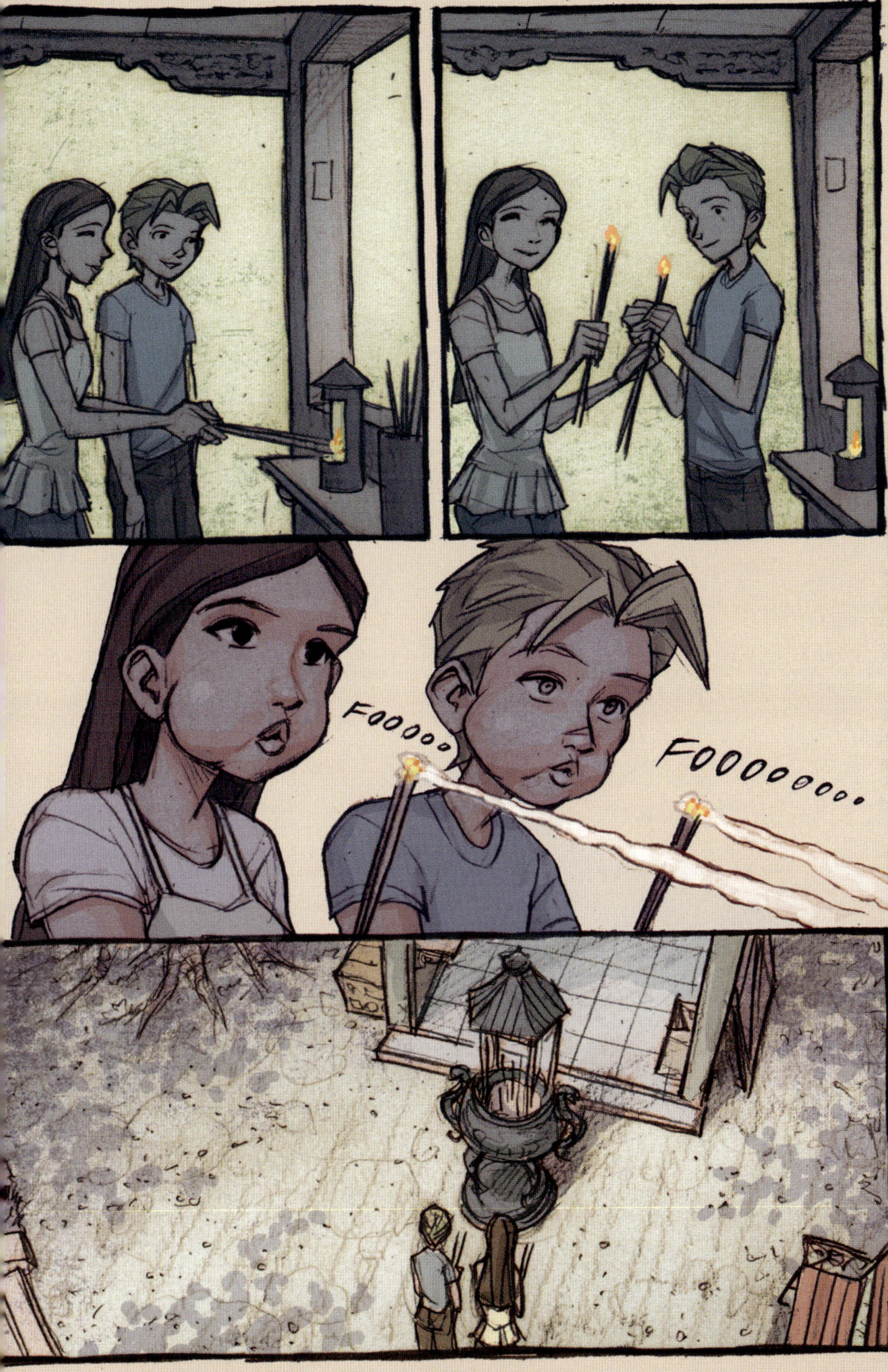

FOOOOO
FOOOOOOOO

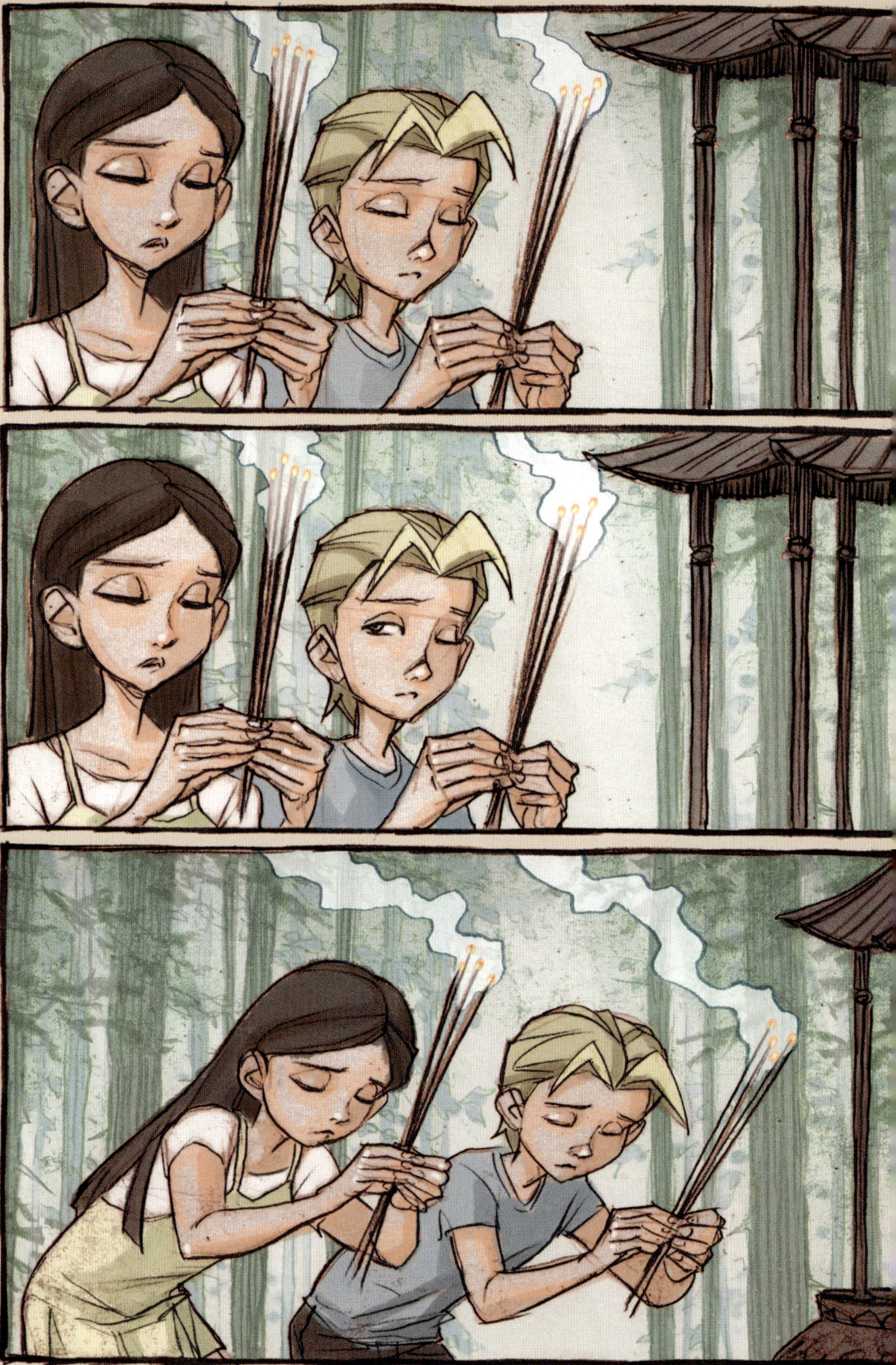

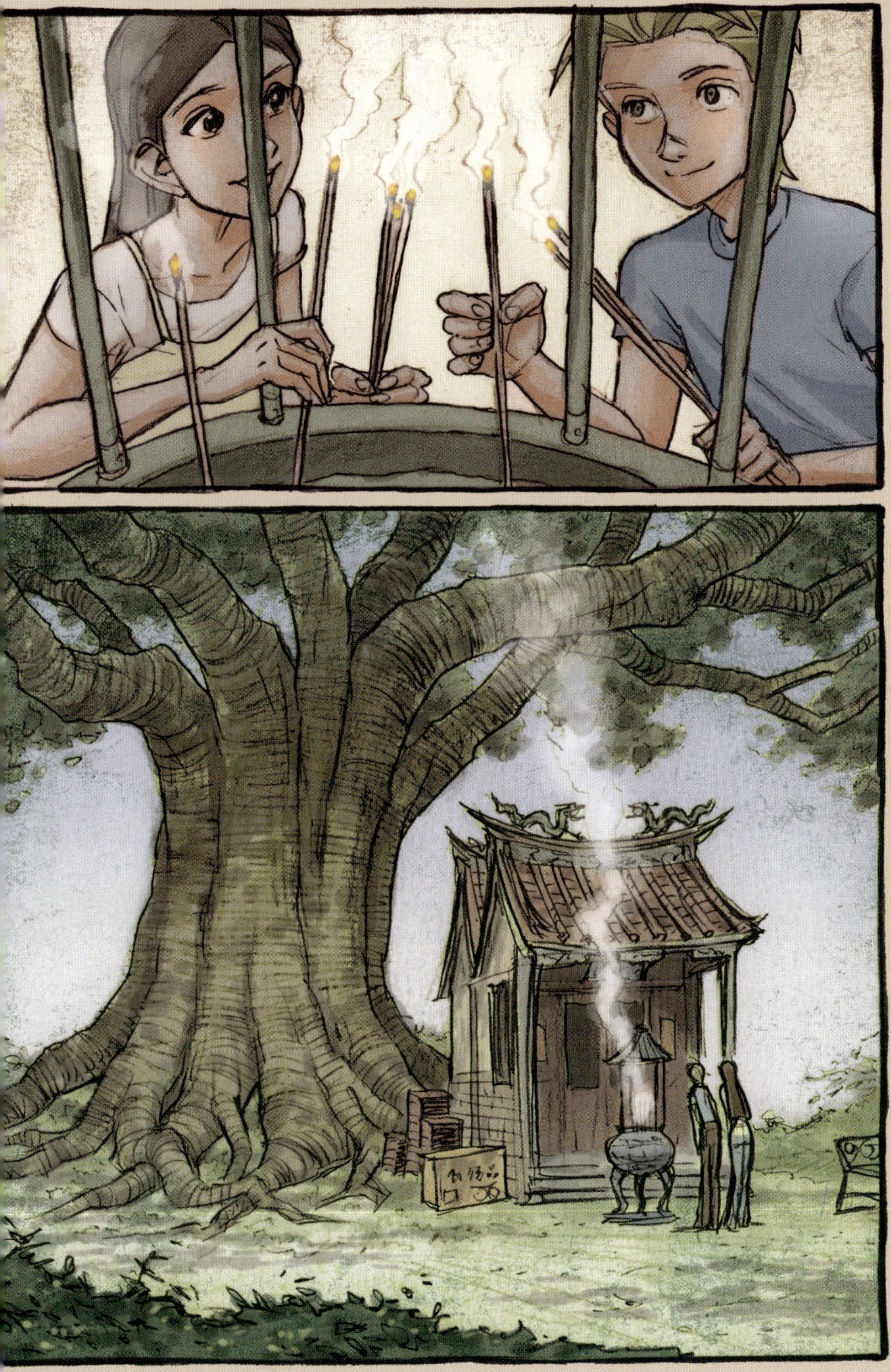

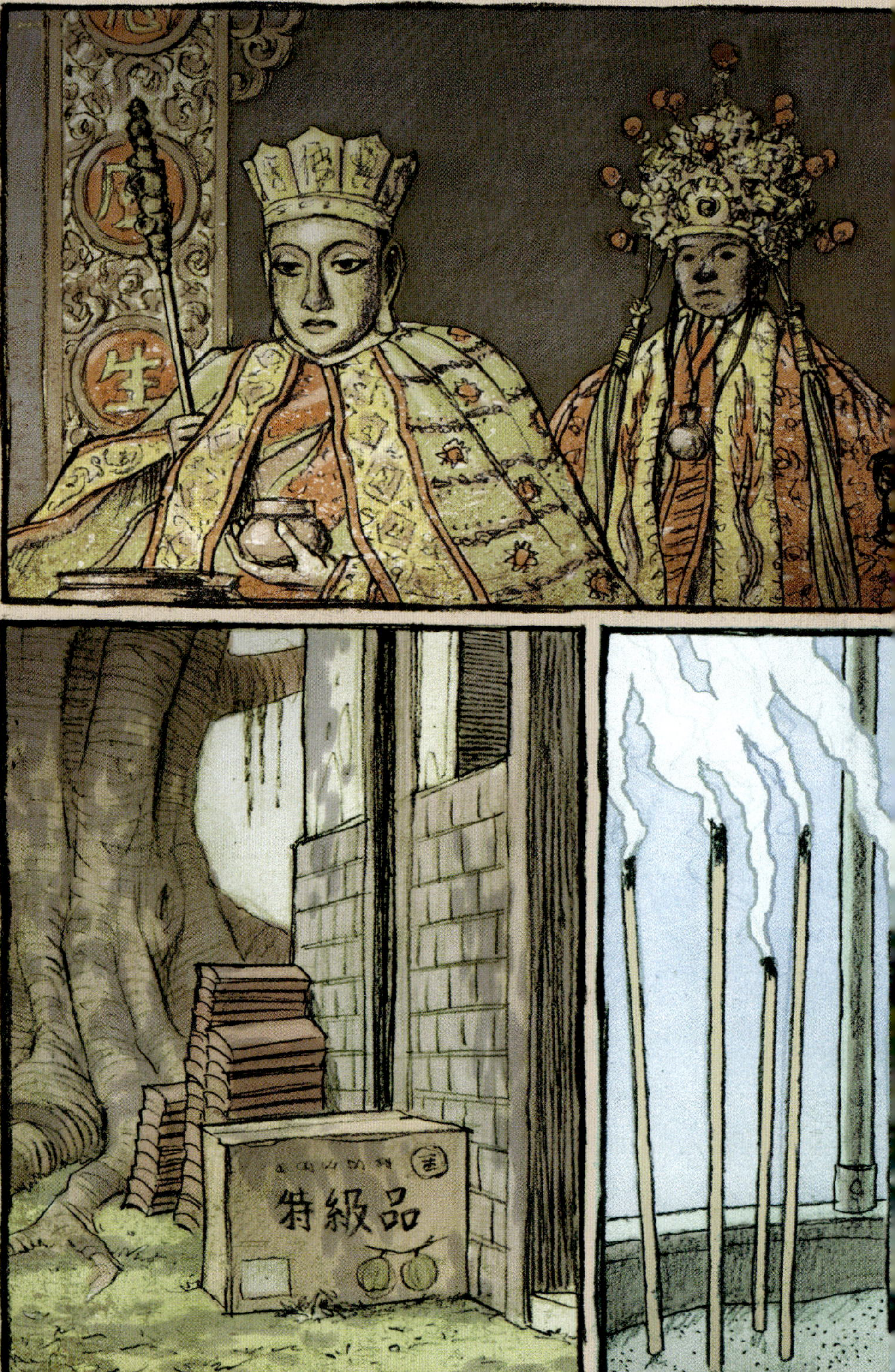
生
特級品

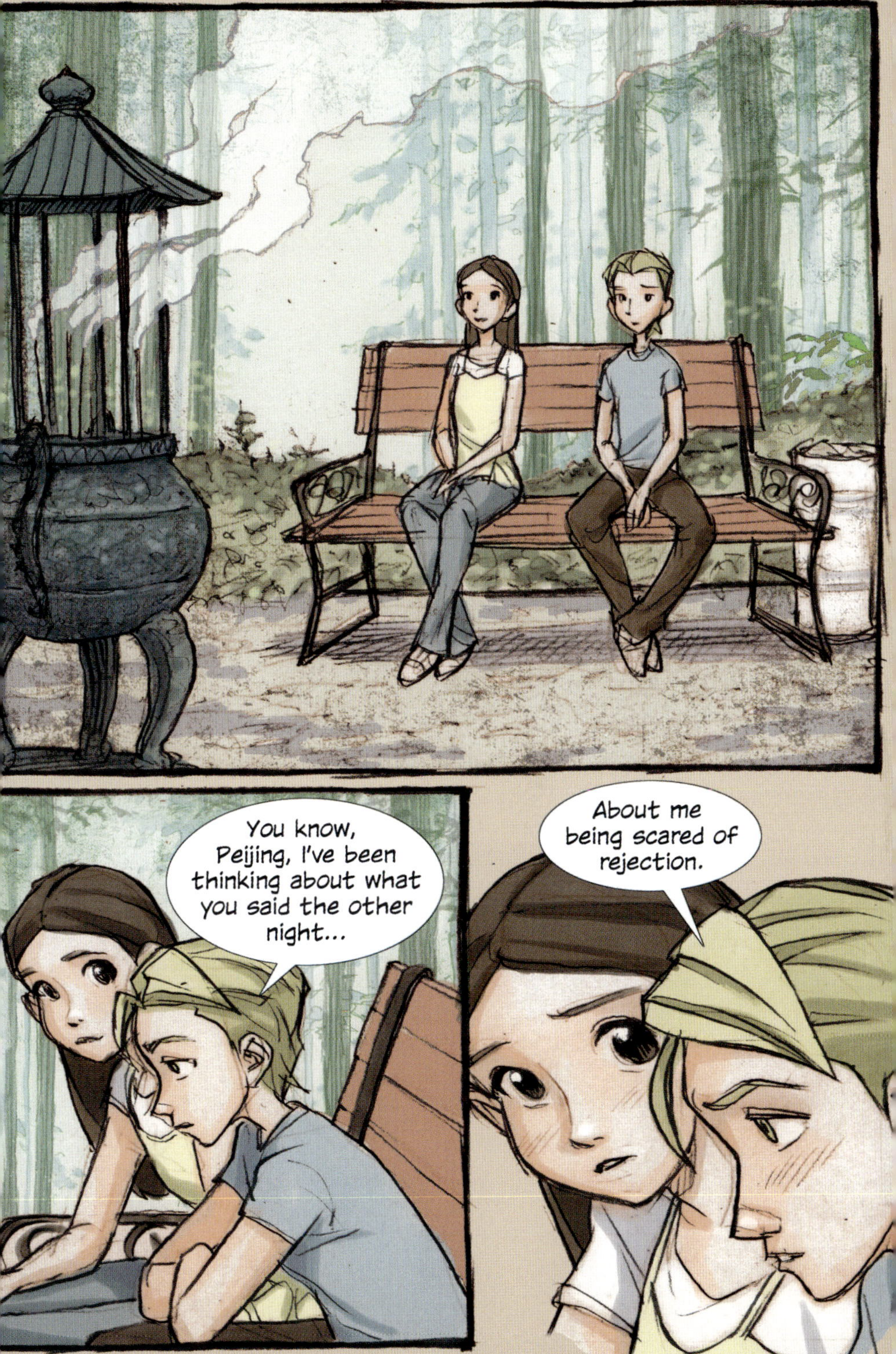
You know, Peijing, I've been thinking about what you said the other night...
About me being scared of rejection.

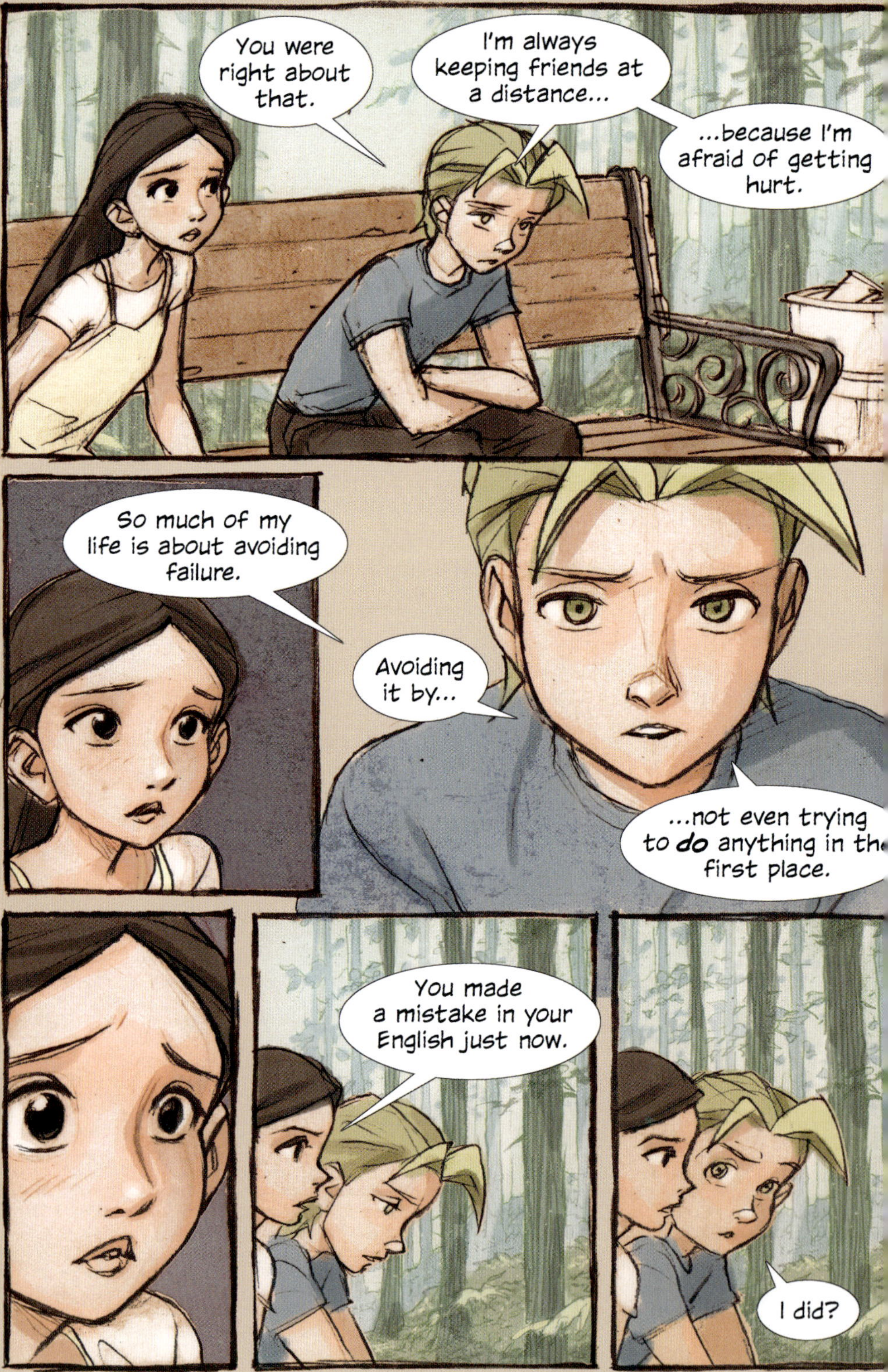
You were right about that.
I'm always keeping friends at a distance...
...because I'm afraid of getting hurt.
So much of my life is about avoiding failure.
Avoiding it by...
...not even trying to **do** anything in the first place.
You made a mistake in your English just now.
I did?

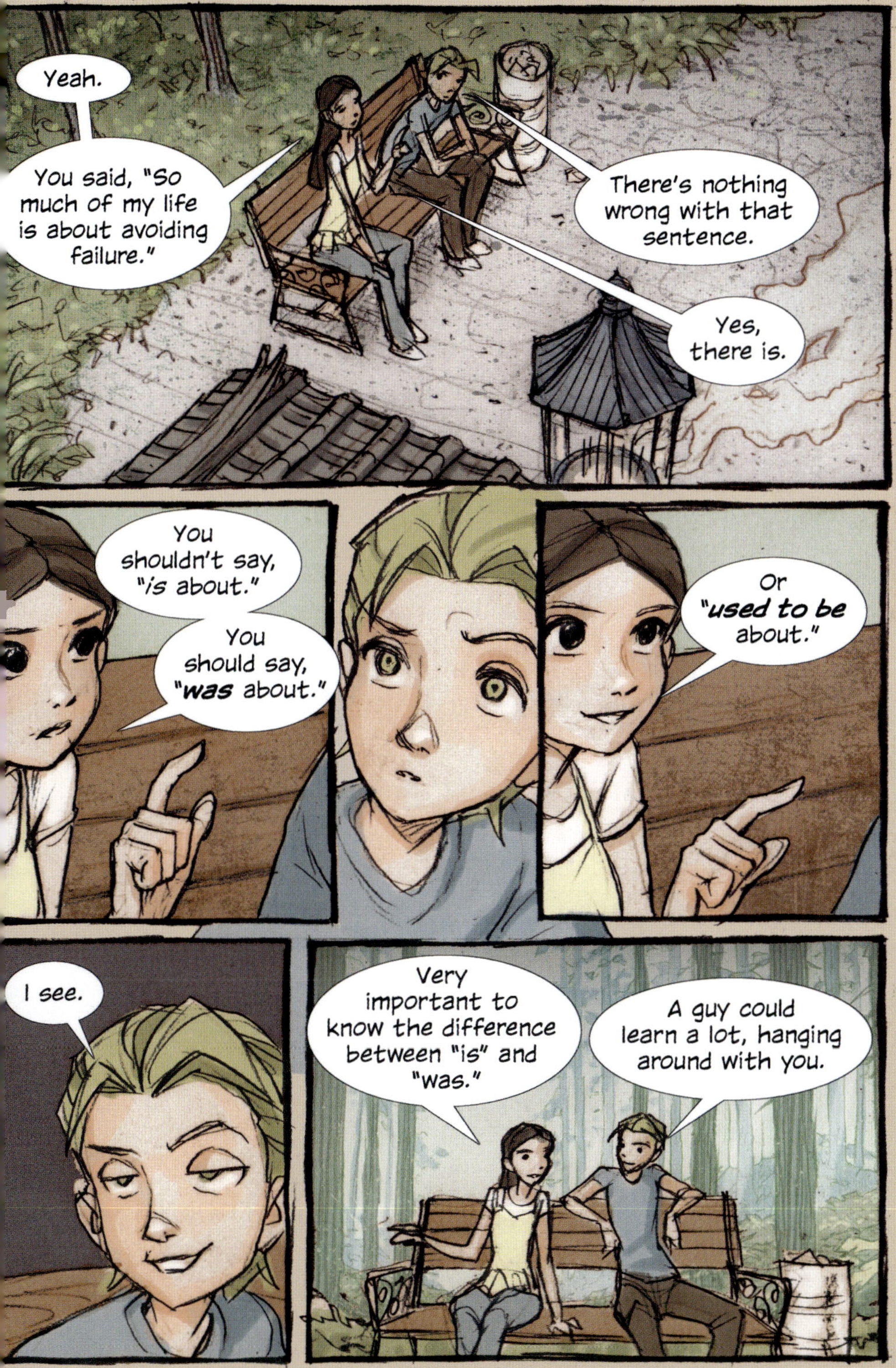
Yeah.
You said, "So much of my life is about avoiding failure."
There's nothing wrong with that sentence.
Yes, there is.
You shouldn't say, "*is* about."
You should say, "***was*** about."
Or "***used to be*** about."
I see.
Very important to know the difference between "is" and "was."
A guy could learn a lot, hanging around with you.

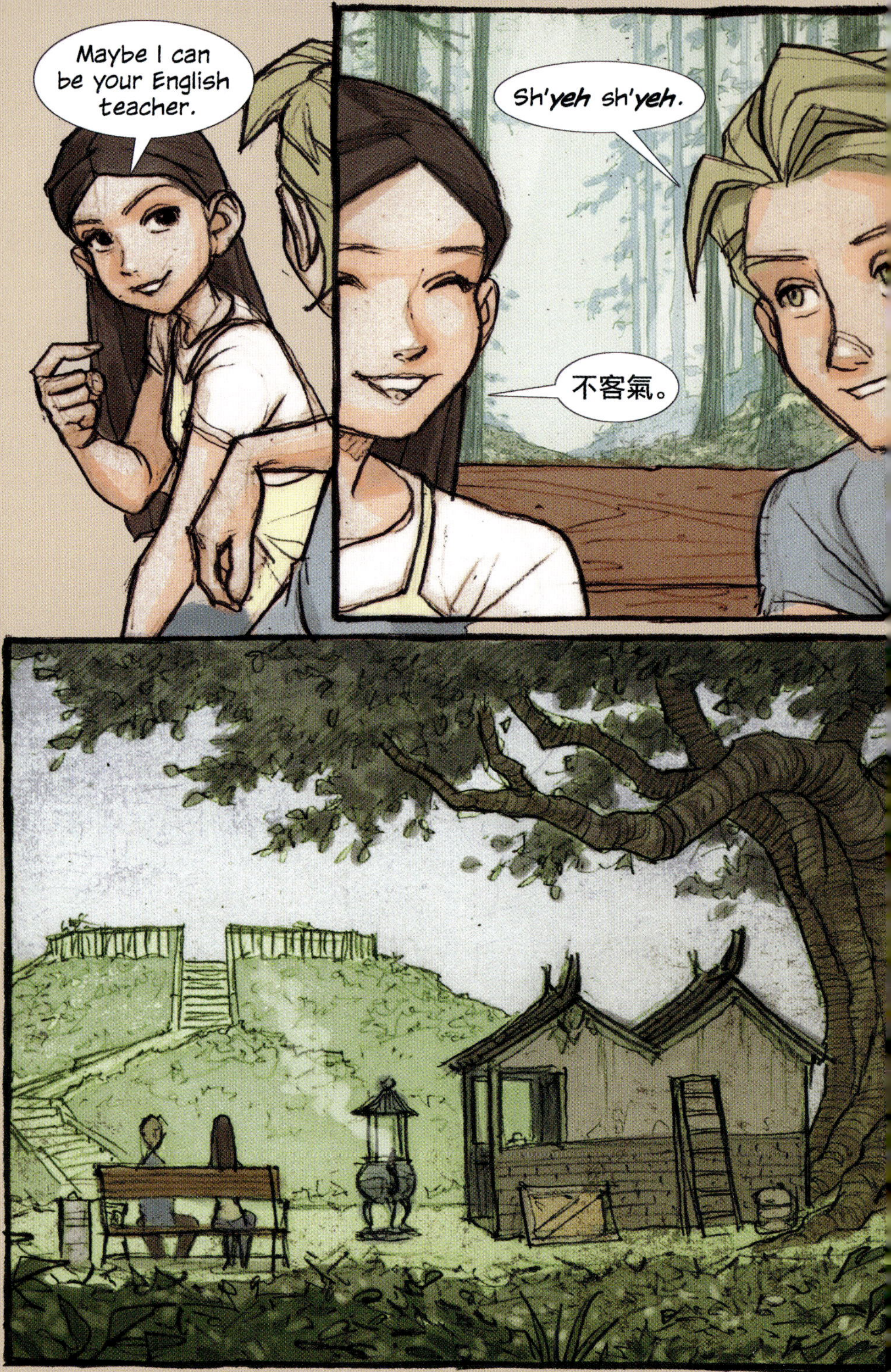
Maybe I can be your English teacher.
Sh'*yeh* sh'*yeh*.
不客氣。

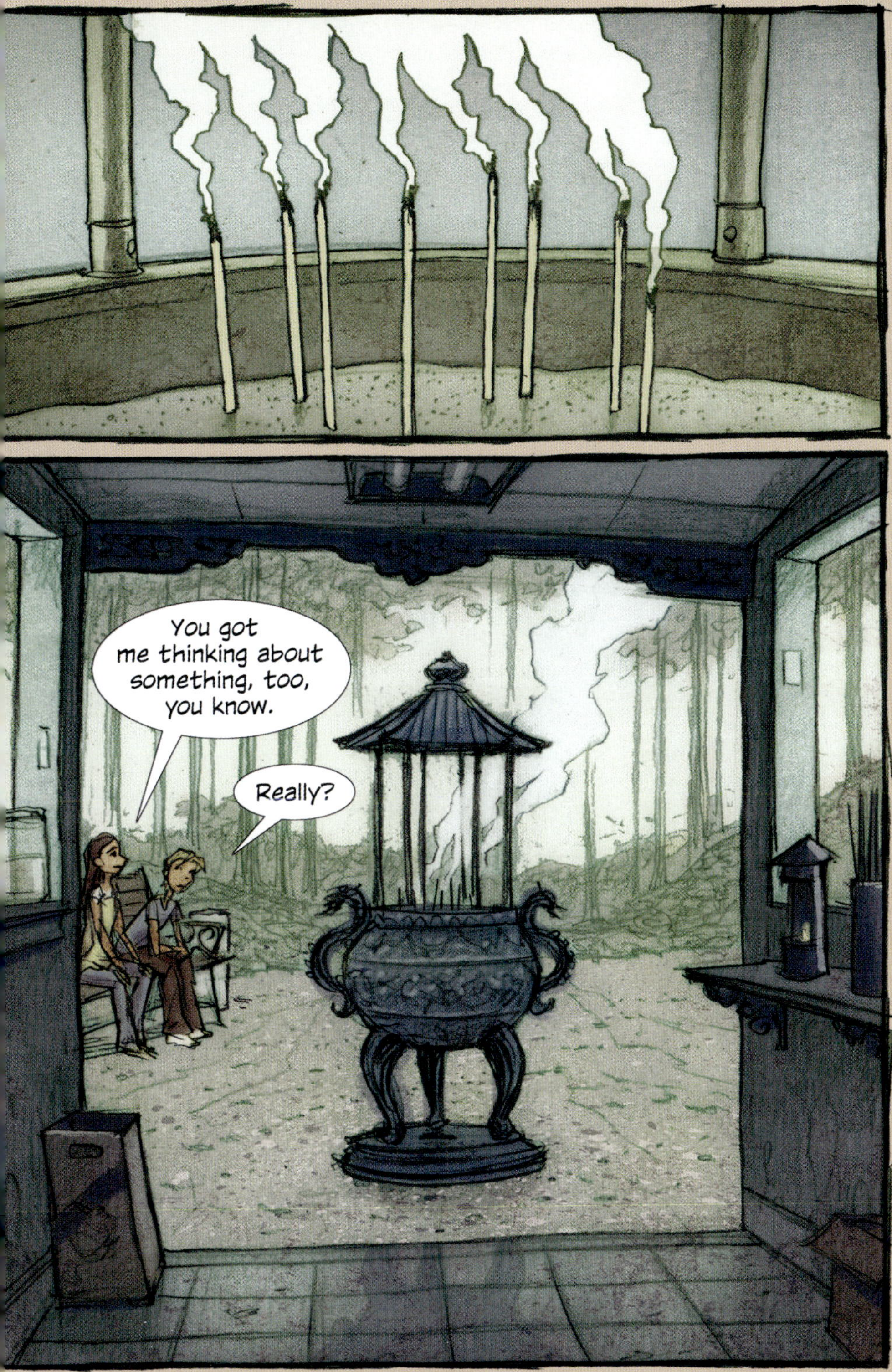
You got me thinking about something, too, you know.
Really?

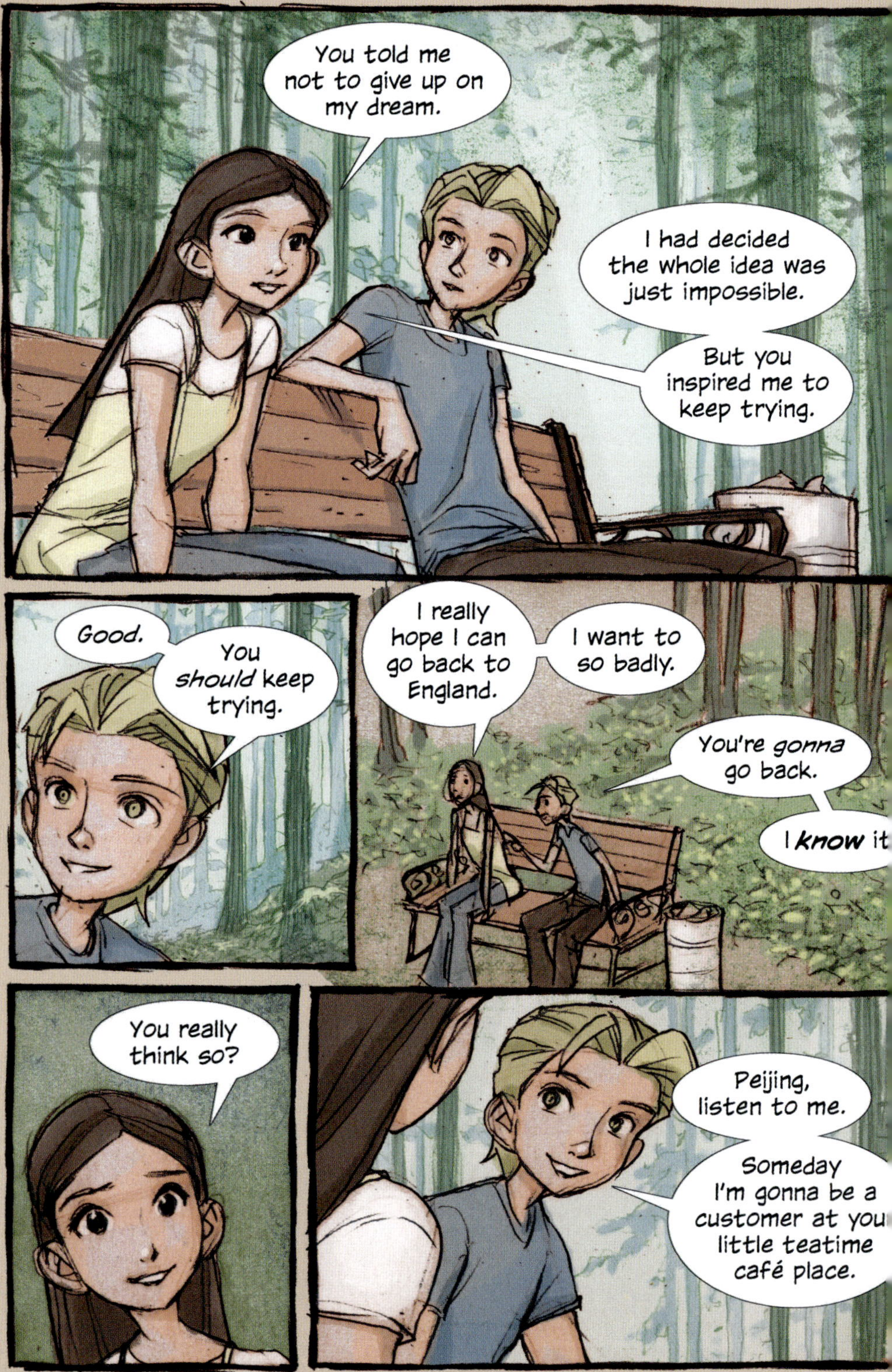

You told me not to give up on my dream.
I had decided the whole idea was just impossible.
But you inspired me to keep trying.
Good.
You *should* keep trying.
I really hope I can go back to England.
I want to so badly.
You're *gonna* go back.
I ***know*** it
You really think so?
Peijing, listen to me.
Someday I'm gonna be a customer at you little teatime café place.

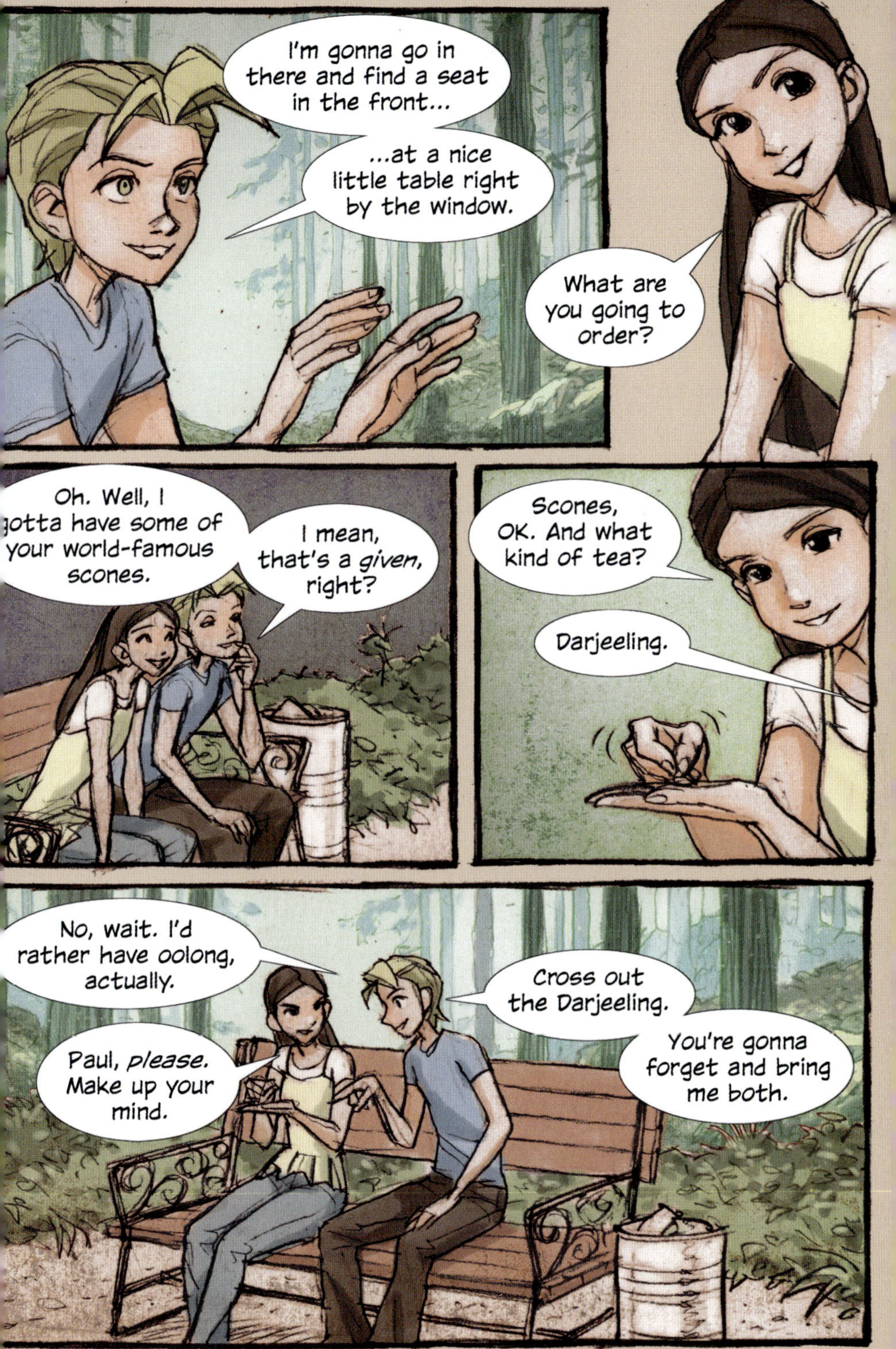
I'm gonna go in there and find a seat in the front...
...at a nice little table right by the window.
What are you going to order?
Oh. Well, I gotta have some of your world-famous scones.
I mean, that's a *given*, right?
Scones, OK. And what kind of tea?
Darjeeling.
No, wait. I'd rather have oolong, actually.
Cross out the Darjeeling.
You're gonna forget and bring me both.
Paul, *please*. Make up your mind.

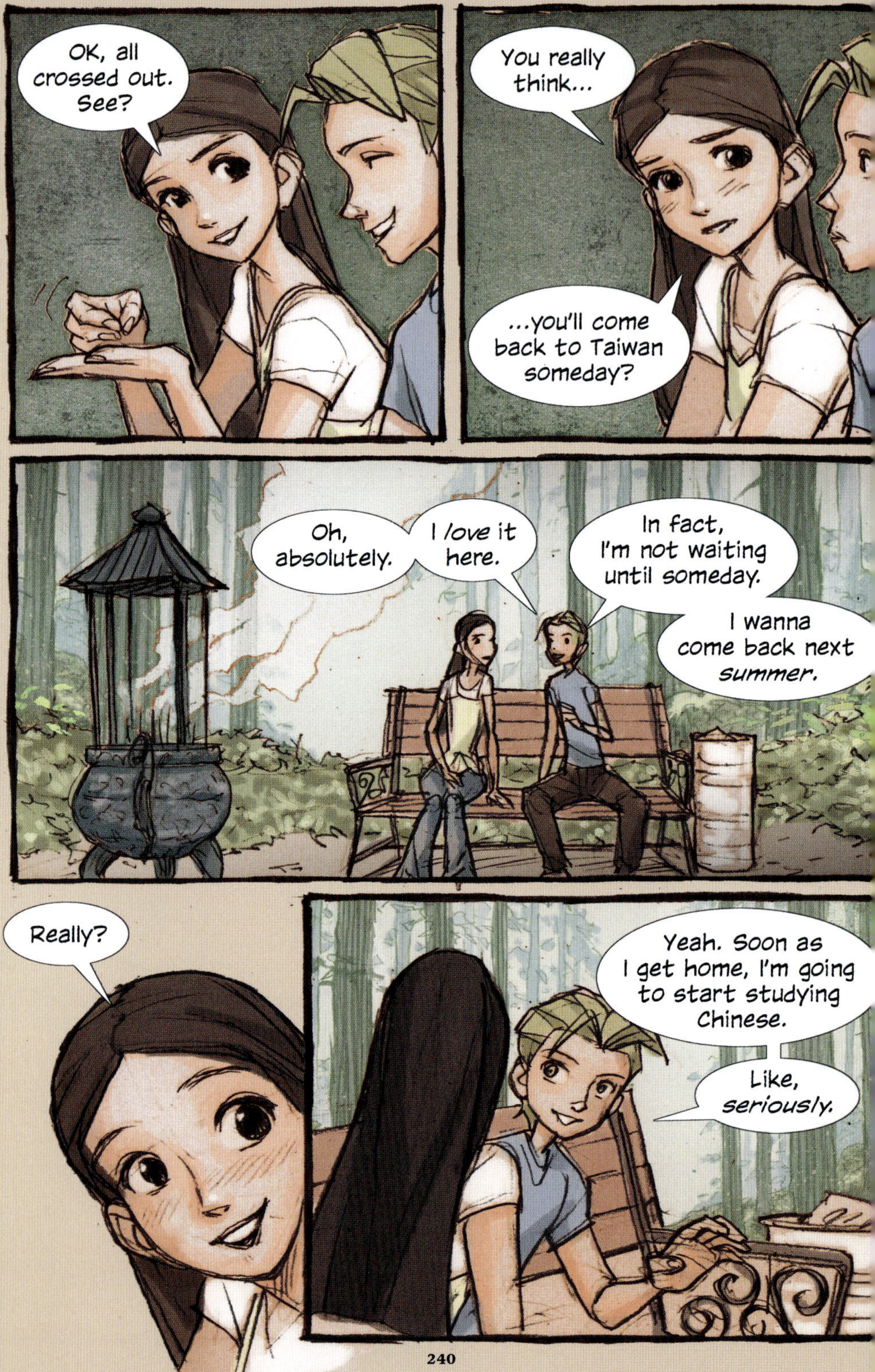
OK, all crossed out. See?
You really think...
...you'll come back to Taiwan someday?
Oh, absolutely.
I *love* it here.
In fact, I'm not waiting until someday.
I wanna come back next *summer.*
Really?
Yeah. Soon as I get home, I'm going to start studying Chinese.
Like, *seriously.*

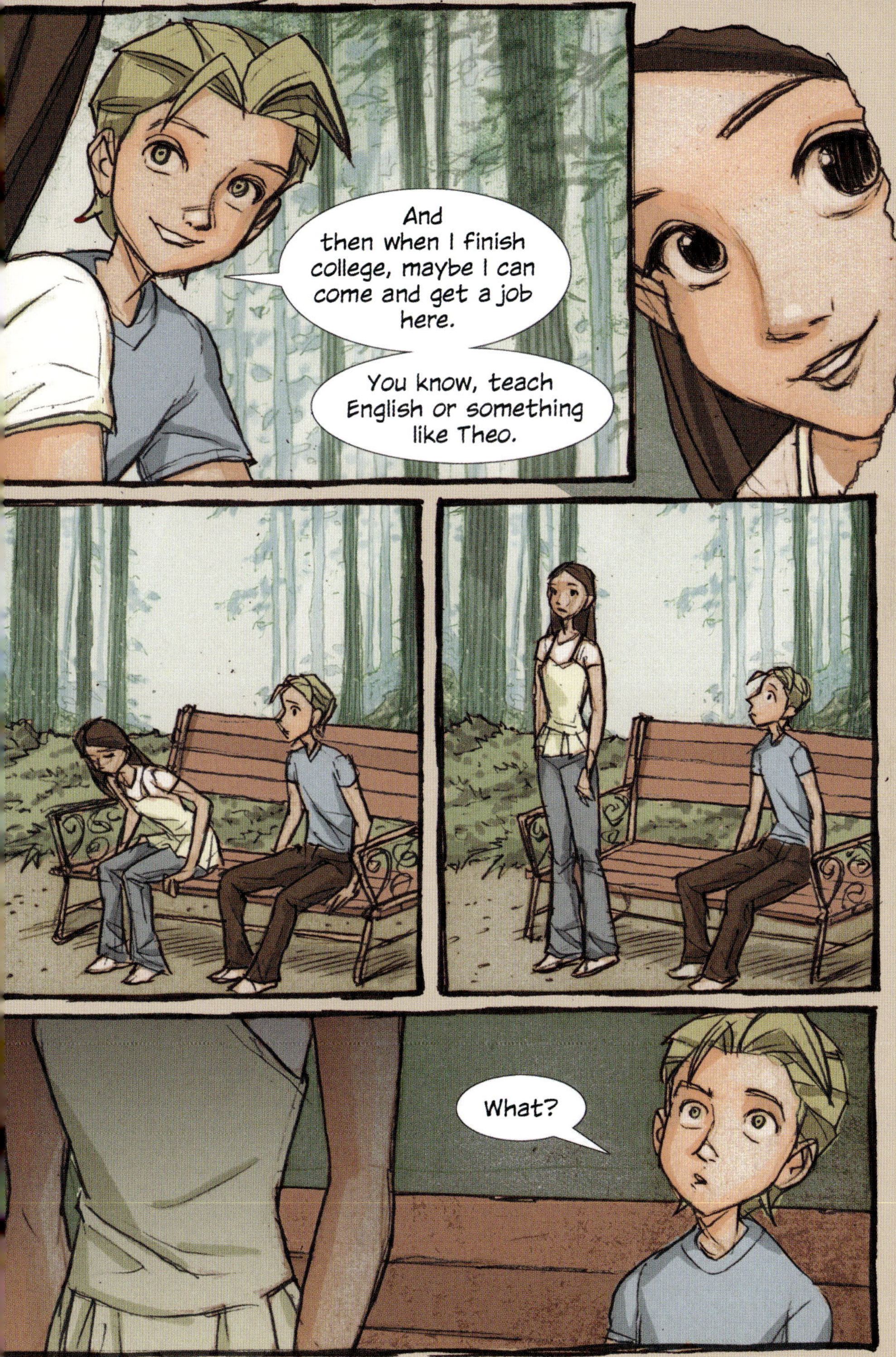
And then when I finish college, maybe I can come and get a job here.
You know, teach English or something like Theo.
What?

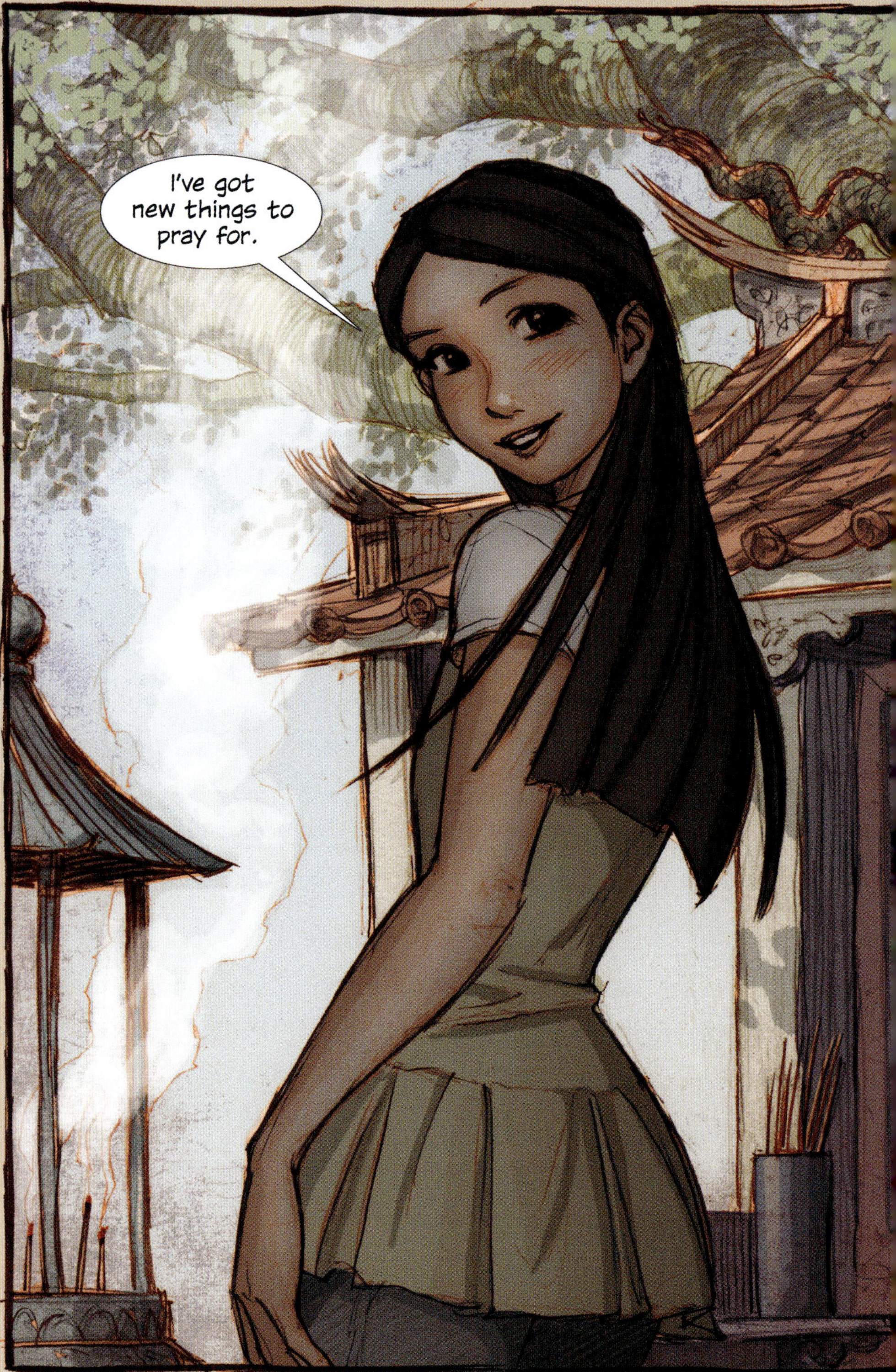
I've got new things to pray for.

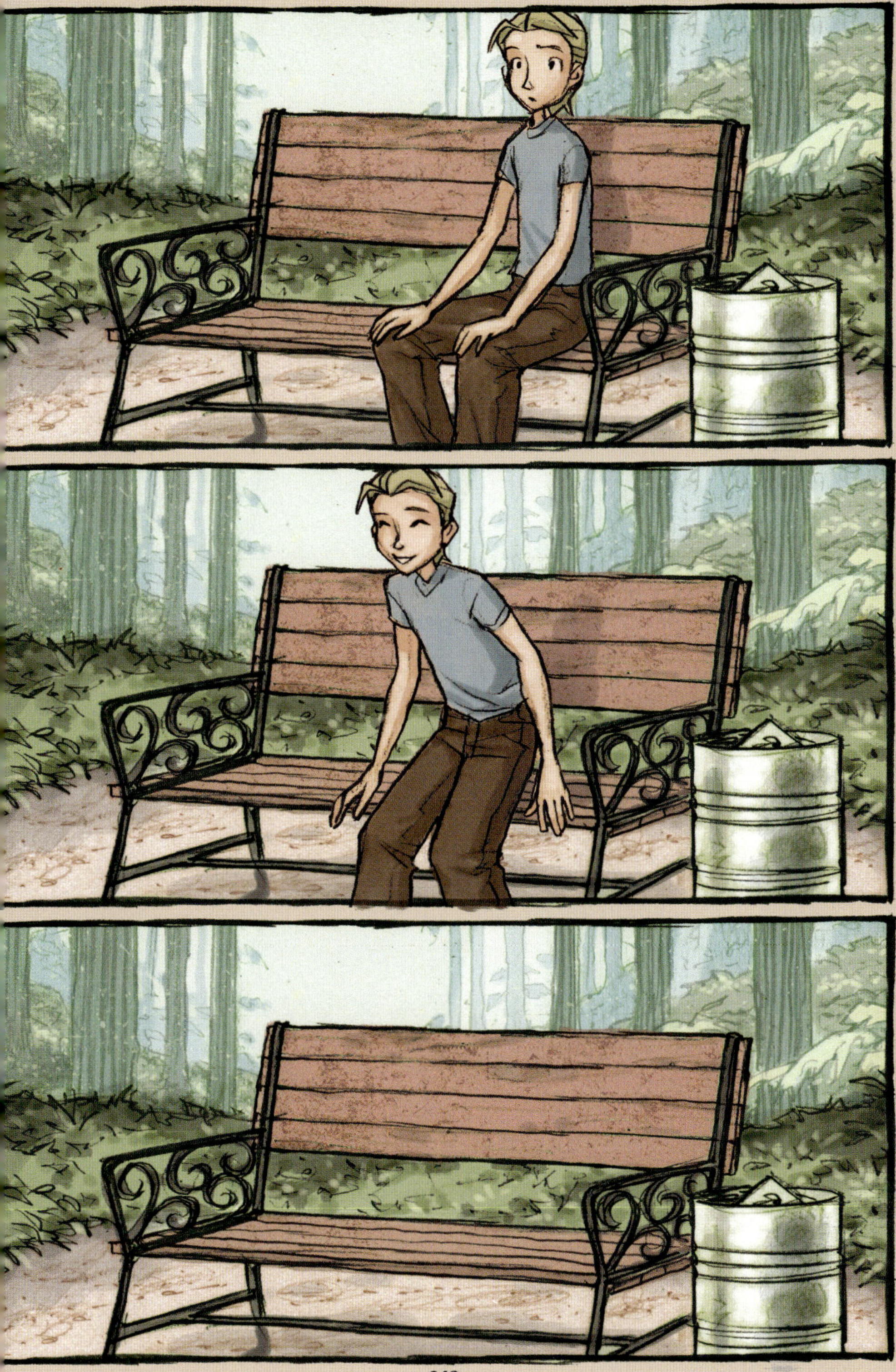

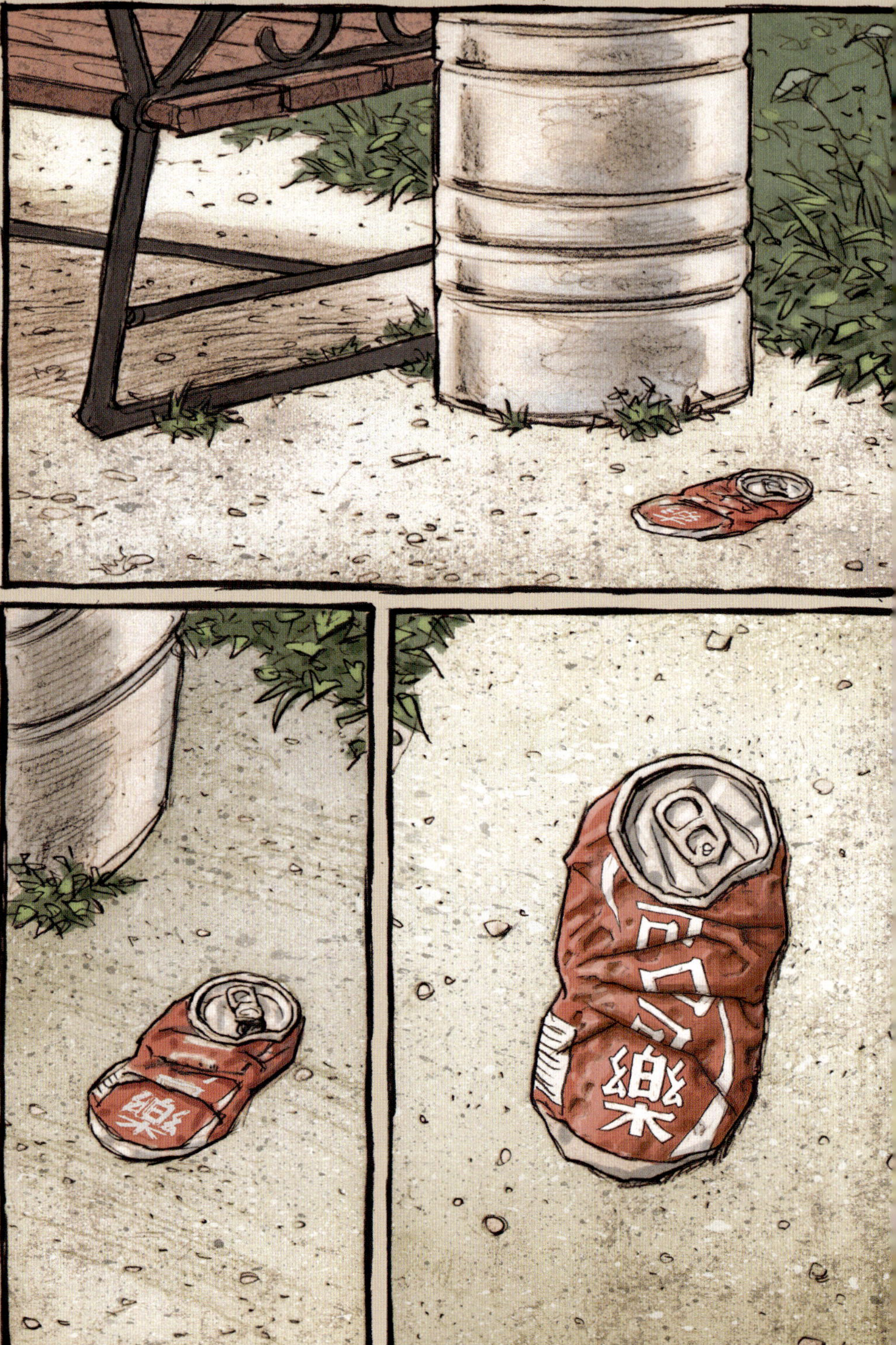
樂
樂

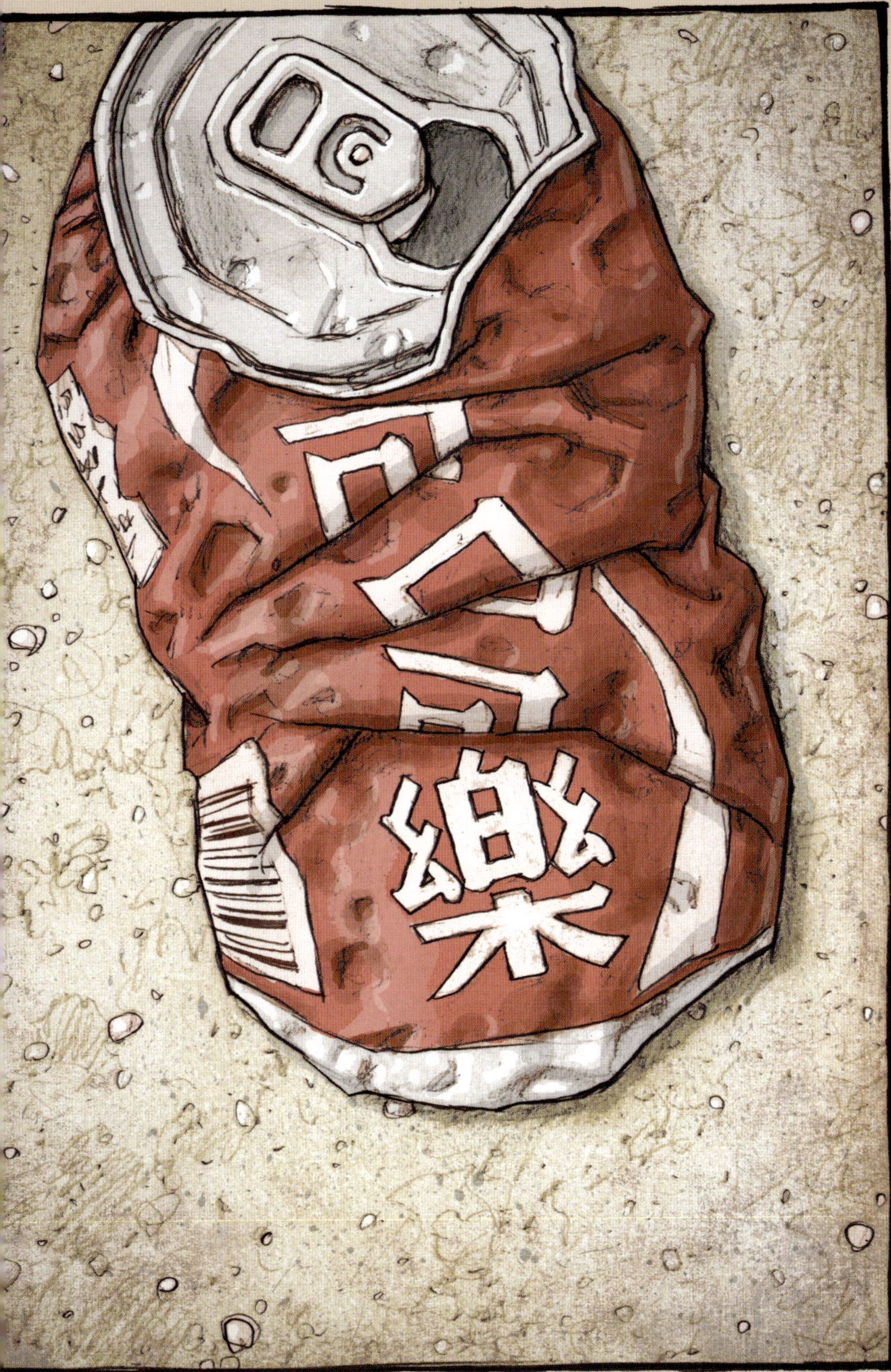
可口可樂

AUTHOR'S NOTE

No one should mistake this book for being autobiographical. I mean, it barely even counts as "inspired by a true story," since nearly everything that happens in it is complete fiction. But there is at least one line of dialogue that refers specifically to my own life (in a slightly embarrassing way). At one point when Paul is telling Peijing about his brother, Theo, he says, "When he first heard about the teaching job over here, the dude couldn't even find Taiwan on a *map*!"

That was me, I'm sad to say.

My senior year of college, I found myself nearing graduation without any idea of what I was going to do. By sheer luck, I had a professor, Scott Friesner, who had taught English in Taiwan with the YMCA back in the 1970s. With his help, I was able to line up work doing the very same thing a few months after I got my diploma. And yes: When I first heard about the possibility, I would have struggled to find Taiwan on a map.

Talk about a great first job, though. I'd done a fair amount of traveling up until that point, but this was my first time in East Asia. I'll never forget what it felt like to step off the bus that had taken me and my fellow teachers from the airport all the way into downtown Taipei, and to gaze up at all those neon-lit Chinese characters that surrounded us. The sights and sounds of Taiwan fired up my imagination, and I immediately set to doing pen-and-ink drawings everywhere I went, some of which you can see between the chapters of this book.

Flash forward thirty years or so, and I found myself with quite a different opportunity: the chance to create a graphic novel that would pay tribute to Taiwan and convey to others the many joys that await you if you go there.

There didn't seem to be much drama in basing the main character, Paul, directly on myself. I was what you would call an "enthusiast": eager to learn the language and soak up as much Taiwanese culture as I could. Surely it would be more interesting storywise to watch Taiwan cast its spell upon an unwilling visitor.

I lived and worked in Taiwan for two and a half years altogether. The sprawling series of experiences I had over there would be impossible to capture in graphic-novel form. I needed a more condensed time frame to work with. As I played around with different approaches, I hit upon the idea of having most of the story take place over the course of a single day. That would allow me to give readers an immersive, nonstop experience in which they accompany Paul every step of the way, seeing, hearing, and tasting everything that he does. (Well, I *wish* you could taste it, anyway!)

So, no: I never got lost in Taiwan, and I don't have a whole lot in common with this story's protagonist. If anything, Paul's older brother plays the "Crilley role" in this story, memorizing Chinese characters and singing the praises of Taiwan to anyone who will listen.

But did I have days in Taiwan that were every bit as magical as the one Paul experiences? You bet I did. Plenty of them. And as for the kindness and generosity displayed by Peijing and Wallace...well, there's nothing fictional about that. You could circle the globe forever and never find friendlier people than the Taiwanese.

So please do add Taiwan to the list of places you'd like to go someday. You'll have an amazing time there—guaranteed. And take it from me: being able to find it on a map is strictly optional.

ACKNOWLEDGMENTS

Many thanks to my editor, Andrea Colvin, who believed in this book and guided it with a steady hand, all the way from when it was little more than, "Hey, I should do a story set in Taiwan!" Thanks also to Ann Dwyer and Megan McLaughlin, whose art direction and design made this book the best it could be. Thanks to Lindsay Walter-Greaney, Jill Freshney, and Lillian Sun, who lent their expertise to the editing and production of the book. Much gratitude to my copyeditor, Danielle Moran, and proofreaders, Starr Baer and Rebekah Wallin, who caught many a foolish mistake before they could go out into the world. Thanks to Shenwei Chang, who went over the manuscript and alerted me to cultural aspects of the story that could be handled more sensitively. Very special thanks to Teresa Lien and to Tom and Ula Cain, who graciously went over my clumsy Mandarin Chinese dialogue and fixed its multitude of errors. A hearty round of applause to my agent, Ammi-Joan Paquette, who wisely said, a few years back, "We need to get you making graphic novels again." And finally, many, many thanks to my wife, Miki, who makes sure I never get lost, every day of my life.

MARK CRILLEY

is the author and illustrator of more than forty books, including several acclaimed graphic novels, for which he has received fourteen Eisner Award nominations. His work has been featured in *USA Today*, *Entertainment Weekly*, and on *CNN Headline News*. His popular YouTube videos have been viewed more than 400 million times. He lives in Michigan with his wife, Miki, and children, Matthew and Mio.

樂

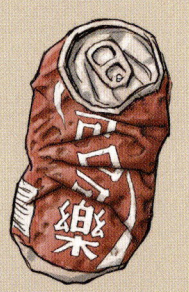